# AWAKENING OF THE STARBORNE

THE GAME OF ENDINGS AND BEGINNINGS

BOOK 1

LOUVE -CH

First edition

LuxsulaVerse Publishing



Developmental Edits: Sarina Leo

Edited by Becky Sweeney & Isabella Friemann

Cover illustrator: @Sajrafox

Chapter Header illustrator, Ruthless, and Kiss of Chaos: @Aeridan_

Map created with Incarnate by Louve -ch

Gildorea illustration by @Jeremyadams.ink

Map of Gildorea & ornamental illustrations by N.Errico

Savaé Mosaic illustration: @Crow__V

Calais, Pip, Savaé, Sølas and Nyxara illustrations by @Elzappata

Shadowveil illustration by @KotiKomori

Nyxara portrait illustration by @Sakurumi.art

Mosaic heart and dragon fang dagger by @WisteriaRoad

ISBN

979-8-9931780-0-4 (*Paperback*)

979-8-2186730-5-5 (Hardback)

❀ Formatted with Vellum

# TRIGGER WARNINGS

This book is intended for audiences of 18 years and older. This story—though one of triumph—is dark. It contains limited but graphic child abuse and neglect, mature language, suggestions of rape, graphic murder, blood and gore, knife play, strangling, biting, branding/marking, licking of blood, possessive characters, unhealthy mental coping strategies including casual sex, LGBTQ representation, female-female and male-female explicit adult content, alcohol consumption, hallucinogenic experiences, graphic battle scenes, acting under compulsion/without consent, depression, PTSD, suggestion of trafficking/slavery, passive thoughts of suicide, and potential emotional devastation for the reader—therapy not included!

CASCARA
HIGHLANDS
ELDORIA PEAK
ESTRELA
SNOMAS
DRAGON SPINE
FROSTMA
N
W E
S
DRAGON SPIRE
EMERALD LAKE TOWER
DORAAN
GILDOREA UNIVERITÁS OF WAR
MYSTHOLD
RAEYA'S FORTRESS
MIDLANDS
STERMA
LOWLANDS
RIICAH
ABBERDEAN

# Gildorea Universitás of War

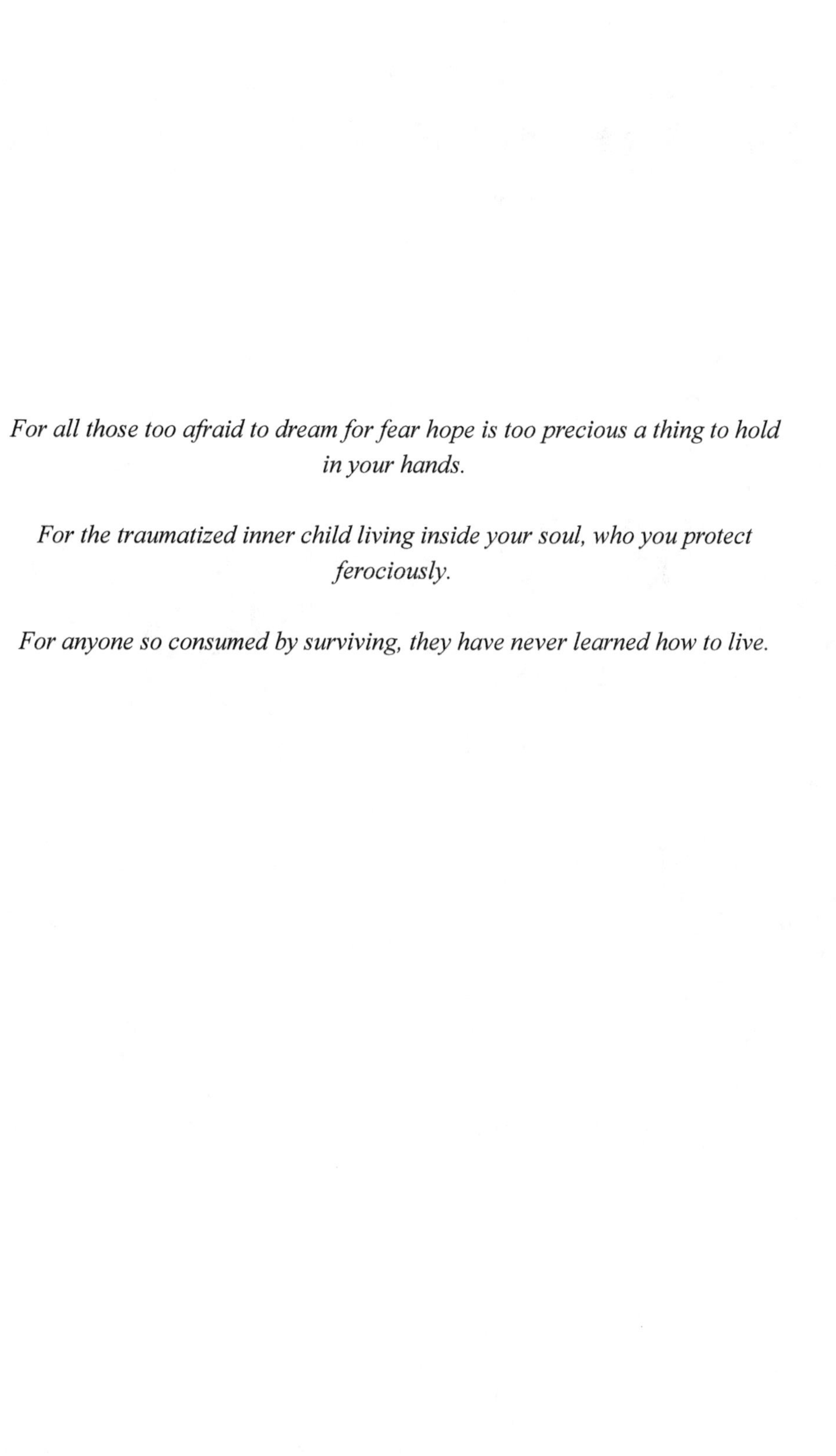

*For all those too afraid to dream for fear hope is too precious a thing to hold in your hands.*

*For the traumatized inner child living inside your soul, who you protect ferociously.*

*For anyone so consumed by surviving, they have never learned how to live.*

◇ FLIP TO THE LAST PAGE ◇

TO FIND YOUR WAY INTO THE

◇ APPENDIARY ◇

# Wing Structure

## Ground Unit

### Savant
MASTER STRATEGIST. POSSESSES UNPARALLELED BATTLE HISTORY RECALL AND TACTICAL INSIGHT. THEY LEAD THE WING. COORDINATING GROUND AND AERIAL MANEUVERS TO EXPLOIT ENEMY WEAKNESS AND MEET THE ASSIGNED OBJECTIVE.

### Spycraft
SKILLED IN DISGUISE AND DECEPTION. GATHERS INTEL UNDETECTED THROUGH STAYING HIDDEN IN PLAIN SIGHT OR CHANGING THEIR APPEARANCE TO BLEND INTO ENEMY RANKS.

### Runic Engineer
SPECIALIST IN RUNE TECH. THEIR ABILITY TO CAST AND INSCRIBE RUNES CAN BE DEFENSIVE OR OFFENSIVE. MAINTAINS BATTLEFIELD TOOLS. REPAIRS RUNE TECH MID CONFLICT AND DEVELOPS CREATIVE SOLUTIONS UNDER PRESSURE.

### Scouting Rogue
QUICK. AGILE AND SILENT. THEIR OBJECTIVE IS TO SNEAK AHEAD OF THE UNIT TO ASSESS THREATS. ENEMY POSITIONS. AND INCOMING DANGERS WITHOUT EVER BEING SEEN.

### Healer
FIELD MENDER ON THE FRONTLINE. PROVIDES ON-THE-GO HEALING TO ALLOW MEMBERS TO QUICKLY REJOIN THE FIGHT.

### Marksman
PHENOMENAL SIGHT AND TRUE AIM. OCCUPIES A HIGH VANTAGE POINT TO ELIMINATE DISTANT THREATS AND PROVIDE COVERAGE FOR SCOUTING MISSIONS WITH DEADLY ACCURACY.

### Ground-Combatant
CLOSE-QUARTERS WARRIORS WHO EXCEL IN HAND-TO-HAND COMBAT AND BREAKING DEFENSIVE LINES. POSSESSES A STRONG NATURAL RESISTANCE TO PERSUASIVE POWERS.

### Kinetics
DEVASTATINGLY POWERFUL MAGIC WIELDERS. SHIELD THE GROUND UNIT FROM ENEMY ASSAULTS AND RANGED ATTACKS. WHILE THE CHIVALRY LEAD THE ATTACK FROM THE SKIES. KINETICS ENSURE THE LINE IS HELD AND THE TEAM IS DEFENDED.

### Persuasives
EXPERTS IN MIND WORK. PSYCHOLOGICAL WARFARE AND INTERROGATION.

## Aerial Unit(Chivalry):

### Ellian Knights:
LEAD THE ASSAULT FROM THE SKIES. BOUND TO A FLYING MAGICAL CREATURE BY WHICH THEY ARE EACH GIFTED AN ARCANE GLYPH. PROVIDING AN ENHANCED MAGIC TO AID THEIR OFFENSIVE.

# PROLOGUE

A blur of gold whirls for my face, punching through my translucent strands as I narrowly dodge the package chucked at me by a frantic Carrier-Drake. I might pity the poor Drake, if I had any fucks left to give. I unravel the folded parchment to reveal my new uniform. *They're cutting it awfully close.*

The door exhales a creaking complaint as I enter one last time to slap on my new outfit. My nostrils flare. Gloom hangs heavy in the air as the memories I've tried to repress creep up the walls like haunted vines, gouging out to drag me into their clutches. I imagine another layer of frost sprawling up along my ribs as I slip into my new leathers. The door slams shut behind me, locking away those pesky emotions and serrated memories—beyond the broken mosaic window in my mind. Now looking the part, I tread steadfast towards my future with a resolve sharp enough to make even marble flinch and shadows kneel.

Eyes wide, I drink in the gleaming white and gold rotunda, its peaking spires carving into the hill before me: Gildorea Universitás. The war university of Cascara. The only place to be formally trained to join the elite front, keeping our civilian population safe from the corruption of the Wuvon threatening to devour us all.

An exasperated sigh mashes my lungs. *Stars above…* Already, I've stopped on three separate occasions just to dust myself off. Kicked-up soil. Breezing pollination. Each determined to cling to me like a useless, spellbound lover. *What fucking genius chose white aerial leathers for a Celestials be dimmed war university?*

I grind my molars, begrudging how impossible it'll be to keep these things clean, even with water magic. I give it two whole days before I'm scrubbing my fingers raw, prying splattered blood from the seams. Maybe I'll ploy a Runic Engineer into etching me a clever rune for spotless enchantment. The Fates know these leathers won't survive me otherwise.

My muttered curses echo through the palatial Grand Conservatory as I fidget defiantly with my attire, struggling to break in the new material. Wiggling, twisting, tugging—grief needling just beneath the surface of my skin, making everything uncomfortably tight. I meld my trauma into a more familiar temper: rage. Yet each chafe kindles my fury, sparks licking up the edges of my composure, threatening to incinerate my icy demeanor.

I clench my fist, trapping the shiver that dares slither down my spine as I walk through the arched doors of the Gilded Amphitheater. My shattered soul—still too raw and frozen to weave back together—bristles on my skin like armor. Sharp. Jagged. Slicing into anyone who gets too close.

The grand lecture hall is silent as I arrive early to claim the best seat. I'm not here to make friends. I'm not here to impress anyone. I'm here for me, holding on to the only tether I have left: my goal of becoming an Ellian Knight.

A twitch tugs at my lower lip as I leer down at my armor. Pristine, gold-laced. Too perfect. My unique form, especially in this drag, appearing more like a statue—a decoration at home among these ornate walls—rather than a Fae of blood and bone. My golden-olive skin is the only hue preventing me from blending into the alabaster façade entirely.

Each footstep resonates across the sea of white marble, which splashes up the walls. Geometric details glint back at me, mirroring the markings on my flesh: two golden bands spill down the back of my neck, cascading over my shoulders. They nearly kiss above my heart before streaming down my center, bowing out to meet the flare of my hips, feathering into gilded wings.

No one has ever been known to carry gold woven into their skin, forever branding me as different, curseborne. Yet they never cease to glitter and gleam, forever mocking the darkness pooling inside me from all the suffering they've wrought.

I tilt my head up, drinking in the lavish decor gleaming with Celestial worship. My long hair waterfalls with the movement, translucent strands snatching every color, spooling like liquid crystal.

I'm not the only Elarian who has white hair. But I am unique: I was not born this way, a fact betrayed by my dark brows and eyelashes. The rumor in my village was that the fear of whatever killed my parents turned my hair wraith-white. Typically, pale starlight hair belongs to Arabellians, Elarians thought to descend from the very Celestials who created our world. While mine… mine is nothing more than pastel ruin, the ghostly echoes of rainbows once bright with hope.

And me? I'm an orphan with no history, only the story I've carved out of this world for myself with nothing but my own blood and grit. Yet I'm finally here, taking a breath for what feels like the first time since that wretched day.

The edges of my skin bristle, freezing me in place. I know exactly who stalks the shadows. His gaze gnawing at my nerves like a starving beast, waiting for my guard to drop so he can devour me whole. I roll my shoulder, slipping off his grating presence along the ice of my hollow core.

I flit down the steps with deadly grace, mind swirling with memories of the three trials I clawed my way through to stand here. The sacrifices etched into my bones. The loss echoing in the silent screams of my marrow. All of which is now comfortably numb.

My bottom sinks into a golden velvet seat, center row with a prized view of the stage below. I inhale the air thick with the weight of all those who have sat before me: warriors of the Golden Legion, molded in magic, cast in strategy, forged for war. Here, all my abilities will be honed into the ultimate weapon.

But becoming an ensign here requires more than just magical prowess. All the Fae species of Cascara have varying abilities to practice magic. It's strongest in the great bloodlines, the pairings of Fae with powerful magic that complement one another. Some civilians even believe them to be divine, like the Arabellians. But I know better. It's simply breeding for genetic selection. The same logic farmers use to create hardier stock for the unforgiving mountains of the Highlands.

Today is the magical entrance exam. My worth dissected down to a score. The moment that determines the threaded path I'll be spun upon. There are eleven different tracks, but you can only be selected for one: Healing, Ground-Combatant, Savant, Persuasive, Spycraft, Runic Engineer, Kinetic, Scouting Rogue, Marksman, and the Ellian Knights—the masters of all, blessed with a sacred bond—taking flight to the skies.

# CHAPTER 1

I am considered a curse upon Estrella. As the barmaid so kindly reminds me. Her fist tangling in my hair, ripping at my scalp as she plucks my unwelcome body from the shadows beneath the table.

*Bitch.*

I *had* been quietly minding my own business, scrounging for crumbs. Broken, forgotten bits, just like me. But if she wants to make a scene, I'll indulge her.

A feral growl escapes my mouth as I feast on the pain needling my skull, mincing deeper as I thrash like an animal swallowed alive. I buck wildly, gouging my claws up into her skin where she twists my hair tighter. My roar falters into a whimper, a searing kick to my ribs smoldering my flames, her only pause as she rakes me along the ale-sodden floor.

"Sneak into my bar again, and I'll have my husband whip you like the dog you are," the barmaid threatens. Her dark hair curling like snakes around her bosom as she tosses me into the darkness. I contemplate biting into her plump, overfed hand, wishing it could fill my empty belly. As though I truly am one of the animals I prefer over the wretched citizens of this town.

She turns, slamming the door, while muttering something under her breath about how she's certain my curseborne presence will spoil all their ale.

I crumble to the frozen ground, alone once more. My dark brows pinch above gold-flecked cheeks twisted into a sneer. My loathing spearing into the gold woven through my skin. Mocking me as it glitters through peeking holes of my tattered clothing. The gleaming bands lining my body are easy to hide, but the tiny golden squares on my face, just below my lower lashes, are ever-present. Aligning perfectly with my obsidian irises, shimmering like midnight pools eddying with gilded waves. I've never minded my black and aurelian eyes. They serve as a warning of the darkness lurking beneath.

The unimaginative residents here believe my gold brands me as a jinx, misfortune unfurling in my wake like a malignant mist of chaos. I wish they were right. Instead, my bad luck clings to me like a jealous lover, unwilling to share her affection.

The villagers need someone to blame for their miserable existence, and unfortunately for me, *I'm the fucking one*. I stand out. I'm different, painting me an easy scapegoat for town woes. It's clear to everyone I don't belong here—even me.

Yet here I am, trapped with these wretched fuckers. In a crater carved from the earth by a falling star's last breath. An ancient prison, pinned in by the unforgiving peaks of Eldoria.

Estrella. *What a pretty name for a shitty fucking place.*

I scrape the ground, gathering the remnants of my mettle, snapping each vertebra upright as I bolt into familiar shadows. Yet my darkening thoughts dig in, dragging me back to the first memories I possess.

I was three years old when the town elders found me and plopped me on the stoop of a wooden shack, a typical abode for this abysmal village. Yet there was something particularly haunting about the way the weathered timber wailed in the wind. A warning of what lurked inside: a morbid fate gleaned to swiftly sever my curseborne existence.

My innocent tears were greeted by a string of curses lashed into me from my venomous foster parents. I'll never forget the way his soulless eyes scraped over my flesh with disdain.

"Fucking curseborne! Don't you fucking look at me with those demon eyes," he seethed as he dragged me to a dark corner. His words festered in my young, squishy heart. Spreading like rot.

In that somber crook he left me in, the twisting shadows welcomed me with open arms, curling around me as though I was theirs to hold. They taught me how to become as cold as the darkness that cloaked me, heart barely beating, lungs breathless. Hidden. Out of sight, out of mind.

Now, I use them to travel unseen, threading in and out of shadows cast by rickety buildings and windswept merchant stands. I scavenge what I can to survive, piecing together scraps. Just like I piece together my soul after my foster father's done with me.

I am a fucking mosaic mess of sharp edges.

A feral Faeling with nothing to lose, not even my dignity, clinging to the foolish notion that one day, I'll escape this icy cage.

My only escape, my only reprieve, is the uncorrupt patches of Mysticwoods nestled around our town: my sacred refuge. The creatures who inhabit the magical forest are the only kindness I've ever known. Perhaps that's why I've grown to act more like a beast than a Fae child.

I needle through the shadows, making my way to the violet sanctuary of the Mysticwoods. I often spend my nights among their twisted limbs, sleeping below a forever lavender and indigo orchid canopy. Despite the beautiful view, the bitter frost slices through me, carving me out hollow, too numb to feel the echoes of his torture on my skin.

The icy cold is my kindred.

Locking my heart away in her glacial palace, ensuring my foster father can never fully break me. Oh, but how he endeavors, ripping me to ribbons like a monster spawned from the corrupted Blackwood. He has cultivated an endless abyss of darkness within me, twisting me in unnatural ways.

I often wonder how my golden markings still gleam, when he has stolen all my fucking light. Leaving me with nothing but feral rage. Layers and layers of rage. Bristling on my skin like invisible dragon scales.

*If only they were real.* This thought curls the shadows of the snowy street around me, tightly, as if to shield me.

Their darkness suits me. Their darkness becomes me.

I now know, the elders left me to those monsters in the hopes their demons would consume me. And oh, how they did. Just not in the way those old fuckers hoped.

A wicked smile kicks up on my lip. It's been five years since that day. Five years of stumbling to grasp my Shadowblending ability, befriending the darkness they sought to ruin me with.

The shadows are now my home. My solace. My only embrace.

A pit groans in my stomach, gnawing hunger reminding me of my failed attempt to scavenge dinner. I curse my iridescent white hair for giving me away to the barmaid. My Shadowblending has improved over the last five years, but I let my overzealous hunger get the best of me, moving when I should have been still.

Food is a scarcity, a luxury, and one of the most pressing problems of being a feral Faeling in the unforgiving ice tundra of the Highlands. In the warmer months, I can at least forage the Mysticwoods for gorgon nuts, atria berries, crunch plumes… Emberhell, right now I'd even settle for the mind-bending neon green mushrooms I ate once that made the world fold in on itself.

My exasperated sigh blooms a cloud of white plumes into the frigid air. Tonight, I'm shit out of luck. It's the dead of winter, and I minced my only chance at a bite to eat. I tuck my tail like a feral pup, shame and exhaustion hanging heavy on my face as I retreat into the beckoning shadows.

I'm almost at the edge of town when something snags my eye. My stomach churns, leering at a waste bin tipping in the whipping wind. My sickening reality gutting me while hunger whittles my bones.

My eyes widen on a moldy loaf of bread beside the bin, glowing in the light of the blacksmith's forge. *Thank the fucking Celestials.* My stomach badgers me forward, growling like a wolf, drool pooling in my mouth despite the green and grey fungus desiccating my find.

Hunger devours my typically calculated stealth. I lurch forward, snatching my lucky break. The fuzzy, rotten loaf is almost to my mouth when a large shadow swells before me. My gaze rolls up to the giant, towering grizzly bear figure, looming menacingly above me. I topple backwards, trembling, the feral need for food overtaken by self-preservation. Frantically, I claw for the embrace of darkness to hide me once more.

*What the actual fuck is a bear doing in the middle of town?*

Instead of a roar punching through my eardrums, a male voice rumbles—gravelly, but warm, like it's been slicked in summer honey.

"Come, sit here by the furnace, little one." Cascading moonbeams spill over him, revealing his almost seven-foot-tall frame. *No wonder I mistook him for a bear.* His voice tumbles from the depths of a dark beard. The comforting tone scrapes along my icy skin, his kind words more menacing than a hand raised to strike me.

"I have an extra bowl of stew to share. By the looks of you…" He pauses, stepping further into the light, his warm honey eyes sweeping over my emaciated form. "You'll need the extra meat on those bones to survive this winter."

There's a gentleness laced between each of his words, but habit curls my lip into a snarl—a conditioned response to being noticed at all. I've grown quite attached to my well-made mask, one fitting of the feral dog the town folk see me as. A carefully crafted façade, tucking the real me away in the shadows, deep within my layered darkness. Guarding what little I have left from this cruel world.

My mind's a muddled mess trying to unravel his kind words. *Why is this male willing to offer me help?* I've survived this long without so much as even a smile tossed my way. My scrutinizing gaze reluctantly narrows on him, studying his upturned mouth, the subtle wrinkles extending to his eyes. I have a knack for reading others, sometimes even *feeling* intense emotions bleed through me, as if they are my own. Perhaps because I'm so hollow, locking up my own feelings deep within the darkness, out of sight, out of mind. Their absence leaving space for others' to seep in.

I assess his full face. A scar cuts across one side of his features, disappearing beneath the angular beard hugging his jaw. His warm brown hair is tied back in a loose bun at the nape of his neck. He holds a bowl of soup in one hand, attached to an arm as wide as me. Although with my gaunt form, that's not really saying much.

His words appear genuine, matching his at-ease posture. There's a soothing feeling rolling off him that I can't quite place. It pools around me, beckoning me, making me all too reluctant to trust his oddly inviting presence.

I crouch on my hands and feet, a stray mutt ready to dart, when a glimmer in his honeyed irises pulls me back. Hesitantly, I prowl a step forward. Beneath their warmth hides a subtle pain. An unspoken history flickering, one that has him seeing the little child veiled behind all the icy walls of my feral exterior.

Patiently, he leans against the wall, as if he already knows my decision and he's merely waiting for me to catch up. It makes the silence… comfortable. I swirl my tongue along my teeth, tasting the odd notion of being seen as a child for the first time instead of the town mutt they've convinced me I am. It tastes foreign, almost challenging, but lacking any bitter undertones, like when I've eaten something poisonous.

Silently, I nod, tugging my patchwork cloak over my head, ensuring my markings remain hidden so he won't rescind his compassion. Because the only way this foolish fucking giant would offer me any kindness is if he's new to town, unaware of the curses marring my skin.

Or maybe he's poisoned the fucking soup, determined to finally free this shit village of me. That's just as well; the few dead bodies I've glimpsed always looked somewhat peaceful. Though, based on the luck I've had, I'd surely end up in Emberhell. *At least I'd be warmer there.*

Another wave of warm reassurance rolls off the towering bear of a male. My gut twists with hunger, but there's another feeling there, spurring me to give him a whisper of trust.

He turns away from me, waving a silent hand to follow.

I sway as I stand, shadowing him into the unfamiliar warmth and light of his forge.

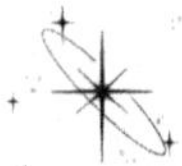

WINTER MONTHS BLOOM INTO SPRING, and a friendship grows between us, blossoming into something I struggle to comprehend. I split my days between climbing the untamed limbs of the enchanted Mysticwoods and watching the blacksmith at his craft.

I become his shadow, hovering in the cracks of his towering frame, obsessed with memorizing how he works metal into creations of beauty and power. My hungry belly particularly relishes his daily mistakes of making too much food, always having some to share. I enjoy his quiet nature; raising myself left me rather lacking in proper social etiquette. There's a silent understanding within our conversations of scarce words and nods. Although we have yet to formally exchange names, from eaves-dropping on conversations with his customers, I deduce the blacksmith's name is Sully.

He's a thoughtful male, always kind and courteous to his customers, who come from all walks of life. The way he treats me—compared to the rest of this shit village—still minces my mind into a slurry mess. To believe I am worthy of kindness and not just a feral dog casting curses in my wake… Well, that… is an entirely new reality. One I refuse to let settle into my marrow just yet. Or maybe ever.

As I'm finishing my stew of mooca beef, fire roots, and red tubers, I watch Sully pull out a small bar of metal. Confusion contorts my face; it's unusual to start a new project this late in the evening.

"Come here, little dragon. Let's see what you can make with all the fury and fire I know hides within you," he says softly. His voice is woven with a subtle hope while his eyes blaze with pride, ruffling my imaginary dragon scales of rage.

I take the cold steel in my hand, watching it glimmer in the dancing flames of the forge. A funny feeling tugs at the corners of my lips, contorting them upward, as a flash of all the things this steel can become pours through my mind. I smile, a genuine smile that reaches my eyes, allowing myself only a moment of the foreign sensation before resuming my well-worn scowl.

Sully sits patiently with me as I fumble through the basics of his trade. He's made it look so easy, yet my scraggly muscles burn, quickly comprehending the strength of his build.

In all the times I've witnessed him work, he's never forced the metal against its will. Instead, I've watched in awe as he whispers to the glowing steel with each strike, shaping it, molding it, blending the atoms into shapes that sing to him.

The same grace does not come naturally to me as I attempt to beat the metal into submission with my frustration. My muscles beg me to cease lifting the hammer, yet I do not relent.

Instead, I repeat the mantra I've branded into myself. *Mind over matter.* A trick shared with me by a creature known as a Mistling, whom I'd met once in the Mysticwoods. It's a secret she whispered to me when I asked how she shifts from her small faerie form into pure mist. Her words resonated with me, guiding me in the darkest of times when I was certain my foster father would break me. The kindness of the creatures of the Mysticwoods had been my only reprieve, my only guidance. Until I met Sully.

My frail body may falter bending the metal, but I can still bend my body to my will, refusing to yield. The iron hisses in protest, another burn from my impatient nature, but I hiss right back. Matching its fury. Refusing to surrender.

"Fucking Emberhell," I curse, licking my wounds like a winged wolf of the Mysticwoods before continuing my work. I catch Sully nodding off to the steady beat of the metal as I continue my endeavor.

Manically, I cackle at my pain, as if I'm laughing at the Fates themselves. At last, I hammer the steel into a thin triangular blade. Instead of a traditional hilt, I use a mold for a circular tool loop, smelting it to the dagger. Shaped to hide within my palm. Perfect for sneaking up behind someone or anchoring myself as I fall from a branch.

The untraditional blade fitting my untraditional nature. A story born between us, small, sharp, and hidden.

The sun's rays curl like fingers over the Eldoria Mountains, grasping the snowy peaks before hoisting itself up into the sky. Light glistens down on my hands, revealing dripping blood from pushing my body beyond its natural limits. The blade now shimmers with a crimson hue from the blood forged into its creation.

A grumble rumbles from my left as the burly male rises with a yawn, a grizzly bear waking from hibernation. Bones creak beneath heavy muscles, born of battle scars and hard labor, in a lengthy stretch.

He meanders to my side, and I catch the prideful grin from the corner of my eye as he murmurs, voice heavy with sleep.

"A dragon fang." He pauses with a hearty chuckle. "Well-suited for the spirit of a fierce little dragon." His smile falls into a frown seeing the state of my marred hands. "Now it's time to rest, little one. Even dragons must know their limits."

Only I don't want to be pulled from the trance I've lulled myself into, rejoicing in the simple focus of sharpening the blade to perfection. This is the first time I have experienced pride. And the confidence that comes with creation.

I snap without thinking, as if I truly am a dragon, "I cannot rest until it's finished. It must be perfect."

His eyes grow wide, mouth slightly agape in his lengthy beard. A roaring chuckle cleaves the silence. A big barrel laugh, joining the fire in warming the air. He tilts his head with a soft smile, nudging my foot off the wheel of the grinding stone and gently taking my wrist.

I flinch at the touch of another, trembling until he quickly releases his grip. The blade tumbles from my hand with a *clank* as I stare at my wrist. Confusion brewing as I study the echo of his grasp, bracing for the familiar bite of pain.

Yet the pain doesn't come.

My mind minces, caught between disbelief and silence of my surely broken nerves. For a long moment, I wait. Rigid. Untrusting. Until my muscles finally unspool. I chance a glance up at the bear before me. The warm honey of his gaze seeps deeper than the fire at our side, thawing my frosted bones as I accept the impossible truth: there will be no pain.

Hesitantly, I nod, spreading a smile across Sully's face. I shift my weight, unsettled by the strange sensation gnawing at the glacial palace of my icy heart.

The village begins humming with waking activities. Doors groaning, mud sucking at boots. My gaze drops to the blade on the anvil. I could take it. But it's his metal, his forge. I decided it's not worth the risk. It's better to never have it at all than to have something worth losing.

A gasp rips my attention to the female freezing mid-step beside Sully's open-air forge, her face twisted in horror.

"Curseborne!"

Her words lash into me, casting my gaze down. My eyes widen in terror at my exposed skin, unaware I'd shed my cloak and scarf in the heat of the forge. I dart for my clothes, scrambling them on as I lunge for my home amongst the shadows, safely out of sight.

Sully's words call out behind me, musing along the wind.

"Be back tomorrow for your next lesson, little dragon."

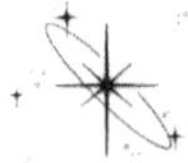

WEEKS SLIP by in the glow of the forge. Under Sully's guidance, I learn not only how to craft different blades and tools, but the secrets of fusing them with magic: gems, runes, enchantments, and rare components from the natural world that create unique powers.

One might add firelight glow to create a blade that hums with electricity, sharpening itself with each cut. Another option is the down feather of a phoenix to ignite a blade in flames. My favorite is imbuing different poisons, requiring only a single cut for devastating effects.

Fae travel great lengths to obtain a weapon from Sully, as it takes years to gather the right ingredients. His customers are among the very few visitors that risk the dangerous, remote path to our hidden village, besides the traders and the queen's tax enforcers.

Our shit town is unsurprisingly poor. Thanks to the rising taxes each year and our short growing season, leaving folk to scrape by on inflated goods. The village doesn't have much going for it, other than the ancient patches of uncorrupted Mysticwoods and the beautiful prison bars of the Eldoria Mountains. Their icy peaks severing us from the rest of Cascara, sparing us from the Blackwood's slithering corruption and the monsters who feast beneath its black branches and crimson canopy.

After showing up to work too many times with my face swollen and contorted beneath mottled bruises—reminders of my failed efforts avoiding my foster home—Sully makes me an offer.

"How does becoming my full-time apprentice sound? I even have a spare room. It's tiny, but it'll fit a small bed, where you can stay, if you so choose."

My eyes widen in disbelief. I blink. Certain I've misheard. Maybe I'm imagining things. After all, last night's blow from my foster father fractured more than just a few bones in my face as the world went out around me.

A grizzly chuckle warms the air, rattling me with a gentle comfort. An odd sensation of almost feeling safe wriggles in between the crevices of my icy heart. I roll my right shoulder, casting off the emotion of the impossible thought. My natural reflex to rid myself of feelings that don't quite fit within my understanding of the world.

Sully tips his head with a sly look, adding, "My only condition, little dragon: no burning down the house with your fierce flames."

That seems like an easy enough promise to keep. A smile tugs at my lips, the muscles sore from disuse. I nod slowly, grappling with a strangeness bubbling in my chest. Perhaps this is what hope feels like.

He chuckles again. "Well, it's settled then. Tomorrow, I want you up extra early, because I'm finally going to teach you how to use all these blades you've created." Then Sully straightens, his posture somber. He adds in a serious tone I've yet to hear from the kind bear, "And when we're through, no one will ever be able to turn you black and blue again. I promise you that."

I tense slightly at the tone of his last words before letting them sink in. There's a power to them. And I believe him. A warm silence lingers between us before he asks softly, almost as if he's asking me to reveal a secret, "What is your true name, little dragon? The one your parents gifted to you, when you were starborne into this world."

My gaze meets his, the embers from the forge flickering amongst twinkling gold in my obsidian eyes. I whisper, as a subtle power simmers in my veins, guarding the only thing that is truly mine in this world.

"Savaé."

# CHAPTER 2

A knock rattles the thin door to my tiny room. It's been several years since I moved in with Sully, but he still insists on waking me at the crack of dawn for training.

"Can't you let me sleep in for one cursed day?" I groan, dragging the pillow over my head.

"I'll let you sleep in when you can beat me in sparring," he teases, opening the door. Which I promptly blow shut with air magic, using manipulation magic to twist the lock into place.

"Alright, alright. I'm up," I grouse.

It turns out the quiet, burly blacksmith of our hidden village was an Ellian Knight before being granted his request for early retirement.

So, naturally, our schedule is a bloody military routine. Mornings consist of hand-to-hand combat followed by physics. And if working at the forge wasn't sweaty enough, it's now accompanied by a grilling on battle strategy and tactics. Weekends serve no reprieve—covering the art of healing, review of magical creatures, and training courses to hone my agility and coordination. Even when we hunt, he has me reviewing monsters that lurk in the corrupted Blackwood, along with their weaknesses.

Yet I wouldn't change my time with Sully for anything in the world. He's planted my withered shell of a body in warmth, cultivating me with unconditional love, patience, and safety—all while letting me be unapologetically me. My body has transformed from that of a feral, starving creature to a weapon to be wielded. He's sharpened my confidence while also softening me, bit by tiny bit, over the years with his honey-laden kindness. He has grown and nurtured light in the endless abyss of my darkness. Coaxing nebula orchids to bloom under rays of pastel starlight.

As we jog to the clearing before the Mysticwoods for sparring, he harps on his favorite topic: the balance of magic. The guiding force of the magical world. The more powerful the magical item you seek, the more difficult it is to obtain.

"You never take from nature without consent, for then you tread the path of the Wuvon."

The Wuvon are Fae corrupted by the same dark source mutating the Mysticwoods into the infectious Blackwood. Black and crimson vines mar their skin, branding their use of black magic: the forbidden art of grinding up pieces of magical creatures and beings without their consent.

Power corrupts them, driving a hunger to consume any wild magic for their gain. Their bloodshed mirrored in their garnet eyes as they cast, controlling Blackwood and the monsters lurking within. To escape, countless creatures evolved wings, fleeing the spreading plague of Blackwood—rot and nightmares devouring the whimsical lands of Cascara. Our greatest defense is the Golden Legion and their heroic Ellian Knights, working endlessly to keep the blight at bay.

I plummet from my thoughts, the world tilting off axis from the force sweeping against my ankles, knocking me on my face with a perturbed gasp.

"You need to be aware of your surroundings always, little dragon." Sully laughs, bending down to give me a hand up.

"Cheater!" I snarl, grabbing his arm, levering my weight to pull him off balance as I spring up, landing a cheeky sucker punch into his ribs.

"Good," he wheezes. "You need to expect the unexpected. Life doesn't play by the rules." He feigns catching his breath, only to throw a sly swing at me as he whirls around.

I block, my forearms groaning under the impact as I attempt to dodge his next blow. But I'm too slow. Searing pain erupts across my abdomen, a knee smashing into my stomach. Nausea and hot bile claw up my throat—I'm not entirely sure my guts aren't lodged up right alongside them—as I stumble back, desperate to create distance and catch my breath.

"Get your mental shields back up, block out the pain, focus your air magic around your muscles to make your movements quicker. It's the only way you will outmaneuver my brute strength," he commands. Ever the strategist and always annoyingly fucking *right*.

The golden light shields rise, casting a protective dome over my mind. Locking my emotions on the outside, sealed behind a mosaic-star window. A numbness I know all too well seeps out between my ribs from my glacial heart palace. Frost permeating deep into the crevices of my marrow, leaving nothing but jagged ice. My mind clears as the chaos of feelings become distant echoes beneath an icy tundra of quiet, cold, sharp precision. Turns out…

Shattered ice bites just as deep as steel.

First, I heed Sully's advice, bending air to quicken my strikes, which fails to yield the desired result. Failure will not best me, for I am her tamer, her master. All my past defeats and victories whip into a mental blizzard, crystalline structures of angling strategies. A frozen scheme unfolds, which I pluck from my mind, brandishing it like a dagger in my palm.

Air magic whirls through me, wielding me like a jagged icicle, whipping along a frozen gale. Each strike is more precise than the last. Swifter. Brisker. Until I'm no more than a frenzied fury of striking gusts, pummeling muscle before landing a lashing uppercut.

Sully staggers back, panting, but not before flicking a powerful wall of fire right at me. The clever fiend uses my choice of elemental magic against me. The air billowing around me rapidly stokes his honey-colored flames into a roaring blaze, Emberhell-bent on devouring my flesh like kindling to a dry season wildfire.

"You're an ass," I growl through gritted teeth as I utterly drench myself in water magic, just barely avoiding crisping into a molten, roasted mellow. Which is great, since I'm sure I'd make a mockery of the delicious campfire treat; instead of gooey insides melting into sweetness, my bitter, sticky mess of broken bits would mince your tongue and cut you apart from the inside out. I am not made to be savored.

"Again." Sully's words lash me from my spiraling metaphors. "Until you learn to expect the unexpected." His words, the order of a commanding warrior. *So much for his early retirement.* He's ceaselessly persistent when it comes to our lessons. Likely because my stubborn nature often leaves me learning the hard way.

After slipping on conjured ice and tripping over the ground he breaks beneath my feet, anger simmers along my golden mental shields, threatening to liquify them into a molten muss. I let the strategic mind blizzard free once more, the pattern to his movements forming a crystalline map, allowing me to predict his next use of magic.

The way he's twisting his fingers tells me a slew of ice daggers are going to be slashing my way. Flames lick up my body, forming a physical shield, melting his ice as I lunge right, faking him out with a punch I never intend to land. My flame shields vanish, switching to water, pooling at his feet before freezing into perfectly slick black ice.

He slips, adjusting his still-moving body further to dodge my mock punch, sending him perfectly spiraling onto his ass. A smug smirk hooks up at the corner of my mouth, proud of my victory as I watch him wobble, trying to stand up before melting the ice with honey flames, but the sound of rustling leaves nicks my attention.

"Like I said, you're an ass." I swing my small crossbow off my back before I load a bolt. I cast two simple illusions of wooden objects landing in front of a fleeing pheasant. His long tail feathers twirl like purple ribbons as he changes directions, allowing me to land a devastating crossbolt through his heart. I pull the arrow from our dinner, grasping it by the feet.

Sully chuckles, dusting himself off. "You're a natural with your elemental magic! Even the way you used your minor magic to distract the pheasant was instinctual, demonstrating your close connection with the power welling inside of you. I can't wait to see what you do when you come into your Celestial Gift."

My shoulders stiffen. I'd come into my elemental magic quite young. All Elarian Fae have access to elemental and minor magic for the mental manip-ulation of objects, simple illusions, and Sangre healing powers. We also have innately superior sight, smell, strength, and speed. However, all Fae receive the blessing of a Celestial Gift, a magic unique to them. The strength varies, from the ability to see in the dark to being able to wield plasma, the very energy of the sun.

I sigh, releasing the tension between my shoulder blades. My Celestial Gift will come to me, eventually. Late is better than never.

"Race you back to the forge, big bear!" I shout over my shoulder with a head start, changing the subject. I utterly loathe things I have no control over, and manifesting my Celestial Gift is out of my hands. Fucking Celestials Blessings and all that—maybe curseborne don't get gifts. I shake my head and pick up the pace, adrenaline melting my irrational worries away.

Sully curses under his breath as he lumbers after me.

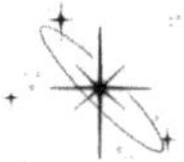

THE SUN IS ALREADY NESTING WELL past the horizon as we sit by the embers of the dwindling forge, enjoying roasted pheasant. Yet there is an unspoken weight in my chest, building up like tumbling boulder trolls. A dream I've hoarded away like a dragon, in fear Sully may reject the notion, given his resolute refusal to speak about his time in the Golden Legion.

Between bites, I muster my dragon courage, spewing words out like vomiting flames. "I want to go to Gildorea Universitás of War. And be an Ellian Knight like you."

Sully sits in silence, hard lines rolling through his jaw as his brow twists into knots with an almost… sadness.

"It's not everything it appears to be, little dragon."

"How can you say that, when it's made you everything you are? Everything you've trained me to be?" I snap. *Maybe his term of endearment is giving me an actual dragon-complex at this point.*

His eyes drop, shadowed in thought. Then he mutters in a whisper of admittance, "Pure opulence draped in claims of protecting the land with profound righteousness. Their obsession with power and bloodlines… but with many things that gleam too flawlessly on the outside, there is well-hidden rot festering within."

"Well, that's some cryptic Ritherin-shit," I mutter under my breath. The Ellian Knights of the Golden Legion protect Cascara. I mow his words over like a mooca grinding up grass. They don't make sense within the confines of everything he's taught me. They are the good guys, fighting the Wuvon and the monsters in the corrupted Blackwood. Obviously, they're not infallible. I'm not so naïve as to think no corruption lies within their ranks. But his words suggest something more profound than that.

He continues gazing at the embers, his beard moving in a way that tells me he is clenching his jaw. A clear signal this topic is not up for further discussion. He never likes speaking about his time as an Ellian Knight, beyond the core subjects he educates me on. Whenever I ask, I can feel the pain needling his features, hidden memories bristling to the surface. I have my suspicions as to why.

As an Ellian Knight, he would have been bonded to a magical flying creature for battle, yet he does not have one. He's on the younger side to be retired from the Golden Legion, which can only mean one thing: his bonded creature must have died. It's no doubt the reason he keeps the memories of his time in the Golden Legion locked away—a loss one can never truly recover from.

"One day, I would like to hear the story of the magical flying creature you were bonded with."

Sully shifts his elbows onto his knees, clasping his hands. He seems to hesitate, but then his lips twitch into a subtle smile.

"His name was Xeno. He was a great winged badger." A sense of peace seems to cascade over Sully as he thinks back on his companion before he continues, "The Arcane Glyph of our bond increased my physical strength, especially when it came to manipulating the earth." He pauses, the smile evaporating as he clenches his hands tighter, silver welling in his eyes. "He died saving my life in the battle against a shadow Wuvon and his Crowven at the stronghold of Sternma."

Only top-ranking Wuvon fly on Crowven. They're giant crows, the flesh rotted away on their head, leaving a bare skull with an obsidian beak. It's said to be sharp enough to pierce anything. Even dragon scale.

I reach out without hesitation, holding the back of his hand. Sully knows how hard touching another person has been for me. He knows how meaningful the gesture is. I have gotten better over the years, but let's just say I'm still not the touchy-feely type.

We sit together in silence until I attempt to unravel it, asking him to recount his favorite memories of Xeno. I listen quietly, allowing my friend to lose himself in the past. Little does he know that their stories only solidify the choice he so desperately wants me to reverse.

I want to be an Ellian Knight. Just like him.

He saved me. Who knows, maybe I could save someone too. Or at least protect other younglings from losing their families.

A sly smile creeps up my lips as I think about how his great winged badger reflects the best of Sully. Strong, stubborn, grounded, patient. Painted in a slew of colors, but only if you look closely, and a downright savage fighter. I wish I could have seen them together.

There's clearly a hole left in his soul without him in his life. A cold washes over me, like melancholy snowflakes sneaking down the gaps of my clothing on a winter day, and for the first time in my short life, I feel true loss through my friend. When Xeno died, a part of him died too.

It turns out my theory is, unfortunately, correct. In the aftermath of Xeno's death, Sully asked for early retirement and hid away in our poor, isolated village, far away from the borderland battles. Far away from other Ellian Knights, leaving it all behind like another life.

Until he met me.

He ruffles up my hair as he says goodnight, a fair price to pay for the hoarded memories he was surprisingly willing to share. It was hard enough nudging Sully to open up just a little about his time as an Ellian Knight. I can't imagine it coming up again.

As I am falling asleep, the floorboards creak. I keep my eyes shut as I recognize the sturdy sound of his gait.

Sully comes in, pulling up the blanket, thinking I'm slumbering. He gives me a soft, fatherly kiss on my head and whispers to himself.

"You are too special for them, for all of them, little Starborne dragon. You deserve more than this world can offer, but I will prepare you the best that I can. I wish I could forever hide you, but I cannot save you from your fate."

His warm voice ebbs away as I'm whisked off to sleep. Despite his words, I feel safe, knowing his training gives me the power to protect myself. Regardless of what the Fates plan to throw my way.

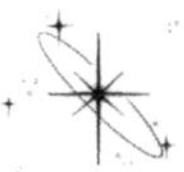

*I'M BACK in that fucking wooden chair again.*

*My child form, sallow with starvation, struggles against the ropes that bind me. The wood creaks beneath my frantic wriggles, groaning like haunting ghosts come to watch the show.*

*A spindly male looms above me, his broken-teeth smile peeking out through long, greasy dark hair. Pain slashes through my skull as I look down from my swollen eye, barely recognizing my body. My shoulder crunches beneath another strike from his fist that glistens garnet, painted in my young blood.*

*His screams, a verbal lashing. "I'll beat those markings from your cursed skin and soulless eyes!"*

*Manic laughter creaks from my ragged throat as something deep inside me shatters, becoming as dark as my obsidian eyes. Yet my markings only grow brighter the more he persists, as if they're cackling with me.*

*In his failure, he slashes on to his next endeavor: attempting to fucking carve the markings right out of my skin, every gleaming line on my body, every golden fleck sprinkled along on my face. When that fails, he resorts to taking long drags off his ope cigar.*

*Between puffs, his smile turns venomous. Carefully and methodically, he burns every inch of the two solid gold bands that draw down from my neck, over my shoulder blades, barely grazing the other as they run down my middle before bowing out to my hips. Then a fit of rage consumes him as my gold endures, mocking him with their gleam as he breaks my bones right along with the chair I am trussed to. Left a tangled mess of a shattered child, bent at unnatural angles.*

*I hack up blood curdling in my lungs like spoiled milk. My body pooling on the floor as I watch with dread. Each* snap. *Each* grind. *Every slithering strand of sinew weaving together. I heal before my very eyes, reliving each horror in reverse as my form threads itself back together. I'm certain my unnatural ability to heal so fucking quickly is a curse. Any other child would have succumbed to death's sweet embrace from these injuries. For too many nights, nights I never want to remember, I begged for death to claim me. But she never showed.*

*I descend into a sickening madness as my golden markings stitch themselves anew out of blood and shredded tissue. A lunacy festered from a beautiful dream I once had. My mother, with gleaming starlight hair cascading over her shoulders, smiles at me as though I am the most precious thing she has ever beheld. Her cupid's-bow lips dance as she tells me about the beautiful gift she is giving me.*

*My eyes widen as all her love and power pours into me, wrapping around me in one golden embrace. Her golden eyes dim, as if she knew she was dying and there was nothing she could do. So, she marked me with all the love she had hoped to give me in an entire lifetime in one single moment. She couldn't change her fate but dreamed with all her heart to change mine.*

*A manic smile curls across my cracked lips. How could anyone who loves me curse me so? Though it fits the twisted games the Fates adore playing, endlessly toying with the balance of magic. My markings being cast with love, only to be the inevitable cause of so much pain, the reason others think*

*I'm unnatural, unlovable. Gilding me as curseborne, but also the very reason I have survived. As if her light weaves me back together each time.*

*I slowly crawl out of the shack, hoping to retreat into the solace of my shadows. Even as a babe, I'd rather shiver to death in the dark than have his twisted hands ensnare me again.*

*The nightmare restarts, just like my days as a child.*

*I am back in that fucking chair. Forced to endure another night, as death is too sweet a relief for me. So, I convince myself to revel in his crushing defeat. He lost. Yet again, he fucking lost. My skin gleams in pure spite of him.*

*I treasure this win, rendering the pain worth it, forging me into something so dark, he can never shatter me completely. Yet my psyche still splinters. Severing—giving me control to break myself apart, allowing my mind to fracture from my body, dissociating.*

*I leave a smile on the husk of my body as his torture begins once more. Taunting him. Letting him know he's lost before he's begun. He taught me how to thrive through physical pain, consuming it whole to feed my feral rage.*

*Even if I'll never know what it is to be truly safe, nurtured, and loved... I sure as fuck know how to endure, how to survive.*

*I raise my mental shields, blocking out the pain with glacial frost. The magical hum of friendly creatures beckons me as I follow my familiar shadows out into the Mysticwoods. Leaving my physical form behind entirely, ensuring he can never wholly shatter my mind as I let my imagination take flight.*

*I become a flying armored bear, then a phoenix, then an iridescent dragon, just like the one I once saw flying through the peaks of Eldoria. Freedom flows through me as I catch an updraft, gliding into buttery clouds, pretending the thundering is from distant lightning instead of my bones breaking once more.*

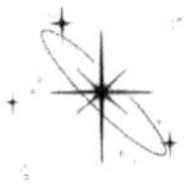

A SCREAM CLAWS its way out my throat, heart bruising itself, thumping against my ribs like a caged bird. I stick like sap to my sweat-drenched cotton sheets, my skin boiling like a hissing kettle. My eyes snap open, latching onto reality as nightmares and memories meld, threatening to drag me back under as their talons sink into my fluffy pink brain, mincing it apart.

I twist my searing flesh into the sheets as my vision comes into focus, revealing white flames slithering up the surrounding walls. I gasp, only to suffocate on clotted smoke. Sully bursts through my door with tidal wave after tidal wave of water until the flames sizzle out.

My eyes grow wide. There's nothing but ash where the wall of our cottage used to stand. I shudder at the devastation of my uncontrolled magic lashing out during my nightmare. My gaze falls on my trembling hands, waiting for Sully to bellow at me to get out.

I broke his promise. I burnt the fucking house down. Part of it anyway.

I am a fucking curse.

A deep laugh rumbles out into the chilly night air of my now open room. I stiffen, gaping up at Sully, sure I've lost my mind.

He drops his large hand to my shoulder and smiles. "That's what I get for letting a dragon sleep under my roof."

A laugh bubbles up in my chest at his silly comment, while tears prickle the back of my eyes at his continued kindness and patience with me.

We move my charred bed to its temporary new home in the living room. Sully brings out a fresh blanket from the closet, tucking me in tight.

I twist and turn restlessly, afraid of falling asleep and burning down the rest of the house. The scratching of a chair has me sitting up as I watch Sully sit beside my bed.

"Let me tell you a tale, little one. The story of the great Eclipse War." He speaks softly, his voice brimming with a dreamlike presence.

"Once upon a time, there were great Celestial bodies who could control matter, creating stars and worlds alike. Our world, Elyndor, was created and ruled by a Celestial named Savorah Arabella. Each of the Celestials governed the worlds they created, controlling the very balance of magic and power. They rode on great Celestial Dragons, beasts bigger than the mountains of Eldoria, allowing them to travel the heavens."

"Is that why those with white hair are called Arabellians?" Sully nods. His sweet smile wraps around my heart like a soothing hug. "What happened to the Celestials?" I murmur, conjuring dreams of Celestial beings riding cosmic dragons, soaring through the stars.

"The moon became ice blue, eclipsed in shadows. Then a darkness followed. Celestials dimmed from the sky, falling with their dragons, their worlds losing their magic along with them. This cataclysmic event is known as the Celestial Dimming."

I attempt to picture a world without magic, shuddering at the possible loss of what links all living creatures, a part of the very life source of their souls. I'd be utterly hollow without it. I wonder if that's what it feels like to be a corrupted monster of the Blackwood.

"What happened to them? The worlds without magic?"

"They became what we now know as humans, those who have lost the ability to wield magic. They look similar to Elarians but are shorter, with round ears, dull-colored eyes and hair, muted senses, and their strength and agility weakened."

I gasp at the thought of transforming into a magicless form. A part of your soul forever lost. I can't begin to fathom their ache of emptiness, how hard life must be for them.

Sully continues, "The change in the moon brought with it monsters of pure pitch. The remaining Celestials were terrified of leaving their worlds without magic. So, they rallied together to fight in the battles of the Eclipse War. It waged for many millennia as more and more planets were lost to the monsters. Meanwhile, on Elyndor, chaos broke out between the warring Fae species vying for power in the absence of Savorah, who had left to fight in the war.

"As the stars aligned, creating a Celestial Convergence, the Celestials hoped this would empower their magic, allowing them to recharge their fallen kin and end the darkness for all. Instead, a great power awoke deep in the darkness: the Voidbringer. This unknown being sucked all the life essence and light out of anything he touched."

"He sounds terrifying. How did Elyndor survive?" I ask, pulling the blanket to my chest, attempting to cast off the chill the name sends shivering down my spine.

"In a desperate attempt to save the worlds they created, the Celestials sacrificed their immortality. Falling down to their planet as their magic rippled out, cloaking their creation in a magical shield. Protecting them from the Voidbringer's touch."

"That's why we say Celestials Blessing! An homage to their sacrifice, their blessing. But wait, what happened to Savorah?"

"She lived a long mortal life. It was said her Celestial presence gleamed through her skin as if woven with the heavenly night sky, marked by the constellations above. Her eyes were said to be made of gold, and her hair shimmered like starlight. Her once mighty Celestial Dragon, guardian of the skies and keeper of ancient magic, fell into a deep slumber as her powers dimmed in the broken bond from her rider. It's believed that the towering mountains that divide the Highlands from the Midlands rest atop her sleeping beast, hence the name Dragon Spine Mountains."

"But the shield must have failed! Parts of our Mysticwoods became corrupted, turning into the Blackwood," I argue with frustration.

"That's a less happy story, little dragon." I cross my arms and huff, waiting for him to continue despite his warning. "Well… after Savorah's sacrifice and ascension, she united the world, bringing a prosperous time of peace. Then, a thousand years after the Eclipse War—1000 AE, After Eclipse—it's believed the Voidbringer found a brief crack in Elyndor's protection. Just enough for a single drop of blood to land on the surface before sealing back up. No one knows what caused that brief moment of shield weakness, but that's all it took. Corruption propagated in the soil; political unrest spread across the world. Parts of the Mysticwoods became contaminated, becoming the Blackwood, growing ravenously across our lands."

"This is when the Ellian Knights come in!" I chime.

"Glad to see you do listen during my history lessons." He smiles before continuing, "A faction of exceedingly strong magic wielders teamed together in 1200 AE, forming the first ten Ellian Knights, who were all Elarians, the dominant Fae race of Cascara. They bonded with magical flying creatures, and this bond was forged with an Arcane Glyph, giving the Ellian Knights another magical power beyond their Celestial Gift. It allowed them a tele-pathic connection with their mount, too. The earliest bonds were so strong that death of either beast or knight would lead to equal demise. They fought back against the Blackwood, slowing its growth."

I sit up in bed, jumping into the story. "On the night of a Bloodmoon, the Voidbringer's corruption made its way into the Ellian Knights. Five of them sought more power, upsetting the balance of magic. Then the other five attempted to kill them by severing their Arcane Glyphs, killing magical beasts and riders alike. Unfortunately, one escaped: Vyzon. He retreated to the Blackwood, entrancing Elarians and other Fae species through the power of black magic. He became the leader of the Wuvon. This marked a dark period in the Great War of Cascara. Many cities vanished off the map in the bloodshed of the battles between the Ellian Knights and the Wuvon. The Blackwood rapidly expanded, dividing into tendrils, snaking across the continent."

I let out a stretching yawn, cueing Sully to take over as I curl up in my blanket.

"Gildora, one of the most powerful descendants, was a Phantom Veil manipulator, a unique subset of Shadowmancing. She could create illusions that deceived all senses, indistinguishable from reality. This allowed Gildora to trap Vyzon long enough for Raeya to wield her plasma, burning him into oblivion. Without a leader, the remaining Wuvon were disorganized, suffering heavy losses, retreating back to the deepest depths of the Blackwood. They knew the threat of the Wuvon remained, so they founded Gildorea Universitás of War, to train all those willing to join the Golden Legion's efforts, ensuring no more civilian life was lost. During this time, Savorah was lost, believed to have died in the Great War.

"Thankfully, before this, she anointed a queen to rule in her stead, keeping the political peace allowing Cascara to prosper..."

His words continue as my mind drifts off into dreams of Celestial Dragons and brave Ellian Knights who protect all those in need.

# CHAPTER 3

The next several years of my life are full of training, preparing me for the important coursework I will be tested on at Universitás and the trials I need to pass for acceptance. The training Sully gifted me has transformed me into a confident young lady. I have definitely come out of my shell during my years with the gentle giant. People in town even manage to act civil around me, due to the respect they have for him.

Don't get me wrong, this town is still an utter shithole, but being Sully's apprentice has definitely improved my tolerance of other Fae.

As my body matured, I learned to use it as a weapon in a different way. I got even with the nasty barmaid, who had a particular hatred for me, by seducing her daughter. I did feel a tinge of remorse for breaking her heart in the process, but to be fair, I had made it clear to her from the start that I don't do attachment. Really, it was her own fault for falling for me. That was nearly a year ago, and now, what we guesstimate to be my seventeenth birthday is fast approaching.

Any free time I find between training sessions, work, and Sully's teachings is spent in the only good part of our village: our ancient, uncorrupted patches of Mysticwoods. Today, I visited one of my favorite creatures, the armored flying polar bears. Their fur is translucent, like my hair. They love teasing me, saying someone in my family lineage must have bonded one of them, giving me my iridescent hair that shimmers like starlight.

The bears believe the color signals warrior's blood coursing through my veins. However, I think they just enjoy telling me fanciful stories in hopes of extra ear scratches. Many creatures in Cascara can speak in some form or another: telepathy, body gestures, or oral language.

I lost track of time in the Mysticwoods with the bears, hurrying my way back into town. I peer down at my sketchbook of magical creatures as my boots slosh in the mud of the rutted road. With my focus on the pages in my hands, I fail to notice the stumbling man's path swaying into mine as I bump into him.

The hairs on my spine rise like the hackles of a wolf. I know exactly who I've collided with as the stench of vomit and cheap beer stings my nostrils. My eyes snap up to see the slithering bastard swaying in front of me.

It's been so long since I've seen him, bile instantly crawls up my gullet at the sight. In the time since I left, his wife had died. The rumor was that a monster had gotten into their house after they drunkenly left the door open. Which never made sense to me, given the blistering cold of our winters. She was said to have been ripped apart, blood spattering the walls in a frenzy. The local healer couldn't even identify the body, but when her face was never seen again, the town knew.

But I know differently. It wasn't a monster from the woods but a monster from within that haunted the house I had been left to.

A cold grip around my neck rips me from my thoughts. "My, how you've grown, *vermin*," he spews each of his words between his broken teeth, a grin peeking out from the lengths of greasy dark hair. His breath foul with decay. His six-foot-tall, gangly form reminds me of a misshapen tree, like the one that grows out of a swamp, never forming quite right. But I can see that half of his putrid smile reaches his bloodshot eyes.

His eyes get lost in mine while his suffocating grip tightens around my throat, as if he is reliving his fond memories of his favorite bloodletting activities. Fear seeps through my veins, as if I am still that tiny child in his hands again. A little thing whose only desire is to melt into the safety of her shadows once more.

Power wells inside me, reminding me of all I have become. I grab the forearm attached to the hand constricting around my neck and shove. My other elbow swinging up, smashing the spot right before his wrist. I take advantage of the physics Sully taught me, creating torque. *Snap.* The satisfying sound sunders the frozen air, twisting my face with a wicked grin—his bones shattering beneath my strength for the first time.

My frame—now 5'11"—is cast in pure muscle from years of training and working as a blacksmith. I devour his cowardly screams as he stumbles back several steps. Taking note of the changing position of his feet.

Sully's words echo in my head. *"Watch the direction of their feet, the momentum of each part of their body. Mass times velocity. Let your opponent show their cards, then wield their own hand against them."*

The subtle change in his positioning signals me he's reeling up to charge at me. The sway to his left side shows me he will come at me with a weak left hook, followed by a knee to the gut. A smug smirk kicks up at my lips as I take in the tremble of his right hand, thanks to my gift leaving his right arm hanging with an unnatural bend.

I counter his moves, allowing him to reach maximum velocity before leaning my weight backwards. I sidestep as he leans into me; gravity does the rest. My smirk twists into a wicked grin as he falls face-first with a *thud*. I step on the back of his neck, pinning him down as the muck *squelches* into the side of his mouth, placing my other boot on his newly deformed forearm.

He whelps in pain, writhing further into the filth. I crouch down, my whisper slicing his with a chill sharp enough to make ice envious.

"Who's the vermin now?" I mutter under my breath. "Fucking scum."

Deciding I've had enough of his slurred curses and pitiful attempts to break free as he chokes on more and more mud, I quiet him with a blow to the back of the head with the hilt of my short sword. Dragging him into the woods to a known Ronew hunting ground.

He wakes up tied to a tree, deep in the woods, bound by magical vines that tighten the more you move. Which I strategically positioned around the soft parts of his neck, stomach and groin.

He spews toxic words as he gazes into my obsidian eyes, gilded in vengeful gold. "You rotten piece of shit. You think I won't kill you for this? You are a curse upon this world, you—" he hisses before his words are cut short. Vines slithering tighter. Gnawing through his flesh with his every movement.

"Mmm. Please, do finish that sentence, darling." I beckon with a feral grin, twisting into a predator's smile. "Vines snagging that foul tongue of yours?" Without remorse, I look down on him. Blood trickles down his neck to meet the pooling garnet below his groin. "Not so tough now that you're picking on someone your own size?" I laugh, but there's no humor in it.

I falter, the manic grin threatening to slip from my face. *Does this make me as evil as him?* Giving him a taste of what he did to me all those years… I sigh dramatically, quickly concluding that I frankly don't give a fuck.

Karma's a fickle bitch. But I must admit, Karma is my favorite of the gods. The balancer, the enforcer of good and evil, decider of souls in the Ever After. She is the weighted scale between her older sisters, the Fates: Beaságe of Beginnings and Endara of Endings. They are believed to be the children of the power who created our universe, Saool. The Fates and Karma, born of divine conception. The Celestials were created as amusement for her children's immortal lives. They lit up galaxies and molded stardust into worlds of celestial wonder. Most importantly, they created a diverse array of life, each one a thread for the Fates to spin in the wicked games.

A raspy wheeze claws me from my thoughts. *Ugh, how fucking rude.* I look at the pale, greasy male before me with no guilt for the vines ripping him to ribbons. Only disappointment I didn't make his suffering last longer.

"Pity." I click my tongue, the darkness inside me brimming with utter delight. It revels, feasting on the bloodshed and carnage before me. Yet quickly, it grows restless. Snarling and bucking against the confines of my corporeal form, always craving more. *More.*

I clench my fist, stifling the beastly energy within.

With his last full breath, he seethes his dying words, "He will devour you, starb—" before the blood gurgles from his freshly exposed trachea, vines severing his tissue into muscle threads and macerated cartilage.

*How typical.* Still trying to lash me with his hollow, delirious threats. Even with his last fucking breath. I turn, pulling up the hood of my cloak as my cape twirls behind me in suit. Just before a shower of tainted blood rains down from his diced carotid artery. Thank the Celestials. I loathe scrubbing blood from my iridescent hair.

With the scent of a fresh kill on the breeze, I don't have time to waste thinking about his last words. Nor do I care. I know all too well the speed and hunger of the Ronew, who will be ravenously approaching to bring his soul back to the soil. They shred through flesh with five hundred teeth layered in three disturbing rows. Their long bottom jaw splits down the center, so they can engulf prey much larger than themselves. Their skin is a patchwork of devoured flesh, recycling leftover nutrients.

I have a feeling Karma is on my side for this kill. May he journey to the pits of Emberhell on his venture to the Ever After of the Underrealm, to finally atone for his demons that mar his soul.

The next morning, Sully doesn't fail to notice the fading bruise around my neck, fading fingers outlining the haunting shackle I'm finally free of. I catch his eyes lingering on it. Jaw clenching. Rage fires in his eyes, and it's not just the reflection of the furnace. He turns away when he realizes my attention.

We are both silent for the rest of the day. He never asks when word spreads around town that the monster who fostered me hasn't been seen in over a week.

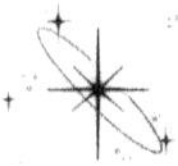

I'M SHARPENING A NEWLY FINISHED GREATSWORD for a customer on the grinding stone when Sully walks out of the side of the blacksmith shop into our outdoor workspace. In rough hands are several items wrapped with fraying cloth. I pause, setting my work down as he makes his way to my side.

My eyes drift up to find a giant, ridiculous grin on his face.

"Set the blade down, little dragon. It's time we celebrate your seventeenth birthday."

I stand up, taking a step back from him, shaking my head no. We live a simple life. Much of the coin we earn goes into running the business. "Sully, one gift a year is already a stretch, especially as the queen continues to raise the taxes for the war effort this season."

He chuckles like I am not absolutely correct. His only response: offering the gifts to me once more. "Have you lost your ever-loving mind, or did I just hit you too hard in the head the other day during combat training—?"

He cuts me off. "This old bear still has a few tricks up his sleeves," he says with a grin peeking through his beard. That damn smile will always warm my soul, just like the bear hugs he gives me when I master a new skill. He insistently places the first gift in my hands.

I unfold the cloth to reveal translucent cuirass armor. It glimmers in the light, picking up the colors surrounding it, almost camouflaging it. But it doesn't move like armor; it moves like scales made of silk, responding to my every movement. My jaw drops, an abnormal break from my typical steely expression.

Sully laughs at my unusual display of emotion.

I shoot him a glare as sharp as daggers, to which his laugh trails off quietly. "First, what the heck is this made of? Second, this can't possibly be for me?" I demand, unable to process the special gift.

"Basilisk scales… And trust me, you don't even want to know what kind of favor I had to do for them to amass such a quantity of scales." He raises one eyebrow, tilting his chin. The look convinces me that I really don't want to know. Some magical creatures have extremely peculiar taste when it comes to consenting to the use of their naturally powerful parts. Even if these scales were naturally shed and no longer of use to them, one still needs permission, freely given. The balance of powerful magic sometimes likes to snicker in your face.

I remember one time, Sully told me how he had to clean the gills of mimic fish for nine weeks to finally get a pearl that grows in their deeper gills. All to forge a rare blade he was crafting. The magic from the pearl of the mimic fish gives the blade the ability to change shape based on the wielder's desire. He sold it for a pretty copper to an Admiral of the Ellian Knights. But the fish made him agree to four additional weeks of gill cleaning, even after he retrieved the pearl. There must be balance, for such a powerful item. A grimace creeps at the corner of my mouth while vividly remembering the details he shared as he described the tedious job of cleaning those slimy gills. *Yuck.*

I examine the magical armor. The movement and the strength. Then, I notice the fine details of how the scales extend up the back of the neck, just far enough over the shoulders… My eyes widen. A glimmering hint of a tear twinkles in them but dares not leave my eyes as I look up at Sully.

He sighs deeply. "I know you prefer to keep your unique markings hidden. I may not understand why you choose to hide what makes you, you. But I figured the extra scales in those areas will make you feel more comfortable. And I know it will keep you safe. A blade cannot penetrate the scales, nor can fire or magic. When you wear it, the scales will mirror the dominant color of your skin in the light and your surroundings in the dark." He pauses for a thoughtful minute before remarking with a soft pride, "Now you have scales, almost like a real dragon." He laughs, honey eyes alight, reminiscing on the night I made my dragon-fang dagger.

"Is my subsequent gift dragon fire? So I can light up your stubborn ass the next time you get me into a headlock? Because then you'll never be able to beat me in sparring," I tease. Dragon fire is extremely powerful, impossible to put out by the elemental magic innate to all Elarians.

"My, what a cocky dragon you have grown up to be!" He chuckles deeply, putting his hand on my head and roughing up my hair to annoy me.

I huff, blowing the hair out of my face as I cross my arms in annoyance. Yet, a small smile slips onto my lips listening to Sully's rumbling laugh hug the air. He's always had a way about him, luring out a bright hopefulness in me.

He hands me the second gift. My eyes widen as fraying cloth falls open to reveal a cloak. It glimmers in a vast array of pigments, made of small feathers delicately spun together.

My heart sinks. The feathers of a great winged badger.

"*No.* I couldn't possibly take this."

Sully insists, pushing it back into my hands. His eyes swell with reverence, thumbing the feathers one last time before letting it go. "These were the molted feathers of Xeno. He had me collect them for many years before he brought me to a peculiar crone's house in the woods. She wove them into this cloak. It's a secret—no one can know. When woven together with lavender spider silk, this cloak will render you almost invisible. If you wear it with the feathers out, that is. With the feathers on the inside, it appears as a normal cloak."

He smiles, reminiscing softly. "Xeno always wanted me to be safe. He realized in his long life that sometimes staying hidden is not only a strategic advantage in battle, but also for survival. Now, I pass his secret gift to me on to you. So I always know my little dragon will be safe. Even when I am no longer with you."

My heart lurches. Sully is the rock that grounds me on the few occasions I've let my temper flare, when I push the limits of my physical and mental boundaries. The only person I have ever allowed to see me vulnerable. He is more than my teacher… He has become my father. I leap up, squeezing him as he gives me his big bear hug in return. But there is a subtle sadness to it, like a goodbye unsaid. I shake the notion from my mind.

Lastly, he hands me a small, light gift. "Your dragon-fang dagger, so you can always bite with a deadly might." He snickers. "I weaved several symbols into the center of either side of the dagger. Drawing one drop of blood will paralyze your opponent. So, *please,* don't cut yourself." He tilts his head with a smile.

I look over the dagger in the light. Intricate small runes dance along it. It still has a glimmer of crimson. Yet, oddly, a new iridescent glow now settles into the metal.

"I also adjusted your blade design to give you a full set of six throwing daggers." Sully pauses, pulling out several attached pieces of leather. "These straps attach to your armor, allowing the blades to be sheathed along your ribs."

I peer down at the beautiful, powerful magic he has metal-worked into the blades I hold in my hands, in awe of his mastery. Perfectly balanced. A handle with a circle at the end allows me to palm the dagger, hold it traditionally, or throw it at my target.

I gaze up, staring into his comforting honey-brown eyes. "Thank you. Truly. I owe you more than my life."

He gives me a genuine, heartfelt smile in return, reaching out his hand to my shoulder. "Today, we celebrate the Starborne little dragon. Tomorrow, we begin our preparation for the acceptance trials for Universitás."

That night, we drink ourselves silly by the hearth. It's always been easy to smile with him, his honey-warm aura softening my heart. With Sully, the world doesn't feel so horrible. He brings light to my life where once there were only shadows and pain.

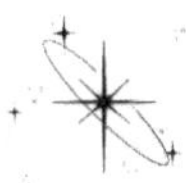

"Run it again," Sully orders.

It's the fifth time I've run the mock obstacle course. It's set up like the second trial, mirroring the borderland of the Blackwood battleground obstacles I will need to overcome.

This tests my endurance, agility, strength, and physical willpower.

The point of the trial is to ensure ensigns won't make it through all the coursework at Universitás just to end up immediately killed once they're stationed for battle, given that our enemy can manipulate the Blackwood. Our enemy exploits the natural landscape to their advantage, able to control the Blackwood and expand it at will. We need to adapt as quickly as they manipulate the surroundings in the woods, where their wild black magic is the strongest. Their control of the Blackwood is why the Golden Legion can never find their stronghold; they're able to literally move the entire structure through their manipulation of the forest.

I stand up and dust myself off, throwing a middle finger at Sully for knocking me down with a large rock to the gut.

"That type of attitude won't be enough to get you through the course." He chuckles, flicking his wrist, liquifying the ground to quicksand beneath my feet. I let out a string of curses while I lunge for a low-hanging branch, hoisting myself out and swinging to safety. A whirling *hiss* cleaves the air. I duck and dodge through a storm of daggers whistling towards me.

"Sully! What the fuck!? There're no flying daggers in the trial," I screech.

He shrugs. "I'm not a naturalist. I can't control the course like they will, so I'm taking creative liberty."

"Creative liberty, is it?" I smirk, slinging a dagger at him, slicing the sleeve of his shirt.

"This is my favorite flannel!" he grumbles as he hurls a ball of fire at me, then a gust of air, followed by cracking the earth beneath my feet as I stumble trying to dodge his last two magical attacks, ending his tirade by drenching me in water.

I growl at him, summoning fire magic. The flames lapping up my body, evaporating the water until I am dry once more. I still haven't come into my Celestial Gift, but thankfully, I'm strong in all my elemental magics. Plus, my natural ability to shield my mind is invaluable. The third trial will test my emotional control and strength against Persuasive mindwork.

We sit down, drinking from our canteens, a much-needed rest from physical training. However, Sully never lets a moment go to waste. Our breaks entail reviewing potions, topics of the natural world, and battle strategy.

"When you become an Ellian Knight, you'll be part of a group of five called a Chivalry, a group of Knights. You will be the aerial unit for your Wing, the combination of both your Chivalry and your Ground Unit."

"Yes, yes, I know." I wave my hand dismissively. The Golden Legion is divided up into two sections: infantry, our first line of defense; and our aerial Knights, combined with their ground elite force, known as Wings.

"You need to listen to this. I know you like to do everything on your own, but you will be part of a team, trained together and stationed together for the rest of your career. You need to let them in. You need to learn how to use each other's magical strengths to a team advantage. If you try to fly into battle and handle everything yourself, you won't survive long."

"But my lone-wolf vibe is so alluring." I wink sarcastically, and before he can even think up a retort, I lunge. Air magic whirls around me, increasing my speed. I switch to earth magic, shoving the boulder he's sitting on as I snatch his arm, taking advantage of his imbalance to pin him to the ground.

"I've trained you too well." He chuckles as I release him, helping him up.

"Let's hope it's enough to get me on the list for the first trial," I murmur. Being an orphan with no family line to open the door for me will make it difficult to even be admitted to the first stage.

Over the years, fewer trials are held in the outlying areas of the continent of Cascara, since too many of the attendees die with no one to train them appropriately. This sharpens the competition to secure a spot on the list in these areas. You essentially must prove you're at least a descendant of one of the many known, powerful, magic-wielding bloodlines or trained by someone with an important name. Compared to the same trials in the cities, where hundreds can prove their worth, only twenty applicants will be accepted in each of the smaller towns. If the infrastructure wasn't already in place, I don't think they would even bother holding the trials in the border-lands at all.

After a long day of training, my sore muscles moan as I roll into bed, slumber consuming me with ease. A serrated cough followed by several wheezing breaths slashes me from sleep's sweet embrace.

I've never heard Sully cough like that. Another rib-rattling rasp crawls down my spine. The sensation claws its way through my sinew, settling deep in my bones. Like a winter chill that refuses to relent.

# CHAPTER 4

I marvel at the hard cobblestones beneath my feet. We traveled two months to reach Snomas, the only area in the Highlands where the first trial is held. Excitement and trepidation coil in my stomach; it's my first time in a new town. I clutch my cloak tighter around me. It's held up remarkably well despite its daily use since Sully gifted it to me nearly five years ago.

Here in Snomas, we are still far from the hilly Midlands, dripping with waterfalls and meadows, where Gildorea Universitás was established. And farther still from the capital, Riicah, in the rich old-growth forest of the Lowlands, where the Queen's emerald castle sits atop cliffs that give way to the ocean.

The last rays of sunlight twinkle goodnight over the jagged fangs of mountain peaks. I take in the single-story stone buildings lining Mainstreet, dimly lit by the faerie light lanterns strung along metal posts peppering the walkway. Each building is filled with various goods: fabrics and leathers, books, spices, herbs. There's even a bakery still alight, displaying window shelves overflowing with so many colorful desserts, I start drooling. I imagine what the sensation of sweet icing would be like melting on my tongue. That's as good as it's going to get though, since I'm certain I don't have enough coins to afford anything.

I wonder how Sully is faring. After we initially arrived, he told me to explore the town while he went off to talk with every military person he could find in an attempt to get my name on the list. I don't know if Sully is well-known from his time in service, but he was an Ellian Knight, and that has to matter. Plus, he killed a Wuvon and their Crowven before he retired. That must be a big deal, right? I shake my head. Of course it is. I shouldn't doubt his ability to get me on the list. He never seemed worried about it.

The racket of a group of drunk Elarians screaming at each other causes me to lengthen my strides, avoiding all the noise I'm not accustomed to. The shadows cast by the buildings here are large enough for me to dance through, but I ignore their call to meander on the main road, absorbing everything new and foreign.

I snarl at a male air Pixie, who knocks into me in a hurry, fluttering on translucent wings. Shifting my attention to the shop he was leaving. It's filled with fabrics strewn together to create eccentric outfits. My eyes catch on a black dress made of shimmery material in the shop window. I walk into the store with an undeniable urge to touch the fabric.

"That black velvet dress would look absolutely divine on you," an odd, jovial voice muses from behind, startling me.

I turn to see a male-like figure with long, metallic gold hair, done up in a high braid. Their face is painted in makeup that makes them almost look like a female; they are stunning. Their form is of a Fae, except their arms are covered in purple scales with ears shaped like fins. My eyes widen; they're a Pesche, a fishlike Fae subspecies I've heard Sully talk about. They're originally from a continent that lies further south, called Perch.

Unfortunately, political unrest and pirates plague their country, leading to some Pesche splitting off to make Cascara their new home. I recall Sully harping on how they're excellent swimmers and insanely quick on land thanks to their scales, reducing turbulence and drag. I clench my jaw, preventing it from gaping, as I curiously glare at the being before me.

Canary-colored eyes look me up and down. Taking in my disheveled appearance from months of traveling on the road, the weapons sheathed along my body and peeking out of the large bag slung over my shoulder.

"Well, this attire and your… lack of *hygiene* certainly won't do, darling. Not in my shop." They flick their wrist, and water washes over me, drenching me as I gasp. *What the fuck is going on?* I don't even know this Fae. Their fingers twirl, wringing the water from my clothes and hair into a muddy, suspended puddle, floating beside me before splashing it out on the street through the open doorway I'm still perched in.

I look down to find I'm spotless, my hair and clothes clean. Their flagrant use of magic on a stranger alarms me. I'm glad Sully isn't here to see this. He always scolds me for using my magic frivolously. *You never know when you will need all your reserves to save your life.*

"Ah, that's much better. Now let me get this dress off the display for you."

"Do you normally go around bathing your customers without permission?" I scowl, checking my weapons to make sure they didn't abscond with any.

"I have a reputation to uphold, and you smelled… well…like a vagrant. Now that you're clean, let's get you into the dressing room!" They beam.

I eye them suspiciously. Why are they so set on getting me into this dress? "No, that won't be necessary. I don't have that kind of coin," I grumble, turning to leave.

"Nonsense. Clothing is my art. By the looks of you, perhaps metalcraft is yours? You're certainly drenched in enough weapons." Their eyes drifting down, splaying their fingers to inspect their nails before they continue. "It just so happens that I'm in need of a short sword. One can never be too careful, you know, with the Blackwood advancing every day. Do you have an extra one you'd be willing to part with for a trade?" They flit around me, blocking off my exit.

"Blocking my way is very unwise. It would displease me to mess up your beautiful makeup," I growl low. I don't like this stranger trapping me.

"Apologies. I didn't mean to upset you. I can get a little overzealous. It's the artist in me. Especially when I find a being who… *completes* the image in my head."

I pull my large bag in front of me, rattling around to find an extra short sword. I crafted several, since I knew I couldn't access a forge until entering Universitás. Short swords are my preference over long or greatswords. I snatch the weapon by the hilt, shoving the flat side against their chest.

"Take it, give me the dress, and stay out of my way."

"Oh, yes! 'Tis a shame I won't get to see it on you… but, alas, my mind can dream," they squeak as they take the sword, prancing over to remove the dress from the mannequin before delicately wrapping it and handing it to me.

I trudge towards the inn, more than done with people for the day. If only there was a stretch of Mysticwoods close enough to slip away to. I miss the soothing hum of nature. A frown folds over my lips. I may never see some of my favorite alpine creatures again, who once made the wild feel like home.

I enter through the loud bar of the inn, heading upstairs to our room at the end of the hall. There is a quaint, round, wooden table in front of a shabby couch by the metal hearth, with a small window looking at the wall of another building over the sink. I hear a rattling cough from one of the wooden doors off to the side. I guess Sully went to bed already.

I head to the other door. My body collapses onto a wooden bed with a stiff mattress stuffed with wool as I drop my pack on the floor. My head falls to the pillow, letting sleep consume me.

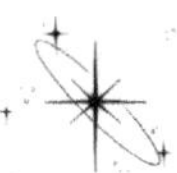

I SHOOT out of bed like a forest sprite rising in spring. My blood humming with adrenaline. The first trial is today. A pit tightens in my stomach, despite Sully training me since I was nearly eight years old.

Or maybe the pit is from the sound of Sully's cough that tortured me throughout the night. The cough has lingered and continues to worsen, despite me trying every magical healing herb Sully taught me.

The last few years have been like a vice slowly spinning. Constricting. Tighter and tighter around my heart. I watched Sully retire earlier and earlier each night from our training session, as his overpowering grizzly bear form dwindled, more akin to a brown bear now.

His demeanor changed during training, too. I could see a hidden sadness in his eyes, just for a second, as I mastered harder and harder skills. It was almost as though he felt making me stronger was putting me in more danger, rather than keeping me safe. But he still refused to elaborate on his cryptic words that night by the fire and kept pushing me harder. Some days he pushed me so hard, I think he was hoping I would quit. But I enjoyed the challenge.

When I tried to pester him about traveling to find a stronger healer for his cough, he waved me off, saying, "Focus on your first trial. This cough is nothing to worry about. Just too many years of inhaling fumes from the forge, and now I finally got to cough it all up."

Even I could tell he didn't believe his own words. I spent all of my free time delving deeper and deeper into the Mysticwoods, speaking to any plant, mushroom, or creature who would listen. Trying to find a cure for a cough that wouldn't relent.

I sip on a warm cup of silk bark and frostflower tea, steam rising between my eyes as the cup sits between my hands, braced against my lips. The warm liquid slinks down my throat, heating my muscles, while racing thoughts of the first trial consume my mind.

I will be dropped into a pit where one of three monsters could be released. I either win or become dinner. *Simple.* A nervous laugh sneaks out as I gulp my tea. My next sip balls up in my throat, refusing to submit. *I will fucking survive today*, I repeat to myself as my grip tightens on the mug.

I spread my knees, grounding my feet, clenching the warm mug tighter as I swallow harder. The tea abides, settling heat in my stomach, casting off the chill lingering on my skin.

"What is the weakness of the Casin?" Sully chimes as he grabs my shoulders, shaking me, causing me to spew my next sip on the table.

"For a big old man, you sure can be quiet, Sully! Wait, were you trying to sneak up on me? You know you don't always need to keep me on my toes…" I stick out my tongue at him, wrinkling my nose as I wipe up the mess.

"You didn't answer my question. Are you getting slow and dull-witted at your age? Already?" he teases.

I sling him an annoyed scowl, but a smile curls on my lips at seeing him so full of energy, like he used to be before that fucking cough. "My failure would only be a reflection of you, big ol' bear! Now let a lady drink her tea in peace." I sigh.

"Ouch. That may have actually hurt my feelings if I didn't know who trained you." He smiles. "And I still expect an answer." A knowing brow arches at me.

A Casin is an undead, humanoid-like creature with hollow white eyes, elk antlers, and poisonous, rotten flesh. "A Casin's weakness is their unsteady shoulder joints before their disturbingly long arms. Two daggers to the shoulder, and one to the knee. Then slit its throat, but don't let its skin touch you, and mind the antlers. They are fast once they get moving, so distance and not missing your targets are key. If you do miss a target, create distance, and strike again."

He smiles with pride, taking his big hand and ruffling up my hair *again*. I cross my arms, blowing the hairs out of my face as I huff. "Bone-thresher, a creature made of thick bones with long bone spikes down its back into its tail. Its skull has a lockjaw. If it bites down, you're as good as dead.

Normally, it prefers pouncing on its prey from high places. Weakness: less agile in tighter spaces like the pit, without the high ground, but the only way to kill it is the soft gullet, the finger-length unprotected area down the underbelly of its neck. The key is sliding under the beast to cut its throat. This is your only chance."

Sully manages to ruffle my hair *again*! I scowl at him, unamused, as I blow even more hair out of my face this time, twirling like beams of rainbow light trapped in a crystal prism.

"Now you're just showing off, huff the little dragon." He scoffs before continuing, "Remember: no use of magic in the pit, or you will be disqualified. But wear your armor. It will keep you safe."

I pause before looking up at him, leaning back into my chair. "Isn't that kind of cheating?" I shrug. I'm not opposed to breaking a few rules, as long as I don't get caught and screw up my one chance of getting into Gildorea.

He smiles slyly. "Only if you get caught. But I made it to not be seen. Plus, I'd rather you lived through the trial and be disqualified than be cleaning your bloody mess off the pit floor." He winks at me.

I stand up and try to shove him for suggesting there's even a chance I could lose today. Despite how much he's withered in the last six months, it's still like pushing into an old tree, firmly rooted. I change the position of my arms, falling into him with a big bear hug instead.

He whispers over my head, "I don't doubt you for a second."

My heart is almost full at that moment as I push his sickness out of my mind and savor this memory, breathing in the familiar smell of metal and soot.

# CHAPTER 5

I prowl up to a harsh lady with grey hair shorn to her chin, standing with the roll-call list for check-in.

"Name," she says coldly, as if everyone on this list will die today. I know she frankly doesn't care what my name is, but this is what she is paid to do.

"Savaé."

Her dark brown eyes look up at me, pausing as she gazes over the gold squares in my obsidian eyes and the gilded flecks across my cheeks. Clearly, I did a lackluster job in my attempt to cover the latter with soot from the fireplace this morning.

"Full. Name." She punctuates each word as if exhausted she must clarify her previous statement. I haven't thought of my full name in a long time. I suppose it's one of the only things my birth parents left me. There is almost a power behind the words that have rested unspoken for so long, grazing my lips like an unavowed promise.

"Savaé. Entropaé."

She pauses again, staring at my odd eyes before returning to review her list. "You are fifteenth today. Wait over there." She waves me off with a dismissive hand.

I sigh, fighting the urge to flip a rude gesture in her direction for her tone before stepping to her left. The waiting area is filled with Fae around my age. You must be twenty-two years old to enter Universitás. Some people attempt the trials earlier, to have the extra year for a third trial repeat, where you must survive the mindwork of a newly graduated first year Persuasive from Gildorea Universitás, who needs to pass to make it to second year. Needless to say, they are very motivated to see you fail. This is the hardest trial to pass for many.

I am twenty-one years old, and with my strong ability to shield my mind, I figure I don't need the extra year. My presumed birthday is soon, so I'll be of age by the time all three trials are completed.

Most of the trialists are average-looking, with dark hair and pale skin typical of the Highlands. One girl, unique in her appearance, has long, wavy blonde hair, contrasting her emerald-green eyes. Another girl on the upper row of seats stands out with short, angular lavender hair that matches her sharp features, one side shorn to her skull. Her most striking feature: stunning violet eyes deep in focus. The color of her eyes is mesmerizing. I get lost in thinking how they'd look deep in the waves of bliss. How they would gleam as her blood heats beneath mine.

She awkwardly catches me gawking at her, and I give her a roguish smirk, raising my brow as she blushes, twisting her hands in her lap. Perhaps I can make that fantasy a reality, if she lives through the day. Nothing like a much-needed release after skirting Lady Death's clutches.

I walk with newly boosted confidence to an open seat in the front row. There weren't many opportunities for romantic liaisons in my small village, but I found occasion to enjoy the bodies of a few of the queen's guards on quarterly tax collection. I enjoy the raw beauty of both females and males and the wide array of Fae Cascara offers. Why limit yourself?

My pleasure comes from others' satisfaction. I enjoy being in control, limiting how much they touch my body. The added perk of them only being in town for a few days increased the thrilling pleasure of the moment with no strings or ridiculous attachments. Connection more than physical pleasure is beyond my wheelhouse and, frankly, something I am not sure my glacial heart is capable of.

I make sure not to look back at the violet-eyed girl, following my rule: 'always leave them wanting more.' I glance at the opposite side of the pit and see Sully seated in the watching area, giving me two big thumbs up and grinning. The corners of my mouth curl up, happily annoyed at how ridiculous he looks.

As I sit, the hairs prickle on my neck, just like before you get a static shock from a blanket. I turn to the side where the charge is coming from, swearing I catch a glimpse of a shadow racing under the amphitheater steps. *Odd*. Shadows have never tried to play games with me before. I shake my head. Great, now I'm seeing things. It must be my nerves. Yet I can't shake the feeling of someone's heated gaze on me. I know my markings are hidden, so I brush it off as the heat of the midday sun warming my cloak.

The third creature of the pit is a worm-like centipede—a Tieped—with large, piercing jaws and hard armor covering its back and underbelly. It has a weak spot where its legs enter its body. Ideally, one gets on its upper back to avoid it twisting around to snap off one of your limbs. You then cut off one of its legs, about four armored plates down from its head, and shove a sword straight through, skewering its heart.

*Crunch* is the only sound we hear from the trialist frozen in fear in the pit below as he loses his head to the Tieped's large pincers. Yet another trialist to be collected by Lady Death; that makes thirteen so far. My stomach flops as the waterfall of blood shoots from his neck, while the darkest parts of me find an unsettling thrill in it. The dark parts of me I try to keep locked up and hidden, only to be released when I need to draw extra power in a fight.

Oddly, in the squirting of his blood, I notice a fourth entrance to the pit that isn't how you enter the arena. This pit has recently been adapted. You can tell by the green hue of the gate's sharpened tree trunks. An additional gate doesn't make sense to me. There should only be three gates for the three trial monsters. And one smaller door for trialists to enter the pit. They wouldn't add a new monster, would they? That hasn't been done in recorded history. It must be for some other function.

My contemplation is interrupted by the call of the next name to enter the pit. A shadowy figure walks out in a form-fitting black leather vest, accentuating his broad shoulders and rippling, thick arms. I don't mind his snug leather pants hugging his shapely ass. A smirk tugs at my lips. At least it will be dinner and a show as we watch this one die. At that moment, his gaze snaps to mine, as if hearing my sarcastic thoughts. A wave of wildfire sweeps through my body. It's unlike anything I've ever experienced. Maybe I'm going to be sick?

His eyes are ice blue, almost white, like a frozen lake, or perhaps... moonlight. I swear there almost appears to be shadows swirling in them. His eyes fixate on mine, unwavering, and my heart almost forgets how to beat.

The light moves over his warm umber skin, like an oil painting beneath the shadows of wavy black hair framing his soft but angular face. My breath catches. Something is clearly wrong with me. I break his gaze. My eyes drift to his thick lips, a decadent finish to an artistically sculpted face. He is too handsome. He belongs in a museum, not a pit full of monsters. The hairs sway on my neck as my lips curve at the edge. *Why the fuck am I smiling?*

My eyes immediately lock back onto his. He appears amused to be drinking in my gaze once more. The rising gate groans in the distance. His moonlit irises linger on me. Unwavering. Almost pleading. Like it's impossible to pull his gaze from mine. Then, he gives me a sly wink just before turning his focus away, facing the opening gate. As his gaze leaves mine, there is a strange feeling of… What is it? Absence?

*Wait.* Did he just wink at me!? My blood boils for a whole new reason. Who the fuck does this fuckboy think he is? I huff, rolling my shoulders, trying to shake the unsettling feelings off. He's probably just looking at someone seated behind me. Probably the emerald-eyed blonde I couldn't help but notice on my way in. She is the classic beauty standard of the Midlands. Now that I think of it, what is she doing this far north?

My skin is still oddly hot. A new feeling tightens deep in my stomach. I loosen the cloak around my neck to release the heat. Hormones. This must just be my fucking hormones. I clearly need to get laid.

The snarling and clattering of an armored skeleton nips my attention back to the fight below—the Bone-Thresher. The male has two broadswords crossed against his back. A hint of relief drifts inside me when he doesn't unsheathe them; that would be certain death.

*Shit.* What's wrong with me? Why would I even have an inkling of relief that this random fuckboy might not die? He means nothing to me. Let's just tuck these feelings into my favorite box in my mind. The one labeled: 'never going to open that shit again.' And chuck it right out my mosaic window.

I quickly note the other weapons he has at his disposal: a short sword on one leg, and two daggers sheathed on the other. And the idiot goes for the short sword.

The Bone-Thresher stalks around the edge of the circular pit, lined with thirty-foot-tall trees sharpened to spikes at the top and slicked with tar so no monsters or contestants can get out. The creature prowls, searching for the nonexistent high ground. Realizing this, the beast lunges for the trialist. He dodges like shadows escaping the rising sun, narrowly escaping its snapping maw.

He's quick but doesn't account for the length of the thresher as it crashes into the wall with its momentum. The Bone-Thresher's body pins him with the less-sharp bony protuberances jetting out from the side of its body.

My heart lurches as he thrusts his short sword in between the vertebrae spikes of the creature's back. Hoisting his immense body up onto its spinal column, using his sword as leverage. The right side of his pinned leather vest rips to shreds, exposing the lines that carve his abdomen. He latches onto the spikes of the beast's back as it bucks wildly. I almost can't watch as he reaches for one of the long swords from his back. His luck has finally run out, and it's time for him to meet Lady Death.

My eyes go wide, breath held prisoner by anticipation, as he uses the long sword as bait for the Bone-Thresher's death bite. The beast snaps down, bending the steel in its lockjaw. Then, gliding through the beast's dorsal spikes in a sideways dive, he grabs onto the hilt of his long sword for torque, guiding the swinging migration of his body. The lethal precision of his movements make me swallow. In one fluid maneuver, as if dancing with the killer beast, he unsheathes his dagger and slides under its neck, slitting its throat open. Appearing on the other side as he lands perfectly on his feet.

My skin crackles with delight as I glare at him, swallowing again in the heat of thinking about how effortlessly his body moved. He knows how to wield his frame, and my traitorous body wants to find out just how deadly he can be.

A trail of splattered blood leads me from his chest up to his face. His gaze claims mine. The contrast of his icy eyes against his umber skin and black hair, now dripping with crimson, awakens a feral hunger in me.

A sly grin kicks up at the corner of his mouth. My lips part, his eyebrow arching in response as his gaze shifts to my lips. *Fuck.* He is trouble, and I can feel it in my bones, despite how my skin warms under his piercing gaze. There is something almost challenging about his smirk. Celestials, why does my body feel so drawn to him? Must be the adrenaline.

"Next trialist: Savaé Entropaé." My gaze unwillingly pulls away as I hear my name called from the dais of administrators overseeing the spectacle.

I reach for my mental shields. Nothing and *no one* will distract me from my goal, from everything Sully and I have worked for. And definitely not whatever the fuck just happened to me when he looked at me. With my shields up, I let an all too familiar numbness seep deep into my marrow.

Now, I am the weapon. With unwavering focus, I walk down the steps.

Sully grabs my cloak as I descend. I send a silent *thank you* to him for the armor that will keep me safe and hide my markings from the onlookers.

I can almost hear the words as he mouths, "Give 'em hell, little dragon," before falling out of sight above me. Then I hear the creaking of *that* gate.

The one that gave me the eerie feeling earlier. The one *out of place.* Yep, that checks. Perhaps I truly am cursed.

Of course, the Fates are laughing at me, giving me the proverbial middle finger. Of course, the rules of the game change when I come into play.

Well, bring it on, because I play to *win.*

A cold smirk grazes my lips as I reposition myself in the pit. There's a smoldering gaze on my neck again. Odd. This time, I am fully cloaked in the shadows; no one can see me. I find the hole in my shields where the feeling of that branding gaze sneaks in, adding another layer to my shields as the feeling drifts away.

I pause. Do I want distance or surprise?

I have no clue what I'm going up against. A warm feeling along the back of my neck nudges me to the notion of surprise.

Darting to the shadowy edge along the rising gate of thick wooden beams, I rest my body flat. *Mind over matter.* I will my heart still as I close my eyes. The beat slows as I breathe out, opening my eyes to the calm of control.

A nude, almost-wet, contorted arm slinks out of the gate. Claws as long as my hand glisten at the second elbow joint. I follow the arm to its end, where long fingers with one too many joints reach out. I track the path of the arm to see a skin-colored wing attached between its third elbow. An oval face with no eyes kinks its head at the crowd above.

*No. It can't be.*

Goosebumps prickle my skin as a staccato of clicks chatter from its teeth-filled mouth, confirming my suspicion. Echolocation. My heart screeches, begging to race, but I imagine my fist clenching around, holding it still. I cannot lose control. Mind over matter. I focus.

*Shhh.*

This is a Ritherin, a favorite among Wuvon for scouting missions. They leave their victims withered husks, hence the name. They excel at sightlessly finding their prey, no matter how well-hidden. On top of that, they can fly. It has long, contorted arms with four joints to grasp you into its wings, filled with hooks. Hooks that are actually small mouths for draining your blood. Or ripping you apart in the blink of an eye. And if that isn't bad enough, it has long, agile legs, so it's even fast on foot. I remember Sully's words: "Every monster has its weaknesses. Nature insists there is always a balance."

Clicks ricochet in all directions as the monster continues to slink out. I have to think *fast*. My position is to my advantage, praise the Celestials. The circular structure will cause its clicks to bounce back; plus, all the noise from the people watching above the pit, combined with the hustle and bustle of city life beyond, should distract it. I'm thankful for the noise I was cursing earlier. If we were in my isolated village, I'd already be Ritherin meat.

I pause. They couldn't release this thing into the pit without clipping its wings, or everyone who showed up today would be dead, plus countless others in the city. I notice its right wing has a large slit through it, so it can't fly. The slit will reduce its balance but also give it more mobility.

I hold my breath as I slowly reach for my dragon-fang dagger, paralysis poison imbued into the metal. Even if I don't kill it, the beast will be paralyzed. I just need to stay alive for a few heartbeats. Every monster's metabolism is different, and against a predator like this, the time it takes may not be enough to save me.

My focus is on only moving when it sends clicks out and not while listening for the frequencies to come back. Before attacking, I have about three leaping steps I need to make—soundlessly—before I can jump on the back of its left wing, going in for the throat. I wrap the circular hilt of my dragon-fang dagger around my middle finger, resting the large part of the circle against my palm with the short triangular blade parallel to my wrist. I listen, attuning myself to the rhythm of his clicks. Gliding one step, with my toes barely touching the ground, before I make the leap of my second step.

On my third step, I barely feel my toes graze the ground before using all my weight to create momentum, swinging my arms up into the air for extra lift. The shift in the air snags its attention. It turns, body twisting to assess the change. Its eyeless face snaps over its right shoulder at me, shifting its position, causing me to crash-land further out on its left wing than intended.

*Son of a bitch.*

The little mouths under its left wing wriggle up, snapping at my fingers. I swing out with my dagger, jamming it into the side of its neck but too far back to slit its throat. I let go with my left hand, reaching over its shoulder as I try to grab under its neck, hoping I don't tumble into its mouth.

The Ritherin wails as it swings side to side. Searing pain pierces my back as the claws of its gangly hand slam into my armor. Two talons filleting my flesh as they make it past my armor in the part without scales, allowing me to lace it tight. I ignore the slashing pain, positioning my left hand on the right side of its jaw with my forearm, thankfully under its mouth. I use the momentum of it trying to rip me off its back with the force of my hand, snapping its neck. Gravity catapults us towards the ground.

I fucking play to win.

I rip the dead weight of its claws out of my back before pulling my dagger from its neck and sheathing it at my ribs. I look up at the humming crowd; the spectators are busily whispering to each other.

What? Is there something on my face?

My eyes dance around the circle above me before meeting *his* piercing gaze. Pinning me in place. A shiver caresses my back as he arches his left eyebrow at me, almost looking impressed. I huff, determining it's just the shiver of blood dripping down my spine.

I shift my gaze to the opening exit, grateful only a few of the claws pierced my back. Luckily, my vital organs are unscathed.

As I walk, my mind races with thoughts of how I can fix my armor. Then my legs sway a little, hit with the magnitude of what just happened. I defeated a Ritherin—a wounded Ritherin, but still. This is one of the deadliest monsters on the continent. That was fucking wild, but I did it!

My brief elation plummets along with my stomach as I hear Sully raging at someone about how the fuck this could have happened.

# CHAPTER 6

"What the fuck were you thinking, releasing a Celestials be dimmed Ritherin!?" Sully roars as the ground outside of the pit rumbles in his rage. A guard goes flying as he tosses them aside like a rag doll on his way to the council, perched upon their dais.

I've never seen Sully so infuriated. I'm stunned by his strength, even after how much the cough has weakened him. He'll tear apart the administrators if I don't get to him in time.

"Come on, grey ol' bear, you'll get me in trouble. I survived. We're okay. I promise," I whisper, grabbing his shoulder.

He roars, "This isn't right. They can't just do this. Adding a monster at the last second. A Ritherin at that!" Silver tears pool in his eyes. He's terrified and worried about me.

A darkly dressed, thin male rises into a tall figure, standing out of the slew of administrative representatives. With his pale skin, white hair, and light blue eyes, his Arabellian lineage drips off him with the superiority of his presence. Slowly, he drags his icy gaze over us. As if he's mesmerizing every detail.

"Correction. We *can* administer the trials however we please." His cold and uncaring voice grates on my nerves. "With the enemy strengthening their efforts each day, the stakes are higher than ever for new trialists and recruits alike." He scowls directly at Sully. "And since this one got her name on the list by being trained by the great Ellian Knight Sully Stonewall, I had no doubt your apprentice would be capable of rising to the challenge. As Fate would have it, I was yet again *correct*."

The way he said the word *correct* makes me want to punch the word right down his throat for his asinine remark. I'd fucking love to show him the *correct* way to land a punch.

I have half a mind to act on my violent thoughts, but I'm too busy holding Sully back. It's clear Sully and I agree this administrator needs to be taken down a peg or two. But I am not going to risk my chance of getting into Gildorea because of my short temper—or Sully's.

I whisper in Sully's ear, "That pompous ass isn't worth everything we've worked for. Let's go celebrate my win, big ol' bear."

His muscles finally relax under my death grip. He turns for the exit as I bow to the Arabellian administrator, showing my respect to his royal blood-line and whatever position he holds.

"Thank you for the chance… and challenge. We will take our win and leave now," I say coolly as we retreat.

"I look forward to seeing you at the next trial, Savaé Entropaé. It will be my delight to watch you rise to my next challenge," he quips.

Sully rips his head around, showing me he's about to lunge at the guy. I place one hand on his right shoulder and pull his wrist behind his back before pushing him forward, making sure he knows leaving is the only option I am giving him.

Just outside the inn, a coughing fit rips at Sully's lungs, painting the snow in crimson splatter that plunges a dagger right into my heart—twisting deeper and deeper—as I usher him into the warm pub. I follow him up the stairs, my eyes drifting over the five trialists who lived, celebrating with friends and other local folk. I guess I won't be getting any sleep tonight with all this racket.

"Typical," I mutter to myself as I take in Mr. Fuckboy standing on the bar, twirling the classically beautiful blonde round and round as everyone cheers. His eyes meet mine, an odd longing in them as they linger on me, settling like a swift kick in the ribs, hacking at my racing heart and seizing the air from my lungs.

*What the actual fuck?* I sling a scowl at him as I throw up my shields, my old friend, numbness, seeping over me.

I don't have time for whatever Ritherin-shit that was, not with Sully all wound up. I need him calm and resting, especially after the blood he just coughed up. We head to the end of the hallway, to our adjoining rooms. Sully sits down on the chair by the table while I open the window to let in the fresh air.

White fire magic blooms from my hands, igniting the hearth beneath a hanging kettle. Steam billows from the brassy pot as I sprinkle a slew of herbs inside.

I set down the full mug in front of him. "Drink. It will help with the cough."

He won't even look at me. He's never behaved like this with me. After a long silence, he finally mumbles out some words.

"We are going home tomorrow."

"We're what? I must have heard you wrong. Because I know you didn't just say what I thought I heard. Not after all our work," I seethe. A strong emotion is a sure way to let your shields slip. I don't have many strong emotions, but I already know this conversation will be an exception.

"We. Are. Going. Home. Tomorrow." He punctuates every word to ensure there's no mistaking him this time. My blood turns to liquid fire inside my veins. I want to scream and throw the Celestials be dimmed kettle at his head. The thought causes a crackling beneath my skin, purring at the feelings of destruction.

Instead of giving in to the brewing darkness, I take a deep breath, calming myself as I raise my shields once more.

My voice is low as I say, "We. Are. *Not.*"

"I did not stutter. And this decision is final. I won't let them take you." His anger lashes me like a whip.

I wince, and a deep sorrow furrows his brow. His odd choice of words rumbles like unturnable stones in my chest. "No one is taking me anywhere. This is *my* choice. I don't know what you're going on about. I still have two more trials to pass. We are a team—"

"This was a mistake. We need to go home. I shouldn't have brought you here."

The fury in my blood simmers into violent rage as I stand. "No one forced me to be here! We came here together. This is everything we have worked on for nearly eleven years. You can't be fucking serious, Sully. I know you are mad about the challenge, but because of your training, I won. I will take on whatever they fucking throw at me. Just like you trained me to."

He just stares down at the mug clutched against his chest.

"Sully. Look at me!" Then, softening my tone, I plead, "You can't mean this."

He finally looks at me, silver streaming down his face. "I can't lose you, too, little dragon."

My heart wails seeing him weeping silently. I grab a cloth from the table, getting down on one knee next to him, softly wiping the tears from his face. I sweep over his beard, which is now salt-and-pepper grey, matching his hair. I take his hand and give it a squeeze.

"You are not going to lose me, grey bear. You trained me too well. I promise." He squeezes my hand back before wrapping his arms around me, suffocating me in a hug that nearly snaps my ribs. "Can't. Breathe," I squeak out.

He chuckles softly, letting me collapse to the floor. I stand. His sullen face needles my heart, which has become far too squishy and vulnerable around him. My voice softens into a plea once more. "I want to do this. Please. Let me do this."

Another tear tumbles down his face. Defeat highlights the wrinkles dragging at the corners of his eyes. "Okay."

He finally drinks his tea as I leave to change into something nicer to wear out. I have a few options: two black leather outfits which I frequently wear, a blue tunic, and the black velvet dress that wraps around my neck with a slit up one side—the one I traded for yesterday with the eccentric Pesche.

Since I'm behind closed doors, I allow myself to use my water magic, pouring over me, cleaning off the blood, dust, and sweat, before fire magic licks up my skin, drying me and my armor. I decide to wear the dress over my basilisk armor, which will blend with my skin in the light of the pub and appear dark in the night's shadows.

I fix my kohl, connecting a black line on my upper lid, extending it out at the corner. My gold freckles shimmer uncovered along my cheeks. I don't know what it is about the darkness of the night that gives me the confidence to let them shine. Maybe it's the comfort of the surrounding shadows, knowing I can easily slip away if someone makes an untoward remark.

I return to the common space between our rooms. "Want to come grab a beer to celebrate with me, Sully?" I ask while crossing my fingers in hopes he's too distracted by our earlier conversation to realize I used magic to clean myself off quickly. I really don't want another fight with him tonight.

He's deep in thought when he looks up at me. "Stay away from that boy who fought before you in the pit. Promise me. He and his blood lineage will bring nothing but trouble."

"I could have told you that he's trouble. It practically ripples off of him." I laugh.

He grabs my wrist. "They will try to break you for what you are, for who I am to you, and for who you are to become."

Oddly cryptic, but that's the Sully I know and love. I place my hand over his. "They won't be the first to try to break me. Or the last, Sully. I know you think you can, but you can't protect me from everything. I love you for trying, but remember: I am not easily broken."

I lift his chin up, making sure he looks at me. "The fury of this little dragon is an Emberhell all of its own to be reckoned with. You taught me that. You taught me everything. You're my father and, apparently, the famous Sully Stonewall. Even if your name puts a target on my back, I wouldn't trade you for all of Elyndor."

I have no bloodline, and being trained by someone well-known will already mark me as needing to prove my worth. I could tell by the way the administrator glared at Sully, he didn't retire from the Golden Legion amicably.

Sully smiles at me with glowing pride, wrapped in a delicate sadness and drenched in love all at once. Yet my heart hangs heavy with the melancholy in his eyes.

I change the subject before my heart splinters under the weight of his pain. "Are you coming to get drunk with me, ol' bear? I don't know about you, but I need to celebrate defeating a Ritherin!" I smile.

He shakes his head silently as he looks down at his tea again.

"I won't be gone long. I promise," I say softly, pressing a gentle kiss to the top of the head. I hesitantly close the door behind me as the sound of his cough lances my heart like a Ritherin claw.

I remind myself there is nothing more I can do. It's far beyond my Sangre healing powers, and I have used every herb I know that might help. I pause outside the closed door before striding down the hallway. I can't look at him anymore tonight without my heart breaking from his disappointment that I insist we continue with the trials.

I don my mask, letting my feelings about the argument melt away as I walk down the steps in a sultry rhythm. I am hunting for prey, something to distract me from the chaos of the evening. Who knew defeating a Ritherin would be the easiest battle of my day?

# CHAPTER 7

After grabbing a beer at the bar, I stifle a gag at the emerald-eyed blonde hanging on to every word of the male who fought before me in the pit. His head turns my way. I quickly look the other way, the heat of his gaze painting the side of my cheek with an unsettling intensity.

I will not give him the time of day, especially after what Sully said upstairs. Although I never actually agreed to his request, but that's beside the point. If Sully is warning me about him, he must be real fucking trouble.

I rake my gaze across the room of swaying drunk Fae, spotting the violet-eyed female from the pit. Lucky me, she survived. She must have gone after me while I was rushing Sully off before all Emberhell let loose. A bored expression paints her face, which is propped up on her fist as her finger twirls the rim of her flute filled with sparkling Moonwine. Adjacent to her is a burly blonde male, laying it on thick.

I prowl to her table, scraping a chair along the floor as I drag it next to hers. I plop down, resting my elbow on the table and my chin on a closed fist as her eyes snap to mine. It's time to have some fun. Time to pretend I'm not a broken mess on the inside.

"Glad to see you survived, Violet." I smile with heat in my eyes as I watch her pulse along her neck quicken under my gaze. The guy next to me rips my shoulder so I face him. *Big mistake.* I don't indulge people touching me without my permission.

"Hey, we're having a conversation here. Get lost."

"I think you're mistaken, Blondie. A conversation implies two people are involved. You were simply talking this stunning lady's ear off, and she, politely, didn't leave." I glance towards her; a blushing smile paints her cheeks. I've certainly got her attention now.

Her rosy hue heats my skin, giving me the reassurance I wasn't wrong earlier when I sensed she enjoys my face as much as I enjoy hers.

The smug blonde male's voice starts again. "You clearly don't know who I am—"

I use my air magic to pull the oxygen from his lungs as he grasps for his throat, eyes wide in terror. "Let me stop you right there. I don't give a fuck who you are, and I rather think you have squandered enough of this lady's time." I release my hold on the air; he gulps and gasps like a fish out of water. Very few Elarians can master that level of elemental air control unless they have air Pixie lineage in their veins.

He stands up, shoving his chair from the table. I listen for his movements. By the sound of the positioning of his feet and the way the cloth of his shirt creates friction against the leather, he has the gall to try and punch me.

I stand spinning, catching his fist in my hand. Now we are eye-level, my height matching his in my boots. Still holding his fist, I yank him into me, grabbing his shoulder.

I whisper into his ear, "Don't pick a fight you know you can't win, or I will further your embarrassment in front of everyone." There's a strange draining sensation in my palm right before I shove him back. His face ignites in flames with fury as he clenches his fists and storms away.

The pub is eerily quiet as I turn back to the violet-eyed girl, smiling at me with beautiful, generous lips. I bite my lower lip slowly, plopping back down in the chair with a confident lean. Finishing off Blondie's beer before working on my own. I'm not above free alcohol.

"My name is Winx. Yours is Savaé, right?"

"Uh, yeah, actually. How did you know that?" I run my hand over the back of my neck. I'm not used to anyone other than Sully knowing my name, and he rarely uses it.

"Defeating a Ritherin kinda makes you a big deal. Plus, everyone saw the ex-Commander Sully Stonewall going up against Chancellor Ashfel."

Ex-commander? Wait, *that* was the Celestials be dimmed Chancellor of Gildorea Universitás of War? *Son of a fucking bitch.*

My mind muddles like I've taken a blow to the head, trying to mince through the mindfuck of facts she just casually stated. I manage to choke out, "That skinny Arabellian?"

"Yep, that's my dad… unfortunately."

That comment has me spitting out my beer. "He's your dad? But your eyes… your hair… uh, sorry about calling him skinny."

A beautifully warm laugh bubbles up from her chest, warming me like glowing embers. "Don't apologize. I'm skinny, too." She giggles. "I got my eyes from my mother." She twirls her fingers through her lavender hair in a way that drives me wild with lust.

"As for my hair, I dye it, silly. Having white hair really makes the pigments pop. I change the color quite often." She gives me a flirtatious half-smile as her eyes drift up, like she's pondering the next color she'll dye it to suit her mood.

"So, let me guess, with eyes as striking as yours, your mother is a Pixie?"

"Nailed it!" she says with a wink before taking another sip of her Moonwine.

Elarian- or Arabellian-Pixie crosses are a common bloodline choice, known as Lilliac. Named for the various hues of purple that glimmer in their blood, this unique power allows their eyes to flare neon colors.

Pixies' elemental magic is so strong, you can literally see it simmer through their veins, but they can't practice the wide variety of minor magics like Elarians. Cerfios harness the element of earth; they have stone-like skin, almost as though they are sculpted from marble, nearly impenetrable with unnatural strength.

Those born of fire are known as Pyros. When channeling, they can levitate from the heat. Their hair shifting into roaring flames, while their skin becomes extremely hot to the touch, almost glowing. Some of the tax-collector guards passing through Estrella told me how they are known to be fierce and eccentric lovers.

Visci have the zeal of water. They gain unusual flexibility, their bones becoming fluid, nearly impossible to strike on the battlefield when trained. Some can even fit through small places and shapeshift. These abilities make them a favorite for the Spycraft division.

Last are those borne from the sky, known as Airrias. They conjure air, flying on translucent wings powered by storms, while their hair appears like clouds. Some can even divine the whispers of the wind, the strongest Airria manipulating the weather.

My eyes flick up from my beer to Winx. She is clearly waiting for my next move. I notice a subtle beating glow in her violet eyes, quickening my pulse with the heat of desire. I imagine it will be quite fun to watch her power flare as waves of pleasure take hold of her body. The air shifts between us, molecules vibrating in her radiating heat.

To ease the temperature, as I'm still debating whether she's worth the risk, being the Chancellor's daughter and all, I ask, "Did you fight today, or are you just here with your father?" I try to act nonchalant about who sired her, taking another sip of beer. Her dad must be the one and only Chancellor of Universitás. I regret my earlier snide comment to him and the fact Sully nearly fucked up my chances by cursing at him. Maybe I should tread lightly with his daughter before he ensures my death at the next trial.

"I went last today. Killed the Casin with a crossbow bolt through the eye. My father and I aren't close, but he said I had to do the trials with him in the outlands, where he is trying some new experiments. Apparently, he needs to keep a closer eye on me. I have a knack for getting into trouble in Riicah. I love the electric nightlife. Plus… I like to make things go boom. Tends to be frowned upon in a big city," she muses with a flash of darkness in her eyes that pauses her finger, circling the rim of her Moonwine flute. Her gaze climbs with anything but an innocent blaze, the pulse of her flaring irises speeding up. Slowly, I exhale, realizing it is giving away the beat of her heart. How divine. I savor the control this tell gives me.

"A crossbow to the eye. Sexy and deadly." My eyes lock on hers as she drags her teeth along her lower lip. "Plus a Pyro. I guess that makes you a triple threat."

She grabs my hand, which rests on the handle of the beer tankard. Heating up, I gaze into her eyes, which are flickering faster, glowing brighter as my beer sizzles.

I smirk at her. "Impressive fire magic to not burn my hand while ruining my beer. Excellent control."

She pulls her hand away. "Oops. Sorry, I didn't think about the hot beer. My father always says I think about the consequences of my actions too late." She looks at the table. I can still see the flicker of her eyes, more erratic now she's nervous. Almost guilty, as if she's expecting me to chastise her.

I lift the curve of my index finger to her chin, forcing her to peer up at me as I move in close to her. There it is, that steady beat again, flickering like embers of a slowly building flame. Heavens, she's a fun time I'm struggling to resist. I know there are safer females to sate my need for distraction tonight, but I'd be lying if I said the Chancellor's daughter doesn't seem like an Emberhell of a good time. One that can burn right through all the things I'd like to forget, even if just for a moment of reprieve.

I lean in even closer. "My beer isn't the only thing that's hot now."

Her lips part, just inches from mine, her chest rising and falling, breath quickening. I arch my eyebrow with a sly half-smile, moving another notch closer. With the placement of my finger, I can feel the shiver that dances through her, the air molecules vibrating into a mesmerizing hum as the atmosphere swelters between us. I lean my cheek parallel to hers, tucking the long part of her lavender angular bob behind her right ear.

"Wanna get out of here?" I whisper along the pointed cusp. Her breath catches as she nods wildly.

I grab her hand, whisking her to the door. So much for treading lightly. But Emberhell, if she doesn't look worth the trouble. Pyros are powerful fire wielders, and something tells me she is a fire worth setting ablaze. If Pyros become Ellian Knights, they often bond with other flying creatures that wield fire so they don't get burned in battle. The latter makes me glad I kept my basilisk armor on in case things get too fiery.

I lead her into the shadows with me. Throwing her playfully against the wall, tugging her close just before she lands, making sure not to hurt her. Then I let her relax against the wood panels, which sizzle from the heat of her skin. My hand weaves through her lavender hair, grasping it just above the nape of her neck. I devour her neck in untamed kisses, her pulse quickening beneath my lips, matching the beat of her flickering eyes as she lets out a whimper.

I growl in return, continuing to kiss down her chest. She's wearing a short dress of thin silk that clings to her petite body, with a deep V between her petite breasts. To my pleasant surprise, she isn't wearing anything underneath. Her peaked nipples catching the moonlight under the soft sheen of the dress.

I bite into her bottom lip, my thumb brushing over the peak of her breast. My other hand tugging her hair back slightly as she moans. We're both panting as my forehead meets hers, our lips only a whisper apart as I move my hand down the outline of her carved stomach, dipping between her thighs.

Her breath catches as my hand slips under her dress, lazily grazing up her thigh. Her back arches, rolling her hips forward to crash into my touch. A subtle violet glow emanates from the heat consuming her flesh.

Her lashes flutter open as she thrusts my hand into the wetness pooling for me. Her hunger for me. I growl at her fiery greed. The pad of my thumb teases over her plump clit, summoning a soft rumble from her vibrating chest. Then, I indulge her wanton need. Slipping my finger through her throbbing dampness. I partially enter inside of her, teasing her entrance as her nectar drenches my fingers with her gasp.

I lick the bottom of her lip before nipping at it as she tries to kiss me, but I relent, pulling the nape of her neck back, giving me all the control.

"Not yet, Violet," I purr. Her eyes blaze as her body grinds against mine.

I continue to tease her until her movements become wild, frantic, feral. Begging. Then, at the same time, finally giving in to her demands, my lips crash into hers. I kiss her deeply while my finger slides into her just as deep. My tongue's rhythm matches the motion of my finger as it curls at just the right spot. My thumb swirls at varying pressures around her swollen clit. Waves of tension curl inside her, building up, ready to crash in release.

She moans into my mouth. Then, slowing the rhythm, my lips trail down her neck, kisses alternating with delicious bite marks. Every time she gets close, I pull back, keeping her on the edge of pleasure as she begs for release. "Savaé. More. Please."

The fire in her breathless plea causes me to slip a little in my control, now entering her with both fingers, curling pressure on just the right spot.

"Be a good girl, and come for me," I susurrate along her neck; without hesitation, she obeys.

A heavenly sound leaves her lips, which I capture in a kiss. She comes on my fingers, her body dancing like blissful flames of wildfire, ready to consume everything in her wake. I moan with her, feeling her pleasure as if it's my own. Consuming it raw, coming from the pure ecstasy of feeling her release. Both of our breaths become ragged in the moment. Gently leaving her delicate, sensitive area, I give her one last deep kiss. I feel her move her hand up the slit of my dress, but I quickly halt the motion.

"Your pleasure is mine."

She nods in understanding as I lean my forehead against the wall, steadying my breath before helping her neatly fix her dress. I've always found it easier to feed off others' pleasure rather than be vulnerable, giving in to the chaos required for me to feel it firsthand. It's too much, too... intimate.

The flicker in her eyes slows as she looks at me. She tries to take a step closer, stumbling a bit under the weight of her own body, and I catch her.

"You are quite the little firelight," I whisper in her ear as she falls into me, her skin still flaming to the touch.

She smiles at me. "Firelight?"

"Bioluminescent creatures. They pollinate flowers at night. They make the forest dance in the moonlight."

"That sounds magical. Maybe one day you can show me? Father has never even let me get close to the Mysticwoods."

"Love to. I'm surprised your mother never took you?" Pixies are beings of the Mysticwoods.

"Oh. She died in battle when I was young. I barely knew her. Then my father moved us to the capital with my aunt and cousin, Flint. He's completing the trials in Riicah. He'd like you, a Cerfios. He would have had a blast watching you fight today. Ground-Combatant is his forte."

"I'm sorry for your loss... A Cerfios and a Pyro? I bet you had some pretty wild fights growing up."

"It's okay, hard to miss someone you never knew... and we most certainly did, yes. He swore I almost turned him to lava one day!" Her head tips back in a laugh, reliving the memory. I can tell she's hiding her grief behind her own mask, bright and fiery, compared to mine of ice and steely control. I can feel her disconnect with her father, cold and calculating, the complete opposite of her wildfire, her explosiveness.

"I can relate to that sentiment. I never knew either of my parents... Lava? I guess this wall got off easy then." I nod my head to the wall behind her that has faint scorch marks from where her body had been.

She giggles nervously at the sight, her eyes flickering fast. There's that anger and fear of trouble again, tearing through her. I understand her struggle in my own fucked-up way.

I pull my arms tighter along her waist.

"Let's get you home before your dad tries to murder me in cold blood," I whisper in her ear before releasing her from my grasp.

She nods, grabbing my hand. I have never held anyone's hand before. I feel almost shackled by the gesture, but I can tell she needs this feeling of safety more than the discomfort gnawing at my ribs pains me, and I'm not about to let her walk home in the dark. I may be an ass, but Sully raised me to be better than most. That is, when I'm feeling generous.

The fleeting glimpses of her broken bits have me extending myself outside the boundaries of my comfort tonight. I can give her the gift of this small moment. We continue, and I let her lead the way.

"You'll be at the next trial in Frostmar, right?" Winx asks. I nod. "My dad mentioned something about releasing a monster during the course. He didn't say what kind. I overheard him talking to one of the majors about where they are going to keep the beast. I figured I should give you a heads-up after today. I caught a glimpse of what went on after your trial. Seems he has it out for you already."

My brow kicks up at her. "I hope you didn't come with me just to piss your dad off?" I don't want to be the dagger she twists into his side; that will only ensure he strings up a noose with my name on it.

"I won't lie, it definitely made you hotter, but it's not the only reason." She winks before turning her head to the building beside us. "Well, this is me."

We stop in front of a white stone building with gold-framed windows and a copper roof that's weathered into a textured seafoam green. The building is three stories, and you can see the glowing faerie light chandeliers from the street. It's a stark contrast to the one- and two-story stone and wood buildings surrounding it.

"Quaint accommodations." I nudge her with my elbow as I take in the beauty of the building.

"The inside is just as cold and sterile as my dad. You want to come in for a nightcap? We could torch the place after. It's in dire need of some warmth," she teases, nudging me back. I swallow at how quickly she escalated to destruction and violence. She's fucking mad, and it's kinda hot but absolutely terrifying. I may have killed my foster father, but arson on the first night is a bit much, even for me.

"Yeah, that will be a hard pass for me." My generosity is worn through as

I regret not listening to the gnawing sensation needling between my ribs that told me not to hold her hand. My fingers drop from hers, turning to walk back before anyone sees us together. She may have helped me forget the agony of Sully's cough and our argument tonight, but I have a feeling she's strung me up for more than I've bargained for.

# CHAPTER 8

I slink my way up the stairs, weaving over piles of vomit from the dwindling pub crowd, who are blissfully obliterated. I creak open the door that leads to the hallway of rooms, finding it darker than I remember.

All the candles that previously lit the hall have been snuffed out. My hackles rise on the back of my neck. Attention narrowing on twirling shadows at the end of the hall, revealing two pure white eyes fixed on me.

I quickly reach for my poison dagger, still sheathed along my ribs, and shift my stance with a slight bend in my legs, poised to strike.

"Woah. Woah. Woah. Settle down there, savage." A smoky voice breaks through the darkness as the candles ignite once more. Shadows melt away, revealing a tall figure, arms crossed, with one leg kicked up, bracing his weight.

It's *him*.

He's much taller now that I'm not above him. I guesstimate about 6'4" of sculpted muscle resting up against the wall, with a not-so-subtle confidence to him. He has that stupid half-smirk on his gorgeously carved face, framed by soft black waves dancing in the candlelight. His icy eyes are transfixed on mine, the hairs along my neck instinctively prickling under the intensity.

Being only a few feet in front of me, I can see his arctic blue eyes, splattered by flecks of crimson, swirling with smoke-like shadows. I look away, afraid I might fall into them and never escape. My gaze drifts over his muscles, barely contained in his black leather outfit, which is newly adorned with thick leather stitches, fixing the rip on his side from his battle earlier today.

"What are you doing here? I could have killed you," I hiss.

"I highly doubt that." He arches a brow, to which I raise my chin, beckoning him to test his theory of who would win. He lifts his hand, gazing over his tattooed knuckles as he continues, "Yet it does appear you're working hard to be on someone's death list. I saw you walk out of here in a heated hurry with the Chancellor's daughter after embarrassing Commander Bragen's son. A ballsy move, especially considering the rumors they are a Bloodline pairing."

His voice is smoky and smooth, like fine Smokewhisper libation. He lowers his knuckles, rubbing at his heart like it's hurting for some reason.

An exasperated, "Fuck me," leaves my lips as I rub the bridge of my nose, comprehending how much trouble I've managed to get myself into in a single evening. So much for treading lightly.

"That's a little forward, but I wouldn't say I am totally opposed to the idea." A devilish twist curls at his lips.

"Ugh. I wasn't talking to you," I growl. Fucking *males*.

"I don't see anyone else in the hallway." He shrugs nonchalantly.

"Celestials, you know what I mean," I snap, debating if I should slit his throat and be done with this ridiculous conversation.

"Oh, do I?" he purrs with a feline grin curling up on his full lips.

"Shut up, before I smack that stupid grin off your face." My blood boils in aggravation. Yep, slitting his throat is looking more appealing by the moment.

"Fun. I like it rough." His eyes darken as the shadows pulse within them, cracking something deep within my darkness. I refuse to explore it, instead slinging verbal daggers his way.

"Trust me, whatever your name is, you couldn't handle me. Even in your wildest dreams."

"Sølas Zyon. I'm a fast learner, if you're offering to teach," he muses with a *fucking wink*.

The blood boiling in my veins shifts into a different heat as my breath catches on the glimpse of our bodies colliding in my mind. *Fucking lovely.* Now, my mind is joining my traitorous body. No one has ever affected me like this, mincing my mind into a useless slurry. Just one more reason to be all the more wary.

I shake my head, flinging the delusions from it.

"I'm not on the class schedule for today," I sneer, but my body has an agenda all its own. I screech internally as I watch myself unwillingly stepping closer to him. *What the actual fuck is going on with me?* Sweat beads my brow as I regain control, halting myself before I take another step.

"What are you even doing here?" I snip, hoping my advance appears threatening, rather than revealing my clearly unsatiated hormones. Yes, that has to be it, although they've never been this difficult to control.

"Waiting for you, of course," he purrs. My gaze snaps to his, wishing my eyes could burn him to ash on the spot.

The thick air between us freezes. I don't like the idea of anyone waiting for me in the shadows, no matter how fucking jaw-droppingly handsome they are.

"Choose your next words carefully, or you won't be surviving to the next trial," I purr right back, lethality dripping from every word.

"Bloodthirsty, are we? Don't worry. I would have kept the element of surprise in the shadows if I planned on picking a fight with you. I just wanted to meet the mysterious female who no one has ever heard of. Savaé Entropaé. Who, I might add, took down a Celestial-damned Ritherin today. Let's just say curiosity got the best of me. Plus, I didn't mind how you looked at me in the pit today."

I debate kicking myself for ignorantly hoping he was looking at the pretty blonde behind me. Things would be so much easier if he had been. Things would make sense, instead of this snowballing mess bludgeoning in my chest.

I chew on my bottom lip; the way he says my name in that smoky voice echoes in my head. He pronounces it properly, holding the 'ay' of *Sa-vay*, which is how my name is said in old tongue. Most people just pronounced my name Savæ, *Sa-veh*. My reckless heart skips a beat at the taste of my name on his tongue. A primal urge courses through me, craving something more, like an invisible tether pulling us together.

I take another step closer, as if to fight the challenge in his eyes... those mesmerizing shadows swirling within, pulling at something deep inside me, grasping hold of my body once more, willing another step closer to him.

I should gut him for the control he wields over me, or at the very least turn and run. Those would be the logical things to do. Instead, my breath quickens, sinking further into the quicksand I've found myself in. My lips part as if I can't get enough air, a response that could kill me as I drown in the invisible ocean he pulls me under.

There's the softest of velvet whispering a caress along my cheek, whispering a promise that rattles the walls of my glacial heart palace. The danger finally snaps my mind from its trance as I realize it was a smoky tendril of one of *his* shadows.

I move like lightning, my dagger poised at his throat.

He's a Shadowmancer. An extremely rare power. One that hasn't been seen in the last fifty years, though there had been one in the last generation of Wuvon. He had died in the battle of Sternma—Sully killed him and his Crowven before their horde descended on him, when Xeno sacrificed himself so Sully could live.

I recall the icy fear in Sully's voice as he recounted the eerie description of the Shadowmancer consuming all light around him, nothing reflecting off. The only way he was able to see him was the faint hue of garnet that outlined his body—and the crimson-drenched night sky of his eyes.

This must be why Sully warned me to stay away from him and his bloodline. I should fear Sølas, but why is my body unsettlingly at ease so close to him?

The shadows in his eyes whip violently now, becoming darker. His emotions are harder to read than most. Typical for a Shadowmancer, exceptionally good at hiding things, including their own mind.

His skin radiates heat, despite his cool demeanor. I'm now only inches from him, allowing me to glimpse the shadows swirling beneath his skin: a moving tattoo, tracing from his steady pulse below my dagger, down to his knuckles. A subtle aroma of amber and spruce trickles into my lungs.

An electricity builds in the air between us, like right before lightning strikes. I don't understand how I can be so close, yet long to be closer.

He is *absolutely* trouble.

"Shadowmancer," I hiss.

He swallows. His shadows swell, darkening the space around us, like when I first entered the hallway. His eyes turn ice white, no pupils or irises, reminding me of moonlight peeking through stormy night skies.

Chilling.

Spellbinding.

His power envelopes me, all at once, coating all of me in a sea of velvet.

I steady myself in the odd comfort of his darkness. I suppose it makes sense; I've always felt safe in the shadows. A part of me knows I need to break free of the darkness consuming my body, but I savor the serenity, craving to hold on to this foreign energy between us just a little longer. Although I should be dissecting it with my dagger, finding a way to slice myself free of it.

Power like I've never felt before crackles beneath my skin, reaching for him, splitting my ribs to escape. In total darkness, I notice a light coming off my body—before I can investigate, I'm jolted by his words.

"Has anyone ever told you, you have the most breathtaking eyes?"

*What the fuck did he just say to me?* My eyes mark me as cursed, warning of the darkness within, something he's failing miserably at heeding. Fucking shadow *prick*.

I shove my body off his, sheathing my dagger. I need to get away from him and his strange fucking antics. The lights return to the room once again as the shadows retreat back into his chest.

"I need to go to sleep." I turn towards the door of my room before I scoff under my breath, "Hope I was worth the wait."

"You most certainly were."

There's a chill in the air. I look back over my shoulder, and he's already gone.

I close the door behind me. Open the door to Sully's room, pull the blanket up around him before closing the window I'd left ajar earlier.

In my room, I lie in bed, replaying the day in my head. The fiery pleasure with Winx that was apparently not so secret, according to Sølas. The Chancellor's words hit me, reminding me he's already planning his next challenge.

I appreciate the heads-up from Winx. It gives me time to prepare. But seducing the Chancellor's manic daughter and pissing off a Commander's son will likely make getting into Universitás even more difficult. I have a feeling it won't get any easier after I arrive if my debut with my future class-mates is any indicator.

I'm at a loss to describe what happened between me and Sølas in the hallway. I roll the syllables on my tongue, *soul-luss*. His name means *dark-ness* in the old tongue—a forgotten language from before the Eclipse War. I wince at how I lost control near him tonight. I never lose control like that. Okay, maybe I do, when my temper boils over, or I let my darkness out to play.

This was different, though. There was a tingling energy twirling inside, drawing me closer; an inescapable gravity, longing to explore every inch of his shadows. Then there's the matter of figuring out where that glow came from when I was with him, cloaked in his shadows.

In all my life spent in the familiarity of shadows, they have always hidden me, kept me safe, the companion to the darkness of my soul. I have never experienced a light like that from within. Was it something about him that made me glow? Or was it something about my body in his shadows, almost resisting his darkness with my own light? Although I wouldn't say that I found myself resisting anything about his darkness. Savoring it is, unfortunately, more accurate. And that's precisely the problem: the way his presence commanded my traitorous body. I need to steer clear from his chaos.

I'm likely overthinking the strange light thing. The glow is, most logically, from his moonlit eyes when they went all eerily white. That has to be it. Or maybe it's my Celestial Gift finally manifesting... No, it wasn't anything like casting elemental magic.

This whole losing control gnaws at my brain, making it a stringy mess. Why had it been so much harder with him? What makes him so different? Unlike with Winx, when I'd been in total control and only giving in when I wanted to. Something about him riles me up in all the wrong ways, distracting me—more than the endless ocean of shadows in his eyes that seek to drown me.

Sully's wretched cough fillets me from my thoughts, flooding me with the image of blood-speckled snow, frost spreading across me, casting a chill deep into my marrow. Maybe in the next city, we can find a Mycelium Nymph. They're a mushroom-Faeanoid species, having two arms and legs with various species of mushrooms growing from their skin, their hair, a mix of lichen and fungi. Mycelium Nymphs are naturally strong healers, especially Helios, who can wield the mycelium network to mend just about anything organic. Sadly, few Helios exist. Even fewer reside in the cold Highlands.

Hopeful thoughts of finding a Helios wisp through my mind as weariness weighs on my eyelids. A tidal wave of exhaustion consumes me as all of the tiredness of the day hits me at once, and I am out like a faerie light.

# CHAPTER 9

After a month of traveling, we finally reach the city of Frostma. There were times during the treacherous travel through the snowy, mountainous terrain I wasn't sure Sully would make it. Razors churn in my stomach, lapping up my ribs, remembering the endless number of blood-drenched rags. At one point, I was half certain a Ronew might eat us in the night, smelling his crimson-soaked pillow.

By the time we reach the inn, he's hacking bloody clumps.

*Fuck*, this is really not good. The vice around my heart twists and twists, tightening with each step towards our room until it threatens to fracture at the seams.

I need to find Sully a healer. *Now.* I tuck him into the bed, ensuring the hearth toasts up our rooms, leaving him with a cup of Midnight Bark tea on the nightstand. I kiss him on the forehead.

"I'm going to find you a healer."

He grabs my wrist, tugging me close to him. "You need to stay focused, Savaé, to pass the Trial of Tenacity. You only have a week to practice the terrain. I know this is what you want. My cough will get better out of the cold air."

There's a chill in the way he says my name. He always calls me his little dragon. Hearing him say my name is odd, especially when I'm not in trouble. A thought ignites a feral rage in me.

"Don't you dare give up! I could pass this trial in my sleep." That's a lie, but I'm making a point. "You coughed up enough blood on this Fates-be-damned trip that you might even need a blood-succubus transfusion. And don't you dare tell me you are fine because we both know you're not. You have lost at least another thirty pounds. You're so thin, you might blow away with a gust of wind."

Seeking out a blood-succubus is an absolute last resort. I sigh at the thought, softening my tone. "I am really worried about you, Sully. I can't lose you. This cough is serious. We need help. You need help. *Please* let me help you. Let me do this for you."

Taking my hand in both of his, he says with a wisdom and sorrow that breaks my limping heart, "Little dragon, some things can't be healed. Some things just have to be accepted as they are. All the power in the world cannot defeat death. She comes for us all."

Tears gush down my gold-flecked cheeks.

He struggles to sit up from the bed, a whisper of the male he once was. His big bear hands, now withered fingers, cup my cheeks, wiping the water-falls away with his thumbs.

"I will always be with you, in this world and the next. Every moment with you has been a treasure. Thank you for bringing laughter and love back into my life. When you watch the stars twinkle above you, know I am smiling down on you, always, my little Starborne dragon. You made my heart whole again."

His words are so full of love that my heart heaves against my chest. As if breaking free from the cage of my ribs will grant her the ability to give her own life to mend his. I wrap my arms around his neck as he wraps his thick bones around my body with a hug I never want to end. Unfortunately, it's interrupted by that fucking wretched cough, like nails scraping along the surface of my heart.

"I need to rest now, little dragon. Tomorrow morning, I will be in better sorts. Then we can review the course together."

I tuck him into the thick wool blanket as he wheezes, trying to catch his breath. My heart falls to the floor, shattering into a thousand pieces as I watch the male who raised me struggle to live. He is always strong for me, so I muster all my strength and stand.

My legs feel rickety, like all the blood has been drained from them. I summon strength from a place I don't even know I have, because it's Sully,

and I need to find a healer. The universe is going to have to wait to break me.
I have a mission to complete.

I scour the town in a frantic rush. Racing from one white stone store to
the next, all the way down MainStreet, speaking to anyone who'll listen.
Until I'm finally pointed towards a retired healer from Gildorea. Her name is
Kanuvwoodi. Kanuvi for short. She is a Mycelium Nymph but not a Helios.
She's been brought into town at the request of the Universitás administration,
healing for the trial, no doubt. Even for those who survive the deadly
obstacle course, their injuries can be quite significant.

I rush into a slate building with a carved sign above the wooden doors
that says 'Healing Ward.' The front desk is tended by an Elarian with fair
skin, long black hair, and a white tunic. Unfortunately, she tells me Kanuvi is
off-duty and unavailable for healing requests. After I lie my ass off and
convince her Kanuvi is a family friend and I just want to see her before I
leave town, the Elarian reluctantly agrees to bring me to her.

She takes me to a corridor upstairs with a common living space, likely
where healers reside between shifts. The walls are lined with anatomical art
of various species. There's a diagram of a Müra, a moth-like Fae. Their eyes
are set on upside-down moth wings, the tips pointing upwards, blending into
a head full of small wings at odd angles. Their noses and lower faces look
Elarian but are covered with soft moth fuzz. They tend to be slender and
more willowy in appearance, with intricately painted wings on their backs
for flying.

The anatomical art depicts the deeply grooved nature of their brilliant
brains and their bioluminescent antennae that glow in the dark. They are a
favorite at Gildorea for the position of Savant, being the team leader, masters
of battle strategy, seeing the complete picture, and calculating every
possibility.

Several doors are placed around the room; the Elarian from the front
desk points me towards a blue one. I knock on the door with the determination that no matter how this conversation goes, I am not walking away
without her help.

A female covered in various orange and red fungi—teal lichen filling in
the spaces between—answers the door. She swipes long enoki mushrooms
away from her sage eyes as she adjusts her circular spectacles.

"Apologies. I am not on-duty tonight. Come back tomorrow. May the
Celestials bless you." Her voice is earthy and melodic.

"My father is dying. I need your help. I've tried every magical herb and potion I know of. My Sangre healing does nothing, and now he is coughing up blood clots. Please, help me," I plead.

"I am sorry. The Elarian at the front desk will direct you to a healer on-duty."

"He needs a Mycelium Nymph. Sully trained me as well as any other Elarian healer here." I'm about to kneel and beg for help when curiosity peaks her tone.

"Sully Stonewall?"

"Yes! Sully Stonewall."

"You say you are his daughter? That's impossible."

"How is that impossible?" I ask.

"Because everyone knows his Bloodline-pairing offspring died as a child."

I snap my jaw tight, refusing to let my mouth gape like a fish on dry land, despite her comment stealing all the air from my lungs. *Everyone knows except for me!* There is so much Sully never told me about his time at Universitás and in the Golden Legion. He gained and lost so much in such a short amount of time; it's no wonder he never wanted to speak about it. He came to a literal ice tundra to forget his past life, just like the metaphorical glacial palace in my chest I use to keep what's left of my heart safe. The only difference is, he cracked through my icicle ribs, blooming warmth and all these dainty fragile flowers that will wither away into ash without him.

Tears prickle the backs of my eyes. I fight the welling silver threatening to gush from my lashes like the cascading waterfalls of the Dragon Spine Mountains. I will not yield to these ridiculous emotions or the thousands of questions festering on my tongue, craving to be spat out.

Right now is not the time to search for answers. Right now, I must stay focused. Right now, I only need one thing: her help to heal Sully.

"He took me in when I was eight and had nowhere else to go. He's the closest thing I have to a father. I'll do anything for your help." I lower my mask, allowing just a smudge of my sadness to paint my features, baring this one glimpse of my vulnerable, wilting bits, so she can see the pleading desperation hidden beneath all my armor.

She looks me over with an assessing gaze. "Taking in an orphan and raising you as his own does sound like Sully…" She pauses, lifting a dainty finger covered in shades of ruby lichen to tap her lip. A small smile perks up the corner of her mouth.

"Our service overlapped. He was the best of us. An exemplary commander. He always put the good of his soldiers first, never risking those stationed under him to meet an objective. He and Xeno were so close, I thought his death would take his life, too. In a way, I suppose it did. He was never the same after. Our fleet admiral was extremely disappointed when he refused to continue his service in an administrative role when he was no longer an Ellian Knight. He saved a great many lives with Xeno's sacrifice, killing the last shadow Wuvon." She pauses thoughtfully, as if lost in a memory, before adjusting her spectacles and continuing, "Let me gather some supplies. I will be right out."

Even if Sully never wanted to share his experiences with me, I thank the Celestials his name carries so much weight. She described him exactly as I imagined he'd be during his service. I really hope Sully lives long enough for me to pester some stories out of him—although after this many years of holding them close to his heart, I doubt anything will change.

I return with Kanuvi to the inn and bring her to Sully's room. He wakes briefly to smile at us between ragged breaths.

"Thank you for your honorable service," Kanuvi hums, crossing her arm with a fist over her chest in salute. Sully gives her a weak nod as his honey-brown eyes flutter shut.

Her fingers drift over his chest, a white glow emanating from them, humming at various frequencies as she assesses him. Her hand freezes over his right ribs, and we both jump slightly, ears clawed at by the screeching pitch.

Her shoulder blades tense, eyes growing wide, her fear twisting around a subtle anguish. At that moment, *I know*.

She turns to me slowly and looks up with eyes drenched in regret.

"I am sorry. There is nothing I can do about his affliction. All I can offer is a salve to ease the pain, allowing a more peaceful passing."

The heavens themselves come crashing down, dragging my howling soul to the pits of Emberhell with them. After a long second, I whimper, "What if we brought him to the woods? Your magic is stronger there, yes?"

She stares at the floor. "Regretfully, I don't think that will help. His condition is beyond my abilities. I will bring you the salve tomorrow. May the Celestials bless you both." She quietly leaves the room.

I'm frozen. Waves of shock, horror, and despair crash through me, but I don't shed a tear. I stay absolutely frozen as the storm threatens to consume me. I cannot break. Not now. I raise my mental shields, a calming numbness taking their place as I become a hollow ghost.

I sit by Sully's side for the next four days, applying the salve as directed every four hours without fail. I watch him wither away as his respirations become quicker, more uneven. He's awake for less and less time each day, unable to speak in more than two-word sentences due to his shortness of breath. On day five, he stops eating and drinking altogether and doesn't wake from his suffering slumber while he continues to gasp for air.

I go back to Kanuvi and beg her to meet me in the forest the next day, to at least try to heal him. She initially protests, but when I make it clear I won't give up, she gives in to my pleas.

The next morning, I place Sully's withered form into a modified chair with wheels on either side, which I borrowed from the Healer's Ward. To my surprise, even with barely any meat on his bones, he is still so heavy. I wrap him up in several wool blankets.

I meet Kanuvi at the location she marked on a map deep within the Amberwood—a unique forest where it's always autumn, between the Highland's tundra and the Midland's golden meadows. She makes me dig a shallow oval into the ground where I place Sully, intentionally disturbing the dirt that exposes the mycelium network.

My strong muscles softly lay his skin and bones down on the bare soil. It's odd how he now resembles the form he found me in. Spindly. Holding on by a thread.

Kanuvi kneels over him, placing one hand on his forehead and one on his chest while I hold his right hand. Then, the earth beneath him moves ever so slightly as a wild array of mushrooms spring up from the soil and cover his body.

Under their growth, his breathing seems to ease; only his face and hand in mine are still exposed. His eyes flutter open for the first time in over twenty-four hours. In that moment, hope dares to trickle into my heart.

He squeezes my hand as he gazes up at me. "It's time to let me go, little dragon. The stars are calling my name."

Tears pour from my eyes like they intend to flood the entire planet in their reckoning.

His eyes become pure, iridescent starlight, and he squeezes my hand tightly as he draws his last breath.

"I love you. Always."

"I love you, big bear," I whisper.

Then his eyes close.

Kanuvi removes her hands as the mushrooms continue to grow. Their spindles flourish between my fingers and Sully's. I refuse to let go until nothing more than soil remains in my hands. The mound of mushrooms grows over him and collapses into spores before twirling towards the sky.

I wail to the heavens, my cry so thunderous that it shakes the earth beneath us. After I quiet, in the eye of the storm, Kanuvi's footsteps trail into the distance, leaving me in mourning. The cyclone swirls up inside me once more. I wrap my arms around myself as I scream with the pain of a pack of ravenous Ronew, shredding my heart to ribbons. Agony fractures through my bones in the wake of my powerful sorrow, splintering the surrounding trees into shrapnel—a reflection of my shattering heart and soul.

I lie there on the ground next to where his body returned to the cycle of the earth. I weep as all that makes me tame and kind dies with him.

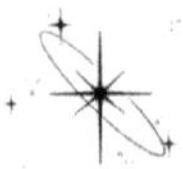

WHEN I WAKE the next morning in the Amberwood, my skin is chilled, and it isn't the air. Yesterday feels like a distant dream. I am a haunted shell of a being. The only thing left inside me, still tethering me to this realm, is my mission of becoming an Ellian Knight. A glorious suicide mission, to die one day in battle and join Sully once more.

My body is nothing more than a jagged dagger of ice for my mind to wield. The eerie silence is thick as I pack mine and Sully's belongings. I am numb to it all. It's as if my humanity departed with him at his eternal resting ground. After all, he was the one who brought me up from a feral creature hiding in the shadows to become something more, something whole. In his absence, I am fractured once more, as if I'm still at his grave, screaming and shattering along with the trees around me.

Tomorrow is the Trial of Tenacity on the edge of the Amberwood, closer to the city of Frostma. Every trialist journeys here for this challenge, which is too elaborate to recreate anywhere else. I'll be going in without a practice run. A shudder crawls down my spine at the barren room. I can't stand being here anymore.

I move to a different inn on the other side of town, closer to the Amberwood. To save some coin now that I only need single accommodation. The world seems to fall still as I fall asleep, part of my soul wishing I never wake again.

# CHAPTER 10

Rising with the sun, I don my basilisk-scale armor before slipping on my black leather fighting vest, adorned with the six daggers at my ribs and a short sword strapped along my left thigh. Something in my gut tells me to strap my small crossbow to my back, with the quiver pouch on my right thigh.

I fold my cloak, leaving it for safekeeping in my solitary room. I don't bother covering the gold flecks on my cheeks today. I will just sweat the soot off during the trial, and frankly, I don't have any more fucks left to give.

I arrive and check in for the trial. The same cold, bitter lady is begrudgingly present at this event. Her eyes appear more tired, no doubt from the many days she has been at work with the entire continent of trialists arriving for the event. She will be here for the next three months until everyone on the list has a chance.

She looks up at me and then returns to her scroll as she writes something.

"You are last today." There's a ghostly inkling to how she said 'last,' but I already suspect it has to do with the extra challenge Chancellor Ashfel will send me. I know it involves another monster, thanks to Winx's warning.

It makes sense they will have me go last—assuming if I can't kill the beast, it won't unintentionally kill anyone else for the day.

I have nothing left to lose at this point. I'm not saying I have a death wish, but my gut tells me the universe and the Fates enjoy torturing me too much to let me off easy with an early death. Plus, this is everything Sully and

I worked for. Even if he didn't want me to go to Gildorea, I know he wouldn't want me to just give up.

We're seated in order today; our times are spaced out by one hour. Being last means the sun will set during my trial. Commander Bragen's son goes first, his name being called as I walk to my seat. Apparently, Blondie's name is Chet. Chet Bragen. Sounds about right.

He glares at me as I walk by, raving, "You're as good as dead this round, Savaé Entropaé." Celestials, I wish my name was sharp enough to cut the tongue out of his mouth and leave him choking on his own pompous blood. *If only.*

"I'll ink you in for this evening, right after I leave Lady Death moaning my name," I say with a sarcastic wink. Out of the corner of my eye, I catch a shadow reaching up behind Chet, shoving him forward. Before he can catch himself, the side of his face smashes into the railing.

I sling a dagger-like glare at Sølas, who's sitting next to him, reclined, hands clasped behind his head with a smug smirk on his face. I grit my teeth. I don't need him or his shadows fighting my battles for me.

He gives me a lazy perusal. I curse my heating skin, which only intensifies in the electricity of the air between us as I walk by. I really loathe how he affects my body. I hate not being in control.

I roll my shoulder in an effort to roll off the sensation as he says, "Good luck, though something tells me you won't need it."

The emerald-eyed blonde is next. Her hair is spun into two buns at the top of her head. I pass several other trialists before I see Winx, with a big grin on her face as she sees me. I don't bother to smile back—there's no kindness left inside me. I have nothing left to give. Her smile falls to the floor, brows pinching with confusion.

I take my seat last in line.

First is the crucible of thorns. Chet struggles clumsily due to his oversized build as thorns and vines try to drag him under, mimicking the ability of the Wuvon to manipulate the ever-changing landscape of the Blackwood. For this trial, they use Elarian-Naturalists, a hybrid subspecies with strong druid magic. Allowing them to manipulate nature. During the obstacle course portion, Chet triggers a fire trap, burning half his hair off. The sight of his fuming, singed face would have made me laugh if my insides weren't lost to a blizzard of grief I'm barely holding at bay.

The crowd cheers from below, seated in rows of amphitheater seats for everyone to watch the spectacle of misfortune. Next, Sølas dances through the entire crucible of thorns and obstacles with ease, like this is just a game. He plows through the mountainous climb, designed to test your endurance. His tall body making quick work of the ascent up the steep rocky cliff. He slips out of sight over a ledge midway through, where he enters the Ethereal Maze of Whispers.

The blonde is quick and agile on her toes. However, the three trialists after her all die. One succumbs to the quicksand, the next falls from the tightrope, and the last almost climbs to the maze but loses his footing on the final ascent before tumbling in a twisted, broken mess to his death.

The course blazes violet in Winx's glow—a living flame racing like forest fire. Vines shrivel and blacken just from the heat radiating off her in a shimmering wake.

Next is an Aetherhawk called Highin Heathrow. Aetherhawks are a hawk-Fae hybrid species with exceptional vision. His face is that of an Elarian Fae, though his nose is narrow and flat. Two small wings jet from his temples, made of sepia-colored feathers that descend his back into powerful wings. His build is lean, with scaled legs shifting to birdlike feet ending in talons. He moves with precision. It's extremely rare for Aetherhawks to enter the trials and join the Golden Legion. Their species has been hunted near extinction as they are a coveted prize for the Wuvon. Clearly, some parts of them harness extremely potent magic. Despite the unwavering lines of his stoic face, there is a sad determination to his eyes. As though the Wuvon have stolen someone important from him and he's here to make them pay.

Well, would you look at him. Climbing the mountain instead of just flying to the maze. He's a better Fae than me, no question. If I had wings, I wouldn't hesitate, taking flight without a second thought.

The following Fae is a feline-like species known as Mao. Her name is Kissa Mrow. The announcer pronouncing her name *Keyssah*. She has cat-like eyes the color of striking chartreuse and enormous ears that twitch to follow sounds in all directions. Her face is structured like an Elarian Fae, but her nose ends in a pink cat's nose. Rich mauve fur, dappled in speckles of white and mulberry, covers her tall, muscular frame. She has toned arms with fingers ending in retractable claws, and lanky legs meet her paws. A fluffy tail whips behind her, dusted in violet spots with white centers. Her cat-like dexterity is stunning to watch. White feline canines glint as she smiles, showing off on the tightrope with an acrobatic cartwheel that has me holding my breath.

Finally, my name is called overhead. I hit the ground running, not giving the vines beneath my feet a second to catch up as I quickly scale the ten-foot wall. Next, I cross four-inch disks, balanced on rickety beams. I barely touch them as I leap off, moving like lightning, never giving the vines a chance to snag my ankles.

Then, I make my way to the end of the crucible of thorns, a narrow corridor of vine-like walls closing in as I run through and avoid vines snapping out at different angles. I duck and dodge, twirling my short sword to make quick work of them before they get too frisky with me. Suddenly, a giant stone boulder swings towards me, suspended by chains. I slide underneath, a breath away from losing my nose.

I turn the corner onto a stone pathway and face another agility course. My weight will trigger tiles to fall, so I glide over them, my first toe skimming the surface before leaping for the next one. Next are the swinging bars, spaced too far apart above a pit of quicksand. Thankfully, my arms are just long enough to make the gaps somewhat manageable as I hurl my body from beam to beam.

Then I'm swinging from vines that try to creep around me the longer I hang on to them while fire bursts from the walls, avoiding the death drop below. Sully did his best to mimic this in the courses he created for me growing up. If he were still alive, I'd definitely have some notes for him on this one. The thought of him threatens to tug my grief out of its locked window, but I raise another layer of golden light, reinforcing the shields of my mental fortress. I bring my focus back to my swinging momentum. I just have to hold it together for a little bit longer.

I make it through without any singed body parts or hair. Climbing up the large tree is a breeze for me, just like being in the Mysticwoods. I hop from the branch to the tightrope, arms out, one toe in front of the other, moving quick enough to never give myself a chance to look down.

I don't mind the ride of the bucking cylinder, squeezing my thighs tight, my upper body swaying with the motion rather than resisting it. I fly off in a rolling landing, gazing up at the towering ascent before me. My muscles sing with fire as I sling my grip to the next hold. Before I know it, I'm halfway up the mountain when a shiver slowly ticks its way down my spine.

I chance a glance below me to see a Pykavow hurdling towards me.

Shit. Shit. *Shit*. How the fuck do they keep catching all these Wuvon monsters!?

This creature is composed of ten arms, walking on its ten large, muscular, three-fingered hands. It looks as if it has a severed neck, but that's actually where five small, hungry mouths are. A long, snake-like tongue flicks out into the air, tasting my scent as a horrendous screech rattles my bones. It picks up the pace, teeth-like spikes along its elbows glinting red in the setting sunlight.

*Fuck*. This thing can definitely climb faster than me. Holding my body weight with my left hand and foot, I reach for one crossbow bolt and put it in my mouth for backup. Then, using my right hand, I free the crossbow on my back, which I had pre-loaded—a dangerous choice, but it hadn't misfired along the course. Loading even a small crossbow with one hand is a bitch.

The ball of arms and hands is hurtling towards my sweaty scent—where to aim? I slow my breath as the monstrosity moves closer and closer, the gap between us shortening, just like the gap between my shaky breaths. I notice pumping veins coursing up each arm, all meeting in one spot. That has to be the heart.

It's closing in on me fast. My skin pebbles in the wake of a howling screech of delight, as if it can already taste my sinew along its whipping tongue. I steady my right arm as I gaze down the sight.

Trying to land on a pinpoint spot in a sea of moving arms is no fucking easy feat. I focus. Becoming the weapon Sully trained me to be, honing in on a rhythm to its movement, a pattern where my target becomes visible, again and again.

I breathe out. Three. Two. One. Shoot.

The bolt lands slightly to the right of my exact target. I spit out a string of curses. *Celestials be dimmed*. The fucking Fates are never on my side.

The pain rattles the Pykavow, freezing for a beat before its arms crawl up at a slower pace, black blood dripping from its wound. I lodge my crossbow on my thigh, dropping the arrow from my mouth. I need to climb—and *fucking fast*. I won't survive if this thing catches me in its clutches.

I sling myself up to the next hold and then the next, rallying all my strength to bound upwards to the next rock jetting out of the mountainside. The loud cracking of rocks crumbling beneath the monster below gets closer and closer. I don't have time to look down as I leap for the next rock and propel myself to the next hold.

I grasp the edge of the cliff, heaving myself up and over as I see the Pykavow just three feet below me. I sprint to the stone door before loading my crossbow again and shooting another arrow slightly to the left of my previous mark. Bullseye. It slows, blood now pouring from the second wound. Surely I can use magic up here. Who would see? Ugh, it's not worth it. I'm not getting disqualified after all this Ritherin-shit.

My furious scream cleaves the air. Grabbing my short sword in one hand and my poison dagger in the other, I run straight at the beast. I leap onto the center mass of the Pykavow, using my poison dagger as a landing anchor. Its hands violently grasp my legs and arms—my joints groan, burning in the stretch as it pulls me apart, its tongue slithering putrid, digestive slime along my neck. Its five mouths snap greedily at my chest. I jam my short sword into the space between my arrows, gutting its heart wide open. I dislodge my poison dagger from its body just as we begin to… *fall.*

The world spins in slow motion as my gut bounces from my head to my toes, over and over again. *Maybe the Fates want a short life for me after all.* I ponder my new fate as we tumble down the mountainside, the Pykavow's arms still tearing at me, hunger consuming its last heartbeats.

I drop my sword, trying to grasp onto the rocky mountain with one hand, while frantically stabbing the cracks with the dagger in my other. Rock after rock crumbles beneath me. Crumbling like the broken bits of my shattered soul.

Finally, my dagger catches, snapping my middle and ring fingers backwards under the weight of the circular hilt.

*Damn, I really liked those fingers.* I let out a manic laugh as I consume the screech of pain that wallows in the back of my throat.

I find a hold for my left hand and both my feet. I'm about halfway down the mountain. *Again.* I glare upwards, unamused. No problem. Just have to climb the fucking mountain again, with a broken hand. Sarcasm drips with the sweat from my brow as I sheathe my dagger.

Holding my weight on the left side of my body, my teeth rip a piece of leather from my vest, and I wrap it around my fingers. After making sure my mental shields are solid, I start to climb. Yep, that fucking hurts, but I summon my darkness to feed off the pain. Eventually, I become numb to it. I lumber on at a dreadfully slow pace. But hey, I'm still climbing.

Not today, death. Not today.

I sling myself over the cliff once more, narrowly avoiding slipping in the giant puddle of black blood on my way to the entrance carved into the mountainside. A stone door groans open, mist uncurling from the pitch within. Now for the hard part. A sardonic laugh creaks out of my chest.

I carefully maneuver through the Ethereal Maze of Whispers, navigating around the constantly changing stone walls, moving in all directions. The magic is tugging at my mind, scavenging for my worst fears in an attempt to break me just like a Wuvon would.

My next turn brings me into an open space. A spotlight strikes, lighting up a wooden chair. A chair I know all too well. My foster father's laugh echoes.

His gangly body crawls around the edge of a wall. I dart straight for him, slitting his throat, and the illusion dissolves in front of me.

I come around another corner to a female with long, translucent hair and a dress adorned with the heavenly constellations from the night's sky. She's standing beside a male with dark hair and dark eyes. They're smiling and singing to a baby in their arms.

Wait, is that supposed to be me? They look happy. *Good for them.* Maybe it would mean something if I ever knew them. I quickly walk through the illusion, waving my arms dismissively as it dissolves into dust.

A colorful, bright mist billows in front of me. I'm dressed in a stunning gown, smiling up at a dark-haired male. Are those tears of joy coming from my eyes? A dark laugh resonates from my hollow chest. The male is drawing a vow rune on the back of my hand.

Oh, no. *Fuck this.* I tear through the mist. It evaporates around me. Crackling sparks slash between my ribs, as if that illusion was something special. This maze is going to have to try harder to break me. I am not meant for pretty endings.

The twisting passages blur with each dizzying turn. Turn after turn. I suck in a breath, shimmying between two walls right before they finish their turns, severing the passage. My eyes squint as a light cleaves the eerie umber, pupils finally adjusting—the exit! I'm so close, just another step, when a towering figure swells before me, taking on the shape of a bear with a smaller shadow below it. I teeter closer and freeze, the illusion shimmering to life. The smaller one is me, the night I met… Sully. He stands young and healthy, full of life, with that big, stupid grin. His hearty chuckle coils around me as my heart sputters and limps, attempting to beat again.

*It's not real Savaé!* I scream to myself. *But I want it to be real.* I want it to be real more than anything I have wanted in my wretched life.

A new memory shimmers to life. Sully messing up my hair and calling me his *little Starborne dragon.* I want to reach out, wrap my arms around him, and never let go. It looks so real.

My heart fractures into a million pieces, slashing the inside of my chest into a stringy mess of sinew and crimson.

I miss him so much. Maybe I can just stay here, with my memories of him, in utter madness. That wouldn't be so bad…

A haunted sound sunders the illusion—his serrated cough.

No.

*No.*

Not that fucking sound. Anything but that fucking sound.

I howl in agony. The walls of my glacial palace splinter under the weight of that sound, smashing what's left of my frozen heart until the pieces are too small to ever hope to put back together again.

"Make it stop!" I scream, covering my ears.

But it doesn't. The images uncurl. Him withering away. Second by second, in front of my eyes. I slam them shut, only for the sound of his labored breathing to scrape across the seams of my soul.

Then, a twisted version of my voice echoes across the moving walls.

"Why didn't you do more for him? Why didn't you bring him to a healer instead of continuing to train for the trials? You're a selfish bitch."

The voice morphs again, into my foster father.

"You are a curse upon this world. A vermin to be exterminated."

The voice shifts into a warped version of Sully's voice.

"You were just using me. You never loved me. *You don't even know what love is.* All you do is take and take."

"No, no, no! That isn't true," I scream in protest, covering my ears harder and squeezing my eyelids tighter as tears rip down my cheeks.

"You can never love or be loved. You have no soul. No heart. Anyone close to you dies. You are a curse. You beckon darkness to consume everything you hold dear." The words of Sully's warped voice reverberate in my head, like a broken melody, hauntingly stuck on repeat.

Perhaps the voices are right after all. I am curseborne. I didn't force Sully to go to a healer sooner. I do not know how to love or be loved. How could I when all I have known is how to survive? Maybe my love for Sully is just a well-crafted lie I told myself. How could I let someone I truly love wither away like that? My presence is a corrupting darkness, consuming all the light around me.

As the words repeat again and again, I latch on to the last sentence of his distorted threat, slashing me from my spiral. I have already lost everything I hold dear. I have nothing left to lose but my will to fight. And oh, how the darkness inside loves to fight. I suppose I do have something left after all.

A wicked grin curves up my lips. Sully taught me there is more to this world than darkness and terror. He taught me how to become a weapon. The villagers say fear turned my hair translucent, like a wraith. Perhaps I was the wraith all along. Forever a harbinger of death and destruction.

I will not let fear paralyze me. I need to fight. For him. For me. Just like he taught me. I have to get out of here alive.

I need to keep moving. I listen to my intuition, humming a song Sully used to hum by the fire at night, keeping the voices of the illusions out of my head.

"From the mountain tops to the valley low. The moonlight guides us as the Mysticwoods grow. A symphony of silence, the world holds its breath as the heavens crumble, a Celestial death. Oh, the stars are falling. Hear their call. Dancing like firelights in the night's soft thrall. With all their shimmer, a wish takes flight, in this enchanted realm where day kisses the night. And with their love, a power born, full of dreams they do not mourn."

A rough surface bites into my palms, fingertips fumbling along chilled crevices and notches. Searching for any chance of escape. *Click.* A stone door releases with a grumbling groan as light spills in. I open my eyes to a beautiful view. Snow-capped peaks of Eldoria pierce the late sunset clouds to my left, curving to fall into the Dragon Spine Mountains before ending along the eastern border of the Amberwood below.

I have survived my second trial.

*Or have I?*

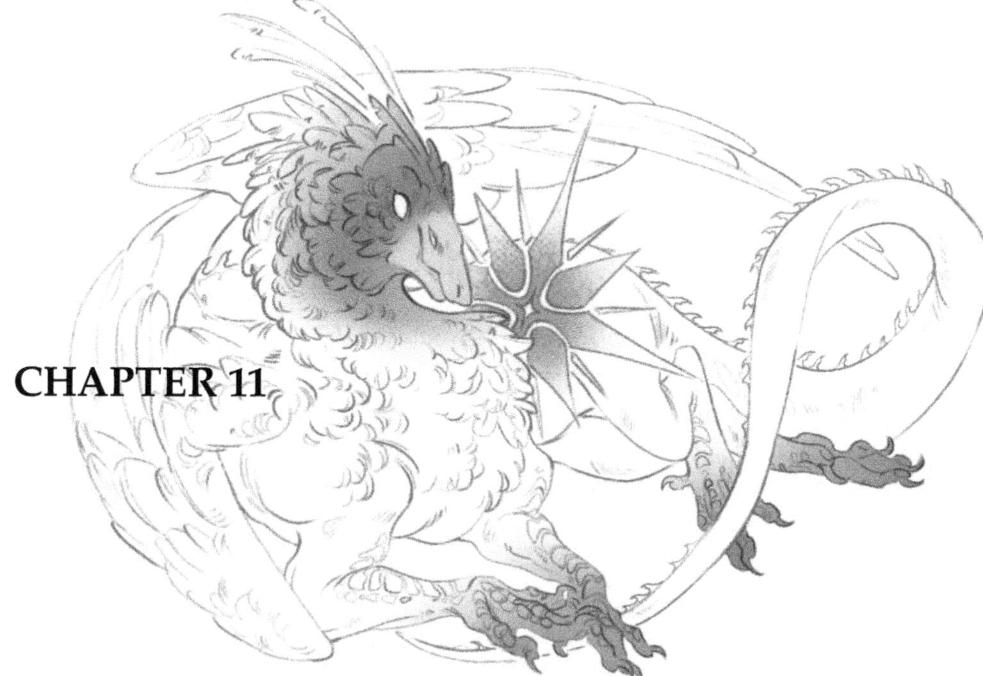

# CHAPTER 11

My legs tremble as I struggle back to the inn on muscles screeching for rest. My name drifts on the breeze. I drag my eyes up from the ground. Someone is running from outside the pub across the street. Violet eyes pierce me in the darkness.

Oh, she is running *at* me.

Winx leaps onto me with a spinning hug, unabashedly blazing through my boundaries. I freeze, not quite sure what to do. I'm not the touchy-feely type—and I'm *definitely* not one for public displays of affection.

She lets go, finally sensing my tense body. She clearly disregarded my lack of smile today, and based on her greeting, she mistakenly thinks our night of pleasure is more than a one-night stand.

"You're alive!" Winx exclaims, bright eyes flaring.

"Yeah… I think so," I mutter as I look down at my body. Yep, it's mostly intact, although I don't think I can say the same about my mind.

"Everyone is talking about how you defeated that Pykavow. And I mean *everyone*. I think I even saw a slightly impressed glimmer in my dad's eyes —that or some dirt got in there—before he slinked off. Ya never know with him." Violet flames spark in her irises with an envious glint. A craving for her father to look at her the same. No wonder she wants to torch him.

"Uh, thanks, I think?"

"You need to come celebrate with us! Come on, come on, come on!" She beckons, trying to snatch my unbroken hand before I jerk it away.

"I really should get to bed. It was a long day," I grumble, wanting to be left the fuck alone.

"I am not taking no for an answer!" she squeals, snatching my wrist and dragging me into the pub with such fervor, I don't even get to reply. Shaking my head, I accept the truth of her previous statement. Something tells me it's never been one of her strong suits.

The pub roars with hollering and singing drunk Fae while I gag on the scent of piss and ale. I just want to go to bed. Before I know it, there's a shot in my hand. Then everyone is cheering.

"Drink, drink, drink!"

Well… I guess this will help ease the pain in my hand until I can see Kanuvi in the morning. *Bottoms up.*

And, likely through some deranged form of enchantment magic, there's another shot in my hand, and another, and another…

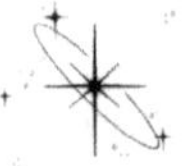

MY EYES POP UP, awaking in a strange bed. Based on the moon's position out the window, it's sometime around three in the morning. I am not alone in my debauchery, accompanied by two females, a male, and a splitting headache. What the fuck did I get myself into last night? I can't even make out their subspecies in the dark. I groan at my poor choices, stumbling into my clothes before lurching across town to my room at the inn. Puking my guts up all along the way. I roll into bed, twisting and turning, unable to fall into the peaceful slumber I crave.

Sully's warped, distorted words echo in my mind, mincing deeper, maggots savoring the festering rot.

*You can never love or be loved.*

*You have no soul.*

*No heart.*

*Anyone close to you dies.*

*You are a curse.*

*You beckon darkness to consume everything you hold dear.*

I can't stand the racket in my own mind. Each time it's repeated, the words squirm—munching deeper and deeper—my remaining sanity slowly putrefying. So, despite my aching body's lingering protests, I settle on going for a walk. Maybe some fresh air can temper my noxious thoughts.

As I saunter down the street, the hairs on my neck prickle. The shadows shift behind me, almost imperceptibly. Ever so slowly, I ease out my dagger. The shadows swell, growing closer. I lunge at them, my eyes widening as I pin Sølas against the wall with a dagger to his neck. *Again.*

"We really need to stop meeting like this. Is this how you greet all your friends?" his smoky voice purrs with a devilish smirk to it. Amber and spruce bludgeon my next snarling inhale. I grit my teeth, resisting the urge to breathe deeper, to indulge his smell and the comforting memories of the Mysticwoods it elicits. If this scent had come from anyone else, I would have gladly wrapped them around me. Surprisingly, the unrelenting torment of my mind quiets in his presence.

"You're the one lurking. And we are not friends," I hiss.

"Sheesh, tough crowd. I'll settle for acquaintances then," he muses.

There's that senseless electricity in the air between us, and I fucking hate it. The ache in my chest soars and eases all at the same time when I look at him. Like he holds the ability to soothe the hurricane of my broken soul. *If only.*

His shadows swirl around me. An odd, aching sensation lingers in their echoes, like they're tugging my ribs apart, cracking my chest wide open, searching for my heart. Well, *he* can't have it… *There's nothing fucking left.* An exasperated sigh mashes my lungs, mind muddled by whatever oscillates between us. Celestials, why couldn't it just be lust? Lust is simple. Lust I can fuck away, but whatever eddies between us feels anything but simple. And I want *nothing* to do with it.

I want absolutely nothing to do with him tugging at things he has no right to when I barely know him. Speaking of which, I also don't want to know him. Not now. Not ever.

I don't want to feel anything. I want to be numb. I want him gone before I let my darkness out to silence him for good.

I snarl my upper lip at him. "Stop following me, and go find someone else to bother."

My words summon his hand, rubbing at his chest again. That spot seems to bother him quite often. Maybe he should see a healer about that.

His hand drops, a cocky smirk kissing his insufferable lips once more.

"Why would I do that when you're clearly the most interesting person to bother?"

"What the fuck is wrong with you? I'm not in the mood for whatever game you are trying to play with me." I spin, striding away from him.

He follows me. Of fucking course, he does.

"Stop making a scene at every trial, and maybe you won't be so intriguing."

"Are the females you like normally into this strange stalking behavior?"

"Hmm. I believe they call it dark and mysterious," he croons.

"Pfft. Mysterious is playing hard to get. You're more like a gnat that won't stop hovering."

"Ouch. Ladies and gents, she's a feisty one." He extends his arms out as if speaking to an invisible crowd. Stars above, he is full of himself.

"Buzz off, would ya?" I wave my hand dismissively.

"And she's got jokes. C'mon, where would the fun be if I left now?" he asks, appearing out of the shadows next to me.

"I don't know, wherever the fuck you're not."

"Someone's in a bad mood. You seemed much happier when you were dancing on top of the bar tonight. And leaving with what appeared to be several romantic liaisons." His eyes seem to darken at those last words as he slips his hands into his pockets. The shadow prick can fuck right off; he doesn't get to judge me. Or perhaps that's a flash of jealousy in those stormy eyes?

*No.* Absolutely not. I shake the thought from my head, hoping to also rattle back my common sense.

"Winx got me obliterated. I don't even remember what happened. Was she there when I left?"

"No, Chet dragged her off. I don't think he wanted to take the chance of you stealing his thunder again." He winks, but his mask falters, revealing an unexpected melancholy. Expertly, I chuck those nipping feelings right out my fractured mosaic window, because the fuck am I touching that.

I opt to focus on my rage, a safer emotion if I am going to have to feel shit, growling, "Just because they're possibly a Bloodline pairing doesn't mean he owns her."

"I agree. But try telling that to the male whose father is a cousin to the queen and whose mother is commander of the Golden Legion."

"Entitled Ritherin-shit." I pinch the bridge of my nose. "And I'm on his hit list. *Great.* Should make for a thrilling Universitás experience."

"You sure know how to piss off the right people. Don't worry, I'm taking notes."

"Are you always this annoying?"

"Only when you make it so much fun." He smirks.

"You're being really frustrating, and not in the sexy kind of way."

"Disappointing. I normally aim to please," he says with a roguish tone, kicking up his brow.

Celestials, he's sexy, but I'm not in the mood for his shenanigans. Not now. Not ever. He's a liability waiting to happen with how my shields melt around him.

The air is uncomfortably thick. The energy between us curling around my chest. Needling between my ribs, searching for a way into my glacial palace. Prying at the vulnerable parts I keep hidden. But all he'll find are broken bits. Too jagged, too small to ever foolishly hope to fit back together. Maybe I *should* let him in. Let him tear through the ruin of me—if only to watch him bleed, gutting himself on my shattered remnants. Yet even my frozen wasteland is too vulnerable and raw for me to expose. I shove and cram all this Ritherin-shit he's dredged up straight out my mosaic window— more panes fracture, splintering under the weight of everything unfelt. I roll my shoulder, sending the burden slipping off my icy façade.

"You have a strange way of flirting, has anyone ever told you that?" I scoff.

"Oh, trust me, this isn't flirting. You'll know when I'm flirting with you." The shadows in his eyes whip violently as his gaze collides with mine.

Nope, not tonight. He's not going to charm me again with those eyes. My focus darting straight down to my feet.

"You hide your sadness well, behind that mask of yours."

"It's none of your damn business," I growl low with warning.

"True. But there is no one else around. I'm here if you want to talk."

"Talk? To you? After I asked you several times to bugger off?" A humorless laugh laced with venom seeps from my lips. Who does he think he is, asking me to bare my soul to him? My darkness would send even his shadows cowering for the light.

"Well, I couldn't let you walk the streets at night alone."

My humorous laugh becomes sarcastic. "You saw what happened today. Do you really think I need *you* to protect me?"

"Valid point." His hand clutches at his heart, wincing as he steps back, vanishing into a plume of shadows.

Celestials be dimmed, it took him long enough to take a hint. But in the silence, there is absence—a feeling akin to loneliness. I shake the feeling from my head. I have been alone for many years in my life… before Sully.

I will survive alone again just fine. But the feeling festers in my throat, making it hard to swallow.

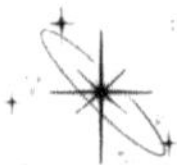

AFTER SHOWERING AND A QUICK NAP, it's mid-morning as I head to Kanuvi's lodgings.

"Good morning. Mind mending my hand?" I greet her.

"Straight to the point. Good morning to you, too." She places her hand on mine, spores cascading out around twinkling light. Pain burns through my fingers as they snap back into place, the tendrils of the mycelium network weaving my bones and sinew back together. Then, the ache from my hangover magically melts away.

"Thank you. For this, and for what you did in the woods. I can never repay you for trying."

"He did a great service for Cascara. The least I could do was try. It's clear he loved you very much. You're a ferocious fighter, just like him. He is still alive, in you."

Her words make the shattered bits of my heart hurt, but I shove the emotion out my fractured mosaic window, slapping a polite smile on my face.

"Make sure to visit him before you leave. It looks like you are well on your way to being in the next class at Gildorea," she says softly.

I nod in thanks and leave, unable to bear the way her kind words stir the grief of my soul. She's right, though. I should visit him before I continue on my journey towards my goal of becoming an Ellian Knight. The only thing I have left to hold on to.

I pack up all the belongings from the inn. Warmth tickles me as I don the cloak Sully gifted to me, almost like he's here, hugging me. I smile before a single tear kisses my cheek. I raise my shields up, reinforcing them. There's no room for grief where I'm going, while I wait for the third trial to begin.

But first, there's something I must do. Visit the place where Sully left this world. As I walk alone in the woods, I hear something digging, right in the mushrooms that returned his bones to the earth.

I sprint at the creamy-orange creature, screaming, "Shoo, shoo!"

It turns around, looking utterly unfazed. It's a small, bright orange dragon with four cobalt-colored eyes and five leaf-shaped tendrils framing his head, like the points of a star. He's pretty adorable, with four dull-clawed paws and a long tail, whipping back and forth. I've never seen or heard of a dragon with four eyes, nor one without wings, never mind one this small. He almost looks like an overgrown salamander.

"Go on, get out of here," I say, shooing it away once more.

It cocks its head to the side, looking at me like it's confused. Trying to figure out what I'm saying. I let out a frustrated huff.

"You have no clue what I am saying, do you? You don't know any better, hmm, little guy?" I sit down next to the mushrooms of Sully's grave, trying to put them back as they were. The next thing I know, the little thing is running up my arm to the top of my head.

"What are you doing? Get off!" I snap, reaching for it on my head. It jumps and ducks over my hands, making cute chirping sounds like I'm playing a game. Then I open my bag, grab half of a sandwich, and throw it into the woods. It takes the bait and runs after the food.

Finally, some peace and quiet. I lie next to the mushrooms, talking to them as if Sully is still here, recounting yesterday. Leaving out the part about where I woke up later that night.

Then there's a sad silence. I am alone. Sully isn't coming back. My mosaic window shatters, the hurt flooding in, crashing me beneath an infinite tidal wave of grief. A wave I cannot fight, only succumb to. I lie there, crying until my chest aches. Until I can't breathe. Until I'm drowning.

"Goodbye."

I leave a piece of me with him as I close my bag.

The rest is up to me.

Me, alone.

# CHAPTER 12

I make it to the town hosting the last trial, just outside of the Gildorea Universitás of War. Doraan. At one point, I was certain the journey itself would kill me. Alone, with echoes from the Ethereal Maze of Whispers taunting me, filleting my mind into broken slivers since there's nothing left of my heart to destroy.

One night, I even tried to cry again, to let myself grieve. I lowered my shields, freeing my emotions from the broken mosaic-star window. I sat there as grief gutted where my heart should be, ripping through my ribs like a ravenous beast. I screamed. I wailed. I pleaded to the Celestials to ease the suffocating weight of unfelt emotions as I punched the cold soil until my fists shredded into a bloody mess.

But not a single fucking tear.

The rest of the journey, I was a hollow ghost, a husk. Too broken to even grieve properly. Thankfully, I found some work as the local blacksmith in Doraan to distract my fractured self while waiting for my assigned slot for the third trial. And to afford my drab accommodations in the bustling city.

As I unpack, a little orange blur runs out of my bag.

"You have got to be kidding me! You've been a stowaway all this time?"

For being bright orange, the little dragon is exceptionally good at hiding and so fast, I can barely see it. I pull out some bread and lure it out from under the bed. In the shadows, it almost seems to change shape.

Odd.

The creature scurries out, snatching the food in its mouth, and then runs up my arm to the top of my head, messing up my hair, before crumbs tumble down my face. I cross my arms and huff. Not this again. I shoot my hands up towards him, trying to catch him. The creature does his avoidant dance, continuing to mess up my hair.

"I guess you're coming with me to work then, little guy?" I don my cloak as he scuttles down to my shoulders, hiding at the nape of my neck. He's too quick for me to catch. I sigh; I guess that means I'm stuck with him.

I head over to the blacksmith forge and get my work done for the day. To my surprise, the creature stays on my shoulder, and no one notices him. I guess city folk are just too wrapped up in their own lives to look up around them. I stay at the forge to start on a new short sword since I lost mine in the battle with the Pykavow.

It's quiet now, and most of the city has bustled off to bed. The little creature scurries down to my hand, appearing very interested in what I'm doing. Almost inspecting my work. The audacity of this little fellow.

He scurries around, here and there, very curiously moving his way through the tools. As I beat the metal, he slips into a trance, mesmerized by the blade taking shape. Then, I lift the metal, setting it back in the forge for reheating before finalizing its shape. The creature crawls up the metal, spitting a puff of flames. Silver flames curl, the steel instantly glowing red.

My eyes grow wide. "I guess that works, too." I pause, appreciating the blade heated to the perfect temperature in one breath. "Thanks."

The metal is so hot, it bends easily beneath my hammer, each strike shaping a beautifully shaped short sword in record time. The blade glimmers orange in the light, resonating with a subtle hum, a sound I've never heard before. I move to smelt the simple hilt onto the blade. The creature leaps up, exhaling a small blast of fire on it, with some added threads of dangling liquid spit. The ridiculous sight cracks a laugh from my hollow chest.

He looks up at me, a happy crinkle around his four cobalt eyes; one might almost call it a smile.

"Okay, I think we're done for the night, little drago—"

The air rips from my lungs as the words sink in. Yet the creature doesn't give me a chance to tumble into my thoughts, scampering up my arm and wrapping around my neck again, like the strangest scarf I've ever worn.

I haven't really felt any emotion since I left the Amberwood.

A whisper of sadness blends with a delicate happiness. Almost as if Sully is here with me after all. Reincarnated in this strange little orange dragon, who refused to leave my side since offering him a sandwich at Sully's grave.

It's the day of my final trial, and I'm scrambling to get my little dragon sidekick to stay in the room so I can leave.

"Stay here, Pipsqueak. You cannot come with me to the trial. You'll get me disqualified." I snatch him up and plop him onto the bed as I walk to the bathroom to cover the gold flecks on my cheeks, finishing the kohl under my eyes that swoops up at the edges.

And guess where Pip is by the time I finish my makeup? Right on top of my head, messing up my hair. I've gotten quicker at catching him, but when he doesn't want to be caught, he's positively impossible. I find myself wondering how Sully stayed so patient with me for all those years.

"You cannot come with me. They will see you and lock you up."

He tilts his head to the side, looking at me in the mirror, then twists down to my neck and wraps himself around it. Before my eyes, he changes into a dark cobalt-blue scarf.

I blink, rubbing my eyes as I gaze into the mirror. My fingers run along the scarf to reveal four cobalt eyes opening up, looking back at me. I jump.

Pip chirps happily, and then his eyes flutter shut. He appears exactly like a regular scarf. My brain hurts trying to wrap my head around what I've just witnessed. I've never heard of a creature who can change into inanimate objects. Sully trained me on all the known, catalogued mystical creatures, a vital part of my entrance exam before I officially become an ensign at Universitás. Our continent is full of creatures, but it's possible we haven't catalogued them all.

"I suppose you can come with me, Pip, but you can't move an inch while we're there. No matter what they try to do to me." He chirps in a tone that I hope is agreement.

It's an unusually warm autumn day, making my new scarf appear a little out of place. I walk through the edge of town along the pathway that leads up to Gildorea Universitás of War.

Even from here, the white marble campus, topped in gold, sparkles in the sunlight. The multi-tiered walls cascade down the hill it's carved into, like layered terraces of a cake. As I journey closer, each layer comes into focus, like steps climbing a slope.

The campus is diamond-shaped. The top, flat edge of the diamond is along the eastern rocky cliffs of Cascara, meeting the ocean far below. This border holds the heart of Gildorea, the Grand Conservatory, a large circular building of white marble decorated with three balconies. The rotunda, capped with a golden dome, is adorned with an eight-pointed star, an ancient symbol thought to mark the Celestials' blessing. This building is where most classes are held.

Extending out from the cupola, on either side, are ornate multi-tiered walls, meeting spires tipped in gold. These wings are brimming with the offices and homes of those who work for the school. The wings meet the diagonal, multi-tiered walls, coming to a point facing west. Their tops are decorated with extravagant penthouses, reserved for powerful Bloodline pairings, ensuring the next generation of Ellian Knights. The many floors below are cozy with dormitories for ensigns. You can enter through the walls framing the central diamond-shaped courtyard one of two ways: the stairs of the main entryway or the north and south archways.

On the outermost and lowest tier, lined with round-arched entryways, are the buildings that house Faelings raised by the Maidens. They raise the offspring of Bloodline pairings of Ellian Knights, so our precious warriors are not taken from battle. There is, of course, the option for Knights to request to be stationed at or nearby Gildorea to be a part of raising their offspring. This is a rare occurrence in newer generations; those who sought this life understand this obligation as the military tactic to increase our power, to even the playing field against the Wuvon. Most of the Ellian Knights today have been raised by the Maidens, not their biological parents.

I'm destined for a location through the columns below the entry courtyard, which leads to the underbelly of the campus, housing the infirmary, holding cells, interrogation rooms, and barracks for the infantry—those who become meat-shields as our first line of defense. It's unsettling to think you can pass all three trials and still end up there if you fail the magical entrance exam.

I shove the thought out of my head; fear can kill your mind if you let it, especially when walking into my last trial, which is all about mind games. I can't let emotion tear me from the only thing I have left to keep me going. Powerful emotions are the quickest way for your mental shields to falter. The fact that I hate emotion—and the lack of control associated with it, instead enjoying the comfort of being numb—is part of why I know I will succeed in this last trial.

You have to show the capacity to resist a trained Persuasive to be further trained on the subject. Wuvon are known to all have a strong capacity for exceptional mindwork. They can pull out your deepest secrets, obtain confidential information on battle strategies and Ellian Knights' unique magic. Some even control the ability for compulsion; they can inhabit your mind, controlling you like a puppet, even at long distances. The ultimate infiltration tool.

If you don't have a natural ability against Persuasion, you're a liability to the entire front. Luckily, you can reattempt the final trial the following year if you are unsuccessful the first time. No doubt to allow more cannon fodder for the first years to work through.

An eerie darkness settles over me as the light from the glistening world behind dims as I venture past marble columns. I finally reach a door, where a scribe cloaked in red awaits me. A peculiar green flame flickers above their head as they scan the parchment for my name. They nod, scratching something along the scroll with a golden quill.

I enter the gothic arch stone doorway, the carved slate doors moaning along their hinges. I envision the golden dome shield that surrounds me in my mind. My fingers trace along the gleaming walls, humming with my strength, searching for cracks. I raise another layer of golden light, just in case.

Then, using the sound of the doors as cover, I whisper quietly to Pip, "Remember. No movements. No matter what." He doesn't make a peep, so I take that as him acknowledging my command.

An endless hall jets out before me, lined with green flames, casting a queasy-colored light along the passageway. I see another scribe ahead, this time in a golden cloak, shimmering like a beacon. As I reach the tall figure, they open a wooden door carved like a portcullis—how fitting. It evokes the feeling of being trapped in a cage, but I won't let their attempts to rattle me succeed. *Mind over matter*.

As my eyes adjust to the dark room, I make out a chair with metal shackles attached to the arms and two front legs. *Charming*. I reach into my mind, making sure the latch to my broken mosaic window of emotions is shut tight.

A petite figure emerges from the pitch, followed by a tall, slender form. With the sound of a sharp tap, a crimson flame lights up above the chair, revealing the two people in the room with me.

The petite female has chocolate-brown hair and olive skin a few shades lighter than mine. Her hair is shorn to the skin on the sides. As she comes further into the light, I notice she has silver, jagged scars running across the sides of her head.

Scars are uncommon in Elarians, given our ability to heal quickly or use Sangre magic. She must have intentionally blunted her power while they healed slowly without any magic. The only other time this can happen is if you are poisoned or become almost drained of your magic and cannot find a healer.

Next, a slender figure comes into light behind her, revealing long white hair and sharp features… Chancellor Ashfel.

"Greetings, Savaé Entropaé." His icy tone might've chilled my skin if I weren't so delightfully numb.

"Greetings. What an honor to have the Chancellor at all three of my trials," I lie tastefully with a bow, despite the quills prickling at the back of my throat begging to spear him with what I really think.

I take a breath, unraveling the lace strings of tension binding my shoulder blades like a corset. I didn't make it this far for my sharp tongue to ruin it all… the night with his daughter in the alley doesn't count. I cage the snicker accompanying that thought behind a glimmering smile. Not the time to be pissing off the Chancellor.

"You did such a gripping job with my last experiment. It will be my delight to watch you rise to my next challenge, Starborne."

My eyes whip to his. No one has ever called me Starborne except for Sully. I never asked him what it meant, figuring it was just another nickname of endearment. He told me once, while looking at my gilded markings, the gold on our planet wasn't created on Elyndor. It's finite, and thus all the more valuable, a gift from fallen stars. I figured it was just a pleasant fact to help me feel more comfortable in my own skin.

Clearly, this male is trying to get under my skin, like a weasel nipping at tattered walls, gnawing on a weak spot in hope of getting through to find its feast. That smart, weaselly fuck knows exactly what he is doing because I can feel the molten rage leaking from the mosaic window of my mind. It takes all my strength not to smash his skinny bones against the wall and rip the secrets he's keeping right out of his illustrious Arabellian head.

I breathe in calming blue. I breathe out flaming red, numbness cascading over me once more while raising yet another wall of shields, this time on the inside, putting a layer between me and any reckless emotion attempting to escape that Celestials be dimmed mosaic window.

This is all just a part of the trial. He's not even worth another thought. And I sure as Emberhell can't let him rattle me, wielding my easily triggered rage to his benefit.

I am no one's puppet to be strung up and played with.

"Please, take a seat. Get comfortable." His slithering words catch on his tongue as he pauses. His eyes narrow on my neck. "It's warm out for a scarf today, is it not?"

I nod. "Feeling a little under the weather is all, sir."

I don't let my thoughts fester on the prior memories I have shackled to a chair. Donning my mask of cool indifference as I take a seat in the chair. Without hesitation, the female locks me in. The cool metal inscribed with runes traps my magic beneath my skin. My strength extends beyond my magic, though. Using my hidden skill, just like I did when trapped in a far more wicked chair as a child, I dissociate—leaving a smug smile on my face for the Chancellor.

In my disjointed state, my mind is free. I find myself back in the Mystic-woods of Estrella. This time, Pip is with me as we race through the twisted branches of trees beneath a lavender canopy, jumping from limb to limb without a care in the world. We roll along multicolored mosses and lichen carpeting the cool soil. Snowmelt streams carve through the forest floor, the edges brimming with fauna and creatures of all shapes and sizes, which light up and smile as we dance among them. Pip and I get into a growling competition with the armored polar bears, our faces covered in their slobber as we laugh ourselves silly.

We slink into a cave filled with crystals of every color imaginable, humming wildly to the sounds of Pip's happy chirps, which echo off the walls, harmonizing, unleashing ricocheting rays of rainbow light.

In the back of my head, I can feel the ensign smashing against my shields, her finger screeching along tempered gold, failing to dive deeper into my head. I hear a faint, disgruntled voice off in the distance.

"Push harder. You are stronger than this; if not, you will fail your exam."

My smile grows with the blossoming scent of frost lilies bathing my mind. The aroma brings memories of Sully flooding back, crashing over me in an unleashed tempest. The last remaining light of my soul sputters, threatening to extinguish. Frantically, I grasp for something to keep the flame lit as grief swells up with a consuming hunger.

A piercing sound grinds my molars, the ensign's nails scraping along the fracturing seams of my mind. The glow of my mental shields—flickers—potent emotions spreading like cracks along thin ice, splintering under the suffocating, unyielding weight of everything unfelt. All at once, every feeling I've managed to chuck out that broken mosaic window hails against my shields—with the fury and wrath of Endara, Fate of Endings, set on shattering my very existence.

I open my eyes in the golden dome of my mental fortress. Thousands of hands claw at the walls. Nails dig in. Corroding an open fracture. Splitting wider and wider into a gaping chasm. Lapis blue liquid waterfalls in, flooding all around me. Tears prickle at the back of my eyes as I realize it's my grief pouring in.

I race towards the hole, clasping my hands over it. I scream through gritted teeth as the painful feeling torrents through me like a flash flood. My knees buckle with a splash. My ribs crack and bow under every unfelt emotion bludgeoning my chest.

Each new blow splatters the walls of my glacial palace with warm blood, melting my strength, threatening to capsize my withered black heart in a sea of crimson it's too weak to pump against. Her fractured pieces—messily stitched together—a tapestry of limping beats and weeping holes. A sad and pitiful sight. But it's all I've managed to piece together. All I have left.

My shields flicker.

I cannot fail.

Mind over matter.

I will not have another chance to repeat. I was too confident in my abilities to give myself that chance. A string of curses slings from my lips for being so fucking foolish.

But I have no other choice. I have to do this. I *can* do this.

Mind over *fucking* matter.

This will not be the end of my story. Becoming an Ellian Knight is all I have left to hold on to now that Sully is gone.

A deep breath steels my resolve. I harness the jagged ice deep within my marrow. I imagine wall after wall of golden light reinforcing my shields. Hoarfrost seeps out from my bones, freezing my grief, creeping along the walls. Shattered ice bites through the fingers probing my mind. Ice and gold mix, hardening into something new, an impenetrable gilded frost, numbing my soul just enough to *focus*. I corral all my emotions back out their window as this new substance spreads like liquid light, filling the fractures of my mental shields. Reinforcing them.

Then, after some time, my mind releases from the ensign's grasp. I drift back into my body, opening my eyes. The shackles are undone, but a shadow looms over me. The towering spire of Chancellor Ashfel.

"Oh, how I do enjoy being correct. I will see you in class next week. Congratulations. You have been accepted into Gildorea Universitás of War."

I stand up and give a half-bow. "Thank you. I look forward to all you have to teach me." I smirk and walk out, feeling lighter than I have in weeks.

Once we are outside and heading back to town, I look down at Pip. "I did it!"

He opens his four cobalt eyes in succession, looking up at me, chirping happily. I smile and then gaze up at the sky.

"We did it, Sully. We did it!"

My chest deflates in the deafening silence, the terrible weight of his absence crumpling me once more.

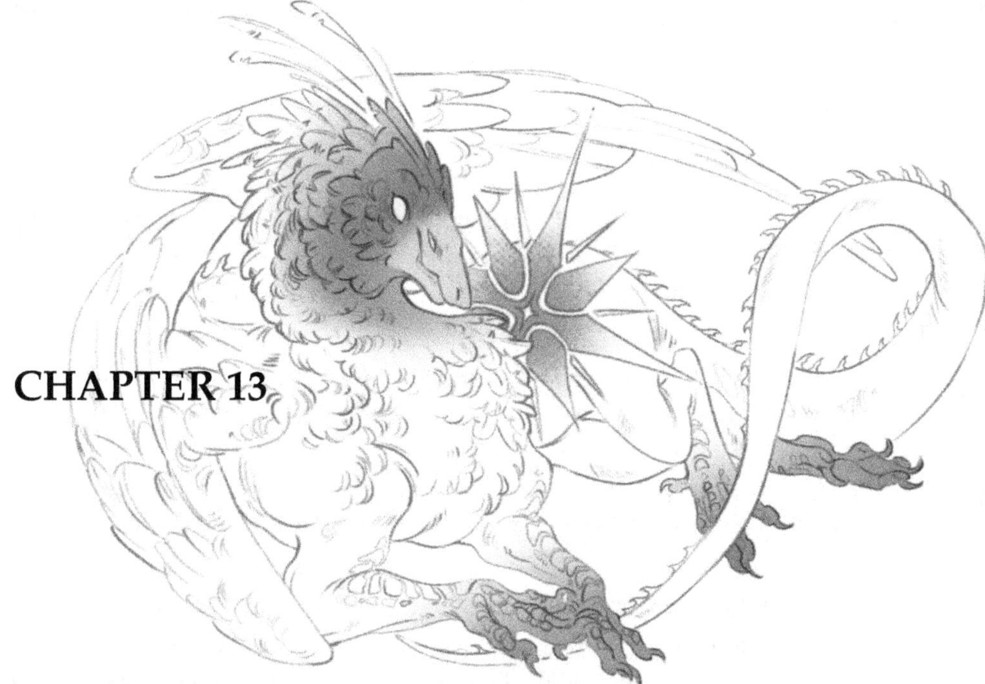

# CHAPTER 13

Waking up early was worth Pip's grumbles as I settle into my prized seat in the middle of the amphitheater. The thought that my body's gilded markings, wrapped in white and gold aerial leathers, are more at home as a statue decorating these ornate walls than as an ensign training for war still sits bitterly on my tongue. Maybe I should take it as a sign that I belong here. *After all, I do match the decor.*

In the low hum of recruits trickling in to take their seats for our entrance exam, thoughts of my magic tumble through my mind. At only eight years old, ice and fire bristled through my fingertips, elemental magic awakening in my blood at an unusually young age. Allowing me more time to master each element.

With Sully's help, I've become proficient in minor magic: manipulation, simple illusions, runes, enchantments, Sangre healing. I have a strong foundation in potions and deadly poisons. The Mysticwoods being my second home granted me fluency in all things natural and magical creatures. I may not be a Shadowmancer, but I can dance among the shadows in a way others can't, an ability called Shadowblending. Maybe that is my only special talent.

Yet everyone has a unique magic, their Celestial Gift. I hear there's a Chronosense in this year's class, with the ability to sense more than just random moments in time, able to reverse or speed up time by several seconds. An insanely unique skill. Emberhell, even Sølas is annoyingly powerful with his Shadowmancing skills, able to manipulate them as an extension of his own will. I'd love to have his power, minus the part of being branded as an outcast, just because the last-known wielder of shadows was Wuvon. However, it certainly didn't seem to scare the ladies away from what little I witnessed during the trials.

By my age of twenty-two, everyone here will have already come into their Celestial Gift. Perhaps mine is just Shadowblending or being strong in all Elarian magic. I guess for the first time, I won't be standing out, which is pretty amusing now that I think about it. The Fates are known to be fickle, mischievous entities; I suppose that's where their younger sister, Karma, gets her sense of humor.

A happy squeal tears through my thoughts as Winx finds me in the auditorium. I look over my shoulder to see her smile radiating beneath striking violet eyes. Our gazes collide, hers flaring neon, glimmering through newly dyed rainbow hair. Her lean, muscular body and slender legs move with a Pixie-like flutter. She's modified her uniform to a cropped leather corset, tightening across her petite breasts and exposing her midriff. So impractical, but she does love standing out. The high cut showing off the carved lines of her lower stomach, cutting in a V. Everything about her is petite, except for her personality and the flames roaring through her blood.

I catch her blushing, curling a smirk at the corner of my mouth. I may not be one for attachment, but I can admit it's nice having such a beautiful, familiar face excited to see me in the sea of strangers. Especially when I'm not used to being around so many Fae at once.

"I am so happy to see you! I knew you would make it, of course." Her words come out so fast, it's hard to keep up. "Last week, I heard my father mention your name angrily in his office, talking with Commander Bragen. They could have only been that upset because you made it here." She snickers with a coy smile.

"It's good to see you, too. I like the new hair. Brings out your eyes," I say with a wink, donning my mask, using the numbness to help me pretend I'm not a gutted, hollow ghost.

I have to play the part, a confident weapon ready to bloody my way through a Wuvon horde. Tucking the real me deep within the darkness, which happily coils around it, a dragon of shadows hoarding her treasure. Hidden even from myself.

Winx's eyes flare brighter as she glances at my lips. "Oh, I almost forgot. This is my cousin, Flint Rockwell. He's been dying to meet you since I told him about how you slayed the Ritherin in Snomas."

Flint pops out from behind her. Winx quickly whirls aside, making room for him. He's taller than her and a Cerfios Lilliac, a stone Pixie-Elarian hybrid. His skin is carved of white marble with grey veining. His muscles are chiseled into broad shoulders, his left arm bearing a crack filled with gold veining. His face is carved for the heavens, with striking emerald eyes framed by windswept white hair. He's a walking piece of art.

I swallow at the sight of him. If my body looks more at home amongst the ornate walls of this theatre, he is the centerpiece.

He shyly glances my way with a sweet smile as he says, "*The* Sa-Savaé Entropaé. You're already the talk of the class. I can't wait to sa-see you in the spa-sparring ring. I'm hoping to be placed in the ground-combat division." He glances down nervously, as if his stuttered words sputter out on the floor.

There's a subtle beauty in the stark juxtaposition of Winx's vibrant, fiery confidence against her cousin's cool, quiet shyness—like a magnet's north and south poles.

"Glad to see Winx hasn't melted you to magma yet." I throw a smirk at Winx before continuing, "I'd love to train with you in the combat arena anytime."

His eyes flare neon green as he nods excitedly before taking his seat next to Winx, who's sharing her experience of the third trial. He seems eclipsed in her presence, fading into the background he's accustomed to, while Winx shines on the center stage.

The open seat on my other side is taken up by a familiar face. It's the Mao who went right before me in the second trial. What is her name again? A laugh tugs on my mind, rumbling up her last name, as she is of a feline-Fae subspecies. Mrow, that's it! Kissa Mrow. I silently chuckle to myself before painting on a smile as she takes her seat.

"Hey, I'm—"

"Yes, Savaé Entropaé. Trust me, everyone in this room knows who you are." Her ears shift in different directions, consuming all the conversations around us. "You are currently on everyone's lips," she says, unamused.

"Um… sorry, I think?" I'm not quite sure what the fuck to say to that.

The white and gold leather illuminates the different hues of purple in her fur as her chartreuse eyes narrow on me before softening. "Sorry. It's not your fault. The racket of the room just has me on edge. I'm Kissa Mrow. Laugh at my last name, and it will be your last breath."

I smirk at her. "I'd prefer to make it through orientation with my trachea intact, thank you very much. But I'm glad I'm not the only one unnerved by being around this many Fae at once."

She laughs, and there is almost a purr to it. "I guess you're alright, then… and it *was* pretty fucking badass, the way you took out that Pykavow. I thought for sure you were minced meat when you went rolling off the cliff. Nice moves. Glad to also know you have a clever head on those broad shoulders of yours. Not all stab first and ask questions later."

I laugh dryly. "Don't be so sure about that last part. It's far more fun to stab first."

She rolls her chartreuse eyes before lifting a finger to her lips as her ears lurch towards the front of the lecture hall. Steps ring out across the amphitheater stage, silencing the recruits. A thin, short male with disheveled brown hair and an ill-fitting tan tunic strolls to the podium.

"Welcome, new recruits, all five hundred of you. I am Professor Alaric Teak, scholar of Magical Theory and Arcane studies. I will be teaching you how to hone your Celestial Gift. And, if you become an Ellian Knight, your Arcane Glyph. But first, you must pass the written entrance exam. The papers will appear before you, starting the three hours you have to finish. The results will be posted this evening. Each of you who pass will receive a letter from a Scroll Owl with your assignments."

The entrance exam decides your fate. Not just with ink and parchment, but with magic. At the end of the written portion, each ensign nicks a small cut on their finger, placing it on the parchment—mentally teleporting to a magical room where all their abilities are tested to their limits. Powerful Runic, Illusionary, and Sangre magic combine to create the entrance exam. Regardless of whether we pass, we're all considered ensigns in the Golden Legion now. Those who fail this part are still trained, but for a shorter time before joining the infantry. They are not weak—having proved their strength in the trials—but they don't have the strategic fortitude for leading assaults.

The Golden Legion, Cascara's shield, divides its strength up into two arms. The infantry is our first line of defense. Our advance force is broken up into an aerial military structure: a Wing is the combination of our tactical Ground Unit and our Chivalry of Ellian Knights. The former rides volunteer Pegasuses and the latter on their bonded flying creatures. Wings soaring together in coordinated mission forms a Command, capable of devastating or defending entire fronts.

Everyone who passes will be assigned a division based on their exam scores. Savants' profound memories are deployed using history and information to help adapt movements, leading us on the battlefield. Spycraft stay hidden in plain sight or change their appearance, working in tandem with sneaky Scouting Rogues to gather intel or for covert missions. While having phenomenal sight and true aim targets you for Marksman, natural abilities for mending brings you to the Healers. A passion for Rune Tech and weaving runes lands you as a Runic Engineer. Strength and mastery in hand-to-hand combat are naturals for the Ground-Combatants. Persuasives are exceptional at mindwork and interrogation. Kinetics are known to be extremely powerful magic wielders; their job is to protect the Ground Unit while the Chivalry leads the attack from the skies.

Each division has their strengths, but they're not as adept in the other areas. Being proficient in every category marks you as a recruit. This group of ensigns has the chance of becoming Ellian Knights. Some will fall along the way, while others who fail to progress as predicted will be reassigned into other divisions.

Recruits who prove their mettle have one last hurdle to survive: the Celestial Bonding event, a daylong affair where all the recruits voyage out into the Mysticwoods south of campus. They will either die in the woods or come back as Ellian Knights, bonded to a mystical flying creature. Those who succeed are marked with an Arcane Glyph, forging an ionic bond that lasts a lifetime. Followed by celebrating the Celestial Dawning Festivities throughout all of Cascara, paying thanks to the protection of the Golden Legion.

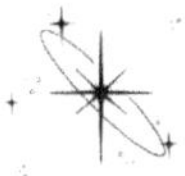

As I LIFT my hand off the parchment of the exam, I'm left with a heady feeling from the powerful magic, like I've drunk one too many flutes of sparkling Moonwine. A purple spark shimmers as the parchment spins into a roll, disappearing. The purple light swirls around me, leading me out of the auditorium to the rotunda before winding through the endless white-marble and golden corridors of Universitás to find my room in the first year's section.

I peer up to see the glass-domed ceiling, inlaid with intricate swirling golden runes. The campus appears more like a castle for the heavens than a place to be trained for war. Part of me feels the opulence—the gilded white battle leathers we are adorned with—is to separate us from other Fae, making us appear almost Celestial-like. Yet we are not. We're all simply mortals.

The queen's tax increases snag my mind as I take in all the luxury. If I think this place is lavish, her castle must be beyond words. Bile rises in my throat. Poverty racks our continent, and yet we could solve it with all the gold here on campus. If I weren't so numb from forcing down the crippling grief of losing Sully, my heart might cry for the indignation.

Every year, more and more children are being born without magic, their ears completely rounded, signaling the loss of part of their soul. When I was in Doraan, the town outside of Gildorea, I saw a human child smile. Despite everyone else's beliefs, I know humans still have magic in their veins—hope is a power all its own.

The loss of the Celestials is no doubt the cause of waning magic. I remember hearing stories in the bar while I hid under tables, eating crumbs that tumbled to the floor. Patrons recalled fables of a time nothing short of a fairytale—when the Celestials ruled and there was only peace.

Everyone had full stomachs, every crop bore a bountiful harvest, every being had a roof over their head. People worked with smiles on their faces, honoring our Celestial by sharing goods and services with everyone. One particularly drunk old lady crooned over how you could go to the capital and watch the Celestial create things of pure dreams. She said that's why our world was full of such a wide array of magical creatures and different Fae species: their imagination and powers were limitless. She raved about how there was no illness, and even death was rare, filling Cascara with endless love and mirth.

I wonder what kind of person I would have become, growing up in such a world. One where I was whole and full of light and love. A world where I could dare to dream, dare to hope. A dry laugh escapes my chest. *Broken things like me should know better than to indulge in fantasies.*

The purple spark zips up a golden spiral stairway in front of me. I bound up the steps, two at time to keep up. It fizzles out in front of the middle door in a small hallway. I stand outside, taking a deep breath, not sure why I'm hesitating opening the door, when the hairs prickle on the back of my neck. Fucking Emberhell. What is *he* doing here?

I lean my forehead against the cool wooden door. My heartbeat picks up as smoky shadows curl around the one I cast below me. As if my shadow is something precious to hold.

An odd feeling kicks up in my chest, as if I am worthy of feeling precious. Indulging such thoughts would only lead to my ruin, especially where this male is involved. A pang of longing scratches the surface of where my heart should be.

"I need you to kindly fuck off." Right along with the strange way my body reacts to his presence.

"You need me? My, how things have escalated. I rather like this forward side of you," Sølas croons from behind me.

A mix of a grunt and an exasperated sigh escapes my chest regarding his selective comprehension. I lazily turn to face the obnoxious male behind me. My eyes drag up his tall, muscled frame, wrapped in black leather, leaning against the wall. Of course, he's the only one of us who gets to wear fucking black.

"You need to learn how to take a hint."

"Oh, but I am. Don't think I can't hear your heartbeat from here?"

"That happens when you find someone aggravating." I roll my eyes as a cloud of shadows swirls beside me to reveal Sølas leaning with his arms braced behind his head. Heat skitters through my veins with his proximity.

"Are you going to tell me that scent you're giving off is aggravation too?" He arches a dark brow at me.

I want to kick and scream at my traitorous body. Instead, I shrug, trying to breeze over the statement. "That scent means nothing, other than my hormones have... pretty low standards." I rake my gaze over him with a venomous smile.

He clenches his jaw, lifting his tattooed knuckles to rub at his chest—as if I actually wounded him with my words. *Good.* Maybe he'll finally leave me alone now. Then something shifts in him as his full lips kick up at the corner.

"The lowest." He winks before he vanishes in a plume of shadows.

The wild swing of his emotions leaves a subtle dust of chaos in his wake, stirring something deep within my own darkness. As if it's waking up to take note of someone important.

I drag my hand down my face. *No.* Absolutely not. He is no one to me. He's nothing more than a distraction.

# CHAPTER 14

I open the door to my cubby-like room. The walls are layers of wavy slabs of Mysticwood, mahogany brown with vibrant lavender veining. Slats jut out of the wall on one side to make a bed and on the other to make a desk. There's a golden velvet chair beneath the workstation.

The empty space under my bed is already filled with my belongings, thanks to the Elarian who collected them at check-in. Several planks jut out of the wall, creating shelves for my books. There's an oval reflective glass on the back wall, but no window.

As soon as I shut my door, Pip is swirling around my room. I'd almost forgotten I was wearing him. He's mastered the skill of staying breathtakingly still. His colors appear to shift with his excitement exploring our new space.

"This wood will heighten magical powers while also shielding it from magic. So no breathing fire inside, mister." He tilts his head to the side and then scampers off to continue his exploration.

Most of the magical creatures of our world can speak through either words, telepathic connection, or body language. Typically, dragons use telepathic connection. Yet Pip only speaks to me in body language, mannerisms, and chirps. I appreciate his quiet nature. The notion of voices booming in my head leaves me uneasy, but it's an inevitable fate for me once bonded. It doesn't mean I can't enjoy the peace that is still currently mine.

"When I'm in battle, you're going to have to find another shape to shift into. I can't be wearing a scarf in the arena or on the field," I say, placing my weapons on the shelves, finding a place for my sketchbook among them. My cloak hangs on a small wooden spool poking out of the wall.

I slide my armor off, kick off my boots, and tumble back on the bed with a *thud*. I lie there in my white and gold leather pants, with several layers of fabric bound around my petite breasts, flattening them, creating a more masculine shape that matches my broad shoulders and carved muscles. Gold silk sheets caress my skin in the softest embrace of a bed I've ever felt. *Geesh, they really spared no expense.*

Before I know it, there's a scratching at my door. I throw Pip a look, and he knows to hide. I wrap my cloak over my body, hiding my markings, then open the door to see a Scroll Owl. An odd creature that appears to be an owl made of a robe. When standing, they have the silhouette of a slender human draped in a cloak that goes over their head, hiding their face, with just two yellow eyes staring at you from within the darkness.

As they lift their arms, the robe splits into wings; the back of the robe becomes their tail, revealing two owl legs. Typically reserved for conversation between the queen and the Golden Legion, it's said they can carry hundreds of scrolls beneath their wings. This Scroll Owl drops a piece of rolled parchment at my feet before flying off. I slink back in my room, my cloak pooling at my feet as I unroll the parchment and read:

*SAVÆ ENTROPÆ Species: Elarian.*
*Division: ENSIGN RECRUIT*
*Wing: I. ZENITH*

*Ground Unit*
*Healer: Kivi Shaw Species: Mycelium Nymph, Helios*
*Ground-combatant: Flint Rockwell Species: Elarian-Pixie,*
*    Lilliac Cerfios*
*Savant: Atlas Ailanthus Species: Müra*
*Persuasive: Orion Nightshade Species: Pesche*
*Spycraft: Seraphina Denova Species: Elarian-Pixie, Lilliac*
*    Visci*
*Runic Engineer: Gearin Griswald Species: Automaton*
*Scouting Rogue: Eko Lightfoot Species: Yassur*
*Marksman: Highin Heathrow Species: Aetherhawk*
*Kinetic: Fenwick Brightspar Species: Elarian*

*Potential CHIVALRY:*
*Cinder Ignis Blazeheart Species: Elarian-Pixie, Lilliac Pyro*
*Juniper Stormfel Species: Elarian-Naturalist*
*Kissa Mrow Species: Mao*
*Vex Boomer Species: Infernai*
*Sølas Zyon Species: Elarian*

*Son of bitch,* they spelt my name wrong but... I've made it to Ensign Recruit! Not that I doubted I would... Okay, maybe when I was tumbling to my near-death down in Frostma, a smidgen of doubt crossed my mind.

I am almost an Ellian Knight.

For the first time in what feels like forever, a genuine smile twists at the corners of my mouth. I'm so close! And yet, a delicate sadness laces my happiness, knowing Sully isn't here with me to see this moment.

I scroll through the rest of my assigned Wing. Our Wings are named based on our aerial formations in the skies; their names come from being an observer looking to the stars. The number 'I' represents primary. We will be the first group deployed to the roughest battles.

Zenith means we will be the forward topflight, leading the way into battle. Nadir flies underneath and behind us. Declination Wing flies in the left-middle, Ascension Wing parallel to them on our right. If we are deployed to a close location, Ground Unit members travel by horses. If our mission brings us far away, we have an entire herd of Pegasuses to carry units with their assigned Chivalry, a group of Ellian Knights. Pegasuses cannot form Arcane Glyphs, so this is their contribution to the war effort, as their breeding grounds reside in the grassy fields adjacent to Gildorea Universitás.

Our Ground Unit is made up of a war beast of exceptionally strong species; just having a Helios on our team lets us be mended and sent straight back into battle. I smile as I notice Flint's name, thinking of his quiet nature, yet his body is a pure weapon of strength and unbreakable marble skin.

Müra are a race of moth-like Fae. They are the strongest of Savants, a walking weaponized encyclopedia, known for their quick, decisive battle strategy in combat and on the field. When not in battle, you can find them deep in the catacombs of the archives, finding peace in cataloging events from current battles and memorizing every confrontation that ever occurred before, as well as reading a wide array of history.

They weren't playing any games when they added a Visci to our team. They are the ultimate spies, especially those who can shapeshift. This allows them to be sent ahead, infiltrating camps and strongholds. They are almost impossible to kill, given their ability to bend their body like liquid. They will be sent ahead with our Scouting Rogue: a Yassur, the Fae species with large, ribbed bat ears, a purplish to brownish hue to their skin, covered a thin layer of fur. They have small, residual flaps of skin connecting from below their elbow to just above their hips, allowing them to glide from high heights. They move in a fast blur and possess exceptional hearing, making silent clicks at a frequency beyond most species' hearing range for echolocation.

I remember the next name from my second trial; he had gone before me. Aetherhawks are on the brink of extinction thanks to the Wuvon hunting them, so it's a privilege to have their ancient Fae lineage as part of our team. I remember the unique sienna color to his feathers and skin, almost as though he were colored by flying too close to the dawning sun.

Moving on to the names of our potential Chivalry—assuming we all survive until then—a grin crosses my lips at Kissa's name. I'm excited to have a familiar, fierce female to ride with into battle.

The last unique species on the list is an Infernai, known to be absolute barbarians in a fight with strong magical abilities, including the ability to see in the dark. They're said to be descendants of demons who once walked this world before the Eclipse World War, originally hailing from a continent to the east of us known as Emberhell. They appear like Elarian Fae, but their skin is leathery. Their heads are adorned with horns of all different shapes, abutting their pointed ears.

My heart stops when I reach the last name on the list. *Not him.* Sølas Zyon.

There is just something about him, striking a nerve deep within me. Trouble practically drips off him; I remember the swirling shadows in his ice-blue eyes flecked with crimson, like blood splattering across moonlit snow.

An enigmatic shiver foxtrots along my spine as I think of him. My heart seems to bow to this shiver as heat kisses my skin. *No, sir.* All these feelings are going straight out my favorite broken mosaic window. Heeding Sully's warning will be even harder with him in my Chivalry for the rest of my life. Yep, we will train together and be deployed together. Bonds forged here are for life.

Well, I guess that settles it.

I will need to end him before or during the Celestial Bonding event. The effect he has on me will otherwise be a liability to our Wing, and I refuse to have him distracting me for the rest of my career. I won't let anything stand in my way. Maybe that makes me unhinged—evil, even—but maybe that's all that's left of me now that I've lost Sully. A broken, crooked thing, holding on to the only tether I have: becoming an Ellian Knight, no matter the cost.

It has to be done before he bonds, making him even stronger. Killing a Shadowmancer is already a near-impossible feat, but I'll have no chance once he's bonded. His powerful Celestial Gift will draw an exceedingly powerful magical flying beast.

It's grounds for expulsion to kill any other ensigns and forbidden within our own Wing. This ensures trust in the connections we forge with one another during our training here. Especially since our bloodlines could be paired within our Wing. And since Chancellor Ashfel and Commander Bragen already pinned a target on my back, they'll leap at the chance to expel me.

I'll have several opportunities, however. One will be during training drills in the wilds of the borderlands, where it'll be possible to make it appear as though he simply got in over his head and the Blackwood claimed his soul. Shit—never mind, that will be after the Celestial Bonding event...

Perhaps sneaking into his room and killing him while he's sleeping would work? I'm sure there are at least a few ensigns who would rise to the chance to take out a Shadowmancer, just for the glory it would raise them to for killing such a powerful wielder. Although I don't particularly like the idea of having to indulge his endless flirtation to get me into his bedroom, especially with the way my traitorous body responds to his presence.

Lastly, on the day of the Celestial Bonding, *I could* make it look as though he approached the wrong creature, leaving him ripped to shreds. Come to think of it, actually killing him will be the real challenge, especially since I have no real Celestial Gift of my own yet. I'll need to be cunning. As long as I can survive long enough for my paralyzing dagger to drop one ounce of blood, I should be able to pull it off.

I'm jolted from my murderous plotting by a knock on the door.

"Open up! It's Winx."

Looks like alone time will be a rare occurrence here. When I led Winx outside that bar in a lustful frenzy, I never meant it to be anything more than a one-night stand. An impulsive thrill to fulfill a need, subtly loosening my own noose of control without losing the reins entirely.

I didn't realize how reckless my choice in vice would be. Her being the Chancellor's daughter definitely complicates things. I need to handle her wildfire carefully, or she'll burn me down with her. Wary of getting on the wrong side of her wrath spurs me to leap to the door without remembering my current brazen attire.

Winx busts into my room, her blatant disregard for boundaries continuing to rear its head.

"Guess what? My room is right down the hall from yours. I'm sad we're not in the same Wing. Let me see your assignment!" She snatches the scroll from my hand before I have a chance to respond. She moves like a wildfire: fast, without thought, full of consuming energy. Her vigor and self-indulgent approach to the world around her are sexy but also worrisome.

"Celestial's tits! You're in primary Zenith Wing... and *damn*, this Unit is unbeatable! I'm so jealous you get to be with Flint, but I'm glad you two will have each other's backs. They don't let relatives be in the same Wing for fear our focus on keeping family members alive could risk the mission. Which is definitely valid... I would let them all burn before letting *anything* hurt Flint."

There's a coldness in her last sentence that makes me uneasy. She isn't lying; the tone reminds me of her father's voice, which is uncharacteristic as everything about her is more fire Pixie. She even has a more pronounced angle to her ears than most other Lilliacs.

Winx continues, "And Vex Boomer is the Chronosense everyone has been talking about. I can't believe that sly bitch didn't tell me her Celestial Gift." She scoffs with devilish amusement before continuing, "Ooh, *and* you have this year's heartthrob in your Chivalry. Sølas. I caught him staring at you in the Gilded Amphitheater this morning before entrance exams. I have a sneaking suspicion he's into you. If you leave me for him, I'll burn him alive just for the show of it." Her eyes flare violently at the teasing remark. I'm sure she'll make good on that threat, leaving a muddling worry to tug at my chest. I debate using her to kill him for me, but that's too low a level even for me to sink to.

"Jealousy is unbecoming, and don't be lewd. I'm sure he's been with half the class already. That blonde female from our trials has been following him around like a lovesick puppy dog." I lean in, twirling a strand of her hair. "And I can't leave you if you never had me in the first place."

She swats my hand away, not even bothering to pry her eyes off the parchment. "I make it my business to know all the tea party gossip—that's why I can't believe Vex held out on me. Perhaps I owe her a singe as well. Rumor has it, Sølas is a total flirt but never takes anyone to bed. Nothing worse than a tease, in my opinion. Plus, his bloodline is unknown. I don't care how powerful he is; he's not worth the risk, although my dad seems to disagree. Him and Seraphina were always getting into trouble when I had to stay here, and they barely got a slap on the wrist."

Her eyes darken at the last part; apparently, her father's punishments were more severe when it came to her. I don't need her broken bits tugging at me, so it's time to distract from this line of thought.

"Why am I not surprised that you're the queen of gossip? And to think you tricked me into believing you were a sweet little thing. A wolf in sheep's clothing. How could anyone resist you?" I take a step closer. "Do your eyes flare neon violet when you use Persuasive abilities? Or is it only when you heat with power?"

She's still distracted, reading the scroll.

I take another step closer, my voice low and sultry. "Perhaps they flare brightest when I make your heart race?"

Her eyes dart up from the parchment for the first time to meet mine. They flare a vibrant hue of violet, then back to magenta, racing with the beat of her heart. Then they widen, her gaze dragging over my shoulders and collarbones.

I'm distracted by the beat of her eyes as she reaches out with dainty fingers, touching my bare skin. I lurch back from her touch, grasping for my cloak, covering my bare markings on display. I hadn't realized I was so exposed.

She pulls her hand back to her chest. "I have never seen skin like yours. I noticed the gold flecks on your cheeks, but I thought they were just an edgy makeup choice. Why are you hiding them? They are… stunning. I want to see the rest! Please? Please, please!" She jumps up and down like a child on Blessings Day morning.

I can tell from her excitement that she's genuinely curious. I've never had anyone look at my markings with… glee? It's unnerving. I fall another step back, watching the neon violet fade to solid magenta.

"They are nothing, other than one more thing marking me as cursed. That's why I keep them covered. They're meant to be hidden, not seen. Just like me. Out of sight."

I curse myself for letting a piece of me slip out, exposed and vulnerable, waiting to be minced to pieces.

Her rainbow hair suddenly turns into purple flames with her anger. "That's not true! They make you unique and striking. They should be flaunted. Fuck everyone else. You're different. Your skin has been blessed by the Celestials. Make the world weep in the shadow of your beauty."

I tumble another step backwards, almost certain she'll set my room ablaze with the violet flames emanating from her. Her power dims, realizing the discomfort in my rigid posture and clenched jaw.

She gently grabs my hand. "Sorry. I have a quick temper. I get it from my mom. I can get a bit dramatic." She laughs almost manically, as if she wasn't just literally on fire. "I'm definitely not used to the amplification of the Mysticwood walls yet. Listen… what I'm trying to say is: being different isn't a bad thing. It's what makes you beautifully *you*."

She smiles big, eyes glowing with wildfires.

"Remind me not to piss you off," I whisper, pulling my hand from hers slowly, surprised it's not burnt to a crisp.

"See? You're already the smartest in our class." She lets out a beautiful laugh. "Wait a minute, how come I've never seen your markings before toda—?"

I cut her off with a knowing distraction. "Maybe you can help me figure out something to wear tonight to the celebratory festivities?"

She squeals with excitement. "Let's open that bag of yours and see what we're working with."

I'm thankful she's easily distracted. She's already seen my markings. I don't want her knowing about my basilisk armor, too. I like my secrets; they belong to me. I'm not used to being close to people, especially someone I've slept with.

Winx throws various things out of my bag in frustration, clearly disappointed at my extremely limited attire. "I don't know what you expect me to do with this. Next weekend we have off, I'm taking you into Doraan to go shopping. Or better yet, maybe I can convince my father to let us go to Riicah for the weekend!" She seems tickled violet at that thought.

I'm not used to seeing a sexual liaison more than once—and definitely not used to being around Fae of the aristocracy. I'm not even really sure what this is between us. But whatever it is, it's going to take some getting used to.

"Can't I just wear my new uniform? It's the fanciest thing I own."

Her violet eyes narrow on me like I just cursed her family. I swallow the uneasy glare with a gulp.

"You're insane, simply insane, if you think I'm letting you walk into the party beside me in aerial leathers," she says, mumbling a string of curses as she paces my room, tugging at her hair.

I'm rethinking my choice in females at this moment. I should've known getting involved with an Arabellian aristocrat with a flare for explosive fire was a bad idea. Never mind who her father is. Now I'm starting to wonder if I'd given myself too much credit in the smarts department. I guess I didn't really think things through when I whisked her away. Nothing like the pleasure of skin to wash away the sin of battle.

I watch her gears turning, hand rubbing her chin.

"I've got it!" She pulls out my one black velvet gown and glamours it into a chiffon dress that clasps around the back of the neck, draping the fabric in a deep V before rejoining to form the bottom, with large gaps that extend up the thighs on either side.

My jaw drops. "The fuck am I wearing that thing! I'd be practically naked. On second thought, maybe I'll just stay in tonight."

"Ugh, you're no fun!" With another twist of her finger, the dress magically changes back. She grabs my battle leathers next, and she twirls her fingers. A black leather romper now appears before me. Tight leather pants attached to a strapless leather bustier with gold embellished down the center, fanning out towards my hips. Clearly, she's trying to mimic my markings, but the patterns are more ornate than the simple thick bands on my skin. But it will cover most of me, and from the look she's giving me, I'm not getting out of wearing this or going out tonight.

"Put this on, and I'll be right back after I change," she chirps, skipping out the door.

I take the private moment to unwrap the banding on my chest because there's no hiding it in the deep V of that bustier. I dress in the clinging leather romper and tighten the strings of the strapless corset, gasping for my last deep breath. This tightens much firmer than my basilisk armor, accentuating the curve of my waist before it meets the bow of my muscular thighs. I do my makeup in the mirror, adorning kohl along my bottom lash, contrasting against my golden squares.

My hair takes on an almost lavender hue from the Mysticwood veining along the walls, glowing with a powerful, soothing light. I debate putting on my basilisk armor. But I have a sneaking suspicion that after Winx's burst of anger about hiding my markings, I'd regret it. I guess since everyone will be dressed nicely and the outfit continues the pattern of my markings, I can probably get away with brushing them off as an edgy makeup choice, like Winx said. Hopefully, everyone will be too drunk to look at them closely. I send up a blessing to the Celestials that no one I've pissed off decides to kill me tonight.

Before I know it, Winx bursts through my door without knocking. *Note to self: enchant the door so everyone can't just come waltzing in as they please.*

She looks stunning in a dress similar to the one she had originally glamoured for me. Showing off the fine curves of her lean, muscular body, which reminds me of a dagger: small but deadly. Her golden eyeshadow accentuates her violet eyes, stealing my breath.

"Keep looking at me like that, and you may get your wish of staying in your room." A sly smile paints her lips as her irises begin to flicker like violet embers amongst the gold.

The heated flare only makes me crave her all the more. I crave to sling her petite body, pinning her down on my bed. I want to mark her throat—not in possession, but in reminder that her fire is untamed and wild. My fingers gripping her thighs, with my mouth taking everything it wants. While I keep her on the edge of bliss until she loses her fucking sanity, and I drown in the crashing waves of her pleasure.

I grab her waist, spinning her in front of me; her bare shoulders graze across my lower chest. On the side of her head, where the hair lengthens, I breathe a lustful growl into her neck as her body arches into mine with a moan. I have half a mind to bend her over and take her right now.

As quick as a spark, she snatches the dagger off my desk, spinning around, grabbing my jaw in one hand with the tip of the blade at my throat.

Well, this is *unexpected*.

"Behave," she hisses before smiling sweetly. "I promise you can devour me after we have graced the celebration with our presence."

I make quick work of grabbing my hands around her ass, pulling her off the ground closer to me. Thankful my paralysis dagger is sheathed at my ribs under a glamour of my own and out of her sneaky little fingers.

A nip of sweet pain pierces my neck as I drag her closer into me. She isn't playing with that dagger. She meant what she said. Her eyes flicker wildly, locked fiercely on mine.

"Why wait when I already have you all to myself right now?" I respond to her daring threat in a low, guttural rumble as magenta fire blazes in her irises.

"Patience is a virtue," she purrs, pressing the dagger in, ever so slightly. A warm drop of crimson drips down my neck.

I release my grip, letting her feet plop down to the floor. She slings the dagger back on the desk before spinning back to me, standing on her tiptoes to lick the blood off my neck. The hum of her Sangre magic echoes along my flesh, healing the wound with a kiss. She looks up with her own hunger, her lips stained in my crimson blood.

*Fucking Emberhell,* she's sexy. Darkness curls deep inside me, ready to be released to play with the wildfire before me. It takes far more strength than I care to admit to resist the crazy eroticism of her. I grasp for her, and she twirls wildly away.

"Now, sit. Let me do your hair. Or I'll break my promise of letting you have me for dessert." She snickers with a devilish smile that only stokes the flames of my lust. Her eyes narrow as she nods her head to the chair. Letting me know that, right now, she's the one in charge, and I need to obey if I want to enjoy her. She knows how to get exactly what she wants, I'll give her that.

I sit with a disgruntled huff. She works meticulously, delicately pinning my hair up on the sides, leaving several loose strands. She curls them with the heat of her finger. My hair is feminine but powerful. Her talents continue to surprise me.

I stand up, ready to leave, following her out the door, when I notice something warm around my neck. Celestials be dimmed. *Pip.*

Winx senses my hesitation, whipping around, her eyes almost constricting on my neck as she visualizes the scarf. "You are not hiding your markings with me. Take that scarf off, please and thank you very much." She scowls.

"Sorry, I slipped it on out of habit. It is fall, after all." I turn away from Winx, taking Pip off my neck, mumbling quietly, "You can't come with me. I'll be back later." I place him on the bed. In a blink of an eye, I have a matching leather bracer on my left arm, adorned with four fire-opal jewels down the center. My lips tip into a smile. *Clever little dragon.*

Winx grabs my hand as she trots into the hallway so quickly, I'm forced to use magic to close my door behind us. I try to tug my hand away, but her grip only tightens. I don't have the energy to make a big deal out of it and decide to go along with it. At least I'm too numb to fully feel that gnawing sensation at my ribs this time.

# CHAPTER 15

We enter through two huge arched doors into what I imagine is normally the dining hall. The towering domed ceilings are adorned with faerie chandeliers dancing above us, cloaking the room in a romantic ambiance. Ornate floral centerpieces don all the tables, which are dressed in golden silk linens. Each porcelain plate detailed with ornate golden patterns around the rim.

There's a handsome Infernai bartender behind a golden counter along the wall with curved horns adorning his skull and slicked-back indigo hair. Red sparks fly from his fingertips as he creates a show of mixing and pouring drinks. Various Elarians of different shapes and sizes scurry about with innumerable appetizers held on baroque silver platters.

The decadence of it all sours my stomach, knowing this is all paid for by the high taxes on the hard-working civilian population. We're supposed to be here training for war, not schmoozing like aristocrats.

Chet simmers against the wall with a group of males. He glares at me, clenching his jaw, and I swear his head is going to burst into flames. Even if he and Winx end up as a bloodline match, we aren't supposed to catch feelings; it's meant to be a simple exchange of genetic material. Or several exchanges, depending on how long it takes. It's quite frowned upon to develop feelings for your match. It makes things… too complicated. Once a fetus grows, it's magically teleported out of your womb into an artificial one for continued incubation and protection. A clever design of the Runic Engineers, so Knights are not taken out of battle during gestation.

When the Faeling is born, it's raised by the Maidens, who dedicate their lives to their upbringing. It's up to the sires if they want to be a part of their life when they grow up. Either way, they're essentially property of Universitás, raised to be weapons. This is our sworn contribution to the line of Ellian Knights; other students do not have to partake in Bloodline pairings if they do not wish to.

After Universitás, we can get vow runes and have our own offspring if we desire. Though that's definitely not in the cards for me. I know better than to think of happy things like family and a place to call home.

I'm unsure whether Chet actually has feelings for Winx or if it's a dominance thing, like a dog marking his territory. Based on how he's puffing his chest up at me, I suspect the latter. He doesn't threaten me. I shoot him a wink, and boy, does that make his skin turn beet red.

His friends turn around to see what's caused his new coloration. I don't care; it's clear Winx doesn't give a shit about him, either. She doesn't even seem to know he exists tonight.

Suddenly, I'm surrounded by a group of Fae. That's what I get for walking in with the life of the party. I don't enjoy everyone's focus on me, like I'm a prize to be shown off at the fair.

I'm rapidly introduced to a slurry of people, hardly hearing the first one's name before the next. My head spins as I gulp down another glass of sparkling Moonwine. I'm clearly not meant for this type of socialite life.

As the introductions continue, I recognize one of the names from my Chivalry, Vex Boomer—the Chronosense. She has a similar body frame to Winx—slender—and her leathery skin is a hue of vermillion scarlet. Delicate features make up her face, with scattered freckles across her nose and temples and grey lips matching her deep, slate eyes. Her face is framed with a head of tight black curls with braids on either side, showing off her rounded spiral horns that remind me of the mountain goats that traverse Eldoria.

Another face I recognize is the blonde with emerald eyes, her hair strung up in ringlet curls. I believe Winx said her name is Tyranny Everclaw. Next to her is a tall, slender Arabellian male with pink highlights in his long hair tied up into a bun. He has a feminine beauty, with a melodramatic queerness to his voice. I nudge Flint as he clearly eyes the other male like a schoolboy crush.

"How do you put up with this?" I whisper to him over my shoulder.

"Just nod your head, sa-smile, and find something more interesting to distract your mind," he mutters back. It's clear his quiet nature has left him on the sidelines, watching a world he's not wholly a part of.

"By something distracting, do you mean something tall, pink-haired, and pretty?" I snicker as I swear his marble cheeks faintly blush a pale pink. "You should go talk to him," I urge.

"I wouldn't know what to sa-say to Rizz," he whispers back.

"Yeah, I'm no good at small talk either." I huff.

Winx looks at me, squeezing my hand. I can tell I missed some important cue by the feeling of anticipation that falls over me but isn't my own.

"I was telling everyone about how you defeated that Ritherin and your close call with the Pykavow." Everyone is looking at me, waiting on my words, like I'm some war hero to entertain them with my epic clashes sung in bardic melodramas. I don't enjoy having everyone's eyes on me, yet Winx thrives under their scrutiny.

Tyranny looks unamused and sardonically asks, "Regale us of your secrets. How did you manage such feats?" Something's hidden behind her question because she witnessed both fights, but I can't put my finger on her intentions.

"You just find a weakness and kill it. Otherwise, it kills you."

The pink-haired male, Rizz, gives a giddy clap. "Darling, you're simply vicious. I'm positively gagging. I see why Winx has grown a shine to you."

I nod, mustering a half smile, attempting Flint's advice. Heat radiates off Winx's skin, a rosy hue painting her cheeks as the neon violet flares in her eyes.

"She was trained by the legendary Sully Stonewall. Of course she's vicious. Anyone trained by a fighter like him would have to be. It doesn't make her special, just well-taught. What I can't figure out is why they only chose *you* for these monsters each time. What have you done, other than fucking the Chancellor's daughter, to merit his special challenge?" Tyranny quips.

She has dealt her hand, and now her emotions are plain as day to read. She's jealous and clearly doesn't find me worthy of anyone's attention. I find a twinge of pain in her words about Sully. *He was more than my fucking teacher, you twat.* The words coil like venom on my tongue, burning to be spat in her face, but she isn't worth the effort. I don't even bother looking at her. I know ignoring her will fester far deeper under her skin. And it does.

Her eyes bore into the side of my face, begging for me to acknowledge what she clearly thought was a clever question. There's a truth in it. Why did he challenge me and no one else this trial season? No one else faced the same *experimenting*, as Winx had put it.

"Tyranny, why do you have to be such an insufferable bitch?" Winx jabs.

I squeeze Winx's hand in thanks for saying what I'm essentially thinking.

"Oh, honey, we all know she's just mad Sølas won't give her the time of day. She's been practically throwing herself at him for months like a cat in heat." Rizz turns his head towards her, giving a mocking pat on the hand. "Now, now, Tyranny. It's unbecoming of a lady such as yourself. What would the queen say?"

Tyranny rebukes him with, "He's just playing hard to get. It's his thing. He can't say no to me forever. He knows who my aunt is."

"What are you going to do, Tyra? Have your auntie declare a royal decree to make him love you? Even the queen has her limits. No one wields the power of love, or have you let being spoiled rot your brain, too?" Rizz laughs, and the others chuckle in.

Tyranny is the queen's niece? Ugh, one more person not to fucking piss off in this place. And she's already clearly unhappy with me, likely noticing Sølas staring at me today, just as Winx did. Not to mention my secret mission to take her not-so-interested loverboy off the map.

Speaking of which, I may want him dead, but I still detest the way she felt like she could force someone's hand just because of who she's related to. The thought of it leaves a bitter taste fermenting in my mouth.

I'm not sure which is worse: what Tyranny said, or how mean her friends were to her. I'm no fan of Tyranny, but the whole scenario is off-putting. They're her friends, and yet they're bullying her. I guess this is how aristocrats treat one another. Everything for them is a power play, just like Winx walking in with me on her hip.

Winx pulls me in closer, whispering, "Sorry about Tyranny. We only put up with her because of who she is, not because any of us like being around her." I try to give her a reassuring smile, but bile curls my stomach.

"You're one to talk, Rizz. We're all spoiled rotten. That's what makes us so much fun!" Vex Boomer snarks, and they all laugh with a maniacal delight.

A suffocating wave crashes over me; this socialite scenario is too much. I enjoy the raw lust I share with Winx in private, but that's all it is. What we share isn't meant for the test of her society. I have no intentions of being in a relationship of any sort.

The obligations of being a part of Winx's world start to outweigh my craving for a fun distraction. She's intoxicating, but being around the aristocratic society is far too sobering. Companionship beyond the battlefield only serves to make us weak. I'm not here to lose myself to the vice of lust. I'm here for me. I'm here to be all that it takes to become an Ellian Knight. Holding on to the one thing that seems to be gluing my sanity together.

I look at the obscene decadence surrounding me and think of the coal workers caked in black dust as they cough their lungs up at the bar, spending what little coin they make on a beer to drown the pain. The farmers who break their backs in the fields each day to feed our kingdom while they starve, barely able to afford a loaf of stale bread. The queen's taxes make life extremely hard for the civilian population, barely able to make ends meet. Is sleeping soundly on hay beds really worth all their sacrifices?

Then I think of those human children I saw in Doraan, running down the street with rags for clothing. They'll die before adulthood without magic to get by. Surely, this decadence is unnecessary for a war university? We can still be trained just as well and sacrifice many of the luxuries afforded to us, so the civilians we boast about protecting can go to sleep with full stomachs and have days off to rest. Suddenly, suffocation cinches tightly around my throat, drowning in the wealth surrounding me while remembering what it's like to be cold and starving with no one to give a shit if I make it through the night or not.

My eyes wander around the room, looking for an escape. I eye Kissa and give her a pleading look that says *save me*. She rolls her eyes and, to my relief, starts to slink my way.

Finally reaching me, Kissa purrs, "Sorry ladies and gents, I need to borrow my Chivalry pal."

I start towards her, but Winx tugs at my wrist. I look down at her disappointed face, feigning a half-smile. Thankfully, she finally lets me go. I'm not her precious prize to garner the spotlight with her friends, it's like a dagger twisting in my gut that she sees me as such.

"You're a lifesaver," I say once we're out of earshot.

"Don't get used to me saving you. You're the dumbass who decided to sleep with the Chancellor's daughter. You made the bed you're lying in.

You're in *way* over your head with that one, and I'm not getting in the middle of you two."

"Yeah, I know it wasn't smart. You know males are not the only ones to think with a brain that's not between their ears," I retort.

Kissa rolls her eyes so hard, I think they might tumble right out of her head. "Just keep it in your pants when it comes to our unit, or I will claw out those unique eyes of yours," she hisses. She's kind of terrifying... which makes me like her all the more.

"I will hold you to that. I have a feeling you and I are going to be friends."

She gives me a side eye, but I see a subtle smile hinting at the corner of her mouth. She brings me over to the group of Fae along the wall. They have a decanter of Smokewhisper libation on the table.

I notice a Pesche pouring the amber liquid into an empty glass. The aquamarine scales of her sylph-like frame shimmer beneath the faerie lights as she moves. Darker blue scales appear in a pattern, forming eddying shapes, almost like a tattoo. Her hair—waves of candy red with matching eyes shining bright across the scales that frame her forehead—stops at the right side of her shaved head, revealing a fin-like ear. Her neck is bejeweled by an obsidian and citrine choker, mirroring her jet blazer with sulfur-yellow embroidery. Her fashion sense is impeccable. She slides the full glass across the table to me.

"Drink up. I can tell by your Aura that you need this after dealing with that bunch of self-indulgent Nightbloods. They'll suck the life force right out of you if you're not careful. I'm Orion Nightshade. Welcome to the team."

I *clink* the table with the glass and then lift it up to her with a tilt. "May the Celestials never dim."

I recognize her name from the scroll; she's our Persuasive. I heard some have the ability to read Auras, the energy radiating around you, displaying your emotions like a waving flag. They're extremely powerful; even the strongest mental shields cannot hide one's Aura. At Gildorea, Persuasives are not allowed to read others' minds without their consent, unless it's in their specific training sessions, but an Aura reader would not be held to this same rule since it's impossible. They definitely weren't playing around when they made our Wing designations. If we survive as a Zenith until graduation, we'll surely be stationed on the frontlines of the Blackwood.

I peer to the side of Orion. Leaning against the wall is an Elarian with short, messy hair, the bright color reminiscent of fall pumpkins. Which matches the freckles strewn across his face. His cheekbones are chiseled above hollows that meet his defined jaw, leading up to his pointed ears decorated by glittering piercings. His muscular shape is painted in tattoos that peek out along his chest and up his neck, where his red-and-black checkered flannel shirt is unbuttoned. I'm glad to see someone rebelling against the dress code.

His eyes flare bright amber when they meet mine; he's a powerful Lilliac, like Winx. He lifts his chin up and down to me in a smooth nod.

"Cinder Ignis Blazeheart." There's something about how he pronounced Ignis that pulls at a string in the back of my mind, like a memory just out of reach. I remember his name from the scroll as well; he's part of my Chivalry, a Pyro, but there's something more I can't put my finger on. Something Sully had told me about the Ignis family line. Oh well, I'm sure it will pop back into my head at some totally useless point in time.

On the other side of Orion, a male finishes his drink. He's much taller, more slender than me, with a head full of short white dreadlocks that appear dipped in gold. His hazel eyes are framed by round, golden spectacles, shimmering against his ebony skin with a jaw made of gold that only makes his debonaire imperial mustache stand out all the more. He's clearly an Automaton, a subspecies of Elarian so enthralled with Runic magic, they replace parts of their body with Rune Tech. They're consigned from a young age to become the very best Runic Engineers. Consecrated to the craft.

"Pour me and this one another, Orion," the Automaton grumbles.

"She has a name, Gearin," Orion scolds. I remember his name from the parchment as well. Gearin Griswald.

"My name—"

"We know," the group says in unison. *Geez*, okay. Everyone knowing my name dredges up being curseborne all over again.

"I'm Fenwick Brightspar," a surprisingly short but muscular Elarian says on my right. She jumps slightly up and down, almost like she can't wait to finally introduce herself. She's bright-eyed and bushy-tailed. Her hair shorn just below her jaw in a straight bob, parting it down the center: one side is white, the other sable. Sunburst eyes gleam against her warm skin and soft features. The energy of excitement is practically radiating off her.

"I'm so, *so* excited we have you on our team! We are going to totally kick ass during Fortress Battle this year." Fenwick beams. Literally. She's a

Radiant, able to harness the power of light and solar energy. I can't help but smile down at Fenwick. Her happiness is almost infectious.

The hairs on my neck prickle. I peer behind Orion to a mass of unfurling shadows. Ugh. *Not this fucking guy.*

"Finally, the fun has arrived," a confident female announces—her voice almost masculine—walking in next to Sølas. Shadows cascading off the pair like smoke.

"I found this little gem playing a prank on a second year. Disguised as Chancellor Ashfel. The poor ensign nearly pissed himself. But her cerulean eyes flared at the sight of me, giving her away," Sølas jabs.

"The kid didn't even notice until you blew my cover, ya fuckwit," the female argues, flipping Sølas a lewd gesture. Jostling her powder-blue hair, woven along one side of her head, snarling into a group of long war braids down her back. Zaffre-blue tattoos swirl up her left arm to the bottom half of her scalp, shaved into an undercut beneath her braids.

"You're going to have to get better at shielding so you don't blow your cover when you're on mission. Or we'll be in need of a new Spycraft for Zenith Wing." Sølas elbows the female at his side.

"Well, if it isn't the Savaé fucking Entropaé. As I live and breathe," she says with a feigned bow. The female is clearly a Lilliac by the neon blue flaring in her eyes during her perusal of me. With the facts Sølas has previously said, I surmise she is Seraphina Denova, our Unit Visci. Designation: Spycraft.

"Yeah, everyone knows me. I fucking get it. Tell me something I don't know." I huff, bristling as I down the rest of my Smokewhisper libation.

"*Damn*, Sølas! She's as feisty as you said. You're lucky ya only ended up with a dagger at your neck and not at your balls, my friend." Seraphina smacks his back, knocking the wind out of him. It's clear they're thick as thieves, but she comes off as much more fun than her intolerable shadowy counterpart.

A jagged, hyperpigmented scar transects her chiseled face. It's at home alongside her sharp, angular features. Her eyes are a deep cerulean, flaring ultramarine when she catches my appraisal of her rippled, battle-hardened body. I'd heard those raised by the Maidens with exceptional powers could be deployed for missions before Universitás, but part of me always hoped it wasn't true. I can see the subtle pain hidden behind her mask of brash jokes and flirtation. Broken things tend to recognize one another… I wonder what broke Sølas to make them so close, hiding behind masks of similar construction. *Nope.* Not going there.

Seraphina is dressed in a black woven turtleneck with the sleeves cut off. Her tattooed arms are interrupted by black leather straps spun around her hands and wrists. She's armed to the teeth. Multiple daggers strewn about, a crossbow on her hip, and two battle axes slung across her back. I'm not sure if I want to take her to bed or take a step back. Given I never back down from a fight, I have an inkling to my true intentions.

"Ugh, not these two. Loud is an understatement. If you don't behave—both of you—I'll have to leave or claw your fucking throats out," Kissa hisses.

"Aren't we starting the rough foreplay a little early, kitty cat?" Seraphina winks.

"I can't believe I'm stuck with you two for the rest of my nine lives. If one of you wasn't bad enough alone, the both of you will be absolute fucking torture," Kissa laments.

"My heart. You wound me, my love." Seraphina clasps her hands to her chest, feigning a deadly blow from Kissa's comment. Then she prowls over to Kissa, slinging an arm around her waist. "But you know I'm always down for some torture."

Kissa bares her fangs in a growl. "Fuck this. I'm getting us all shots. I'll need to be smashed to put up with this."

"I'll come help," I say. I'm all too excited to get away from Sølas, turning to follow Kissa, only to be met with a hiss from snarling canines.

"Or not," I murmur, backing away slowly.

"Don't mind Kissa. Once she's drunk, she's much more agreeable." Gearin twists the side of his imperial mustache.

"Shucks, I was looking forward to her clawing out their throats. I do love a good show." I smirk. Plus, that would have taken Sølas off the playing board for me. Instead, I'll be exploring just how dirty I'm willing to get my hands.

"No, please. Too messy for me. Remember, guys, we're a team now! Save the slaughter for the front! Plus, I *really* don't want to spend this week cleaning their blood out of my new dress," Fenwick warbles, our self-declared team sunshine. She's wearing a beautiful white dress, decorated with dancing shapes of her weaving light magic.

"I'm just here for the booze and the view," Sølas hums as his eyes drift to mine.

I snarl in return—but there's something about him, keeping my gaze locked with his, almost as if it's impossible to look away. *To my fucking dreadful lament.* Maybe it's his spellbinding eyes swirling with smoke-like shadows on fresh fallen snow, a haunting darkness—matching my own.

His presence eclipsing everyone else in the room. He stands with the effortless confidence of someone who's untouchable, despite his dark aura and unknown bloodline marking him as an outcast. His very existence simmers my blood. His eyes dance over the markings on my collarbone, leaving an uncomfortable heat searing along my skin, making me shift my weight.

Celestials, I need to shake him off, squashing the *feeling* of him, like a bug crawling its way up to bite me. I finish my second drink, slinging the empty vessel on the table. Sølas disappears, leaving me looking at Orion, who is eyeing me suspiciously.

*Fuck.* She can read my Aura. I really hate that. Don't much care for how intrusively she can see through my mask, watching me grapple with these pesky emotions that won't fucking stay in their boxes long enough for me to chuck them out the broken mosaic window. Nothing's been quite right in my head since the Ethereal Maze of Whispers. Everything's messy—harder to control.

The ringed curls on the back of my neck move. Sølas is suddenly right behind me, his touch so delicate, I can barely feel it, arcing electrifying tingles across my skin. A reedy breath leaves my lips before I come to my senses, elbowing him in the gut.

"Who the fuck said you could touch me?" I snap, more alarmed at my body's response to him than anything else. And just like that, he's back on the opposite side of the small table, shadows swirling around him.

Seraphina smacks her leg in a laugh while Fenwick, Gearin, and Orion try to hide their snickers. I even catch a subtle half-smirk on Cinder's broody face. Glad everyone else is having a blast while I shove all those tingly feelings in a tight box and light it on fire before chucking it out my mind window.

"You're a curiosity to me. I couldn't help myself." Regret painting his face in realization of his mistake.

"I am not some oddity here for your entertainment. If I'm forced to be stuck with you, the least you could do is learn to keep your hands to your-self," I snarl.

Sølas bows his head with an odd melancholy and anguish to his features. Like my words are daggers, twisting in his side. He wouldn't look so pitiful if he knew of the real dagger I have planned for him.

"Let me apologize for this fuckin' brute. I think you're the first female he's ever met who isn't begging for his touch. How's the sobering chill for ya, Sølas?" Seraphina smacks him on the back of the head, his raven waves tumbling into his face.

I want to slap him upside the head for touching me, even if it was barely a graze. I don't need him mincing up my already muddled mind, not with the effect he has on me.

"Touch me again without my permission, and I'll remove your pretty little tattooed fingers."

"So you think my fingers are pretty? That's quite the revelation," he purrs with a chaotic shift in his emotions. What the fuck is wrong with this male? I understand using flirting and confidence as a mask but can't begin to comprehend his tumbling emotional kaleidoscope.

"Be careful. I've heard what he can do to ladies with those fingers. You'd be doing a great disservice to femalekind, removing them so hastily." Seraphina laughs.

I cut a glare at Sølas with a look that could slash his beautiful, oil-painted face. To my dismay, it doesn't.

He runs his tattoo-covered hands through his hair. I catch myself wondering the meaning of the various runes inked along them. *Best not to know.* The less I know, the easier it is to sever him from my world, cutting away the infection before it festers.

My eyes go fuzzy as Seraphina changes into Tyranny, attire and all.

"Ohhhh, Sølas. You're soooo dreamy," Seraphina coos in Tyranny's voice. I honestly wouldn't have known it wasn't her if I didn't watch her shift. She's incredibly gifted.

"Knock it off, Seraph. That's fucking mean, and you know it," Sølas scolds.

At this moment, I hate him a little less. Maybe even respect him. I've always loathed bullies.

"Yeah, Seraphina, it's my job to mess with minds." Orion winks as Seraphina changes back to her natural form. There's a flash of fear in Orion's eyes, like she's worried her role to fracture someone's mind may break hers too.

A shuffle of drunk stumbling skids behind me. Fuck, what now? I sigh. Before I can turn, two fingers slither down the back of my exposed neck and over my shoulder, tracing the gold lines on my skin.

"What the fuck are these? Guess you're as much of a freak as Chet says you are."

I whirl around, ready to break the fingers of whoever fucking touched me, but I'm too late. Shadows slice through tissue and bone, severing the male's two fingers. Crimson squirting in a beautiful arch, stirring the darkness inside of me.

He clutches his wrist, screaming like a bitch, as another male runs over to help him. The bleeding male's voice trembles as he tries to shout, "Have you lost your fucking mind, Sølas? They should never have let you in here. You're exactly the monster we all think you are!"

Sølas' face is positively feral as he growls low, "No one touches her."

I try not to roll my eyes at the fact that *he* just touched me, although barely. His feral growl cuts through my ribs, sending my pulse skittering before I trap it like a moth in my clenched fist.

"C'mon, Brock. Let's get you to the healers. They'll be able to reattach your fingers if we hurry," the second male with slate-blue hair says as he picks Brock's fingers off the floor and drags him out of the dining hall.

I cross my arms, scowling at Sølas. "I don't need you fighting my battles for me."

"Surely if I'm not allowed to touch you, I won't be allowing any other males the pleasure either," he says nonchalantly as he finishes off his Smokewhisper libation.

"That's not the point," I growl as he fucking shrugs.

Seraphina and Orion hold glasses up to their lips, attempting to mask their smiles, while Fenwick throws napkins on the floor to cover up the blood. Meanwhile, Cinder and Gearin look utterly unfazed, as if this behavior is totally normal. *Unbelievable.* I'm not used to spending so much time around other Fae my own age, and after tonight, I'm glad of it.

"I'm back with the good stuff... Why the fuck is there blood on the floor? Ya know what? No. I don't want to know." Kissa huffs as she drops a tray on the table, nearly spilling the nine shots of glowing green liquid.

"That looks ominous," I say hesitantly, but all too ready to forget everything that just happened. I roll my shoulders, the feeling of two strangers touching me rolling right out my mosaic window.

"Savaé, you've never had Hallucina's Delight before?" Orion remarks with shock.

"You're in for a wild ride, then. Don't try to fight it. Let go, go with the flow, or it will eat you up. No one wants a bad trip." Cinder's lips twist into a devilish smirk.

"That sounds like a terrible idea for me. I already make bad enough choices sober. I can't imagine what situation I'll wake up to if I drink this shit." I huff.

"It makes me feel a butterfly," Fenwick chirps cutely as she sways. She already pretty drunk, and I'm worried about her drinking more. Ugh, since when do I give a fuck? I guess tipsy Savaé is sentimental tonight. Another reason not to indulge in a mind-altering substance.

"Maybe I should take Fenwick to bed and leave you heathens to your debauchery," I comment.

"The Emberhell you are. If I have to put up with this lot, so do you," Kissa hisses.

"Unfortunately for us all, it's a traditional bonding experience for the Wing, although not everyone is here for the experience," Orion chimes in.

Seraphina whistles. "Flint, Vex, get your asses over here. It's Hallucina's time!"

The room is cast in an eerie green glow as the drinks appear on all the tables across the room. The color matches Flint's eyes, flaring over the shy smile he throws me as he joins the table. I have always wanted to blend in, and I guess this is what blending in feels like. Although I definitely didn't think this is what it would entail.

Everyone holds up their drink, creating a circle in the air.

"To good times, fucking, fighting, and staying alive. One. Two. Bottoms up!" Seraphina broadcasts. The liquid tingles, sliding down my throat. Then I'm tumbling through the floor before coming to a swirling stop as a kaleidoscope of colors fold into me. I'm clay being molded, my body losing shape. I hate being out of control, but I try to remember what Cinder said.

I let go.

I'm floating through space, dancing in the stardust of the cosmos. My body moves, twirling the dust around my fingers. I watch worlds being born into the darkness before crumbling out of existence. There's a steady beat, thrumming against my ribs, echoing in my chest. I bite my lip until a metallic tang fills my mouth. I don't need this drug giving me delusions that there's something left beating in my chest.

The effects dwindle, everyone around me coming back into view, but all their colors have changed, so I know the tonic is still in effect. They look absolutely ridiculous—dazed, interacting with their hallucinations. My unusual healing ability must metabolize the potion quicker than most.

I recall the map of the campus. There's a door to the back of the dining hall opening to a rotunda, leading to the Pavilion of Heroes, an open-air pathway carved with the statues of previous famous Ellian Knights.

I stumble my way to the cool, crisp air. I'm not dressed for a fall night, but the cold is refreshing after the stuffy air of the party. The first two statues are the largest. Gildora mirrored by Raeya on the opposite side. I continue to sway down the lane of towering effigies… I fall to my knees—stone piercing my flesh—the view before me ripping my hollow rib cage wide open.

A statue of Sully Stonewall. Towering above me with a marked resemblance. My hand drifts out to the foot of the statue, wishing I could feel his warmth once more. A tear slices down my cheek, fracturing the mosaic window in my mind. All my emotions pouring out. Drowning me. Crippling me.

It's too much all at once. I slam the window shut, but liquid rushes around the edges. I envision a drain to catch them, funneling them out, too, while I gasp for air.

I look up at the statue wiping away the silver tears. "I did it, grey ol' bear. I made it. Thank you for everything, all that you have gifted me." Clearly, Sully was far more well-known than he had ever let me know. Only thanks to Winx did I find out he'd been a commander. With me, he was always so humble. I figured by the way the Chancellor had spoken of him, he was more renowned than he let on.

My little orange dragon appears, taking his natural form, scurrying up the statue.

"I guess you recognize him too, Pip." I gaze up and watch the stars twinkle brighter, almost like Sully is smiling down on me.

"Who are you talking to?" A smoky voice interrupts the moment. One I know before even looking at him.

"Don't you have someone else to bother?" I sneer at Sølas.

"Hey. I promise, I come in peace. I saw you leave and wanted to talk to you alone."

"You know, not every lady is leaping at the chance to be alone with you," I verbally stab, hoping the wound will leave him limping back to the dining hall.

"No, not like that. Give me a chance. I am trying to be serious here."

"Okay. Say your piece, so you can leave me in mine," I relent.

"I'm sorry."

"Come again?" I'm not sure what he's going on about now.

"Usually, that would require a first time," he purrs, but then, noticing the unamused expression on my face at his cringey joke, he drops his hands in the pockets of his slacks before he continues.

"I'm sorry I touched you without your consent. You're right, that was wrong. I… have a feeling I can't shake. Like I hurt you somehow. I really am sorry. I just wan… I had never seen skin like yours. But that is not an excuse. Forgive me?"

"Must hurt you to admit I'm right. Well, I can admit when you're right, too. It's not an excuse. You didn't hurt me, but in my life, another's touch has never been a comfort for me. It just caught me off guard is all… I guess, since you came out here to apologize, I can forgive you. This once. Don't push your luck, though." I sit down, resting my back against the square base of the statue, peering up at the constellations decorating the clear night sky. Turns out, it's easier for me to forgive him when I know it will be short-lived, given the expiration date I have planned for his heart.

"I have a feeling admitting you're right will be the least painful thing I experience around you. And I promise not to make that mistake again. Thank you for forgiving me. Can I sit with you?"

"Pushing your luck, are you?" I smirk.

"Always," he croons.

I'm too exhausted to fight with him as the elixir continues its lingering effects. A cool gust of air catches us in a shiver, pebbling my skin.

"Here, take my jacket," he says with an almost-sadness in his eyes.

"I'm fine," I grit, trying to mask my chattering teeth.

"You being stubborn won't make you any less cold. C'mon, it's the least I can do."

I nod as he slides his black-and-gold embroidered suit jacket over my shoulders, the scent of amber and spruce wrapping around me. A smell I savor like a fool.

We sit in peaceful silence as we gaze up at the stars together. I blame Hallucina's Delight for my newfound tolerance of him.

"I saw you crying when you saw the statue. I may not have known him, but from what little I saw, Sully seemed to really care for you. I'm sure he will come visit. I saw him almost tear through the Chancellor for you at that first trial. He must have been some teacher."

"Sully was like my father... But he can't come visit me. Not anymore... Now, he is always watching over me." I lift my head up to the stars.

"My parents are gone, too." He clenches his fists until they're almost white. *Touchy subject.* There's a long silence before he finally relaxes and adds, "I bet he's incredibly proud of you."

A sad smile kisses my lips as tears begin to gently stream down my face. Celestials, I'm never drinking this stupid shit again. Only two people have ever seen me cry like this. Why does he make it so easy for me to feel things?

I think of asking him about his parents, and then I think better of it. I've already revealed far too much of myself to this distraction of a male. Asking him questions will only lead to him thinking he can ask me to bare more of myself to him. I don't want to get to know him; I need to keep him as a stranger. I know better than to indulge in whatever this is between us.

I hear Sølas move his hand next to mine, careful not to actually touch me, though he's only a whisper away. His small gesture stirs an unsteady beating sound in my chest, like my shattered heart is piecing itself together, limping to life.

Perhaps there's hope for me yet.

That glimmer cracks through my darkness, weaving its way around my heart.

And suddenly, the world doesn't feel so impossibly lonely.

I'm not sure what comes over me, as he unfurrows an inextricable vulnerability from within me but... I lean my head over onto his shoulder, and he leans his onto the crown of mine.

His touch warms me, soothing me in the strangest way. A flutter bubbles in my stomach. Perhaps the drink has decided to work its way back up out of my body.

Yes, that's it. That horrid drink has to be the reason I've allowed myself to be this vulnerable with someone. I know I'm strong enough to resist if I truly want to. Yet, somehow… I find myself enjoying the company of not being alone. Especially tonight, when the weight of Sully's death threatens to shatter my chest, a wreckage my limping heart will never survive.

No matter how much we like to keep things in neat little boxes, sometimes they seep out of the shadows. And what a handsome, broad-shouldered shadow I find myself in tonight. I breathe in his warm scent of amber and spruce. The smell of him reminds me of home, my sanctuary in the Mysticwoods outside that horrid village.

He's pleasant at this moment, maybe because he's finally quiet for once, not hiding behind his own mask. However, I remind myself, he's a distraction nonetheless, one that can get us both killed. One that decimates my well-placed, icy walls, seeing a vulnerable side of me no one ever should.

My moment of weakness only solidifies his fate. It's too bad once I'm sober, I'll still have to kill him.

# CHAPTER 16

A queasy stomach awakes me the next morning. My head pulsating like a hammer on an anvil, while slobber slicks up my cheek from a hungry Pip.

I attempt to burn off my obnoxious hangover with a run through the Mysticwoods south of campus before classes. Hitting the bathing chamber just in time. I'd rather not have the entire university gossiping about my markings. Surely, I've given them enough to keep their tea parties amused.

On my way back to my room, last night's vulnerable moment with Sølas fillets my mind. How did he slip past my glacial walls? Effortlessly ripping my broken shards to the surface. Bleeding and raw. His effect on me is a liability. A deadly distraction I desperately need rid of. I'll gut him, and everything between us, before it guts me. His death now sits at the top of my slate.

White leathers with gold detailing slip over my muscles. I almost like how my body looks in them. Tempting me to let my markings show before common sense kicks back into my hungover brain. To survive my first day of class, my basilisk armor is the smartest move given I've already made a few enemies here.

I sheathe my daggers along my ribs—hidden beneath a twist of glamour —and my short swords across my back in an X pattern. I'm not sure which will be more uncomfortable: blades on my back or my legs throughout a day of lectures. I think of Seraphina's large battle axes strewn in a similar pattern across her back; perhaps I will need to carve out some time to make a smaller version for myself at the Universitás forge. I do enjoy my throwing hatchets.

I beckon my spiky-headed companion. "You're going to turn into a chubby ball, sneaking back all that food from meals. Don't think I didn't see the trail of crumbs leading under my bed."

Pip huffs at me. I swear he even rolls his eyes. Can dragons even roll their eyes? I'm rubbing off on him—and not in a good way. My jaw drops as he drags an entire meat pie from under the bed and pops it into his under-sized mouth.

"If I keep trying to figure out how you do the things you do, I'll surely go mad. Assuming I haven't already." I laugh. Emotions always feel safer, easier to hold, in the company of animals. They've never hurt me like people have. A smile crinkles my face as Pip's tongue swirls the crumbs off his.

"Alright, chubby critter, time to go."

He happily chirps and scurries up my arm, turning into a white leather bracer this time with four cobalt stones down the center. I close my door, awe-struck. I'll never get over how he can do that. Who knew a dragon would have a fantastic, innate sense for color coordination?

I suck in a sharp breath. Chet is waiting outside my door, his beady green eyes level with mine. His light blonde hair is slicked back, doing little for his forgettable face. He flexes his broad shoulders but fails to muster even a fraction of the towering menace Sølas casts effortlessly. Chet is painfully readable, veins bulging their way up his neck. My icy face gives him nothing, holding his glare.

"Just the *girl* I was looking for," he snarls.

"Just the *boy* I hadn't even bothered to think about," I retort.

"Do yourself a favor. Stay away from Winx. She's not your plaything."

"Winx is not *anyone's* plaything. She's a strong, independent female, who can make decisions for herself."

"Well, this choice is being made for you."

"I know it must be hard to get through that thick skull of yours." I tap my finger dead center on his forehead. "But you're not in charge of anyone here —and I sure as fuck don't take orders from the likes of you."

His hand darts for my neck. I'm quicker. I bat him aside, grabbing his shoulders and slinging my weight forward. I headbutt his nose, manically smiling at the satisfying *crunch* as his blood gushes down his chest. Before he can even gasp, my knee swiftly drives into his balls. He crumples, tipping over, grunting on the ground in riving pain.

I bend down, ripping a strip from his shirt. "You don't own females, Chet. We are not your playthings or your property. Do yourself a favor, and learn from this experience." I wipe his blood from my white leathers and toss it at him.

"Use this to stop the bleeding, and stand up. We have class to get to." My voice is pure ice as I walk away. I'm sure I'll face the Chancellor's own version of Emberhell for my actions, but fuck, did he deserve it. If I hadn't enchanted my door, I bet he would've jumped my sleeping form. *The fucking coward.*

I saunter the upper balcony towards the gold-plated stairwell when a tingling sensation stirs along the back of my neck. I spin around, certain Chet is as stupid as he looks.

My eyes go wide.

Sølas.

My body instantly softens—*traitorous bitch*. That cursed fluttering tumbles in my stomach again. Perhaps it's my hangover clawing its way up to purge the memories of last night.

Stars above, of course he looks beautiful. His umber skin glows in the warm morning rays spilling in through the glass-domed ceilings. Raven waves slide into his face from the momentum of my whirl, contrasting against his arctic eyes dancing with flecks of crimson. I grit my molars, fighting the Celestials be dimmed instinct to swipe the lazy ringlets out of his eyes. *What the fuck is wrong with me?*

My breath catches, drawing me out of my red fury to realize—only leather stands between us. My petite breasts pressing into his carved chest. My lungs drenched in winter, amber, and spruce. I bite my bottom lip, heat skittering through my veins. His neck muscles flex beneath a clenched jaw, pulse thrumming so fast and hard… I can feel his heart beating against me. Knocking at the gates of my glacial palace. My mind minces, walls trembling, caught between warring desires. Rage and want tangle until I no longer know whether I want to push him away or pull him closer. And this—this is exactly why I need to cut him out of existence. I don't have time to untangle this stringy mess, nor do I care to. I prefer a sharper method to solving my problems.

One hesitation. One distraction. And my entire Zenith falls. Perhaps it's just my icy logic, but I think I'm being rather reasonable. *Look at me,* already a natural at prioritizing my team.

I let out an exasperated sigh, and Sølas wisely steps back. I turn, rubbing my temples as I stomp down the spiral stairs to the hallway below. I'm too hungover for all this shit mincing my brain. Today is going to be a fan-fuck-ing-tastic day.

Lungs expanding with a deep breath, ceasing my thunderous steps. I'm better than this. I won't let him or anyone else rattle me. My cold and unyielding demeanor returns, as I imagine sharpening a greatsword. The slow, steady strokes gliding against the wet stone. The metal sings of the blood she will spill with her new deadly bite. The rhythm reforges control from the wreckage of this loathsome hangover. Golden light knitting together to repair my fractured mental shields. I still feel the emotions crashing just outside. Echoes bellowing through me. A brewing flood waiting to drown everything beneath its wake.

Sølas follows me, *of course.* With long, perfect strides, as if he's immune to hangovers, catching up beside me.

"You technically touched me that time," Sølas remarks, with far too much amusement for my liking. His eyes flash with something else. Agony? Longing? The flicker is gone before I can dissect it. His mask back in place, curling his full lips into that half-grin I hate. The one that twists me with unfamiliar feelings.

"You have a habit of sneaking up on me. Actually, at this point, I'd call it a hobby. Or maybe *obsession* is the better word for it? Either way, I am too hungover, so go find someone else to buzz around." I shoo him off like the bothersome gnat he is. I don't need him stirring up last night. I thoroughly intend to keep existing like it never happened.

"Or perhaps I just keep falling into your orbit, like a moth to a flame."

Wow. This is the male all the ladies are after? What some females will swoon for never ceases to amaze me.

"Well, that moth is going to get *burned* one of these days." I raise my hand, igniting dancing white flames in my palm.

He steps closer, ripping a warning snarl from my lips. I avoid meeting his gaze, but it burns through me all the same.

"If we are starting things *this hot,* this early in the morning, I can't wait to see what you have planned to do with me after lunch." He winks.

He's inflaming! I have half a mind to burn him right here. The only thing saving him from a crispy fate is the witnesses pouring into the hallway.

"Fuck around, and find out, loverboy," I hiss.

"Jeez, now we're in love? This escalated quickly. At this rate, we will be vowed by dinnertime."

The fire he spurs within me is a catalyst, summoning waves of unfamiliar power. Not my well of magic, but something wilder. A caged beast thrashing against my skin like the bars of its enclosure. Clawing and snapping to be released. It feeds on his insufferable presence, whittling my control. Perhaps it's not magic at all, just a lifetime of repressed emotions finally bursting at the seams. If only I could drown him in them—instead of myself.

I splinter, my fist arcing for his face.

He catches my hand.

"You're fast, little savage." He smirks. "But I'm faster." He winks. I rip my hand free and give him nothing. My face a sheet of ice, refusing to crack for him once more.

"And clearly," he adds, "we're both faster than Chet." His arctic eyes ebb and eddy with shadows, like he's struggling between warring emotions.

"By the way, that was pretty gallant of you back there. Chet was in way over his head, knocking on your door. And stars above—" his eyes darken, voice dipping lower "—watching you smash his face in? Fucking turned me on."

Fumes are no doubt radiating off me at this point. I don't want to turn him on. I want to turn him off! I snarl at him before pacing down the hallway. Why is he always around me? Why me? Tyranny is beautiful and practically falling over herself to get his attention. Take her bait for Celestial's sake, and leave me be. I realize too late that giving in to the train of thought is a mistake as a powerful surge swells up within me. I grasp at the very seams of my skin, clutching at the frayed edges as they unravel.

Suddenly, I'm aware of everything. All of it. Every connection, every energy, perceiving it down to a molecular level. Atoms dance on swirling electric fields. Threading the world together in impossibly small bonds. The sun's photons bounce off my skin. Air molecules spiral and collide around shuffling legs as potential energy transforms into kinetic energy. I can even feel the strange electromagnetic pull of Sølas' body sauntering beside me. Heat radiates off him in the blaze of his racing pulse, searing deeper than sunlight could ever reach.

Gravity itself hums at the edges of my nerves, spinning Elyndor around its seasonal axis while our galaxy spirals through the cosmos. The power thrumming beneath my fingertips is wild, infinite, bound to the very chaos of the universe. One spark, and I'd tear it all apart. Atoms. Bonds. The foundation of life itself.

First day of classes and…What the actual fuck?

My hand drags down my face. It's too much. Too fucking much, and I can't chuck it out my mosaic window fast enough. More and more Fae nudge in around me, bustling to class. Their footsteps and voices smashing off the hard marble walls. My head throbs. Each sound another hammer, splintering my skull. I dart out a side door, fleeing the crowded hallway. I am never drinking Hallucina's Delight again. Even with a hangover, I've never struggled like this to maintain my shields.

Crisp air kisses my skin. I greedily suck in a breath, the chill expanding my chest—coaxing my icy composure back into place. The kindred cold settles in, easing my mind. Inhale: cool, calming blue. Exhale: red fury, boiling my blood. Each breath raising the golden light of my mental shields and stuffing these absurd emotions back out my mosaic window. I return to order. Control, my mission, and the routine of a set schedule.

*Breathe in blue. Breathe out red.*

Our class will be about half the size of yesterday. Everyone who didn't pass the entrance exam now training in the catacombs for infantry positions. There are typically twelve Wings for every class, numerically marked I–XII, with fifteen members of each team.

Gilded Auditorium hosts the curriculum intended for our entire class, typically in the mornings. For the afternoon, we break up into divisions for education specific to our role. Essentially, the specialists go to their focused courses and the Ellian knights to theirs. Any classes involving magic or target practice, beyond hand-to-hand combat, are held in the Warded Hollow. A space where we can train with our magic on inanimate targets or illusions created by Runic Tech while protecting the rest of Universitás if we lose control of our magic.

The voice of Kissa breaks my concentration. "Hey, what are you doing outside?"

"Trying to avoid killing people."

"Shame. I would have enjoyed seeing you on a murder spree. May have even joined in."

I chuckle. "I'm really trying to not get kicked out on my first day."

She laughs, but it falls silent when she catches up to me. "Savaé, you have blood on your face. After your earlier comment, do I even want to know?"

"You're right. You don't want to know." I wipe my face, hoping it's clean now as I ask, "Why are you walking outside?"

"I'm outside because the hallways are too noisy for these obnoxiously large ears of mine. Plus, I have a massive hangover." Her purple hair, shorn at her shoulders, glimmers in the morning rays.

I smile. "Talk about a massive hangover. Remind me to never drink that stuff again. I feel like it's still messing with me."

We both laugh, entering the Grand Conservatory through two ornate, gold, arched doors. The racket from the hall pins Kissa's ears flat along her head.

A loud voice booms from one of the balconies of the domed atrium. "Please, align yourself with your respective Wings for your morning classes. Today, academics will end earlier for the first round of sparring in the Combat Arena."

In the full atrium, we slowly gather our entire Zenith. Fenwick spots me and Kissa. Skipping over to us with a bright smile, her sunburst eyes ablaze against her unique half-white and half-black bob. Enthusiasm suits her.

We find fire-haired Cinder brooding against the wall next to the aquamarine scales of Orion, contrasting her candy-red hair. They've already found Highin Heathrow, the Aetherhawk, pruning his sienna-colored feathers beside them. I take in the various shades of red shared between them; the only other red-hued one missing from their gang is Vex Boomer.

Speak of the demon. Vex bounds in from a group that includes Winx, who's shooting me a disapproving glare. For not showing up to her room last night as planned, or for beating the shit out of the arrogant ass Chet this morning. I assume the former. I give her a half-smile and mouth, 'I'm sorry.'

Her gaze softens as her irises flare neon violet before returning to magenta, blowing me a flirtatious kiss, clearly forgiving me for ditching her last night after the party. I will say, she's a pretty problem to have on my list of troubles.

Gearin Griswald and his spectacles come sauntering in as he twirls his mustache. Next to him are the sculpted Flint Rockwell and a Fae I haven't met yet.

He's a male, with gloomy amethyst fur and a face of hard features meeting his pink nose. Large, bat-like ears sit on either side of his head. His eyes are striking, limerick-green eyes, darting around the room as his ears twitch, taking in all the noises. I don't envy him or Kissa at this moment. He's a Yassur, a bat-Fae hybrid species, making him the Scouting Rogue of our Zenith Wing. His name is Eko Lightfoot. He tosses me a fiendish smile, revealing his very pronounced fangs.

The hairs spike on the back of my neck. I already know who's arriving behind me as I turn to meet his gaze. Or so I thought. Instead, I'm met with a jarring slap on my back from Seraphina, Sølas sauntering in behind her.

Her powder-blue war braids jostle in the movement as she hollers, "Emberhell of a job you did on Chet! Sølas gave me details. I'm jealous I wasn't there to join the fun. Remember to invite your favorite teammate to your next ball-busting soiree, will ya? I saw Chet hobbling through the Great Hall with a busted nose, and Brock and Victus almost had to carry him! I nearly pissed myself laughing. You're one piece of fucking glorious, bloody work." Seraph jabs me in the side with her elbow. I'm going to have to get used to Fae touching me now that I'm on a team with Seraphina.

"Great." Orion rolls her candy-red eyes. "For someone who hates attention, you sure know how to make yourself the center of it. Zenith Wing will have a target on its back with you raising Emberhell for Commander Bragen's son. No wonder his Aura was roaring flames when I caught a glance of him earlier."

My hand rubs the back of my neck as I shift my weight. I guess I was a little overzealous earlier in my claims of being a natural at prioritizing my team.

"That self-important dickbag needs to be taken down several pegs. You've got my respect, Savaé." Cinder tips two fingers off his brow in salute.

"Pray tell, what merited such violent hostility?" Gearin enquires.

"He called Winx my plaything. So I taught him a lesson: females are not anyone's property." I shrug. The group chuckles in agreement.

"Oh, *that is* a very important lesson indeed!" Fenwick beams.

"Now the blood makes sense, troublemaker. Knew I didn't want to know. Still wish I didn't." Kissa sighs.

Sølas shifts his position unreasonably closer to me. My breath falters, held hostage by the scent of winter spruce with a pinch of amber, stripping me of logic.

I transfer my weight onto my leg nearest to him, collapsing the space between us. My gaze flicks up to his face, carved in temptation. A thick brow kicks up at my change in position, while shadows swirl in his eyes with amusement over the inch I've foolishly surrendered to him.

The fluttering stirs in my insides again. I beg the Celestials for the strength to resist whatever this is. Stars above, *what the fuck is wrong with me?* Me, begging, when I prefer it the other way around.

Energy hums in the small gap between us. Thick and heavy. Storm clouds swelling with lightning, ready to strike. Maybe I just enjoy the challenge, seeing how close he'll get without touching, now that he's promised not to without my consent. I do like toying with my prey before the kill. A little torture, light or otherwise, is always fun.

He takes the bait, leaning his weight, tipping closer to me. We are a mere whisper apart, amplifying the storm crashing between us. Never breaking his gaze, I arch my brow right back.

He's shown his cards. I can wield his infatuation with me to his weakness, luring him into a trap. Oh, the delicious irony of his *moth to a flame* remark. He has no idea how close he's flying to the flames that will consume him.

A new face arrives in the group. She's a tall Elarian-Naturalist with long, forest-green hair, growing with various leaves and flowers. Her skin is pale as birch, with almond-shaped ombre eyes, fading from grey to blue.

The contrast of her features is striking. Our white battle leathers almost match her complexion. She darts towards us, so eager she collides with me—knocking me into Sølas.

Velvety shadows wrap around me, catching me with his powers. The sensation is overwhelming. Magic crackles beneath my skin, aching to be released on his shadows. Fucking great. Even my power is betraying me for him. Nothing about this can be good.

The shadow prick must think this doesn't count as breaking his promise about touching me. To be honest, his Celestial Gift is the only thing I don't mind about him. The shadows have always kept me safe. *Fuck.* Not that I'm thinking I feel safe with him or anything like that. I regain my balance and roll my shoulder, slipping away his shadowy embrace.

"Oops, sorry about that, and hi, everyone. Name's Juniper Stormfel." She smiles brightly, petals floating on an invisible breeze around her. Now our full Chivalry is here.

"The last two members of Zenith Wing are right behind me. Kivi Shaw and Atlas Ailanthus," Juniper says as she turns, beckoning them this way.

The first to arrive must be Kivi. Her dainty, thin body is strewn with various breeds of mushrooms growing through moss-like armor. Her skin appears a faint beige color. Her eyes and lashes remind me of the lilac bioluminescent spores that dance through the Mysticwoods.

Power radiates from her as blue spores swirl about; a Helios healer is quite the magical sight to behold. Appearing like part of the forest with thin white mushrooms blossoming from her head of lichen in different shapes and heights. Her pointed ears have thread-like gills, the kind you'd find on the underbelly of mushroom caps.

I thought I was already awestruck, but my eyes widen as our last member approaches from behind Kivi. A Müra, a moth-Faeanoid species. He's a tall, lean male, with a taupe tunic beneath his battle leathers. His skin dusted in fuzz, the color of the pages of a book. His maroon eyes set into two upside-down moth wings, as if you are looking at a moth's back as it rests on a tree. Instead of the illusion of eyes to warn predators, his are real.

His head is decorated by various moth wings, coming out at different angles and shapes. Two feather-like antennae jut out of his forehead on either side of the wings framing his eyes. They can glow in the dark, providing their own light to read. I catch a glimpse of the moth wings that fold on his back. I inhale deeply, taking in the view of him next to Kivi. It's fantastical.

They greet us in a coordinated bow. Kivi speaks first.

"I am Kivi Shaw. It will be my honor to heal you through battle."

"You may call me Atlas Ailanthus. Celestials Blessings to you all." The grace in his movements reminds me of the ballet dancers I glimpsed in the town outside Gildorea, sneaking in the wrong back door searching for Pip after he scurried off one night.

"Looks like the whole gang's here. What a bloody sight we are. Let's give them Emberhell in the sparring arena tonight," Seraphina cheers, raising her fist into the air.

"Let's get to class first, before we end up on dish duty for being late," Kissa scolds as she turns to lead the way through the large ornate doors of the Gilded Auditorium. We all follow suit, finding several rows empty, marked with 'I. Zenith Wing' on gold brocade.

I'm glad Sølas is seated behind me and not next to me. His glare is distracting enough; I can't even imagine what it'd be like sitting next to him. I happily settle between Kissa and Orion.

A short, wispy Müra sashays on stage, taking the podium. The upside-down wings that mark her face are golden fawn, her eyes a shimmering indigo, with skin shaded slightly darker than her wings. She's dressed in a parchment-colored tunic embroidered with gold, matching her golden feathered antenna.

"My name is Professor Polyphemus Gloomnight. Welcome to Countering the Wuvon, a course focusing on learning their strategies and tactics so you may better prepare yourself for the battles once you leave these hallowed grounds of Gildorea Universitás of War. Let's start simple. What are some of the strengths of Wuvon in a fight? When called upon, please introduce yourself to your fellow classmates before answering the question."

Enthusiastically, Fenwick raises her hand, practically bursting out of her seat. The professor nods at her.

"Hiii, my name is Fenwick Brightspar. Wuvon are extremely powerful magic wielders, even stronger than our best Ellian Knights, due to their black-magic enhancements from ingesting different parts of magical creatures, which is super gross." She sticks out her tongue, physically disgusted by imagining the taste.

"Correct. Next time, personal commentary is not needed. How does this put us at a disadvantage when in battle?" Professor Gloomnight queries.

She calls on a girl I recognize from my third trial, the one who failed because I passed. Her short, dark brown hair is slicked down the center; I can see the jagged scars along the sides of her shaved scalp.

"Farrah Sinvoy. If alone, it's almost impossible to take one on with casting alone, hence why we have a group of Ellian Knights for each Wing and we train to work as a team. If we try to beat them alone with casting, we will burn out, using up all our magic in one battle. In addition to magic, we are trained in combat, and the Knights bond with magical creatures, giving them the aerial advantage, along with the powerful magic of the Arcane Glyph. The goal is to damage their hands or cut off their head to interrupt their casting. The strength of their magic is why Bloodline pairings are so important, creating stronger and stronger generations of Ellian Knights to combat their corrupt power."

"Excellent. Your team is your greatest asset. Later this year, you'll receive a unique piece of Rune Tech. A button on either side. The purple button allows you to communicate with the entire Command. The blue button allows you to communicate with your Wing. Conversation among team members, especially your Savant during battle, helping you turn the tide, creating coordinated attacks. The closer your team works together, the better you all fare. Your deepest bonds should be to your entire Wing. If you get singled out, call on your team for help. If you burn out your magic because you are too proud to ask for help, you're worthless and a liability to your Wing. Teams with the strongest bonds are the Wings who excel in the end-of-the-year Fortress Battle."

As she continues, I don't take notes. Sully has imparted his wisdom from his education here. I reposition myself, my quill rolling off the desk onto the floor. As I drop down to pick it up, a smoky shadow wraps around it, raising it to my hand, where it lingers before retreating. Okay, now he's pushing it with the not-touching-me Ritherin-shit by using his powers. I turn around, casting a hardened glare at him, like molten ore dropped in a cooling bath.

He, of course, winks at me, unaffected by my gaze. I want to set him on fire right then and there, but I take a deep breath, steeling my face and emotions. My distraction doesn't go unnoticed as I hear my name called by Professor Gloomnight.

"Savaé Entropaé, what is another fatal mistake when encountering the Wuvon?" Her tone is evidently perturbed by catching me distracted by the Celestial-forsaken shadow prick, who's clearly proving my point about being a liability.

"Entering the Blackwood. Their magic is at its strongest there; they can manipulate the forest around you. Never mind all manner of monsters they can choose to devour you."

"Beauty and brawn but no brains. Such an obvious answer," jeers Chet from behind me. His posse lets out a sound that makes it seem like he had just leveled a great insult. I don't bother to glance his way, remaining sitting up straight in my chair. His words mean nothing to me. I know he's just trying to restore his bruised ego.

"Just because Savaé made a fool out of you on the first day doesn't mean you get to be a twat in class, Chet," Orion sneers, flipping him a middle finger.

"Enough! Ensign Chet Bragen, since you seem to know so much, please enlighten us to the knowledge you think is superior to that of your counterpart," Professor Gloomnight reprimands.

"Letting them injure or kill your bonded magical creature. It takes away your aerial advantage and your enhanced powerful magic."

"I dare say, that is yet another obvious answer, and one that only applies to Ellian Knights, for the most part. I would expect a more in-depth answer from the son of Commander Bragen. Your answer, while elementary, is correct. Losing your bonded magic creature does create a huge weakness for the Wing, as Ellian Knights are the main attack front. If you find yourself caught in the Blackwood, your team should consider you as good as dead and not merit a rescue. This would put the entire Wing in jeopardy. There is another clear advantage they have that has not yet been stated."

"Letting those fuckers fuck with your head if you're caught with your shields down," Seraphina calls out.

"Language, Ensign Seraphina Denova! You are correct, though. Their mindtraps are extremely powerful. If they catch you with your shields down, they can not only obtain endless amounts of classified information, putting the entire warfront at jeopardy, but they can compel you to attack your teammates. They will know your weaknesses because they have been in your head and have seen your training. There is no greater pain than having to kill your Wing member, realizing they have been compromised by compulsion."

Her eyes cast down to the podium, as if reliving a painful memory and speaking from experience. Her wings nervously flutter before she settles, focus returning to the rest of the class. She inquires, "What are some of the favored monsters of the Wuvon manipulation?"

"Why don't you ask Savaé? That badass bitch has already defeated two of them," Seraphina boasts.

Fucking stars above, I'm tired of being singled out. I'm jealous of Sølas' powers, wishing I could slip away into the shadows, unseen. But it's far too bright for my Shadowblending. So I settle for glaring back at Seraphina like a whetted dagger. If only looks could kill.

She shrugs, giving me two thumbs up. I huff, turning around. I appreciate her compliment, but this is neither the time nor place.

"Ensign Seraphina Denova, you will respect the decorum of Universitás while in these hallowed walls. This is your final warning. Surely, there is someone other than Ensign Savaé Entropaé who can answer my query."

"Winx Ashfel. Ritherin, Pykavow, Crowven, Merdervin, Ocularis,

Feverin, Eskera, Manasin, Rowwer, Scorphia, Slairix, Zikra, Fakatyia, Horisp, Spindhorrow. To name a few," she answers before turning back to give me a smile.

"Thorough answer from the exemplary Ensign Winx Ashfel. I expect nothing less. Remember, a Wuvon who can tame a Crowven is your top priority. They even the playing field when it comes to your aerial advantage. Crowven beaks are made of obsidian, sharp enough to pierce even dragon skin. What is their weakness?"

Another student answers as I answer in my head. A Crowven's weaknesses are their wings and their neck. Additionally, heavy rain can take them out of flight but will also take out any other heavily feathered flying magical creatures, so this is only an advantage if you have multiple flesh-winged creatures on your team.

Unfortunately, the many different breeds of dragons have stopped seeking bonds with Ellian Knights. Too often their riders die. Dragons form strong bonds with their Knights and are unable to rebond after the loss of their rider. The advance of the Wuvon has meant more and more riders are dying, so most remain in their breeding grounds, high in the Dragon Spine Mountains.

The thought reminds me of the dragon that would fly over Eldoria, the tallest peak in Cascara, right next to my home village of Estrella. A white dragon, with four wings and an eel-like tail. As the dragon flew through the sky, you could see lightning emanating from its wings. The townsfolk said the beast was a bad omen, but I could never understand how something so beautiful could be a harbinger of darkness.

I remember lying in the snow, closing my eyes, and imagining myself flying next to her as a bird. Enjoying the gusts created by those enormous wings. I envision the way my stomach might dip, flipping and diving towards the ground before pulling up. What it would be like to be uninhibited by my Fae form, to leave behind the pain of my existence, to be truly free. The brisk winter air dancing its way between my feathers and nipping my feet. To be able to fly through the sunset clouds of pink and blue as their moisture condenses ever so lightly on my beak.

Even though I know I should be paying attention, I lose myself to the freedom of my beautiful daydream as the professor's words fade away.

# CHAPTER 17

"Savaé, are you coming? I wasn't sure if you were concentrating really hard or daydreaming. Now I know which." Kissa sighs, grabbing my arm up, almost as if she's yanking me out of the dream itself.

I daydreamed through the rest of our morning classes.

"Let's get some food in you. That hangover is rearing its ugly head, isn't it?" Kissa remarks.

"Yeah, that green stuff definitely muddled things up," I confide to Kissa. A strange familiarity growing between us. Is this what it's like to have friends?

"That's what makes it fun. Ya gotta let loose! You're no fun when you're so serious," Seraphina teases. I spin to lance her with my glare, but she's already darting up the steps, her blue war braids slashing between the battle axes crisscrossed against her back.

"Just depends on your definition of fun, Seraphina," I call out behind her.

"Call me Seraph. As much as I love your ball-busting excursions, there are much more exciting things to fill up your free time with than just more fighting." She elbows Sølas, turning her head to throw a wink over her shoulder at me.

I roll my eyes. I don't think I even want to know what fills her wild free time. I don't appreciate her horrible attempts at trying to be a wingfemale for her friend.

We make it to the dining hall. Though no longer decorated for the celebration, it is still incredibly beautiful. The walls are made of sandalwood, with beautiful carved murals of famous battles embellished with accents of gold. Kissa tugs me from my gazing to a table with our entire Zenith Wing.

I plop my ass down, a grumble brewing in the back of my throat as Sølas takes the seat right across from me. A fetching smile grazes his lips. I steel my expression as a wave of warmth courses through my body. I don't know what's between us, but it's nothing I can't suppress or stab out of existence. A subtle sadness falls over his face when I clearly don't give in to the acknowledgment he's looking for. I guess me not fawning over him is hitting him hard.

A golden plate steaming with more food than I can eat in a month appears before me. Beyond the few cured meats, I don't recognize anything. The combination of savory and sweet things has me salivating. I pick up a flakey, doughy triangle, my mouth bursting with flavors as melted cheese slides down my throat. I savor each bite.

I'm pretty sure I'm full-on drooling as I pick up the next thing on my plate. A small cake with layers of fudge and pink icing, covered with heart berries dusted in edible gold. The eruption of flavors on my tongue rolls my eyes back. Simply divine.

"This is a first. I never thought I'd find myself jealous of a cake." Sølas' smoky voice wakes me from the delight dancing on my tastebuds.

"If a dessert can do *that* to her, imagine what you could do," Seraphina teases Sølas. The faintest hint of crimson kisses his cheeks, while shadows swirl violently in his eyes. I cut right through Seraph with an ice-shard glare.

"Yikes. See, this is what I mean, Savaé. No fucking fun. Lighten up. I'm just providing the entertainment for lunch. I've been told I'm an excellent wingfemale. Some even beg me to join the liaisons." She winks.

I'm pretty sure my eyes nearly roll out of my head at her brash remark. I have a dirty mouth, but I'm civil in public in comparison to Seraph. I continue to enjoy my food until I'm interrupted by a kiss planted on my cheek.

*Fuck.*

Winx and I clearly have very different interpretations of what is shared between us. I'm not looking forward to that clarifying conversation. She slinks her way in between me and Kissa.

Palpable anger radiates off Kissa; she likely would've punched her if she was anyone other than the Chancellor's daughter.

Winx's hand grasps onto my leg before sliding up between my thighs. I try my best to muffle the blaze on my cheeks and not cough up my food from how forward she's being. I'm more of a giver than receiver, so this is uncomfortable to say the least. Plus, I've never had someone show affection like this to me in public. I'm not sure what to do.

I look straight ahead to Sølas—to my surprise, he's glaring at Winx with a hateful scowl. Is he jealous? Celestials, everything here is far more complicated than I want it to be. He's just a flirt; I didn't think his cake comment had any truth to it. And we were both high last night, so that hardly counts.

"Winx, you're not allowed to sit at our table. Fuck off back to your Wing," Vex grumbles.

"Chet is being insufferable. I need my knight in shining armor to put a smile on my face."

My fingers rub my aching temples as I pray to the Celestials for it to be sparring time so I can beat the shit out of something and forget everything else that has happened today. And last night.

Winx catches Sølas' scowl, which only emboldens her. She pulls back my hair, tucking it behind my ear as she whispers, not breaking Sølas' glare, "Meet in my room tonight. I'd like to *thank you* for defending my honor with that insufferable twat my father is set on vowing me to."

Sølas' eyes are almost entirely black beneath the storm of smoke torrenting through them. Then I look over to Winx; her eyes are vibrantly flaring neon violet at an erratic rate. Whatever the fuck is going on between the two of them, *I want nothing to do with it*. I don't want to understand it or be a part of it.

Instead of indulging this madness, I stand up, face cast in steely ice. I'm not going to be caught in the middle of some pissing contest. I head to the door, hearing my Wing erupt into bickering behind me.

A brunette male with short hair stands up from Chet's table before walking right into my path.

"Hey, cutie, you can call me Lorgan." He grins. "You left a nasty mark on Chet today. I'd hate to have to mess up that beautiful face of yours."

I nearly vomit up all that delicious food listening to the words crawl out of his mouth. He's strongly built, but something about his appearance reminds me of a hairy gorgon spider. My skin hums with an insane well of power brimming to the surface again, begging to be unleashed. I clench my fists at my hips, hoping to quell it.

I lift my lip in a snarl. "I am incredibly hungover. I will only ask nicely once. Please, move the fuck out of my way." It feels as if I'm holding an avalanche at bay—just the tip of my fingers between me and devastation.

"I'll move when I damn well feel like moving and when I'm sure you have gotten the message. I could always relay this message to you out of aerial leathers, if you prefer?"

And just like that, I snap.

No longer able to hold back after what that disgusting filth said to me. There is clearly no room for consent in his tone; thus, my magic believes his consent is not needed for what happens next. Without even thinking it into being, I watch a whirlpool of food whip around the room, off everyone's plates as it flies at him, covering him in a mountain of fancy baked goods.

Then I hear the shattering of hundreds of plates against the wall. The fractured pieces swirl in a cyclone around Lorgan, slowly inching forward, superficially slashing across his skin, slowly gashing their way deeper.

I inhale, filling my lungs, releasing the tension in my muscles as the shards fall to the ground on my exhale. I definitely do not want to get expelled for killing someone who isn't even worth another thought. The dining hall is dead silent as I walk out the door.

I don't even know what kind of magic that was. Normally, you need to envision what you want to do in your mind before you move your hands, listening to energy, casting your vision into light. Sully had never taught me about a type of magic that could be cast without even forming an image in your mind, never mind not using your hands to bring the magic into being. Unless, of course, you're a master magic wielder, but I don't even know what magic I just unleashed. All I know is, right now, I need to get away from everyone.

When did I become so horrible at keeping a low profile? I'm not sure how I managed to keep out of sight back in Estrella, but clearly, those skills are lost to me here. I don't even want to think about the trouble I'll be in for casting like that against another ensign outside of the Warded Hollow.

This will make two students I've injured outside of training. Commander Bragen is surely going to ask for my head. And to add to my list of transgressions, I'm going to have to tell the Chancellor's daughter she can't go around kissing me in public. The chances of me surviving to graduation are getting slimmer and slimmer, and it's only the first day.

I find myself outside by Sully's statue. It's lightly snowing. The flakes melting against my skin are a cool relief. I didn't even know my body could get this hot.

"I really wish you were here to tell me what the fuck is going on with me. Although you'd also probably be pretty disappointed. So I guess it's better you're not." I reach my hand out, grazing the rough, frozen stone of his statue's boot. I could really use some of his wisdom right now.

The wind picks up, breezing a chilled shiver down my spine. Pip must sense it, because the next thing I know, he is scurrying up my arm, around my neck. I nuzzle the warmth of him mimicking a scarf.

"Thanks, Pip," I say with a small smile. Goosebumps rise on the back of my neck. I figure they're from the snow gale but turn to find a mass of smoky shadows taking the shape of Sølas. I twirl back around towards the statue. Can't people just leave me alone for five minutes? For Celestial's sake...

"Are you okay?" he asks quietly, as if he's afraid to speak for once. *Am I okay?* No. Obviously not.

"Yeah. I'm always okay. I have to be. Now shadow off to wherever it is that you came from."

"It's okay to not be okay, Savaé. You're not alone. You have me and the rest of Zenith to support you. We're stronger together than alone."

*No.* No more tugging the vulnerable bits of me to the surface. No more making me feel like I'm not alone. He doesn't get to have these broken pieces of me. *No one does.*

I snap around at him, shoving him a step back. "Are you saying I'm not strong?" I grit out with a deathly cold stare, my steely calm slipping once more.

"No, no. Of course not. I would never say something like that, unless I had a death wish. It's been clear since the moment I first met you that you can take care of yourself. But being a part of a team requires more than just brute strength. It requires trust. Being able to lean on each other. Knowing when to ask for help."

"I don't need *your* help," I hiss.

"That outburst would suggest otherwise."

"I will show you an out—"

"Savaé, let me finish. Please." He pauses, running his inked fingers through midnight hair. "I know how strong you are. I've seen you defeat monsters. Cool, calm, and collected. Something is clearly up with you if you're willing to lose control for the likes of Lorgan. None of us know how you did that, either. Your hands didn't even move."

The way he says my name causes calm to cascade over me. Another beam of light, zipping through my darkness, swirling around my heart, holding it together.

Tightly.

I gaze up at his stormy eyes, snowflakes glinting across his thick black lashes. The contrast of his chilling arctic eyes, so blue they're almost white, against his umber bronze skin, stirring something deep in me. It's as if I can see into his soul of shadowy storms swirling between the shimmering crimson flecks.

Before I know it, my hand's in his wavy raven locks, dusting frozen crystals away. He tilts his head into my palm, his eyes fluttering shut.

I recoil slightly at the warmth of his skin, suddenly realizing what I've done. Yet I can't pull away. I find myself memorizing the features of his perfectly handsome face. The way the warm tones shift along his high, chiseled cheekbones, like a moving oil painting. His nose is straight, leading down to full plum-colored lips that make my toes curl.

He nuzzles his jaw deeper into my palm, like he's nuzzling his way right in between my ribs, curling up around my heart. A dragon protecting his precious treasure. A peacefulness falls over his face, as if he's always imagined this is how my touch would feel, as if it's all he's ever been searching for, all he will ever need.

*What a foolish thought.* Still, I can't ignore the fact that I have touched him without thinking—as if there's an invisible thread intertwining us together. Twice now, I've touched him, instinctively, without thought. As if it's the most natural thing in the world.

I've never, in my life, touched someone without a serious amount of consideration on my part. The thought severs me from my daze, and with it, my hand from his face. A longing sadness flashes in his eyes as they open with my movement. That fleeting look is like an icepick, nailed right into my limping heart. I clench my fist, catapulting that raw, bloody feeling right through the mosaic window before locking it shut.

I recover the steely mask I wear as I continue our conversation, trying to distract us both from the unusual moment we just shared.

"That makes two of us. I don't know how I did that. I've never cast magic like that. It was… like it happened without even thinking it into being. But I also haven't come into my Celestial Gift yet."

I pause, turning around to narrow my eyes on him, realizing what I've accidentally exposed. "If you tell anyone that, I'll slit your throat while you sleep and feed your corpse to the Blackwood." He's silent, but a flicker of surprise toys in his eyes as he nods, agreeing to keep my secret.

A deep breath fills my chest, thankful the prick so easily agreed. Doesn't change my murderous plans though. This only adds one more reason to kill him, on top of all these vulnerable moments he keeps plucking from me like petals from a flower.

I sigh. "Even if that *was* my Celestial Gift finally manifesting, I've never heard of a power that can be cast without you listening to your energy, moving your hands along the current, manifesting it into reality. Unless, of course, you're a master wielder, which only requires thoughts. But I'm nowhere near that level in anything other than elemental magic."

The thought that I can magically hurt someone without so much as thinking terrifies me. It means I'll have no control over my Celestial Gift and could be a liability. How can you control something that happens without thought, that happens by chaos of an emotion unchecked? How can a magic like that ever be mastered? I look over to Sølas, who's pacing with his hands in the pockets of his leather pants, framing the carved muscles of his ass in a far too distracting way, causing my gaze to linger.

"I mean, I *have* heard… never mind." His words trail off quietly as his thick, flat brows meet in a furrow, contemplating far too many secrets for my amusement.

"If you have something to say, spit it out, *shadow prick*."

He arches a brow at my nickname for him. "It's a folk fable my mother told me, when I was young. Just fairytales, there's no truth to it."

"Then why are you wasting my time?" I scowl, wishing he'd tell me anyway, but I'm not willing to look weak and appear too interested. I've already exposed too many vulnerable areas for him to pierce. Exactly why his death is a necessary evil, even if a small part of me is screaming at the thought of taking his life for some reason unbeknownst to me. I squash that voice in my head like an errant ember on the hearth.

"I just wanted to make sure you're okay." His voice seems genuine, but I can't help but notice something deeper lingering between his words, unspoken.

"Well, you have your answer then," I snap, freezing a layer of ice over my limping heart, layering up along the ribs of my chest, restoring my glacial palace.

I gaze over his face, expecting a snarky rebuttal, but all I find is a cursed sadness. I'm not sure why. And I sure as Emberhell am not going to let myself explore it. I don't need anything causing my hesitation when it comes to eliminating the clear threat in front of me.

The sound of snow *crunching* under fast-paced footsteps coming our way snags my attention. Seraphina is trotting our way, and I'm grateful for this moment with him to end.

"C'mon, lovebirds, you're gonna be late to your magical creatures class, and I have my own training to get to." A confident grin on her face.

"Lovebirds?" I roll my eyes, "Celestials, one of these days, I'm going to smack that smug grin off your face, Seraph." I lift my upper lip into a snarl, shoving my shoulder into her, walking back towards the school.

"It wouldn't make you bristle if you didn't feel something for him, too," she teases, lowering her voice for the second half of her sentence, as if she knows her words are jabbing me like a dagger.

*Well played.*

I huff loudly, refusing to let her statement gash me open into a festering wound. She's really getting on my nerves, mostly because she's right. It wouldn't have bothered me if there wasn't some strange thing between us. Luckily, once he's inconspicuously disposed of, it will no longer be a problem. Maybe I should have started stabbing away my problems sooner in life…

Sølas and I are breathing hard as we enter class right before the doors magically shut. We're here to train, and being late is unacceptable. I caught a glimpse of Seraph making it to her classroom door as we made it to the fifth floor, where the Ellian Knights' classes are held.

This classroom is much smaller, only meant for seventy-two of us. I take my seat next to Sølas with the rest of our Chivalry. Due to our almost-tardiness, I don't have another option. The heat between our bodies is unbearable. I can't tell if it's the eldritch energy pulling us together or the growing anger at Seraph's words.

Pip wriggles, trying to move, and I gently stroke him, looking down and ever so slightly shaking my head 'no,' so he knows it's not safe to move. I don't want 'harboring a magical creature' added to my tally of fuck-ups for punishment.

"Welcome to Magical Creatures of the Realm. My name is Professor Yuri Smeltfire. In this class, you'll learn of all the spectacular magical creatures you can bond with, as well as what takes place on the day of Celestial Bonding."

He's a fit-appearing male, with deep brown hair waving over his shoulders. He wears black-framed spectacles, and his high-collared blazer is the color of deep magenta; a mirrored pair of golden phoenixes are embroidered on each shoulder. His maroon eyes flare deep red, letting the class know he's a Pyro Lilliac. I wonder if a phoenix is his bonded? The professor has a shapely beard, peppering to grey along his chin.

He starts by recounting the various breeds of gryphons, which come in numerous colors, from pink and violet to bluejay and cardinal. They can be more feathered or have a more scaled appearance. They all boast sharp beaks of various lengths and deadly claws. Some even have vibrant plumage, like the peacocks said to frequent the queen's royal gardens.

"Just this month, we discovered a new breed of hybrid gryphon, with scales that transitioned to feathers on the wings and large armor-plated scales along the neck," Professor Yuri regales us before jumping to describe the next beast.

"Another unique breed is the snow leopard owl. It has the head of a leopard but with a beak-like mouth, which molds into fangs on either side. It has giant, paw-like wings that stretch out to claws at the end and two enormous legs that look like they belong to a snow owl. Oh, and a long tail that flares out at the end." He seems tickled pink by the description, despite having taught this lecture hundreds of times.

He has a metal object over his finger that appears to have similar runes to the metal object in the middle of the room. When he presses the metal on his finger, moving images of the beasts are projected in front of us. The runic engineers never cease to amaze me with their creativity.

He ends the class reviewing the types of dragons. Dracos are a more common creature, a distant descendant of the much larger four-legged dragon. They are big enough to support the weight of a large warrior but no more. They come in all sorts of varieties.

I enjoy seeing the unique mycelium breeds that mimic the large mushrooms of the Mysticwoods, like the Chantrelli, whose head is adorned with a

Chanterelle mushroom that flares like a frill around its neck. Its mushroom-shaped wings make it easy to hide in the forest.

"Here is a Blightedbrew. It's a long-snouted Draco with wings speckled in burgundy spots. That right there," he points with his golden rod at the mouth of the illusion in front of us, "is its poisonous saliva, dripping from a mouth of overlapping, jagged teeth. It's native to the toxic swamps west of Cascara along the Blackwood. This is the same Draco bonded to Commander Bragen, as it's immune to the noxious vapors of her Celestial Gift. On Celestial Bonding Day, when you listen for a bond, make sure not to approach any creatures that do not match your Celestial Gift. Or you may end up losing more than a limb." Professor Yuri laughs.

Then he mentions the Wyverns, a type of fur-covered dragon with just two legs, resting their front weight on the knuckles of their wings. They're much bigger than Dracos but pale in comparison to the four-legged, traditional dragons. A smaller breed of dragon, known as Coata, having a body and wings coated completely in feathers.

The chimes sing from the Grand Conservatory, queuing us to break from class.

Next, it's time to hit the combat arena, and I can't get there fast enough.

# CHAPTER 18

I dash up and out of the room, down to the end of each balcony of classrooms. The burning in my lungs feeding a crackling beneath my skin, craving something I can't quite yet understand.

We had been briefed that there are to be no weapons in the Combat Arena, which only serves to assess our hand-to-hand combat skills. Magic and weapons practice are typically reserved for the Warded Hollow.

The far too beautiful distraction of shadows that have ceased to leave me alone comes to mind, remembering a tiny icepick dagger I have in my room. It's one of the more advanced blades Sully taught me in order to hone the delicate touch needed for woven metal runes. This combines both elemental and manipulation magic to thread extremely thin pieces of hot metal with excellent control into intricate patterns. This isn't as strong as imbuing a blade with an ingredient from a magical creature; however, these ingredients are rare and harder to come by.

The unique dagger Sully had me make was an introduction to delicate metalwork. The blade is only two millimeters, thinner than a writing quill, and fifteen centimeters long, about the length of a toothbrush. The design is meant for only one purpose: a precise stab between the fifth intercostal space, right between the left ribs, where the lungs expose a vulnerable area of the heart.

A sinister plan brews in my mind. I can use this blade to eliminate my strongest threat, the shadowy male strumming my heart to life. I'm not going to let him weaken me, make me vulnerable and distracted, just so he can dice me up later and serve me to the enemy.

No one will hold me back from my only goal in life, the only thing holding me together right now. With Sully gone, becoming an Ellian Knight is all I have; it's what he trained me to be, even if there was always a part of him that didn't want this life for me. I have nothing else left but this mission. I also have Pip, but a shapeshifting dragon has no need for me, other than all the free snacks he gets from sticking around.

After getting to the ground floor of the rotunda, I take the northeast wing towards my room, weaving my way through the crowds of class change. My long legs burn, but I make quick work of the journey. I grab the deep steel-blue icepick dagger from its hidden compartment, carved into one of my books. I know they'll likely pat me down before entering the combat arena room. Sneakily, I use my magic to sheathe it on the inside of the bracer Pip is disguised as.

Pip seems to wriggle at my magically hidden blade against his skin.

I pull my arm closer, offering a bribe. "I promise I'll bring back extra bacon tomorrow morning for you. Next time, you can choose how we hide the weapon." The guarantee of food is always a sure way to get him excited. His magic stops rebelling against mine, and the weapon is hidden.

I sprint back to the rotunda. The room that houses the Combat Area is directly underneath the Grand Conservatory. I descend the white marble stairs, curving down to reveal the dark underbelly of endless halls jetting out from a circular room, lined with eerie green flames. The naturally dark-hued stone is at odds with the glamour of white and gold embellishments above.

Across the room, the stone is carved out for two arched doors hewn from slabs of carnelian. Their bright red color engraved with the battle of two Elarians, one on each door. Without wasting another second, I barge through them.

On the other side, I find a room cut deep into the ground. The top floor of the square room has different weights equipped to strengthen various muscles; layered below are rows of seats, giving you a view of a large, square arena filled with crimson padded mats. A strategic color to hide all the blood.

I spy my Zenith Wing at the center mat next to Nadir Wing, which includes Chet, Lorgan, and Winx among others. I enter the Combat Area floor to meet a towering figure of pure muscle blocking my entrance, long silver hair braiding down the center of his head.

"No weapons in this area. Raise your arms for inspection," he says curtly.

I roll my eyes, raising my arms as he pats me down. I think I'm home free, but then he grabs my wrist, inspecting my bracer. *Shit.*

He looks it over, turning my wrist around in the light of orange flames that illuminate the room. Then he grabs the bracer with his hand, his palm right over where the blade is glamoured. It takes all of my strength not to punch him for touching Pip so roughly, but I'm thankful the little dragon doesn't budge.

"You're free to go," he says gruffly, shooing me away with a dismissive wave of his hand. I hurry along impatiently. Things to punch. A handsome distraction to kill.

My plan is to challenge Sølas to combat at the end of the session. All I need is to pin him, slicing the discrete blade into his heart, using my elemental fire to heat the blade on the way out of his skin, cauterizing the flesh so the blood doesn't squirt out, painting my guilt in crimson. His skin should heal quickly enough not to leave a mark, since no poison is involved. His heart will be beating fast enough from the battle that the blood loss will be quick. As long as I break his ribs right before I pin him, the murder will be seamless. And no one the wiser.

I make my way over to the center mat. Kissa eyes me once over, as if waiting to find me covered in blood since I disappeared between classes. I shoot her a smile, which she returns, revealing feline canines.

Cinder's bright orange hair looks even more brilliant in the lighting of the orange flames overhead. The various piercings that line his pointed ears are removed, preventing them from being an easy target for an opponent.

Juniper bounces in place, her deep forest-green hair wound in two braided buns on top of her head, decorated with lilac flowers. Her body is willowy, made of lean muscle; agility is her prowess. Just like Kissa.

Fenwick's black-and-white cookie bob is tied back at the top. Her short, muscular frame means she needs to use her low center of gravity to her advantage. Gearin, Eko, Flint, and Atlas are stretching at the edge of the mat with Kivi, Orion, and Seraph.

My breath catches as I take in the sight of Sølas standing there with his shirt off. My body betraying me only serves to solidify my plan. His wavy raven hair is cut in layers to frame his ice blue eyes, chiseled cheekbones, and strong jaw. The light cascades down the large muscles of his chest, emphasizing the warmth of his umber-toned skin. He turns his upper body, stretching the carved muscles of his back.

As I follow the swirling black ink that moves from his fingers, up his arm, and across his defined shoulder blades, my gaze snags on his low-hanging leather pants that expose the curved V leading beneath them. I bit my bottom lip while taking in the muscles of his well-defined ass and thickly toned legs.

My eyes wander back up as his movement stills. His lips are twisted at one side into a wicked grin as one eyebrow kicks up at me, clearly catching my perusal.

Whoops.

I lift my top lip and snarl at him.

He just bites his bottom lip, slowly, in return. Heat courses through my veins, watching his thick lip roll beneath his seductively defined white canines. I flip him a middle finger as I walk towards Kissa's side. *Yep. He definitely needs to go.*

The gruff male who inspected me clears his throat. "My name is Zander Atreides. I will be overseeing your hand-to-hand combat instruction. This is your last form of defense against the Wuvon. If you're on the ground with a Wuvon fighting hand to hand, they will be using the Blackwood against you. In the rare likelihood you are fighting them outside the Blackwood, they will be using their enhanced Persuasive powers with every touch of your skin to wreck your mind." He pauses, silver eyes looking around pointedly.

"If you fail to keep your shields up, they will leave you a drooling, blubbering mess on the ground. Death is a mercy to anyone found like this, as they trap you in your mind with your greatest fears. Make every hit count because it may be your last. Today, you may challenge anyone. If there's anything you need to work out with fists, this is the time to do so." He laughs dryly, but no one joins in.

"I will see how you fight, making note of your weaknesses for future sessions. If anyone uses magic in my arena, they will be facing me on the mat and finding themselves housed in the infirmary for the next few days, recovering from the beating they receive."

His thick jaw clenches, matching the flexing biceps of his bare arms crossed in front of his chest. His arms are as big as my thighs put together; one punch could crush a skull. I swallow, thinking of my plan. Hopefully, the small bit of elemental fire I'll send down the tiny blade won't get caught.

I tie my hair up in a tight bun behind my head as I join Juniper in the same motion, bouncing from foot to foot, warming my blood. My body is more muscular than hers and Kissa's. However, my build is not as robust as Cinder's wide frame. I'm somewhere in between brute strength and agility. A more feminine version of Sølas, whose tall, carved build is a deadly combination of speed and force. We may be equally matched on the mat, but I know I can use his irresistible urge to flirt to my advantage.

My scheming is interrupted by hearing my name from a voice that slithers around my neck like a snake. "Challenge Savaé. That's an order, Draven. I want to watch the bitch bleed." Chet's sour voice is directed at a tall Elarian male with slate-blue hair, the waves shorn close to his head. His skin pales as his stormy grey eyes meet mine. Conflict is worn in the soft features of his face as he hesitantly steps my way.

"I, Draven Bane, challenge you to combat." His voice cracks along the words. It's clear he doesn't want to obey Chet. I recognize his last name; Major Bane is known for his ability to cast storms. A Stormcaller. Their friendship is no doubt due to the association between their parents, since Chet has no authority to be giving orders.

I raise another internal wall of golden mental shields, the world around me melting away as a lethal focus sings through my marrow. I nod, stepping onto the mat, circling him like prey. Observing his every muscle, listening to the sound of his steps on the mat. I hear the pattern of his movements through the air as his heartbeat hums to me.

The speed of his pulse picks up as the sounds of his steady pattern shifts, giving away his plan to strike. I block his punch with my forearm with ease as I use his exposed side to my advantage, landing a blow in his ribs.

He stutters, catching his breath. I use his distraction to swipe my feet underneath him, knocking him to the mat with a *thud*. He gasps with the wind knocked out of his lungs, still trying to catch his breath from my last hit.

An overconfident kick to his side allows him to grab my ankle, yanking me to the ground. With one leg already over him, I try to land, pinning him down, but he has the same idea. We roll across the mat together, struggling against one another to get the upper hand.

I hear a satisfying *crunch* as the air hisses from his lungs, with my punch to his ribs in the same spot as before. I use the rolling momentum to my advantage, letting him spin as I get up, pinning him on his stomach with his arm pulled tight behind his back and my knees digging into his spine.

He growls in pain as I yank his arm back tighter, hearing the slow rip of tendons as his free arm taps the mat three times, signaling my win. He stands up, taking short breaths beneath his broken ribs, cradling his injured shoulder.

"If you got into a rolling match with a Wuvon ensign, you'd be dead. I hardly consider that a win," Instructor Zander scolds dismissively as he walks by. He's right; there's no arguing with his logic. "The goal of your next fight should be to take them out in three hits or less," he commands, continuing to the next mat to observe.

Chet's voice is full of disdain as he serves up his next friend. "Victus, it's your turn. Don't be such a fucking disappointment like Draven."

Well, it turns out Chet treats everyone like shit. Here I was thinking I'm special. I smirk as my next victim strides up to me with more confidence than the last. Victus is a wall of muscle, brute strength I doubt I'll be able to overtake if he pins me. I will have to be very strategic with my hits.

"I, Victus Eldrin, challenge you to combat," his deep voice grunts out. He clenches a muscle in his jaw, shooting a side-eye in Chet's direction. His hesitation tells me he doesn't like being under Chet's thumb, either. His last name is another famous one of the Golden Legion, this one belonging to the commanding officer of Commander Bragen.

XO Eldrin is known for his Naturalist powers on the frontline, helping prevent the Blackwood from gaining more territory at the Wuvon's behest. This means Victus is an Elarian-Naturalist hybrid. Which is pretty obvious from his legs, thick as tree trunks, his arms like thick branches. His deep brown skin almost has a bark-like appearance under sage-green hair of leafy vines, matching his eyes.

We start our dance along the mat; his movements are slower than Draven's. He flexes his forearm, wrapped in a spiraling vine tattoo, as his fist goes for my face. I duck, side-stepping. He stumbles with the momentum of his large build as I slam my foot down at an angle along the weak fibula bone on his lower leg, hearing it crack. It's not a crippling blow, like a broken tibia, but it will surely hurt like the demon fires of Emberhell.

He curses as he regains composure; he can't hide that he is favoring his weight on one leg now, which gives me the upper hand. He comes at me again, swinging. I dodge again, but this time, he anticipates it, hitting me in the gut. I smile manically at the pain, letting it fuel the dark, feral part of my soul that has survived far, far greater horrors. I avoid his grasping attempt to trap me in his arms.

As his weight falls on his injured leg, I take advantage of his pain, faltering him in an off-balance step to land a devastating uppercut, sending him reeling backwards. I kick him in the stomach as he flies off the mat from the extra momentum, smacking his head so hard on the floor, he goes unconscious.

I'm breathing hard as I become more and more feral with each hit I land, bathing in the anger of Chet's vicious eyes, narrowing on me.

"Why don't you come over here and be my next plaything?" I spit in Chet's direction. The bruising from the earlier blow to his nose blooms under his eyes, making them appear all the more hollow.

He snarls, "Blackbriar, you're up. Put that bitch in her place," as he shoves Brock my way. He has dark hair shorn to his scalp. Brock Blackbriar is shorter than the rest but just as muscular. His eyes are a light turquoise, falling into a dark blue, but beautiful colors fall flat in the lack of soul behind.

He doesn't bear a surname I recognize, meaning this male actually has something to prove to Chet if he's putting up with him. He doesn't wait to circle me on the mat, doesn't bother to even formally challenge me. He just lunges straight for me.

I spin away from his hands, but his shorter center of gravity allows him to rebound quickly; I'm still huffing from the last match. A part of me wants to release the feral, chaotic demon I know hides deep inside of me. A dark child who will do anything to survive, even tear someone to shreds with her bare hands. I try to keep her safe from the world now, deep in the confines of my mind, protected from any more suffering. Yet, as my adrenaline continues to rise, I can hear her clawing to be released. Her serrated screams begging to wreak vengeance on a world who'd forgotten her. Who left her to fend for herself in a den of monsters.

The distraction of her screeches echoing in my mind leaves me open for him to land a kick to my cheek before I can complete my duck. The sound of bones *crunching* reverberates through my skull. To my opponent's soon-to-be-lament, my head injury causes me to lose the reins on my tight control.

The beast is released.

My movements becoming feral as I lurch forward, punching him in the throat, then spinning around him, wrapping my arms around his neck as he gasps for air. I use my body weight to bend him backwards in an unnatural way, kneeing him in the spine as he howls in pain. He stumbles to his hands and knees, unable to get up despite two attempts.

I stand above him. "Do you yield?"

Patiently, I wait for his response, but when he attempts to stand again and fails, he reaches out for my leg closest to him. I step out of his reach and strike him in the side several times until he falls to the mat once more. A smug smile kisses my lips at his satisfying three taps while Chet curses in the background.

I wipe the blood from my nose as the wind leaves my lungs, a terrifying *crunching* sound as someone lands a sucker punch along my back ribs, right over my right kidney. Without my muscles clenched to protect my ribs, my armor alone isn't enough. I snarl as I catch myself before stumbling off the mat. If I wasn't wearing my basilisk armor, that could have been a devastating blow, taking out one of my kidneys.

I turn to see Lorgan's slicked-back hair and eyes of currant red narrowed on me. It's a coward's move, sneaking up behind me without a formal challenge. Even worse than Brock, who at least had the gall to take me head on. I hear Chet's words over my shoulder.

"Finish her."

Lorgan attempts another punch, but I block him with my forearms, trying to spin out his momentum so the punch doesn't break my forearm. I twirl, but he reaches for my bun. He rips me back by my hair, and I use the force inwards, against him, landing a backwards kick in his stomach. I turn around as he staggers a step back, landing another blow across his face, splitting his lip.

He uses the closed space to strike the same punch I just delivered. I cackle viciously as the metallic taste of blood fills my mouth.

"You'll fucking pay for marring my handsome face. I see why your parents abandoned you. You're worthless—or will be soon," he threatens. I don't have time to digest his words, dodging his side kick.

I spit my blood at him. "Missed me." Winking at him as he lunges for me again. The quick movements are taking a toll as each deep breath I take shoots fire up my right side. I try to let numbness sweep over me, but each inhale pulls me right out of it.

I just need to keep dodging his hits. He's much larger than me and will tire quicker; it will also give my body some time to heal my ribs before the next blow. He plays right into my hands. His strikes becoming less strategic as he continues to miss. His eyes become torrents of violence scowling at me, trying to figure out why I'm not attacking.

I can finally take a full breath in, thanking my body for its quick healing. It still hurts like Emberhell, but then again, all my muscles are screaming from lack of oxygen, burning more than I can breathe in with my shallow breaths.

The change in his arm positioning signals he's going to go for a double jab. He lunges. I attempt to block with my forearms and then my leg. But I walk right into his trap; he changes his movement after the first hit, grabbing the loose strands of hair falling down my neck. He uses my hair as leash to spin me against his body. His heavy arm wraps around my neck, squeezing the air from my throat.

"I like my females unconscious." His hot breath crawls along my ear like the hairy spider he reminds me of. The little demon inside screams to be released once more; as my eyes darken, she takes over. I kick back and upwards, landing a blow between the legs. His knees bend in natural response. His grip around my neck loosens.

I grip my weight on his arm, using it to hoist my feet up on his slightly angled thighs like a ramp before flipping over his back. I land on my feet, losing control in a frenzy as I land strike after strike in the ribs. I bathe in the sound of his *crunching* bones after the third hit, but I don't stop; the darkness inside me wants more. It wants to see him pay for what his words mean. It wants to make him pay for every female he has ever touched without their consent. I'm lost to the darkness, now straddling his back as I continue my frenzy, unfazed as he lies face down on the floor, coughing up blood.

Then Kissa and Cinder are dragging me off him, the red bleeding from my vision. Their voices piercing through, unified and frantic. "He yielded! He yielded!"

My breathing is ragged as I whip myself from their grasp, reeling in control from the darkness I've let win. This is exactly why I hate feeling my emotions. They are reckless. Uncontrollable. Utter chaos. There is too much darkness inside me from years of torture by those who were assigned to take care of me, nurture me.

Eko's smug grin cleaves open his split lip, blossoming crimson as Kivi works to heal it. At least someone is having a good time watching me unravel at the seams. Chet and Draven help Lorgan to his feet. The amusement in Chet's eyes tells me this is far from over.

I spit blood in his direction as his glare bristles the darkness inside me. Sending his friends to fight a battle he knows he can't win is repulsive. I want to rip his throat out with my bare hands, but I know that will only make things more difficult for me here. His mother finding a fate much worse than expulsion for me.

Cinder shakes me, waking me from my haze. "Let it fucking go. He's not worth it. You have more than proven your skill today. I honestly don't want to know how you're still raring to go."

I look into his amber eyes with a crimson smile, wiping the blood dripping from my lip. I reply, "Aw, c'mon, Cinder. I'm just getting started."

"Well, now I know why you and Winx are into each other. You're both fucking mad," he says as he shoves a metal canteen of water into my hand. "Now, drink, you feral fucking wildcat," he commands as he strides off, mumbling to himself as he takes his usual place leaning against the wall. His mask of unamused boredom firmly back in place.

"I understand where that feral darkness comes from inside you. You need to learn how to tame it, rather than let it rule you when it comes out to play," Kissa mutters next to me.

I shrug. That's a clever plan, except for the part where I have to release it to learn how to tame it.

Cool water slides down my throat like the first snowfall of winter as it tempers my scorching body. I peer across the room to see Winx's violet eyes pinning me down. A wicked smile curls on her face as her eyes deepen. She's clearly aroused by the sight of me tearing through all these males. Or perhaps it's the thought that I might be just as twisted in the head as she is.

I can't deny that the dark part inside me finds her wildness alluring. I never quite know what to expect from her, but I know she's an untamed wildfire who will set the world ablaze just to watch it burn. Perhaps that's why I've hesitated having a conversation about boundaries. She's sexy *and* terrifying. I'm not sure I'd survive the blaze of breaking her wildfire heart.

The moment's interrupted as I see Sølas making his way off the mat, having easily taken down a bulking Mao male with pink fur, just as tall as him but twice as muscular. The way the sweat glistens off his rippling muscles makes me glad for the cold water I'm drinking. Kivi tries to step into my line of sight to heal me, but I shrug her off. Simmering rage burns in my veins, thirsting for more carnage.

I step into Sølas' path, remembering I have a plan that still needs finishing. I let the numbness flood my veins once more.

# CHAPTER 19

"I, Savaé Entropaé, challenge you, Sølas Zyon, to combat," I say without a trace of emotion marring my face.

"I was hoping to be fighting you between the sheets, but I suppose if you like an audience, I can make this work, too," he finishes with a wink. Before I can respond, he tugs my arm, gently but firm. Pulling me close. *Guess he does break promises.*

He tucks my loose hair back, whispering along my ear, "I see you, and I am not looking away." He pauses, as if hoping his words will dissuade me.

The darkness purrs inside me, but it does little to blur the red in my vision. After holding my silence for long enough, he continues.

"You tore through four males already. You have more than proven your worth. Do not think I will take it easy on you, little savage, just because you refuse to know your limits," he growls low as the smell of amber and spruce fills my ragged breaths.

I shove him away.

"My challenge stands," I snarl, refusing to let my plan be foiled. He snatches the canteen from my hand, taking a large sip as beads of water trail down his face, cascading over every curve of his muscled torso. I remind myself of the threat he poses to my goal and Zenith. I roll my shoulders, clearing the sight of him from my mind as I take the mat.

He prowls around me; each step is calculated. The shadows storm in his eyes as he assesses my every movement. In my lust to see his heart still, I hadn't even bothered to fix my hair, which streams down either side of my blood-splattered face.

We both stalk around the mat, waiting for one of us to make the first move. I grow bored and lunge towards him, slinging a fake punch, but it's really a kick I'm intending to land.

He dodges my moves as if they're nothing.

I growl at the wicked smirk that teases his lips, knowing I missed my mark. We each take turns, trying to land hits, each of us missing, dancing with each other between the movements.

Each time our bodies get close, he finds a way to gently graze me with a touch too lingering to be accidental. He's enjoying the excuse to touch me far too much, playing with me, trying to use my hormones against me. I need him off his game.

"I'm surprised a flirt like you hasn't taken advantage of my challenge to pin me to the mat," I purr with a devious smile as we circle one another.

"Oh, trust me, there are all manner of things I would love to pin you to. But I'd prefer to hear you screaming my name in a much more intimate place than this pit of sweat and—"

Before he can finish his sentence, I dart one way, my toes barely touching the ground as I lunge the opposite way, landing a jab across his jaw, splitting his full bottom lip. I bet even Kissa's impressed with my feline grace after that set of maneuvers.

"Look at you. Sneaky little savage Savaé. That's your one free hit," he says as he slowly licks the blood from his split lip.

"One free hit?" I croon sarcastically, ignoring the way my name rolling off his crimson lips sends lightning skittering through my veins. "Come a little closer, darling. I'll give you a black eye even your shadows will be jealous of." I wink.

"I can't deny that I have a soft spot for a dangerous female with a tongue as sharp as her daggers." He slings me a cocky smirk and lunges for me. I attempt to spin out of his way, but his hands spin me an extra rotation as he uses his lunging momentum to pin me down on my back, straddling me between the weight of his legs. Thick arms knock down on either side of my shoulders as he leans over me.

I gasp from the blow as I watch the crimson flecks twinkle with amusement in his ice-blue eyes. He shrugs, then purrs with far too much delight.

"This is definitely not how I imagined the first time having you beneath me would go. But I'll settle for it, since you seem to like a show."

I wrap my hand around the back of his neck, dragging him in closer to me. "What if I prefer being on top?" I purr right back along the corded muscles of his neck, leading him into my well-laid trap.

Without hesitation, he spins us both, placing his strong hands around my hip as he secures my position on top of him.

My hair is wild now, and I brace my arms against his chest, holding my upper body weight close to his to hide my movements. I slip my weapon out of my bracer, shifting my right arm to position the icepick dagger above his fifth intercostal space. My hair now creating a curtain, I lower my weight into him, my mouth a whisper from his as the dagger begins to pierce his flesh.

"*Do it.*" A feral growl escapes his lips, his eyes darkening with a never-ending storm of shadows.

His comment catches me off guard. There's a lighter part of my soul screaming for me to stop. *Hmm, didn't realize there were any light parts left. Well, that certainly muddles things.*

The male beneath me is not a monster like Lorgan, Chet, or my foster father. I suppose he doesn't deserve to die just because he's a distraction. Nor does he deserve to meet death just because he has a way of scraping my vulnerable bits to the surface, nestling in between my ribs and curling around my heart in the most terrifying fucking way.

My soul screeches, begging me not to let the darkness win. A part of me knows killing an innocent being is something I will likely never come back from. The darkness in me begs to differ; she's craving the kill. Certainly, he can't be that innocent then.

"You'd be saving me from a lifetime of heartache. *Do it,* before my own monsters come up to play." His words are laced with longing and agony, pecking at my dark bits—like our monsters play too well together already.

In fact, it's as if my monsters know his all too well. The feral darkness inside me grows quiet as I search the hurricane of shadows that swirl within his eyes. Perhaps I'm not as broken and evil as I think I am.

Perhaps there's still hope for my soul. For my ragged heart, limping to beat.

I hold his gaze as I sheathe the dagger. I linger, hovering above his face, studying the curiosity before me. I reach my free hand out to the mat, striking it three times.

Disappointment flashes across his face. Then his typical smirk tugs at the side of his lips. Before I can even blink, he lifts us both up to our feet in one graceful glide. I stare at him, waiting for him to make a move; after all, I just tried to kill him.

"If you wanted a moment alone with me, all you had to do was ask." With an arched brow, he lazily looks me up and down. My body simmers beneath his lustful gaze, but I don't move an inch. I'm stunned. I cannot comprehend what just happened between us.

I blink, and he's right in front of me, raising his tattooed knuckles, stroking my broken cheekbone. I'm waiting for the pain of his touch to come, taking advantage of my sore spot, gutting me with the vulnerability I've foolishly bared to him.

My breath staggers from my lungs as his soothing Sangre magic heals the residual swelling lingering above the already mending bones. Not an ounce of pain follows; something quite the opposite blushes my face.

Sølas clearly notices my shock, leaning his head down, his minty breath caressing my cheek.

"I could never hurt you," he whispers. So quietly, I'm not sure he even spoke.

I close my eyes, not fully able to take in the weight of those words as they chisel along the glacial palace of my ribs, leaving fissures in their wake. The air escapes my lungs, leaving me breathless, wondering how he knew exactly what I was thinking. I open my eyes, hoping to study his face for answers, to catch his features in a lie…

But he's already gone.

I look over to Juniper, stumbling in shock, jaw gaping wide. Both Kissa and Cinder are rolling their eyes as they head for the stairs. Clearly, we've been quite the spectacle.

I run my hand over the back of my neck, unsettled by not only whatever the fuck that was but having witnesses, too. I didn't even hear the bell chime to signal class was over, but by the way everyone is clamoring for the stairs, the session must be done.

Kivi stops me, mending the rest of my injuries before we both head to the stairs. I'm almost at the steps when a large hand grabs my wrist. My eyes snap up to silver ones framed by the same shade of metallic hair as Zander rumbles, "Sully trained you well. I heard of his passing. I'm sorry for your loss." He pauses, his eyes searching mine before he continues, "but know that he lives on, inside you."

He releases my arm, and I nod, thanking him for his words. I dart up the steps two at a time, blinking away the tears threatening to fall from my eyes.

My limping heart is flooded with emotions. The loss of Sully. The kindness of Sølas. The shit Chet put me through today. It's all too much. My mind is a fucking mess. I should have shoved those feelings—along with Sølas—right out the window when I had the chance. But now it's too late. I'm drowning.

My skin burns like the sun as tidal wave after tidal wave crashes within me. My control continuing to slip, too wrecked to grasp onto my reins.

I need to get outside. Fast. I need to breathe before the waves threatening to consume me drag me under.

Every emotion crackles through my veins. A building storm. Demanding release, destruction, mayhem. The power welling inside me seems tethered to my emotions. Which is fucking horrifying in this moment when I can't reach my mosaic window to shove them out and lock them where they belong.

I'm almost out of the Combat Arena when Chet and his lackeys hustle past me, going out of their way to bump into me. A pinching sensation digs in on the side of my arm where one of them nudges past me. One of the buckles of their armor must have snagged my exposed flesh. That's the least of my worries as storms of chaotic emotion splinter the walls of my chest wall. I'm unsure of what will happen if they manage to get free, but I'm not willing to find out with anyone nearby who could end up hurt.

I yearn for the snow. To run to the Mysticwoods and just lie in the ice, cooling my skin, mending the fractures of my glacial palace walls. I try to focus on the pain of my body, rather than drowning beneath the emotions flooding my soul. My muscles moan and ache from the lactic acid that built up from pushing my body through every fight. I'm sure being hungover only adds to my loss of control.

At last, cool air collides with my skin. I'm not even sure how I've gotten outside. My mind is hazy. The Dragon Spine Mountains pierce the horizon, placing me on the north side of campus.

A deep breath inflates my chest, suppressing the screaming emotions crawling up my throat. The clouds above clot and curl with storming darkness, mirroring the tempest inside me as lightning splits the sky.

A heady sensation waterfalls over me, leaving me almost delirious. Perhaps it's the joy of surviving my first day here. Or dehydration.

I'm not sure at first. Then it hits me like a wave all of its own. My knees buckle under my own weight. Arms out, I stumble forward, unsettlingly off-balance as I attempt to regain my footing and grasp onto my spinning thoughts. This is more than just exhaustion from one too many fights. This is more than lack of sleep and a bad hangover... Kivi had healed me after all my fights... I shouldn't feel like this. I shouldn't still feel hungover. Nor should my body be exhausted and weak.

My mind reels, connecting the dots.

I've been poisoned.

The pinch must have been a stab-like delivery system. Clever, but cowardly for a group of males who easily outsize me. I guess they're afraid they can't best me at my full strength, even if they're fighting me all together.

I mean, I did take down four out of five of them... I crumple forward. The soil digs into my hands and knees as I try to crawl my way back to the Universitás. My head is spinning; I don't know which way is up. I hear steps coming towards me, but my senses are muddled. The sounds splinter. Coming in all directions.

A rush of pain pummels into my left side. I gasp for air. Then another hard kick to the same spot, sending me hurtling down a sloped incline. A hill? The world twirls in a blur now. I can't even make out shapes. I close my eyes, reaching for the moist, cool ground. I find purchase, pushing myself back up on my hands and knees.

Sick, twisted laughter ricochets around me. Their familiar voices crawl like maggots along my skin. Yet there's one among them that seems much farther away, one that's unfamiliar.

"Not so fucking tough now, bitch," hisses a snakish voice I know all too well. *Fucking Chet.*

I sigh, wincing slightly from the pain piercing my left flank. I hack up spit, slinging it in the direction of his voice. "You had to poison me like a little bitch just to land a hit on me? Pathetic," I seethe.

A swift kick cracks under my chin, rocking my spine in an arch as my body flies backwards. A *thud* resonates through the occiput of my skull, colliding with the ground.

Hmm… that headache I was groaning about earlier really wasn't bad, in comparison. Manic laughter bubbles up from my chest. I smile, licking the new metallic taste from my teeth, glinting in crimson.

"I told you this bitch is fucking crazy." Lorgan's hideous voice is clear as day.

*Crack.* Throbbing pain fractures through the side of my head from another kick. My cackle becoming positively feral. "Even with my face covered in bruises and blood, I could still get more females into bed with me than you ever could. They come willingly, too. You're a disgusting excuse of a male," I spit out. I lose myself to manic laughter, rocking on my back like a beast lost to madness.

Another kick slams my ribs, accompanied by Lorgan's colorful array of curses. Despite every searing breath, my feral cackle grows wilder. I suppose it's fun to join the Fates in their laughter, rather than cursing their continued attempts to bring about my early demise.

"Isn't this fun? This fun little back and forth we play. A game for just us. Let us play!" I rave to the heavens above, as if the Fates and the universe can hear me, descending further into delirium.

My gasping, maniacal laughs of my flexed core painting me all the more deranged. I have no intention of relaxing my muscles and making it easier for them to damage my core organs.

Several more kicks bludgeon my sides. Only pausing once they finally realize my ribs aren't breaking as expected.

The silence is sundered by severing layers of sinew.

A sharp cold slashing into my right inner thigh. Burning. Twisting. Shredding my muscles as they spin like tangled twine. A warm gush of blood, saturating my leather pants, sticky with warmth.

I don't scream or cry. Not even a whimper or a wince. I won't give them the satisfaction. I may not have control over anything around me, but I still have control over my body. *Mind over matter.* Instead, I just smile like a wildcat with crimson-stained teeth, going mad in the darkness.

"My next cut will make sure you're a barren waste to the Bloodlines, ensuring you're worth nothing to us here. You will never be an Ellian Knight, you self-righteous whore," Chet snarls.

This guy is one sick fuck. *I mean, come on!* Rather than just getting me expelled—which frankly, at this point, would be pretty easy given my slew of misdoings to pick from—he's concocted a vile plan to make me sterile? Just so I can no longer perform my service and donate genetic material to the Bloodline pairings?

I know it's our obligation to provide the next generation of powerful wielders, but would they really expel a potential, strong warrior if such a horrible thing happened? I shudder, unwilling to continue the line of thought. I don't want to find out. This is a new, profound level of evil, and I've met my fair share.

I need to distract him, but I'm so swimmy-headed, it's hard to think straight. I blurt out, "You'll have to try a lot harder than that to kill me, Chet."

"I'm not planning on killing you. I plan on savoring your suffering. But now that you put the idea in my head… how can I resist a begging female? Better yet, why kill you when we can have the Blackwood do it for us. A perfect crime, with no body or evidence to ever be found."

Fear slithers down my spine. Curse my Celestials be dimmed fucking mouth. The edge of a weaving track of Blackwood isn't horribly far from here, although they'll need horses or a Pegasus to get me there, even if I wasn't injured.

I am definitely in no state to survive the possibility of them ditching me near the Blackwood, not with the blood gushing around the knife in my leg. I need to get away from them. It doesn't matter where. Anywhere but here will do. Adrenaline ripples through my veins.

I ignore the pain, the lightheadedness begging to break my will, and roll on to my stomach. I lurch my arms and feet under me in one swift movement before lunging straight ahead. A flash of light flares beside me. Thunder splits my ears as the world rumbles around me. The wind whirls, gusting behind me, pushing forward. The soil beneath my feet shakes, sliding into a ramp, adding speed to my sprint.

The darkness is only a blur of shapes. I summon my magic to increase my agility and strength, whatever power I have left as I bolt for my life. I've never been known to run from a fight, but I'm no fool. I can barely see, let alone land a strike, so I go with the only option the Fates have divined for me.

I fucking *run*.

I run with the will to survive.

I run with a force inside me that refuses to break on anyone else's terms, other than my own. I run as if the stars above fuel my very soul, and I don't stop until their light dims around me.

I have no clue how long I've been running for, but I keep going, stumbling up and down hills and tumbling over unseen obstacles. I don't let anything stop me until my body is no longer my own to control. I topple, pitching over what are possibly roots. I'm not sure, and nor do I care. I just pray to the Celestials I've run fast and far enough away that the gang of monsters who dare to call themselves Elarians are no longer in my wake.

My heartbeat sputters, the edges of my vision darkening. I'm dying from blood loss. I can feel it. My connection to magic drifts off into the distance. I have nothing left to give this world. I've defeated some of the deadliest beasts of Cascara, but a couple of over-privileged brats will be the end of my curseborne story.

The story I have worked so hard to forge into something more, now slipping out of my hands. Spilling between my fingertips just like the blood from my wound. My skin is clammy. My heart slows down, down. Breathing uneven. *I hope Pip finds a new pawn to steal bacon from.* I smile weakly, but it doesn't quite form. My thoughts drift to Sully. At least I'll see him. Soon. Perhaps I'll even get to meet my real mother. My real father. Soon. The shadows beckon.

The world is silent now. Darkness swallowing me whole.

# CHAPTER 20

"Savaé! Stay with me. Please. Just hold on a little longer…"

A smoky voice curls around me like a velvety embrace. I know that voice. *Fuck.* I guess I ended up in Emberhell after all, to be tortured by Sølas for eternity. *Seems a fitting punishment.* At least he's easy on the eyes; there's always a silver lining if you're willing to look for one, I suppose… I hear a faint ripping sound as I start to drift off again.

"I'm sorry I have to break my promise to you." Sølas' smoky voice drifts through my ears like a dream. He seems so far away…

My hazy mind catches on his words. I wonder which promise he's going to break this time: touching or hurting me?

"Fuck!" I scream. The pressure of something wadded up is packed into the wound on my thigh. *Okay, hurting me it is.*

"I'm sorry. I have to pack the wound to stop the bleeding. The tourniquet wasn't enough. I don't even fucking know how you're alive right now. Can this thing breathe dragon fire?"

I'm fading through the pain. The call of peaceful darkness is luring me, the sultry voice of Lady Death singing my name. Beckoning me. I must be losing myself to hallucination… Who would be breathing dragon fire?

"Pits of Emberhell!" I screech. Searing heat courses over the wound on my thigh, burning away the haze of death. Oh, I am definitely *fucking alive.* A shattering bellow erupts from my chest. Fire lashes through my veins, searing more than just my flesh. Awakening me. The pain reforging very seams of my soul.

"This is not how I imagined I'd be making you scream. But screaming is good. Screaming means you're alive." His flirtatious voice is threaded with a nervous undertone.

I'm now awake enough to realize we're moving, amidst a cloud of shadows. I peer up to see Sølas' face chiseled with tension. Fury and fear well in his tormented ocean eyes. Massive arms tighten around me, cradled under my shoulders and legs. I try to use what little strength I have left to push him off me.

"Let go! I am not some damsel who…" A wave of nausea curls my stomach, darkness creeping back in along the corners of my vision.

"Save your strength. You can kick the shit out of me later. But first, we need to get you to Kivi or Helios," he replies. His voice lowers to a feral growl. "Then you're going to tell me who the fuck did this to you, or I will kill every last Fae in this cursed place until I find out my-fucking-self."

He doesn't break my gaze as he says those last words. Maybe it's the blood loss, but he fucking lights a fire deep inside me as he says them. I've never needed anyone's protection. I don't need his protection … okay, maybe just to survive *this particular shit day*, I do. And, to be totally honest, my half-dead self oddly doesn't mind the possessive nature of his words.

The darkness inside me seems to revel in the idea of someone being willing to slaughter masses to keep me safe. What an odd feeling. Apparently, being this close to death is making me weak in more than just a physical sense.

I'm jolted from my thoughts as an orange figure appears on Sølas' shoulder.

I buck, reaching for him.

"Pip!" My weak cry expending the last bit of effort in me before darkness falls. The smell of blood, burning flesh, and spruce is the last thing I remember, as shadows consume us all.

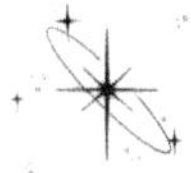

I DON'T KNOW how much time passes, but I do remember familiar voices buzzing about me. Vague bits and pieces of conversations as I ebb in and out of consciousness.

"How the fuck did this happen?" Kissa hisses.

"How in Emberhell did you even find her?" Cinder broods. Feigning disinterest.

"How did she end up with a dragon burn?" Atlas inquires.

"Woah, look at these cool markings on her leg!" Fenwick pips.

"Her Aura is so faint. Are we sure she is going to make it?" Orion asks hesitantly.

"Please. Let her rest. She's lost more blood than I can heal. The mycelium can mend tissue and bone; however, replacing blood is not within my abilities," Kivi's even-toned voice echoes.

Then there is quiet as I fall in and out of a slumber. Yet there's warmth wrapped around my hand that never wavers. That warmth is a guiding light, a thread thin as spider silk, pulling me back from Lady Death's siren call.

I swear, I hear a faint voice, a whisper vibrating along the thread, a note just to me.

"Come back to me, *Luxsula*."

The words a humming tether as I fall into deep slumber once more.

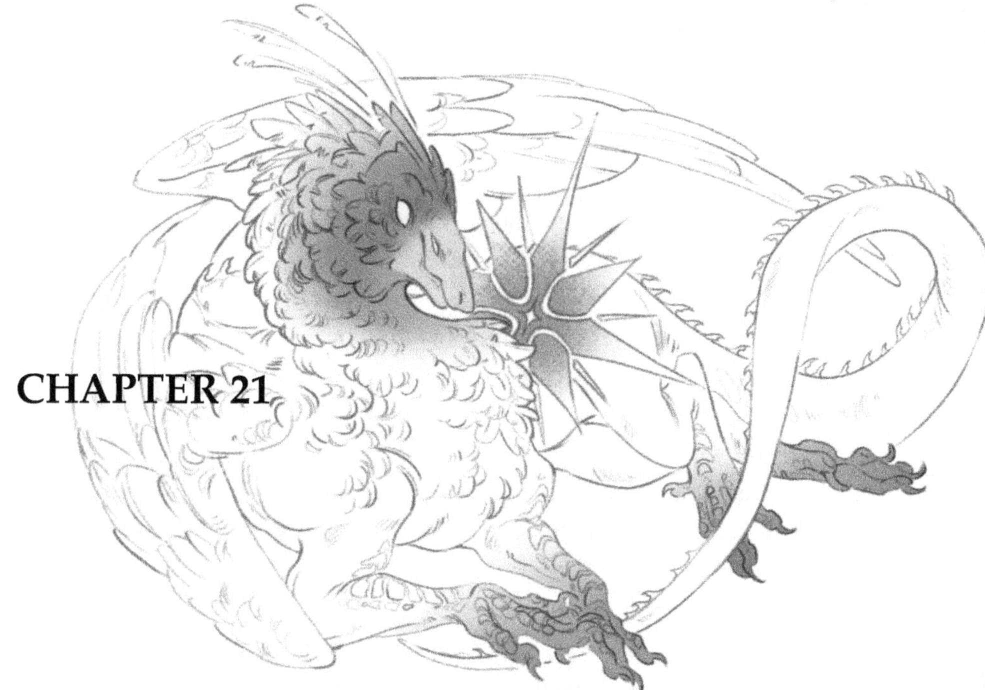

# CHAPTER 21

I soar through the stars on wings of raw energy. I gaze down at my body to see the celestial night sky adorning my skin, outlined by my markings of brilliant gold. Galaxies swirl on my flesh; nebulas churn, creation humming inside my marrow. I glide through the cosmos, witnessing the birth of worlds, the collapse of ancient stars, and the blooming of supernovas. Clouds of stardust trail in their wake, the echoes of their stories ready to be woven into new ones.

An eerie shiver whips down my spine, lashing me in place. In the distance, there's a darkness. Its black draining tendrils reaching for me, growing stronger as I journey closer. All the light is swallowed whole by it, nothing escaping its clutches. A chilling fear grasps at my soul. I recoil, whirling to fly in the other direction. Faster and faster I fly. Light unravels, wisping into ribbons all around me. A blur of endless color.

I'm released from the beams of light into a beautiful nebula. I watch as stardust swirls all around me. My breath is stolen by the beauty of new stars born within the chaos of collisions, each one glowing with newborn hunger.

Then that eerie feeling prickles along my skin—the darkness catching up. I take flight again, leaping from galaxy to galaxy in an instant. I am searching for something amongst the stars twinkling around me—though what, I cannot be sure. My heart is leading the way. She longs for something. *No.* Someone...

"It is not your time, Starborne," booms a cutting voice. And I awake.

The light burns my eyes as I adjust from the darkness of my dreams. A warmth drops from my hand, its absence leaving an aching pain in my chest. I lift my weary hand, rubbing the pain away.

"Ah, good. You're awake," a familiar voice hums.

"You heal remarkably quick. It is likely the only reason you did not die from your wound before Sølas found you." She pauses thoughtfully, looking me over from the foot of the bed. The blurry figure of Kivi takes shape.

"Please, move slowly. You have a concussion, and although your wounds have healed, your body will still take some more time to replace the blood you lost. I tried to heal the concussion as much as I could, but even my power has limits." She inspects me once more before continuing, "We voted to keep what happened a secret."

Kivi then displays her mushroom-covered arm, moving it across the room. "Welcome to my chambers."

I struggle to sit up, bracing my arms underneath me as I will my body to conform and listen despite the nausea that whirls inside me.

"How long have I been out for?" I ask, a shakiness to my voice I'm unaccustomed to.

"Two days," a silky-smooth voice replies. It's so close, I startle, rubbing my eyes to reveal Sølas sitting in a chair pulled beside the bed. A brief memory of a warm hand laced in mine flashes through my mind before I shove it away. *Out the window you go.*

Then the realization of how long I have been out for hits me like a brick.

"I've missed two days of class? I am so screwed," I groan.

"Don't worry, we all vouched for you. I informed the council you had a nasty stomach bug, and you were too stubborn to let me heal you. It seems none were too surprised by your stubbornness. As soon as you're well, Chancellor Ashfel has summoned your presence," Kivi says calmly, without any hindrance of emotion in her voice.

"Guess I'm dead after all," I grumble with a sigh.

"It would rather displease me if you died after all the work we put into saving you. Now I must get to the library to meet Atlas. I imagine you two have much to discuss. Celestials Blessings to you both," Kivi says as she turns, heading for the door.

"He and I have much to discuss? Oh no, no, no." I try to stand to follow Kivi leaving the room. I wobble, struggling to catch my bearings. Before I can take a step, a trail of spores shuts the door behind her.

Sølas' arms brace my shoulders, a steadying force gently guiding me back down to safety.

"You're barely alive, and you're already raring to go. Nothing stops you, does it?" he inquires with a cocked brow. I've forgotten just how beautiful his face is. I will the thought from my mind.

*I definitely don't want to be left alone with him.*

"No. And I don't need you in my way, either," I snap, but my threat falls flat with the tremble in my voice.

"I will get out of your way once you can walk without falling over. And once you answer two questions."

"I am making no such deal. I'm fine," I growl as I stagger, trying to stand again. This time, the world spins before I'm tumbling back to my seat.

"Let me know when you're done being stubborn. I'll wait." He sits back in the chair, crossing his rippling tattooed arms across his chest.

"You'll be here a long time then." I scowl, rubbing the sore spot on the back of my head.

"I'll wait. I've got time. I've already been here for two days. What's a few hours more?"

"You've been here the whole time? Why?" I ask through gritted teeth. I certainly do not need a sitter.

"Someone had to stand guard since none of our Zenith know what happened to you. Luckily, everyone believes you gave me that stomach bug of yours." He winks.

I roll my eyes before responding. "Okay, I guess guarding my unconscious body is a fair play," I admit unhappily before I continue, "How did you even find me?"

"That brings me to the first of my questions. I believe you called him 'Pip' right before you passed out?"

As Sølas says his name, Pip comes scurrying over his shoulder, straight into my arms. He's gobbling down a piece of bacon that still partially hangs out of his mouth.

I squeeze him tightly, so relieved he isn't harmed. Everything happened so fast, I didn't even have time to check if he was okay. I hold him up, giving him a once over. Not a scratch on him.

He chirps in amusement. I swear, I can feel his happiness that I'm awake.

"I was asleep when this little orange thing found its way into my room. He bit my hand, trying to drag me out of bed. He got *frantic* when I refused to follow. The little critter stole one of my swords and teleported through my door. I chased him all the way to you. You were bleeding out at the edge of campus. By the Mysticwoods. I tried to pack your wound, but the bleeding wouldn't stop, even after I placed a tourniquet. Even my Sangre magic wasn't strong enough. As soon as I mentioned dragon fire, he seemed to know what to do and seared your wound shut. He left a wild scar on your leg. I've never seen anything like it," Sølas explains.

"It was so bad, you couldn't use fire magic combined with Sangre magic to seal the wound?" I inquire. We are taught all manner of healing. The wound would have been major for someone as strong as Sølas not to be able to heal it.

"You were practically drowning in your own blood. I still don't understand how you're alive." He looks me up and down. There's subtle marvel in his face, as if I'm some kind of miracle.

"I've always been a quick healer." I shrug. I'm not really sure how I'm alive either. I felt Death's voice calling to me. I remember feeling ready for her to take me.

He gives me a suspicious look before he continues, "So. Let's start with my first question: how have you been hiding a small dragon on campus?"

There's no way I'm getting out of answering this question, and Pip clearly thinks Sølas can be trusted. He's the person he found to come save me.

I need to add giving Pip a stern talking-to to my list of things to do once I am up and about. Out of all the people in my Zenith, I can't imagine why he found him. Surely Kivi would have been the most logical choice?

"He has… some really unique magic. I can't explain it. Trust me, it's better to just show you." My eyes land on Pip, and I point to my neck. He gives me a side-eye before begrudgingly crawling up onto my neck, transforming into a scarf.

Sølas' arctic eyes widen, and I swear, the crimson dances within them. Then his gaze hardens, piercing me.

"Next question. Who the fuck did this to you? I want fucking names."

"I don't know," I lie as I peer down at my toes, stroking Pip. He turns back into his natural form, curling up at my side.

"You're lying to me. Don't do it again," he commands in a lethal tone.

"Is that a threat?" I growl as I lift my chin to him. He may have saved my life, but that doesn't give him the right to boss me around.

"I saved your life. It's the least you could do," he purrs.

"I didn't ask you to," I hiss.

"You didn't have to." His words caress my skin.

"You're infuriating!" I roar. Trying to rattle the sensation from my body.

"Birds of a feather…"

"They are not your battle to fight."

"Names!"

"I am not some damsel in distress for you to save."

"Damsels aren't my type. And trust me, what I have planned for them will certainly make me no prince."

"I can handle them myself." I stare at my feet, fury seeping off me.

He takes the side of his knuckle to my chin, tilting my eyes to his. "I know. I have no doubt of that, you little savage." He pauses. His eyes search mine, storming with shadows swirling into a vortex, almost lost completely to darkness.

"I want to fillet their flesh. Just slowly enough that they have time to heal. So I can do it all over again while I bathe in their screams for mercy. I want them to choke on the pain that bludgeoned me while I held you dying in my arms." His voice is quiet. A deadly rasp.

I've never seen this dark side of him. He is the very essence of violence before me, yet he holds my face so delicately on his tattooed knuckle. His menacing words slipping like liquid silk between my ribs, stirring my own darkness, waking the shadow dragon curled around my misshapen heart, her prize treasure deep within her glacial palace.

I'm not sure why I suddenly mean so much to this male I don't even know. His words should elicit fear, the desire to push him away—only… they don't. He saved me. A fuzzy memory tugs at my mind—the boundless safety permeating deep into my marrow as velvety shadows wound around me, nuzzled tightly in his protective embrace as he whisked me away.

And he stayed.

He stayed by my side for days, his fingers threaded in mine, a lifeline pulling me back from Lady Death's sweet siren song. I barely know him. And suddenly, I want to. I want to know him deeply.

All common sense hemorrhages from my brain. I reach out to Sølas, placing my hand along his chiseled features as I soak in the shadows storming in his eyes, calming to an ethereal moonlight blue.

He draws closer to me with a longing in his gaze as his full lips part, his hand roaming to cup my face.

My hand trails down his neck, lingering over the center of his perfectly carved chest. My heart limps frantically, my breath becoming unsteady as his heart pounds like a steady drum beneath my palm, a balm to my fraying nerves.

He's dangerous. Not because of the violence he threatens or his unknown bloodline, but because of the control he effortlessly wields over my body. My misshapen heart flutters like a sick bird, bruising itself against my ribs, heat ravishing my blood as a deep ache throbs between my thighs, flushing my pallid cheeks.

His thumb glides over my bottom lip, parting my mouth, molten desire pooling at my core. He leans in close, his lips feathering my ear, releasing a subtle tremble from my wonton body. My flesh becoming lightning beneath his touch.

His voice is sultry as he whispers, "I want… their names."

I shove him away. "Prick!"

"What? You were being stubborn. This seemed like a much more fun way to tease their names from your lips. I get what I want."

"You're unbelievable."

"You didn't seem to mind my presence a second ago."

"I was willing to look past the whole breaking-your-promise-not-to-touch-me thing, since you saved my life and all, but I'm alive now, and I'd like to reinstate that promise of yours."

"It's far too late now. I don't make promises I can't keep," he croons.

"Fuck right off then."

"Right here in front of you? If that's your kink, I'm sure I can make it work." He shrugs as if he's actually thinking about doing it.

"You have a dirty fucking mind, ya know that?"

"Oh, you have no idea," he growls primally, and I can't help the heat that skitters through my blood in response to his feral tone. He's an emotional roller coaster. One second, he's kind; the next, manic with violence; and then the next, he's luring me into a lustful frenzy, just to get what he wants from me. He feels more emotions in five minutes than I feel in an entire month.

*He is utter chaos, while I prefer control.*

The stormy shadows in his eyes become more erratic as his lust takes over. He's a walking crimson flag, stained with my own heart's blood, untethered emotional chaos threatening to pull me in with him and spit me out, unsalvageable. I bash my mind with the thought, hoping for it to cement, despite how my traitorous body aches for him.

I know better than to give in. He'll be the death of us both, distracting me and dredging up emotions beyond my control. Plus, I desperately want to get out of telling him who did this to me. Partly because of the shame of needing his help, and partly because I was foolish enough to let it happen. And lastly, because it's not his vengeance to take. It's fucking *mine*.

Although, admittedly, I'm in no shape to be making any plans of murder at this point.

"In your dreams, Sølas," I scoff as I try to inch myself further back on the bed, escaping his menacing presence. My body may feel weak right now, but it's doing very little to dampen the lustful connection we share, despite my best efforts to block him out. Why *is* he so hard to block out?

The small amount of space I create rips at my chest like a chasm. I find myself longing for him to be closer again, like he can soothe this ache that lashes my rib cage. His warmth, the kindling to the invisible sparks that smolders between us.

As if he can read my mind, he pitches in closer to me. His strong hand finding purchase on my thigh. With the slightest movement, his knees nudge mine, parting my legs.

The rush of desire thunders through me, rumbling my pain away, threatening to melt me into a muddled mess. I long to trace the lines of his muscles, the tattoos that weave their way up from his hands, tumbling over his rippling arms, broad shoulders, peeking over his corded neck. His black battle leathers are unkept, worn loose from his unrelenting presence at my side, allowing me to see the shadows moving beneath the sun-kissed umber skin of his chest. The scent of spruce and amber sends my pulse skittering as the air becomes unbearably thick.

If I did cross this line, giving in to my dark desires, perhaps it will only be my body on the line. My broken bits hidden from his disarming touch. Perhaps I can indulge in the consuming lust, dissociating just enough to enjoy the pleasure without any chance of emotion creeping in to gut me like a fool.

I lean in, challenging his advance. I'm normally the aggressor, but something about his dominating presence makes me want him to ravage me right here.

A clawing sensation pricks and gouges at the back of my mind, scraping his earlier remark to my attention: *I want them to choke on the pain that bludgeoned me while I held you dying in my arms.* Warning me that he craves more than just my flesh. My close brush with death should not have affected him so deeply; we don't even know each other. I'm something more to him. What, I'm not sure. Perhaps I can use my Persuasive powers to figure out why exactly he said those words. That is, once I'm strong enough to stand on my own two feet without swaying like a new sprout threatening to crumble in a light breeze.

Frost curls along the walls of my glacial palace. This makes his previous attempts of weaving his way around my heart all the more threatening. More terrifying. More messy.

My thoughts are interrupted by his breath on my neck. Another small shiver sneaks its way through my grasp of control.

"Say my name again, and you'll find out exactly what my dreams entail." His growl rumbles from deep within his broad chest, resonating into my bones, stoking the unbearable tightness in my lower belly.

The goosebumps prickle along my skin as the throbbing between my thighs begs for him to be between them. What little control I have left burns to ash. Tilting my head, baring my neck to him, I beckon his kiss while revealing my manically racing pulse.

His grip on my thigh tightens, pushing in so close, I can feel his every breath. His roaring heartbeat drums mine into synchrony. A deep, guttural groan gnaws along my exposed flesh, vibrating my very being.

To my odd displeasure, he doesn't move any closer.

I smother the whimper threatening to escape my panting lungs. His twitching lips brush against the shell of my ear. My knees fall weak, crashing into his with an uncontrollable quiver. My weakness fueling his delight as his grasp tightens on my thighs, lazily sliding further up.

"I need you… at your full strength for all the things I will do to you," he rumbles.

My body arches closer to his at the salacious promise of his words. In my carnal state, a roar builds in my chest. I can handle him, and I want him this instant. But before it can tear into him, he vanishes into shadows, reappearing on the other side of the room, leaning against the wall with his hands in his pockets, ankles crossed. I watch the muscles tick along his perfect jaw.

*What the fuck?*

Garnet betrayal rises to my cheeks as he leaves me here with a facial expression that says nothing less than *stay with me*.

He clenches his jaw so hard, I'm surprised those pretty white teeth don't shatter. I wish they would, slitting his mouth apart, shredding his throat like he's gutted me.

I showed him where to cut, and he impaled his sword right where it hurts. Leaving me a wrecked, wanton mess of thawing frozen bits, pooling like a fool for him. If I was stronger, I'd march over to him, fuck him, and then slash him into dinner for Pip.

*Fucking shadow prick.*

My rage storms, shifting on searing winds of disappointment in myself. How am I suddenly the one lacking control, acting reckless, while he's across the room, the very essence of restraint? I can't even blame it on my lack of circulating blood; I'm smarter than this lustful beast he's brought out to play.

This is exactly why I don't get close to people. Letting emotions get involved only shows them where to cut to leave the most devastating wounds.

Sølas leans against the wall, smoky shadows twisting all around him, his eyes glowing solid white. Even his pupils are lost to the blizzard.

"I need you strong enough to survive all that I want from you. Now. Tell me their names!" he roars across the room.

Celestials, like I want him anywhere near me again. Or do I? *No.* No. I don't. My mind's a fuzzy mess. Too many pesky emotions running around, not enough time to catch them all and chuck them out the window in my mind and seal it shut forever.

Something tugs at my chest, his distance suddenly tightening like a vice. My ribs creak and moan, their impending fracture looming like spears menacing to lance my limping, misshapen heart. *What new Emberhell is this cursed feeling in my fucking chest?*

I sigh, drinking in a deep breath. He isn't wrong. I'm in no state for any form of strenuous physical activity, including beating him into a bloody pulp, but it still doesn't make me any less annoyed at his sudden show of restraint. Or his insistence about the names.

Maybe I should have killed him when I had the chance. *Why are his eyes so white?* I shake the thought from my head. I can't spiral. I need to focus to distract him from his mission.

"For someone so clever, you'd think you would have already figured that out," I snip as I pick at the dirt underneath my short nails, trying to feign that his sudden distance isn't affecting me.

"Oh, I have my suspicions. But I want to hear *you* say it." His tone is utterly lethal.

I shrug, continuing to toy with my nails, disinterested. They're utterly filthy. Should keep me busy for a long while.

"Well… that concussion must have rattled their names right out of my silly little head," I say with mock innocence, twirling my finger next to my temple like there's a few loose bolts up there.

*Too many to count, actually.*

Then I flash him a wicked grin, biting my bottom lip before giving him a sarcastic pout as I purr, "Oh, how I do so hate not giving you what you want."

Swiftly, the room becomes absolute darkness. Ribbons of black velvet wrap around me, lifting me up from the bed. His violent presence is in front of me, yet he continues his gentle hold, raising me with his shadows to look him in the eye.

"There is a time and place for games. *This* is not one of them. Now give me their names," he growls before continuing in a sharp, flirtatious tone, slashing at my resolve. "I made a promise to the rest of our Zenith I would surmise them. Do not make me break another promise, *Luxsula*."

Sølas' eyes become foreboding as he lifts my chin with the softest shadowy touch. That word. I vaguely remember hearing that word but can't place it. I'm too faint from the lack of circulating blood scrambling against gravity to perfuse my brain.

I summon what strength I have left and raise my chin to fight him nonetheless. "I will not—"

"Sølas! Put her down this fucking instant! Have you lost your ever-loving mind? She nearly just died, and you are throwing her around with your powers like she is a Celestials-damned doll!" Kissa hisses. Her claws gouge out, wrapping around his neck.

"She refuses to tell me their names." He scowls, disappearing in a cloud of shadows to reveal himself leaning back against that damn wall once more.

Kissa helps me settle back into the bed, checking me over for new injuries before whirling back to him. "I know we agreed that you would be the one to ask her their names, but not like this! We all just figured since you were the one who found her and you refused to tell us how, that you were the one closest to her. We didn't want you to bloody kill her all over again, especially when it's pretty damn obvious who did this to her. You're a fucking idiot, Sølas Zyon." Kissa is practically snarling at this point. He vanishes out the door in a fury of lashing shadows.

Kissa's ears twitch in my direction. "Your pulse is far too fast. You need to lie down, or you're going to pass out again."

"I'm fine. What's up with him? I've never seen him act like this… I mean, not that I know him very well," I murmur, finally able to shove everything that just happened with Sølas right out the window.

"Celestials, he has been on a whole other level since he brought you here. I think you almost dying switched something on in him." She gives me a suggestive look.

"Stop. Nothing has happened between us." I wave my hand dismissively at her.

"The smell of this room would say otherwise. I half thought that when I walked into the shadows, I was going to see something I couldn't unsee… but then I smelled your fear." She pauses, looking me over once more. I smirk, as if her superior feline vision could have missed something the first time.

"Don't think for a second I believe that Ritherin-shit he spewed about just coincidentally taking a stroll in the Mysticwoods at night. Right where your body was lying." She gives me a knowing look before she continues, "We are a team. You can't lie to us. We're supposed to trust each other. In addition, you have a dragon burn on your leg, according to Atlas. Nothing but a dragon can make that mark. And you oddly always smell of dragon. Did you bond with one before the Celestial Bonding event? That would be sacrilege!"

Her chartreuse eyes narrow on me. She's putting the facts together in all the wrong ways. Trust doesn't come easy to me, but if we're going to be a team, she's right. I have to tell her the truth.

I pull the blanket up towards my chest, almost hoping it can shield me as I gather my words.

"Pip? Come on out."

"Who's—?"

A little orange dragon springs from the corner of the room, running up my leg and on to my shoulder, tilting his head at Kissa.

"This is Pip. He's a type of dragon I've never heard of. He can shapeshift and apparently teleport through doors. At some point, when I was getting the shit kicked out of me—after Chet poisoned me, I guess—Pip ran off and found Sølas for help. And no, there is nothing between us. I don't know why this little guy decided to find him of all people. I guess maybe because he is always hovering around me or whatever. I mean, I guess I have known him since the first trial. Anyway, that's not important. I vaguely remember Sølas trying to pack my wound. He said his Sangre magic wasn't powerful enough, then he asked Pip to breathe fire on it to sear the wound. He might be small, but he's a powerful creature."

Kissa's furry jaw drops, revealing her sharp bottom fangs. Her chartreuse eyes dart from me to Pip and then back again. She blinks in disbelief.

"Let's hold on to the whole shapeshifting mini-dragon species no one has ever heard of. They fucking *poisoned* you?"

"Yeah. I felt a prick on my arm as they jostled by me leaving the sparring arena. I didn't think anything of it at first. I was too exhausted from pushing myself through one too many fights in the Combat Arena. My brain didn't put two and two together until I was outside on the ground with my head spinning. Then they took turns kicking me, and Chet stabbed me in my leg. He said he was going to stab me again… to make me barren. So I'd get kicked out of Gildorea and would never become an Ellian Knight," I continue, recounting the rest of the story.

"I am going to fucking rip out every one of their cowardly throats. Other than Chet, who was there?"

"It was four different voices. Chet and Lorgan spoke. I recognized Brock's laugh. The last one I didn't know. It was distant, and I only heard their laugh."

I reach out, grabbing her arm. Her fur is soft beneath my grasp. "I know they are cowards, but you and the rest of our Zenith cannot fight my battles for me. I am the one who brought this on myself. I antagonized them. I can't risk the rest of the Wing for my stupidity."

"Savaé, an attack on one of us is an attack on all of us. It's not who we stand against but how we stand together. That is the true power of the Ellian Knights and our Zenith." She pauses, looking down angrily before continuing, "He should be expelled for what he did, but his mother, Commander Bragen, will never let that happen. From what I've heard, that's where he gets his evil streak from. We won't fight this battle for you, but Celestials be dimmed if we aren't going to protect our own. You need to rest today. You'll be expected in class tomorrow and will need to talk with Chancellor Ashfel. You'll need all your strength for that encounter, no doubt about it. I need to go update the rest of our Zenith on what happened." As she starts to stand up, Pip prances up her arm, grabbing on either side of her enormous ear.

He peers down it like he thinks there's some surprise waiting for him. A smile curls on my lips at his wild sense of curiosity.

"Is he always this invasive?" she hisses as she pulls him off her, plopping him on my lap. The five prongs that jut out from his head are down initially, like an animal tucking its ears along its head. I smile at him, and the spikes jet up, framing his four-eyed face like a star. I swear, there's the slightest crinkle around his eyes, like he's smiling back.

"He is just curious." I laugh. "Please, make sure Sølas doesn't do something stupid when you tell the rest of the group."

"I know better than to waste my time trying to control that beast, but I'll talk to Seraph. She's pretty good at keeping him on a leash, when she's not off getting into her own troubles. I swear, some of the Bloodline kids raised by the Maidens are the worst. I wish they all could be as respectful and diligent as Atlas and Kivi."

"Oh. I didn't know they were all raised by the Maidens." Then I remember Sølas mentioning his parents being dead. I suppose he must have been raised by the Maidens after their passing.

"Yeah, most of our team was. That's why we're such a powerful lot. You, Cinder, Flint, Highin, and I are the only ones who were raised the natural way, outside of a Runic Tech artificial womb," Kissa replies.

"How do you know them so well, if you weren't raised with them?"

Kissa pauses for a second, her hackles raising before she sweeps her hands over her neck.

"When I was little, I was stolen from my family. They put a chain around my neck and locked me in a cage. Apparently, some rich king from another continent heard of Mao and wanted one as his personal pet. Luckily, my parents and village tracked me down and freed me from the smugglers. My parents took on full-time administration jobs here, so something like that would never happen again. I spent a great deal of time in the same classes as the Faelings raised by the Maidens. I never want to be that powerless again. That's why I want to become an Ellian Knight. To keep other Faelings safe."

I reach my hand out to hers, understanding all too well the feeling of being powerless. "Do you ever wish you had been born and raised like them? Trained for this since you were born without the hindrance of familial attachments?"

"Not a chance. The Maidens practically give them a Celestial complex. They think they are Celestial's gift to Faekind. Untouchable. Some are too powerful for their own good. For example, Commander Bragen's Celestial Gift is Toxic Miasma, right? She can breathe out a cloud of toxic gas that suffocates all within it. She is bonded with a Blightedbrew, which can withstand her poisonous vapor. Their bonded gift is that her nails can become poisonous darts she can shoot off at enemies."

Kissa extends her claws, and I flinch at the thought. Pip curls up beside me as she continues, "Her abilities and ruthless nature are why she's invaluable on the battlefield and ascended to Commander quickly. She was Bloodline paired to a powerful Siphon named Rex Renfield. Now Chet has the ability to not only Siphon magic but to siphon power from poisons, too. Rumor has it that *his* Celestial Gift is the ability to poison people with the nick of his fingernail. I think that's what he did to you. He thinks he's invincible because of who his mother is. Unfortunately, she has been here at Universitás enough to rub off on her son during his upbringing."

"Wouldn't it be incredibly stupid to use his own magic-bound poison on me? If I had died, a strong Sangre would have been able to determine whose magic was responsible. Also, if he was willing to risk getting caught, why not just siphon my magic and leave me there as a husk?" I ponder aloud.

"I don't think he cared. Sadly, I think he is a sadist fuck, and siphoning your magic seemed less painful than what he had in store for you. To be honest, I wouldn't be surprised if his mother would have been proud of what he did to you. An uneasy feeling always settles in my fur when she's around." She shudders. "Look, you're safe for now. Rest. I'll see you tomorrow. I have to meet with the others." The sounds of Kissa's words chase her as she pounces out the door.

A pit builds in my throat that I struggle to swallow. I know people can be above reproach because of who they are related to, but to get away with murder? As if my life meant so little?

I suppose it makes sense. I'm no one to these people, just an orphan from a small village. Although I've made waves with my fighting prowess, I'm nothing in the grand scheme of the bloodlines they've worked on for generations. Especially when my Celestial Gift has yet to manifest. You can train

Fae with the skills I have, but without a unique magic ability to contribute to the Bloodline pairing, I'm meaningless.

I haven't felt this small since before I met Sully. The moment is sobering. Or, better yet, harrowing. I lie down, staring at the ceiling as fear creeps into my mind. Pip scurries up, wrapping himself around my neck, chirping into a soothing hum. The sound calms my restless mind, and eventually, I drift off into exhausted sleep.

# CHAPTER 22

I awake to a humming sound radiating from Kivi's chest as bioluminescent spores vibrate above me like the night sky full of blue stars. Her magic is breathtaking.

"Celestials Blessings, Savaé. There is food for you on the table. I wouldn't wait too long. Your dragon has already eaten half the plate."

I sit up. My eyes trail to the table with a plate and a small orange trouble-maker, who turns around to look at me with a face covered in crumbs.

He chirps with excitement. I tilt my head down, giving him a disapproving glare, and grunt. He grabs an additional biscuit before scurrying off.

"Atlas would like to meet with you and the dragon later this week, to see if he can explore further details on its origins based on some supplementary information he will need from you and inspecting the creature. Additionally, I worked with our Runic Engineer, Gearin, to create this unique ring. It's imbued with magic so the effects of Chet's poison should no longer affect you, or at least affect you to a lesser extent in case he tries a stunt like this again." An odd beat hums in melodic voice.

No one other than Sully has ever cared for me like this. It's an uncomfortable feeling, having everyone joining together to help me. Is this what it feels like to be a part of a family? I imagine it's something like this. Individuals you can trust, lean on in times of need, who always have your back. Even when it doesn't serve to benefit them as well.

I'm so used to being on my own, to fending for myself, that it always made me feel weak to accept someone's help. Until I met Sully. Yet this is different.

It's more akin to a tapestry; we're all interwoven together. I'm the thread that has been picked at, becoming unraveled. This threat risks the entire tapestry coming undone. But the rest of my Zenith has come together to restitch me, securing me in place so we remain neatly interwoven together. Becoming stronger with each challenge we face and rise above. Or maybe I'm just still slightly delusional from the lack of blood coursing to my brain…

"This is incredibly generous and thoughtful. I… I don't deserve this kindness," I say, my eyes widening as I look over the delicate runework of the golden ring in my palm.

Kivi tsks at me. "Nonsense. We are one, we are each other, we are linked. If one of us is a target, we are all a target. We battle as one. We live as one."

"But I just met you a few days ago. My death would take the threat away, and eventually, I would be replaced. The Zenith would be safer for it."

"We would be weaker for it. If we cannot rise to the simple challenge of one young male within our own ranks, then our Zenith has no business meeting the Wuvon in battle. We rise together, we set together, we are one or none at all." Her melodic voice echoes with power, yet the frequency of her voice never wavers.

*A tapestry it is then.* I suppose my delusional musings are rather on point after all.

It's clear Kivi's connection with nature—deeply interwoven with the mycelium network—shapes her voice into something other worldly. Her connection to the vast cycle of life and death altering the very perception of reality.

The notion of *we are one or none at all* resonates through my mind. This is a new concept to grasp, but one that feels like power in my hands. If I'm strong on my own, I can only imagine how it will feel when we fight together as a united force—we will be glorious.

But then Sully's distorted words from the second trial slash my mind.

*You can never love or be loved.*

*You have no soul.*

*No heart.*

*Anyone close to you dies.*

*You are a curse.*

*You beckon darkness to consume everything you hold dear.*

For someone so confident in their skills of shoving things away in little boxes and discarding them out a window, I am having some real fucking trouble ridding myself of those cursed words. So convenient, when I finally think about letting someone in. I wonder if I can get Orion to remove the memory from my head. I'd be elated to never hear those fucking words again. I know they're just an illusion, one based on my worst fears, but Celestials, how true they feel.

"Class is soon. Please bathe, and ready yourself. Orion waits outside to chaperone you to the bathing chambers. One of us will be escorting you at all times. May the Celestials give us strength and bless us from the darkness," Kivi blesses with command laced in her words as she turns.

I reach out gently, grasping a part of her delicate arm where no mushrooms grow.

"I do not need an escort. You already made this ring that will protect me from his poison. That's enough." I'm standing now, without even realizing it. My knees beg to buckle under my weight, but I clench my fist, refusing their plea.

"You are weak. Which means we are all weak." Her voice is low, drawing out each word as if it's a threat. I quickly let go of her.

She straightens her shoulders and lifts her chin as she continues.

"Until your blood recovers, and possibly after, you will abide having an escort. Our Zenith has voted, and so it shall be. This is not negotiable. Do not protest that which you have no control over. There are Fates at play above your ego of solitary strength, beyond what you are. You shall accept your fate is tied to us. Resisting is foolish; I know you to be more intelligible than this. I will not waste time on repeating myself. There are new leather pants for you on the chair. Get dressed, eat, and meet Orion outside, or I will have her compel you to do so." Lost is the melody of her voice. Now, a monotonic command braces the room.

I almost fall backwards thinking that a member of my team would use her Persuasive powers to compel me, never mind the fact that she's strong enough to do so. The thought of being compelled definitely sizzles out any semblance of my rebellion.

I peer down at my leg. My leather pants are ripped high, and there's a scar on my leg from where Chet stabbed me. Except it isn't a scar. It's a glowing, iridescent tattoo of a twelve-pointed star. As my fingers graze it, it shines brighter. I rub my fingers over the bridge of my nose.

*Great. Another strange fucking marking.*

I know dragon fire burns hotter than any fire we can produce, even the strongest elemental-fire Pixie, but this is on a whole other level of odd. Fire-wielding dragons supposedly have remnants of Celestial fire from the Celestial Dragon that rests beneath the mountains. I expected there to be a huge chunk of my leg missing from the scorching, but I guess they can control the power behind their fire.

Come to think about it, Pip did seem to have amazing control of his fire when he was working with me at the Blacksmith shop as he heated the metal for my new short sword. I'm thankful his flames somehow were just strong enough to stop the bleeding without maiming my leg. I never thought a dragon-fire burn would look like this, though.

I'm lightheaded as I don my new pants. They're made of a much thicker leather than our standard issue uniforms, yet somehow just as light. I also notice they have several sheaths built into the legs and waist with small runic symbols on them that I don't recognize.

The Automatons are always finding ways to invent more and more complex runes. It makes sense we have specialists dedicated to just being Runic Engineers. They devote their life to runework. Looking at the pants, I surmise these are another extravagant protection gift from my team. I add asking Gearin what the markings mean to my ever-growing list of priorities.

I shove the rest of the food in my mouth, practically drooling on myself from how delicious it tastes. It's a combination of buttery spices, cheese, and flakey dough. If I could ever be mad at Pip, this would be one of those times. After not eating for two days, I could've eaten the whole plate if Pip hadn't already absconded away with a full belly. I'm ravenous, but I don't have time to stop for more food.

"Little dragon, it's time to go." I beckon. My orange friend comes scampering out from under the desk and up my leg, leaping to my arm, where he settles as my white leather bracer. I open the door to find Orion leaning against the wall, twirling her candy-red braid through her matching nails. Her aquamarine scales shimmer on her sylph-like frame, dressed in her white battle leathers. The contrast really makes the red pop against her varying shades of blue scales.

Her piercing candy-red eyes meet mine. "Your Aura's a little brighter, which is good. Means your blood is getting stronger. Don't get me wrong, though; you still look like absolute trash."

"Good morning to you, too, sunshine." I squint at the bright light diving in from the cathedral ceiling topped with domed glass.

Orion links her arm with mine. "The bathing chambers in this corridor are down this hallway. Let's get you cleaned up. You smell even worse than you look. I don't know how Kissa managed to be in the same room as you for any amount of time with her nose. She must really like you." She taps me on the nose with her free hand.

I huff at her in response, but I am glad for the support her arm offers my swimmy head after being bedbound for the last two days.

She brings me to a bathroom with walls made of beautiful slate-blue tile and golden fixtures for the plumbing. There's a different rune on each handle of the shower as I undress myself while Orion waits outside the stall. They're similar to the ones in my first shower here a few mornings ago. One handle has the rune for hot, and the other the rune for cold. On the ceiling, there is a circular piece of metal with holes in it. So much more convenient than a bath heated by fire magic like in Estrella.

I turn the knob for hot, and steaming water cascades down from the metal disk above, soothing my aching joints. I scrub the dried blood and dirt from under my nails. I'm elated to remove the crunchy blood from my scalp and see it hasn't stained my translucent hair crimson.

I turn off the water and dry my hair with my fire magic. Orion throws some new fabric over the crystal stall door to bind my breasts and a clean pair of underwear that are surprisingly my own.

How did she get my underwear from my room when I have a runic lock on the door? Orion senses my confusion, no doubt noticing the shift in my Aura.

"I had Gearin hack the lock for me. Your runic magic is decent, but he said it definitely needs work."

"Well, right now, I'm thankful for my lackluster job allowing him to hack his way in," I say with a dry laugh. Then I quickly use magic to clean my basilisk armor and boots. I emerge from the shower stall in my white and gold leathers, my secret armor underneath and Pip hidden on my arm. My body is steadier; I'm less lightheaded after scrubbing the memory of that night from my skin.

"Spick and span. Next, we meet the others in the Grand Conservatory before morning lectures. If you need to run to the bathroom, Kissa will go with you, since she's with you for all your classes. Sølas is your escort for meals because his shadow powers are a force no one dares to mess with. Do be a dear, and try not to provoke him… He's been in a particularly foul mood lately."

I roll my eyes at Orion regarding that last comment. He is the one who's always provoking *me*, but I don't need to bring that to anyone's attention.

Orion continues, "Fenwick and Juniper will escort you to and from your room at night and morning. We talked to Winx, and she convinced her dad to let them be roomed on either side of your apartment. So, make sure to thank her for her kindness. After classes today, Cinder will escort you to your meeting with Chancellor Ashfel. He insisted the Chancellor wouldn't fight him on joining you for the meeting. Don't ask me why; he's always so cryptic. He likes taking his whole dark and mysterious bad-male vibe to a whole other level."

"Any idea on when I'll no longer have to be shepherded around like a sheep?" I regret the comment as soon as it slips from my lips. They've clearly put a great deal of thought and effort into keeping me safe. I'm sure they have better things to do with their time.

"Just because you fought off some wild monsters during your trials doesn't make you the strongest one here. You may have trained with Sully, but you were isolated in your backwoods village. There are games afoot in these halls, secret agendas. You're out of your element when it comes to the scheming of high society. Yes, this is a war university, but it's also a place where bloodlines are vying for control and the queen's favor to grant them power beyond magic. You have managed to make yourself the target of some very powerful players."

I open my mouth to apologize for my indignant comment, but Orion's not finished.

"We're all working to survive this battle, just like we'll have to work together to survive the battles out there against the Wuvon. It's time you start learning how to play nice with others. Trust our knowledge of the skirmishes between the walls here, and we will be able to lean on your battle prowess for the war out there. We are one or none at all," she says fiercely as she grabs my arm, her patience lost.

There are those words again. I guess they've become the Zenith motto while I was unconscious. She's right; it's a recurring theme of the day. I need to stop thinking like a feral, lone dog and reframe my point of view to that of a member of a well-honed wolfpack.

Orion's tone softens.

"I can tell by your Aura that this is new for you. I promise, you'll never be alone again. You really need to start thinking of us as one. The rest of our lives, we are bound together by invisible threads. To sever one is to weaken us all." There's almost a plea to Orion's words as she opens the ornate golden arched doors to the rotunda of the Grand Conservatory.

She leans her head to my ear. "I know it's not easy adjusting to being part of a team. The other Faelings never wanted to play with me because of my powers. Then one day, I accidentally compelled someone, unaware the power manifested. After that, I was put in separate classes. That ability is kept secret. It's hard being around Fae for me, in a different way. Seeing all their emotions and not saying a thing. I make other Fae uncomfortable, but not in our Wing. We're stuck with each other; we will eventually know one another better than anyone in this world. We're stronger together because we are a part of something bigger now. I'm here for you, when you're ready, to help you sort out that messy Aura full of emotions you think you've cleverly stuffed away."

*I'm surprised she can handle looking at that shitshow.* I squeeze her arm, thanking her for sharing her own vulnerable bits, tucking them somewhere safe so they can never harm her in my hands. It seems like our team is full of broken pieces, fitting together in a powerful mosaic. Ready to channel our darkness into something good, for once.

Our entire Zenith is standing close by, waiting for us. The skin on the back of my neck prickles as I see the broad-shouldered male leaning against the wall with his arms crossed against his black aerial leathers, which barely keep his muscles contained. My pulse dares to quicken, remembering his grip sliding up my thigh, a smoky whisper on the cusp of my ear.

I roll my shoulder, brushing off the thought; after all, he was just using my forsaken hormones to pry information out of me. The way he looks at me is different this time. He appears lost as I search his ice-blue irises, the flecks of crimson hidden behind swirling smoke. His jaw clenches, the bands of muscles popping in his neck. I think I catch a glimpse of a new tattoo there that I don't remember from when his shirt was off in the Combat Arena.

His focus darts to a door opening across the rotunda. His gaze sharpens, irises pure white as his raven hair billows into smoky shadows coiling above him. In a blink of an eye, he disappears. I find myself jealous of his ability to melt into the shadows and port anywhere at will. I follow where his previous fixation led as I walk forward to my team. To my dismay, it leads to Chet and his cronies. Power crackles and sizzles beneath my skin as his beady green eyes lash to mine.

Chet grits his teeth.

My face: a mask, pure boredom and indifference. I won't let him know he nearly killed me.

An unsettling grin takes over his face as he runs his fingers through his slicked-back blond hair.

I want to mince him apart, cut off his precious bits, and watch him choke on them for what he did to me. But a petite hand grasps my arm.

Fenwick's smile beams beneath her black-and-white cookie bobbed hair. Her sunburst yellow eyes twinkle in the golden light spilling from windows of the Grand Conservatory.

"He isn't worth it, Savaé," Fenwick warbles. She has a way about her. So much gleaming light, so full of hope and happiness. It would utterly gut me to see her frown. She is everything bright and good in this world. Every wholesome thing I've never had. I want to keep her this way forever. A shining beacon in this wretched world.

I smile back at her. "You're right. He isn't."

She jumps up and down in excitement. The large single broadsword on her back sways with her movement. She's short, fiery, and full of light, just like her magic. I wonder how she's stayed so chipper despite being trained as a weapon for war by the Maidens.

"Good to see ya alive and kickin'. Ya know, that slithering coward doesn't even deserve the fate of Emberhell," Seraph jests, blue war braids swaying with her typical greeting—a slap on the back—before her eyes widen in apology, remembering I just nearly died.

Vex flips the black curls around her curved horns with a sigh.

"You do realize my family is *from* Emberhell, right?" Vex asks with a furrowed brow across her freckled red face.

"Yeah, and there's a reason they *left* that burning shithole full of demons, ain't there?" Seraph chuckles.

Vex huffs. "You're right. It is a scourging pit of death and destruction, infested with all manner of horrifying demons. Unlike the beautiful demon you have at your leisure now." She feigns a curtsy to the group. Her black horns shimmer with the movement, contrasting against her leathery scarlet skin.

Emberhell is thought to be an extension into our world of the Underrealm itself, where souls too corrupt to find redemption transform into all manner of demons made of pure pitch. The continent itself is believed to be a barren wasteland of burning flames, filled with tarry pits that allow the dark demons from below access to our world.

Infernai are a demon-Fae hybrid species hailing from that region. They're not the only demons to reside in Emberhell—apparently, there are many species of demon who have souls and are not made of pitch, although no texts exist on them. Probably because a realm of flames makes book-keeping a rather arduous task.

"I am glad to see you in better spirits. The Celestials have surely blessed you to make such a recovery. Along with the wonders of Kivi's abilities, of course." Atlas bows, revealing the intricate beauty of upright moth wings laced about on the top of his head. It's clear he and Kivi are both devout in the worship of the Celestials who once bore our planet and ruled the lands.

Fewer Fae worship them nowadays, thanking the Golden Legion and Ellian Knights for their safety. How easily they forget the sacrifice our Celestials made in an attempt to save Elyndor.

Even if corruption has still found its way to our planet, it's a preferable fate to losing magic altogether. Like in the worlds where the Celestials dimmed, losing their magic before they could make the sacrifice like our Celestial did. Part of me wonders if it's the growth of the Blackwood that is causing more and more children to be born without any magic at all.

I pull myself from my thoughts, remembering my manners and bow in deference. "Thank you for the kind words. May the Celestials bless us all."

As I return to standing, I'm met with a warm kiss on my cheek as slender arms wrap around my waist.

Winx squeezes the air out of me. "Thank the Celestials you're alive! I made them tell me everything when they asked me to speak to Father about a room change. I wanted to burn Chet alive, but your boring gang said I wasn't allowed."

She lets out a pouty *hmph*. Her short, angular hair is now neon pink, almost as vibrant as when her eyes flare bright violet. Winx bats a hand at my Zenith as she continues, "They are simply no fun! So, instead, I left a little magic bomb I created in his room. It exploded, covering him in pink glitter. He was furious yesterday while everyone laughed about the glitter he didn't manage to scrub off."

"Honestly, I thought the pink glitter was a big improvement on his usual look," Vex mumbles as she grabs one of Winx's arms. Flint grabs her other. Together, they pull Winx off me and hold her back.

"Hey! What's the big idea? I'm just saying 'hi' to her. She nearly died. I missed her!" Winx hollers as neon violet eyes flare viciously beneath locks of pink hair, flying across her face in the jostle.

"Exactly. She nearly died, and you're over here squeezing the life out of her," Vex snaps as she mutters under her breath how unbelievable Winx is being.

"Oh. Right." Winx giggles. "Well, sometimes, I just can't help myself around her," she muses. Violet flames roar as she drinks me in.

Seraph rolls her eyes. "She'll be better soon enough and back to knocking you against walls and leaving scorch marks in no time. Don't you worry your flaming little head."

Now I'm rolling my eyes because clearly everyone knows about the rendezvous between me and Winx outside the pub in Snomas. *Lovely.*

Seraph bites her lip as she flicks her gaze lazily over Winx. "But if you're in need of a distraction in the meantime, I'm happy to lend my services." She winks.

Emberhell, the thought of a fun night with both of them in my bed? *Fucking Tempting.* But the embers of that fantasy fizzle out quickly. Winx isn't after a casual burn, and I'm not forged for anything more than passion without promise. Too sharp and jagged to be held in the confines of a relationship. Yet I need to handle letting her down carefully or she'll burn us all in the rage of her wildfires.

I turn my body to face Winx, giving her a sly half-smile. "I promise, I'll visit once I'm strong enough. I know I need to make time for us to catch up."

"Can't wait." She winks at me and then scowls at Seraph, sticking her tongue out before she prances back to her Nadir Wing.

My eyes follow her back to see Chet fuming at the sight of what has just transpired between Winx and me. It's clear he doesn't care that it's obviously Winx who came for me and not the other way around. I guess it's easier to make me the bad guy than accept that Winx just isn't interested in him.

"You do realize she is just making everything worse for you, right?" Eko states the obvious. His limerick-green eyes are piercing against his grey fur.

His ears are down against his skull, due to the noise that reverberates through the conservatory.

"Obviously. When you figure out a way to break it gently to a powerful Pyro Lilliac—who just *happens* to be the daughter of the Chancellor—that you're not interested in a relationship, please do let me fucking know." I huff before grumbling on, "I swear, I had no idea who she or Chet were when I stole Winx away from that table. She was just a pretty face I wanted to get lost in after a harrowing battle against a Ritherin."

"Hey, don't look at me. I'm not the strategist. Maybe Atlas has some words of wisdom for you?" Eko nods to Atlas, whose eyes widen as his cheeks peak in a rosy hue.

"Romantic relationship strategy is far beyond my expertise. Apologies, Savaé," Atlas murmurs as he shifts his willowy weight uneasily and chances a glance to Kivi. *Interesting.*

"Figures." I sigh, as the chimes overhead sing, letting us know class is beginning.

# CHAPTER 23

We find the seats allocated to Zenith Wing and sit down together, ready for the knowledge of today's lessons to be imparted to us.

A large figure walks out onto the stage; he's tall, broad-shouldered, with leathery skin and a buzzcut that makes his large, curly Angora horns appear even more menacing. His mink-colored skin is strewn with battle scars. His deep slate eyes match Vex's, and they have a distant familial resemblance to their face. Perhaps an uncle?

I glance over to Vex, who actually looks studious for once. Her face is sketched in longing for approval, shaded in fear. He must be someone important to her.

"This is Warrior Physics, and I'm the unfortunate soul who gets to teach it to you." His voice is rough, bellowing and abrading against the marble walls. "Name's Reginald Hadron, but it's Professor Hadron to you lot. If you want to survive out there, then this class is just as important as sparring and battle magic. If you waste my time, I will kick you out and let the others eat you alive using the skills they gain from my training." His commanding tone leaves no one questioning his threat.

"The physics of battle is a complex interplay of forces, motion, and energy, each governing the dynamics of conflict. In this class, I will teach you how to bend these principles to your will, giving you a sharp edge to wield in battle. Especially if your Wing plans to win the Fortress Battle at the end of this academic year." Excited murmurs regarding his last comment build into a low hum.

Professor Reginald stomps his foot. The room instantly falls to silence.

"When a warrior swings their sword, the kinetic energy generated is merely a product of their mass times the velocity of the blade, equaling their lethality upon impact. Similarly, the trajectory of an arrow is dictated by gravitational forces and air resistance, which affect its range and accuracy."

Professor Hadron pauses, whipping a bow from his back, slinging an arrow into place. "One must account for these as they nock their arrow to their bow, mobilizing the potential energy from tension, pulled taut in the bowstring." The arrow releases, piercing a target on the side of the stage with such momentum, the stand tumbles over. My eyes widen at his strength before I go back to jotting down notes.

"When two forces collide, momentum and impulse come to play with the outcome determined again by the mass, speed, and angle of collision. An object in motion stays in motion, or that motion is transferred to another object. If you don't understand momentum and force trajectories, even being bonded to a dragon won't save you. In the air, casting magic without considering Knights' movements around you will end in you slaughtering members of your own Wing. Doing the Wuvon's objective for them."

Professor Reginald Hadron snaps his finger as an illusion of the Blackwood forms on stage around him. Haunted black trees twist and screech upward to a crimson canopy.

"The battlefield itself is an arena of friction, where the very ground beneath your feet can be harnessed by the Wuvon to give them the upper hand, leading you into their well-laid traps." The illusion of the forest shifts around him, vines lashing out as tree branches grasp for him, coming alive with vengeance.

"Understanding these physical principles enables combatants to exploit weaknesses, anticipate enemy movements, and maximize their own efficacy as they transform the fight into a calculated dance of force and energy."

The physics of combat was one of my favorite topics for Sully to review. I scribble endlessly as Professor Hadron continues. Even though I know much of it already, there's always more to learn. I'm able to visualize the transfer of energy, see the manipulation of the forces, adjusting and accounting for the different elements of nature that could hinder me in battle.

I'm almost in tune with the physics around me when I'm fighting; it's just something that's carved deep into my bones.

The rest of the classes of the morning drag on, and I realize just how weak I am. All I've done is sit and listen, yet my body groans for rest. It's unsettling to be so powerless when I've spent so many years training to never feel that way again. Yet, with time and continued training, I'll get back to my former self.

I praise the Celestials that we don't have another round of sparring until next week. I never thought I'd be thankful to not have my favorite class, but I'm in no shape to enjoy the adrenaline or the challenge.

Lunch comes, and Sølas never leaves my side, yet he's eerily silent. None of the typically obnoxious, flirtatious banter I've come to expect from him. He doesn't even bother to look at me. His focus is elsewhere, like a shadow panther on the hunt, stalking its prey.

I imagine he's searching for Chet, but he and his lackeys are nowhere to be found. His change in demeanor is unsettling. I never thought I'd say this, but I think I might actually prefer his reckless, flirty side to this focused silence.

Afternoon classes start, and Kissa stays close by my side. It's strange having no alone time, but at least Kissa and I seem to understand each other. She never insists on filling silence with idle small talk, one of the many things I've grown to appreciate about her.

Instead of battle magic in the Warded Hollow, we have a guest lecturer from the frontlines coming to speak to us.

Our afternoon class is held on the top floor. The ceiling is the domed gold of the central building of Gildorea. The circular room is filled with tables, aligning the center dais made of crystal to let the light flow to the grand conservatory below. The circular pattern of tables is broken up by a central passageway from the door to the heart of the room. The space is intimate due to the rainbow-colored lighting that paints everything, radiating from artistic stained glass set in gothic arched windows.

A smile curls at my lips. The colors reflecting throughout the white marble construction are alive and vibrant. The display reminds me of a time when I felt that way. Before I lost Sully. Before my heart shattered and pieced itself together, not quite right, before I encased it back in ice. Before I left a bunch of vulnerable bits for Sølas to peck at until he found the right time to stab me where it hurt most. I roll my shoulder, brushing the memories aside.

From this view, I can see the terracing levels of Gildorea. Sometimes, I wonder how they managed to find enough white marble to build this enormous campus. I shudder to think about the poor souls who had to carve it out of the earth and then haul it here.

"It's my pleasure to take a day of reprieve to give you updates from the frontlines of Cascara. My name is Captain Maya Maza."

She's Mao, like Kissa. Her undone tangerine hair sweeps over her shoulders with petite ears peeking out, marked by golden piercings. She has chocolate-colored fur, with orange stripes instead of spots. Rainbow irises encircle her black slit pupils. A wrapped-up whip sits on one hip and a chakram circular blade on the other. Sickle blades glint over her back. She picks her teeth with a bone, a pure warrior presence cascading off her; she's a force to be reckoned with.

"I will not lie to you. The Wuvon advance the Blackwood every day, despite our efforts to keep them at bay. This is why the Bloodline magic we foster here is more important than ever. We need warriors and even stronger magic wielders to keep them back. We lost an Ellian Knight this week at the fortress of Mysthold fending off a horde of monsters that climbed the walls. They killed his bonded creature before he could take to the air. Despite his years of combat, he was quickly overrun, separated from his other Wing members." Captain Maza's jaw clenches, lips almost twitching into a snarl before she swipes her claws into her hair, pushing it back, gaining her composure once more.

"The Wuvon who attacked seemed to sense his isolation, focusing all the monsters on him. After they had nearly eaten him alive, leaving his mental shields vulnerable, a pale female shrouded in darkness sauntered in, lifting him off the ground. The rest of us arrived to see the last of his bones breaking before she disappeared into black mist. The monsters that had heeled while she finished her torture then descended on us. By the time we got to his body, he was unrecognizable." Her gaze becomes hollow, grappling against the haunting memory she's struggling to wrangle.

It's very uncommon for the Wuvon to directly assault a stronghold without extending the Blackwood closer to the grounds of the building. This attack is so odd, bubbling my brewing thoughts aloud without even thinking.

"There has to be a reason for the Wuvon to attack the stronghold. They normally keep the fight in Blackwood, or at least on the borderlands of the wilds that surround them, where their magic is the strongest. It doesn't make strategic sense to risk themselves out in the open like that. Mysthold is at least six hundred paces from the wilds and even further from the Blackwood."

"A very astute observation, Ensign Savaé. I see ex-Commander Sully Stonewall trained you well." Captain Maza's compliment prickles the back of my eyes with tears, which I blink right out my mosaic window as she continues, "While they have extended the Blackwood closer to Mysthold by about two hundred paces, you are correct: that's still too far for them to typically risk an attack. They seemed to counter this exposure with over a hundred monsters, overwhelming the infantry quickly. The only survivors were those who made it to the skies. As for the Wuvon who walked the corridors, it appears she stole several maps and scrolls from the executive officer stationed there. Obviously, all correspondence and maps are coded so she won't get much, but it's clear they were willing to take a big risk looking for something."

A male Pesche with merlot-colored scales that glisten on the pronounced ridge of his scalp is next to speak. "Have we sent any Scouting Rogues or Spycraft lieutenants into known camps of the Wuvon to determine what the female is looking for?"

With a feline smile displaying her sharp canines, Captain Maza responds, "I know, you know, that is classified, Ensign. Rest assured: we are doing everything possible to investigate this new behavior and prevent future aggressions such as this." It's clear from her tone no more questions on the topic will be answered.

Another ensign asks about the scariest monster she's ever seen, but I'm too distracted by thoughts of what they could be possibly looking for.

I tap Atlas on the shoulder, whispering in his ear, "Have there been other attacks like this?"

He twists around, brows pinched in annoyance by my interruption. "No. If they truly are looking for something or someone, this will not be the first attack of its kind." He shushes me off with a wave of his hand, implying he's done talking about this here.

What did he mean by 'someone'? He clearly knows more than he's letting on. Luckily, I know he's interested in Pip; hopefully, I can use the time he wants to investigate him to further suss out whatever he's hiding.

Frustration suddenly licks up the seams of my composure. The Zenith want my unyielding trust but seem not to trust me. I let out an exasperated huff in Atlas's direction, crossing my arms. To be fair, I haven't been the most forthcoming, nor have I done anything to earn their trust. Surely, saving my life and taking care of me for the last three days merits the trust they're asking for? Earning their trust is a challenge I am willing to take on.

# CHAPTER 24

After a delicious dinner, stuffing myself so full I can barely walk, I'm ready to pass out in my own bed.

Then I meet Cinder's glowing amber eyes as he leans against the bracketing of the dining hall doorframe. His broody face reminds me of the unfortunate meeting I have with the Chancellor. I suddenly regret eating so much as my stomach plummets thinking about Thorne Ashfel.

Electricity spikes the air behind me, telling me Sølas is looming. There's clearly some exchange I miss because Cinder nods to the male over my shoulder, and then his shadowy company drifts away.

"Make sure your mental shields are high. And please, for the love of the Celestials, watch your tongue. He barely believes our story, and even I can't save you if you piss him off." Cinder's voice is deep and gritted with charcoal, amber eyes flaring bright with warning.

Silently nodding, I follow him. His orange hair rustles like fall leaves as he heads out of the dining hall. My eyes roll. I can hold my tongue… *Most of the time*, I smirk to myself.

We arrive at two gothic cathedral-like doors. Instead of gold, like most of the entrances here, these are carved into onyx stone. Their color is out of place, casting the entrance in a menacing façade.

Without even a knock, the doors groan open to looming vaulted ceilings, creating the ambiance of what I imagine a haunted castle would feel like. The air is thick with the smell of ancient texts and ink. Crimson rugs pool over the white marble floors. A tall spire pins the corner, brimming with books. In fact, all the walls are lined with tomes. Perhaps he was a Savant before becoming Chancellor.

The pathway is lined with dark stone carvings of various species of gargoyles, believed to reside in Emberhell. *How fitting.* Two chairs, trimmed in deep purple, cower before an oversized mahogany desk, carved with an array of haunting creatures.

"Please. Sit. I have been waiting patiently for your recovery."

His icy tone prickles a shiver to crawl down my spine like a spider has caught me in its web. Light purple eyes level a chilling glare at Cinder. He's clearly unhappy at his presence but refuses to tell him to leave. Cinder must have some status I'm ignorant of. We take our seats as the Chancellor's pale hand smooths his slicked-back, long white hair.

"Do enlighten me on what you could have possibly eaten to put you out of training for three whole days? Dare I say, you look awfully pale for a stomach bug. Are you sure you're not mistaken about what ailed you? Perhaps it was a blood-sucking monster instead?" He's amused at himself, obviously not buying the excuse. He stands up, circling us like a vulture ready to devour his carrion prize.

"One of the other ensigns clearly tried to poison her. Just some hazing for her being a showoff at the trials is all," Cinder deflects, his mask of nonchalance perfect as always.

"I wasn't speaking to you, Ignis. I know this one can speak. I hear she has a rather sharp tongue at that. If it was simply a poison, why not go to the infirmary for an antidote to be healed?"

I maintain a steely expression. "I'm not a coward, unlike some of the other ensigns in our class. I would not show weakness, requiring healing in the infirmary. I made my own antidote and suffered the consequences of my foolish mistake of not smelling the poison on my food in the first place."

"A foolish mistake indeed, especially when you have two species who can smell better than Elarians in your Zenith. I imagine you will tell me that, coincidentally, neither Kissa nor Eko were present for that specific meal? Now, I would like the cowards among your rank of which you speak. They must be rooted out."

Ritherin-shit, he's already caught me in one lie. He's right, Eko and Kissa would have been able to smell poison on my food. I have to be careful about my next words.

"Why waste your precious time, Chancellor? You have designed the curriculum of Gildorea Universitás well; they will meet failure soon enough. If not, surely the Fortress Battle will make quick work of them." I smile sweetly, despite how foreign it feels on my face.

"Perhaps." He pauses right next to me, pinning me under his frosty gaze. "Please *do* be careful, Savaé. I have so much more in store for you. I'd hate for your foolishness—or someone else's—to rob me of your presence." He spits my name like it's poison on his tongue. I don't even try to unpack his noxious words, twisting at my gut and begging me to run.

Cinder stands and bows. I follow his lead, and then we turn to leave.

"I'd make sure those legs of yours have extra armor next time I see you." His words slither from the serpentine smile curling on his face as the doors hiss shut. I swear, that smile will haunt my nightmares.

"He fucking *knows*, Cinder," I growl when we're far enough down the hallway.

"He doesn't know shit. Calm down. You're wearing new pants, and they are covered in custom runes that signal protection. It's clear we're trying to protect you from something. And you were really pushing your luck with that coward comment. We're fortunate he didn't pressure us for names. You know, for someone who was clever enough to pass the entrance exam, it's amazing how stupid you can be."

"We all have our flaws." I laugh dryly. He isn't wrong; I'm exceptionally good at screwing myself over. Maybe that's my Celestial Gift?

As we make our way up the winding gold steps to my room, the hairs on my neck sway. I twist, peering over my shoulder across the corridor, but if he's there, he isn't planning on being seen.

I spin forward to see Fenwick and Juniper's faces painted with huge grins.

"Why don't we have a slumber party!?" Fenwick cheers, and Juniper nods excitedly, flower petals cascading from her forest green hair. Then they grasp hands, leaping into a swirling circle of dancing mirth. Their endless energy and chipper demeanor never seem to wane. Juniper stumbles, and Fenwick catches her with her light magic as they continue to prance.

Cinder runs his pale, freckled hand down his face, eyes flaring neon yellow. "Absolutely not. She needs her rest and won't get any with you two yapping away like night goblins."

They both sigh in disappointment.

Cinder rolls his eyes and continues, "Just stay on alert. Gearin and Sølas did some combination magic on your door, combining runes and shadow magic. Now, only you can enter your room, unless you invite someone in. The magic will sense if you're under duress and blast the person trying to threaten you." He points to his ring finger and taps on the door, twice.

"Tap just like I did, and it will allow you to hear and see what's going on outside your door. The people outside the door will be none the wiser. If you tap on it three times with your ring finger, the entirety of Zenith Wing will receive an alert only we can see and hear. So, if those fuckers show up outside your door trying to ambush you, you better tap three times. Because if they don't kill you, I will," he finishes, mumbling a slew of curses under his breath.

"Yikes. Okay, Cinder, message received." I loosen the collar around my neck. His anger raised the temperature a few degrees. I muster a genuine smile as I continue, "And thank you for everything. It really means more than you know, being with me to face the Chancellor."

"Don't mention it. I've known him for a long time. He doesn't scare me anymore." He throws me a slight wave as he starts down the stairs. I wonder what in life led to him growing up around the Chancellor. I do remember Kissa saying he's one of the few of us not raised by the Maidens.

"Thanks, gals, but I'm going to go to sleep. I'm exhausted," I say to Juniper and Fenwick, who are back to dancing.

They pause, frowning with puppy-dog eyes, as if their expressions can change my mind.

Fenwick sighs. "Aw, shucks. Well, we'll see you in the morning. Extra early to take you to the bathing chambers and then breakfast."

Juniper tsks her ashen finger at me. "Don't you dare think about leaving without us. If you wake up before us, we're just a knock away."

I nod, and we all head for our doors. I hear Juniper and Fenwick giggling about if they think I'll let them braid my hair up in flowers. I laugh, opening my door.

The powerful magic brushes over my skin as I walk through. The velvety shadows of Sølas' magic ignite the blaze in my veins. Another nick at the wound as my body betrays me.

I'm too exhausted to fight the ache for his dominating presence on top of me, his weight pressing in against my body. I wish there weren't emotions simmering below the surface for both us, that all this could just be fucked away and forgotten. Then I wouldn't have this gaping wound from him leaving me like he did. Too bad there's just enough light left in my soul that I couldn't kill him in the Combat Arena. Things would certainly be less messy. And I wouldn't be left with this icicle storm prickling my chest without an end in sight.

Thankfully, those thoughts are interrupted by Pip scurrying off my arm—going straight to the door, which is odd. He never asks me to go outside. I never even bothered to think about how he relieves himself before now, in fact. I pace to the door and tap on it twice as Cinder instructed, using my ring finger.

Before my eyes, the door becomes a see-through shadow, allowing me to make out a chaotic shape leaning against the wall. Sølas helped imbue the door, so there's no doubt he knows I can see him standing there. His raven hair has morphed into pure shadows above solid-white, moonlight eyes.

Shadows swirl like smoke through his rippled arms, crossed over his chest. What I thought were tattoos on his fingers now dance with the rest of the shadows beneath his skin.

Agony and longing etch his features as sticky pitch pools at his feet. I've never seen his shadows appear like tar; the eerie sludge raises my hackles.

His hands come up, covering his ears, pain contorting his face like he's fighting his own demons. After a few dragging moments, the pool of pitch melts away, exhaustion hanging heavy on his brows.

He looks so broken. So fragile. One of those broken bits slits it way right between one of my ribs, fracturing through my glacial walls, scraping along my pitiful, misshapen heart. Digging its way in, urging me to comfort him.

He did save my life. But he also managed to be an ass afterwards.

I hesitate. Should I open my door and ask if he's okay? He hasn't spoken to me in over a day, since Kissa caught him entrapping me in his shadows.

I do want to ask him about the new tattoo I saw on his neck earlier, but now it appears to be gone. Without thinking, my hand twists the door open.

"You should be sleeping." His smoky voice is right by my ear, although he's still leaning against the wall on the other side of the small hallway.

"You should also be sleeping," I parrot.

"The monsters in my head make it hard to sleep some nights." His voice fades, distant and gravelly. I look down, kicking the tip of my boot against the floor.

I understand those nightmares all too well.

"I have those monsters, too," I admit quietly.

He takes a large stride towards me, closing the gap between us. My body heats far too quickly in his closeness. I avoid peering up at his ice white eyes. They have a way of slicing right through me, plucking out the bits I try desperately to hide.

"Yet another thing we have in common." Again, his voice plays, whispering against my ear, but he hasn't moved any closer. Smoky shadows swirl around us both, towing an invisible line, as if he's holding them back from reaching out to me.

"I'm glad to see you're talking to me again. I was worried Kissa ripped out your vocal cords, finally." I smirk, still not daring to let his eyes whittle right through my walls. I enjoy watching the smoke move through his skin. The power beneath my own almost searching for his. Calling to me. Begging me to let go of my hold on my magic. Sølas is like the kindling, always igniting when he's near.

"I was talking to you today. *You* just weren't listening in the right way," he rumbles, as if disappointed in me for something I have no clue about.

*Rude.* I knew I should've stayed in my room and left him to fend against his own damn demons.

"Okay, whatever the fuck that means. I'm too tired to play these games with you," I snap.

"Then rest, *Luxsula*. I will keep watch," he whispers softly.

"I don't need you watching over me. I can feel the powerful magic you and Gearin have cast upon my door. I'm safe in there, at least," I retort.

I look up at him to find an arched eyebrow above arctic eyes storming with shadows. He stares *into me*, as if he's looking for something. Or perhaps waiting for something. The intimacy of his gaze settles into my bones, thawing their ice into a steady stream, trickling onto my heart like life can grow there.

I can't bear this silent heat he's melting me in, so I finally ask, "Why do you keep calling me that word I've never heard of? You know my name."

"Exactly. That's just it; everyone knows your name. This name is mine."

I've never been one to blush really, but I'm suddenly glad at the lack of blood circulating through my body. Hoping the heat in my currently pale cheeks cannot paint them in a rosy hue.

The way that word slips off his lips, I... I don't mind it. For some reason the thought tightens my chest, like something taking root, trying to grow along my disfigured heart. Maybe it's the exhaustion, or lack of blood, begging me to lie down.

"Are you going to stay out here all night?" I murmur.

"No. I always know where you are," he says smoothly, as he takes a step forward, leaving a whisper of space between us.

"Alright. That's not creepy or anything." I try to force a laugh, but my body has other priorities, craving to lean into him. But I am not going to fall for his lustful tricks again.

My mind wills my body, and I take a step back into my room, still facing him. There's a solemn sadness to his eyes as he melts away into the shadows of the hallway.

I close the door. Part of me is cursing him for the way he always slips away. The nipping sensation ripping open the wound of abandonment that has no right being there in the first place. I walk backwards, too drained to process anything about the mysterious male who continues to taunt me, wound me, in ways he shouldn't be able to. Yet I gave him the blade and showed him exactly where to pierce.

I fall onto my bed, wrapping the sheets around me tight, hoping they help hold me together as sleep claims my soul.

# CHAPTER 25

The next few weeks, my schedule is like clockwork with all of the escorts from my team. The only time I have to myself is in my bedroom. I'm not used to being so surrounded by Fae all the time. Every day, I get stronger until I'm finally back to myself, but my cohort refuse to break their schedule of chaperoning me.

They know Chet will make another move if given the opportunity before Celestial Bonding Day. And he won't make the same mistakes as last time.

Juniper and Fenwick hate me waking them up early in the morning for extra training and my morning jogs, so everyone takes turns now, waking up at the crack of dawn and waiting outside my door for the extra sessions.

I think the only one who ever arrives that early with a smile on their face is Flint. He enjoys the extra sparring practice, and so do I. He's insanely strong—and most days, impossible to beat—but occasionally, I get the upper hand on him. I also enjoy our silent jogs. I've slowly gotten to know him more on our cool-down walks afterwards.

"It's been weeks now; *please* tell me you have finally made a move on Rizz." I arch my brow at Flint, breathing hard next me after our run.

"I'll ma-ma-make a move when you admit you feel sa-sa-something for Sølas." A coy smile tugs at his lips.

I elbow him in the side, which only hurts my flesh against his marble skin. I look away, trying to hide my emotions. His stutter always gets worse anytime I bring up the pretty boy with pink hair, Rizz Pinkerton. In his quietness, he observes many things and has discovered teasing me about Sølas is the quickest way to get me to shut my mouth.

"You need to spa-speak with Winx. You can't avoid her forever."

I run my palm over my sweaty face. "I'm not sure I'm ready for her to burn down the entire campus."

"The conversation won't go well, but you're making it worse the longer you avoid it. Sha-she may love to light things on fire, but she has never burned anyone alive… No one that I know, anyway." He shifts uncomfortably at that, his words oddly chosen. The air becomes stiff between us. Winx is an unhinged firecracker, but surely she's never killed anyone? At least, not someone who didn't deserve it?

"You're not inspiring me into action with those last words, Flint." I wave goodbye as I hit the showers to wash off the unsettling thought.

Atlas arranges several sessions to examine Pip, the dragon fire marking on my leg, and the gold woven into my skin. He appears more and more frustrated after each session, unable to find anything in the archives that explains any of it. I try to pry information from him regarding his comment about the Wuvon female looking for someone, but he always concocts some riddled answer, like I should know what he's talking about.

I can't entirely avoid Winx, but I'm always able to come up with an excuse to stay out of her room. With our busy class schedule, she's often too exhausted to protest much.

Luckily, Gearin enjoys the heat of the forge, and he spends many nights with me there, teaching me more intricate runes to imbue magic on the weapons I create.

I've crafted several more dragon-fang-like daggers but with a flat, T-shaped hilt that wraps around my fingers. It's also known as a push or punch dagger. One that is held in between the fingers of a clenched fist, landing a punch with a hidden, deadly edge.

I imbue the blade with potent magic from a small creature made of stone. It lays stone eggs, and not all of them hatch. I bargained a nest I made out of metal, designed to keep predators away, for an infertile egg. I ground it up and refined the particles to work into the metal of the blade. This added ingredient turns your blood to sludge and, eventually, your body to stone, if you don't get the antidote. The poison is known as the Petrifying Kiss.

I work with Pip to practice him sheathing a similar type of blade without poison to ensure I don't kill myself or him during training. Over time, I'm able to get him to release the blade, sheathed underneath him shaped as my bracer, with the flick of my wrist in a particular way. I figure it's a good fail-safe to have in case Chet tries to sneak up on me again.

Sølas remains broody and distant. He comes to my door every night, standing guard for varying amounts of time, but I don't bother to open it. I need to stay focused. The Celestial Bonding event is in just two days' time. I still haven't figured out what my Celestial Gift is, which puts me at an insurmountable disadvantage for bonding. Surprisingly, no one has noticed. *Not sure what that says about the teaching staff here.* Sølas seems to have managed to at least keep that secret as promised. And I've discretely found ways to always be helping someone else when Professor Alaric walks by during our Combat Magic course in the Warded Hollow.

Most magical creatures can sense your Celestial Gift, as well as what kind of person you are. They want to bond with someone they can make stronger, whose magic can be enhanced by them and not get them killed in the midst of battle. So, it's not unheard of for an ensign who's marked as a potential Ellian Knight to complete the day of the Celestial Bonding without finding a creature to bond with.

Last year, this occurred to a male Yassur, who was reassigned to Scouting Rogue regiment. He was trained without a Wing until one lost their own scout in aerial training when he fell off his Pegasus in a particularly intense maneuver. I start to wonder where I will be reassigned if I fail. I hope it's to Ground-Combatant.

There's also the chance that you approach the wrong creature, and they eat you instead of bonding with you.

My heart aches at the thought of losing the team I have grown closer to in the last few weeks. I've even spent several nights having slumber parties with Juniper, Fenwick, Kissa, Vex, and Orion. I let Juniper braid my hair and grow numerous flowers through it, while Fenwick did my makeup and Orion dressed me up. I have to admit, Orion has a wicked sense of style. I even told them all I'd let them get me all done up for the Dawning Festival event after bonding my magical creature.

Kissa and I went for a few adventures out to the Mysticwoods south of campus. We raced one another through the branches, but with her feline grace, she always wins.

Tonight, we convinced some of the others to join us for a race.

"The course starts from this branch. Whoever makes it to the big tree ahead first wins. Ready? Set. Go!" I shout, leaping from limb to limb as Eko climbs straight up the tree we started at.

I'm swinging to the next limb while Highin flies past me and Eko is gliding down from above.

"Cheaters!" Kissa hisses between ragged breaths as she jumps to the next limb.

My feet slip on the knobby branch, my arms snapping up to grab on to another. I swing, perching on the next branch, looking up to see Sølas and Seraph waving at us from the big tree at the finish line as shadows fade away from them. Highin lands next to them, shortly followed by Eko.

Kissa and I let out a string of curses as we tie for last place.

Eko cackles wildly, and I can't help but join in, followed by Kissa and Seraph. Even Highin smiles and lets out a faint laugh. I tuck the sound of all our laughter somewhere safe, a precious memory. It's rare we all get to be happy and have fun with how intense our schedule is.

That night, the world doesn't seem so gloomy. The light parts left of my soul shine a little brighter, a little stronger. A sliver of happiness I grasp, nestling it like a treasure inside me. Happiness to have friends, ones I will spend the rest of military life with. I let the fear of failing to bond a magical creature slip away, instead focusing on the happy memories with my Zenith as I snuggle Pip tight and fall asleep.

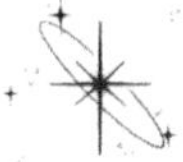

*A sea of bright stars glisten around me as I fly through the night sky. I am snatched from the beautiful sight. A shiver prickles down my spine.*

*The moon howls. Shadows slither around it, suffocating its light with a crimson eclipse. Screams echo all around me. My eyes well with tears as the stars dim and fade before me. An endless sea of black as stars weep from the sky, streaming down like crystal tears.*

*Their cries pour into my soul. Their heavenly forms shifting into beings of faded starlight, raining down all around me. The air grows thick with their wailing pleas for aid. I try to catch them, but their dimming light fades between my fingers as I beg them to tell me how to help.*

*Then my wings of pure energy flicker. Flickering again before dimming out completely. I'm in free fall, joining their tumbling fate to death. Agony pours from my lungs as my connection to magic rips away from my soul. The land below grows closer. Closer and closer. I welcome the sweet relief from the searing pain whittling my bones to ash.*

*An eerie darkness reaches to me from the skies, consuming all light around it, and suddenly, the ground below can't come fast enough.*

*I shift my gaze away. I am heading straight for the heart of the Blackwood. Either direction is a fate I don't want: a hungering darkness above and, below, a forest of monsters and Wuvon.*

*As I descend, someone in a small clearing takes shape. A tall slender figure, with long, metallic black hair, billowing on black mist that emanates off her feminine form. Her silver piercing eyes become solid crimson, drenched in a bloody night sky. She's gazing right at me, smiling with long white fangs.*

*Just before I hit the ground, I'm suddenly grasped between giant white claws that meet iridescent scales. It's an enormous dragon with four feathered wings, just like the one who flew above Estrella. Up close, I can see her large crescent-moon-shaped horns, almost kissing at the top, making an incomplete circle. Multiple spikes make up the crown framing her face. Lightning radiates all around us as we soar.*

*Her deep raspy voice booms in my head. "Not yet, Nebulight."*

The sound of the dragon's voice echoes in my head, awakening me from the dream. My heart thumps wildly against my chest, remembering the wicked, fanged smile on the mysterious female's face, deep within the Blackwood. She's stunning, with an ominous draw to her, an indescribable pull. As if, had the dragon not caught me, the female would have. Which is absolute madness, because I would have left an enormous crater in my wake falling at such a speed.

The beautiful, iridescent dragon was larger than any other I've ever seen fly over me in the sky. Her size would dwarf the more common breeds. Not that dragons are as common as they once were.

I peer at my Rune Tech alarm to see it's not set to go off for several more hours. I decide rather than trying to fall back to sleep, I'll rouse one of my neighbors to run off the adrenaline scorching through my veins. I think back to the rotation. I believe it's Juniper's turn. I appreciate that the friendliest of our team got stuck with rooms next to mine. They were likely just too nice to say no.

I get dressed quickly. Brushing my hair from the twisting and turning of the night. Pip has already jumped on my arm, ready for the day. I guess my bad dream woke him up too.

I open the door, and to my surprise, Sølas is leaning against the wall. I've never seen him stay this late, although I guess he may have just arrived. It's hard to tell with the heavy shadows that hang under his eyes. The look he is going for certainly doesn't shout *well-rested*.

His eyes widen, drinking up the surprise sight of me.

"Monsters keeping you up?" I whisper.

"They seem to have found their way into your head as well." His voice wraps around my body like smoke. I suck in my breath at the sensation.

"I was going to wake Juniper to train with me… I bet she'd be thankful if you took her place, since you're already awake?"

"Are you sure you can handle being that close to me? Lately, you seem to avoid my company," he quips.

*Quite strategically, in fact.* I needed some space to heal the wound he kept picking at.

"Psh, you are literally always around me, whether I like it or not. I, for one, have been focused and not giving in to the little mind games you love to play with me. So do you want to train or not?"

"Are you not at all concerned that you have not manifested your Celestial Gift? The bonding event is awfully close."

My eyes narrow on him, his ice blue gaze piercing deep into my chest. Sometimes, they're difficult to look at, as though the shadows swirling within might pluck me right off the ledge and I'll never stop falling. But with my blood brimming with adrenaline, I hold my stance and square my shoulders.

"It's been weeks since I let that slip to you. How are you so sure that's still the case?"

"I'm more than a Shadowmancer. I am the shadows themselves. They whisper to me. I see everything hidden beneath the umbra."

"Where was that ability when I was getting ganged up on by four males?" I mumble under my breath.

He clenches his jaw and then dips his head low in defeat.

"Maybe your shadows missed it. The Warded Hollow is well lit after all." I shrug.

"I've been watching you in Combat Magic. I've never once seen you use a magic that is unique to you."

"Well, maybe my magic is just being good at every kind of elemental magic." I huff, knowing even I don't believe the words I'm saying.

"You're wound up so tight, trying to control yourself rigid, rather than feeling any emotion. It's no wonder your Celestial Gift hasn't been able to break through. You keep yourself barricaded to the world. You're likely blocking out the very emotions that would let you wield your magic." He's now pacing before me. "I'm willing to bet that, on the first day of classes, when you were past your breaking point and finally lost some semblance of control, that's when your magic was released."

I don't do feeling. *Feeling is messy.* Feeling is what led me to being vulnerable with him in the first place. And a whole lot of good that did me!

I deflect with a scoffed lie. "Manipulation of objects is hardly a unique and powerful magic. We all have that ability. Plus, magic is not supposed to be tied solely to your emotions."

"It was something much more than manipulation magic or even telekinesis. I felt the waves of power cascading off you in the hallway earlier that day."

"Let me guess," I say, continuing sarcastically in air quotes, trying to mimic his smoky mysterious voice, "'*You have your theories*' on what my unique magic is?"

"First of all, my voice is much sexier than that. And of course I do. I've discussed them at length with Atlas. Not that you'll believe me, but he concurs."

"You're obnoxious, you know that? Why are you just now telling me this?"

"I told you. *You* just haven't been listening to me."

"Not this again. You have barely spoken a word to me in weeks. In fact, I take back my invitation to train with me. I'm going to get Juniper." I wave at him dismissively, heading for Juniper's door.

Then a whirling mass of shadows unfurls in front of me, revealing Sølas conveniently blocking my path as he leans his shoulder against the wall beside me.

"And ruin all my fun? Come on. I want to take you somewhere. An experiment much more important than sparring, which we already know you're deadly at."

"A fun experiment with you sounds like the very definition of a bad idea," I snarl.

"Live a little, Savaé," he purrs. The sound of my name on his lips whips another ray of light, sneaking through the glacial walls, right into my heart, shifting its shape a little, giving it life to beat a little more steady. My chest tightens, holding on to the morsel of light.

I close my eyes and sigh, wondering how that will come back to bite me later.

"Fine," I agree sourly and against my better judgement. But I know there's no way Juniper will wake up this early to go anywhere with me, so he's all I have to distract me from my nightmares. If there's some chance he's right, I guess my heart will be a worthy sacrifice to complete my dream of becoming an Ellian Knight.

I follow him out to the edge of the Mysticwoods. The cold winter air bites at my skin beneath my magical cloak, blending me into the shadows of the early morning before the sun has woken. The moon is almost full; we don't even need fire magic to light our way.

He moves with long, tall strides, one with the night. I can hardly keep up as he leaps amongst the shadows.

Suddenly, his hands are on my shoulders, bracing me to a halt. The warmth of his touch fans the embers, relighting them aflame. I try to push the feeling right out my favorite window.

"Stop." His words are a daring command.

"Stop what?" I enquire. I have indeed stopped moving.

"Stop pushing away your feelings."

"How do you know what I'm feeling? I don't feel your Persuasive powers at work."

"Celestials, you're terrible at listening, even when I use my words aloud. In the shadows of the night, I become the shadows. I open myself up to my feelings to sense everything around me. I can feel the shadows whispering to me, allowing me to sense things deeply, especially in the dark. Just as I can sense the creatures as they move in the woods, I can sense your feelings here, as you are drenched in the umbra of the forest. Or better yet, your *lack of feelings*. Shadowmancing is rare. You're the only one who knows I can do this, knows the secret of my Celestial Gift. My ability to sense people's emotions when enveloped in shadows. So, I've told you one of my secrets. Now, trust me. Close your eyes."

"This feels like a rather invasive experiment."

"Close your eyes, and stop talking." His glare deepens with shadows.

I suppose he did tell me a rather revealing secret. Perhaps I can let my guard down a little. Especially if he and Atlas are right about my powers. Although I don't like the idea of his shadows whispering nothings about me alone in my bedroom. I guess I'll be sleeping with the lights on from now on.

He continues to glare at me, tilting his head slightly with a curve to the corner of his lips. Challenging me with his request.

"Fine." I huff and obey, closing my eyes. I shift uneasily as the golden light wall of my mental shields falls.

I let the feeling of his touch sink in instead of rolling it off. Indulging the feeling effortlessly sends my pulse skittering as his muscular, tattooed hands grasp my shoulders tighter. His thumbs skim down my arms, finding their target of bare skin beneath my cloak. His index fingers gently shifting in small rhythmic circles. The touch is so faint, I can hardly feel it, leaving me craving more.

"Stay focused only on what you are feeling right now," he whispers.

I squint one eye open to see a smug half-smile on his face, but his eyes are shut. Mine flutter shut again. I soak in the rhythmic circles on my skin, the warmth of his body close to mine.

I can hear the rustling of the forest, the sound waves bouncing about the trees. The sun's photons springing off the moon, lighting it up in the night sky. I sense the moisture in the air as the molecules kiss all around us, turning into early morning fog. I enjoy the pull of the polar bonds of the water molecules as they dance in the air, lacing around my fingers, responding to my movement.

"*Good.* Now try to feel the molecules heating up." He almost hums the words.

I don't bother asking again how he can practically read my thoughts. I'm sure I'll get another Ritherin-shit excuse about the whispering shadows. Maybe he's just sensing the environment alongside me. I guess I don't really know the extent of his shadow magic.

I get back to the task of feeling the water molecules around me. I take advantage of the heat he ignites beneath my skin, letting it reach out, warming the air around us as it crashes with the cooler air. The collision of opposite temperatures transforms the invisible gas into tiny water droplets in the air. I control the new molecules, not letting them cluster into clotted droplets of rain. My lashes flutter open to reveal mist swirling around us, waltzing to my desire as I move my fingers.

"See? You do have a Celestial Gift." He looks down at me with a devilishly handsome smile on those full lips, making my chest tight. "Now let's see if we can push you further."

"But this magic makes me a Stormcaller. Isn't that strong enough?" I petition. My gaze meets his deepening leer. He's peeling away all my layers, all the walls I have worked so hard to build, uncovering my tattered soul.

"Trust me." He smirks with smoldering blue embers peering down at me.

*Easy for you to say.*

"That is asking a great deal from me," I plead, eyes wide.

My chest creaks under the vice of his request. Trust doesn't come easily to me. It makes you vulnerable, and I have enough of that to deal with around him as it is. I trust him to have my back in battle, but this moment is already too intimate, too raw. Too close to these pesky emotions that make everything far too muddled.

Then I remember the terror drenching his eyes the night he ran with me dying in his arms. There's something more to him, a tether beneath my attraction to his divinely carved beauty. It calls to me, imploring me to throw caution to the wind and give in to all of him.

Yet the one time I did exactly that, he fucking left me. Sure, I wasn't in any shape to be wildly ravaged by him, but it somehow hurt deeper than expected. Now I'm leery of letting him close again. That wound is still healing, can't have it ripped wide open again.

He leans his head down to meet mine. My breath freezes in my chest as he wraps his large hand around the side of my neck, the pad of his thumb braced beneath my jaw. He gently tilts my head, iridescent hair cascading back like tumbling starlight. Then moving to my exposed ear, his lips grazing my skin as he whispers.

"Trust me."

With my shields down, his commanding grasp tugs the invisible tether taut between us. As if, somehow, my foolish heart already implicitly trusts him, strung up in all this golden light he's weaving through it.

Rather than focus on pushing him away, I decide to play along for the time being. Closing my eyes once more, and letting myself feel *everything*.

The electricity of his breath on my neck, eddying waves of power simmering beneath my skin. Instead of fighting to bottle them up, I let them crash into me, galvanizing me. They roar through my veins, clawing to be released.

I stumble a step back from him, fearing I'll hurt him. It'd be a shame to kill him accidentally after committing not to.

He steps towards me, wrapping his strong arms around my waist. His embrace overwhelms me. Power cascades off him, a rushing waterfall I'm struggling not to drown in. Velvet ribbons of shade reach out, far beyond my vision, shielding us in his shadows. The scent of amber and spruce filling my gasping lungs.

My magic pours out, trying to intertwine with his. The lightest touch of my power against his melts me from the inside out. I wobble in the heady sensation. This is way more intense than I've come to expect being close to him. I'm going under, forgetting how to swim. How to breathe.

He uses his shadows, pulling me back closer to him. Then the wall of smoke retreats, expanding outwards all around us.

"You won't hurt me. Not like this. Not with your magic. Now, I want you to focus on that rock." He nods to a boulder to our right.

I'm not going to lie that I'm slightly disappointed that his sentence began with *I want you* and then ended talking about a cursed rock.

"Focus on its structure, and concentrate on unraveling the bonds."

I should probably ask him what he meant about my magic not being able to hurt him, but his eyes suddenly turn solid white again, glowing like the full moon. I follow his gaze to a large boulder that's now in his Shadowveil alongside us.

I sigh, shifting my focus, peering deep within the rock, envisioning the crystalline matrixes bracing its structure. Then I visualize a beam of pure energy coming out of my lifted hand, tearing through the bonds. The boulder begins to fracture before my eyes, its splintering cry tearing through the silent night.

Sølas squeezes me tighter, lowering his head more, breathing heavily along my neck, his lips grazing my skin, teasing, torturing me with temptation.

My craving for him becomes crushing. Overpowering.

*And I let go.* I arch my body into his, savoring the swell of his endowed length against my lower abdomen.

He responds in kind by releasing a guttural growl against my neck. The sound of his pleasure unshackles an untamed wildness deep within me.

Any semblance of control unravels along with me.

I wrap my arm around his neck, running my hand through his hair as I pull his head back, biting his exposed nape, rabid in my hunger for him. His body rocks against mine, hard, as I gasp for air. I cling to him as his power consumes me, touching me everywhere, all at once. The otherworldly pull of our connection, a force all its own.

I shatter.

And the world along with me.

Explosions bursting all around us.

I immediately jump back, unsheathing the two short swords from my back, ready to fight as the shadows retreat. My eyes dart all around, waiting for something to move.

But all I hear is a warm laughter filling the air. A genuine laugh. One that cracks my ribs open, like my heart recognizes the sound that can wake my soul. One that I want to bottle up and swallow like a cognac on a cool winter night, satiating my very being. I've never heard such a laugh from Sølas.

I look at him with his head dipped back, raven waves twirling from his face, revealing a pure smile of amusement. The sound of his happiness flutters in my chest. Golden light slings through my ribs, curling around my heart, as if they can mend all the misshaped parts.

Until I realize I have no clue what he's laughing about. There's nothing worse than being left out of a joke. He finally composes himself, tucking strands of hair behind my ear.

"I do enjoy being right, *Luxsula*," he purrs.

There's that fucking word again, but the way he says it with heated eyes pries my ribs open further as more rays of light flood me. I sling him an unamused glare, ignoring the muddling mess of light in my chest.

He steps back, waving his arm in a long arch in front of his hips as if he's presenting me with a grand dinner spread.

I take another step back, truly taking in my surroundings. The boulder is shattered into a million pebbles. But it's not the only one. We are left in the bottom of a crater with thousands of tiny rocks strewn about. My mouth falls open, fully appreciating the havoc my magic wrought. Thank the Celestials the protection of his shadows held against the wreckage around us.

His presence is suddenly behind me.

"Chaos Magic," he susurrates along my bare collar as he sweeps my hair away.

"Chaos Magic?" I'm awestruck and don't have the slightest idea what he's talking about.

"It's why you have so much trouble accessing it. You thrive on being in control of yourself. You hate to feel your emotions. With magic, there is always a balance. It makes sense someone who loathes chaos would be granted the power to wield it."

"I've never once heard of 'Chaos Magic.' You're just making shit up now."

"It hasn't been seen as a gift since before the Celestial Dimming. That's why you've never heard of it. But I sensed the wild, untamed disorder radiating off you that first day of classes, in the hallway when you threatened to burn me like a moth. Chaos thrives in the shadows. Atlas theorizes this is why I could sense it. We found an ancient carved stone that was hard to translate, but it briefly mentions the might of chaos wielders in the Celestials' fight against the darkness. The inscription was on a tablet from Emberhell. Atlas wasn't sure of the translation, but it said something about how only a being of demonic blood could wield it. Clearly, he got that part wrong. Look at you!"

"Are you telling me you just held me like that as part of an experiment to get me to unleash my magic?" My fists curl, nails digging in, slashing crimson from my palms and slitting wide the wound from him I worked so hard to heal.

I want to rip out the stringy golden mess he's made of my heart, chuck it right in his face. He can fucking have it; it's no use to me anymore. Leading me right into his manipulative snare, snagging my feet right out from underneath me. How many times is it going to take me to learn this lesson?

Grey clouds tumble in, blotting out the moon, rumbling with the fury building in my chest. Lightning flickers in the distance as shards of ice pelt from the sky, nipping at my skin in futile attempts to cool my boiling blood in his silence.

This is the second time he's pulled me in with the energy between us just to get what he wants.

He asked me to fucking trust him, and I did. How fucking foolish. Lightning cracks outside the crater, splintering my soul into another fragment, blinded by pain that whips in the blizzard's building wrath.

I manage the strength to finally walk away, and then I'm enveloped in black velvet smoke. There's only darkness around me. Until I see him stepping out from the shadows, prowling towards me. I want to eviscerate him.

His shadowy figure reaches out to me, cupping my face in his hand. Thunder roars along my bones at how safe his touch feels. I hate myself for letting his touch soothe me in a way I can't even begin to comprehend. He may have saved my life, sitting guard over my unconscious body, but none of this makes sense, not after he continues to manipulate me. His touch should bring me pain, not comfort.

He wraps his other arm around my waist, pulling me tight, all my sharp edges going blunt in my feeble efforts to push him away.

Silver tears pool in my eyes. How can I continue to let him touch me after what he did, yet again? Perhaps now I'm the tragic, fragile moth, attracted to the heat of his body's embrace. A fire that will surely end me, but I fly towards it nonetheless.

"I'm sorry. I never wanted you to feel the pain you are feeling. You can trust me. But I will not take what is not mine." He pauses, as if searching for the right words. "I shouldn't have used what we share between us to bring out your power."

With my hands still braced against his firm chest, I dare to look up at him. He gazes into my soul, considering me, like I'm simply the most astonishing being he has ever encountered. I falter in his embrace, but I steady myself for the answers I seek.

"Then why did you?"

"It was selfish of me. I never meant to take it that far. I promise my initial intentions were… well-mannered. I was only going to use the faintest touch to bring out your magic, to help you lose control just a little. Time is running out before the Celestial Bonding; you needed to release your magic. I didn't mean to lose control in the process. But… watching you reborn into the fury of your powers is a marvel unlike any other. I became intoxicated by you, *Luxsula.* I couldn't help myself."

"You keep pulling me into your snare, only to release me. Eventually, I will stop falling for your traps," I whisper as warm tears slash my face.

He wraps his shadows around me, keeping me close. His hands free to clutch my face as his thumbs wipe my tears away.

His eyes pour into mine, unwavering, as if he holds my very soul in his palms. "I only wish to trap you for good. For once I have you, I will never let you go. You will be mine for eternity. Not even the Celestials themselves will pry you from my being. I refuse to take only part of you, if I cannot have all of you."

His words are a blow to the head as all the pieces click into place. Too messy, too tender, too raw, *too real.*

The reason my sharp words seem to wound him more than she should.

*One of the golden light strings slung around my heart freezes.*

The reason for his terror when he held me dying in his arms.

*The frost spreads, creeping along another golden thread.*

The reason he kept pulling away from me.

*Black ice races along the remaining golden strings, spreading like wildfire.*

His distance after, knowing I didn't feel the same for him.

The frozen golden threads of light around my heart quiver in an ache to give in to what he wants while my mind buckles, knowing I wasn't made for such things.

Sully's warped words from the Ethereal Maze of Whispers echo along the broken pieces of my soul like shrapnel. The strings shatter, climbing up my ribs in jagged ice, a glacial palace of frozen thorns.

*You can never love or be loved. You beckon darkness to consume every-thing you hold dear.* Fear coats everything in black frost.

I'm too terrified to find out if those words are true. A risk I'm not willing to take, because if they are, the Fates will finally break me beyond repair. As strong as I am, to give myself completely will take a strength I do not know. How can someone who knows so little of love even begin to know how to give it to someone else?

The invisible tether between us loosens with my thoughts.

I peer up into his longing eyes. The crimson shimmers like his bleeding heart against the snowy background, consumed by a shadowy eclipse.

"I am sorry." I exhale as my words push into his heart like my icepick dagger, agony washing over his face. Perhaps my real blade would have been a less cruel fate.

"I know," he replies as he lets me go, and the shadows return to their host. Head bowed with the heaviness of his heart, he turns to face the build-ings and holds out his hand.

"Come, *Luxsula.* Let me walk you to your room. It's the least I can do. And please, don't argue with me. I don't have the strength for it. Give me this final gift." Melancholy laces his every word.

I want to scream at myself for not being able to even try to give him what he wants. But I know I can't.

Despite me stepping towards him, the distance grows between us. I grasp his hand tight, wishing I could be what he desires. Someone who understands emotional attachments, who can even dream of what love might be like.

His shadows creep out before us, taking the shape of a staircase, allowing us to walk out of the cavity I have created. The sky is still stormy, but it's too cold now, even for snow.

As we step onto level ground, I know this is not the only crater I leave in my wake tonight.

# CHAPTER 26

Sølas returns me to my room in silence. As I open the door to my room, I turn around to say goodnight, but he's already gone.

My heart slams against black ice, shredding herself in the glacial thorns of her new cage, pleading with me to change my mind, to run back to him. To take a chance, throwing caution to wind, giving in to my feelings and exploring what we could be.

I shut the door, gently resting my forehead and my palms against it, wishing he was still on the other side, like every other night. Wishing I could step out and say I will try…for him. Giving my fear a middle finger and letting myself dream of something more for myself.

But I'm no dreamer. I know better than happy endings for myself. Perhaps that's exactly why I'm unable to escape those haunting words from the Ethereal Maze of Whispers.

When you spend every day of your life surviving, you forget how to dream, how to hope, how to find the light in the darkness.

In all honesty, even if I did want to try, I wouldn't even know where to begin. This isn't like all the other skills I've honed my body to know with diligent practice. What he's asking of me is uncharted territory. The thought of giving my heart to him consumes me with more fear than any monster ever could. Things are simple with monsters: I either live or die.

But with him, it would be pure chaos of the unknown, of emotions, of vulnerability. Celestials, what we already share is overwhelming enough; I can't imagine letting it grow into something precious. The potential loss is too great a risk, especially with the life we've set out to live.

It's tragic that I'd rather walk hand in hand with death herself than give myself completely to him. I know, deep down, that life has broken me beyond what anyone's love can ever heal. Beyond what I could ever curse someone to try to love.

I fall onto my bed, mapping the purple veining of the Mysticwood walls with my finger. It's for the best that I don't even try to give him what he's asking for. At least, that's what I manage to convince myself. I need to stay focused on things I can actually achieve, like becoming an Ellian Knight. I'm so close I can taste it, especially now that my Celestial Gift is fully manifested.

My golden mental shields rise, appearing slightly dimmer tonight. I turn off my emotions, shutting the mosaic window so hard it cracks, dissociating from all that has happened in the last few hours.

An icy calm freezing around my bleeding heart, silencing her pleas. I start to drift off to sleep's embrace.

*Knock. Knock.*

I jolt up, wiping my weary eyes from the fading lull of just falling to sleep.

*Knock. Knock. Knock.*

I stumble to answer the door, realizing I haven't even taken off my cloak.

"Ready for a morning jog and some combat practice? I learned a new move you're sha-surely going to enjoy!" Flint's emerald green irises beam with enthusiasm.

"Of course I am. Today is the last day we have before the Celestial Bonding." A familiar mask drapes over my face, pulling my lips up in a weary smile, casting the real me in shadows too dark to see through.

"I have no doubt that the strongest creature will bond you. My coin is on a dragon." He tosses me a big reassuring smile.

I elbow him in the side. "I hope you didn't place too much silver on that bet. Even if I don't bond, at least I'll be joining you as Ground-Combatant."

"Don't sa-say that. Zenith Wing can't lose you. Plus, it ruins the fun if I get to kick your ass every day during Ground-Combatant training classes."

"Rude!" I scowl before we both break out into laughter. We walk down the spiral steps out into the courtyard for our warm-up jog before going down to the Combat Arena for sparring. I make it back just in time to shower before I race to the Grand Conservatory with Juniper and Fenwick. They swirl with so much light and happiness, I wish I could soak it up into my soul, but I know that's not what's waiting for me outside the mosaic window in my mind. I can feel Pip's stomach growling along my arm. We grab our breakfast to go with some extra for him as we meet up with the rest of our Zenith.

Before our first class starts, Orion's candy-red eyes keep darting between me and Sølas.

He's against the wall talking with Seraph, his back towards me. He turns to head to class and won't even look at me. I don't blame him. If the roles were reversed, I wouldn't want to look at him either. I honestly don't even know how he has the strength to be in the same room as me.

Our normal afternoon division classes were switched to the morning today to allow an extended session of Combat Magic this afternoon.

Professor Yuri Smeltfire steps out onto the dais of the small circular room as rays of colorful light dapple the room from the stained-glass windows. Today, his chestnut brown hair is tied back into a neat bun at his nape. He adjusts his spectacles as he begins.

"Welcome to your last class of Magical Creatures of the Realm as it's now focused on beasts you have the potential to bond with. After the Celestial Bonding, we will change our focus to different animals with different magical properties that, with their consent, can be used to enhance certain magical properties for battle. Our last class today will focus on reading the signs of different animals that you might approach tomorrow."

Kissa lowers her head down to me and whispers, "I bet Cinder will find a creature brooding up against a hill somewhere. *It'll be love at first sight.*"

I feign a snicker, the response she'll be expecting. I wonder what fierce creature will seek Kissa out with her ability to Beastshift.

"Remember: listen to your gut. Be open to their connection. The right one will sing to you like a siren song, leading you to it. I warn against approaching animals you feel no connection to. Trying to force a link will lead to a fate worse than being unbonded. Also, it's highly recommended not to fight among yourselves during the event. The temperamental creatures will not waste their time on the squabbles of Cascarans fighting one another. They're sacrificing themselves to help our warriors for the good of the realm. Do not squander their time."

It's more than just the good of the realm. The largest grove of Mysticwoods is south of campus. It's where most creatures go for their young to be born. The sacred nesting grounds. It's at the farthest point away from any snaking paths of Blackwood expansion. We have an entire command of Wings stationed at campus, plus a slew of infantry to protect everyone here and the Mysticwoods besides us. If attacked, our priorities are to get the Faelings out and protect the sacred grove of Mysticwoods at all costs.

There's a question burning like molten ore on the back of my tongue. I want to know about the dragon from my dream, the one I saw fly over Estrella when I was young. We've never covered it in our class about the different breeds of dragons. I assume because they're not known to have ever taken a rider. Maybe I'm a fool to ask, but curiosity claws the question from my maw.

"Professor Smeltfire, have you ever seen a white dragon with four feathered wings that seems to be attracted to lightning?"

"Please call me Professor Yuri. A rare creature indeed!" He presses a finger covered in Runic Tech to his head, and the metal box at the center of the room depicts an illusion of the dragon from my dreams, but slightly different than I remember it.

"Moonstorm dragons are an extremely rare form of Lunaria dragons, believed to be hatched from the chaos of moonbeams trapped in the lightning of full-moon storms. They have the unique ability to wield blue fire and lightning from their mouths. Their scales are actually translucent and can blend into the colors surrounding them. Their nests are believed to rest in the clouds themselves. There are very few in existence today, if any at all. Their blood is ancient and said to be born from the Celestial Dragon's tears as they wept lying down for the infinite slumber at the loss of their Celestial rider. They bear a unique biologic metal along their back ridges that allows them to conduct lightning, storing its energy for later use. Over time, the tips of their wings evolved feathers to sustain longer flight and faster speeds. Ensign Savaé, you hail from the remote village of Estrella, correct?"

"Correct." I nod. Does he know where all his students come from?

"You are likely one of the few of us to have ever had a chance to see one. The steep cliffs of Eldoria, the tallest peaks in Cascara, are rumored to be their breeding ground. Alas, this species of dragon has never shown for a Celestial Bonding event; it's only been known to eat any who approach it. They are very aloof creatures, thankfully. Some ancient texts said they have the ability to shoot spikes of ice from their tails. I pray to the Celestials none of you ever find out if that's true."

He continues on about several other dragons, including a Mountain Laurel Draco, with its green body and poisonous vines that whip out from its legs. It has a frill that, when agitated, forms deadly flower petals around its neck. The end of its tail is covered in small jimson weed pods, which can induce you with the intoxication of belladonna, causing temporary loss of vision.

He elaborates on several other flower Dracos with far less menacing descriptions; one even has wings that look like rose petals melded together. He finishes with discussing a Sunkissed Draco, a creature with heavy, armored spikes across its chest and a tail shaped into a circular metal shield. It has eight pointed horns, giving its face a star shape. It's golden like the sun, occasionally seen basking near the cascades of the Dragon Spine Mountains. I find myself wishing everyone in our Zenith got the chance for a Celestial Bonding. The Sunkissed Draco seems like the perfect fit for Fenwick and her light magic.

Then there are the different breeds of phoenixes, covering their unique colors: carmine red, burnt orange, amber, boric green, violet, lilac, white, and even black.

Next, he reviews the species of Chimera, creatures with the head of a lion but with horns and dragon-like wings, some of which even breathe fire. Their skin is a mix of scales and fur. Some have jagged, sharp spikes that jut off their legs, while others appear to blend in to the natural foliage around them, growing leaf-like objects off their body.

The creatures less likely to show up for the Celestial Bonding Day are covered more quickly to leave time to get to know the more likely candidates.

Lastly, we review other types of flying mammals, like the Orcalia, which has the body of a killer whale but giant fin-like wings covered in feathers. It's believed they can wield ice magic. Or the Alpe, a species of flying wolf, typically with the silent wings of an owl, though some are graced with dragon wings.

The chimes come and go.

I wait for Sølas at the top of the stairs to escort me to lunch, which is the typical schedule. I'd felt his presence behind me in class, but now he's nowhere to be found. A finger taps me on my shoulder; I spin to meet

Cinder's amber eyes as he brushes his unkempt bright orange hair back with his other hand.

"Sølas has somewhere he has to be during lunch and dinner. He asked me to take over his escort for the rest of the day."

"Did he say where?"

"He's being even more cryptic than me with his answers today. I didn't bother pressing him on the issue. The guy needs some sleep. He's more grumpy and broody than usual. He's kinda stealing my vibe," Cinder gripes.

Black, tarry regret slowly seeps out of the box I try to hide the stirring emotions in. I quickly envision another box around it, chucking it out the mosaic window, leaving things tidy and under control. It's for the better we have some space after everything that happened this morning.

We all eat lunch together, minus Sølas. Seraph seems to be in a mood as well; she isn't her typical boisterous self. I catch her leaving halfway through the meal.

Orion's suspicion only grows, as if she can see my Aura frozen over in ice.

I watch Fenwick tease Juniper animatedly about which magical creature she will bond. "Maybe you'll bond a gross worm, or even worse, a giant flying spider!" Fenwick teases.

"Praise the Celestials, no flying spiders exist." I sigh in relief. I loathe spiders.

"I like spiders. Their silk is so beautiful and strong. It kind of looks like your hair, Savaé."

I cringe, gagging on my drink at the thought of my hair feeling like sticky spider webs on my flesh.

Kissa looks less than amused with our conversation.

"I am pleased to announce, mine and Sølas' hypothesis was correct, and Savaé has manifested Chaos Magic as her Celestial Gift. It is uniquely tied to her emotions, rather than how we conjure: picturing in our minds and moving our hands to release our power."

"And what exactly is Chaos Magic? Atlas… are you just making shit up because you've run out of things to read in the archives?" Eko quips.

"Entropy, otherwise known as chaos, is the natural disorder of the universe. The degradation of matter and energy, the change of state from ordered to turmoil." Gearin twirls the side of his mustache beneath his golden spectacles, his biomechanical jaw glinting in the sunlight.

Kissa spits out her drink at his statement. "You're telling me that the most tightly wound one of us here gets the magical ability to create disorder? And this emotionless ice queen has to use her emotions to cast? We're going to be totally fucked on the battlefield. The Fates must be laughing themselves into tears with this one." She cackles at her own remark.

*Bitch.* I shoot her a dagger-like scowl. "Yeah, yeah, real funny," I disparage with a flat tone, wishing I could slink away from this conversation. I barely understand my magic myself.

"There's always a balance to magic." A small twist kicks up at the side of Kivi's mouth as she continues humming.

"She should also be able to wield hot and cold, transferring them to create an equilibrium, without the use of fire or ice magic." Atlas' eyes crinkle with amusement, likely planning his next manuscript.

"That's *skraith.* Savaé, why do you always have to be an oddling? I'm glad I got magic that makes more sense." Vex sighs as she twirls her red finger through one of her black ringlets.

"*Oh yeah*, because being able to fast-forward and rewind time three seconds is so simple and straightforward, Vex?" mocks Eko.

"It is to me!" She lets out a *humph,* crossing her arms.

"I'm the oddling? When you're using words like 'skraith'? What in the stars above does that even fucking mean?"

"Maybe if you didn't go around snarling at everyone but us you'd know." Vex rolls her eyes.

Flint whispers to me, "It means not normal. Winx and all her friends from Riicah use it." I give him a small smile in thanks for not making me feel any more like an oddling.

"I think it's neat, Savaé. We'll make a nasty combo together. If I remember from physics correctly, you should even be able to manipulate the plasma I can wield." Fenwick beams. I can't believe she has the same Celestial Gift as Raeya. She only ever practices with her light magic.

"Now *that* I would pay to see," Cinder says as a smirk curls on his lips.

"It hasn't been wielded since before the Celestial Dimming, so we will become enlightened together." Curiosity blazes across Atlas' face. Ugh. He's *definitely* planning to write his next textbook about me.

"I can't wait for you to *enlighten* me during combat magic," Kissa teases. "C'mon, it's time to head to the Warded Hollow. All hail the wild Chaos Magic of Savaé Entropaé." Kissa's practically drowning me in her sarcasm.

"Laying it on a little thick, aren't we?" I roll my eyes at her.

"Just how I like my males." Kissa winks as she darts in front of me to the door of the Grand Conservatory.

"Well, that was an overshare." I laugh.

I hear a wild cackling behind me. It's Eko. He's laughing so hard, he can barely walk. "Entropaé has *entropy* magic." He gasps for air in between fits of laughter.

"I don't get why you find it funny. It's quite convenient to have one's last name match their Celestial Gift. Imagine how organized things would be if we were all born knowing our gift." Gearin taps his mouth in contemplation, Eko's sarcasm flying right over his head.

Orion drags her hand down her face at Gearin's comment before placing it on her hip. "Eko has a point. Does seem a little too on the nose to be the work of the Fates. Although requiring her magic to be powered by emotions when Savaé would rather cut off her own hand than feel anything… Definitely the Fates laughing their asses off."

"Glad I can finally make everyone laugh." I huff.

Flint walks to my side and adds, "It's unique, just like you." He is simply the sweetest.

I muster a smile. "Glad I know I always have you on my side."

Highin joins us. "I concur with Flint. Don't let the racket of the others get to you."

"Or maybe you should. I am pretty sure anger is the only emotion I've seen on you," Eko jabs as he catches up to us, still wiping the tears of laughter from his eyes.

"Don't antagonize her, Eko. She can use her magic to literally rip you apart, bond by bond," Gearin deadpans.

I level a crippling glare at Eko.

He adjusts the collar of his battle leathers. "Well, when you say it like that, it definitely loses its humor. I rather like all my parts bonded the way they are."

Now I'm the one laughing as we make it outside. We head to the gardens of the central courtyard. The site of the Warded Hollow still takes my breath away. The golden orb structure is covered in guilloché golden enamel, laced with intricate platinum runes. My skin buzzes with the power radiating from it. There's an oval-shaped door carved into a hollowed-out space along the side.

As I step through, the potent spellwork tickles my senses. The unique magic here can simulate reappearing practice dummies that move all about, target ranges, illusionary combatants, and battle scenarios. The inside is exponentially larger than the outside, changing the illusionary environment depending on what's required for practice. For marksmanship, it creates long distances with moving targets and distractions. It even can recreate the Blackwood, Wuvon, their monsters, and all. It allows us to hone all our magical skills in an illusionary environment before we face any real threats. It's also warded, so if we lose control, we won't kill each other.

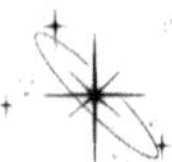

Professor Alaric Teak is required elsewhere today, so his understudy is filling in. Assistant Professor Layla Emberleaf marches to the center of the room. She is an Arabellian with short white hair and snow-white skin.

"Today's agenda entails honing your Celestial Gifts in a scenario that includes moving enemies and flying friendlies. The goal is to practice control, not missing an enemy target as the friendlies—representing your teammates—fly around them. Combat is layered; missing your mark means you can end up hitting your partner as they fly, moving behind or in front of your target. That's why understanding the physics of battle is so important, being able to predict different trajectories in space and time. Let's see how well you paid attention to Professor Reginald Hadron."

A shudder teeters through my body at the thought of controlling my Chaos Magic in a literally chaotic environment. Professor Alaric's attention was always all over the place, no doubt how I'd gotten away unnoticed only using my elemental magic. But Professor Layla Emberleaf is eyeing us down like she's part Aetherhawk.

At least this building is warded, so if I lose complete control, I'll be surrounded in a pink bubble of magic that shields everyone from me and dampens my magic. I swear, one session, Winx appeared to almost turn into a phoenix when she lost control. It was beautiful and terrifying as she levitated above us, radiating flaming wings. Her connection to fire magic is unrivaled and suits her personality perfectly.

We've already done many sessions on training with weapons and combat magic at close and far distances. Today's lesson is about taking it up a notch by adding targets we *shouldn't* hit. The design of this initial lesson is a bit easier, with our enemies being marked red and our teammates blue. On top of that, our Chivalry will be casting from the ground, rather than in our typical aerial position. I guess they don't want any of us injured before we actually attempt to take flight tomorrow for the first time during the Celestial Bonding event.

I would much prefer using weapons or practicing magic that comes to me more easily than my Celestial Gift, but I know my entire Zenith is waiting for me to show off my new ability. Thankfully, I won't be able to kill anyone here while I explore a magic literally only meant for destruction. After hearing Gearin's definition of chaos, it's a miracle I didn't kill Sølas and myself earlier today. I still can't believe that was less than twelve hours ago. The new distance between us makes it feel like a lifetime has passed.

Cinder is lucky that his unique power is heat vision so he doesn't have to create a spectacle, but he's paired next to Fenwick. Which makes sense; her plasma and light magic make it difficult to use his vision without being blinded, so they need to be totally in sync.

I stand there, unable to do anything as I watch Juniper control the environment around her targets. Quickly shredding enemies with spiked vines while raising the illusionary soil to form a wall, protecting her allies from injury. She makes the horrors of battle look like an artistic dance, completely in tune with nature and waging war.

Next to her, Kissa shifts into multiple different animals, slaughtering her victims without a single scratch on the blue dummies that twist and turn around her every move.

I try to focus on just one target. I picture my arm becoming a sword of pure energy again… but nothing happens. I grow frustrated, thinking of how Sølas confirmed last night that I have to let go of control and feel the chaos of emotion and my environment to use my magic.

I know if I switch back on my emotions, everything that happened last night will come avalanching back. It's not that I *can't* feel emotions at all; they're just severely blunted, making them easier to control. Raw emotions are just too overwhelming. Yet I know I need to get it over with to access my magic.

I retreat to the golden domed shields of my mind. I swallow at the cracked mosaic window, with far too many emotions lurking behind it. *Definitely not opening that nightmare.*

Maybe I can slowly organize my emotions, controlling which one and how much I feel? I imagine piercing a tiny needle through my shield. A small ribbon slowly trickles in through the hole, the color of amaranth.

I reach out to it, letting it curl between my fingers, heating my skin. It's my feelings of lust. I envision a small upside-down, heart-shaped window with a golden latch, letting me close away the emotion.

I prick another place in the wall of golden light. A honey-colored ribbon twists around my hand; it's warmth and happiness. Memories flash into sight: carefree days with Sully exploring the Mysticwoods, hearing my Zenith laughing together at lunch and racing through branches with Kissa. Then the sound of Sølas' laugh before dawn echoes through me, sneaking through the ice, tightening my chest as flutters fill my stomach. I let go of the honey ribbon, envisioning a circular window, yellow like sunshine around it, closing its latch.

The next slash brings watery, dark blue ribbons cascading in. I bend down, letting my fingers graze over the puddle that forms. Sorrow and misery ripple through me. The loss of the parents I never knew. The shame of failing to heal Sully. I'm overcome with the regret of not being able to even try to give Sølas what he wants from me. I slam shut the teardrop window that forms over the hole.

Bright red ribbons whip out of the next rift I open. Anger courses through me as I remember what Chet and his groupies did to me that night. Followed by the unrelenting torture of my foster father's blade carving into my skin. Then the hideous remarks fill my mind, the voices of the townsfolk of my village when they caught a glimpse of my golden markings. I envision a window shaped like a flame. I don't close this one.

Out of nowhere, a large starburst-shaped window appears next to me. I can see the outside world around me through it. I open it wide. Innumerable energies channel through me, becoming acutely aware of every molecule around me. I focus on the structured red shape in front of me, its plea to be broken free of its bonds. The physical world's craving for disorder. I grasp the red ribbon of fury, letting it boil my blood.

I can hear the screeching of broken, frozen bones, the pain of my burning, frostbitten toes. I let my anger radiate out of me, hitting the first red target in front of me, splintering it apart, then the next one, and the next, and the next.

I become lost in my rage until *crash*, my knees smashing the ground. In my mind, I run to the flaming window, locking it shut. Next, staggering to the starburst window, falling against its panels as I seal its center clasp.

I peel my eyes open, and the room is utterly silent.

There are no targets left.

Just a slurry of splintered particles hovering in the air. I breathe, sweeping numbness over me like an arctic breeze. The broken fragments clattering to the ground.

Slowly, I look around, clenching my jaw to keep it from gaping. I not only decimated my own targets, but everyone else's as well. This is well beyond what I believed I could do. The smile falls from my face before it even begins to form—wind kicking out of me. I destroyed literally *every* target in the structure. The blue ones, too. I released pure chaos, leaving nothing in its wake. I utterly failed the point of the exercise. *Control.*

I'm a fucking liability.

My eyes drift to see a menagerie of appalled and gawping faces. Even the stern face of our Assistant Professor is painted with wide eyes.

Kissa rushes over to me. I'm still on my knees, shame casting my gaze down, unable to take in the horror of the aftermath of what my magic reaps. I tremble as images of a true battlefield littered with blasted parts of bodies flash through my mind, shredded monsters alongside the members of my Zenith Wing. The image of their eyes, cold and grey, sears into the backs of my eyelids.

Kissa crouches down next to me, wrapping her furry mauve arm around my shoulder.

"I guess there's a reason it's called *Chaos* Magic." She pauses, grasping for her next words. "But if there's anyone who can control it, it's you, Savaé Entropaé." She squeezes my shoulder tighter and commands, "Now get up. I've never seen you let anything defeat you. You'll master this, too."

The rest of my Zenith surrounds me. All placing a hand on me, lending me their strength to stand.

"We will figure this out together! And when we do, we'll be *unstoppable!*" Fenwick beams with a jump. I'm not quite sure how such a petite structure can contain all her vibrant energy. I give her as much of a smile as I can summon.

The hairs on the back of my neck sway. I turn my head to see Seraphina and Sølas joining the circle around me. He has his classic smug curve to the side of his full lips, but it does little to mask the melancholy in his eyes when they meet mine. At least he's able to look at me again.

They all come in to give me a group hug; their united compassion is overwhelming, yet exactly what I need. They're willing to support me in spite of all the danger I reap. Claiming me without falter.

They are my new home, my new safety. Kivi's words resonate in my heart.

*We are one, or none at all.*

# CHAPTER 27

The raucous dining hall is alive with the thrill of the Celestial Bonding event dawning tomorrow and the party to celebrate after.

As we walk into the room, silence falls. Ensigns give me an unusually large berth, refusing to make eye contact with me. Fae I know and don't know alike.

"Fucking freak. I didn't realize being a grim reaper was considered a Celestial Gift," Chet condemns loudly for everyone to hear.

Swiftly, Sølas positions himself between me and Chet while Flint comes around to protect my other side.

I notice Seraph walking close at my back, while Atlas and Kivi lead the front.

Gearin, Highin, Fenwick, Juniper, Eko, Orion, and Cinder fill in the gaps. Kissa walks right next to me, holding my hand. They create a living shield around me. Normally, I'd be irritated by being protected; instead, their proximity is grounding, comforting, allowing me to retreat into the shadows their bodies cast. Despite their unwavering support, I'm still grappling to block out the terror of my Chaos Magic.

"She's more like a walking curse. Maybe you should let her have Winx after all. Jinx and Winx has a nice ring to it," sneers Brock. Chet's face twists in disagreement, elbowing Brock hard in the gut for that comment.

"Looks like Zenith Wing just went from our leading asset to our ultimate liability," Lorgan denounces with a chuckle that grows boisterous as the adjacent males join in.

A blur surrounds Kissa, her form shifting into an enormous Chimera, colored in turquoise fur and a sienna mane. Towering horns pierce out from her head, mirrored by elongated fangs extending beneath her maw. A long black tail ending with the head of a snake snaps at Chet's neck.

"Say one more fucking word, and half of Nadir Wing will be in need of replacement," Kissa roars, shaking the faerie chandeliers overhead, splattering Lorgan in thick, dripping saliva.

The color drains from their faces. Victus and Draven actually jolt up and run for the door.

Another haze whips around Kissa as she returns to her natural form.

Even the quiet Highin extends his wings to them, creating a giant gust that causes their plates to blow off the table, shattering on the floor.

"Ya hear that? Ya mess with one of us, you mess with the whole fuckin' lot of us. Don't tempt me with the fun of spilling your blood on these floors. The white marble could use a little color." Seraphina cuts the entire room with her glare, battle axes raised in each hand. She chuckles, sheathing them along her back.

We sit down at the table. Instead of sitting tall, I want to crumple into the shadows, and my team seems to sense it.

"Savaé, your Aura's a fucking mess. I'll drop off a grounding crystal to your room after dinner. It'll help you focus on one emotion at a time," Orion whispers. I can't even rally the words to tell her I had been focusing on *one emotion* when I obliterated every target in the Warded Hollow.

"There's a reason this magic was gifted to you. You are appropriately terrified of its immense potential," Atlas astutely remarks.

"I shudder to think what someone like Chet would do with that kind of power. It picked the right being; we all know it!" Fenwick gleams. I can't argue with either of their points, but nonetheless, it still feels like a curse. The universe and the Fates are certainly laughing at me in their endless ploy to see me break.

Part of me wants to give up and crumble, but as I behold the smiling faces of my Zenith, I know I have to be strong for them. I can't fail them. Not after everything they have done for me. Unlike what Sølas asks of me, this is another skill I *can* master. Just like all the rest.

My resolve cracks, a seam splintering in the glacial palace, letting enough light in to melt the icy thorns; even the black ice retreats. I sit up straight in my seat, throwing them a devilish grin.

"Ladies and gents, I do believe Savaé is back in the game." Seraph raises her powder-blue, tattooed arm in a cheer, her matching war braids tumbling behind her.

"And she's ready to play." Sølas winks with a smug grin. I swear the sadness melts from his eyes for just a moment.

"So, who's volunteering first for early morning training?" I ask with a newfound determination.

They all let out an exhausted moan before erupting into laughter.

"Why do you have to be such a morning person? We need our beauty sleep." Vex pouts.

"Vex, when have you ever made it to morning training with her? You have always convinced someone else to take your rotation." Orion throws her a side-eyed accusation.

"It's hard work looking this beautiful all the time. Something the rest of you mangey lot clearly don't appreciate." Vex flips her mane of perfect black curls around her curved matching horns.

She isn't wrong. We all look a little worse for wear after a day of training, but not a single black curl is ever out of place on her red head, and her makeup is always flawless. I guess being a Infernai from Emberhell, she has a higher tolerance for breaking a sweat than the rest of us.

"Fuck it, I volunteer. At least with my Visci abilities, if you shatter me into a bunch of water molecules, there's hope I can put myself back together again." Seraph chuckles as she smacks me in the back. My laugh's a little more nervous in response. Would she even be able to put herself back together again afterward?

"First things first: Zenith Chivalry must bond their magical creatures," Atlas levels.

Gearin's lips curl into a smile beneath his imperial mustache. "Then we work on controlling that which, at its very nature, cannot be controlled. However, I have just the rune in mind that may blunt your powers a bit while you're learning to control them, making them more manageable as you learn the mechanics." His white dreadlocks are worn down today instead of his typical ponytail. The gold-dipped ends glimmering against the deep tones of his skin.

"Thanks for giving me hope, Gearin. You always have something up your sleeve." I toss him a side smile.

My tastebuds erupt as I scarf down savory meat stew and several small cakes before shoveling a few into a napkin for Pip.

We make our way out of the dining hall into the Grand Conservatory before splitting off to head to our rooms. I walk with Juniper wrapped around one arm and Fenwick around the other. The hairs on my neck lift ever so slightly, telling me Sølas is keeping his distance but still around.

My door shuts, and I soak in the peace and quiet of my room. I unravel the napkin on my desk as the ravenous little orange dragon swallows up the food like he has never been fed.

"I wish you were bigger and had wings. Then we could be bonded and fly through the skies together."

Pip tilts his head so far to the side in response, I think it might just fall off his neck.

"I know it's a silly idea, but we're already such a good team. You're my family. It'll be strange being bonded to a different creature instead of you. Plus, then I could hear your thoughts."

He tilts his head to the opposite side now, no doubt thinking I'm crazy.

"Who am I kidding? I already know what I'll hear. Endless conversations about food and when our next meal is." I chuckle.

He licks the remaining crumbs off his face, confirming my hypothesis. I remove my battle leathers and the tight cloth that binds my breasts. For once, opting for a silky nightgown left boxed on my bed a few weeks ago. There was no letter saying who it was from, but I imagine Winx left it for me. I can't envision the hulking frame of Sølas walking through a shop of dainty lacy things. The silk on my skin reminds me of the conversation I need to finally have with Winx.

I'm utterly spent from the long day that started well before dawn. As soon as my head hits the pillow, I'm out.

# CHAPTER 28

Nerves gnaw at my stomach like a trapped rodent eating its way through my innards. I can't believe it's already been four months since classes began.

I weave my hair into a loose side braid, instead of my typical straight hair. I don my basilisk armor and runic leather pants, which recently received an upgrade of lightweight chainmail hidden between the layers of leather around my femoral arteries. Just in case Chet tries for a low blow again. It's not as strong as my basilisk armor, but it will certainly make the area harder to slice through.

Sharp metal blades glint across my body: daggers along my ribs, short swords crisscrossing my spine, and a small, double-edged battle axe buckled on my thigh. Then I adorn my magical badger-feather cloak; being invisible in a forest teeming with magical beasts for the event seems a clever backup plan in a pinch.

Two knocks sound at the door, one high and one low, telling me it's Juniper and Fenwick without having to use the shadow magic to see through. They're practically champing at the bit; as soon as I step through the door, they grab my arms. Everything's just a little brighter with them around. Thankfully, Pip quickly scurries up my arm, carrying the push dagger in his mouth, taking his bracer form.

It's frivolous to use my magic to shut the door, but the ladies leave me no choice; we're already halfway down the stairs. The act stirs up memories of Sully.

*Don't use magic if you can do without it. You never know when you'll need all your power. Nothing worse than burning out because you used your magic to heat a kettle while the hearth is already warm.*

I laugh silently at the flashback of him burning his hand on the overheated kettle he forgot to pick up with a mitt.

We gather outside the sacred Mysticwoods to the south of campus. Its boundaries stretch beyond the Midlands, all the way to the Lowlands, stopping right outside the capital, Riicah. This is the most well-protected stretch of Mysticwoods in all of Cascara. Where many magical creatures come to have their young before taking them back to the home territories.

My breath catches on the chromatic sky of flying creatures, casting us in dancing shadows of all shapes and sizes. The earth rumbles my bones as several larger beasts land amongst the towering trees.

Professor Yuri takes the makeshift dais, his auburn highlights catching on rays of sunlight, glimmering through his chestnut hair.

"Congratulations on making it to the Celestial Bonding! Today, the members that make up your potential Chivalry will journey into the Mysticwoods with the hope of coming back to you as Ellian Knights, bonded with a sacred magical creature." A winning smile paints his face as he continues.

"Remember to listen for their song. When you return, please head to the scribe in the golden cloak so they can record the name and species of the bond. This is taken into account for the Bloodline pairs you will have by next week. Those who do not bond by sunset can see the scribe in the sapphire cloak for reassignment. We will all gather here to watch your bestowal of the untold magical power in the form of an Arcane Glyph." He adjusts his spectacles as a giant carmine Phoenix lands on the boulder to his left.

"Ah, I see Belenus has come to wish you luck. May the Celestials bless your way!" A cheerful screech bellows from Belenus, beginning the event.

My classmates scurry like mice into the woods. I wait. This is the first time in several months I won't have an escort. I need to be aware of my surroundings.

*Rather be a drag if I died now…*

Murderous plans tinker in my head. What an opportune time to get my revenge on Chet. I can scorch the body, and no one will be the wiser.

As I enter the woods, there's a distant sway on my neck telling me I'm not completely alone after all, but Sølas needs to focus and not worry about me.

I close my eyes, opening the starburst window just a crack. Several velvety black ribbons dance their way in. I glide my fingers above them, sensing the direction they come from. I'm tempted to hold them, but even just hovering above them, I can feel the torrent of emotions that ripple off. Surely, that would be an invasion of privacy I'd never live down. Furthermore, I'm not sure I can handle what they will reveal. I coax the ribbons back out the window before shutting it.

I jaunt in the opposite direction I felt the ribbons tugging me in. I shuffle into some overgrown bushes, turning my cloak around so I can blend into my surroundings.

Then I enter my mind, opening the starburst window again, just a peep, so I can listen for any type of song or frequency. There're many different noises but nothing calling to me.

My eyes widen at a shell lifting off the ground, revealing a slimy, two-legged snail-Faeanoid figure.

"Bugger off. This is my home. Unless you bring little cakes? Only then will I share my bush," the creature bargains.

"Apologies. I'll be on my way," I grumble, rustling out of the bush as the creature lets out a slew of curses behind me.

Leaves rustle to the right of me beneath a strong gust. I smile, hoping it's someone from my Zenith Chivalry taking flight with their new bond.

I journey deeper into the Mysticwoods. The older trees here have bark that shimmers silver and emerald, spiraling upward to canopies woven together into a vast tapestry of lilac and violet orchids, pierced through by an ethereal dappling of golden sun rays.

A myriad of colorful mosses and lichen blot the forest floor. I name the colors as I walk: damask, zaffre, celadon, xanadu, gamboge, glaucous, and cyan. I'm in my element, surrounded by nature. A diverse range of mushrooms and flowers sprout around the bases of the trees. Some fluctuating bioluminescent colors of blue, green, magenta, and pink. The forest is a living, breathing entity of its own, responding to my every movement.

The sweet scent of the cinamellion flowers fill the air as they vine up the trunks in search of sunlight. My feet trail along a babbling brook of glimmering liquid crystal. Several breeds of winged fish leap from the stream, their crystalline bodies disappearing beneath the pastel water.

Whispers dancing on the wind lead me deeper, singing of hidden glades where mystic creatures dwell. The air grows thick with magic, instinct telling me to change course so I don't trespass on the sacred nesting grounds.

An enormous tree, appearing to have no end, spears up in my path. I reach out, connecting to its life force. The energy of the Mysticwoods pours through my blood. Life and death, birth and growth, serenity and chaos.

Something calls to me. It's not a melody, like Professor Yuri described. More akin to a frequency, resonating deep inside of me. Each step closer syncing more in tune with my heartbeat, beckoning me to forge a bond that transcends the ordinary. My legs begin to dash towards the frequency, my soul harmonizing with it.

The sound of an all too familiar slithering voice strangles me to a stop. I duck, finding cover behind a tree, as I listen.

"She has to be here somewhere. We'll find the bitch," Chet snorts.

"I saw her magic in the Warded Hollow yesterday. She has the power to obliterate us. It's not worth it, Chet," the voice of Victus pleads.

"I'm with Victus on this one. She's terrifying. I'd like to live to graduate," Draven sighs.

"You're fucking cowards. She won't use her magic here. She'd kill us and every other living thing here. It's too big a risk. You all saw how she had no control over it. She would never live down that massacre." Venom seeps from Chet's voice.

"Why don't we focus on finding our bonded creatures? The song I heard is getting more distant here. You're becoming obsessed with her. It's getting kind of skraith," Brock retorts with a subtle tremble to his voice.

"No. We have to do it today. My mother said this is the smartest move. There is no chance they can pin it on us."

Chet's words send a chill slithering down my spine. His mother fucking knows and is helping him plot my death. I really shouldn't have made such a fool of him, which reflects poorly on her, pinning me within her vicious sight.

"We could wait until she finds her bond and kill the creature before she even has a chance to bond. Then she could never be an Ellian Knight," Lorgan suggests. That's a horrible thought, possibly worse than death after all I've worked for.

"Too risky. We don't know what she'll bond with, and I don't want to take the chance it's something hard to kill. We need to stick together. We stand a better chance against her," Chet replies.

"Chet, there were three of you last time. You poisoned her, slit her femoral artery open, and she still lived. I don't see how two more of us will suddenly change the odds," Draven protests.

He's right; their chances aren't any better, and now they don't have the element of surprise like they did last time. But there were more than three of them—I heard the fourth person's laugh in the distance. If it wasn't one of them, who was it? The subtle feminine lilt to the laugh slashes through my memories. Frost spreading through my veins in realization of just how involved Commander Bragen has been.

"If you dare leave right now, I will have my mother station you on the worst assignments for the rest of your life. You sniveling vole," Chet chastises with a hiss.

I guess those threats are how he keeps his so-called friends tolerating his presence. Maybe when Sully was talking about the rot in the Golden Legion, he was speaking of Commander Bragen and her insufferable spawn. After all, she did take his place, so she must have been next in line underneath him.

The humming frequency snatches me from my thoughts. They're right in the path of the calling tune. I can go around, but I don't want to chance them sneaking up behind me. I have to be strategic.

There's a chance I can survive a fight against all of them.

I have a feeling Victus and Draven will dart immediately, especially with the way they ran yesterday at dinner. That leaves me to fight Brock, Lorgan, and Chet. Even if Chet hits me with his poison, my new ring will dampen the effect. If I can get one hit in with my paralysis blade, I can take him off the table. There's also the fact that I don't know what Brock and Lorgan's Celestial Gifts are, which leaves me with two wild cards.

The safest thing will be to go the long way around. Today, I will be smart and do the safer thing.

I start to move silently away from them until I remember how close the power of the sacred nesting grounds are. *Fuck.* I wouldn't put it past Chet to Siphon its magic. He has a pure evil streak to him. I wouldn't be surprised if his biological father is actually Wuvon. Commander Bragen seems like she would have no qualms taking a monster to bed.

I sneak back to where they're still bickering about which direction to head in next. Silently, I climb a tree behind them, careful to brace my weight slowly on each branch. I perch myself like a Bone-Thresher, ready to pounce. I have a partially mapped-out plan in my head; the rest I'll figure out on the fly. Maybe I'm more chaotic than I give myself credit for after all.

My goal is to throw my dagger down at Chet's neck; being so close to his heart will ensure the paralysis works in one to two heartbeats but missing his carotid artery.

A deep breath fills my lungs; I steady my hand as I hold the blade at its tip. I exhale, slinging the dagger, slicing into my mark just above his collarbone. His echoing howl claws at the air as I leap down, casting my arms out wide, taking Lorgan and Brock to the ground.

Lorgan lands a right hook into my ribs. I swear that male has an obsession with my right ribs at this point. It's blunted by my basilisk armor and clenched core, but I still gasp from the force.

I move like lightning, pinning Lorgan with my legs before stabbing my short sword through his shoulder into the ground below. With my now-free hands, I snatch two more daggers along my ribs. Chet comes timbering down on my back with his only step before the paralysis sets in. Brock's still stumbling to get up when I use my other dagger, slitting the back of his calf, which is just in reach as I'm sandwiched between Lorgan and Chet.

"Ow! You fucking witch," Brock hollers. The slice gives me a sliver of time to wriggle out from under them, a position I hope never to find myself in again.

Lorgan reaches for my leg as I stand up. I twirl, using all my force to jam my boot down on his hand. The satisfying *crunch* of bones ripples up my leg.

Lorgan screeches in pain. "My fucking hand, you whore!"

I hear footsteps trailing off in the distance—Draven and Victus fleeing, curling my lips into a smug smirk.

But I make the mistake of leaving my back towards Brock, who wraps his arm around my neck in a headlock. I try to break free, but he's too strong.

I grab the battle axe on my leg, hacking it into the side of his thigh. Brock roars in agony, releasing my neck as he stumbles backwards. I whip around, kicking him in the gut, sending him barreling into a tree. The momentum snaps his head back against the trunk, knocking him out.

To my surprise, Lorgan has pulled my sword out of his shoulder, leaving me with my own blade at my neck.

*Son of a bitch…*

# CHAPTER 29

Well, it was a good run while it lasted.

Lorgan's nostrils flare, huffing in the scent of me. Even with his injured shoulder, he manages to rip my left arm tight behind my back, pinning me against his body. The only way he could be able to use his mangled arm is if he's a Bloodsinger: a strong form of blood magic that lets you manipulate the blood of a body, willing movement with your mind.

I hate to think what someone like him enjoys doing with a power like that. It's odd he hasn't used his magic on me yet, but I'm not waiting around to find out what that experience is like firsthand.

"It's too bad you wrecked my good hand. I could have really showed you a good time before I killed you." His threat crawls along my neck with his repulsive breath.

He reminds me exactly of the kind of company Chet fucking keeps. I'm going to die killing this disgusting waste of space if it's the last thing I ever do.

My right hand is free, allowing me to flick my wrist, signaling Pip to release the blade from my bracer, just like we practiced. I reach around my side, jamming the dagger right into his dick, which is revoltingly hard, making the tiny thing an easy target.

The dagger in his hand slits my neck slightly as he timbers backward, cursing with furious pain. *Good for me.* The braid was a clever choice, or he'd surely have shorn my hair asymmetrically.

A familiar, sticky warmth trickles down my chest. I'll deal with that later.

I tower over Lorgan, looking down on him with uninhibited disgust.

"I hope you enjoy that Petrifying Kiss. You fucking sicko. It'll be the last time your small dick is ever hard." An evil laugh bubbles from my chest. I feign a pout. "There's no way you'll get the antidote in time; we're too far out." A wicked grin dances on my lip as I purr, "It would be the civil thing to slit your throat, but where's the fun in that?" I shrug.

His breathing shifts to short gasps. The blood that pours from his dick thickens to mud, then hardens to solid stone.

"You'll fucking die for this!" he rasps between *crunching* coughs, each inhale scraping grit across solidifying crimson mortar.

"Been there, done that. Death takes me out for dinner now, thanks to you lot." I wink, garnet sludge *squelching* as I wrench the dagger from his crotch. My lips curl into a sneer as I wipe his disgusting filth off my blade on the remaining leather of his pants.

My undivided attention pivots to Chet.

His eyes are wide with terror, unable to look away as Lorgan rasps his last breath.

I fetch the blade from above Chet's collarbone, thankful I missed his carotid artery. There's no chance I'd escape the Commander severing my head for killing her son; their combined plotting likely put me first on her suspect list. I use my Sangre magic to heal the wound from the dagger, knowing well the paralysis will still take time to wear off. I can't leave a scar on him as evidence now, can I?

I pick up my remaining weapons, cleaning them on Chet's cloak. He doesn't protest, given he's barely breathing. Taking small, pitiful gasps. Lucky for me, he isn't totally paralyzed; I didn't account for asphyxiation in my plan. I notice a quiver at his lips, signaling the toxin is wearing off. *Time to go.*

I freeze.

Even my heart seems to still.

My every cell lulled by the crackling frequency from before, now soaring in the clotted clouds above me.

*Thrump. Da-bump.*

Each thundering beat of wings zings electric impulses, thrumming through my nerves, harmonizing with the alluring siren call. Overhead, hues of lavender dance in leaves that quiver and quake. Then drafts of wind bellow, swaying me like wheat in a brewing storm. I coil my arms around a tree, narrowly avoiding being whisked away like a leaf clutched in a gale.

Branches *snap*.

Trunks bow and buckle.

An iridescent dragon splinters the canopy, folding the forest like the binding of a book to reveal her enormous form. Dwarfed trees cower in her wake as my neck cracks, craning to look up at her.

"*Bathed in blood already, I see.*" Her voice cuts like daggers, flaying the fluffy parts of my brain.

"You're the dragon from my dream," I breathe, eyes pooling wide in awe.

"*I have been waiting for you for a very long time, Nebulight. I grew impatient for you to find me.*" She pauses, tilting her head to fully take in the sight of the carnage I've wrought. "*I see you decided to have all the fun without me.*" Her sharp voice slashing through my mind becomes less rattling with each word, but no less sarcastic.

"This bunch are horrible excuses for Elarians. I was afraid what they might do if they found the sacred nesting grounds."

"*This pet looks already dead. Shall I erase the remains for you? It's only fair you let me join in on the fun.*"

I trail her gaze to Lorgan. Yep. He's solid stone. Definitely dead.

Taking a stride back reveals Chet gulping up air. Thankfully, the chilling terror of my dragon seems to be keeping his tongue quiet for once.

"*What about the other two? I am feeling a bit peckish.*"

Her massive snout is square in shape; above are two piercing rainbow eyes slashed with black slits down the center. Her face is framed by spikes of varying sizes. The horns crowning the top of her head form two crescent moons facing each other, almost kissing at the top.

Her lips curl with a low growl, revealing eight-foot-tall fangs. Blue lightning brews in her throat, peeking through her teeth, casting an ominous shiver down my spine.

"If we kill that one, Commander Bragen will likely skewer my head on a pike. I could care less about the one passed out against the tree." I throw a pointed thumb over my shoulder. "Dead one didn't understand the concept of consent, hence his current state."

Then I step over to Chet. Anger and dread swirl in his hollow green eyes.

The blood staining the white streaks of his blond hair prickles me with utter delight. A vicious smile peaks at my lips as I savor the visual.

*"Should we make this one beg for his life?"* the dragon hisses in my mind with far too much shared amusement.

"As much as I do love to make a male beg, he isn't worth the air he now breathes."

I lower my head, releasing a snarl like a feral wolf. "Know that you only live because of my mercy. Know that your life is a gift I will not give again. Your futile quest to kill me is over. Death *knows* my name. Yet she does not call it. And nor shall you." I spit on his face before spinning on my heels, plotting course towards the gleaming dragon.

A maniacal smirk curves on my lips, snaring my momentum as my head hooks over my shoulder. "And I wouldn't tell mommy dearest about this. She may very well disown you at the shame of your failure."

I don't spare another glance back. A thought congeals; perhaps we should finish off Brock just for the fun of it. The idea fizzles out as the dragon suddenly darts her head up, snapping to the side like she senses something.

*"Quickly now. Get on my back. I will torch the evidence of the deceased. No time for snacking. I'm not the only thing looking for you in the woods."*

I'm not going to argue with those ominous words, nor bother wasting time thinking about what could spark fear in a monstrous dragon like her.

I back up to get a running start. Using the spikes on her legs as anchors, I hurl myself up her almost two-story leg before reaching her back. Then I settle into position, resting my spine against the icicle spike that makes up one of her three lightning conductors. My eyes drift down to see two curved spikes as the base of her neck, positioned perfectly for me to hold on to.

I watch a bundle of lightning arc out of her mouth, melting the stone carcass of Lorgan into a puddle of molten glass. I find myself wishing I had better control of my Chaos Magic so I could shatter him to nothingness.

*"One day, you will. When that day arrives, you will be a fury to be reckoned with."* She dips, her legs crouching. *"Now, hold on tight."*

"Wait, did you just read my thou—?"

And just like that, we're hurtling into the sky. The muscles in my arms and legs screech, consuming all my strength not to fall off with the sudden momentum.

*"Astute observation of you."*

"I was taught that it took at least a few days for that to happen, as the bond strengthens," I scream over the air rushing past me.

*"As I told you, Nebulight, I have been waiting for you for a very long time. Do not make me repeat myself again. You don't want to see me when I'm cranky. Just focus on holding on for the next part."*

She extends out her four enormous wings, covered with iridescent feathers. We fly straight up, slashing through blush and lilac clouds, the chroma of her scales shifting, reflecting the colors all around us. An electric energy pulses within the spikes behind me, causes static to charge my willowing hair.

Her long tail is almost eel-like, with two thin ribbons rippling along the top and bottom, waving in the wind. My hair swirls in the gusts of her wings. She spins through the air, diving down to the ground, twirling around the other magical creatures flying around us.

Utter, careless freedom soars through my blood, melting the ice shackles of control anchoring my mind, shattering my glacial palace as my heart sings to life.

I've finally done it.

I'm an Ellian Knight.

The clouds remold around me, revealing the blotted outline of Sully's smiling face. An armored flying polar bear dives beneath us, as if Sully is here with me, soaring with pride. An endless weight crumbles from my chest as I revel in the beauty of the moment. My hair spins, its last strands freeing from the braid, joining in my liberation.

Calais ice, cerulean flames, and shattering lightning summon my Chaos Magic, tangling together in fractals of pastel rainbows. The feeling of everything around me seeps into my flesh.

I am alive. So very alive.

Black velvet ribbons flutter at the edge of my mind, sneaking through on the rift of my newfound freedom. I picture a beautiful arched window of stained glass adorned with the night sky and close it. I'm not ready for what those ribbons could mean, what lies hidden in their seams. Or how they've lurked past the defenses of my mental shield.

This magical moment isn't for thinking. It's for feeling - feeling alive and free for the first time, and I never want to let this sensation go. White light shimmering in pastel rainbows leaks out from my veins, melting the remnants of my glacial palace, my ribs cracking, setting my heart free to soar.

We dip again, twirling and dancing, whipping the clouds up into new shapes.

"*Now you're just showing off,*" I say in my mind, hoping the dragon below can hear my thoughts. That it's truly that simple.

"*We are a sight to behold. They should be honored by our presence.*"

"*I am noticing you are as large as your ego.*" I smirk. She lets out a sassy huff, and I can't help but smile. I would get a feisty dragon.

"*You may call me Calais Lauoona Kaosa. Calais for short.*"

"*Calais.*"

She growls. "*Don't butcher it. It's pronounced Kah-lay.*"

"*Calais, I'm Savaé Entropaé. But I have a sneaking suspicion you already know that.*"

"*Good, your assumption is correct. Your true nature, Savaé, has been long awaited.*"

"*And I doubt you care to elaborate?*"

"*Patience, young one. All in good time.*"

Figures. I've heard dragons love their secrets, hoarding them like treasure, I think to myself, despite how futile that seems now.

"*There is only so much your young corporeal mind can handle. We do it for your protection. You'd be wise to be thankful for it.*"

"*Shit. Sorry. Still getting used to this whole hearing-my-thoughts thing.*"

I close my eyes, enjoying the wind in my face. Her movement pattern shifts, circling to land. I notice within the shielded walls of my mind there are now white, effervescent ribbons wrapped around me. My hand reaches out to touch them, sparking blue lighting, and I immediately know the energy belongs to Calais.

"*Clever girl. Our bond is remarkably strong already. Because of this, I will be able honor you with an Arcane Glyph that will shake the realms. A gift foretold by the heavens.*"

"*Are you sure? I already kinda have my hands full with my Celestial Gift.*"

"*I promise you, you can handle more than you know, Nebulight.*"

I've already caught on enough to realize not to waste my energy trying to ask about what any of that means. She lets out an unamused snarl as we land.

"*I am honored. Thank you,*" I finally reply.

*"Better. Now, cement our legacy in ink. Tell the scribe my name."*

I slide down her leg to the ground. I'm met by her breath on my face, nearly knocking me on my ass. *"You might want to clean up the blood on you. Can't go around having all these little pets thinking I ate someone in front of you."*

*Fuck. Double fuck.*

My cloak. I hide behind her enormous leg and turn my cloak back to its normal position. Grabbing some leaves and dirt off the ground, I attempt to wipe the blood off my face and battle leathers. Why did these Celestials be dimmed things have to be white of all colors? Someone clearly didn't think that one through. Calais lets out a sound that remotely resembles a chuckle. I guess she agrees. I walk out from behind her leg and head towards the scribe.

*"You still have blood on your face, and now you're covered in dirt. You're making me doubt my decision."*

"I doubt that with your foreboding '*I have been waiting for you for a very long time*,'" I say aloud, with as much sarcasm as she likes to chuck my way.

She huffs so violently behind me, she sends me stumbling forward. I turn around to glare at her, my fists snapping to my hips.

*"You're not the only one who gets to be sassy."* I think loudly in her direction.

She retorts by lowering her head and snarling her lips, showing off her treacherous teeth, gleaming larger than me.

*"Okay, okay. Message received, loud and clear. Don't pick fights you can't win."* I turn, heading to the golden-robed scribe.

*"Now behave, and do as I command."*

Geez. She's worse than Sully was.

*"I heard that."*

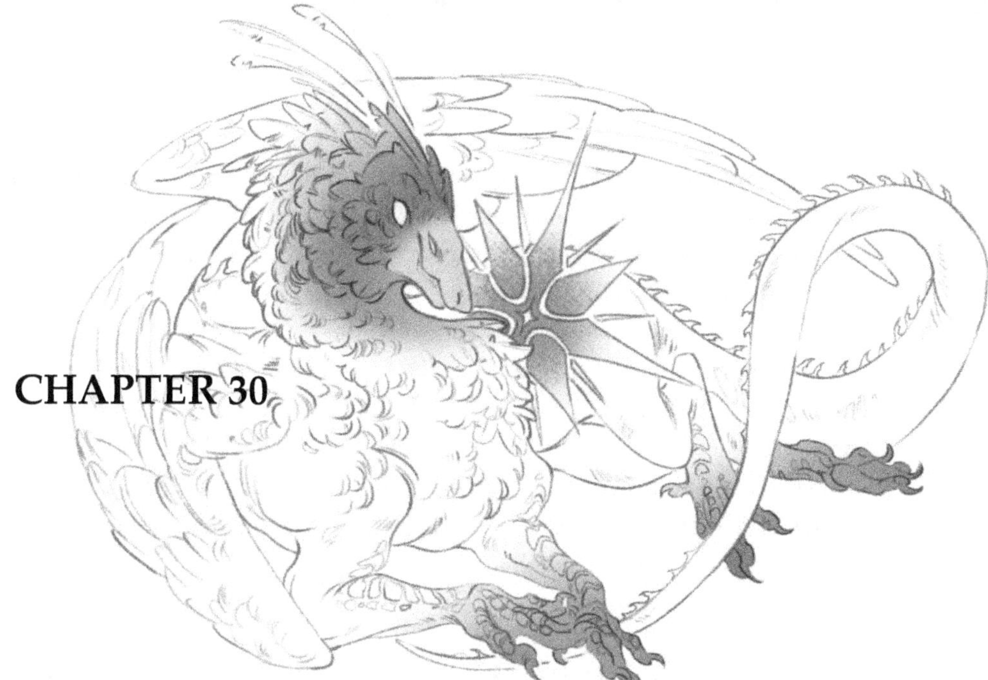

# CHAPTER 30

**E**veryone is backing away again. Except it's not me this time; they're backing away from the sight of Calais. *Good, they should back away.* She definitely won't think twice about taking a bite.

I catch a wisping blur of mauve as Kissa runs towards me. She wraps her arms around me, snatching me up into a hug. After a squeeze, she releases me to look me up and down.

"You're alive. And covered in fucking blood *again*. As well as dirt? Please tell me that's not your blood." She sniffs me. "It doesn't smell much like your blood." Kissa sighs in relief.

"It's not my blood, mostly. I promise."

I try to wipe off more blood and dirt with my hands, but it's futile. Then the hairs on my neck sway. Sølas is exceptionally close to me, closer than he's been since two days ago. The tearing sound of his shirt snaps my spine rigid.

"Take this, and clean off your face, you little fucking savage. I can't leave you alone for one second." His smoky voice feels like a caress I want to fall into.

"Yep. And that's my cue to leave. I can't stand the scent of you two together," Kissa scoffs as she walks away, waving her hand in the air in pure annoyance, her tail following suit, whipping rapidly behind her.

I swipe his shirt, quickly wiping my face and arms. Realizing too late I'm covering myself in the scent of him. My nostrils flare as hints of amber and spruce drown my lungs. My pulse skitters like cold water on a heated iron, my skin searing as he takes another step closer.

In his absence, the feelings he awakes in me have only grown more voracious. My knees plead to buckle, but I refuse to relent, ice clawing up my ribs in attempts to gain back my composure. But then my eyes meet his.

I adore being close enough to see the small crimson flecks dance against the icy blue. With the adrenaline of battle still fresh in my blood, it's taking an entirely new level of restraint to hold myself back from him.

His irresistible lips dare to curl into a smirk, as if he can read my thoughts. He slowly wipes his tongue against his thumb, causing my icy walls to melt like they're nothing.

His powers may be shadows, but all I see is vibrant light and warmth, drunk on his moonlit gaze.

"You missed a spot." He cups my face in his hand, wiping a mark from my cheek.

I can't help but lean into his touch. At that moment, I'm tempted to tell him I'm willing to try—and likely utterly fail, but try nonetheless. After being so free flying, maybe there's more to life than simply surviving.

His other hand gently finds the small of my back, sliding up the gap under my armor. Always finding more ways to disarm me. A Shadowveil rises to shroud us as he leans in closer. His chaotic aura pressing in against me. To my lament, he's careful this time, not letting his lips graze my ear.

"I saw what you did in the woods. The glory of you bathed in their blood with three men destroyed at your feet." He pauses before a growl rumbles along my neck. "I almost lost control and took you right there."

*Fuck.* I let out a dangerous, hushed moan.

His thumb traces over my bottom lip.

I slip, my tongue lazily sweeping out; the taste of metallic blood and soil stirs in my mouth.

His body melds against mine. He's rock hard, making the space between my thighs throb in a slick, wet heat. He tilts his head against mine in a guttural groan. My arms wrap around his towering frame. I never want him to let go.

Sølas lowers his face to mine, hovering above my lips in pure torture. I want him to kiss me, even though I know he won't.

My eyes flutter shut. Velvet ribbons whip violently around me in my mind, making sure not to touch me. I can tell he's barely holding on to control. There's something about him that makes me want to lose exactly that when I'm with him. To lose the precious control that I have clung to like it's the very air I breathe.

To surrender to him.

Letting him ruin me.

Over and over again.

He barely brushes his satin lips against my cheek. Uncontrollably, my hips arch into his. The weight of him throbs against me. I whimper, crumbling under the sensation of it all. He growls in a gasp, as if I stole all the air from his lungs.

"I would worship you until you are high from screaming my name, until you moan with such pleasure, the very Fates bend to your every will. Until we rewrite the rules of physics, galaxies colliding in the wake of your pleasure as stardust seeps from your ribs. You're the reason I no longer ask for heaven, because I've already been touched by a goddess. The hesitation you feel isn't a wall; it's a love note, written in a language I'll gladly spend the rest of my lifetime learning."

*Fuck. He sets my soul on fucking fire.*

"Fucking. Kiss. Me," I growl with a raspy gasp between each heated word. I'm so lost in him, it takes all of me to even speak those words.

He pulls me tight. "I would love nothing more." His lips tracing the words along my neck as my head dips back in a craving that quakes me to my core. The energy of his Sangre magic hums along the slit on my neck, healing, as his tattooed fingers trace over the line of crimson.

He pauses, taking me in with his perusal. Raven locks tumble as his head falls back, gaze cast to the sky. Every muscle in his body tenses, like he's praying to Celestials for strength in making an impossible decision.

And then lets me go.

Catching me in his shadows as my heart stills, quivering to beat. I gasp for air I can't find with the loss of him.

No one has ever consumed me like this, made me *feel* like this. No person has even come close to what he can do to me without even touching me. *What is he doing to me?*

*"Are you truly so naïve? Even I know what you feel for him."* Calais' voice shocks me back to life.

*"You can feel what I'm feeling?"*

*"Unfortunately."*

"I guess we're both lucky Calais came swooping in. So I wasn't tempted into doing something you couldn't take back." His smoky voice is addicting. His hands weave through his hair, doing little to soothe his pacing steps. He's teetering on the edge of control while my request twists that phantom ice-pick dagger just a little deeper. Deeper still in my inability to give him all the vulnerable bits of me he desires. I worry even trying would leave him a bloody, shredded mess.

I'm too fractured. Too sharp. Not enough blunted pieces to safely hold.

I roll my shoulder, attempting to cast the emotions aside, indulging a more practical puzzle to pick at.

"How do you know my dragon's name?"

"Whatever pulls us together appears bigger than you and I." His jaw flexes with dismay, as though thinking of something that can never be.

The weight of it all crushing like boulders on my chest, jagged edges scraping across my flinting heart.

*"The Shadowmancer is not wrong."* Calais snickers with a slight curve to her lips, dangling another secret she hoards in her trove. Confusion pinches my brows.

Sølas is suddenly behind me, tilting my world off axis. He guides my windswept, iridescent hair over my shoulder and whispers, "I have never seen anything more beautiful than you, *Luxsula,* reaping your vengeance like those males were mere mortals in your presence." He pauses deeply, letting out a breathy sigh of control before continuing, "But if I ever see a male *touch you* like that again, I will shred their very soul from existence. From this universe and the next."

His raspy threat brims with chaos, and I have no doubt in the truth of his warning. How can I be mad at him when this surely isn't about protecting me? He clearly could have intervened at any point while watching. The depth of how much he cares for me percolates between each of his words spoken and unsaid.

The strength it took for him to let me have my vengeance instead of taking it for himself, which he clearly wanted to do. Normally, I would protest at a male threatening to protect me, but his threat is something raw and feral. It isn't about protecting me; it's evident to him I can do that myself.

It's about protecting his own heart, tortured in his feelings for me. Feelings muddling my head. Sprouting firelights to flutter about in my chest. A concept too foreign for me to comprehend, while a deeper part of me yearns to understand everything between us.

Yet fear rears its ugly head, fangs sinking in deep. Unleashing its venom, feeding me poison on its obsidian spoon of destruction.

Too afraid those distorted words from the illusion will prove to be right. Too afraid to see if they're wrong. Too afraid to try, too afraid to hope. Too afraid to dream.

Too afraid to fail.

I straighten my shoulders, attempting to let the torment slick off; instead, it seeps into my wounds, new and old.

*Too late.*

*Too fucking late.*

*It's already festering.*

A chasm rips open in my chest as Sølas steps away from me, trailing off through the crowd.

He peers over his shoulder, heaviness weighing in his eyes as he holds back the torrent of turmoil shredding his soul. At my apprehension, he attempts to muster a smile, but it does little to hide the weeping heart behind his stormy features. Waves of darkness radiate off of him, devouring the light around him. In his melancholy, it's hard to see where the shadows end and he begins.

A sane person would fear him and the ominous aura unfurling in his wake. Yet to me, his shadows are the least terrifying part about him.

I saunter the way his head nods, letting my darkness wrap around his fracturing pieces, holding him together, despite the needling mess threaded between us threatening to rip, cleaving the world in two.

Along our way to the head scribe, I see Kissa standing next to her large Chimera. The beast looks similar to the one she had shifted into the night before. Its fur is of teal and midnight indigo, with a mane of mauve and an onyx cobra for a tail. Long horns spiral from its head, mirroring her rider's tall feline ears. Seafoam green eyes with slits at the center mirror Kissa's but lack her vibrance.

It makes sense that a Beastshifter would bond a creature that is not one but many. Its wings flare out wide, veins tracking through the translucent membrane, glimmering in sunset colors.

Next, we pass Juniper and her Dahlia Hypnosis Draco. Mesmerizing colors move through the petals of the frill that cascade around its head: black plum, pine, garnet, dark harbor. Its eyes change colors, matching the rhythmic beat of its tail of vine-like tendrils. I struggle pulling my gaze away from its hypnotic trance.

We find Vex spoiling her Wyvern with chin pets as its purr rumbles the ground. Its head appears like a lion but with a much longer snout, almost like it's combined with a wolf. It perches on two hind legs, which belong to a bear. At the apex of its wings are paws with razor-sharp claws. Its colors are warm reds, reminding me of the heat of summer, blending well with Vex's vermillion skin. Instead of curved horns like its rider, it has two long, straight ones that jut out behind its bat-like, serrated ears. Its head is bowed low, enjoying the scratches of Vex's long black nails, snarling to reveal long, curved canines.

Plummeting down from the sky and scorching the earth as it lands is an onyx phoenix, the tips of its wings marked with amber eyes. The beast seems as dark and broody as our resident Pyro. Cinder causally slides off the creature as if he didn't just come close to incinerating us. He gives us a sly smirk as I make a lewd gesture in return at his ludicrous landing.

Lastly, we pause before a great black dragon, whose face appears to have emerged out of a midnight barn owl. I immediately know it belongs to Sølas from the essence of night that clings to its form like a mist. Its raven-black snout is narrow, leading into a wide, rounded face. Its eyes the color of white snow, surrounded by a second set of owl eyes. No, it's feathers that surround its face, mimicking that of a midnight barn owl with feathered eyes. The dragon's face seeming to have split the owl's face down the middle, emerging from within.

Its head is surrounded by needle-like quills swaying subtly up and down with each breath. The dragon's body and wings are covered with feathers of iridescent, raven black. It splays its wings out wide at the sight of Sølas, revealing a dappling of white, like a clear night sky dusted with stars. The beast is only slightly smaller than Calais, and the sight of him steals my breath away. His wings flap gently; I can feel the wind on my face but hear no sound. They'll be a silent and deadly match, the pair of them. I try thinking back to class and to all the beasts Sully told me about; not a single one meets the description of the dragon before me. I can feel the power radiating from him, old and ancient, vows and promises, stories lost to time.

I move on, finding my way to the head scribe, face masked by the shadows of a large golden cloak.

"Name of your bonded creature and species?" Her voice is soft like a secret.

"Calais Lauoona Kaosa. Moonstorm Dragon." Power crackles beneath my skin just speaking her full name aloud.

The scribe's silver globes flit up to meet mine, topped by a brow bunched in disbelief. At my silence, a subtle tremble ripples through her cloak, likely fear setting in based on the rumor of Moonstorm Dragons devouring anyone on sight.

I give her a confident nod, signaling to her I'm not mistaken, nor will I repeat myself.

She dips her head, scratching her name down on the parchment with a shaky hand, clenching the quill like her life depends on it.

I think about telling her that I'll make sure not to let her be eaten just so she can finish writing Calais' name legibly, but a voice sharp as daggers interrupts my thought.

*"Making promises you cannot keep is unwise."*

I huff loudly as I turn away from the scribe, heading back to my clearly hungry dragon.

A tall, gruff female with a long scar down the right side of her face, slashing through her ghostly grey eye, takes the stage. She's built like an ox, with dark, tawny skin that reminds me of molten chocolate, so at odds with the stern strength that emanates from her.

She's clad in white armor with deep golden embellishments at the edge of each plate of metal. Her hair is weathered grey clouds, hanging heavy around her head. Her eyes flare silver as she looks out at the crowd before us. The color of her eyes tell me she's an Airria, Elarian, and air Pixie mix.

A giant black tiger arises behind her, adorned with golden stripes. Elongated, black, curved canines decorate its maw with silver eyes to match its rider. Quills skewer out from its shoulders and tail, matching the color of its gold stripes. Since Airria can fly by their control of wind magic, they often bond with powerful ground-bound creatures, making them a deadly air-ground combination.

As the sun sneaks past the horizon, casting the sky in pink and cinnamon, she begins to speak. "I am Fleet Admiral Genesis Ragnara. I'm here to extend congratulations to the newest generation of Ellian Knights. May the Celestials bless you."

The crowd cheers into a roar. I remember Sully telling me how Fleet Admiral Ragnara can manipulate air into powerful shields, one time shielding an entire royal escort of the queen, saving her and many others from a surprise Wuvon attack. Her Arcane Glyph gives her the ability to wield blades of air, severing her victims from great distances.

She can even take the air from someone's lungs, leaving a variety of death in her wake. She occupies the highest rank of the Golden Legion, spending most of her time in the war room of the queen. Airria Ellian Knights are known to have wind tunneling abilities to transport them and their beast over great distances across Cascara for battle. Some even claim the winds whisper to them. Allowing them the ability to discern movement of enemies nearby on the battle front.

She raises her hand and silence falls over the crowd.

"Learn from your professors. Master your skills. Be the strength of your Wings. For the darkness threatens our most sacred holds. The Wuvon grow bolder by the day, testing new tactics never seen before. We need all of your power to destroy the darkness coming. May their blood pool at your feet." Her voice is as sharp as a whetted blade. She raises her fist, pounding it across her chest.

The crowd returns the gesture in solitude. It's how we honor accepting an order from a superior officer, known as a Golden Salute. We all bow as she leaves the stage.

Professor Yuri takes the dais for ending remarks.

"Please, take your place in front of your magical creatures to secure your bond. We will see you on Monday for flight training. Now, let the Dawning Festivities begin!"

We all cheer in response, then there's a soft hum of movement as we take our positions in front of our various creatures.

The Dawning Festivities is a grand celebration followed by a weekend of freedom. The beginning of the celebration is marked by our magical creature imprinting their bond upon us. Depending on your creature, it may be a burn, a bite, or a scratch. With this act, an Arcane Glyph marks our skin, taking various glittering markings as our powers combine, imbuing us with a new magical gift.

I can hear the crackle of light brewing in Calais' mouth. I steady my body, reminding myself this pain will forge me anew. Blue light blinds my senses as lightning weaves through my marrow, searing my flesh. Yet it's not painful.

The power is… awakening.

# CHAPTER 31

My eyes roll down, my arms humming with power. I swear for a split second, my skin appears indigo blue like the night sky, dusted in clouds of pink, magenta and flecked in starlight.

I blink to reveal my olive-colored skin is now back to normal but gleaming with new golden markings. Two thin lines glide across my arms, crisscrossing. My shoulders are adorned with mirroring crescent moons, the bows of which curve along the apex of my shoulders. My hands are adorned with the crisscrossed streams of gold from my arms, creating a curved V that meets at my middle knuckle.

Each finger is glazed with a golden star—an eight-pointed star for my middle fingers and four-pointed stars for the rest. I turn my hands over to my palms, thrumming with energy. Each one marked the same: a golden eight-pointed star in the middle with one orbital swirling around it. On the right side, there are two four-pointed stars; on the left lower side, one four-pointed star, speckled with gold flecks. This is far more ornate than any Arcane Glyph pattern that's ever been recorded in the books I've read.

I whip around to hurl a scowl at Calais.

"What is this!? Why is it so big? And how does it mimic the markings of my skin?"

"*Are all Ellian Knights so indignant to their bonded creatures? A powerful Arcane Glyph takes up more space. You should be bowing at my feet, but I will accept a simple thank you."* A menacing growl rattles me as she lowers her head above me, heat radiating from her blue-lit mouth.

*"Since you're in my head, you know that I never wanted these golden markings. Couldn't you have just given me something small and simple?"*

*"Your birth markings and the new ones are a blessing. You should flaunt them instead of hiding them like a coward. Stop acting like a prattling brat."*

She bends her legs and blasts off. The powerful gust of her wings catching me off guard, knocking me on my ass. I guess that conversation's over.

"Well, there's no hiding my markings now, is there!" I huff loudly in her direction.

*"Sometimes, I wonder if you are part dragon. You certainly seem to think you can blow fire with your words, Nebulight,"* Calais' voice growls through my mind.

*"Who knows, maybe once I master my Chaos Magic, I will."* I motion a lewd gesture towards her flight path.

*"Careful, Neubulight. Until you can, I'd hate to burn off those pretty markings on your fingers I just worked rather hard to imbue. Mind your manners."*

She's right; I am acting like a petulant child. The strength of her magic vibrates through my bones, like I'm a tuning fork. She's given me a powerful gift, and I should be thanking her rather than focusing on what others will think of my new markings. I've just spent so much of my life trying to fit in. To blend in. Now that seems impossible. I guess at this point, I should stop trying and take the hint: blending in beyond shadows was never meant for me.

"I don't think you were ever meant to blend in, *Luxsula,"* a familiar, smoky voice whispers in my ear as a shimmery shadow wisps away from my shoulder.

He's doing that thing again, making his voice appear close while he's far away. Never mind the clear invasion of my thoughts. With the sun set behind the horizon, I'm at the mercy of his darkest powers now. His whispering shadows, or whatever he calls it.

I gaze up to see Seraphina's blue war braids whipping in the wind, standing next to Sølas. His white-blue eyes needle my heart. It's possible he's even more beautiful at night. Darkness becomes him.

"Damn! Look at you, tatted up. Lookin' good. I may even have to put up a fight with Sølas to get you into the bedroom." Seraphina's eyes flare neon blue, a wry smile hooking up the corner of her lips.

Sølas elbows her hard in the side, rousing an audible, "Oomph."

I wink and blow a kiss her way, just to ruffle his feathers. Her eyes blaze neon cerulean at the suggestive thought clearly crossing her mind. I jump my gaze over to Sølas, whose arctic-blue eyes are brimming with smoke. His jaw clenching so tight, I'm almost certain the muscles in his neck will rupture.

I do enjoy being a tease. So, I walk over to him and run my newly tattooed finger down the chest of his slightly unbuttoned shirt.

"Jealous thing, aren't you?" I purr.

He growls in response. I've clearly struck a nerve. A pleasant and delightful distraction from the magnitude of what he has been asking me for. His pulse quickens as I circle him like prey. He doesn't seem to mind being hunted by me.

"Settle down, you two. I'm still here. Unless you're gonna let me join?" Seraph chuckles at Sølas' lancing glare. "We need to find the others. There are celebrations to be had."

"I should probably change before we—"

All three of us are surrounded in shadows before I can even finish my sentence. His velvety touch wraps up my legs, cascading over my breasts, my neck, across my lips and eyelashes. Finally, it tangles through my hair; I can't help but let out a small whimper at the sensation. The shadows become more chaotic at the sound that escapes my lips as they begin caressing and teasing my skin. Wild thoughts consume my mind. If he can do this in public, what can he do to me behind closed doors?

"Your thoughts are tame compared to what I would really do to you, if you let me have all you." His smoky voice is startling as the shadows retreat, swirling back into Sølas' chest. Part of me longs for control, like he has over his powers, while the other craves to lose exactly that with him.

I don't fail to notice his eyes darken as he takes me in.

My eyes flutter down to find I'm wrapped in a black velvet evening dress that cuts deep down my chest, ending just before my navel. There are cutouts in the shape of eight-pointed stars along my hips, with a shimmery mesh that reveals my markings. A long slit slashes up the side, freeing my legs for movement. My wrist is adorned with a black diamond bracelet—I assume matching what I can feel on my neck. I realize Pip must have sensed the change of attire and turned into the bracelet to go with my outfit. *A dragon with style.*

I lift my hands to my hair, feeling it pinned up to fall on one side of my head.

Sølas snaps his fingers; a tall, golden mirror appears before me.

I can see I'm right about the necklace. He's even done my makeup, eyes shadowed in smoky black with a gilded finish, matching my obsidian eyes flecked with gold. Kohl lines my bottom eyelashes, curling up at the ends. My lips are black with a thick golden line down the center of my bottom lip.

I look fucking good, despite less clothing, more jewelry and makeup than typical for me. Yet taking in the whole ensemble, he's somehow made my gold markings appear at home on my flesh. For the first time in my life, I'm not ashamed.

He snaps his fingers again. He and the mirror are gone. His presence pushes in behind me.

"You look ravishing." His voice growls in my ear, "Let the world fall beneath your feet as they gaze at you. Let the sight of you hold their very breath your captive prisoner."

My cheeks heat. Deep down, a part of me feels like I can be as beautiful as his words tonight. Rather than slinking into the shadows to hide, I can emerge from them anew.

A low whistle from Seraphina drags my eyes to hers. She clearly approves of the outfit as well. She's in a black shirt with the first three buttons undone. Her black leather pants are held up with coal leather suspenders, two leather straps crisscrossing her abdomen. Her long, powder-blue war braids and neon-blue eyes gleaming amidst the sea of black.

My gaze drifts to Sølas as he falls into step beside me. I swallow in the heat of him. He's dressed in a midnight, three-piece suit. The top buttons of his shirt are lazily undone, revealing the shadows dancing along his skin. Gold embroidery glints across his lapels, mirrored eight-pointed stars. His eyes, pale as starlight, flicker like Celestial temptation against the void. There's clearly a matching theme between our outfits, even though I haven't given in to his reckless demand for all of me. He's playing a dangerous game with this façade—a claim—as if I am already his.

"If I didn't know any better, I'd say beyond jealousy, you have some possession issues. *Both* our outfits echoing my new markings?" I throw him a coy smile.

He slides his hands into his pants, arching a brow at me.

"Sometimes my shadows have a mind of their own. Even if you won't give me what I want, it doesn't mean I am not yours to keep." He shrugs.

The air rips from my lungs. I never asked him for this. He is not bound to me just because he requests all of me.

*Mine to keep.*

No one has ever been mine. And he—he wasn't supposed to mean it when he said he would spend a lifetime unravelling my walls barricading me with hesitation. As much as I want him, I'm not so selfish that I wouldn't let him move on to find another suitable female to fall for. Although something deep inside me screams at the thought of his hands roaming someone else.

"Fucking stars above, Sølas. I forget how much of a hopeless romantic you can be. You're gonna scare her off with that mushy shit."

"Trust me. She doesn't frighten easily."

"You're bloody fucking incorrigible. Sometimes I don't know how I've put up with ya for so long." Seraph laughs. "Save the romance for someone who won't stab you with it, will ya?" She nudges him in shoulder before starting to walk up the hill. "Let's go! I should be halfway to passed out drunk by now." She waves us on with a fiendish grin.

"Hold on. Where did all our weapons go? And our clothes?" Panic sets in, thinking about my gifts from Sully. This will be my second night out without my armor since he gifted it to me.

"Don't worry, *Lux*, they've been portaled to your room. You'll find them neatly on your bed." He pauses, then his voice is right on the cusp of my ear, sultry and low. "Feel free to hold me accountable for each and every one of them."

It's hard to not let the shiver roll down my spine. That mouth of his is going to be a problem for me, especially the way he can play tricks with it.

"Yeah, he's obnoxious with his power like that. One time, he hid one of my war axes. I tore apart the room to find it. It was hidden under the pile of books I never bother to open. Smart ass." Seraph's eyes narrow on Sølas as he raises his hands in surrender.

"Shadow prick indeed." I laugh.

"Celestial's tits, it's getting cold. I'm off to the heated courtyard before my nips freeze off while you two eye-fuck each other under the moonlight...

unless you're gonna let me join." She gives me a pointed wink, and I roll my eyes.

"You're being just as bad as that one." I nod my head over to Sølas, who's giving me a sultry smile with smoky moonlit eyes. Celestials *those eyes*. Too easy to lose myself in them. Stars above! One more problem to add to the lists of why I shouldn't even try to give in… or maybe why I should? I shake my head, trying to clear the building storm of thoughts as the arched side entrance of Gildorea comes into view.

We arrive at the main diamond-shaped courtyard. It's surrounded by the white marble halls leading to our rooms. The main building marks the head of the diamond, the circular rotunda of the Grand Conservatory with its golden domed roof. The walls of the courtyard are adorned with the penthouse rooms assigned to Ellian Knights who are given their Bloodline pairing.

The courtyard is transformed for the festivities. Faerie lights float like Celestials, dancing around twirling gold streams. The globe of the Warded Hollow gleams like a jewel at the center. White and gold circular tables dot about. Oh, and the food! I'm don't know how Pip hasn't run off to devour it all. Molten chocolate spills from towering fountains, cakes of all sizes in impossible colors, roasted mooca dripping in herbs, vegetable medleys, spiced bioluminescent fungi, an endless array of cured meats and spiraling cheeses. Carts overflowing with food from all over Cascara and beyond.

The various Wings and social circles bustle with conversation over vibrant cocktails sparkling with enchantments.

I take the first step. Sølas and Seraphina, a step behind me. I don't lead in crowds, preferring the shadows, but Calais is right—my new markings are powerful. Or perhaps it's the way this outfit sheathes me in a confidence. Who in Emberhell cares? Tonight, I want to soak in the moonlight and dance until I'm dizzy.

I notice smoky shadows trailing beneath our feet, casting a runway of pure darkness. I hook my head to the side, slinging a sly smile back to Sølas. I'm not sure if this is what he meant by worshiping me like a goddess, or if he really wants to ensure he takes everyone's breath away when they look at us. Needless to say, it's working; the raucous crowd hushes to a whispering hum as we prowl our way through. Rather than slinking away to the shadows, I let the ones caressing my ankles empower me.

We pass the table with what's left of Chet's cronies. Brock Blackbriar looking a little worse for wear. I lift my upper lip in a snarl directed their way, reveling in the color draining from their faces.

I'm pretty sure I even saw Draven Bane's hand trembling. Chet won't look at me. I'm surprised he managed enough strength to show up.

As we saunter by Winx, I catch her eyes flaring rapidly at her perusal of my outfit. Clearly, she approves. Her glare hardens to black ice as it lands on Sølas behind me.

We arrive at the five small tables our Zenith Wing has pushed together to accommodate us all.

"Looks like someone decided to embrace their chaos tonight. Your Aura is radiating pure white. You look like a star amongst the shadows." Orion twirls her candy-red hair, her aquamarine scales glistening under the floating faerie lights. She's in a tight red dress that matches her hair and eyes. On the shaved side of her head, her fin-shaped ear is revealed, wearing a large heart-stone earring mirroring the choker around her neck.

"We can radiate together!" Fenwick beams. Her white and black hair shorn to her chin sways with the smile of her round cheeks pinned by dimples. She's wearing a shimmering white dress that flows out at the hips, forming a pleated sea down to her ankles.

"Hey! I want to be included." Juniper smiles as she stumbles into the conversation. Her forest green hair twists in braids beneath a crown of bright green thorns and white roses that matches the color of her skin. Her blue-grey ombre almond eyes remind me of summer storms.

"Savaé, I must request some of your time, along with Atlas, to examine your Arcane Glyph. It's quite the curious masterpiece." As Gearin speaks, light refracts through his spectacles, glinting off his gilded Rune Tech jaw. He's dressed in a white suit with a golden tie, contrasting his ebony skin, emulating his white dreadlocks dipped in gold.

Flint tosses me a wide grin. Emerald eyes shimmering beneath snowy hair with a suit of white and gold, blending perfectly with his marble skin.

Atlas flutters around me, enjoying the exposed skin of my outfit in a purely scientific way as he examines me. "Interesting. Interesting indeed."

His hand takes mine, flipping it over, front and back. Dusting a trail of moth-like fuzz over my skin. "This is by far the largest one in recorded history. The way the Arcane Glyph mirrors each side with the focus on your hands. Perhaps to focus your new gifts?" He tugs my arm like I'm an anatomical specimen, displaying it for Gearin to study.

*"I like this one. He is a clever one. Remind me not to eat him."* Calais' voice booms in my head.

*"You can't eat any of my Zenith, missy!"* I snap.

*"I will most certainly eat you if you call me 'missy' again."*

*"As a dragon, don't you have somewhere else to be other than inside my head?"*

*"I could hunt for dinner at your party if you're already missing my physical presence, Nebulight,"* she snips.

"You okay? You look like you're having a conversation all to yourself." Eko's ears twitch, as if he's listening for the voice I can hear in my head. A growling assortment of sounds that resemble a cackle ricochet in my brain, no doubt belonging to Calais.

"Sorry, it's an adjustment having a sarcastic dragon bludgeoning through my thoughts." I try to smile, like I'm not shaken by the fact that controlling my facial expressions while having a conversation with a snippy dragon in my mind is going to be a tall feat. That thought has Calais laughing even harder.

"It's odd, no, that you and your dragon are so in sync with the bond just being formed?" chimes Gearin, a quizzical look crumpling his face.

Sølas' arm grazes mine as he steps closer to the table. Placing a glass of Firesong agave in front of me and sliding one to Seraphina. "Actually, I can hear Scáil, too. Thankfully, he's rather reticent."

My arm brushes back against his, thanking him for my drink, ignoring the dangerous line I continue to toe along. I'm entangled in his gravitational pull, on a collision course quickly approaching the point of no return. Will I fall from the heavens into him, burning up the last bits of me I've managed to piece together—or will I shatter through him, ruining us both?

"Curious. Not only did you both manage to bond dragons—which hasn't been done in years within the same Wing—but they're both exceptionally rare dragons not known to bond. Further perplexing is that you can already hear them in your heads, which takes most bonds at least a few days. Beyond, of course, hearing their name. We're not even sure what breed of dragon Sølas bonded." Altas drifts off, lost in his own mind.

"Perhaps it's just unique to dragons," Vex sighs, appearing utterly bored by the topic. She's cinched in a black strapless dress, which goes flawlessly with her similar-hued curls and curved horns.

"Cinder, Kissa, Juniper—have you heard from your bonds, beyond their names?" Highin asks, outfitted with an autumn-colored suit modified for his sienna-feathered wings.

"No. And I'll savor every last bit of silence before the bond fully settles." Cinder takes another swig of his amber Smokewhisper libation, which matches his eyes. The bright orange flames trimming his dark suit blaze, bringing out the similar hues in his freckles and tousled hair.

The others nod in agreement.

"Enough of this studious shit. I'm ready to get Celestial's piss drunk! So, let's cheers to our confirmed Chivalry of Zenith Wing!" Seraphina pitches her glass to the stars.

"Wait. Where's Kivi?" Juniper's eyes dart around, concern pinching her brows before melting into a serene smile.

"I have arrived. It appears just in time, too." Heavy crescent shadows hang smudged under Kivi's eyes. She's varied the fungi that adorn her body, weaving the mycelium network to mimic a sheer, satin-like gown. The intricate root system shimmers faintly with life, moisture twinkling along the interconnected pathways of the underground world and the life it supports above.

The mushrooms on her head are now long tendrils intertwined with budding caps sweeping over her shoulder. I imagine it's her take on a side braid. "Sorry, the healers needed extra support today with all the injuries." Kivi's weary eyes flick to me with her last words. Maybe I should have just let Calais eat Chet and Brock after all.

"Yay! I saved you some sparkling fermented tea for the toast." Juniper cheers, her happiness springing petals from her hair, lilting on an invisible breeze, as she passes a flute full of a bubbling pink liquid to Kivi.

"Celestials Blessings, Juniper, and to our newly anointed Chivalry," Kivi toasts.

We all *clink* our glasses in a resounding cheer. Smoky heat slides down my throat, igniting my taste buds with tingling desire. My tongue swirls, pondering if this is what Sølas would taste like in my mouth.

Kissa punches through my molten thoughts, jostling me into Sølas as she claws her way between Seraphina and me.

"So," she purrs in barely a whisper, "am I finally free from the suffering scent of tension between you two?" She nods to Sølas, whose back grazes mine with each breath as he speaks with Cinder.

"I don't know what you're on about." I shift my weight away from him onto the table.

His fingers make a lazy gesture. Slow and deliberate. Rolled-up sleeves baring skin to brush against mine as he braces his arm on the table. Heat flushes my cheeks with the skin-to-skin sensation.

"Why would you think that?" Lifting my glass to gulp away the twitch of my lips, attempting to snap my reins of control. Regrettably, the smoky taste filling my mouth only stokes the flames singeing the fraying straps of my bridled restraint.

"Hmm… well, the giant cloud of shadows in the landing field was *pretty* conspicuous." Kissa raises a knowing brow as I attempt to stifle my whole face from turning the color of Orion's hair. "I'd watch out for Winx if I were you. She combusted into furious flames at the sight of you swallowed up into his Shadowveil. I know you've been dodging that conversation you need to have with her, but something tells me she's not finished with you. And definitely isn't thrilled about someone else touching you." Kissa's chartreuse eyes narrow on me with warning.

It's hard to focus on her words as velvet tendrils of shadow lace around my ankles, continuing their course, curling up my legs.

Kissa doesn't miss my pebbling skin in response. She rolls her eyes, mumbling under her breath as she drains her drink, "I was hoping you two fucked this Ritherin-shit out of your systems. Anything more stays the fuck out of Zenith Wing. If this goes up in flames, you'll burn all of us." Her fur bristles, tail whipping as she storms off to vent to Flint about my pathetic composure.

She's absolutely right, of course; there's too much at risk. I need a distraction that isn't tall, dark, and handsome. It's foolish of me to even consider trying to give in to what he wants. His feelings for me, even if I could be all in, will only put our Zenith in danger. He can't be choosing me over a strategic move that saves the rest of our team in battle. I need to snatch back my reins of control, unhitching the ominous weight of feeling things that require more of me than is safe to give.

"Kissa, perhaps a little chaotic distraction would do me some good?" I wink at her. She huffs in reply, realizing I'll be causing trouble of a different sort by not heeding her warning.

I finish my last sip, bidding my delicious smoky drink farewell as the empty glass *clinks* onto the table, leaving him behind with it. Time to indulge in a fiery distraction that burns with less-frightening promises. The shadows coil tighter around my legs before letting me go as I step away.

I know my distraction will hurt him, but it's for the good of our Zenith. Even if I want to try, failing would be utterly catastrophic for team dynamics.

*"You seem to like to test the Fates. Chaos Magic suits you more than you realize."*

*"Not now, Calais. Trust me, you'll likely want to stay out of my head for the rest of the night."*

*"I would hate to have a dragon come busting through the wall to ruin the mood."* Her voice dripping with sarcasm.

*"Smart ass."* I huff in return.

I prowl over to Winx, managing to grab two coupes from a serving tray along the way. A new color scorches through her hair, back to violet, matching her eyes when her power flares, just like her dress. It has a long slit up one leg and is entirely backless. I take in the view as I walk up. I shift both the glasses to one hand, freeing the other to slide along the small of her back.

"A violet flame of beauty as always. Sparkling Moonwine?" I give Winx a sly smile as I motion the glasses her way. She takes one with delicate ease, her eyes flaring neon as she gazes over my new markings.

"I'm glad you're finally taking my advice about your markings. I like the new ones, too, even if I don't care for the company you walked in with."

"Is that jealousy on those beautiful lips, Winx? You know it's never suited you."

"Oh, and why is that?" She pouts her violet-stained lips.

"Because your beauty and power burn every other female here," I purr.

Her eyes flare to the rhythm of her accelerated pulse, signaling I'm on the right path as she sips her drink. The music picks up, a slew of delightful string instruments. The notes are warm, reminding me of the first days of blooming spring. When the earth is cool beneath your skin while the sun warms your soul.

I close my eyes, letting my body gently sway to the beat as the voices of Winx, Tyranny, Rizz, and the others fade into the background.

A dainty tap to the back of my arm snaps me from the ballad like a misplayed chord. "You never cease to keep us on the edge, whether it's destroying every target in the Warded Hollow or bonding the largest dragon in Cascara. Do tell—what's the next scandal for our beloved Savaé?" Rizz pries, his pink hair swirled into a neat dollop at the crown of his head. Eccentric slate eyes shimmer above a crescent-moon smile, hanging on a cliff's edge, awaiting a bold response to rival his attire.

A sly plot weaves through my mind as I take in his dapper white waistcoat frosted with pink velvet florals.

"Hopefully convincing you to ask Flint Rockwell to dance."

I lean in, chin perching on my knuckles, head titled with a coy smile hooking up, basking in the blush sketching his high cheekbones.

"Oh, stars. I do say, it's never a dull moment with you around." Flustered, Rizz adjusts the high collar of his blazer. "I keep begging Winx to keep you close. Flint *is* quite a sight to behold. Hmm." He taps his chin with a lacquered finger. "I may just take you up on that challenge." He throws me a wink before finishing his last sip of liquid courage.

The walls of my glacial palace chest fracture a little under the undeniable warmth of watching Rizz sashay over to Flint. I didn't think marble could blush, but Flint's chiseled cheeks prove me wrong. His face pinching with a bashful smile.

I bite my bottom lip as I watch my friend nervously take Rizz's hand. With the way Flint's body moves during sparring, I have no doubt he'll be a vicious partner on the dance floor.

Winx lashes a wary gaze at Rizz with Flint, ever the protector of her beloved cousin. I'm more than happy to distract her so Flint has the chance to enjoy himself unshackled from her looming wildfire.

"Speaking of dancing…" I extend out my hand in front of Winx. "Will you grant me this Celestial Blessing?"

"Gladly. My gift is yours." Winx places her hand in mine as we saunter to the dance floor together.

The music quickens, reminding me of a midsummer sun shower. I let the melody seep into my bones, washing away my worries in the flood.

We twirl and swirl, smiling and laughing as we continue to drink more and more Moonwine. I swear the glasses are enchanted to never empty. I'm as carefree as I was flying with Calais, wind spinning through my hair.

I gaze over Winx's shoulder, savoring the smile on Flint's face as he spins Rizz around. Kivi is swaying next to Atlas while Juniper and Fenwick prance in a circle holding hands, dancing to a beat entirely their own.

I find Sølas splayed in a chair with a bright red liquid swirling in his glass. Tyranny is practically dancing in his lap. He has a devilish grin painted on his face, but I see through his mask. There is boredom in his eyes as he stares off into the distance.

As the song changes to a slower pace, I tug Winx tightly into my arms. A part of me wonders what it would feel like to dance with Sølas. To feel his closeness in an intimate moment, to actually let myself indulge a connection that is more than physical lust.

It's something I'm afraid I'll never know.

To be held like I am something precious. To be loved, unconditionally. Just as I am. A safe place where I can shed the weight of all my invisible armor, left pooling on the floor as I let myself rest my weary soul and just *be*.

Yet I can't make sense of how he or anyone could possibly love my wretched, mosaic mess. My shattered edges only serve to sever and shred, flaying and hacking anyone who tries to hold me gently, leaving them raw and bloody. Just as the world has left me.

I'm still bleeding on jagged, broken bits I've barely reconstructed. Each sliver I manage to snap together is met with the haunting echo that continues to shackle my soul.

*You can never love or be loved...You beckon darkness to consume everything you hold dear.*

Every time those words claw at my resolve, another layer of black frost is summoned to creep across the thorny glacial palace of my heart. I cannot beckon darkness if I hold no one dear... if I refuse to let anyone into my heart.

I paint a charming smirk across my lips, hiding what lurks beneath the glittering cage of my gilded markings. I dip Winx, plucking a beautiful laugh from her lips. Drinking in the sound, heady with the sensation of positively too much sparkling Moonwine. I bring her up, dusting her neck in kisses topped with a small nibble. Violet fires blaze brightly around blown pupils as they lock onto my shimmering gold and obsidian irises.

The next thing I know, her lips are on mine. *Chaotic trouble indeed.*

My power rumbles beneath my skin, knowing the repercussion of my choices, almost feeding off it. It calls to me, wanting to be released, craving ruination. Yet there's something different to it now. It's as though I can feel the chaos beyond destruction.

The subtle hum of creation.

# CHAPTER 32

We drunkenly stumble back to her room. I'm already untying her dress as we make it through the door. I slip it off as I spin her around, wrapping my arms around her waist.

She kisses me like her lips are made of fire and I'm her kindling, hooking her legs round my hips.

I playfully sling her on the bed. With the snap of my fingers, her wrists are bound to the wall in my white flames.

Her eyes flare a deep shade of violet, hazy with lust as they tell me *yes*.

I stand up, taking in the sight of her brazen body, basking without shame. There's something so intoxicating about a confident female who knows exactly what she wants.

I trail soft kisses along the outline of her swollen lips, following the angle of her jaw before slipping down her neck.

"I want to savor each kiss until your sweet fury drips down my face and I am drenched in your power," I rasp as her back arches, grinding her body into mine.

I dust kisses across her collarbones, then down her chest to the crested nipples of her petite breasts. My hands take the place of my mouth, pinching her with the perfect mix of pleasure and pain.

Her white skin, fresh-fallen snow, melting beneath every kiss. My lips trace down the carved outlines of her feminine stomach. I pry a whimper from her throat as my tongue lazily licks up the lips between her quivering legs. Her body begs for my mouth to deepen with each torturous pass of restraint.

"Tear me to pieces," she growls, and I obey her plea.

My tongue slips inside her, syncing to her rhythm before slipping in a finger and teasing her clit with my tongue. Her moan fills the air as I savor, devour, and nibble. I drink her in, consuming her pleasure as her body dances beneath my mouth, pleading for more.

I sink another finger inside, curving them in just the right way that makes her delicious cunt purr, tightening around my embrace. Her whimpers are a road map to her desire, her flames guiding me, letting me fuck her exactly as she craves. Her lust is a fiery blaze, just like her.

She burns in ecstasy until she is at her wick's end, melting in front of me like a candle. I melt along with her, moaning into the pure pleasure of controlled bliss. I stay inside her, tracing her body with gentle kisses until the last spasming wave of high dwindles from her body, her legs shaking with gratification.

My drenched fingers twist, freeing her wrists from my icy-white fire restraints. I help guide her stiff limbs to her sides, kissing them as I go.

We lie together, breathy as we both enjoy the last waves of oxytocin and dopamine coursing through our nerves.

I've always found pleasure in giving it to others. The idea of letting someone else pleasure me, though? That's too vulnerable. Too intimate. A shiver trails down my spine as intrusive thoughts flash through my lust-hazy mind. My imagination running wild with what exactly Sølas worshiping me might entail.

Winx's breath steadies, slowing down as she drifts off into slumber, which allows me to quietly slink out of her room.

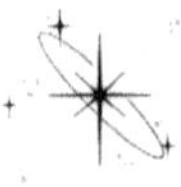

Hot water pelts down from the ceiling faucet, scalding my flesh, as if it can burn me clean of my toxic choices. While Winx was a delightful distraction, getting lost between her legs only provided a fleeting break from the fuckery needling beneath my skin.

Fear. Loneliness. Failure. Longing. They all sledge together, like boulders bludgeoning me from the inside out.

But the real danger is that dash of flickering of hope.

Weaving its way into my sinew with its golden light. Threatening to cleave flesh from bone as it flays my armor, leaving me bare. Letting Sølas know just how to crumple my glacial palace. Slicing my heart upon the broken shards. Bloody. Sharp. Untouchable. A ruin too fractured to cradle. His declarations unraveling in his hands, shredded on my mosaic mess, leaving nothing more than hollow vows—laced in the prettiest words.

Maybe I'd risk the incineration of breathing that burning ember of hope to life if it was just my fate at stake. However, when he realizes I am inevitably too lancing to love, the bitter ripples will taint our every dynamic, risking the entire Wing with ruin.

I turn the water frigid, reminding myself that the cold is my only safety. Only ice can freeze around my sharp edges and not weep crimson.

My worries wash down the drain as I finish cleaning up and head down the hall to my own room. I'm glad when I look down and realize my bracelet is gone. Pip must have portaled off to our room. *Smart little dragon.*

*"At least one of you is intelligent,"* Calais snarls.

I roll my eyes. *"I never claimed I was."* She huffs in response.

I'm almost back to my dorm when the hairs on my neck sway. Before I can spin around, my back is pinned to the wall. My head caged between Sølas' arms.

He's a cyclone of shadows, violently whirling around me, yet somehow not touching me. I can't even make out his face in the storm.

"You reek of her," he growls. "Tell me, did you think of me when you were drowning in her pleasure?"

"Males." I huff.

His shadows seem to recoil from the snark in my remark. His stormy, ice-blue eyes peeking out, but the shadows still rage within them. He keeps one arm braced by my head as he lifts the other to trace the border of my jaw. My heart sputters, pleading to lean into his touch.

"You are not easy to read, my dear. I long for the day the pages of your book become worn by my fingertips, once I've read all your lines a thousand times and discover all that's hidden in between."

The words dance across my heart, spooling strings of golden light. That tugging sensation nips at my ribs, drawing me in with an insensible longing to be closer to him. His aura presses in on mine, stealing the air from my lungs. Suffocating all logical thought.

Celestials, how I crave to know what his lips taste like. My recent release only barely lends me enough control as he dips close. Lips hovering just above mine. I know if I let him linger longer, Winx won't be the only dangerous indulgence of my night.

Fists clenched, I look away, gaze dropping to the floor as I grit out, "In your dreams, Sølas. Even if I wanted to try, it risks too much." I will the shadows to veil the lie etched in my eyes—pleading they don't betray me to the whispers he commands.

His knuckle grazes my chin, tipping my obsidian-and-gold irises to meet his lakes of ice.

"If only you knew my dreams, *Luxsula*."

That word rolls off his smoky lips, tumbling across my skin as my body quivers. How can a word I don't even fucking understand affect me so? I knew he was trouble from the moment our eyes first met. I wanted to stay away. But each time he ensnares me in his gravity, I sink closer. Each time becoming harder and harder to untangle myself from him. Like an invisible string pulling me back into his orbit. Perhaps it's just the chaotic nature of our magic drawing us together. *Fuck.* The thought of our magic unleashed, our bodies colliding bare, is enough to shred the last reins of my restraint.

"Careful now," he whispers darkly against my ear, "with that dirty mind and those wicked lips." His tone ignites the feral beast in me, thirsting to pin him to the wall with far less control than he's exerting.

I lash bitter words to temper the beast, hoping to slash open some distance between him and my fraying resolve. "I'm sure Tyranny would appreciate you warming her bed right now."

Sølas tsks, voice tilting sharp as a blade. "You know exactly whose bed I would be making an altar of right now. But I won't settle for sloppy seconds or mere bits and pieces of you."

"Exactly why I needed a distraction tonight, because you and I... can't happen. Despite whatever this is between us."

"You sure know how to pick a dangerous distraction," he provokes.

"Oh, and you're not? What if I did try, Sølas? What if I did attempt to give you more of me than I've ever given anyone else? What if you're the one who finds the key to my heart? And when you open it, all you find is a black sticky mess. Don't waste your time falling in love with this black tar heart of mine. Don't you see? My darkness is a death trap; not even your shadows can escape."

"Don't say that." His low growl fractures, bleeding out with a pleading sorrow. Hands twitch at his sides, trembling with the urge to reach for me. His shadows falter, wisping into a mourning haze. One knuckle brushes the air near me, only to fall short. His whole body coils with restraint—pleading without words, begging not to lose all he aches to hold.

I sidestep out of his consuming aura, fighting the cracks forming along my glacial walls under the weight of his agony. "You would go through all that, and all we would do is put the entire Zenith at jeopardy in the aftermath. I am too broken to love or be loved. Only a fool would request… all of this." My hand sweeps down, motioning to all of me.

"You can't know that, Savaé." My name on his lips is like sweet honey, almost slipping up my train of thought.

"You're right. We can't know that, because it will never happen." The words drip from my mouth like venom. But my anger is not for him—it's for me.

"Never say never, *Luxsula*." His vow lands heavy on my limping heart as a plume of shadows unfurls. The space between us collapses—he's gone. Leaving me alone in the dark.

Good riddance. He should go. Celestials, why was he even here in the first place? My stupid chest hurts in his absence. The taste of salt slicks my lips. I didn't even realize I'm crying. Why the fuck am I always crying around him? I could blame it on how long this fucking day has been, but in truth, he always manages to make me more vulnerable than I'd ever care to admit.

I bludgeon my door open, but my rage and torment plummet to a simmer as I see Pip waking up with sleepy eyes on my pillows. His face looks stupidly cute when he's all sleepy. He rolls over, trying to stir his energy. Then he's quickly up and prancing around my feet, almost tripping me with his little dance. I snatch him up, squeezing him tight.

"Glad you're okay, buddy," I say as he nuzzles into my face. I'm not sure how such a sweet creature can love a toxic monster like me.

My weapons, armor, and cloak are indeed on my bed, just as Sølas promised. Why did he have to be so annoyingly perfect sometimes?

I clear the weapons off and fall into the comfort of my down feather mattress as the chaos of today crumples into the bed. The humming purr of Pip on my chest lulls me into a sleep where no worries can find me.

# CHAPTER 33

I stir the next morning with a melancholy fermented in my bones from the truth in the words I spoke last night.

I decide there's no better way to warm my soul than to spend my free weekend at the forge, working metal. Something I can actually control. Something I'm good at.

I shower and head back to my room to change, thankful not to have an escort for the first time in months. I'm not sure if they're all too hungover or if being bonded to the biggest dragon on the continent melted their worries away. There's also a loneliness I am unaccustomed to.

*"You'll never be alone again."* Calais' voice booming in my head is as sobering as a hot morning cup of kahvi.

*"Good morning to you, too."* I smile in return.

I bind an extra round of fabric around my breasts since I know the sweat of the forge makes it easier to slip. I opt for a black tank and loose-fitting tunic pants, breathable in the heat of the Universitás foundry. My hair is tied into a tight bun at the back of my head.

Pip is feeling adventurous and turns into a decorative metal pin with a small version of a Celestial Dragon at the end, similar to an image I've seen drawn in ancient texts when exploring the archives. I've learned to stop questioning the magic of my impossible orange companion. I place the pin at the base of my leather-bound updo.

*"Before you head to the forge, meet me in the field outside the Mystic-woods,"* Calais commands. I don't question her, especially after she hasn't

drawn out my suffering with any additional snarky remarks about my poor choices last night.

I head to the dining hall, snatching my breakfast to go, with extra for Pip.

My lungs burn delightfully as I run my morning jog down to the field south of Gildorea just before the Mysticwoods. As I reach the clearing, Calais is already there waiting for me, tail whipping with annoyance.

Fully taking in her presence catches my breath.

Her iridescent scales capture the morning rays from the east, painting her in colors of creamy orange and mauve. On the opposite side, her body is a mirror of all the colors of the Mysticwoods. Her four wings, dipped in white feathers, stretch wide. Blue sparks dance across the biometallic, lightning-conductor spikes dipped in blue across her back. The ribbon-like flesh along her eel-like tail waves in the breeze. Crescent moons bejewel her crown, sparkling in the sunlight, while the large spears that frame her face glisten like ice, rebelling the sun's plea to watch them melt.

As we get close to her, there's movement in my hair. Pip is suddenly crawling down my arm and racing to Calais, whose rainbow eyes narrow on him with an expression I can't read.

"Sorry about Pip." I chase after him, but the little scoundrel is far too fast when he wants to be.

"*You call him Pip?*" she scoffs with an audible grumble.

"What's wrong with Pip?"

"*Has he not told you his true name?*"

"He can't talk."

"*Yet.*"

"Well then, how do you know his name?"

"*That is not for you to know. Yet.*"

"Of course it's not." I sigh, my head dipping back as I pray to the Celestials to give me patience with the lightning-breathing dragon before me. "Well, can you tell me his true name, at least?"

"*Our kind would refer to him as Cadens Regulus.*"

"Seems rather ostentatious for this little trickster, so I'm going to keep calling him Pip. Until he can tell me otherwise." I shrug as Calais lowers her head to snort in my face. This time, I brace myself, so instead of tumbling backwards, I just slide across the dew-covered grass.

"*There is a loose scale on the right side of my chest. Right next to my heart. A new one is already starting to grow underneath it. I want you to take this scale and use it to create a long sword.*"

"I don't like long swords. They unbalance me," I begrudgingly admit. There's no point lying to a dragon who can read my thoughts.

"*It doesn't really matter. It will be as you need it to be. Or make a short sword, to match the one that Cadens Regulus helped you forge.*"

"And how do you know about that?"

"*He told me. Obviously. And I have access to your memories, new and old.*"

"What!?"

"*If you don't know that, then what are they even teaching you at that excuse of a university?*"

"Not that, obviously." I cross my arms, annoyed at yet another breach of my privacy.

"*Well, get used to it. I can already feel what you feel. Soon, you will feel as I feel. You will need to enhance your mental shielding. Might I suggest the Shadowmancer for shielding practice? He has a certain way of getting through the walls of your mind... If only you would listen.*"

"No. I will not practice with him. We shouldn't be near one another. And what are you both going on about listening? I can listen well enough."

"*Then you are not ready.*"

"Ready for what?"

"*Ready to truly listen.*"

"You two are both equally annoying." I huff over my crossed arms.

"*As is your stubbornness, on all the wrong things,*" she growls before continuing, "*Remember to keep that blade with you. Give it to Cadens Regulus. He will know what to do with it.*" She nods downwards, reminding me to grab the scale from her massive chest.

Her scales are enormous, each the size of a cavalry shield. My fingers graze against those covering the right side of her heart until they catch on the loose one. Her enormous heart beats slow and steady beneath my hands. With a good amount of tugging, and some wiggling, it comes free.

Despite its size, it's exceptionally light. She's right; there is another, smaller scale beneath, covering most of her skin, but no doubt this area will be a deadly weakness until the new scale is full-sized. Her skin color reminds me of snow crystals—icy white, almost translucent, but with a sparkle to it. Or perhaps it's more akin to frozen tears of the Celestial Dragon that course through her blood. I step back to examine the translucent, iridescent scale.

With the bend of her legs, Pip scurries down, leaping towards me. I hold out her scale to catch Pip, bracing myself for Calais' take-off. Despite sliding backwards, I'll never tire of the beauty of watching her tear through the clouds, becoming invisible amongst them.

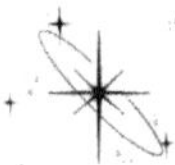

SWEAT DRIPS DOWN MY TEMPLE. I've been sledging away in the forge all day. Calais' dragon scale is exceptionally hard. It took me hours just to figure out how to break it.

It required Pip's dragon fire heating it over and over again until it glowed like hot metal, then shattered like glass.

I've just finished grinding it up and melting it, thankful to find no impurities. However, there's way too much material for a short sword.

She's right; I'll need to make a longsword. I hear her grumbles in my head at my acknowledgement. In fact, the amount of material will require a greatsword for the ratio of metal to imbued ingredient to be correct, so the blade keeps its strength.

As the steel begins to take the shape of the blade, I hear the frequency I heard calling to me from the Mysticwoods, before Calais had arrived. It's subtle but hums louder the more I work the metal, almost reminding me of a song.

I notice myself humming to it. The metal seems to respond, beginning to glow bright white. *Interesting.* I wonder what type of magic will come from her scale. I wait for the sharp voice of Calais in my head, yet it doesn't come. Another secret for her to hoard and me to figure out.

After several more hours, my legs begin to wobble. I take a break to drink some water, restoring the sweat that glistens on my body.

My eyes drift down to Pip, curled up next to the forge. No doubt enjoying the heat radiating from it. He jerks in his sleep, like he's having a bad dream. I shout his name, trying to wake him, but he continues to wriggle frantically. My flesh sears each step I take closer to the forge; I bite back at the pain. Finally, I'm close enough to reach out and stroke him. My touch seems to soothe him, extending his limbs out in a long stretch before curling back in the other direction.

I lurch back from the heat of the forge, enjoying the coolness pooling over my skin in comparison. I watch my seared flesh slowly heal in front of my eyes, as if nothing ever happened, but I can still feel the pain burning beneath my flesh.

Thankfully, the forge has a side door that leads outside. It's on the bottom floor, beneath the north wing of the dormitories. I shakily step out to a late winter night. The skies are clear, twinkling full of celestial diamonds. My gaze drifts to the Dragon Spine Mountains in the distance, glimmering a deep purple under the moonlight. Likely due to the cascading waterfalls that drain from the snow-filled tundra above. The wind whips through the tall grass of the Midland plains. It reminds me of a calm ocean of gold. I follow the current of waves rippling through the golden meadows, as if they are dancing to the sound of the universe.

I sit down, wrapping my arms around my bent knees. My lashes flutter shut, the cool breeze evaporating the sweat from my skin. I swear, for a second, I can hear the melody dancing through the meadow, the very hum of the universe, like it's beckoning me. It reminds me of the only memory I ever had of my mother. Her humming me to sleep in her arms.

I was just a babe though, so perhaps it was just a figment of my imagination. My brain creating an illusion to soothe me on the coldest nights, to keep me from breaking completely. It's a soft melody with a chaotic beat that ebbs and flows, a tune unlike any other. As soon as I open my eyes, the sound fades off into the distance.

Something so close but always out of reach. Secrets I am destined never to know. For I was just a feral beast, discarded for the universe to feast upon. Born to forever walk this world alone.

Yet there's now a persistent part of my heart that begs to differ. Yearning to reach for the heavens. Demanding more for my life. As if it's commanding the Fates to reweave my timeline. Stitching in a love so bright, it threatens to unravel the cosmos at its seams. Untangling the twine of stories untold, the threads of life unfolded, as the price of love is paid. The words of forgotten memories.

An exasperated sigh deflates my chest. It's selfish of my stupid little heart to crave what I cannot behold. Yet I gaze to the stars and dare to ask, "Do you ever think I can learn to love?"

I search the heavens for a response. The stars twinkle in the way they do, keeping their secrets close to their hearts. I rest my forehead against my knees. What a foolish question to ask the heavens and think they would respond. I lift my eyes to the skies once again, irrationally pleading for something more.

As if daring to respond to my desires, a golden falling star cleaves the sky in two. The rainbow aura of colors dancing along its tail brings silver welling to my eyes. Shades of deep violet merge seamlessly into brilliant indigo, transitioning into bright blues and emerald green before flowing into warm yellows, fiery oranges, and finally, a passionate red. Vibrant colors cascade like ribbons in the sky, and darkness seems to weep with me, bowing to its beauty.

The mountains below become luminescent in their glow. For a fleeting moment, time seems frozen in place. The world holding its breath, captivated by the Celestial display. The horizon becomes a kaleidoscope of colors as the ethereal star bursts into sparkling stardust, the wind dusting the heavenly glitter in its blessing. My eyes grow wide as it kisses my skin in its gleaming embrace.

And for the briefest moment, my heart doesn't feel so broken. Its gift: a glimpse of what a full heart might feel like. I tumble back into the grass, the overwhelming sensation of it all pouring from my lashes.

I doze off briefly, feeling as though I've awoken from the strangest dream. I would have been inclined to believe it was all just a fantasy if it weren't for the stardust still sparkling on my skin. I head back to the forge to finish my work with an odd sensation in my heart I can't quite put my finger on. There's something different now. Something magical.

Sweat drips off my brow, sizzling on the hot metal below as I work throughout the night until morning. I once again begin humming the tune the sword sings to me, weaving runes in metal across the blade as if they are the words to a song I don't know the lyrics to. A gentle sort of peace rolls through my soul as I become one with the moment.

One with the blade before me.

As I sharpen the edges of my creation on the whetstone, I notice stardust shimmering through the white metal. This greatsword is imbued with the magic of a Moonstorm dragon and the dying breath of a shooting star.

There is something more to this than my other blades. Something that resonates with my soul, as if we were forged anew tonight in the breathtaking aurora of it all. The blade sings louder to me, its words finally clear.

*Dream Singer*.

# CHAPTER 34

I'm pretty sure the sharp, feminine voice I hear singing in my head is a combination of dehydration and lack of sleep setting in as delirium. Yet I can't help but agree: it *is* a beautiful name for this blade. My finest work of art surely deserves an equally resonant name.

"Alright. I shall call you Dream Singer." The blade hums brightly, as if acknowledging my words with approval. Then sparks begin to crackle off the blade, like small fireworks. It seems amused, celebrating its own creation.

When the great blade cools back to an indigo-blue metal, I take it in my hand. Appreciating it in the light, the feel of it, miraculously lighter than the first short blade I made. It is perfectly balanced. An absolute marvel.

I decide to jaunt outside and practice whipping my blade through the early morning air. The brisk breeze carries the savory smells of morning breakfast from the dining hall. My stomach growls in protest, reminding me I haven't eaten since the morning before. I hear a grumbling louder than my own. I look down to see Pip weaving between my feet in a figure eight. He's so excited for breakfast, I'm surprised he hasn't run off without me.

"Just a few more minutes, little dragon." I lower down, scratching under his chin, when I notice two odd new bumps on the ridges of his shoulders. Before I can inspect them further, he is scampering off after a bug.

My body shifts into a fighting-stance position. I whirl my blade through the air, as if dancing to the song it resonates through my bones. The sword shimmers a brighter shade of blue with every movement until it's almost white. We twirl together, becoming more and more in tune, until the blade is nothing more than an extension of my own desires.

My movements abruptly become more chaotic; sparks fly from the blade, creating a veil around us. As if we are surrounded by invisible enemies, we violently swirl through the chaotic blaze. Light flares, cloaking me in magic, keeping me hidden from what lurks far beyond the seams of our world.

Streaks of lightning pierce the earth, branding the soil in a circular pattern. Runic patterns unfold, weaving a protection spell. Some I know, but many I do not. My form whips into a whirlwind of chaos, lashing between blades of the storm. My movements surrender to the melody, as if puppeteered by the very heavens above.

Yet I'm not afraid to yield control of my body to this force beyond my own. Perhaps it's the ancient energy wrapping me in its sacred force as I let go. Allowing the universe to guide me, for once, rather than having to fight back with gritted teeth. I lose myself as every nerve awakens in my body to the static charge that thickens the air. My magic cascades through me, tunneling into the blade, as if it's a conduit.

My lashes flutter shut. I'm dancing among the cosmos, swirling through the stars. My hands reaching out as I weave gases and stardust together in the clouds of the nebulas, watching stars coming into existence at the tips of my fingers. Humming once again the song the blade sings to me as I weave. Guiding the chaotic collision into a beautiful ballet orchestrated by the movement of my hands.

*Hoot. Hoot. HOOOT.*

My dream is suddenly thrust away as my mind eddies back to my body at the sound of an owl hooting loudly behind me. The sparks dwindle as the lightning ceases. I spin to see a Scroll Owl flapping its robe-like wings aloft.

He spits a scroll at my feet before frantically flapping away. A hint of annoyance prances along his hoots as he fades into the distance. Clearly, he has been there waiting for me longer than I realized.

Without so much as a thought, an indigo leather holster appears, and Dream Singer flies into the sheath along my back. *Maybe I am hallucinating.*

I bend down to pick up my scroll and begin to read.

*TO: SAVAÉ ENTROPÉ*
*NEW ELLIAN KNIGHT ROOM ASSIGNMENT: Penthouse, Starlight Sanctuary*

*Please note, personal items have already been moved to your new location.*

*BLOODLINE PAIR—*

Unfortunately, the rest of the parchment is burnt off in a tree-like pattern. Apparently, I almost struck the Scroll Owl with the field of lightning moving around me. No wonder he was pissed at me. Well, I'm sure I can track down one of my professors to find out my Bloodline pairing.

But first, Pip and I need food and a bath. Excitement bristles through my blood, numbing the exhaustion from lack of sleep and low blood sugar. In my new penthouse suite, I'll have a private bathroom. Today feels like a day to indulge in a shower and then a bubble bath scented with jasmine and eucalyptus, my favorite soapy combo.

Pip changes into the dragon pin strung through my now-messy bun. As I trot my way back to center campus, I try to tuck the hair that comes loose behind my ears, but it's no use. The delicious smell prancing along the air pulls me in like a lure.

# CHAPTER 35

I'm practically skipping to the dining hall, intoxicated by the smell of thin dough smothered in nutty chocolate spread with heart berries, fluffy egg cakes baked in crusts, and mouth-watering bacon on the breeze.

I quickly make my way through the tables of the dining hall, filling my plate with one of everything and a large pile of bacon for Pip and I to devour.

The hairs on my neck dance, and I know all too well who'll be getting in the way of my attempted quick retreat to my new quarters. The scent of amber and spruce fills my lungs as I sigh.

"Already sighing, and you haven't even looked at me yet. How disappointing." I can hear the wicked smile on his lips as he says those last words far too close to my ear.

"I'm hungry and don't have time for your theatrics this morning." I swat his voice away from my ear like the gnat my mind needs him to be.

"I can't help but linger when you look positively ravishing, covered in the darkness of soot." His smoky voice tickles the back of my neck as a finger runs down my upper spine.

I fight the weakness in my knees and spin around to face him.

"Your reckless flirting is going to get us in trouble. Now fuck off."

"Will it? I'd love to discover each and every part of this trouble you speak of." I loathe the way I'd love to bite the devilish smirk right off his face, while my lips savor far more than they should dare to.

Ice-blue eyes lazily prowl over my sweat-drenched body. His hand reaches for my face, arctic irises locking onto mine as he tucks a loose strand behind my ear. My fist clenches, trying to trap the shudder as my body vibrates beneath his Celestials be dimmed fucking touch.

"I was just admiring the marvel of this new blade that stole you away from me for more than a whole day." His voice has a far too irresistible tone for me to trust him as he cocks an eyebrow at me, awaiting my challenge.

"Dream Singer couldn't steal me away from you when I am not yours to be stolen from."

"Aren't you, though?" He snickers, as if knowing something I don't.

My blood heats beneath his words, and I'm not sure if it's lust or fury.

"You're clearly delusional. Maybe you should see if Kivi can unscramble that shadowy mess of a brain of yours."

He leans in close, nostrils flaring, seeming to enjoy the scent of soot and sweat lingering on my body before he turns around with a wicked laugh.

I don't have time to chase after him and demand to know what he's going on about. My stomach's growling, and I'm starting to feel faint. I grab a giant glass of honeycrisp cider and march through the hallways. I twist my fingers along the parchment scroll, enchanting it to lead me to my new room.

The scroll guides me to the northernmost point of the diamond-shaped courtyard, up a golden spiral staircase, until I arrive on the top floor. Before me stands an arched doorway made of a stunning iridescent starstone. It's carved with a scene of the night sky. In beautiful script, 'Starlight Sanctuary' is scrolled into the stone, a word for each door.

The starstone groans as I push through, my breath slipping from my lungs. The square room is open-format, framed with indigo nightstone beams. The ceiling is nothing but glass, so you can see the endless night sky.

Two large doorless openings, cleaved by a corner beam, sway with white gossamer curtains, framing two open balconies. One faces west with a seating area and a glass-vaulted greenhouse. The northern balcony has a large, oval heated pool in midnight blue, surrounded by various planted palms and deep-blue bioluminescent flowers.

White marble with gold veining waterfalls down the one solid wall on the east of the room, spilling out across the floor like streams of gold carving through snow. A slash of indigo carves up the pallid space—an oversized four-poster bed, wrapped in midnight silk sheets, dusted with nebulas of the night sky. Each beam flows with dreamy chiffon curtains. Along the small wall before the opening to the bathing space are two adjacent armoires. One of white wood, carved with the phases of the moon, and the other of Midnightwood, etched with constellations of the night sky.

In the opposite corner of the room sits an oversized copper bathtub, overlooking the perfect vista of the northern mountains. Kitty-corner to the tub is a table for two and a magenta velvet reading chaise with a gold table next to it.

I plop the food down on the table, scarfing what I can before fighting Pip for the last bit of bacon. Which I, of course, let him have. Pip pounces on the bed, stretching out into a puddle of orange, fat and happy. His purring fills the room as I saunter over to the shower.

There are three different shower heads in a large shower tiled in deep blue. The ceiling is speckled silver, twinkling stars peeking through the tendrils of steam. I lather on my favorite soap of jasmine and eucalyptus, spirals of soot swirling away.

Finally clean, I wring out my hair, stepping out to wrap myself in a towel. Next, it's time to indulge in a soak. I make my way towards the copper bathtub big enough for two with the perfect view of the Dragon Spine Mountains.

Every cell in my body stills at my unexpected view.

None other than Sølas is lounging on the chaise. One arm draped across the back, the other swirling an amber-colored Smokewhisper libation in a short glass.

Wickedness curls up at the side of his full lips, eyes tracing every line of my body. With the heat of the shower on my skin, it must have blunted my sensation of his arrival.

"What the fuck are you doing in my room?" I snap, trying to mask my shock with anger.

"Your room?" he purrs with devilish delight.

"Yes, my new room. Get out," I hiss.

"I think you mean *our* new room?" His purr deepens, rumbling within his chest like a mountain cat.

"Oh, I most certainly do not," I snarl, ready to slap that smug grin off his face.

"Oh, you most certainly do," he parrots.

"Get out!" I howl.

"*Make* me." The stupidly beautiful twist of lips quickly falls as I reach for Dream Singer.

"Hey, hey, hey. Easy does it with that thing. I can feel the power radiating off it from across the room. She's as beautiful as her creator." He winks.

Oh, he definitely knows how to press my buttons.

"I will show you just how beautiful she is when she sings dripping in your blood."

"As intimate as you dare to make that sound… that's not on my agenda for tonight." He pauses, running his hand through his raven hair, the violet more vivid in the sunlight piercing through the glass ceiling of the penthouse. "Didn't the fact that there are two sinks and two dressers here give you a clue that this room is meant for two?"

"Well, yes. The room is meant to be shared with my Bloodline pairing."

"Alive and in the flesh." His eyes deepen with the sly curve kissing the corner of his mouth as he feigns a half bow with one arm out and the other bent across his waist.

"No. Absolutely *not*."

"Absolutely *yes*." He swirls the liquid in his glass, amusement dancing in his eyes. "This information was clearly written on the scroll you received when you were assigned this room. Didn't you bother to read the entire thing?"

I look down at my feet, curling my hands into fists as I say, "Well, about that. I may have—*accidentally*—almost struck the Owl Scroll with lightning. So it was a little singed at the bottom."

He lets out a genuine chuckle that warms me to my core, like the music of summer sun rays seeping into my bones. The kind I can sip and savor forever.

I roll my shoulder, letting the thought roll off with it. I need to stay focused with a wolf prowling my bedroom.

"Well, at least we can finally fuck and get this over with. Then we can make our genetic contribution and be done."

Sølas tsks at me. "Nuh-uh-uh. You forgot my promise to you. I won't settle for just one piece of you… I want *all* of you."

"Oh, spare me the melodrama. This is our duty. There will be serious consequences after several months if we fail to conceive what's required of us."

His voice deepens into a feral growl. "I will not relent for some silly rule. Let them come. I will gladly face the consequences."

"I told you the other night. You don't want all of me. There is just noth-ingness inside. And a relationship puts our whole Zenith in jeopardy." My eyes narrow on him.

"Our Zenith is already in jeopardy." Shadows coil up his clenching jaw. "You think I'll be the hero? That I'll save them before I save you? I will slaughter entire worlds before I see you hurt again."

"Fucking great. Kivi is going to kill us both for what you just said."

"Regarding what you said the other night…" His jaw clenches. Tattooed knuckles lift to his chest before drifting up to thread through his raven locks, while I curse myself for my smoldering jealousy of his hands. "The distance you try to put between us will never stop me cherishing all that you are. I want to pin your hesitations to the wall, marked with my bite marks. I want to hold the parts of you that you believe are unworthy. I want to press my lips not against your neck, but to the wounds you swore you'd never let anyone love."

My breath is held captive by his words, soul pierced to the spot under his blue-moon gaze.

"Your thorns and broken pieces are just as worthy of love as the stars that glimmer in your eyes."

My heart forgets how to beat. How can he think I am worthy of love?

I feebly snap out, "You don't even know me," but the quivered words lose their bite on my tongue.

"Then why do I feel as though I have known you my whole life? Why do you consume my every thought? Why can't I breathe when you are not with me? How do I always find you, even when I am not looking? You can't deny you feel the same, despite your desperate attempts to block it out. Do not think I've missed the way your heartbeat races as soon as I enter the room. Even you cannot deny the way your body reacts to my touch, as if it's been missing it for all of eternity.

"Do you wonder why I Shadowwalk away every time we get close? Because your touch has ruined me. With barely a graze, you have touched me so deeply, I will never fit into my own skin again. I want to leave my fingerprints on your soul, messing up the perfectly folded sheets of your control, pressing my palms into your past to pull out your dreams of a future you never dared you could believe in."

My heart bludgeons my chest with its screams to listen to him, but my mind begs to shut him out. I meet him somewhere in between with a trembling whisper. "You don't know me."

He places the glass on the table as he stands up, taking a step closer to me, while I take a step back.

"Then let me."

He takes another step. I tumble another step back, attempting not to crumple under the weight of his request as he continues.

"Tell me every dreadful thing you have ever done, and let me love you in spite of them. Let me unravel your walls and glimpse inside your velvet soul. Let yourself feel the reckless emotion I know you have tried to hide in a maze of boxes."

Sølas reaches out a hand slowly. Hesitantly. "We are cosmic constants, you and I. Where you see darkness, I see nothing but light. Let your soul dare to dream and wonder with me, for I have heard it calling to me in the endless pitch of night. I have been listening to it every twilight, as you continue to fail to listen. You are so brave, yet so afraid. My heart sinks as I watch you in all your strength let your fears win, not logic. Despite what I know you tell yourself."

His eyes pool with longing and sorrow. His hand trying to catch me, but just like water, I keep slipping through his fingers. Always too impossible to hold, forever a glimpse of what can never be.

A warm wetness carves down my cheeks. My soul knows he's right. If only I was as small as a tear, he could hold me tight. Instead, I'm a jagged glacier, carving up and grinding out anyone who gets close. Even if he could melt me into something soft to hold, I'd drown him in all of me.

Anger bristles along my skin, summoning my invisible dragon-scale armor. I cannot possibly be the beautiful, wretched thing he sees. I do not deserve to love nor be loved as greatly as he claims for me. He couldn't know me. He's just a flirt. Yet his words stitch their way between my ribs, slinging golden light around my limping heart in ways that are far beyond flirting now.

Part of me craves to explore the mystery of the male before me, to accept the challenge he lays at my feet. In a fleeting moment of bravery or *stupidity*, I shed my invisible armor and let my mental shields slip. My heart swells, beaming to life, each beat stronger than the last, empowered by the unyielding vows of his words and arctic eyes, who will gladly drown in every melted icy bit of me.

Suddenly, I am wildly unsure and unwaveringly certain of the male standing before me. My body strides a step towards him, and he closes the distance without hesitation.

Gently, he tucks a loose strand of hair behind my ear. "When I look at you, I see colors I have never seen. The scent of you consumes me. Your touch is an echo of something ancient, trying to remember itself, conjured by the stars themselves. What if my fingertips along your skin are just your borrowed stardust, trying to find their way home?" His smoky voice, like a kiss upon my skin.

The hurricane in my chest begs me to take another step closer while my mind screeches to run.

My gaze collides to meet his. I sink as his stare deepens, caught in the undertow of realizing how badly my soul has longed for someone to look at me the way he does.

To see every piece of me as worthy of love. Broken, jagged bits and all.

Yet that little voice of fear creeps along the edges of my thoughts, slithering its way around my mind. Constricting around my throat, suffocating me with the agony of loss. Fear's vicious venom courses through my blood, intoxicating me with dread.

*What if one day that look on his face changes? What if all my worries come true? What if letting out the darkness inside me to be loved destroys us both? Or worse, consumes only him, and I'm left alone and broken with no one but myself to blame?*

Heat slashes through my spiraling terrors, my vision refocusing to reveal Sølas a breath away from me. A shuttered breath whooshes from my lungs as he bends down onto his knees before me. Never breaking our tethered gaze as he peers up at me.

The tempest in his eyes matches the one in my chest, darkness ripping through a background of icy blue, speckled with bloodshed. The depth of which I could easily get lost exploring for the rest of this life, and the next, and every other one after that. Shadows cascade off his shoulders, spilling down his chest and pooling beneath my feet.

He takes my hand with the softest touch. I slip beneath the current of his caress. Drowning. I've forgotten how to swim. I flail, but my strength fails to escape his riptide, plunging me into the depths of him. Wet and all too desperate to let him consume me wholly, caught beneath his feral tide I can never quite resist the pull of.

He tugs my hand, eddying it against his chiseled cheek. His thick lashes flutter shut, sipping and savoring the feeling of my roughness across his velvet skin.

He's kneeling before me, defenseless, chest cleaved wide open, baring his soul to me. He's giving me all of him. I cradle his bleeding heart in my hands, unwilling to close myself off from him for good.

My heart eddies into the irresistible tug drawing us together. No longer caring how to swim, unable to recall how to breathe.

I let go. Prepared to drown in everything, felt and unfelt, for him.

"You are the only being I will ever kneel before to worship. To me, you are sacred. And if you let me, I will surrender to you in ways that would make even prophecies weep."

The thought of fate wriggles the distorted words from the second trial back to life. I step away from his touch, stumbling over thorny threats that slash at my exposed heart.

*Never love.* Ripping. *Never be loved.* Gashing. *Darkness will consume everything I hold dear.* Shredding.

He tugs me back for a second before letting me go. Pure agony mars his face, head bowing in defeat.

My eyes slam shut, unable to bear the sight of him lashed raw by my fear. I turn my back to him. This is too much. We don't know each other. This is just supposed to be a simple fuck and done. I am not meant for some romantic love story.

"I'll wait," he whispers.

I muster the strength to face him, only to find he's gone once more. I raise my mental shields, rage coating my skin in invisible dragon armor as I attempt to slash everything that just transpired into manageable chunks to chuck out the mosaic window in my mind. Yet with each hack, another tidal wave pours out, slamming me with an onslaught of overwhelming emotion I cannot seem to numb away. I wipe the tears from my face, boiling with how I've managed to cry more times around him than ever before in my life. What is he doing to me?

I need to ground myself before I lose all control. Instead of a hot bath, I opt for soaking on the terrace. I lean against the pool wall, head cradled on the edge as I listen to whispering wind through the palm leaves cloaking the border of the water.

Echoes of Sølas' words dance on the breeze. *I want to hold the parts of you that you believe are unworthy. I want to press my lips not against your neck, but to the wounds you swore you'd never let anyone love.*

*To me, you are sacred.*

Is that what love is? Loving someone so much, all their broken pieces seem to meld back together into a work of art? Would I be able to offer him the same vow he's offering me? Perhaps he's just consumed by lust for me like I am for him. *Fuck.* Who am I kidding? His words sledge far deeper than physical attraction. Pummeling through the well-laid walls of my protection, uncovering my most fiercely guarded treasure: my fragile, unbroken bits hidden in a sea of shattered ice. Speaking to my very soul. What we share is definitely something different.

Something more.

*I watch you in all your strength let your fears win, not logic.*

I can't argue with him there. He's absolutely right. At this point, it's no longer just logic that keeps me building walls between us, but fear itself.

I hate fear.

Fear is the architect of paralysis.

I will not be paralyzed by my own fear.

I will not be held hostage by it.

So, I rise from the pool. Gold glistens along my skin, beaded kisses dripping down like dew. I thank the Celestials to have the privacy of my room, even if some irrational part wishes he were still here.

I open the starry midnight armoire next to mine; sure enough, inside hang black fighting leathers I've seen Sølas wear for sparring. The scent of amber and spruce lick up my lungs as I slam the doors shut.

The weight of his words twists with the pressure of failure, constricting like a vice around my heart. My knuckles go white as I fist through the fear, suffocating in the ruin of myself.

I collapse on the heavenly down mattress as chiffon drapes twirl in the morning wind. I watch them dance, weightless and free.

How I long to be like them. Not shackled by the fear of just surviving, but with the grace to learn how to live.

As sleep claims me, I wonder, if—with him—I can finally let myself dare to dream.

Dare to love and be loved. Recklessly wild and untamed.

# CHAPTER 36

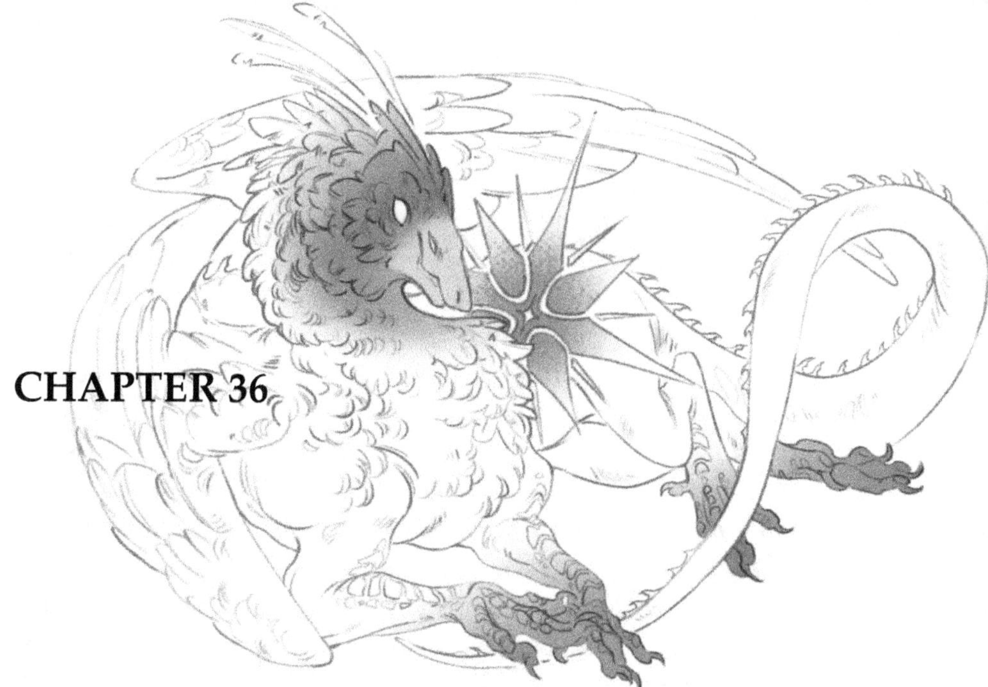

*I*'m *soaring over Cascara once again, the wind twirling in my hair. I spin around, flying with my back to the ground to see Calais high above me, catching glimpses of her wisping between buttery clouds.*

*I whirl once more to peer at the ground below, an ever-growing expanse of twisting Blackwood. I can feel something. No. Someone. Down there, calling to me. Like a humming melody on the wind, repeating my name sweetly, like a honey lure.*

Come to me.

*In the clearing ahead, a tall woman with waist-length, metallic black hair is barely visible. As I fly in her direction, the siren's purr becomes impossible to ignore. My eyes meet her silver gaze; her skin is ghost white, sending a shiver down my neck.*

Come to me.

*I'm close enough I can almost make out her blood-red lips moving in the darkness cascading around her.*

*"Wake up!"* Calais' voice booms through my head, shooting me out of bed like an arrow.

"Celestial's tits, why the fuck are you waking me up right now?" I scream aloud, brain still half-asleep, forgetting I'm talking to a dragon in my head. The sharp trill of my voice sends Pip scurrying under the bed.

*"Meet me in the field north of your room,"* Calais commands.

*"You know I can't always be at your beck and call,"* I grouch.

*"Yes, you can, and you will. We are bonded. We both must come when the other needs us."*

*"You're a dragon; what could you possibly need from me?"*

*"Stop back-sassing me, and find out,"* she snips so sharply, I swear her words could cut my mind if she so pleased. I drowsily draw my body up from the bed.

*"Do I need to wear armor for whatever it is that we are doing?"*

*"Those fire-proof basilisk scales might come in useful, along with that sour mouth of yours,"* Calais snaps with sarcasm.

Alright, so I am definitely going to wear my armor this evening. I guess the time by the sun's position, hanging low in the sky, not yet bursting with the color of sunset.

I don my winter aerial leathers lined with the softest fur and grab my special cloak from the wall. I sheathe my daggers along my ribs, my two short swords along my back.

I reach for Dream Singer, but Pip scurries up the blade, meeting my hand at the hilt. A burst of silver light erupts, forcing me to shield my eyes from the searing pain. Slowly, I open them to reveal a new leather bracer; it's white and matches the golden markings of my arm perfectly. Across it shimmers the shape of Dream Singer's indigo blade, flaring near the hilt, now adorned with four cobalt gems.

I smile down at Pip. "Always watching, huh?"

The gems shift into eyes; two of them wink at me! A wild laugh cracks my chest. Apparently, Sølas is rubbing off on him.

I hurry down the spiral stairs, taking the door on the north side of the corridor to reach a sea of golden grass.

*"Hurry. I grow bored waiting for you,"* Calais clips.

I'm in no mood to argue with her snarky remarks, pressing into a full sprint. I reach her impressively large leg, slinging myself up the spikes onto her back.

*"You know, if you focused your powers, you could glide short distances and wouldn't need to subject either of us to you climbing my leg."*

*"Sure. Let me just add that to my endless list of things to master,"* I mock dryly. And with a bend of her legs, we're flying into the sky, her four wings lifting us up with ease.

*"Where are we going?"* I enquire.

*"Be patient, and you will find out."*

*"You can't ever just tell me things?"*

*"Now, where would be the fun in that?"* She snickers.

After we reach a good altitude with less turbulence, she whisks north through the clouds. I'm grateful for the heat rippling off her body as the air grows colder and colder.

The thick air of Cascara fills my lungs, no doubt what makes it easier for the great many large creatures that inhabit our world to fly. The peaks of the Dragon Spine Mountains pierce the sky like jagged fangs, dripping white in crisp snow.

She begins to dive, weaving between the lower peaks drenched with waterfalls. We come upon a silver lake surrounded by fields of lavender, dappled in dots of fuchsia flowers. The color combination is unlike anything I've ever seen, reflecting off the silver water like a moving oil painting. A large black figure takes shape on the edge of the innermost part of the lake. As we get closer, I recognize the shape of Sølas' dragon.

*"Absolutely not. Take me back right now,"* I sneer.

*"I have brought you to a hallowed place. You will be respectful, or you can walk the rest of the way back,"* she snarls.

I huff, knowing this is a battle I won't win. The lake is tucked between such a rugged maze of peaks, even if I could fly without Calais, I'd still risk falling to my death.

The ground trembles as she lands. Beautiful ripples spread across the silver lake, blending the shades of purple together in an ethereal way. Tears threaten to well, its sacred beauty stealing my breath away.

I slide down Calais' leg to find Sølas lying on a magenta blanket, his upper body perched up on two carved arms. I don't let my eyes linger on him long, rejecting my heart's pleas to skitter at the sight of him.

But I can't help sipping in his beauty. His face is painted with the reflection of dancing silver and purple. He looks like an oil painting. I find myself wishing I could paint so I could capture him like this, to keep it in my heart a little longer. It's the most beautiful pieces that leave you shattered and whole at the same time.

I undo my jacket. Despite being in the mountains, the air is warm and muggy. Yet the cool breeze keeps the air from sticking to my skin.

"What is this place?" I ask in Calais' direction.

*"This is the sacred breeding ground of the Moonstorm dragons. The silver lake before you is called Tearfall Aether. My species is born from the magic of the Celestial Dragon's tears. When the chaos of lightning strikes the pool—filled with our eggs—on a full moon, we are able to hatch. It's a rare event, which is why I am the only one of my kind. My clutch of eggs rests at the bottom of this lake, waiting for lightning to strike, so they may be born and finally join us."*

There's a beautiful sadness to her story. I can sense she dreams of a world full of young ones nipping at her feet.

I walk to the edge of the lake, touching the aether that moves like mercury through my fingers.

I hear steps come up behind me. My breath held captive by his presence.

"It's enchanting, isn't it?"

I ignore him, too angry at myself to speak. For letting my fears rule me; rather than face them, it's easier to be cold and distant. And far easier than letting folk in.

I use my senses to ground me. Twirling my fingers through the aether, soaking in the way the ripples dance across the surface, swirling with every shade of purple.

The soil shifts beside me as Sølas takes a seat. I will my focus to resist the urge to sink into the gravity of this inescapable pull between us.

*"We don't have to talk. As long as you listen,"* a smoky voice says in my head.

I jump, practically falling into the lake, only for his shadows to wrap around my waist and tug me back to safety.

"What. The. Actual. Fuck?" My eyes narrow on him.

He casually sits there, his arm clasped around one leg, staring out along the aether. He's acting like he didn't just magically talk in my head. *That fucker.* Maybe all the sleep deprivation is finally rotting my brain.

*"I see you can finally hear me. It doesn't count as talking if I'm not moving my lips."* The smoky voice echoes in my mind. This time, I see the slightest smirk tug at the corner of his full lips.

"Bastard! How are you doing that?" I demand.

*"Ah. Finally, she listens."* Calais' voice booms in my head. My hands lift to my hair, tugging at the strands as I struggle to adapt to another voice in my head. Why is no one giving me any Celestial-damn answers?

"Are you going to tell me how he did that?" I pin Calais with my glare. I swear her rainbow eyes roll. The audacity of my dragon knows no bounds.

*"I brought you and the Shadowmancer here to train."*

"Train in what exactly? He's not supposed to talk in my head like you can. It's crowded enough with the both of us in there." I scowl.

*"Are you always this petulant? Can't you be grateful for the powers bestowed upon you?"*

"Powers? This is yet another distraction that threatens our Zenith."

*"She can be narrow-minded. I'm working on it."* Sølas' smoky voice caresses my mind like warm silk. That fucking smug smirk of his tugs on my chest in a way it has no business doing.

Perhaps I should have killed him when I had the chance. Now I am stuck forever trying to resist the urge to kiss him as my sanity seems to deteriorate further.

*"Clearly, you need to work harder."* Calais scowls, pointing her head in Sølas' direction.

How is this even happening? Celestials, I really hope this is not the gift of my Arcane Glyph, giving me the power to hear other people's thoughts. Maybe I'll take that walk after all. Right off the cliff.

*"No. This is a gift shared between the four of us."*

"The four of us? You mean, I'll be able to hear Sølas' dragon, too?"

*"Yes. If you would only let your walls down to listen, creating pathways in your mind to anchor the tether to one another,"* Calais snips.

"And what if I don't want to be tethered to those two?"

*"You don't have a choice; the tether is already there. We're just trying to teach you how to listen so all our voices don't come crashing into your brain at once. It can be overwhelming once you can hear all our direct thoughts and feel all our emotions, too."*

"I don't want this."

*"Tough luck, little savage. You're stronger than you think. You can handle this."* His smoky voice is much smoother and more enjoyable than the sharp, raspy voice of Calais, at least.

"I know I can handle it. I just don't need you in my head any more than you already are."

Sølas cocks a brow over his devilish smile. *"Careful, now. I may just think you're finally flirting with me."*

*"Scáil and I don't want to feel your emotions, either, but this is the way*

*things will be. Regardless of our desires. Now, shut your mouth, and listen with your mind. And you, Shadowmancer. Do your job,"* Calais all but barks at us.

Sølas stands to his feet.

I brace myself as he walks towards me.

"Easy. You need to let those golden walls of your mind down. And yes, I can see the color of your mental shields. It's part of my Celestial Gift. I have been exploring them for weeks, searching for a crack. Something I said this morning must have worked; I can finally get through." He has the audacity to end that with a wink. Fucking shadow prick.

"Great. So, now you can read my thoughts." I sigh, hands lifting to scrub my face under the frustration of it all.

"No. You haven't fully let me in, but I catch glimpses of feelings when you do let yourself feel. I stay tethered, though, allowing me to talk to you. I know you want to push me away, but if we fail, Calais may eat us both. She's more savage than you." He smirks, and I can't help but smile back at that remark. He's not wrong; we very well might become her evening snack for disobeying her.

My shoulders relax as I indulge the heat of his presence. I release the tie of the cloak, letting it slip down along with the first layer of my mental shields.

*"Are you trying to distract me?"* he whispers in my mind.

"No." I shoot him an incredulous look—all he has ever done is manage to distract me! "Now. Tell me what to do."

"My unique Shadowsense makes it easier for me to connect with the emotions of others. This is why Calais asked me to help guide you. Close your eyes. Imagine the walls of your mind lowering."

I obey, letting the glowing golden walls fall. I can see the violently whipping iridescent ribbons of Calais. I reach out, snatching one. My knees buckle under the weight of her longing and sadness.

Visions slash through my mind: nuzzling eggs, tenderly, into the aether; blue tears streaming down, rippling liquid as I am gutted by the fear of never seeing them hatch.

My hand drops as I stumble back, overwhelmed. I try to remember where my mind ends and hers begins.

*"You can already sense me. Try to find the Shadowmancer or Scáil."* Calais grimaces. It's unclear if she's disappointed at me or upset I saw her

vulnerable. I'm not risking touching her ribbons again right now to find out.

I roll her response off, cracking my neck as I close my eyes again. Then there's the warm touch of Sølas' hands on the sides of my arms, just barely there, circling his fingers in a rhythmic pattern. My brows pinch as I crack one eye open to scowl at him.

"Is that really necessary?" I whisper, annoyed at how far too soothing his touch is.

*"Yes. Listen for my voice. Touching you will make my connection easier to find. Now keep your eyes closed. Don't make me repeat myself again,"* he says smoothly, but the command in his last statement is not so subtle.

I close my eyes again. Unfortunately for me, he's correct.

I see the same shimmering velvet ribbons as before, tumbling in from the arched stained-glass window of the night sky. They appear slightly different this time; the faintest hue of dark violet catches on them. Rather than making the same mistake of grabbing them, I change up my tactic. My finger slowly glides across the ribbon. A subtle hint of desire and melancholy laces up my hand.

I twirl the ribbon around my finger, prying a subtle purr from Sølas.

I dare to whisper, *"Am I catching on now?"* but my lips don't move.

*"You succeed at anything you put your mind to, Luxsula. I never doubted you. The trick is getting you to focus on the right things,"* he growls seductively across my mind. It's a deeper touch that isn't along my skin. A bellow stoking the flames burning to life through my veins.

*"Enough, you two. There will be plenty of time for that later. Stay focused."* Calais' icy voice cools the heat between me and Sølas. I can't imagine how annoyed she must be trapped in my head all day.

*"You are quite insufferable. Luckily, I can shield myself when I get exhausted listening to your constant excuses regarding the male in front of you."* Calais sighs. To be honest, I wouldn't want to put up with my shit either if I were an ancient dragon.

*"Now, search for Scáil,"* Sølas purrs, sending a shiver down my spine that not even Calais' ice can quell.

I search past the black velvet ribbons, stepping further out from the center in which I ground myself in my mind. I notice the subtlest movement in the darkness: a ribbon that hardly moves, the iridescent black of a raven. I graze it with my hand, and a deep calmness settles along my bones.

*"Hello, little one. You may call me Scáil Cœur. I am the last of my kind. I was born of the darkness of the Eclipse War. There were others, once, but we were hunted and feared for our dark magic. It is an honor to finally meet you. I have heard a great many things about you."* His voice is the peace of darkest midnight under the dim light of a new moon. Humming with an ancient power.

The reverence in his voice spurs me into motion. Leaving Sølas by the lake's edge, I walk over to Scáil and bow deeply as I say aloud, "The honor is mine."

He dips his enormous head, a warm admiration flooding me. I have to steady my feet not to stumble from the sensation.

*"Good. She listens. She speaks. I am glad you have finally met my mate."* Calais' voice is oddly calm.

I whirl around as those last two words sink in.

"Your mate!?" I roar.

*"My patience grows thin for your tone. How else do you think you can hear our voices in your mind? Love tethers us all,"* Calais snaps.

"The last mated pair of dragons and Ellian Knights were Gildora and Raeya, who were also a mated pair themselves."

*"Yes. Which is why they were so powerful together. Their magic perfectly in sync with one another, they wielded as one. Where you see weakness to your Zenith, you are blind to the strength of embracing the bond that links us all. The most powerful magic is tethered in the bond of a mated pair."* Scáil's cadence soothes the fear seeking to creep into my mind.

There's truth in his words. Mated bonds are exceptionally rare. Since the Celestials died, it is believed that their powerful magic is imbued in them. The last-known mated bond was shared between the heroic females who founded Gildorea Universitás, but our lessons did not include how they could share thoughts or wield their magic as one.

*"The Ellian Knights hold as many secrets as dragons do."* Scáil chuckles.

"So, it would seem, *Luxsula,* you are stuck with me. In more ways than one," Sølas whispers along the cusp of my ear, his breath twirling my hair to tickle my face.

"Must be nice, getting everything you want," I growl at him, turning around to face him. He puts his foot out to trip me, catching me in his arms in a low dip. Fucking shadow *prick.*

His head leans down, grazing his chiseled cheek against mine. "Something tells me I'm far from getting *everything* I want from you."

His closeness is like a lightning bolt to my heart with my shields down, electricity ripping through my nerves.

He lifts me back up and spins me in his arms before I can push him away. I sink into him, drowning in his embrace, unable to resist our pull with my shields down. My frantic heart limps to life, beating like a hummingbird caught in a lightning storm.

As if he can sense me not breathing, his arms fall. I gasp, fighting the urge to crumble into the chasm ripped open in my chest at the loss of his touch.

*"Raise your mental shields back up. Now it's time to learn how to control the connections. There will be times when one of us is overcome with emotions, or battle demands focus. You need to choose how much you let in. For me, it's different books on shelves. I can pull one off the shelf, allowing me to open and close it at will."* His voice in my mind feels like a kiss of darkness.

I shake my head, forcing focus. Walls of golden light rise to shield my mind, coolness replacing the heat roaring at my core.

"Windows," I whisper. "Different shapes, each with a clasp, so I can close them."

"Good. Now close your eyes again. I want you to picture a new window for each of us. Save Calais' for last; your strong connection will be the hardest to close." He directs me again. This should be easier since it's something I've already done.

My fingers trail along the golden walls humming with power, dotted with the previous windows of my mind. The upside-down heart of lust. The circular yellow window of happiness. The flame of anger. The teardrop of grief, sorrow, and regret. The most beautiful is the arched window of stained glass adorned with an indigo midnight sky. I coax the black velvet ribbons of Sølas back through it, clasping it shut.

Next, I find the raven ribbons of Scáil. They gently follow the direction of my hands to a window the shape of an eclipsed moon.

Lastly, I shape a window in a crescent moon. I attempt to coax the iridescent white ribbons of Calais to their new home. They whip out, biting my palms. *Bitch,* I sneer in my mind.

*"Careful, Nebulight,"* she hisses. I imagine a powerful gust of wind in

my chest, blowing the ribbons and window shut. Just as I go for the clasp, it bursts open, white ribbons spooling out. I try again. Same result.

"You've done enough for today. We can try again tomorrow. Let's sit down and enjoy the sunset." Sølas' voice is a soothing escape from the fury of failure at blocking out Calais.

I open my eyes to the peaks of the valley buttered in orange, pink, and periwinkle. I turn to face the lake. We can't glimpse the sun from this direction, but the colors reflect from the sky off the aether, stealing my breath away.

I don't hesitate as Sølas' hand tugs on mine, leading me to the blanket I found him on. More and more colors spill across the canvas around us, deepening as the sun kisses the horizon. The aether almost appears to trap the colors inside it. Twilight blue and midnight indigo with fuchsia and lavender swirling on the ripples as the dragons adjusted their body weight.

The world seems to still in the beauty of the sky. I wish I could capture it in a jar and hold it in my heart forever. As the colors fade further into twilight, I notice my hand is still in his, and I don't mind it. For once, it feels right.

# CHAPTER 37

The four of us sit in silence as the moon perches in the sky. The cosmos overhead twinkle to life in the reflection of Tearfall Aether. The lake starts to pulse, a faint ethereal blue, like a heartbeat.

*"Clever girl. Those are the heartbeats of our eggs. We come here often to check that they still beat, waiting for the one-in-a-million strike that will hatch them into our lives."* Scáil's calming voice sighs in my mind.

"But Calais can breathe lightning; could she not use that to help the young ones hatch?"

*"Sadly, no. No magic but that of the Celestials can direct a lightning bolt to hatch our eggs. So, we're left to the mercy of nature."* I feel his sorrow, as if he knows he will not live to see their lives. I quickly realize my shields have fallen slightly in the serenity of watching the sunset, raising them back up but leaving their windows open. Yet his sorrow seems etched in my bones. A feeling I can't shake.

*"You know, Calais, you would be much more tolerable if you were as open as Scáil is,"* I jab.

She lowers her head to snarl at me, *"It's time to return you home. The grumpy one clearly needs her sleep."*

*"And I assume you'll be wanting to sleep in our bed tonight?"* I mock at Sølas, but he's lost in thoughts of his own as he folds up the blanket, melancholy painting his features.

*"Not tonight, Luxsula. Not tonight."* He furrows his brow.

We ride the rest of the night in silence, but I don't feel alone. Each of their tethers anchor deeper than my mind.

Calais and Scáil dip and weave between each other in a dance that twists the biggest smile on my face. Their ancient love radiates off one another. The chaos and the calm of their love saga, forged in years of devotion.

When we land outside of Gildorea, Sølas immediately disappears into the darkness.

*"Where is he off to?"*

*"We all have our demons to fight. He will reveal his when he's ready, young one. He hides much behind his mask, as do you. Rest well,"* Scáil hums. Just as swiftly, he and Calais take off into the night sky.

On the long walk up the spiral staircase, the distance of the three tethers grows as they become farther and farther away. I didn't think I would enjoy being connected to three beings, as someone who's spent much of their life alone. But after letting them in and making a home for their tethers, my heart beats a little fuller.

I arrive in my room to see dinner on the table. The smell of it has my stomach roaring with excitement. A note is placed on top of the silver cover.

'Until next time, Luxsula.'

I definitely can't be mad at him for leaving me dinner. Especially after a long weekend where I've scarcely eaten. It's mooca steak and mashed potatoes covered in butter—my favorite. I don't even want to think about how he knows that.

Pip skitters onto the table, chirping happily as he tries to carry the entire steak off my plate. Dream Singer falls to my feet from wherever he had been holding it when he changed his shape. I tsk at Pip, cutting the steak in half for us to share.

I shower and dress in my nightgown before snuggling up to Pip. I wonder where Sølas is. He wore a different type of sadness on his brow tonight. One I haven't seen from him. Even though part of me scoffs at sharing a bed with him, another part of me craves to know what his body will feel like next to me… at a distance, of course.

I realize I can reach out to him, although I'm not sure if I should. It's clear he wants to be alone. But then I think about all the times I wanted to be alone, and he never seemed to listen to me, so it seems only fair to check on him.

I close my eyes and open the arched stained-glass window decorated with the midnight sky. To my dismay, the black velvet ribbons don't come streaming in. I gaze out the window and can see them twirling violently in the distance.

*"Are you okay?"* I beckon from the window, reaching along the tether I can still feel.

*"No. But I will be."* His smoky voice is distant, which is an entirely new feeling for me, one I'm not entirely sure I like.

*"Is there anything I can do to help? I can listen, if that's what you need."*

*"You can rest for me. Knowing you are safe and rested is all I need right now."* His voice is even more distant, the ribbons disappearing further into darkness. I guess he's shielding me from his mind. I want to be angry at him, as if I'm not safe and need to rest to make him happy, but the sadness that drenches his voice makes me forgive him.

I roll over, pulling Pip into my chest as I fall asleep.

# CHAPTER 38

"Rise and shine, starlight," a chipper, smoky voice purrs in my ear. "What are you doing here this early in the morning?" I mumble sleepily.

"We're heading to the Warded Hollow before anyone wakes to work on training your Chaos Magic. Calais said she's going to roast me over the fire if I don't make sure you have better control prior to aerial combat maneuvers. Something about wanting to keep all four of her wings intact while you're casting on her back."

I groan, pulling the blanket over my head, with no desire to leave the warmth of my new comfy bed. For someone who was so broody and distant last night, he sure is a Celestials be dimmed sunbeam this morning.

"Well, aren't you a grumpy delight in the morning? I can't wait until I'm waking up next to you."

"Over my dead body," I grumble from under the sheets.

"That can be arranged."

"I'd like to see you try. I know I like to wake up early, but you're being obscene." I huff, peeking over the blanket at his perfect raven hair blowing in the breeze.

"Wouldn't you like to know all the ways I could make you die beneath my touch?" His voice growls magically along the cusp of my ear.

"It's too early for your flirtatious shenanigans."

He snaps his fingers; a cup of kahvi appears out of a whirl of shadows next to my bed. The smell raises me from the sheets.

My eyes go wide. He's fucking changing in front of me. I could just about die.

His muscles flex as he takes off his black suit, exchanging it for the vest of his fighting leathers. His body is carved for the heavens, and I'm losing the battle of pulling my gaze from the deep V curving below his slacks.

As he loosens his belt, my skin swelters into molten iron. Sweat beads on my skin, silk sheets clinging to the wetness. I swallow. His pants slip down the sculpted muscles of his perfect ass and thighs. My body goes weak, tumbling the kahvi from my cup.

"Shit," I hiss at the scalding liquid on my leg.

Before I can even blink my eyes, the cup's back on my nightstand, and the fabric is clean.

Sølas kneels beside me on the bed, slowly lifting the sheet, exposing the burn on my leg. Just below the glowing silver star scar from Pip's fire. His eyes lock with mine, pinning me under his blue moon gaze as he lowers his head, never breaking our stare. His lips meet the sensitive, freshly burnt skin.

I almost die, swallowed whole from molten ecstasy searing through my blood with his kiss upon my leg. I crash back into the pillows with a moan, waves of bliss crashing through me. With one fucking kiss on my cursed fucking leg. *Fuck*. I really don't want to know all the ways I can die under his touch. Or do I?

"*I can definitely feel you're awake now,*" he purrs across my mind.

I don't think I can survive the embarrassment of orgasming from a kiss on my leg, but I know his perfect smug ass will never let me live it down. So, I leap out of bed and wobble to the shower on gelatin legs.

There's no door to the bathroom in the open floor plan. He'll have a full view of my body from the bedroom, but I don't care. I need a cold shower. Now, if I'm going to stand a chance being near him after what just happened. I don't fail to catch him watching me walk in my white lacy undergarments that came with the room, leaving little to the imagination.

"*Now who's not playing fair?*"

"*You can watch if you like,*" I purr right back, giving him a taste of his own medicine as I strip slowly. I have half a mind to touch myself in the shower just to drive him mad, but I fear I'll be the one losing control in the aftermath of that stunt.

*Cold shower. Cold thoughts. Cold shower. Mind over matter, Savaé,* I roar at myself.

*"You would have driven me absolutely mad. Even my control has its limits."* His feral growl causes my legs to quiver.

Fuck, fuck, *fuck. Cold shower. Cold thoughts*, I repeat to myself. I have a feeling I'm going to be taking a lot of cold showers from now on.

I jump out of the shower, teeth chattering, relieved to see Sølas staring over the northern glass balcony. His distraction frees me to dress without the weight of his gaze on me. I selfishly use my magic to dry my hair. It's the one thing I'm never patient enough to wait for. Fully dressed in my white aerial leathers and armed to the teeth, I'm ready to go.

I call Pip. "Let's go, little one." I'll never cease to be amazed at his magic as he turns into my bracer.

"He truly is a marvel. Just like you." His voice is suddenly so close, I startle.

"You know, there's such a thing as being *too* flirtatious?"

"You wound me." He covers his heart with his tattooed hand, walking backwards to the door, opening it with a slight bow.

"You're incorrigible." I huff, rolling my eyes at him.

We make it to the Warded Hollow in one piece. I swear if he was walking in front of me, I would have pushed him down the stairs for his comment about how he loved his view, no doubt speaking about my ass. The confident shadow prick. At least my blood is burning in a different way, which I hope makes it easier to cast.

He sets up the Hollow similar to the day I massacred every target: blue and red targets moving, mimicking typical battle maneuvers we're trained for and know the enemy uses.

"Your problem is that you bottle up all your emotions instead of feeling them as they come. You think being numb makes you strong, but it makes you weak." He arches a challenging brow as I huff and cross my arms.

"You're at the mercy of your emotions when they come flooding out after being locked up tight. You think you're in control, but it's an illusion you've weaved for yourself. A wise person feels their emotions, listens to what they are signaling to them, and then uses logic to determine how to act based on those emotions."

"When I tried to feel an emotion last time, it was a murder spree in here."

"Tell me what happened in your mind."

"I grabbed on to where I keep anger and tried to use it to cast."

"And all that pent-up anger came crashing out in a tidal wave of fury."

"I just opened the window in my mind—a *crack*."

"But you can't keep something locked away and not expect it to bite you when you finally release it from its cage."

I can't argue with that analogy. I would bite the hand off someone who caged me.

"I want you to focus on keeping your walls up but not numbing yourself. When you feel an emotion, validate the emotion. Check the facts. Does this emotion make sense? Now what should I do with this knowledge? How does this inform my next behavior?"

He crosses his arms and nods his head to start, ignoring the petulant annoyance plastered on my face at the ridiculousness of his lesson.

Growing bored of my antics, he cleaves the silence. "So very stubborn. Fine. I'll go first." He shakes his head, walking towards the targets. "I'm feeling happy, enjoying how cute your crumpled face looks when you're annoyed at me. How the gold in your eyes glimmers brightly in defiance," he muses while black daggers of shadow smoke twirl above his fingers as they move. He smirks, and the blades dart to the red targets, hitting every single one of them right between the eyes.

*"Show off."*

"I felt the emotion. I validated the feeling. I checked the facts, knowing that the feeling informed me of how you made me feel in this moment, and let the happiness flow over me at the thought of these targets daring to take this moment away from me… Take *you* away from me."

"No one is taking me away from you. I am not *yours* to take."

"True, but the happiness you give me *is mine*. On the battlefield, that can be taken away. Rather than stuffing that fear away, I let the fear guide me to my targets, conquering and savoring the continued happiness of your escalating irritation."

"Well, it must be nice to always be so in control of your magic."

"I have not always been in control of my magic." His tone is pure ice, freezing my bones. Violent shadows twirl like smoke off his shoulders, almost forming wings of death. He's never spoken to me like that, raising my hackles instinctively.

He brushes his hand slowly through his raven hair, as if trying to settle himself from the moment.

"The ease with which I wield my magic came at great costs and many years of practice. You have come into your Celestial Gift late, and you need to catch up. You're always talking about the risk to the Zenith. Right now, you are more of a threat than anything between us." His voice is rough. I can tell he's still reeling from the nerve I struck.

I don't deny the truth to his blunt words; I guess that makes me quite the hypocrite. The thought makes me shift my weight as I take a deep breath and settle myself.

I mow over his words in my head. Maybe if I *thin* my shield, so it's still present, maintaining my focus in battle, instead of completely numbing the emotions? Perhaps I can let them bounce along my shield while keeping the Wuvon out of my mind. It's worth a shot.

"I am going to tell you something, and I want you to tell me how it makes you feel."

"Fine." I close my eyes, preparing for the worst.

"You are beautiful."

I crack one eye open, seeing the coy twist of his lips at one side that I know is there before I even catch a glimpse. My eyelid flutters shut again. I focus on how his words make me feel.

Anger bounces along my shield—but it's not really anger. On the next bounce, I can see it's fear, masquerading as anger.

I'm not afraid of his words; that would be silly. I'm afraid to acknowledge what those words actually make me feel. I validate the fear and let myself open up to what his words actually stir in me. Even if I'm afraid to be as beautiful as he makes me feel.

To my groaning surprise, the next emotion is happiness. I let out an exasperated sigh. Instead of throwing it out my mosaic window… I bask in the warm delight of hearing those smoky words from his lips. How it makes my heart flutter like a butterfly on a gentle spring breeze.

Then I think about those red targets trying to take away this little slice of happiness I desire to keep. Instead of rage consuming me, I let the canary ribbon flutter between my fingers. With each movement, I imagine the red target shattering all around in the splendor of witnessing my secret moment of joy.

Then, the starry stained-glass window opens. Velvet ribbons swirl all around me. I open my eyes to find myself twirling Sølas' shirt between my fingers. I've pulled him close, shrouded in his Shadowveil. My eyes meet his, and for a moment, the world stands still, my breath freezing beneath the arctic storm in his eyes.

The shadows fall, revealing the wooden targets shattered into a million pieces.

My eyes jump around to see only the red targets are gone. Unfortunately, the splinters of the explosion also hit the blue targets.

"Look how much more control you have, *Luxsula*. A little extra bloody, but at least most of the wounds to the blue targets are healable, unlike last time." He winks.

I let go of his shirt, shoving him with a genuine smile pinning up my lips.

He resets the course. "Again."

"No flirtatious remark to inspire me?" I snicker, placing the back of my hand to his forehead, feigning to feel for temperature as if he's suddenly struck with illness.

"Smartass," he purrs. His fingers grasp my chin, shaking my head confidently. "You will practice again until your control is as wicked as that mouth of yours."

I can't help but smile at him. The beautiful, full smile he doesn't hide in return lights up even the darkest parts of my soul.

I let the feelings of the moment rush over me. The mirth between us, hope in mastering my power, my curious nature wanting to know the male that stands by my side, contentment in trusting him. The canary-yellow energy pulses through my veins, frolicking around the moving targets, slipping through the invisible hearts of my enemies, stealing their kinetic and thermal energy as it feeds the life force within me until I can no longer feel the color red in my periphery.

Slowly, my eyelids peep open. Bright light blisters my sight as my vision adjusts. The target parts of wood are mere piles of dust, while the metal parts are cold, molten ore.

The light.

The light of glimmering pastel rainbows is emanating... from me.

Glowing vibrantly through every one of my golden markings.

I turn my hands around. Each star is humming with sparkling, prismatic light rays.

As realization sets in that *I'm fucking glowing*, I lurch back, as if I can jump out of my own skin. The glow vanishes, like blowing out a candle.

The only magic wielders who can glow are Radiants. Like Fenwick. But Radiant magic doesn't do that to targets. And it's golden, not white with pastel rainbows.

"You never cease to amaze me, *Luxsula*." His genuine smile melts into my soul. His eyes. His eyes are the clearest I've ever seen them, like pure moonlight. They drift down to mine, looking at me like he has always known me, like he knows exactly who I'm supposed to be, exactly who I will become, from a million lifetimes of knowing me.

It's my body that closes the gap between us now. My mind searching his crystal eyes for something my heart has already been screaming.

I lean up on my tiptoes, placing my hands on either side of his raven hair. Peering through his soul, praying for something to stop me.

Something to hold me from falling off the edge into madness with him. His heart pounds in his chest, mirroring the beat of mine. And for a second, I swear our heartbeats synchronize.

A mess of golden light strings weaves their way through my ribs, shattering the thorny glacial palace around my heart, wrapping around it with warm light.

Utterly melting my frozen, sharp, messy bits that protect me, protect my mosaic heart.

He has a way of melting everything around us into nothing. It's just me and him in an endless abyss, where nothing seems to matter anymore. It's just us and a force that's pulling us together through space and time.

A force I'm failing to find reasons to continue to deny. As if, suddenly, I can make sense of the pleas of my heart, a little voice inside spills through my veins.

*He's mine.*

# CHAPTER 39

T he bells are chiming, and in the silence of my grasp, my mind whirls to comprehend the two words I have just thought.

A dash of sadness paints his face. Shadows fill my hands, and in a blur of darkness, he is gone.

Part of me wants to be angry that he's slipped through my hands yet again. He has a knack for leaving me at this point. I'm not even sure what would have happened if the bells for class hadn't rung.

Shit. What if he heard my thoughts?

I check my mental shields, hoping they haven't slipped due to the intense emotions I was feeling. Somehow, thank the Celestials, they're still up.

What was I even thinking? He isn't mine. But I hadn't just thought it; I *felt* it. In my bones. In my heart. In my soul. That's impossible! But I don't have an excuse to scuff this off. Not this time.

The next ring of the bells startles me from my thoughts. I don't have time to think about this right now, sprinting to class before the final chime rings. Luckily, the first class is in the Gilded Amphitheater in the bottom floor of the Grand Conservatory.

I make it through the doors in the nick of time, finding my seat next to Kissa. I search around me for Sølas, but he's nowhere to be found. I retreat to my mind, opening the stained-glass window of the night sky, but there are no black velvet ribbons.

I see the subtlest hint of movement, telling me he's alive. I open the eclipsed window, hoping maybe Scáil will know where he is, but no raven ribbons can be found along our tether. I'm disgruntled that I have to talk to my cryptic, cranky dragon, but she's my only hope.

*"Where are Sølas and Scáil?"*

*"Out,"* Calais' raspy voice responds curtly.

*"Care to elaborate?"* I cross my fingers, hoping she'll cooperate for once.

*"No."*

*"Of course not. Are they alright?"*

*"One of them is, and one of them will be,"* Calais clips. Fear creeps into my mind with her words. I know better than to ask her because she's never very forthcoming.

*"Focus in class. I will see you shortly for aerial maneuvers."*

I huff in response, which has Kissa giving me the side-eye. I've been so distracted, I haven't even realized a new professor has already taken the stage. The female is a Yassur, like Eko. Her eyes are saffron yellow, and her fur is metallic silver, which matches the color of her streaming hair, falling between her large bat-like ears. She has a pink nose, and her pronounced canines peek out as she speaks.

"Class will proceed as normal for other ensigns, but your Chivalry will be busy today with flight maneuvers. Tomorrow, they will be returning to class, and aerial practice will continue in the afternoons. The rest of you will also start your own flight practice with the Pegasuses tomorrow afternoon, after their scheduled flight time to reduce airborne accidents. In two weeks' time, you will have your first training together to practice synchronized movement with your Wing. Ellian Knights, you are dismissed. Follow me out to the southern field. Everyone else stays here to continue scheduled morning classes." The professor walks off the stage.

I follow Kissa, Cinder, Juniper, and Vex out of the auditorium and down the corridor to the southern field, a clearing before the Mysticwoods.

I'm distracted thinking about what happened between Sølas and me. Where did he go? Did I do something to make him leave? Did he somehow hear my thoughts? It wouldn't make sense for him to leave, even if he did hear my thoughts, since he's been the one going on about everything he feels for me. The one asking for more than I even know how to give.

Why the fuck is he always disappearing on me like this? *Rude.* If I'm being honest with myself, I'm mostly just worried about him. With my luck, I'll finally feel something more for someone and they'll instantly die.

*"You're so melodramatic. I told you; no one is dead."* Calais' sharp voice cuts through my thoughts like a whetted blade.

*"Rude! You don't get worried about Scáil when you can't hear him along your mated bond?"*

*"Someone had to stop you from your fruitless spiraling. I need you focused for flight training. If you fall off and die because you're thinking of your Shadowmancer, I will be rather annoyed. I can always feel Scáil. If you weren't so recklessly stubborn, your bond would be the same."*

*"He's not MY Shadowmancer,"* I growl before continuing, *"So glad to know my death would annoy you. Kinda sounds tempting, just to ruffle your scales. And what do you mean our bond would be the same?"*

She growls, apparently not finding the same amusement about ruffling up her scales. I would've laughed if my mind wasn't still reeling from her last comment.

*"I certainly heard your thoughts this morning. You said 'mine' loud and clear. You may lie to yourself about what you feel for him, but there's no fooling me."*

*"So, you're just going to casually ignore the last question I asked you?"*

*"I do so enjoy ruffling your hair,"* she snorts in response.

*Snarky bitch.*

*"Call me that again, and you'll be left with Pip for flight maneuvers,"* Calais snarls.

*"He doesn't even have wings!"*

*"He's a shapeshifting dragon. You have no idea what he can do. I'd imagine it would be quite the amusing spectacle."* Her snark trickles down the bond.

The conversation did indeed distract me from spiraling as we walk out to the field, bristling with a wild assortment of flying creatures.

Winx is next to a small dragon, whose wings appear like stained glass, feathering into five points that are layered like dragonfly wings. The dragon is much smaller than Scáil but bigger than a large Draco. Its body is covered in violet scales, its belly shaded in deep turquoise. The bright purple spikes and frills appear like glass, framing its face and rounded snout. Its tail ends with four smaller wings in the same color. I believe this species is known as a Glass Dragon.

I haven't seen Winx since her bedroom that night, and I certainly don't want to have to talk to her while I'm still trying to figure out what's between

Sølas and me. Something tells me she won't be too thrilled about finding out he's my Bloodline pairing. Never mind that there's definitely something more between us…

I casually dip in between a sapphire and golden gryphon, who snaps at me for getting too close, stumbling over a red phoenix while avoiding their beaks. Luckily, I make it through them with all my limbs intact and only a few singed arm hairs.

My luck runs out as I nearly step on the tail of a Draco. Its scales are blended circles of vibrant green and dark teal in a background of black. Clearly sensing my close call, its tail rises to reveal hundreds of barbed spikes, reminding me of a porcupine. It slithers its narrow face to pin me with beady red eyes, flaring a frill made of striped barbs, matching its tail. It's a Poison Dart Draco. And to *no one's* surprise, Chet steps around its head to see what's upset his bonded dragon.

I raise my lip into a snarl at Chet. The Draco snaps for my neck, sharing a similar distaste for me. Its maw shapes into a manic grin due to the white scales extending from the edges of its mouth, appearing like teeth.

The earth rumbles beneath my feet as Calais steps over the beast, causing it to scurry out of the way of her massive claws.

Chet's Draco immediately lowers its quills, bowing its head in reverence to Calais. Chet glares at the Draco, gritting his teeth at its response, yet they both decide to find a new position, farther away from Calais.

I watch the silver Yassur from the Gilded Auditorium take the simple wooden dais. Her saffron-yellow eyes against her metallic silver fur are striking. Her face bears sharp, angular features, fitting well with her diagonal bat ears. She raises her furry arms, signaling the ensigns to quiet. Membranes attach her wrists to her upper hips. The morning light shimmers through them, revealing intricate, blubbery veining.

"I am Professor Reska Swiftsing. Please, call me Professor Reska. I'm tasked with being your instructor for Aerial Combat." Her voice is cool and crisp, reminding me of an autumn breeze signaling summer's end. A large silvery-blue Coata swoops down, landing behind her. She doesn't even waver in the gusts of its enormous feathered blue ombre wings, dipped in deep, dark blue. Its body is the shape of a small dragon with four legs but covered in powder-blue feathers dusted in silver. Its long tail ends in a fan of razor-sharp feathers that resemble blades.

"This is my bonded creature. Her name is Argenta; she is a Bladed

Coata. Do mind her tail if you'd like to keep your extremities in one piece." A laugh bubbles up from her chest as Argenta nuzzles her head.

"Today's lesson will focus on staying mounted through maneuvers escalating in difficulty. As Ellian Knights, you are the forward attack for your Wing. You must clear the path and hold the line while working as one fluid breath with those on the ground. The Wuvon will do everything they can to draw you closer to the Blackwood, where their powers are strongest. If you lose a team member to the dark forest, there will be no rescue. Consider their life forfeit.

"Your role is crucial: attack, defense, crowd control, battle oversight, and keeping distance between your unit and the Blackwood. You should never be dismounting during battle, unless you require healing or you have the ability to fly on your own. Remember: you'll be soaring between various magical abilities being shot in all directions. Your movements must be concise and streamlined, or you risk your life and that of your bonded creature. I will take off, and you will follow my lead. Remember your formations. Zenith will lead, Nadir will follow, Ascension on the right, and Declination on the left."

She leaps onto Argenta's back, boosted by air magic.

I follow suit, and before I can even adjust my positioning, Calais is bellowing to the sky. I nearly slide off under the momentum, having to use all of my upper body strength to get my legs back in position above her shoulders.

*Think happy thoughts, not cursing words,* I remind myself. I'm not going to let my sharp tongue be the reason she decides not to catch me if I fall.

*"Ah, so you can be trained."* Calais snickers.

She's clearly trying to test my ability to hold my tongue with that comment. So, I don't give her the satisfaction.

My eyes drift to see Vex to my right, Cinder to my left, and Juniper and Kissa below me. Typically, we are meant to fly in the shape of a five-pointed star, but Sølas isn't here, leaving us missing the middle of our formation. I take his position as anchor point.

Our formation was decided by Atlas, based on our various flying creatures' sizes, wing spans, and unique abilities using his Celestial Gift of Probabilities magic. He can't see the future like a Seer, but he can see hundreds of probabilities and determine which has the best chance of success.

Calais' four wings tuck close to her sides, sending us plummeting towards the ground, following Argenta and Professor Reska. She whips her tail, slinging us into a spiraling movement. Putting on a show as the world around us spins in a blur of light. My stomach hurls up my throat, spinning with my head.

*"Stop using your vision for sight. Use your magic; sense the world around you. Quickly. I will not tolerate cleaning your vomit from my scales,"* Calais hisses.

I don't waste another second since I'll be the one scrubbing her scales while she undoubtedly tries to eat me just for the fun of it.

My eyelids seal tight, shoving my nausea out my mosaic window. I let my other senses take over. The wind whips past my ears, signaling our direction is still downwards, matching the stillness of her muscles while diving. My magic crackles beneath my skin, sensing the disorder of the molecules spiraling around us. Through chaos, I perceive the collision of atoms, the mayhem feeding my power as it reaches out further, craving even more pandemonium.

The ultraviolet radiation burns my exposed skin at the high altitude. My magic simmers with delight, absorbing its energy, allowing me to determine our position in relation to the sun. Shapes begin to take form under the collision of photons bouncing off objects all around. I can now see the outlines of Vex and Cinder on my flanks. Ahead of me, Argenta's feathered wings flare wide, catching an updraft in an angled ascent. I brace my body tightly to Calais', preparing for the shift in her momentum. In the next second, my muscles screech as I hold on, gravity threatening to claim me. Her large muscles flex beneath my own with steady flaps as we ascend.

*"Your powers are strongest when you let them flow with the natural energy of the world around you. They are not meant to be caged or tightly controlled. Just as the universe around cannot be commanded, nor can your powers of atomics and chaos,"* Calais states with a steadying tone that's almost grounding. My heart rate lowers before spiking again with the realization there's something off about her last sentence.

*"What do you mean by atomics?"*

*"Your unique ability to sense the world at its tiniest level, perceiving atoms so small, they behave as not only particles, but waves, too."*

*"But that sense came to me before we were bonded, so it can't be my Arcane Glyph."*

*"Nor did I say it was."* Her tone's back to her typical raspy sharpness

I've come to know. She's clearly annoyed at my ignorance. It's not like she's the most forthcoming dragon, but I do appreciate her guidance today, allowing me to see without the sight of my eyes.

There are no texts on Chaos Magic. So, it's up to me to explore the extent of my powers. I'm thankful to have someone much wiser than me to help me understand them.

*"As much as I appreciate you admitting that I am clearly the wiser of us, we are a bonded team. I will always be here for you. I will always push you to be more, breaking through your perceived limits, because you are so much more than you know."* Calais' voice is softer now, almost caring, a tone I didn't know she's capable of.

*"Everyone thinks I'm more than I am. It's starting to become a recurring theme."*

*"Perhaps those around you see all that you can be, while you insist on being the one to hold yourself back. You think you're in control, but fear controls you. When you learn to truly let go and become attuned with the universe around you, your powers will be limitless."*

Perhaps the Fates and Saool, the creator of the universe, are not my enemies after all.

*"You're going to give me a complex that gives even the Celestials a run for their coin,"* I jest. A deep rumble and snort emanate from her chest that can only be described as laughter.

Argenta and Reska lead us in various movements of bobbing and weaving. Slowly escalating the difficulty of our movements to sharp turns that have us flying parallel to the ground. I lean my body the opposite way, trying to maintain my seat. The screams of a rider rip through the air as they fall behind us. Luckily, we're so high, the Orcalia has enough time to position itself under her, catching the rider on its back.

I'm thankful to not be bonded to such a creature. I can't imagine it's easy to stay mounted on its rounded killer whale frame, with only its dorsal fin to hold on to. The rider, surprisingly, stays on for the next maneuver as we fly upside down. Her leg muscles are giving me a run for my coin. I hope she isn't using her air magic to stay seated, as we can only cast one element at a time, making her a liability to her Wing.

Several others are not so lucky. A melody of screams burst out from behind me as several beasts break out of formation to catch falling riders. I gaze down to glimpse a rider I recognize from Nadir wing, his pink hair streaming in the wind. It's Rizz Pinkerton, Flint's crush. A beautiful armored Winged Polar Bear catches the nape of his leathers with his jaw. Then, after a few wing beats, he uses his powerful neck to flip him over his head, landing Rizz on his back.

Below this, Winx and her dragon are spinning. She has her arms up, laughing and hollering with joy. Leave it to her wild nature to not even bother holding on. I envy her carefree spirit; she lives every day as if it's her last, full of vibrance and life.

We land for lunch. They bring a banquet of food outside to refuel us, as well as various types of edible items for our winged creatures. My throat bobs as Calais snaps up an entire mooca in one gulp, like it's nothing more than finger food.

I sneak off behind the knoll of a hill, allowing Pip to down the extra helpings. After eating, he's far too interested in meeting all the creatures. It's a relentless battle trying to keep him from slipping out of my hands to meet them.

The ground quakes under Calais' presence. She lowers her head to the ground, snorting at him.

Pip quickly wraps himself around my wrist in a bracer without a second thought. I peer into her rainbow eyes and smile, nodding my head in thanks. I can sense her amusement down our bond at my gratitude. I didn't think I'd be grateful that we can already sense each other's emotions, but it allows her to come to my aid without even asking.

I gaze over the rustling lavender leaves of the Mysticwoods, catching myself wondering: if I speak down our tether, will Sølas even hear me? I keep his window open in my mind, occasionally peeking over to it, hoping to find his black velvet ribbons spilling through.

I don't even bother trying to speak to him in my mind. Him not answering will be accompanied by a slurry of emotions I have no intention of letting myself feel. Sometimes, not knowing is easier than the truth.

I suppose that's why Calais keeps her secrets; she knows some truths I may not be ready to face. I know I need to listen to her advice and stop trying to control everything. But growing up with so little control, I cling to it. Even if it's just an illusion. Even if it's hurting me at this point.

I settle on giving myself some grace. I can't change things about myself overnight. Although, I doubt I will extend that same grace to Sølas when he decides to finally slink back after disappearing on me yet again. Especially while making me actually worry about him all day.

*"You should take it easy on the Shadowmancer when he returns. He has demons that are sometimes hard to escape."*

*"I'm going to try and not be offended that you seem to have more of a soft spot for him than me."*

*"He listens well, unlike you. Plus, I've known him longer than you."*

*"Wait. What do you mean you've known him longer than me?"*

*"I've said too much. That is not my story to share."*

*"Typical."* I huff as I see Argenta and Reska take to the sky. I curse under my breath as I climb the spikes up Calais' leg and find my mounted position. Her annoyance at my attitude is evident in her tight shoulder muscles.

*"You and Sølas keep telling me to feel all these stupid emotions so they stop flooding me, so that's what I'm doing. I'm currently annoyed that you're keeping things from me, and I'm aggravated with Sølas for disappearing all day. I am, in fact, worried about him for some Celestials-forsaken reason, even though I know he's alive."*

*"Yes, you must feel your emotions but also have the wisdom to discern what they're telling you, or you will be ruled by the chaos of them."*

I take the time of ascent to listen to Calais' advice. Yet again.

I realize I'm more than annoyed she won't elaborate. I'm hurt. She can hear all of my thoughts, but I can only hear what she chooses to share. I'm also upset that another Elarian has known my dragon before me, regardless of the consequences that entails.

My thoughts drift to the fact that I'm irrationally worried about Sølas, even though I know he's alive and safe with Scáil, and Calais wouldn't let anything happen to her mate. This emotion tells me I care about Sølas in a way that's more than him just being a member of my Zenith. In a way that's more than just lust. In a way I don't fully grasp yet, but there's clearly no denying it after this morning's events. Despite me initially being thankful that he disappeared so I could process what I had just thought, part of me hates being so far from him.

I haven't realized how much I've become accustomed to him always being around me, feeling the ribbons of our tether always trying to be near me. I find myself longing for the magnetic force that always pulls us together. My chest persistently aches with him so far away.

Then it dawns on me. Those black velvet ribbons have been in my mind since before I bonded to Calais! He'd been trying to speak to me in my mind before our dragons' mated bond tethered the four of us together. I was so busy trying to push him away and ignore my feelings, I hadn't put the timeline together. My molars grind under the tension of my clenched jaw. I've clearly been given an explanation that wasn't the whole truth. I'm not sure what to make of Calais' silence on my thoughts. I suspect nothing good from my brief time knowing her.

I'm jolted from puzzling the pieces together as we hurtle downwards, as if an invisible mountain lies before us. The ground is impossibly close as Argenta pulls up, her claws scraping against the soil in a hovered run before flying upwards again. My guts bound into my chest as Calais shreds the earth beneath her talons before we ascend, my stomach left in the crumbled rocks below.

As we regain altitude, Professor Reska's magically amplified voice lilts on the wind, "Now I want you to continue to follow my maneuvers while switching places with your opposing Wing. Zenith with Nadir, and Ascension with Declination."

Roars and shrieks fill the air with near collisions in the shuffle. It's safe to say, we meet this challenge poorly. Calais leads the way with grace, although a Draco almost flips over from the gust of her four wings after veering too close. Her head whips around, snarling blue light at the poor beast, who's struggling to find its balance, now going pale beneath her wrath. The Draco's color is still better than its Arabellian rider, who's more pallid than a wraith.

I lose count of how many times we practice position changes through alternating maneuvers; each time, less accidents occur. Yet we're nowhere close to a fluid aerial fleet. I look west as the sun sinks low in the sky. Every muscle in my body burns, sore from holding my mount through all the new moves. Even muscles I didn't know could be sore. A thankful sigh crescendos from lungs when Reska and Argenta head back towards Gildorea.

I slide down Calais' leg and nearly fall, my knees bowing under the unfamiliar weight of my body. I'm not sure if my trembling legs will make the journey back up the hill to campus.

*"You did well today, Nebulight. Eat quickly. I will be waiting for you when you are finished,"* Calais says calmly along our bond.

All I want to do is lie down, and now I'll need to come back out here?

I'm too exhausted to argue as I will my limp body towards campus. I'm even willing to table prying information from Sølas until after a good night's rest.

# CHAPTER 40

Remarkably, I make it to the dining hall. Rich smells fill the air, pooling saliva in my mouth as my stomach grumbles. I imagine I look like Pip scarfing down the mountain of food on my plate. I take a break to breathe, peering up to see the rest of my Zenith needling me with their glares.

"What?" I mumble over a mouth full of food. I swear, Pip moves to grab food off my plate, my eyes darting down at my arm, but nothing's amiss.

"Aside from the fact that you just ate dinner like a feral dog… Where the fuck was Sølas today?" Kissa snips.

"How am I supposed to know where the *shadow prick* is? I'm not his keeper." I huff, shoving another helping of food into my mouth. I can't remember the last time I was this hungry.

"Ha! Shadow prick. I'm going to call him that from now on." Eko cackles, landing him an elbow to the gut from Seraph.

"I could smell him all over you this morning in class. So don't act like you weren't the last one to see him," Kissa hisses under her breath, clearly trying to keep it quiet. But from the look on everyone's face, she's failed miserably.

I shrug in response. "Ask Seraph. She's his best friend."

"Oh no. Fuck that. Don't look at me! He's been too busy with your Bloodline pairing to get up to trouble with me the last few days." Seraph smirks as she takes a sip of her drink.

"Of *course* he would be your Bloodline pairing." Cinder's amber eyes roll.

"You should be able to sense him along the tether of your bond," Kivi hums, as if it were just a matter of fact, like she is just discussing the Celestials be dimmed weather. I don't even know how she knows about that. Since I didn't tell her, it must have been Sølas.

Everyone's jaw drops at the table, even Cinder's. Atlas keeps his composure; clearly, he knew. Seraph's guzzling her drink now, also telling me she knew, which isn't that surprising being his best friend.

"Not a bond between us," I snap. "I think what Kivi *meant* to say"—I narrow my eyes on her for not including the part about it being our dragon's bond while she tends to the mushrooms on her arms, unfazed by my glare—"is that our dragons are a mated pair. Their bond tethers us."

Seraph is now choking on her drink while Atlas taps his fingers nervously, and Kivi continues to tend to her fungi, as if she hadn't been the one to even bring up this whole cursed thing. I'm not sure I like any of their reactions to this. Clearly, they know more than they are letting on. Just another reason I need to speak with the shadow prick himself.

"How unusual. We haven't had a mated, bonded pair since Gildora and Raeya." Gearin readjusts his spectacles before curling his white mustache in contemplation.

"Except my great-great-great-great-great-grandparents were the last-known Fated mate pair in Cascara, since the end of the Celestials reign of Elyndor," Fenwick pips, a radiant smile on her face as always.

Everyone's mouth falls open, except for Juniper—her best friend—and Atlas—our Savant, who seems to know everything. I guess it's not that surprising that Fenwick, the most powerful Radiant since Raeya, is her descendent.

"Putting all that aside… it still doesn't explain why Sølas wasn't there for flight maneuvers today." Now it's Kissa's chartreuse eyes narrowing on me. I try not to crumble under the weight of her fierce feline stare. I avoid her by taking a long sip of my soothing frostflower tea. Her whiskers glimmer under her forming scowl. My nervousness failing to slide by unnoticed.

"Did something happen between you two?" Kissa eyes me suspiciously.

I shrug, trying not to let her cutting scrutiny unravel my mask of indifference. The last thing I want is the messy slew of feelings between me and Sølas being dissected by my team in the public setting of the dining hall.

"We were training in the Warded Hallow. He helped me make progress controlling my Chaos Magic. Then he smiled, gave me a look, and in typical fashion, he vanished," I admit, leaving out the part where I loudly thought, *he's mine*. Since there's no way he could have known that, and there's no way in Emberhell I'm bringing it to the dinner table for group discussion.

"Did he give you his classic smirk and a look or a real smile?" Eko chimes in, and I'm not certain I like where he's going with the little bit of information I did reveal.

"Does it matter?" I shrug, hoping to brush it off.

"Of course it matters." Orion's candy-red eyes pin me to the spot. I don't know why I thought I could get away with this, given she can literally read Auras.

"He gave me a genuine smile and a look," I mumble in defeat.

The table erupts in murmurs as if I just revealed the most scandalous fact of the evening. I grumble, seeing Seraphina has managed to sneak off in the kerfuffle. She's exceptionally good at that. Fucking sly Spycraft abilities. I imagine she wants to avoid any further questioning on the matter.

I try to sneak off too, but I'm not as lucky. Kissa grabs me by the shoulder, shoving me right back into my seat.

"Not so fast. Why was he smiling at you, and why can't you reach Sølas through your dragons' mated bond?"

An exasperated sigh whittles my ribs.

"He was smiling because he was proud that he was right and his lesson helped me hit all the right targets in the Warded Hollow. I'm sure I only made his ego bigger. And I can't reach him because he's shielding against the bond. Scáil is, too. Clearly, they don't want to be reached."

Eko and Orion are both shaking their heads. Evidently, that's not a good enough reason for Sølas to have a genuine smile. Kivi mumbles something under her breath about a bond as spores swirl around her fingers.

So I add, "Again, I hit *every red target*, guys. Maybe he's happy I won't be murdering you all on the battlefield when I use my powers."

"I can count on one hand the number of times I have seen that male genuinely smile. And I grew up with him." Eko holds up a fist.

A twinge of sadness tugs at my heart, knowing the world is missing such a beautiful smile. Then I think about how him disappearing afterward is all the more suspicious. He's never been one to shy away from his chaotic emotions.

"You need to let us know immediately if you sense anything concerning down the tether. Let's table this discussion for tonight. I expect you both to report to me and Gearin tomorrow after classes. We'll need to see if this tether will interfere with your Rune Tech communication ring. We can't have you two arguing in your heads and missing important information being relayed regarding the battle. Celestials Blessings to you all."

Atlas stands up with Kivi, and they bow in synch before taking leave. Thank the Celestials for Atlas' decision.

I can't get up fast enough to leave when Kissa stops me, yet again.

"Want me to walk you back to your room?"

"No, I'm good. Calais said I need to meet her after dinner. Don't worry, I don't think Chet will try anything with her so close by."

She crosses her arms, giving me a wary look. "I wouldn't put it past him. It's really no problem, Savaé."

I shake my head in response and will my exhausted body to move again.

Once I am out of the dining hall, I reach out to Calais to confirm where I'm meeting her. *"Northern or Southern field?"*

*"Northern."*

# CHAPTER 41

Slowly, I meander my way down the northwestern corridor. The hairs prickle on my neck, causing me to stop in my tracks. My eyes peer around the quiet marble halls and balconies, only to see a few ensigns making their way back to their dorm rooms. I close my eyes, peeking out the starry stained-glass window to see black velvet ribbons. Tension I didn't even know I was carrying melts between my shoulders as relief floods my veins, instantly sending my heart into a fluttering mess.

That beating relief quickly sizzles up as a wave of anger crashes through me, remembering that Sølas clearly has some explaining to do about our bond. The forefront of my mind bristles with quills poised to strike—he left and then blocked me out all day! My magic morphs into barbs beneath my skin, threatening to rip free, drowning in my anger alongside me.

My legs sling into a sprint, fury and undeniable longing bubbling and spewing inside me, ready to simmer over. To burn. To consume. Fuming as I dart through the arched doors to the northern field.

The cool air unsettles my Chaos Magic, craving to disrupt the low movement of the cold molecules. My power nips at my skin, begging for collision, heat, to make a mess of the world that desires to be untamed. I'm too exhausted to hold it back any longer, and everyone wants me to let go—tonight seems as good as any.

In my wild new state of feeling, I relinquish control. Unleashing my magic…

To let chaos reign.

The wind devours my fury, swirling in a vicious dance around me, twirling to the beat of the thunder booming in the distance. Lightning strikes with every step, the earth quaking and shattering beneath my feet, swaying in gusts of air that caress me. It's nothing compared to the sea of chaotic emotions storming inside me. Icy sleet beats against my sore skin.

Wind violently lashes my hair against my flesh. The weather growing more and more wild as the lightning strikes closer, drawn in by my chaotic magic set free. The next bolt whips down in front of me, illuminating the dark figure below, as I see Calais circle above in the sky. An eerie fog uncurls around my ankles, each step freezing the ground beneath my feet.

A hurricane of weather torrents around me. Yet, instead of being out of control, I am… alive. Free from the shackles of my own design. My own demise.

I hear Calais' voice, faintly. *"She is not ready. She risks ignition."* But it's distant, even in my own mind, as my magic vibrates my bones like a tuning fork, feeding from the chaos dancing around me. Growing more powerful the more I let the world spin out of control around me.

I have no desire to rein it in; it matches the fury within me, kindred to my imprisoned soul set free. My own incessant need for control is shattered, the bars now bowed from my magic's escaping wrath. The earth quakes and quivers beneath my feet, as if I'm as mighty as my dragon. The soil soaring into the blizzarding wind with each step. My eyes can barely see in front of me, but I know exactly where *he* is.

An irresistible pull, like a star orbiting a black hole.

An inescapable fate.

An inevitable destruction.

His shadows whirl around him, ripped apart by my tempest of chaos. Another lightning strike comes in overhead, landing on Calais, sparking along her lightning conductor spikes. I try to gather my thoughts. To remember why I'm so livid …

His blue moon eyes collide with mine, piercing my soul, and nothing seems to matter anymore.

I become the wind, moving wild and swift until my arms wrap around his neck, my lips crashing into his.

Our kiss is frantic, like we're each other's air, gasping one another in, after drowning in absence for far too long.

His full lips part. Our tongues devour one another, consuming each moment like when breath becomes air.

He pulls me into him, his arm around my waist and the other hand grasped in my hair, tilting my head back, deepening the kiss as I fall deeper into him.

He tastes like moonlight and darkness. Hope and dreams.

Our magic intertwines, ripping apart the space between us. To be closer. Interlacing, as if they can't exist without one another.

My skin ignites in such heat, the fires of the forge feel like dying embers in its luster. The fever between us melting away the seams of where I begin and he ends.

He kisses me like the world is ending.

With the way his mouth moves against mine, I'm not entirely sure it isn't.

He grasps me in. Tighter. Stealing my breath away under his strength, as my hand tangles through his silky raven locks.

A moan escapes my lips as the hard length of him grinds against my heated core. The growl that rumbles through his chest resonates through my bones, imprinting on my marrow.

He spins me up and unravels me all at the same time. No being has ever kissed me like him. His velvet ribbons caress my mind, holding me so deeply, I never want him to let go.

Our connection is a magic all of its own.

His black velvet ribbons swirl lazily, weaving their way between my ribs, nuzzling around my heart, finding their way into my soul. Pulling us closer than comprehension. Closer than words exist to describe.

I whimper at the sensation as he groans into my mouth. Melting me like a candle wax into his arms. A flame ignited only by him. For him.

I want more of him.

I want all of him.

*He's mine.*

He grasps at me, as if he can pull me even tighter, groaning at my thought.

My mind shutters as I realize I'm left bare, my shields utterly obliterated in my fury of letting my chaos free.

I try to pull away.

As my lips fall from his, he pulls his forehead to mine. His hands firmly around my waist and neck as his thumb strokes my jaw. His breath is ragged while I barely breathe, knowing the thought he undoubtedly heard.

"*Yours. Always. In every existence that there ever was or ever will be.*" His smoky voice caresses my mind, causing me to sway in his grasp as the weight of his words keep me grounded in this reality, tethering my soul in an unspeakable way.

The exhaustion of the day avalanches over me, my body slackening in his arms. I peer up to see his eyes still closed, snowflakes decorating his lashes as messy raven curls cascade into his face.

He seems to be savoring this moment with his every heartbeat.

The world slips out from underneath my feet, exhaustion and the depth of my magic expenditure claiming my body. The edges of my vision go dark.

The last thing I see is Calais' and Scáil's wings tucked around us as they nuzzle one another's heads. Darkness consumes me as I realize they used themselves to protect us, shielding us from the destruction of my power unleashed.

# CHAPTER 42

I awake to my weakened body in the copper bathtub of our penthouse room. Soap slides across my skin in a soothing, rhythmic motion. Almost lulling me back into the embrace of darkness.

Smoky shadows dance upon my arm. Sølas' fingers move in gentle circles, arching tingles through my nerves.

"You left me," I murmur softly, my voice raspy with exhaustion.

I hear his weight shift, leaning in closer, kneeling behind me. His head lowers beside mine, gathering the damp strands from my face as his lips brush against my ear. The intensity of his closeness spins my heart into a slurry.

"What's that saying again? Absence makes the heart grow fonder," he purrs deeply. His devilish, full lips twist against my ear.

Part of me shudders at even the thought of his absence again. I hadn't been thinking when I kissed him. Only *feeling*. I didn't give myself the chance to dwell on the consequences of my actions.

Oh, but that *kiss*.

It was far more than a kiss.

Our very souls touched.

Endings and beginnings.

It was a claiming.

A branding.

A rapture.

A tremble caresses my body at the thought of just how deeply he kissed me. Smoky swirls spread across my skin, binding me in soft velvet.

His breath caresses my neck, stealing mine away. His lips barely grazing my flesh as he speaks, "Judging by the kiss of chaos you gave me… perhaps I should leave you more often." His voice is nothing short of feral.

My body craves the full weight of his perfect lips on my skin, but my heart aches at the thought of him leaving again.

I gather my reedy breath to speak.

"If you want all of me, don't you ever block me out again." My voice is nothing more than a rasp, lacking any bite, but it hits its mark as the smirk falls from his lips.

I hear his weight shift behind me, positioning himself to the side of me. His wet hands framing my face. Notes of jasmine mixed with spruce fill my lungs.

I'm so drained from pushing myself to the limits. And yet. Under his touch, my power crackles, as though there's an endless well between us. Perhaps it isn't my power that's drained at all, just my physical form. I nudge my magic, beckoning it inside my muscles to give me strength. To my surprise, it listens.

My eyes flutter open, revealing two glowing white, piercing moons. Melancholy crumples around the edges, and I'm not sure why this time.

"I'm sorry, my *Luxsula*. I will explain it all to you tomorrow." His thumbs stroke the gold flecks dusting my cheekbones. I've never felt so safe, so at peace in someone's touch.

"Tonight, let me take care of you," he pleads in a soft whisper.

"I don't need you to take care of me."

"I know, but let me anyway." His words are so gentle, coaxing me to give in.

My lashes tumble shut, and I give him a short nod. Perhaps letting chaos reign left all my walls in ruin. I'm not sure of anything anymore, but I know at this moment, I want to be close to him. And I intend to selfishly let myself enjoy every second of it.

There's a part of my mind that's frightened by everything tonight. The part that always wants to run—it knows once I dive into him completely, there's no turning back.

I let my heart greedily quiet that part of me.

Tonight, I want to pretend tomorrow doesn't exist.

Answers and rational decisions are for tomorrow.

Wafting tendrils of steam bead sweat on my temple as the water heats around me.

Sølas' hands shift with his body. He's once more kneeling behind me. My head now resting on his shoulder, his bare, muscular chest against the skin of my shoulders. My magic rumbles beneath, drawing him closer.

Then, sensation arching my body in an instinctive response. Puzzle pieces sink into one another. I will my weary arm out of the water, sliding my wet fingers over the corded muscles of his arm. I tug his hand, wrapping him around me under the water. Before I can even move to find the other, his arm sinks, already knowing what I want. Obeying my desires as if they are his own.

The fingers of his left hand splay wide against my stomach, dragging me closer to him. His right fingertips skim my collarbone, dipping down the center of my chest. Stalking the golden lines of my markings like a map made for him.

I keep my eyes closed, devouring his every touch, drunk on the liquid bliss pouring through my nerves. It's as if it's the first time I've ever been truly caressed.

And maybe it is.

His thumb sweeps over the tip of my breast, stringing a reedy gasp from my lungs at the electric pulse. His chest breathes unsteadily behind me. Teasing me yet again as he traces my markings along the muscles of my stomach, then out to the flare of my hip. His grip wraps around my thigh, tightening as he grapples for the reins of his control. My fingers weave along his, beckoning his chaos while I relinquish the control I've clung to like the very thread stitching my every seam. Holding me together.

"Unravel me," I breathe.

His shadows obey, flooding out all around me, the dam broken as they consume me. Smoke swirls across my breasts, thumbing my sensitive nipples. I suck in a heady breath. A pinch nips at the peaks; pleasure and pain mix, ripping a whimper from my lips.

A deep feral rumble responds, vibrating my flesh. His aura indenting into me, imprinting his essence as I float lost in my addiction, writhing in my craving, my only thought... *more.*

The sound of a pleading whimper falls from my lips as his large hand makes lazy sweeps along my inner thigh, agonizingly slow. Burning me alive beneath the heat spreading from his every touch. My clit throbs, plump and begging for him. His tattooed knuckles brush over the core of me, my hips jerking into his touch. Lightning rips through my every nerve, bowing my body. With the movement, his lips are against my neck, teeth sinking in, binding me to reality, ecstasy seeping into my blood, leaving nothing free from its blaze.

Full lips drag along the newly sensitive area.

A kiss. A claiming.

"*I am yours, and you are mine.*" His smoky snarl cleaves into my soul.

A breathless moan pours from my throat. His deep growl rumbling along my neck, teeth nipping along the flesh as if he can capture the sounds he strings from me.

Bliss tightens at my core, his shadows teasing my entrance. I can let myself be *his,* for tonight.

His fingers brush up the slit of my center, swirling over my clit. My lips pop open, a wild sound escaping, my back arching, slamming into his touch. *More.* I need more.

He obeys. Prying another feral gasp from my chest as his thumb works the sensitive bundle of nerves.

My hand grasps the corded muscles of his forearm resting along my abdomen, grounding me as heady sensation threatens my understanding of pleasure.

He slips an idle finger into me, a shallow intrusion, keeping me on the edge, but I'm already falling, too lost to hold on, my core tightening around him.

"Look at you. Already unraveling, and I haven't even made you scream yet." His rumbling purr wrings a loud cry of pleasure from my lips. His finger tries to retreat, but I snap my hand up, nails pinning into his shoulder before he can leave me.

My arm trembles under the endless teasing of his shadows, still at work along my nipples and breasts, the soft rhythm of his thumb on my clit. My hips buck wildly, trying to deepen the position of his thick, long finger inside of me, but his arm moves with my body, denying me what I crave.

*Fucking bastard.*

He knows what I want, but I don't know why he won't give it to me. I brush my trembling hand along the back of his neck, drawing him closer. He kisses the side of my mouth lazily, as if my body isn't begging beneath him.

"I. Want. All. Of. You." Each word is punctuated with a feral kiss along my neck, bringing me almost over the edge of bliss again.

*"Please,"* I moan across his mind. I'm too breathless to speak.

"Promise me," he growls. Canines nipping across my neck, the swirl of pleasure and pain have me coming undone as he tightens his arm around my stomach, bringing me back.

*"You are mine,"* I breathe, praying it will be enough.

"Mine," he roars as his finger is joined by another, diving deep inside me. His shadows sear into my skin beneath my breasts, as if they're imprinting his touch. Pleasure consumes me as I cry out, my core tightening around him in waves of bliss as my eyes roll back in my head, body shaking on the tide of dopamine.

His breath panting, heart racing, utterly in sync with mine. Our magic swirls, latching on to one another, sinking in, pooling together. His velvety shadows plunge through the water, wrapping every inch of my skin in silk.

The moans that leave my lips I've never heard before: wicked, wild, and drunk on chaos.

With each thrust, his fingers go a little deeper, a little faster, beckoning waves of pleasure from me I don't even know I have left to give. But I come again and again.

He growls. Low. Guttural. Feral. Possessive. His shadows sink into my core, moving with his fingers.

Stretching me, filling me, consecrating me.

Their velvety touch replaces his thumb, as if he knows it's too rough along the oversensitive center of nerves. Their whispering caress against my clit sends me drowning in pleasure once more.

I greedily devour every wave of ecstasy, certain I will die from the wild-fire that burns through my soul.

"You're mine. All your rage. All your fear. All your darkness. Every single piece of you."

He licks the salt from beaded sweat that drips down the sensitive part of my neck, sending another wave of shivers through my body. Then his left arm comes up, grasping my face as he kisses my lips gently. Nothing like the fury my mouth had shown him before.

My lips part for his tongue, which deepens in synchrony with his fingers. He swallows my moan as I gasp in his words.

"You're taking my shadows so well," he growls, shadows deepening inside my cunt as I moan his name.

"Sølas."

"That's my good fucking girl," he rasps. "Come for me. One more time, *Luxsula*." His free hand wraps around my jaw, snapping my mouth to his. Our lips collide.

His kiss is a pleasure all on its own. My rapture, branding me in fire, burning my soul, becoming a flame of euphoria. My whole body tightens around him, the world unraveling, ecstasy singing through my veins as I come undone around him.

My body collapses, sinking with exhaustion, head falling back to his shoulder as he grasps my waist to prevent me from sliding under the water.

He whispers in my ear, "You feel like heaven along my fingertips." He stills inside of me, unwavering, until the last swell of my orgasm tightens around him. Ever so slowly, he drags his fingers out of me. I whimper softly with each movement.

He redefines the word pleasure.

My body shudders as his presence leaves. His absence causing my heightened nerves physical pain.

As if he can feel it, he's immediately all around me. He lifts my limp body into his arms. Holding my head to his chest as his shadows wrap all around me, wringing each bead of water from my skin, dripping into the tub below.

Safety settles into my marrow, cloaked in his shadows, a home I've always been able to retreat to.

He lays me down in the bed on my side, coiling his entire body around me. I find myself disappointed in the presence of soft fabric briefs around his waist.

Sensing my disappointment, he pulls me tighter into him and purrs along my neck, "Don't think I didn't catch those wicked lips avoiding my promise. I will have all of you, even if it's the death of me."

I hum in response, my nerves still vibrating with pleasure… and something deeper I'm far too heady to explore.

He dusts my skin with soft kisses, each a drop of ecstasy. For once, chaos seems more divine than rigid control.

Perhaps I need a little more chaos in my life.

Perhaps tonight, I can pretend I was born into a different life, with a heart made to love rather than just survive. How much harm can come from living in a fantasy for just one night?

Just for tonight, he is mine, and I am his.

Just for tonight, I can dare to dream what it is to love.

Just for tonight.

Tomorrow is for answers and rational decisions.

My heart sings to the beat of his, to our unfathomable closeness, to the peace my soul has never known. A sleep as deep as death claims me with a serenity I am happy to die in.

# CHAPTER 43

I roll over sleepily in the early morning, swearing I hear Kivi's voice humming softly, "She must accept the bond."

I must be dreaming. I roll over again, finding Pip, tugging him in close before falling back to sleep.

I awake wearily to the sound of morning jays chirping merrily. Pip is curled up in the hollow of my stomach as soft lips graze my shoulder. A heated pleasure simmers in my veins as memories of those lips come flooding back into my mind. I shiver, remembering the recklessness I let rule me last night.

I jump up in bed, slapping the covers across my bare chest.

Sølas stands up, lifting an arched brow at my reaction.

*Fuck.* I raise my shields I left down when I set my magic free.

Sølas takes another step back, feeling my shields block him out. A dash of fear sweeps over his face before he bites down on it, hiding it behind a clenched jaw.

Every muscle in my body aches, but there's a delicious soreness between my legs I try to shove from my mind. But it's too late… I gasp in the flood of intimate memories, blood-simmering, vulnerable passion. It's too much. My legs itch to run, knowing to the depths of my soul, if I give in to him completely, there is no coming back from a love like that.

Ugh, my fucking muddled mess of a brain. I mean a *connection* like that. Yes. A connection because I'd let myself foolishly dream I was someone I wasn't. Someone capable of more than just survival.

Sølas' smoky voice breaks the chaotic storm of thoughts lashing my mind. "You should eat, *Luxsula*." He nods towards the table shimmering with silver-capped dishes. "Before that one figures out how to fly over there."

I follow his gaze to the side of the bed, where Pip is hovering unsteadily. He has wings!

Pip wobbles through the air, trying to synchronize his movements. Quite clumsily. I can feel his hunger as if it's my own.

I wrap the sheet around me, stepping to the side of the bed. I grasp Pip in my arm, his little wings settling along his back. They're speckled with white spots and swirling patterns that remind me of a night sky colliding with the sunset.

"We should both eat," I murmur, padding my way to the table.

Pip doesn't wait for me to lift the silver cloche, pummeling into it, knocking it off with a spine-stiffening *clang* as he scarfs down half the plate.

I grab a few pieces of bacon and a fluffy pastry filled with meat and cheese before it's all devoured.

Sølas saunters over to the table slowly, hands in his pockets, violet and indigo reflecting off his raven waves as they fall into his face. His tattooed fingers thread through his hair, and I heat at the thought of exactly what those fingers did to me last night.

A smug smirk tugs at the corner of his mouth as he sits across from me. His slow perusal greedily takes me in, studying my every feature as his black ribbons caress the golden shield of my mind.

The sensation skips a shiver down my spine, which he takes full advantage of. The starry stained-glass window in my mind blasts open. Black ribbons swirl all around me, gently binding me, preventing me from closing the latch. I think about blowing it shut, but then shadows swirl around my mouth.

"What are you doing?" I snap.

"I'm preventing you from blocking me out," he croons, leaning in, lazily resting his chin on his tattooed knuckles.

I try to fight him in my mind, but I can't budge. His shadows tighten, pulsing a bolt of pleasure through me. My knees tremble beneath the table, a reedy breath tumbling from my lips.

"As much as I'd like to devour your pleasure once more—you yourself said, tomorrow is for answers and rational decisions." His eyes deepen. Mine widen.

"I didn't say that out loud or even think it along our linked tether," I rasp. His face is unamused by me stating the obvious. Apparently, there's more I need answers to than I realize.

"The answer to the questions you seek are one and the same." A knowing smirk heats my skin. His eyes darken with feral desire, a hunger that can never be satiated.

I shift in my seat, holding myself back from the magnetic pull to be closer to him. *Fuck*, sometimes that draw feels stronger than any power I can comprehend. A force that's suffocating to fight. What is he doing to me? I need a cold shower to keep my head straight.

"We should really finish this conversation before you shower," he muses.

I'm too busy trying to keep my traitorous body from pouncing him to figure out how he's using his shadows to fucking read my mind in this bright room. His Shadowsense power Ritherin-shit should not be working right now.

"Why? So I can lose control with you again?" I bite out.

"If I took you fully on this table right now, we wouldn't leave this room for the rest of the day. I'd keep you screaming my name until you lost your voice and every part of you was marked *mine*," he growls. I stumble back into my seat at the thought of it.

Aching heat pools between my legs, my breath becoming unsteady. I'm clearly not the only one struggling with control. I'm far too tempted to let him make good on his threat, but I know he won't let me escape promising him once more.

I close my eyes and will my legs to move to the bathroom. I leave the bedroom sheet on the floor just to torture him.

I hear him coughing up his kahvi as I march my way to the shower.

My shower is anything but cold, despite the freezing water temperature. Every graze of my soapy hands feels like his as black velvet ribbons slip along my mind.

Memories of last night flood my mind. But they're not mine. I feel the way my skin feels beneath his touch. How every kiss he lays along my neck drives him mad with desire. How he imagines how tight and wet I will feel sliding along the length of his cock. He wishes I had promised him what he wanted. What he has been longing for. So he can give all of himself to me. And take all of me. Every last piece.

I feel his control slip when I call him mine. Unable to resist giving in, regardless of the sadness etching into his bones at my continued refusal to make the promise he begs for. I feel his pleasure as if it's my own, drowning in how his heart aches for more of me. I feel him come with me as his mind fractures, and an eerie dark voice beckons to him from a distance. He's shaking in ecstasy with me as the voice grows louder.

I feel him leave to change and raise his shields against the voice, but not to me. His body curls around me, his heartbeat synching to mine as peace and happiness fill his soul, pulling me in tighter as he feels my thoughts about how, tonight, I am his, and he is mine. I feel his yearning for a future where we are together, dreamers full of hope, where anything is possible.

The cold shower does nothing to cool the chaos burning through my veins, experiencing the passion and hope of last night even more deeply than I'd felt it myself.

I step out of the frigid water, trembling from emotions that aren't even mine. My eyes flick to the mirror, going wide at the shadows swirling in my skin beneath my breasts. I almost slip on the floor, scrambling to get a closer look in the mirror at the arched lines dancing *inside* my skin.

*What the actual fuck?*

I try to wipe them off to no avail. A memory smolders to life, the searing pain of his shadows on my skin when I called him mine. Too lost in the heady mix of pleasure and pain to realize he was legitimately marking my skin.

The heat in my skin bristles into rage as mist swirls around me. I thought my words had escaped his promise, but apparently, I'm not as clever as I thought.

But that doesn't make sense. I said he was mine, not the other way around; at least, not in that moment. If I'm being completely honest, I'm not sure words matter, because I did feel like I was almost willing to give him all of me. I should have known my indulgence couldn't escape consequences. Not when the universe revels in her efforts to break me.

The thoughts tumble from my head as a tattooed finger traces the shadows beneath my breasts.

I bite my bottom lip, hard, stifling the moan his touch rouses. The pain clearing my mind as I spin, grabbing my towel and wrapping it around me.

He pins me between his arms against the counter. My breath is held captive, pinned beneath his possessive presence.

His shadows tremor as he grapples to control them around my body. He leans closer, arctic eyes darting to my lips as he tilts his head, licking the metal tang of blood dripping from my bite. Emboldening our darkness in a synchronized groan neither of us can control.

Now, my demands don't seem to care for answers and being rational.

*No. Bad Savaé.*

I need answers, despite the beautiful damn distraction in front of me.

"I told you we should have finished this conversation before you showered," he growls darkly along my neck, like I'm his prey to devour. My hand lurches out, stamped in the exposed V of his leather battle vest, nudging him away, which brings his mind back to me. Clearing his eyes of pooling pitch.

"Are you going to tell me what the fuck *your* shadows are doing in *my* skin?" I attempt to hiss, but his hand finds its way along my hip, dragging the sound into a moan.

"Our bond."

"What do you mean *our* bond?" My voice falters, mind mincing on *that* word.

"I shouldn't have lost control last night before you were ready," he murmurs, foolishly apologizing for something he knows I wanted. Well, maybe not the marking part, but the rest of it I had most definitely recklessly wanted.

"What do you mean *our bond*?" I repeat, summoning more strength to my voice.

"Our mated bond," his smoky voice whispers, as if he hopes I don't hear him. Uncontrollable trembling pitches through my nerves.

He wraps me up into his arms as the strength leaves my legs, realization sinking in. The answer to my questions. Everything suddenly making sense as I struggle to remember how to breathe.

My mind crumbles as all the subtle pieces I've ignored click into place. The air whooshing from my lungs as I gasp in understanding. His conditions —all of me or none at all. *Click.* The melancholy when I told him I couldn't. *Click.* The magnetic pull between us, why our magic is drawn to one another. Why he'd been asking me to listen before I was bonded to Calais. Why I could see his black ribbons swirling around me before we shared a mated bond between our dragons. *Click.*

His plea for me to stab him through the heart to save him a life of heartache because I didn't feel the same way he felt for me. The terror while I bled out in his arms. The fury that someone had nearly killed his mate. The breaking in the eyes yesterday when I saw him as mine but still refused to act on the truth written within both of us. The agony of being infinitely in love with me without mine to ever be in return. *Click.*

I was so obsessed with pushing him away, lost in my fear, that I missed the answer burning right in front of me. *A fucking bond.*

That's why he can read my thoughts. How he could push his memories into my mind, feeling them as if they are my own. Why, even as deeply as I feel him, he feels everything far more deeply. *Click, click.* Fucking *click.*

Perhaps his fingers truly do feel like stardust when he touches me, finding its way home…

And that kiss. When I kissed him, I thought I had imagined our souls touching, but they had found one another.

Two halves of a whole.

# CHAPTER 44

Silver tears cascade down my face. This is too much. I'm not even sure if I can *try* to be what he wants, and now we're bound to one another.

I hadn't realized one night would mean the rest of my life. No, more than that—bound for eternity, in this life and every other until time unravels. Kivi's voice lashes my mind, the words I thought I was dreaming. *You have to get her to accept the bond.*

Sølas' grip tightens around me as he feels my thought.

I can feel his emotions begging me not to ask my next question.

"What happens if I don't accept the bond?" I whisper into his chest.

He draws my face up to him, lowering his head to kiss the tears from my face. His lips send my heart skittering, my magic crackling alive in my bones.

"It will kill me," he breathes.

I'm not sure if he means literally or metaphorically, nor am I sure I want to find out either way. At this thought, he pulls me deeper into his chest, hope rushing through him.

"Why would it kill you and not me?" I ask, already knowing the answer, but part of me needs to hear it out loud.

"Because I have already accepted the bond. From the second I realized it was you." His voice sounds as shaky as I feel.

A warm tear falls on my cheek that's not my own. Without thinking, I free my arms from where they're coiled protectively around myself and wrap them around him. Crumbling the suffocating boulders of fear tumbling in my chest.

I can't bear the thought of his sadness anymore.

He leans down, pressing a kiss to the crown of my head.

We hold each other in silence for what feels like an eternity. The world dissolving away in our closeness.

All that matters is me and him.

His shadows swirl around every inch of my skin, pulling me closer to him. My magic begs to be released to explore him, but I'm afraid I will get lost in it again.

He draws me back, and my heart aches at the small chasm between us. I look down to see I'm fully dressed in my aerial leathers, hair magically dried. I find myself thankful I don't have to leave him to get my sore muscles dressed. Then his shadows beneath my breasts ache deep in my chest, drawing me back to him, but I resist the pull. The action sears agony along my ribs.

"Where's your mark?" I ask with a curious tone, rubbing at the pain in my chest. I sigh, realizing why he was always rubbing at his chest when we first met and I pushed him away.

An amused smile pins up his lips, his head turning to the side. My lips part as I take in his beautiful profile like it's the first time I've truly seen him. His shadows slip down his neck, revealing a golden twelve-pointed star, the same gold as my markings. I'm curious as to why the symbol matches the glowing, silvery one that brands my inner thigh from Pip.

"I glamoured it. I wasn't planning on showing you until you accepted the bond, but I'm at your mercy now." He sighs; he's still worried I won't.

Now I grasp why Kivi is insisting I accept the bond. As much as a relationship within the Zenith can be problematic, losing someone as powerful as Sølas is worse. I also understand that she was actually speaking of a different bond at dinner last night. Not the one shared by our dragons. Based on her reaction, along with Atlas and Seraphina's, they must have all known before I did. So much for blind trust.

"Kivi could feel our bond when she healed you. I told Seraph as soon as I knew. Kivi told Atlas because she knew it would affect the entire Zenith and the decisions he will have to make on the battlefield." His smoky voice answers the questions I haven't even thought along our bond. This level of intimacy is intense, but I appreciate his honesty without me having to pry like I do with Calais.

"*We were all protecting you until you were ready*." Her voice is rough against my mind compared to Sølas. I don't like that I'm being protected, but I can't argue. I would have absolutely lost my shit if they had told me sooner. Knowing myself, I would've pushed him away, no matter the cost. But now, things are different. When I lost control last night, I was the one seeking him, not the other way around.

"Where did you go yesterday?" I murmur, remembering the other question on my list.

"I promise I will tell you after class, but we need to go now, or we'll be late. I don't think I can trust myself having a free hour alone with you at this point." He smirks.

I roll my eyes, recalling how much more control he mustered than I did last night.

That thought has him arching a brow at me.

I huff, prying myself from his arms to find Pip. My legs are as unsteady as Pip's new wings. I try to ignore how the distance between Sølas and me causes my chest to tighten.

"Has it been like this for you since you accepted the bond?" I ask, without thinking.

"Worse. I accepted it without you even knowing about it. Scáil says it will ease with time, if you decide to accept." He leans against the frame to the bathroom with his hands in his pockets.

I shudder to imagine how painful this has been for him. I now understand why he's always around me; it must have been unbearable as I continued to push him away. I can always sense when he is near. I suppose that's the bond. I even remember my neck prickling at the first trial. I shake my head at that because I hadn't even seen him yet, and I place my short swords along my back.

His shadows reach into the armoire next to me. His broadswords slipping against his back, dressed in pitch black.

I take in my star marking him. The gold glimmers along his umber skin as he flexes the muscles along his neck.

"Proud to finally show it off, I see," I croon, though I can't help the rosy hue blooming on my cheeks. I meet his arctic-blue eyes and suddenly lose interest in going to class.

"Proud doesn't even begin to describe how I feel. I am forever yours, *Luxsula*."

He spins me around, his hand at my lower back. Guiding me to the door.

"Let's go before I lose the strength to get us both to class. Kivi will have my head if I miss another day," he rumbles as I snicker at the thought of calm and collected Kivi showing anger.

Pip skitters up my leg onto my arm, which is much more graceful than his flying.

I pause, remembering my last question as Sølas opens the door for me.

"How have you known Calais longer than me?" I ask as I continue to walk forward once more. I hear him curse under his breath.

"*Luxsula*. Tonight. I promise," he whispers in my ear, and it takes all of my strength not to lean into him. I know he will tell me the truth. I can trust him.

I know that I can trust him with all of me if I'm willing to take the leap.

# CHAPTER 45

His hand brushes against mine as we walk next to each other down the corridor. My body smolders at the light graze; without thinking, my fingers weave into his.

A wave of relief and longing floods me from him.

I look up at him to see him smiling. My heart overflows. That beautiful smile he keeps hidden from the world. His eyes are clear of shadows, reminding me of the moonlight once more.

I step closer to him, closing the distance between us as we continue to walk side by side. The happiness that pours through him steals my breath away, leaving me heady.

I find myself thinking: maybe accepting this bond isn't as terrible as I initially thought. The black velvet ribbons in my mind shudder, sensing that thought, loosening their hold on me, as if he's debating trusting me not to block him out.

By accepting the bond, I'll be able to hear all of his thoughts too, beyond just the emotions I can sense. Everything will be heightened. We will be able to share each other's visions, memories. Wield each other's magic, perfectly in sync.

As we enter the rotunda of the Grand Conservatory, the mass of Fae murmuring reminds me that we're not alone in the penthouse anymore. I gaze around the room and catch Winx glaring at me. Her eyes flare a fiery neon violet as she witnesses who I walk in with. *Shit.* My hand immediately drops from his, the black ribbons in my mind instinctively tightening.

I can see the heat radiating off Winx, who clearly saw our hands before I made a move. I'm frozen under the weight of all the times I've failed to talk to her about how things between us are only casual. Always making excuses because I didn't want to deal with the mess I created.

Sølas' hand grazes along the nape of my back, gently grounding me and prompting me to keep walking. I can't pry myself away from Winx's gaze; violet storms fill her eyes as she watches him guide me to our Zenith.

Thankfully, she finally turns away. I'm not sure if I should be relieved or terrified. I'm a fucking coward for not having made time to talk to her.

Kissa links her arm in mine, lowering her head to meet me.

"I see you found him. That Bloodline pairing smells to be working out for you. Maybe you finally won't be such an uptight bitch after getting laid." Kissa winks.

*"You definitely won't be uptight once I finally have you."* His smoky voice is like a kiss along my mind, taking all my strength to will my body still so I don't make a scene. I won't give him the satisfaction of glaring at him.

*"Keep being a tease, and I'll make you suffer,"* I snarl back along the ribbons wrapped around my wrists in my mind.

*"How much pain are we talking?"*

*"What's your tolerance?"* I smirk.

He growls in response, and I peer up to see those feral eyes full of shadows once more.

I elbow him hard.

*"You're making a scene."*

*"I don't remember you minding a crowd before,"* he purrs, stepping closer to me.

Seraphina lets out a chuckle, watching us from across the circle. I shift my gaze to see everyone staring at us.

Kivi is looking at Sølas' marking on his neck, clearly questioning if I've finally accepted the bond. I watch as her spores drift towards us; she's rather determined to find out without even asking me. *Rude.*

Sølas, sensing my thought, shakes his head tightly at Kivi, and her spores return to flitting around her.

Atlas seems to have the same curiosity about the marking's resemblance to the one burnt on my leg by the path of his darting gaze. If anyone will have an answer, it'll be him.

Eko and Orion eye us suspiciously, clearly on to something more between us.

I glare at Fenwick and Juniper, who return to happily bickering about whose favorite color is better. Gearin quickly goes back to fiddling with a rune on an arrow for Highin. Flint gives me a reassuring smile; emerald eyes flaring bright that I seem happy.

*I am happy.*

As soon as I realize I am, it fades right out of my grasp; fear sets in with how easily this happiness can be stolen from me.

Sølas' fear curls around me, tightening the ribbons binding my wrists. He knows before I do that I want to raise my shields back up. He refuses to let me. I wriggle violently in my mind.

*"I am yours. No one will ever take me from you. I promise,"* he whispers in my mind.

*"Don't make promises you can't keep."*

"Is someone going to explain what the fuck is going on between those two?" Eko prods in the background.

Grief swallows me whole. Maybe once upon a time, I could have been loved like Sølas loves me. But the part of me that was bright, lovely, and brimming with hope died with Sully. I know he wouldn't ever have wanted it so, but it's the way things had to be. To survive the fact that everyone I could possibly love and be loved by… dies.

For death is a jealous lover, and she has already claimed my heart. Waves of heartache ripple from Sølas, the depth of his pain dragging the breath from my lungs.

Then Sully's warning echoes: stay away from him and his bloodline. Anger and longing crash into me, storming within Sølas. I thrash, trying to break free to raise my shields, to numb myself from the wrenching pain that's his…and mine.

*"You are my mate. I will always be yours. In life and in death. In this world and in every other. My soul is a part of yours now. That is why I will die if you reject this bond,"* he pleads.

I still. My fight sputtering out.

I don't even know what rejecting the bond looks like, and I surely don't want to kill him, because I don't fully conceptualize what all this means. He doesn't deserve to die because I'd rather be numb than submit to all the emotions he continues to ask me to feel.

Relief trickles through the ribbons, but they don't loosen their hold, and I don't blame him. My breathing is uneasy, and Kissa eyes me, wondering what's wrong. She shoos Sølas a step back.

"You okay?" Orion darts in front of me.

Sølas' discomfort at having to even take a step away from me slashes at my ribs. Orion glares at him, sensing the synching of our emotions in our Auras.

"No. But I will be." I need to be strong. I can't let fear win. It's not only my life that depends on it now. I straighten my shoulders as guilt trickles down the ribbons.

Seraph chuckles, smacking Eko on the back. "Lovers' quarrel."

"Uh, but they aren't speaking?" Eko eyes us, confusion scrunching his face.

"They're using their Persuasive powers to save us from the details." Orion covers for me. I nod in thanks.

*"I never wanted you to have to be strong for me,"* he murmurs in defeat.

*"Everyone keeps telling me I am stronger—and so much more—than I realize. When you looked at me yesterday morning, I actually believed it. I am stronger than the frightened little girl who survived monsters that were far too big for her. If you can bear all this pain for me, the least I can do is be brave enough to try."*

Before I know what has happened, I'm in his arms, his lips crashing into mine. The tension melts from my body, parting my lips for his wicked tongue. I chase each stroke of his, greedily devouring him. His fingers weave through hair and around my waist, deepening the kiss.

He sets my soul on fire.

I don't just want him.

I need him.

I've never felt the need for anyone in my life… but *him.*

He growls into my mouth at the thought, drinking in my moaned response.

The bells are chiming, and my heart hurts knowing this moment has to end. He tugs my face into his chest, kissing me on the top of the head. He releases me as the walls of Shadowveil retreat around us.

"Aw, look; they made up!" Fenwick beams, clasping her hands to her heart with what I swear are literal golden hearts in her sunburst eyes.

Kissa immediately grabs my arm as the bells continue their melody.

"You are *exceptionally* good at making a scene for someone who hates everyone knowing their name," she hisses, dragging me to class.

But I am lost to his gravity, my focus drifting over to Sølas with another beautiful, genuine smile on his lips. My fingers reach up, grazing my lips while still watching him, feeling his smile on mine.

Fuck. I am *totally screwed*.

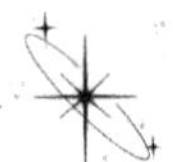

WE SIT DOWN FOR CLASS. Sølas takes his place in the row behind me. His shadows swirl up beneath my chair, threading around my ankles. A nicked moan curls in the back of my mouth; I clear my throat, trying to mask the sound. My concentration skills are going to be put to the test today.

The shadows catch Kissa's eyes, ripping a growl from her as she tries to stomp them away. She turns, baring her fangs at Sølas in a hiss.

"How do you expect her to concentrate like this? You are going to get us all killed if you can't control yourself," she snarls at him.

My cheeks heat, biting my bottom lip to cover my ridiculous smile. Kissa is right, though. I'm struggling to not let the little control I have left slip. I shake my head, hoping to clear my mind as I watch Professor Polyphemus Gloomnight take the podium. The golden, fawn Müra moth wings along her face shimmering in the dancing light.

"I have unfortunate news from the frontlines." Her words chill the air, stiffening my spine. "Last night, we witnessed an unprecedented attack: a coordinated strike against many of our strongholds along the edge of the Blackwood. Several of our Ellian Knights were kidnapped. It was clear they were looking for information they failed to get during their last several assaults."

The warmth plummets from my body, lost beneath a tidal wave of fear wrapping around my throat, suffocating me. Oddly, it doesn't come from the velvet black ribbons tightening over my wrists in my mind. I close my eyes to see iridescent ribbons sparking with lightning around me.

*"Calais, are you okay?"*

*"Yes. Stay focused,"* she clips, yet I don't miss the slightest tremble of terror in her voice.

My teeth sink into my bottom lip, struggling to stifle the trembling terror lashing down the bond from Calais, eclipsing my worry of any possibility of losing Sølas.

I get that this is not good news, but everyone in my mind is freaking out more than is necessary. We are safe at this location.

Suddenly, I'm smacked with why they might be so terrified, blurting out, "Which strongholds were attacked?"

Professor Gloomnight's face pales. "Strongholds: Dragon Spire, Emerald Lake Tower, and Raeya's Stronghold."

I swallow. Kissa's hand clasps mine, claws darting out to nip at my skin as the mauve fur bristles on her arm.

Those are not strongholds deep in the thick of the Blackwood. They're the smallest bases, along the tendrils of the Blackwood closest to Gildorea.

This is no longer a war we bring to them, but one they are waging at our doorstep. They've never overstretched themselves to coordinate such a large assault so far from the heart of the Blackwood. Whatever they're looking for is here on campus.

"Do we have any theories on what they are looking for?" an ensign I don't recognize asks.

"It's obviously something near or within Gildorea. This may even be a distraction. Their real target could be the sacred nesting grounds deep within our section of the Mysticwoods," Professor Gloomnight responds.

Calais and Scáil's eggs. That must be why she's so terrified. Luckily, they are hidden and safe.

"Now, I want to hear from you all. How might we prevent an attack like this in the future?"

"We should have more Scouting Rogues patrolling the corrupted Blackwood nearby so we can have a warning of an oncoming attack," Eko suggests.

"The Runic Engineers can work on the wards to create an early warning system along the borderlands, like we have here at Universitás," Gearin adds in.

"Both great suggestions. Ones we already have in the works," Professor Gloomnight encourages. A sigh of relief escapes me. There are powerful wards protecting the campus and the Mysticwoods. It's why the temperature is always perfect. My thoughts slip to the storm of chaos I released on the northern field; thankfully, I didn't drawn their attention to us.

A shudder skips down the bonds that I don't understand. I guess he hasn't thought about how we could have been attacked last night either.

Several other students suggest ideas, and Professor Gloomnight notes how they'll be pulling Knights from other areas to reinforce the strongholds closer to campus. Which means some of our classes will be shifted this week due to their absence until the new wards are up.

Our next class is Warrior Physics, which flies by. Then we have Defensive Magic, which focuses on ways to strengthen our mental shields and how different types of magic can be used to create a physical shield. Finally, we cover advanced protection wards.

We all have access to elemental magic. We can create temporary shields of water, air, fire, and earth, but we can only wield one type of magic at a time. I wonder if I can create a shield from my Chaos Magic. I doubt it, given it only ever wants to break things apart. However, it will be extremely advantageous if I can physically shield and wield my destructive power simultaneously.

*"Tomorrow morning, we can wake up early, and I'll let you practice physical shielding against me in the Warded Hollow."* Sølas' smoky voice in my mind almost makes me jolt in my seat. Kissa notices me tense and gives me a long look before focusing back on the professor.

*"And what if my magic rips you apart?"*

*"Shadows are absence. There is nothing for your magic to destroy,"* he muses.

I can't help how his shadows felt like anything but absence last night.

He lets a low growl curl around my mind. My skin instantly heats, remembering that sound rumbling against my neck and in my mouth.

Kissa's glaring at me, and Eko whips his head around to sling me a scowl too, nostrils flaring at the lust radiating off us. The combination of their varying shades of bright green eyes pinning me down zaps the heat from my blood.

I can't even think of cold showers after feeling Sølas' bliss as my own this morning.

*Fuck.*

I take a deep breath. Recalling the nights of sleeping outside, ice frosting my bones, dread coiling inside of me, wishing I had a safe home with a family who loved me.

Sadness and anger radiate through the black velvet ribbons, threading tighter on my wrists. I forgot he can feel my memories.

I'm overcome with exhaustion from having too many beings around me and in my head. I need to be outside. Alone in the fresh air, where I can think clearly. It's hard to breathe realizing I won't ever be alone again. I'm now essentially bonded to two beings, even if I haven't accepted the Fated mate bond. It's not like I can ever reject it and kill someone who doesn't deserve it.

His regret seeps down the ribbons at my thought. I can tell the last thing he wants is my pity regarding something he accepted. I wonder if he realized the consequences when he did. How could he have possibly known? The last-known Fated mate bond outside of magical creatures was over five hundred years ago.

*"Knowing the consequences of my decision would have not changed my choice."* His words a mere whisper. Well, now I know he's positively mad. I can't understand how he could just accept something like that without knowing more.

The bells chime, masking my grumbling stomach ready for lunch. I walk up the steps, surprise snipping at me when Sølas drifts farther away with each step. I turn around to see him talking with Atlas. I tug on the ribbons wrapped around my wrists in my mind. I can feel the worry he's trying to block from me.

I swallow the anger threatening to rise with the fact that he's blocking me. *Again.*

I blink, and immediately, he's by my side.

"I'm sorry. I did it without thinking. We were discussing the attack." His hand makes its way to the small of my back, guiding me to walk. I don't want to walk. I want to know why he felt the urge to block me out again.

"He asked me to stay in the penthouse with you, regardless of whether you decide to accept the mated bond or not. He said it would be safer for both of us to be together. He asked me if I am strong enough to do so. I didn't want you to feel my answer."

"And what answer was that?"

"I told him I don't know." His hand threads through his messy raven waves. "It's harder now to control myself after last night. Especially with your shields down and me feeling your every thought."

I gaze up at his eyes, storming with shadows once more. I can feel his confliction: wanting to keep me safe and the fear of losing control.

"What would happen if you lost control?"

"I would make the choice for you regarding our bond."

The air is seized from my lungs, suffocating me. I really had no idea how reckless I had been last night. I gasp, comprehending just how much he could have taken from me without my knowledge.

But he didn't.

He could have ended all his suffering and had all of me, but he is letting me choose. The world falls from beneath my feet. His arm tightens around my hip, reminding me we're still in an auditorium with other ensigns who are trying to get around us.

My hand reaches for his, a profound sense of gratitude waving through me. I don't have all the power in the choice of this bond, but he has gifted it to me anyway.

He stays right by my side as we walk to the dining hall. I fill up my plate and scurry outside. I need a break from everyone, and I theorize Pip growing wings overnight makes him as hungry as I am.

I hide in the shadow of Sully's statue, sharing my plate with Pip, who inhales the food. A laugh bubbles up at the sight of him. He chirps happily, wings fluttering with excitement. I notice his colors have changed. It isn't just his wings that are blue; there are shades of purple and yellow streaking through his scales now.

Everything is changing overnight.

My eyes drift up to the statue of Sully. I wonder if he's disappointed in me for failing to heed his warning. He couldn't have possibly known he is my mate.

*My mate.*

The words are foreign and familiar all at once. I know Sully wouldn't have asked me to stay away from him if he knew. He always wanted me to be happy. After all, that's why he trained me to be an Ellian Knight—even though he didn't want me to be one.

I still wonder why that's the case. So far, nothing seems suspicious here. Maybe he found the opulence here as ridiculous as I do. I am sure he'd agree we could do with less and lower the taxes for the working folks of Cascara. I guess I will never truly know.

# CHAPTER 46

**M**y mate.

The hairs sway on the back of my neck. I peer around the statue to see the tall, dark, and handsome male sauntering my way. I'm jealous that his uniform is all black; he looks far too handsome in it, and you'd hardly know if there was a lick of blood on him. I suppose if my power was controlling shadows, I'd have black leathers too.

The layers of his soft raven waves framing his chiseled face twirl in the soft breeze, shimmering iridescent shades of violet and indigo. His arctic-blue eyes will always be striking against his umber skin. The golden star on his neck glitters brightly in the sunlight, tugging on the shadows that dance along my chest.

A tattooed hand lowers in front of my face.

Pip flashes onto my arm, knowing it's time to go.

I place my hand in his. White light flares, blinding me.

Celestials, I don't have the patience to deal with one more thing today. I slowly open my eyes, expecting my hand to be missing, but my skin is humming in his with a soft glow of pastel light. I immediately let go, and it fades away.

"What was that?" I ask, standing up on my own, leery of whatever just happened.

"You're always full of surprises. It's your magic, not mine; I was hoping you could tell me, but I can feel you're just as clueless as I am." He arches a brow.

I can't understand how he's still managing to flirt with me when I could have just ripped his hand apart.

"Whatever it was… didn't hurt. It was quite the opposite sensation." His voice is low as he brushes a knuckle against the back of my hand.

"What did it feel like?" I'm not entirely sure we felt the same thing.

"It felt like you, *Luxsula.*" He smirks, starting to walk towards the southern field. I hurry to catch up to his long strides.

"Are you going to tell me what that word means?"

"Some secrets remain mine to keep," he hums. I can sense that he only plans to tell me if I accept the bond, but I guess he doesn't want to say that aloud, to make me feel like he's holding it over my head.

We walk the rest of the way in silence, and I'm grateful for the quiet. A rare, peaceful happiness we both share.

We make it through the archway to the southern field. The air roars with the raucous sound of beating wings and different creatures growling and snapping at one another. No one is enjoying the close quarters as we prepare for aerial flight maneuvers.

Calais and Scáil tower above the rest of the creatures; the majestic sight of them still steals my breath away. My mind flooding with the memory of their wings wrapped around us. I still can't believe they risked their wings to keep us safe from my own magic. I'm sure they were not hurt; otherwise, Calais would never let me hear the end of it. My lips curl into a smile. Sølas is with us today, and I won't have to suffer interrogation from the rest of the Zenith again.

My legs and arms moan with the ache from yesterday. I don't even want to think about how they'll feel after today. Yet the thrill of flying quickly blots out the pain; it's worth every sore muscle.

Sølas' hands work along Scáil's feathers. There's such a closeness to their bond, a deep respect and love. I sense he has known him for much longer, the strength of their connection forged well before Celestial Bonding Day.

Iridescent strands tickle my nose, gliding on gusts of my swirling air magic to my mounted position on Calais. Rather than my power being drained from my storm of chaos, it's stronger. It nips and claws. Growling in the confines of my marrow with a bristling ferocity to be unleashed.

"*You're awfully quiet today,*" I jab at Calais.

"*Someone asked me to give you space under the ridiculous assumption I might overwhelm you.*" She shoots a rainbow side-eyed glare to Scáil. I smile at him, bowing my head in thanks. He kindly returns the gesture as Calais lets out a grunt.

I have the perfect view of Professor Reska taking the dais from this height. Her metallic silver fur shimmers in the sunlight, matching the silver that dusts the powder-blue feathers of her Bladed Coata, Argenta.

"Today, we will warm up with escalating maneuvers, quickly moving into switching formations with other Wings while continuing to mirror my movements. Hopefully, today will be a little more... *graceful* than yesterday. We will be staying closer to campus due to the attacks that occurred last night. This means you all need to tighten up your transitions." Professor Reska's air magic waves through her sparkling fur as she glides on top of Argenta, who's already taking flight.

Calais' four massive wings lift, lunging us towards the sky. She may be larger than everyone else, she but flies like she's as light as a hummingbird. We take our place at the point of the star. My head tips over Calais' side to see Scáil and Sølas flipping and spinning through the air.

"*Show off.*" I smirk.

"*I can't help but feel free up here.*" His happiness entangles my heart into a flutter.

A serrated scream rips from my throat as Calais plummets out of formation to twirl around Scáil. Threading through the clouds in a summersault, mirroring his movements.

"*I couldn't let the males make us look bad.*" She huffs.

My lashes flutter shut, magic unfurling, stretching out to be my sight. I sense the hairs on Kissa's neck bristling, snarling at us, creating another spectacle in front of everyone, while a stupid smile pinches my cheeks. I feel free. The worries of the day whipping away as the wind weaves through my hair.

Argenta and Reska tuck tight, diving towards the ground.

Calais and Scáil do the same, spinning around one another. Our tether floods with their love. A love so profound, it transcends time. The magic of their mated bond drawing them together by forces stronger than gravity. They will find one another in any life, in any universe. I wonder if this was what Sølas felt when he realized the bond. I suppose I can imagine him accepting it without thinking. The magic of a love that transcends this plane of existence is all-consuming.

My mind flashes with memories, swelling my heart... They found one another flying in the sky.

Our dragons tear through the ground in sync as I gaze over, arctic-blue eyes locking with mine. The intensity of him presses in on me, makes me shift my weight, yet I can't look away until we're taking off back to the sky. Yet a thought lingers in the background, a constant pecking, needling every happy moment I try to hold on to—why isn't my acceptance of the bond as effortless as his?

*"Time to focus, Nebulight,"* Calais warns.

We've reached cruising altitude. My eyes drift shut again, power fanning out, lighting up every molecule of energy around me. Calais settles into her assigned position as we ready for maneuvering around formation shifts.

My magic crackles, greedily feasting on the ensuing chaos unfolding around us. The air rumbles with roars, grumbling growls, and high-pitched squawks. Scáil shifts with silent grace, disappearing into a cloud of shadows, avoiding the collision path of a tumbling wyvern, Shadowwalking into their new position. The swirl of Sølas' stomach dips down the bond. I silently appreciate that Calais doesn't have that power; I'm not sure I could stomach it.

We practice again and again. Each time becoming more fluid.

Professor Reska's voice whips on the wind, carried by a gust of magic. "Tomorrow, we will be practicing active mounting and dismounting, so come prepared."

Then Calais' claws are digging into the southern field. My legs ache as I slide to the ground, but thanks to today's shorter lesson, the walk back up the hills to campus is slightly less perilous.

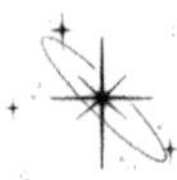

MY SKIN TINGLES as we enter the magic of the Warded Hollow with the rest of our class for Combat Magic Practice. Professor Layla Emberleaf walks to the center of the space. The only color peeking out of her snow-white Arabellian coloring: unmatching eyes of blue and lavender.

"Today, we have set the Warded Hollow to mimic last night's attack. You will be overrun with monsters and hordes of Wuvon. I will remind you that they are not real and cannot cause actual harm if you fail. Many of the Ellian

Knights did not make it to their flying bonded creatures in time because of the attack. This will test your teams' ability to work together on the ground."

I swallow, worry over my Chaos Magic tumbling into a boulder in my throat that I struggle to force down. Sølas' ribbons tighten their grasp on my wrists. I'd forgotten they were there, no longer feeling foreign in my mind.

*"Just like we practiced, Luxsula,"* he hums. His words are grounding, anchored by the prideful smile pinning his lips. Yet it does nothing to mask longing as I search his eyes.

*"You need to let me go in order to wield magic at your full strength,"* I whisper down our bond. His smile falls beneath the fear flooding him.

*"I won't block you out. I promise,"* I admit.

Suddenly, he's right in front of me, arctic eyes wavering as they peer deep into my soul. My heart skitters into a mess under the intensity of his closeness.

"Promise me?" he whispers, not breaking my gaze.

"I promise," I breathe.

Shadows storm, blotting out his moonlight gaze as the ribbons uncoil, hesitantly slipping from my wrists and ankles. Rather than feeling free, an ache lingers in their absence.

I leave open the arched window stained with the night's sky while I raise another layer to my mental shields. His emotions still trickle through, but they're dampened now.

Sølas' jaw clenches, knuckles white, worry twisting him up, worry I'll break my promise. Before I can reassure him, darkness falls.

The room shifting as we all go eerily still in wait.

Distant snarls and screams echo, ricocheting in all directions. My Zenith uses the flash of battling magic to gather into a defensive circle.

Eko and Seraphina sweep out first to assess the situation. Highin, our marksman, follows close behind, providing coverage if things go wrong under the exceptional sight of his hawk vision. Furthermore, his Celestial Gift is true aim, the ability to guide arrows over long distances, unrestricted by the typical range limits of telekinesis.

Eko's body disappears into the faintest outline of ether. His footsteps falling silent, he stills, becoming invisible. Eko's Celestial Gift is known as Ethereal Shifting, a deadly blessing in the hands of our Scouting Rogue. My eyes go wide as floating daggers take shape out of a cloud of purple and indigo Celestial ether, before disappearing with him.

Seraphina shifts as well, taking on the form of a female Wuvon with cardamom-colored hair. Her skin marked by slithering shadows of black and crimson vines. The new form is clever for her role as our Spycraft, infiltration and intelligence gathering.

Atlas' antennae glow faintly, illuminating a green glow over the remaining Zenith. "While they do their job, let's set up in a modified formation to account for our grounded Ellian Knights. Gearin, position yourself further back with Kivi behind a runic shield. We fall back to you if we need healing." A flick of his finger designates their position. Gearin summons a shield of defensive runes around Kivi, weaving scattered attack runes to float above him for quick release. His Celestial Gift, Tinkerer, allows him to fix and create anything involving Rune Tech in an instant. A skill that can turn disaster into survival in a pinch.

"Savaé and Sølas, stay in the center like you would in flight. Vex and I will stand behind you so we can see the battle, and Vex can relay the upcoming shifts of the fight," Atlas adds. This is the perfect simulation to test out Vex's Arcane Glyph of Battlesense, a unique intuition magic regarding glimpses of battle outcomes. This is why Vex and her sunset-red Wyvern are usually used to draw attention while working with Atlas to coordinate our efforts into one fluid movement.

"Flint and Kissa, you head off the attack."

Flint nods to Atlas' command. As our Ground-Combatant, he's the best option in any close quarters fighting with the Wuvon, taking them down in the least amount of hits. His Cerfios form of stone is impervious to their unparalleled Persuasive abilities.

"Orion, you distract enemies with your illusions." Atlas' instruction curls a fiendish smirk on Orion's candy-red lips. She's our second line of defense for the same scenario if Flint is occupied. Her powerful Persuasive skills can prevent Wuvon from overtaking our minds while we battle them at close range or keep enemies distracted in illusion magic, aided by reading their Auras.

"Juniper and Cinder are on crowd control; don't let us get overwhelmed. Fenwick stays back with the rest of us to attack and to defend if our opponent outflanks us," Atlas finishes. Juniper, a naturalist, can manipulate the natural world and counter the same power the Wuvon use. Her Celestial Gift gives her the ability to make creatures out of vines to help fight the monsters the Wuvon control. Her Arcane Glyph allows her to sprout hypnotizing flowers. She's delightfully deadly.

Fenwick, our Kinetic, beams releasing golden light into a shield around us. Her powerful radiant magic spills from her hands, coating plasma along the blade of her broadsword.

"We have company," Cinder calls out. Daggers of amber flames scorch into the air above his palms. "My heat vision is picking up our incoming scouting team with a thrall of monsters hot on their heels." His chin nods in their oncoming direction. I can barely see anything in the pitch dark; his heat vision is an incredibly useful Celestial Gift.

Seraph and Eko come to a sliding stop, panting. The faint outline of Highin is flying behind them, slinging arrows out one after another.

"Report," Atlas commands.

"There are well over a hundred monsters of various forms heading this way," Eko rasps.

"I only saw one Wuvon," Seraph says shakily. The uneasiness in her voice rattles me, so unlike her brass, confident demeanor. "I don't know how, but even from far away, she immediately knew I wasn't truly Wuvon. That's... never happened before. I barely got away from her mindtrap talons lashing into me." Seraph's trembling eases as Sølas comes to her side, squeezing her shoulder. I hate seeing her off-kilter like this. I hate this fear tangling up my team.

The fury brewing in my veins slams my eyelids shut, Chaos Magic igniting my atomic sight. The familiar shapes of my Zenith outline around me. My power prowls out, hunting within the darkness. I snarl at the hurtling mass of monsters roaring towards us.

I bathe myself in the fear of potential harm to my Zenith... to Sølas. I feel the chill of it lash through. I grit my teeth against its attempts to crumple me, clawing at me from the inside out. But then my Chaos Magic snaps back, feasting.

I won't let them take what is *mine*.

Power whips out of me, tracking down the source of my fear. I seep into their bones, shattering the lattice structures that support them. Their wailing roars thrum my craving for destruction. I uncoil upwards to the monsters darting over the formless corpses I've left in my wake. I spill into their blood, ripping it from their veins before they even have a chance to scream from the pain.

More. More. *More.* My power ravenously stalks the darkness. A shift in the air near my Zenith draws me back. Two small orbs appear, speckled in the constellations of the night sky, drenched in crimson. A tall silhouette forming around them. The light from Fenwick's shield catching on the Wuvon male's long black hair as vines barbed in thorns lash out for us. My magic sears into his blood, turning its iron molten. Boiling him from the inside out as garnet bubbles out his gasping mouth.

Two waves of monsters thunder towards us from either side. I sling the shattered bone fragments from my first victim to the right in a hail of daggers. My power devours their pain, arching lighting from one beast to another, stilling their heart on impact. Sølas' shadows slicing through the monsters I miss.

A wave of amber fire crashes into the horde on our left. Juniper's vines slither out, tangling monsters to a halt while Highin's arrows pierce their skulls.

Atlas works with Vex, signaling which direction the next wave's coming from. Fenwick slings a ball of light above Atlas' glowing signal, which erupts into raining plasma. The scattering horde of monsters skids to a stop along the edge of a chasm cracking open around us, an illusion cast by Orion. Gearin slings explosive runes with one hand while the other strengthens the runes of Fenwick's radiant shield. Kivi releases spores all around us, heightening our powers.

Eko darts among the monsters with Seraph. Her axes cut through limbs as his daggers find their weak spots.

My eyes widen as I watch Flint punch straight through the chest of a snapping monster, ripping out its heart before tearing another apart limb by limb with his bare hands.

While everyone is focusing on the threats in our immediate vicinity, I stretch my magic out. There has to be more Wuvon here, the ones that kidnapped the Ellian Knights. I glimpse flashes of ash, blinking its way through the waves of monsters. It's quick, like Shadowwalking, but this power feels different from Sølas' shadows. Sharper. Colder.

I focus on its movement, on *her* movements. A pattern taking shape, allowing me to predict where the next portal will land. I shatter the ground beneath my target, piercing up through the air. As soon as the darkness is in the center, I let the weight of the broken earth come crashing down. My power saving the disorder of her cracking bones.

A black energy whips out against my power, against my mind, fracturing my mental shields. Electricity builds in the clouds overhead. I yank down three bolts of lightning, striking my target.

A screech erupts as black pools over my mental shields, wriggling at the cracks. Then the earth crushing the blackness melts to molten stone, burning her flesh as shadows violently coil around her throat, wringing tighter and tighter until life withers away. An assist leading to a devastating combo from Cinder and Sølas.

A slew of screeching curses cuts from my left, revealing a vine- and light-bound Wuvon male with Orion's hands on his head. She's already starting her interrogation. Seraphina and Orion will tag-team this job, a deadly duo together. Orion sharing with Seraph the memories of their target's loved ones, allowing her to shapeshift into them, playing with their mind until it shatters. A move more tangible than even the Ethereal Maze of Whispers from the second entrance trial.

The lights flicker back on.

The Warded Hollow is reset as Professor Emberleaf claps.

"We may be looking at early deployment for this year's primary Zenith Wing if you continue to show promise like you all did today."

It's unsettling to feel the carnage we reaped but see nothing in front of us other than scattered groups from other Wings. My heart's still pounding with my ragged breaths and adrenaline.

Juniper and Fenwick jump with excitement. The notion of early deployment would have thrilled me, but now… there is more than myself on the line to lose.

Black velvet ribbons caress around my wrists.

I roll my eyes at Sølas. *"I'm not going to block you out. I promised."*

*"Maybe I just need to touch you,"* he purrs.

*"I am not going anywhere,"* I purr right back as I make my way to the door.

*"It doesn't make my need any less,"* he rumbles, catching up behind me.

"We're having dinner somewhere else tonight," his lips whisper along my ear, igniting my skin ablaze.

He entwines my hand in his before I can even respond, and we're bounding back to the southern field. I can barely keep up with him as he sprints. In the exhaustion of the day, I've almost forgotten the rest of my answers are waiting for me.

# CHAPTER 47

Calais and Scáil are already in the field. He tries to nuzzle her and is met with a snap from her enormous jaws. If I wasn't so out of breath, I'd laugh at the sight. He's clearly pissed her off.

"Where are we going?" I pant.

"You'll see when we get there. It's my turn to surprise you." Sølas beams with excitement. However, I'm less amused at the prospect of yet another surprise today.

My air magic twirls me onto Calais. It's far quicker than climbing her two-story leg. Before I can even adjust my position, she takes off.

*"You're in a mood."*

*"This is not safe. We should not be risking this trip after the attack last night."* Her raspy voice is sharp as a blade, her fear slicing right through me. If a dragon as powerful as Calais is afraid, I have to agree with her. Maybe this trip is a bad idea.

*"She's being more protective over you than me, and you're okay with it?"* Sølas' smoky voice coos.

*"I think if the most powerful dragon in Cascara is afraid, I should be too."*

*"Who told you she is the most powerful?"* Scáil's ancient voice hums. Calais snaps at him, missing his neck by a whisper. Scáil is either incredibly brave or stupid. My body vibrates from her grumbling laugh.

*"She may be bigger, but I'd wager Scáil may be more powerful,"* Sølas

jests. Now Calais is snapping at him. Anger bubbles up inside me as Scáil has to Shadowwalk out of her wrath to save Sølas from her bite.

*"Hey! You don't get to eat him,"* I hiss.

*"Oh, please. You haven't even accepted the bond."* She huffs.

*"If I'm not willing to kill him, you don't get to either."* I scowl as she grumbles with disappointment. It seems the soft spot she had for him yesterday has been erased in her anger at this unsupported excursion.

We land by the edge of Emerald Lake, named for its molten emerald water. The setting sun's rays light up the waterfalls of the Dragon Spine Mountains in shades of pink and blue.

I fully comprehend why this is a bad idea as I slide down Calais' leg, wishing I had stayed mounted. One of the extensions from the Blackwood and two of the three strongholds attacked are not far from here.

I'm spun around into Sølas' arms before I have time to suggest going back. His shadows fan out beneath our feet as he pulls my head into his chest.

"Close your eyes, and count to three," he whispers in my ear.

All my worries melt away in the embrace of his arms, heart humming in this pocket of safety. I inhale deeply, savoring the scent of amber and spruce filling my lungs and warming my soul. I count to three and open my eyes.

There's a black velvet blanket set up, covered with cakes and different savory foods. My stomach grumbles as I huff the delicious smells. Pip doesn't hesitate, darting down, inhaling everything as he goes. Candles float all around us like dancing stars.

*"He needs time to practice flying with his wings,"* Calais grumbles. I nod in response as I join Pip in stuffing my face. I'm sure we look like starved stray dogs together, scarfing down the feast.

I gaze over to an amused smirk on Sølas' face, leaning against his elbow, swirling Smokewhisper libation in a tumbler as he watches us.

He nods his head back to the food, spurring us continue.

I curl up on my side facing Sølas as Pip curls up around my stomach for a full-belly nap.

*Those eyes.*

I could fall endlessly adrift in them. I find myself humming happily as I peer up at his dreamy face, gazing over molten emerald waves of the lake.

The ground rumbles, Calais and Scáil lying on either side of us, creating a wall of protection.

Pip's four cobalt eyes pop open in a stretch. He springs up, prances over to Calais, curling up against her chest. I sigh, rolling my eyes, I guess she's warmer than I am.

Shadows swirl around Sølas and me. Drifting away to reveal him in a black button-up shirt with the top buttons undone, and I'm in a black velvet dress. The heat from the dragons around us warms the air.

I tilt my head at him. I'm not sure the theatrics are needed. He smiles in response.

"So. Tell me how you knew Calais before I did?" I ask.

He sighs, moving closer to me, his nerves palpable. Tattooed fingers trace along my arm, swiftly setting the night air to stifling. Yet I can tell he's touching me more to soothe himself, the bond humming with his caress.

"You promised," I purr softly.

He sighs again, sitting up and wrapping his arms around his legs as he begins. Even the slight distance nags the bond in my chest, beckoning me to be closer, but I give him his space.

"When I was a baby, I was adopted by a couple who were madly in love but couldn't conceive a child of their own. They loved me as if I were their own, though. Every day, they shared their love for each other with me. Mother doted on me while teaching her passion for reading, and Father battled me with wooden swords in the field. Each day was full of sunlight and happiness. They never even told me I was adopted—to them, I was their child. Every year, we came to this lake for their anniversary. We'd have a picnic, swim, laugh, chase each other, our hearts always full. I never experienced sadness or pain in their care."

I swallow how very different our childhoods were. No wonder loving deeply comes so easily to him, accepting the bond without worry of consequences.

"The last year we came here, everything was perfect, just as it always was." Sølas starts to rock back and forth. "Out of nowhere, the screams of a thousand suffering souls pierced my ears. I was building mud castles by the lake's edge, my eyes snapping up to see my parents darting for me. Putting themselves directly in the path of a pack of Feverin. To protect me. I watched as a mass of tar bodies oozed, crawling on unnaturally contorted limbs, with rows of razor-sharp, snapping teeth. My parents tried to fight them off, but there were too many. I wailed, trying to run for them, but Mother turned to me, pleading, 'Stay right there, my little star shadow.' In her distraction, razor fangs of the Feverin's smiling maw sliced into her arm. The splintering of her bones, the tearing of her flesh—I slammed my eyes shut, rocking back and forward, back and forward." His own rocking stops for a moment, suddenly realizing his own motion. But just as quickly, it starts again.

"Her serrated screams flayed my heart raw, awakening my magic. Shadows whipped out of me, storming into a blasting wave of wraith. I had no control over my power, shredding through everything unchecked. All I could hear was screaming as I wept, rocking back and forward. Back and forward, until only silence was left." He stills. Silver wells in his eyes, lost to a black storm of shadows.

"In the deafening silence, I finally opened my eyes. A mess of scattered limbs and shredded bodies. And in the sea of tar: the crimson mangled corpses of my parents. I ripped them apart. My wails pierced the heavens at the horrors my magic reaped. I slaughtered the ones who loved me, who cared for me, who risked their lives to protect me… They should have feared me. For I wasn't their little star shadow—I was their death." He begins rocking back and forward again, once more that terrified boy, broken and lost to the weight of his shadows. His violent emotions crash into me, pulling me into his storm. Grief, sorrow, fear, anger, regret.

I sit up, scooching beside him. I place my hand over his, the other tracing rhythmic circles on his back. He continues to rock, sinking in the undertow of his memory. I understand now why he locks this part of him away behind a mask of flirtation. It's too much, too overwhelming, too many sharp pieces to hold, just like me. Yet he is gladly willing to bleed… to hold all of me.

"That's when I heard his dark voice. Calling to me. *'Oh, Sølas, how I have been waiting for you. Look at how you honor me with your gifts. You make me proud, already so devouring.'* I heard the darkness in my mind. Fractured and broken in the weight of my devastation. How could I kill the ones who loved me so? The dark voice told me, *'They never really loved you, not like I do.'* Jagged screams carved up my throat. I covered my ears, hoping to drown out the voice haunting me. Torturing me. I was only eight years old. I didn't know how to shield my mind. So, I just screamed, and screamed, hoping it would drown out the evil inside my head."

He's slipping away, seeping into the distance. I don't want him to block me out again, even if it's instinctual. I lean over, kissing the tear carving down his face, resting my head against his shoulder.

He stops rocking, tipping his head against mine. This action is so familiar to our bodies, so natural. Exactly the same as our first night at Gildorea, as if my body and heart already knew what my mind wouldn't accept. Is his evil voice similar or different from my own darkness that lies heavy in my chest? Is it why his vibrant shadows of curling smoke turned to a thick pitch that one night?

"I continued to scream, even when my throat was raw, my voice nothing more than a rasp. Then an enormous shadow descended from the sky. I was certain it was the demon coming to claim my soul and drag me to the pits of Emberhell. Instead, a warm darkness wrapped around me, and the evil voice finally ceased. I was coiled in feathers and black mist, but my mind was quiet as I wept until I had no more tears left at the loss of my parents. I fell asleep sobbing. When I awoke, my skin was marked with swirling shadows, and Scáil was there. He spoke to me in my mind. He had heard my screams calling to him in the shadows. He brought me to Gildorea, to the Maidens. They welcomed me back, and that's when I discovered I had been adopted." Sølas wipes the tears from his face as Scáil's feathered tail curls around us both.

"Every time I closed my eyes, I saw my parents' mutilated faces, heard their wailing screams and the darkness calling to me, beckoning me to come to him. I couldn't sleep, so I would sneak outside at night. Scáil was always waiting for me. He would take me away, teaching me how to control my magic. My shadows could do nothing to his darkness. I was so exhausted when he would return me, I could sleep without nightmares for the few hours before the Maidens awoke me for training. We continued like this for years. He helped me master my powers. Taught me how to work through my grief rather than letting it consume me." Sølas sighs, releasing the emotions bludgeoning his soul.

"Sometimes, the dark voice that calls to me refuses to be blocked out. It gets louder and louder, summoning me to do dark and hideous things. Especially when I let fear overwhelm me. When you grasped my face and looked into my eyes, you were searching for something. You got so close to seeing the Fated mate bond, to finding it all on your own, and I could feel how close you were, but then those cursed bells rang, and you started to overthink everything. My heart sank as you failed to see it. I feared you never would. That I would always be alone in my love for you while you continued your life without me." His hand lets go of his knee, threading with mine.

"Don't get me wrong—I wouldn't trade a single treasured moment I've had with you. But in my fear of being so close and it being ripped away from me, the dark voice boomed in my mind. It told me you would never accept the bond, that you would rather reject it and kill me, even if you knew about it. That I was nothing to you, and I belong with him, not to you. I called Scáil to come to me. When the voice gets so loud, I lose myself in it. My powers lash out. Scáil uses his magic to quiet the voice. I didn't want to be near you if I lost control... If I hurt you, too..." His voice trembles as more silver tears stream down his face. "If I hurt you, too, I'd be lost to the darkness. I couldn't live with myself." He pauses, raking his hands through his hair before turning to face me. He cups my face in his hand, and I can't help but lean into it.

"I'm sorry I blocked you. I'm sorry I didn't tell you the truth sooner. But I'm sure as Emberhell not sorry you kissed me." A subtle smirk tugs at the corner of his full lips.

"I would live through it all again to find you. Even if you never accept this bond." His words are soft and quiet, like a gentle breeze. I can't believe he's willing to live through all that again to find me. As happy as I feel with him in this moment, I'm not sure I'd relive the traumas of my life to be here with him. But then again, I haven't accepted the bond; maybe I'll feel different if I do.

He chuckles.

"The bond won't force you to love me. It doesn't work like that. That's why the choice is yours. I wouldn't get all of you if I had tricked you into accepting the bond. Other than being stuck with your wrathful hate." He winks.

A smile twists my lips as I nudge him with my elbow for that ridiculous wink. I look over to Calais. "What was it like for you and Scáil when you found one another?"

*"I felt it the moment I saw him, and he did, too. But dragons love differently. Our emotions don't change as quickly and wildly as yours do. I find it exhausting to be in your head, and you don't even feel as intensely as the Shadowmancer,"* Calais answers. I'm surprised she's so open and honest for once.

"It's like an inescapable force always drawing us together. Pulling us closer. I felt it calling to me the moment I saw you. I just didn't fight it like you did. You have so many walls up, I'm sometimes surprised you felt anything at all." He arches an eyebrow, waiting for my snarky response. But I don't have one.

He's managed to melt all the walls away, and I don't mind just *being* with him. It's so different from anything else I've ever experienced.

I still need time to figure out what this all means to me, but I'm willing to try to let him in. I'm willing to stop pushing him away. And I hope that's enough for him for right now.

He brushes the translucent strands tumbling along my face. "You are always enough for me."

I hum in response, uncertain of how to reply to his words, other than just to accept them.

We sit in silence, watching the moon rise, its reflection dancing across the lake. Beautiful waves of liquid emeralds crash along the shore. Candles twinkle around us like stars made just for us. I could sit here with him forever and be perfectly happy.

"We should get back. We both need to rest before class tomorrow," he whispers.

I don't want to go to class. I want to stay here and pretend the war doesn't exist. That the world's a better place than I know it to be. That this is a world where I can have the happy ending I never even dared to dream.

"If you dare to dream of a happy ending for yourself, I will spend every day of eternity trying to make that dream come true." His smokey voice is soft, like a morning kiss.

I smirk. "There you go again. Making promises you can't keep."

"I'm willing to try if you are." He smiles, getting to his feet, extending his palm to help me up.

I take his hand, and it's something more. Like an unspoken promise to dream of a better ending for ourselves.

One where the monsters in our heads don't win.

# CHAPTER 48

I awake tangled with Sølas' body, and I don't want to move. I drink in his slow heart rate and shallow, sleepy breaths along my neck. Then there's the delicious hard length of him against my back. The memories of waves of pleasure heat my skin.

He shifts in the flame of my body, pulling me in closer to him, wrapping his legs around mine as if he can't settle for not touching every part of me. Celestials, *I want him.*

Part of me wishes it could be that simple, that it didn't entail something more. Yet I also can't help but be selfishly grateful that I've found someone who loves me, madly, without reason. I wonder what it would be like to just throw caution to the wind and dive into something knowing there's no turning back. It didn't seem so bad when I did it the other night. It felt anything but bad.

His skin against mine is intoxicating. I crave more. I understand his need to have his body touch me everywhere because I feel it too, tattooed into my marrow. My magic crackles beneath my skin, wanting to explore every molecule of him. I don't trust it or myself.

I reach out to find Pip, tugging him into me. His wings flutter, tickling my nose. This weekend, I'll need to take him somewhere to practice flying.

Sølas reaches out again, wrapping one arm under my neck and across my chest while the other pulls across my waist. I'm plastered to him, and I don't mind it one bit, but I'm struggling to not to think of how hard he is behind me.

Every time I attempt to wriggle any distance between us, he draws me in even tighter. I sigh with a smile, giving up.

Still grappling for any sense of lustful control, my thoughts drift to the freezing winter nights alone in Estrella. My teeth chattering, skin as icy as the glacial palace of my heart. Shadows coil around me, wrapping me up tight, as if they could keep me warm.

Then I realize… the shadows are him.

Always with me, pulling me into them, keeping me safe in his arms. My mind sputters in the realization that I've felt this bond longer than I can comprehend. That Sølas has always been with me, helping me survive in an impossible world, keeping me safe, blending me into his shadows. Always.

He murmurs in his sleep, "Always."

A silver tear tumbles down my face. I've never been alone facing the horrors of my childhood. A part of his soul has always been with me, searching for me, waiting for us to find one another.

I shake my head, not ready to accept what my heart already knows.

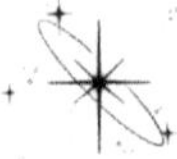

THE MORNING JAYS are chirping insistently as I awake with my cheek on Sølas' chest. My sleepy hands forgetting themselves, tracing the swirling shadow vortex at the center of his chest, which must be his Arcane Glyph marking.

"Good, you're awake. Breakfast's on the table. I'll shower while you eat," he whispers with a kiss on my head. I find myself wishing we could sleep in and the world could wait just a little longer.

"There will be plenty of mornings for sleeping in. We need to find out if you can shield with your Chaos Magic. I have a couple ideas." He hums with excitement, prying my sleepy body off of him.

I grumble, debating if I should stay in bed and watch him shower. He stops, turning to arch a dark eyebrow at me. I think better of it, hearing the *clanging* of silver on the table. Pip's going to eat all the food if I don't get over there.

I growl at him as he tries to steal the last piece of bacon. Snatching a slice and tapping him on the head with it. The scoundrel attempts to abscond with it from my hands. I quickly shove it in my mouth before he leaps for it. His wings look even bigger today. I guess tonight we'll settle for practicing flying around the room.

I hear the shower turn off. I'm slightly disappointed I didn't get to join him.

Sølas tuts, walking in with nothing but a towel around his waist. "You know, you're going to have to keep that filthy mind to yourself if I'm to continue staying in this room with you," he purrs, drying his raven locks with another towel, piercing me with arctic eyes beneath messy, wet hair.

My breath catches on the droplets curling down his rippling form, swirling with shadows. I ache, remembering exactly what those wet hands can do. He moves like lightning, and suddenly, he's beneath me, and I'm straddling his lap. I whimper, feeling his hard length swell beneath my core.

I want him.

I want this.

My hips grind along his cock, growing impossibly harder. His growl rumbles the pebbling skin of my neck, igniting my blood on fire. And before I can make another move, he Shadowwalks me in his arms to the bathroom, turning on a cold shower and leaving me there.

I'm fuming, but I can feel him teetering on the edge of control. So, I suppose I can forgive him for leaving me in another cold shower. After a minute, I turn the heat back on, trying to block out the thoughts of his soapy hands against my body.

Then I remember why I need a cold shower, and I quickly finish up. I may want to wildly ravage him, but he knows I'm not fully ready to accept the bond. That my mind hasn't caught up to the wild nature of my thawed heart. For someone who loves control, with him, I am constantly lost to the chaos of his aura.

Sølas leans on the balcony, drinking kahvi with amusement crinkling his eyes as Pip feebly flies around him.

I quickly get dressed and meet him outside, stealing his mug.

He—surprisingly—doesn't put up a fight, just smiles at me. His full smile melting me on the spot. Without even thinking, I reach up to kiss him on the edge of the mouth. His strong arm weaves around my waist, pulling me flush with him. Swirling shadows caress my skin, blotting out the light, and then my stomach drops. The shadows fall, revealing the Warded Hollow.

Pip screeches and scurries up my leg, flashing onto my arm.

"I couldn't let you keep distracting me, so I took a shortcut," he purrs.

I push him away and instantly regret it. Now my chest sears with agony while my stomach whittles my insides.

"I won't kiss you again if it means we get to walk." I crumple over, clenching my gut. He just laughs because he knows I'm lying.

Fucking shadow *prick*.

"Being a prick would have been me taking you on that chair instead of putting you in the cold shower. Because for someone who loves to be in control, you have certainly enjoyed testing mine." He growls, closing the distance between us before continuing in a seductively threatening groan, "I have half a mind to Shadowwalk us right back to that room and tie you to the chair and show you just how controlled I can be. Keeping you on the edge of ecstasy for hours until I ruin you for anyone else. Your lips forever only knowing how to moan *my name*."

Molten heat pools at my core as I wobble slightly, which he no doubt senses based on the rumble that vibrates through his chest.

If only he could indulge that fantasy, but I know better so I counter, trying to cool my blood. "You asked me not to block you out. I'm not used to having you feel all my thoughts," I hiss, but with the lust flooding my veins, it comes out more sultry than I intended it to.

He smiles, knowing I still haven't done what he initially feared I would. I'm not even sure I could block him out anymore, even if I wanted to. Everything just feels different between us now.

"I'm sorry. I knew it would be difficult, being so close to you. I just underestimated how arduous it would truly be."

"Well, I like a challenge." I throw a coy smile his way, hoping it's enough. I don't want to remember what it's like to sleep without him wrapped around me.

He pulls me in, chest pressing against mine, lazily twirling a strand of hair as he gazes deeply into my eyes. "I like a challenge, too." He leans in closer, his lips grazing my neck as I quiver, craving his kiss.

A kiss that's like lightning in a hot summer downpour. One that is branded onto my lips like a phantom, as if they belong to him now. The throbbing between my legs begs for him to make good on his promise to ruin me as my traitorous hips rock along the hard length of him.

"I was thinking you could use your magic to literally repel other magic away," he purrs, as if he's whispering sweet nothings to me.

I shove him away for letting him ensnare me once again with his tricksy Ritherin-shit. *Prick.* How can I keep falling for this? I release the power burning beneath my skin, vibrating all the atoms around me, creating a field of chaos.

His shadows whip out from his chest, testing it, dissolving to mist when against my shield of chaos. He winces as if my magic actually hurts him.

"Well, that certainly took you no time at all." Clearly impressed I've grasped this so easily.

I shrug. I've always been good at shielding and blocking things out. It comes naturally to me.

He definitely winces at that thought. Which he kinda deserves after luring me in with his lustful words. I can't deny how all the chaotic feelings he brings out in me makes it easier to control my magic.

Rather than the numb flood cycle I've previously known, it's now a constant stream. Easy to pull from to wield my power.

"Try keeping the shield up while you also focus your magic on attacking." He snaps his fingers, and red dummies are lunging at me. I panic but keep the shield up, spooling sharp wind, alternating with fire.

He pauses their movement.

"Again, with your Chaos Magic." He tsks, tapping the tip of my nose.

"Wait. I just casted elemental magic at the same time as my Chaos Magic."

"Yes, you are a marvel, but I need you to focus. Again. Chaos Magic only." He prowls around me, waiting for my obedience.

I'm annoyed how he can be so nonchalant about that, but whatever. I inhale deeply, channeling my focus on my power to master it.

The targets start to move again, and my Chaos Magic crackles, pouring out. The destructive forces seek out the red targets, shattering their wood into a thousand splinters, which I use to stab the next one and the next. A field of sharp wood swirls around me, creating a second shield made of the remains of the targets I decimated. My power instinctively protecting me without me even having to think about it.

He claps his hands as the bells chime and the splinters rain all around me. He follows me out the door, sprinting to class.

We make it just in time, but because we're the last in the door, once again, I'm forced to sit next to him. This will be *beyond* distracting. His shadows hum beneath my skin, begging me to touch him. I struggle to imagine how he focuses in class at all having already accepted this bond. I move my knee against his, and relief settles over us both.

Professor Gloomnight takes the stage, her powdery moth wings fluttering nervously behind her.

"Good morning. In light of recent events, we have decided to move up the Fortress Battle to next week. Today, you will have aerial maneuvers with your entire Wing, and then we will practice aerial combat where you wield your magic while flying." She shifts her weight uneasily.

We aren't ready for this.

Why are they rushing us through this? The Chivalries can barely fly through coordinated formation switching—now we're going to add in the rest of our Wing while we sling magic through the air? This is reckless. Maybe in the past I wouldn't have cared, but now I have one too many fucks to give. One for each member of my Zenith, our bounded creatures, and Pip, too.

My power thrums, feeding on the ensuing chaos as the crowd grows into a raucous fit. Light flares from my hand.

Sølas covers it with his hand on mine, blocking the pastel rainbow light with his shadows. I can feel him not wanting other people to see my light, and I'm not sure why. I can't read his thoughts like he can read mine, unless I accept the bond. Maybe he's afraid I will lose control of it. The light magic that hums beneath my hand is very different from my Chaos Magic. It's like pulling atoms together instead of ripping them apart. That should be the next thing we practice in the Warded Hollow.

He squeezes my hand gently; somehow, anything feels possible with him by my side.

Professor Gloomnight raises her hand, the room falling to silence.

"I know this may all seem rushed, but you are the very best of Cascara, and I have no doubt you will rise to the challenge. We are working on extending the wards around Raeya's Fortress to ensure it's safe for next week. Please, make your way to the southern field for flight practice."

The field is even more chaotic than normal with the addition of the Pegasuses. I enjoy the familiarity of routine, of structure. This is an unsettling change, utter mayhem as we all take flight. Horribly underprepared.

My position at the top of the sky allows me to see the numerous times creatures nearly take each other out while moving through the maneuvers. Every beast flies at different speeds, depending on their shape and wingspan. After two hours of total disaster, we seem to finally find a rhythm.

I'm beyond thankful when we stop for lunch, but I don't have much of an appetite when I remember we'll be practicing wielding magic while flying next. I know we aren't aiming at anything, just avoiding others' magic to start with, but… something's off, and I don't like it.

The hairs on my neck sway as tattooed fingers graze down my arms, sending delightful shivers through my body. No one's touch has ever felt like his. The all too familiar smell of amber and spruce fills my senses as his breath tickles the hairs by my ear.

"You seem lost in your thoughts. I'm almost jealous they're not of me, *Luxsula*," he purrs with a smokey voice that dissolves the world around me.

I'm not sure if I can ever get used to the way he affects me, but I'm not going to let him distract me again like this morning. I elbow him in the taut muscles of his abdomen, hearing an *oomph* from behind me.

"You're a shameless flirt!" I snicker and hear the grumbling laugh of Calais across my mind.

I attempt to walk away, but he grabs my waist, pulling me into him, gliding my hair back to whisper along my neck, "You've done so well with your Celestial Gift. Stop worrying. I dare say Calais' wings stand a chance thanks to your *excellent* teacher." His lips hover near my neck in pure torture.

I'm not sure if I want to punch him or mount him at this point. Perhaps both could be a satisfying combination.

Thankfully, Calais makes the decision for me, snapping next to his head. He has the audacity to wave her off. I guess he's accustomed to her temper, growing up spending time with Scáil.

The grumble that emanates from her chest shakes us both.

I pry myself from thinking of his naked body against mine to see a pair of neon violet eyes flaring like flames in front of me.

*Shit.*

I shove away from Sølas, who reluctantly lets me go, his sadness and longing washing over me. The bond in my chest attempts to tug me back, but I brush it away, gritting through the pain.

I run after Winx. The heat radiating off her sears my flesh as I try to get close to her. I barrel through it. I can't keep dodging talking to her, especially now with our rushed schedule.

"Winx. Please, can we talk?" I beg as I gently grab her wrist, singeing my flesh. She whips around, her pixie-shorn hair now a mess of bright violet flames.

"What's there to talk about?" she snaps, anguish marring her petite features.

"I'm sorry. I didn't mean to hurt you." I can barely look her in the eyes because I know I've done exactly that. And not talking to her about things sooner just makes this so much worse.

"I could tell you felt uneasy about showing affection in public. If you came and talked to me, I would have told you I was okay keeping what we shared a secret while we figured something out that makes us both happy. But you kept making excuses and blowing me off while I kept forgiving you. I'm so stupid, falling right back into your arms, even after you walked into the Dawning Festivities clearly dressed in his fucking shadow magic." Her fists clench tighter, knuckles white as violet flames roar from her shoulders. My eyes water from the heat as I stumble a step back.

"I know he's your Bloodline pairing, so it's not like I can be mad that you're fucking him. What I'm mad about is how easy it is for you to be with him in public. You melt into his touch like the world around you doesn't matter. That's how your touch makes me feel. I want to light this whole fucking campus on fire, knowing that he can do that to you. I wanted to be the one to melt your icy walls, to light up your cold nights. What makes it even worse is you… you look like you fucking belong together!" On those last words, all her fire goes out with her breaking heart.

I want to hug her, but I know that will only bring her more pain, especially as her last words echo through my heart, inappropriately skittering. I'm afraid to tell her about the bond. It may break her. It may bring her father down on me. Or it may finally make sense of everything. I know my Zenith won't be happy with me sharing secrets without talking it over with them first.

She slices through the heavy silence. Wrapping her arms around herself, as if bracing for the answer to her next question. "Is it because he's a male. Is that why it's easier for you?"

"Absolutely not. I don't care what's between anyone's legs. Why would you think something like that?"

"You should be afraid of him, like everyone else is. His bloodline is unknown, and the last-known Shadowmancer was Wuvon. Yet you are drawn effortlessly to him… What does he have that I don't?" she whispers. Winx can't even look at me now. It's breaking my heart that she could even think this is because he's a male, like that can offer me something she can't.

Bloodline pairings can be of the same biological sex. It's the first thing Gildora and Raeya had the Runic Engineers complete, once they created artificial wombs. They retired as professors so they could raise their children together. Even the lay folk can be put on a waiting list, having a child of their own after a few years.

We are free to love how we please, to live a full life free from biological restrictions of conception. It's been like this for hundreds of years at this point.

It's clear her feelings for me are much more than I thought, making me even more leery about revealing the bond. If word gets out, I don't know what will happen. It's not that I don't trust her—or maybe it is. Her natural wildness is exactly what attracted me to her in the first place.

"Sølas is a flirt, but he requires more connection to be intimate for our Bloodline pairing." The words stick to my tongue like putrid honey. It's a partial truth, but it doesn't feel any less horrible.

"And you're telling me that not only are you suddenly okay feeling things in public for him, but your Zenith is okay with him requiring *feelings* from you to meet your genetic contribution?" Her eyes flare neon violet again, clearly not buying my lies.

"We're making do." The words sputter out under my breath.

She cackles in response. "That's Ritherin-shit, and we both know it. Since you are not willing to tell me anything, maybe I'll scorch some answers out of your Shadowmancer you can't seem to stay away from."

"Winx, he is my Bloodline pairing. Stop it," I snap, but she leans in closer, heat radiating from her once more as she scrapes her nail under my chin.

"If all it takes is being your Bloodline pairing to make you mine, then consider it done," she purrs in a threatening way that sends a chill through my chest as she turns and walks away with a prance in her step.

Celestials be dimmed. I just fucked this up even more. Some days, I don't even know why I bother.

*"Hey, you. We'll figure it out together. I snuck away some food for you*

*and Pip, on the other side of the hill. Would you do the honor of joining me? I know you haven't eaten, and I'd hate to see what hungry Chaos Magic looks like.*" A smoky voice slips across my mind, releasing the tension in my shoulders from my last conversation.

I let myself enjoy the sensation, fighting my instinctive urge to suppress it. I already fucked up enough today. Hopefully, I can fare a little better at this.

# CHAPTER 49

Sølas is casually lounging on the hill, looking too handsome for his own good. He tugs me down with grace, his shadows landing me right in his lap.

"What exactly do you think you're doing?" I croon with a scrunched nose. I can't help but smile with how the bond in my chest revels in his closeness.

"Feeding you and my favorite little dragon. And perhaps being a tad selfish, enjoying your closeness, because with our new schedule, I will steal every moment I can with you. You're not pushing me away, so maybe you're feeling a little selfish, too?" He winks as he pops a blackberry into his mouth.

I hear Scáil grumble down the tether of our minds.

"*Hey, I said* favorite *little* dragon. *That's not a word I would ever use to describe you,*" he responds to Scáil, handing me the full plate next to him.

Pip quickly flashes into his natural form, inhaling more than half the food.

Sølas grabs the last blackberry before Pip swipes it up with his tongue.

"Are you going to eat? I am happy to feed you. Some species find it quite romantic." He smirks in a devilish way, and my lips part, knowing full well he's thinking wicked thoughts about my mouth.

"Don't push your limits with these selfish moments. I'd hate to see what you losing control looks like in front of our entire class," I purr, stealing the berry from his hand, biting into it, the juice painting my lips purple. If he can be a tease, so can I. Although we're already walking a thin line. Maybe I don't care if I fall off today.

He growls along my neck, "You're lucky Pip stole the rest of the berries, or you might just find out."

A palpable thrill courses through my blood, leaving me aching in more than just my chest. The same radiates from Sølas, intoxicating me all the more.

"*You two are insufferable.*" Calais' raspy voice chills the mood.

"*Well, if it isn't the pot calling the kettle black. I recall not being able to keep you off me for over a month after we accepted our bond. Not that I'm complaining.*" Scáil's ancient, earthy voice is laced with humor that spreads a wild smile across my face.

"*That was* after *we accepted the bond. I don't want to even imagine what they will be like when she accepts if they're already like this,*" Calais mocks.

"If *I accept the bond,*" I correct, stinging a wave of hurt over Sølas with my unnecessary comment.

"*This one has jokes today,*" Calais taunts ruthlessly.

I huff, standing to finish the remaining food, ignoring the bond whittling at my ribs. I help Sølas up, and Pip jumps to my arm with the aid of his wings, snapping into place as my bracer.

Professor Reska takes the stage, her saffron eyes contrasting against her metallic silver fur shimmering in the breeze.

"We will be practicing a running mount for takeoff and the same for landing. Once in the sky, you will direct a magical blast forward while we rotate through positions. Please, be mindful of the casting around you in relation to the trajectory of your flying creature. Depending on your success today, we will be adding moving targets tomorrow."

Argenta, her Bladed Coata, takes off behind her. Reska sprints on disks of air, gliding onto her back with an easy grace.

We line up in formation, and then all our beasts rumble the ground with a running head start. I mimic a similar pattern, less effortlessly teetering on the air disks before I can glide on to Calais.

Sølas, of course, Shadowwalks right into position. Must be nice. I may just be slightly jealous of the ability now.

He winks at me with a smug smirk before Scáil silently soars off.

After reaching cruising altitude, Professor Reska signals for us to switch formation and cast our magic. I'm not entirely sure what to do with mine.

I look down to see rays of light from Fenwick, whirling spores from Kivi, and vines whipping from Juniper, hovering arrows suspended by Highin matching Eko's spectral blades, bolts of fire from Cinder.

I decide to send a whirling blade of fire in front of me.

Calais audibly huffs.

*"Show them just how beautiful you are when you let your chaos free,"* Sølas purrs, a caress across my mind, sparking my power beneath my skin.

I let his words sink into my soul. He does have a way of making me feel beautiful. Despite what my foster parents said about my markings, strange eyes, and ghostly hair, I deserve to feel beautiful.

I hold onto that warm feeling. I focus on a small area in front of us, an orb to let my power loose within. A circular cloud forms, lightning ricochets in the trapped circle, and ice daggers rain from the cloud, shattering into sharper pieces.

My power nips against my control. I growl back, refusing to release the destruction while changing positions. I grasp onto that happy feeling even tighter, hugging the chaos in warm light. Shifting the lightning to sparks and ice to rain before setting it free. My magic slashes beneath my skin, craving to be released without restraints.

It may feel unsettled, but I'm happy with the progress I've made, and everyone is still alive around me. I think of all the ways I'd like to thank a certain smug, early-morning teacher of mine.

Those thoughts are burned up by searing pain down the bond from Sølas. Calais swerves to the side, allowing me a better view of the madness below.

As our Zenith switches positions with Nadir, Winx bolts violet flames at Sølas.

He quickly wraps them in shadows, extinguishing them, only for her next wave to explode as soon as his shadows get close. They blink in and out of shadows, dodging the bursts.

Sølas almost getting injured erupts a protective fury roaring through my blood, a wild instinct released. Magic tears from me in a wrath of its own. The clouds clot into storming black above us, the wind lashing with violent hail. The soil vibrates, releasing a towering wave of dust.

Why am I so angry? I haven't even accepted the bond yet, but the thought of someone taking him away from me makes me want to cleave the world in two.

Calais weaves, taking on an incoming lightning bolt along her conductor spikes.

*"Luxsula, as much as I appreciate watching you get all riled up over me, flying in your storm is proving to be quite a feat. Especially for those on smaller creatures. Can you do me a little favor? Think of those warm, happy thoughts for me,"* Sølas hums. I look down to Dracos and gryphons spinning, caught in twirling updrafts.

I take a deep breath, letting the beauty of Tearfall Lake, the ripples of lavender and magenta reflected along the aether fill my mind. The happy chirps Pip makes and how adorably ridiculous he looks flying on his wobbly wings. I envision more selfish moments stolen between training and classes, where Sølas steals my breath away with just a look.

My eyes drift open; the sun shines bright, and everyone is touching down safely below us as Calais circles for landing. I use air magic again to glide myself off her as she lands, running as instructed.

She stops notably farther away from the rest of my class.

*"Sølas, do you care to explain why the fuck my rider almost lost control like a feral animal at the sight of you in danger?"* Calais' voice booms across our shared tether. The way she says his name sounds like he's a hatchling in trouble. I sense uneasiness with a hint of fear from Sølas. To be fair, I'd be afraid of her, too.

He drifts out of the shadows as Scáil lands beside Calais. Sauntering towards us, ruffling his hand through the back of his messy hair as he says, "We should probably show them that mark on your chest."

*"What mark on her chest?"* Calais snaps.

"I… slipped up. Lost control. Our magic intertwined, and my shadows found a way into her skin."

*"Yes, she mentioned the mark—the reason you told her of the bond. But she did not accept it, so it should have faded. Unless you lost control once more?"* Calais snarls.

"Well, that's the thing… The mark didn't fade like you guys said it would."

*"Start explaining, or I will be enjoying you as a smoky afternoon snack,"* she growls. Sølas responds with a shrug and then leans against Scáil, hoping to avoid Calais' wrath.

Scáil presses his nose to my body, sniffing. If I wasn't between his nostrils, I'm sure I'd have blown away.

*"She appears to have partially accepted the bond,"* Scáil's ancient voice gravels out.

*"Impossible."* Calais scowls but then adds with a huff, *"It would explain why the bond lashes out at her when he's not near. And her erratic urge to protect him, even though he's safe."*

"You do realize I am right here, right?' I glare daggers at them all.

*"And do you suddenly have something enlightening to add to the conversation? To the last of my knowledge, you know the least about bonds here."* Calais' words are an icy slap across my face.

*"Calais, behave. Perhaps your unique magic gives her the power to accept only part of the bond,"* Scáil cooly replies, trying to ease the rising tension.

I don't know much about bonds, as Calais so gently put it, given it's not a topic important for being an Ellian Knight, and there isn't much recorded history during the time when the Celestials reigned. But I do have a good idea as to how, perhaps, I could have half-accepted the bond.

When I had been thinking to myself that I could *pretend*—just for one night—my heart knew I wasn't pretending at all. I've never had to control my heart before. My mind always leads the way, my heart its silent follower. Until I met Sølas. Then my heart developed a wild mind of her own. I swear sometimes, my heart seems like it will leap out of my chest just to pull me closer to him. Now I know why; it's clear my heart has an agenda all of her own, once she recognized the bond.

Sølas kicks up an eyebrow at me.

"Is it possible my heart accepted the bond, but my mind didn't? It would explain why I can feel his emotions but not hear his thoughts." I raise my voice over the arguing around me.

*"The bond is a connection of souls, transcending the corporeal: time, space, even dimensions. It's your soul that accepts it, not your heart. You feel your pull to him in your chest because for your species, your heart is often more closely linked with your soul than your mind."*

"Well, what if a soul has been fractured? To survive. What if, when I dissociate, it's more than my mind leaving my body, but a part of my soul, too?"

*"That's a thought."* Scáil lowers his head as if contemplating it further.

*"Regardless, if you reject the bond now, both of you could very well die."*

"What?" I shout, then narrow my eyes on Sølas.

He's casually flicking off a piece of dust on his shoulder like I don't exist. *SHADOW PRICK!*

Another thing he carefully avoided mentioning. He continues to ignore me, but I know he heard my thought because there is the subtlest tremble in his hand.

I walk over to him, ready to punch him in the face, but stop a few feet away. I know all too well the control he has over my traitorous body when it's too close to him.

"Sølas… is this why you kept wincing this morning?" I grit out.

He disappears into a cloud of smoky shadows, only to appear right next to me, leaning against Calais' leg. His arms crossed against his broad chest.

"I do love the sound of my name on your lips, even when you're cross," he purrs, ignoring my question.

Calais shifts her weight, causing him to stumble. I shoot a smirk her way in thanks.

"I had my theories that something was off when I noticed the markings still on your skin last night while you were sleeping, and the fact your magic could actually hurt me during training today. Technically, your magic shouldn't be able to hurt me if you love me and have accepted the bond completely. And if you want me to be truly honest?"

"Yes. Complete honesty."

"I've been too busy enjoying every moment of you letting me in. Every smile that sends the darkness in me shuddering for its life. Every time you seek out my touch. I just want to be with you. Yes, this bond links us, but even if it wasn't there, it would not change how I feel about you. Of course, I winced when I heard your thoughts of being good at blocking people out. Because I know if you reject this bond now, it will likely kill you, too."

He sighs before continuing, "Prior to this, it would only be me suffering if you ignored the bond. But now… I hate that because I lost control, you now feel the same ache and longing in your chest." His jaw clenches, hands raking through his raven hair.

"Before, at least, I could find comfort in your heart being full, even if it was not with me. But now, that will never be the case. You talk about fracturing your soul to survive, and I hate to think I could leave your heart fractured. I see flashes of your memories while you sleep. Things no child should have to survive. I understand why it's so hard for you to accept love when you have experienced so little in your life. When those you were entrusted to chose only to show you pain and suffering. As an innocent child."

Sølas begins pacing, as if he can't contain all the emotions bouldering within him. "You deserve to know what it is to be loved deeply, completely. Even if you don't think you do. Even if it's not by me. I won't lie to you, though: *I want it to be me.* The thought of anyone else even touching you makes me want to do unspeakable things, but I would bear that torment if I knew you were happy and whole. The idea that I somehow stole that possibility because your heart will always ache for me kills me. I'm so sorry. If I had known this was possible…"

He's pacing again, arms wrapping around himself, as if they can hold him together. "I don't know. Because I don't regret a single second with you." He finishes, looking lost in his thoughts as smoky shadows billow off his shoulders.

I can sense his guilt, longing, failure, feeling broken, his agony.

*Son of a bitch.* I am somehow messing this up as well. Today just isn't my day when it comes to anything dealing with relationships.

I have to fix this.

I know if he continues down this spiral of self-flagellation, it will only end with both of us pushing each other away, and I don't want to let that happen, even if being numb comes more naturally to me. I may not know much about love, but I never thought it would be easy, and maybe that's why I've never bothered to try. Things are simpler when enjoying someone's company just for pleasure; emotions and attachment are an unnecessary, sticky mess.

But if there's anyone I'm going to figure out this mess for, Sølas is certainly worth the risk. And I definitely can't let him blame himself for losing control when it was me who had accepted this bond, even if only partially and unknowingly.

Something tells me that, even if I'd known the consequences, I still wouldn't change a thing. Maybe I'm going mad, but Emberhell, it feels right.

*Fuck it.*

I may not be ready to fully accept this bond, but I'm willing to finally let him in. Carefully unwrapping and baring all the vulnerable bits I keep hidden from the world. To really give this relationship a try and stop over-thinking every Celestials be dimmed thing. I'll never know if I can truly love someone unless I try, and if anyone is worth falling into the abyss for, certainly it's *my mate*. I don't think I'll ever truly understand the depth of our connection, but surely something so divine, infinite, and painfully irresistible is worth the risk?

I may not know how to love, but I'm willing to stumble through, trying to figure it out along the way. Plus, it seems like he has enough love for the both of us.

He's always patient with me, pushing me to the best version of myself. Maybe this can actually work. Plus, I don't mind putting those pretty decent teaching skills of his to a real test—learning how to love and be loved—and maybe one day, even learning how to accept this bond fully.

He continues to pace, clearly so lost in his own stormy thoughts, he hasn't heard mine.

My hands reach out, grabbing his arms, pulling them around my waist. My touch causes shock to wave over his face. He definitely isn't expecting this. I lift my hand to his cheek.

His face falls naturally into my palm, as if it's his home. I clear the wavy raven locks from in front of his closed eyes. His sorrow pools over me as he nuzzles his cheek deeper, pulling me closer.

He's fearful this will be the last time he will hold me like this.

*"Don't be ridiculous."* I smirk.

At that he opens his eyes, ice blue piercing through long black lashes and so much darkness.

"I guess that means you're stuck with me, then." I wink, hoping my attempt to mimic his flirtations will pry him out of the darkness.

His lips crash into mine. The world melting away around us. My lips part for him without thinking. He devours me like a male who has been starved his whole life. His one hand making its way through my iridescent hair, pulling my head back to deepen the kiss. Our tongues dancing with desire and longing.

I unshackle my magic, wildly colliding with his shadows, an indescribable sensation. Our powers caressing together like souls embracing one another. A touch so deep. So intimate.

The euphoria makes me weak in the knees as I lean back to gasp a moan, but Sølas only pulls me back, capturing my pleasure in his mouth. A satisfied sound rumbles through his chest into mine.

The liquid heat throbbing between my legs spills into my blood, igniting it on fire. The ground lifts beneath my feet, as if we're floating upwards.

His lips on mine make the world feel like it's falling away beneath us. As if our connection transcended this very world, as if we're meant for something more. I savor the taste of him, like a warm spring rain after a bitter winter. Full of life, hope, sunshine, and warmth.

His lips are a promise of undying love, a consecration to reforge me into more than I can ever comprehend. The power between us vowing to remake the heavens. Shatter worlds and recreate them.

Deep in my soul, I know there's nothing we cannot achieve together.

The taste of his essence on my lips melts me into molten iron, ready to take shape into the deadliest weapon if anyone is to tear him away from me.

*"You two are going to float away."* Calais huffs in annoyance.

I pry my lips away from Sølas to see we are, indeed, floating high above them. My marks glowing with white light surrounded by rays of twinkling pastel rainbows. It reminds me of starlight.

I look at Sølas, whose gaze is fixed on me, lust, love, awe swirling in his eyes. While I'm still panting from the world-altering kiss lingering on my lips, I begin to grasp my need to be so protective over him earlier today. My power slowly lowers us to the ground as he leans his forehead to mine.

"I would destroy galaxies to protect you," I whisper.

"I dare say, Savaé, are you flirting with me? We're going to need to work on those skills." He moves his head slightly back to give me one of his dashing winks.

"Well then, I'll need to find a new teacher," I tease, scrunching my nose at him and giving him a playful flick on his.

"Always out for blood, hmm, little savage?"

I *had* almost been out for blood today when I saw Winx trying to hurt him. If I feel this way only having accepted the bond partially, then this is going to affect us on the battlefield.

We definitely need to discuss this with the rest of the Zenith because this pertains to their lives, too. I know Kivi and Atlas will urge me to accept the bond so Sølas and I can wield together. But if he isn't making me choose, then neither can they.

"You're right. We do need to fill Atlas and Kivi in on you being able to partially accept the bond because now, both our lives are at stake. The others deserve to know. There's no going back now. I'll send them a whistle note to meet us at our room for dinner on the balcony. That will give us more privacy and allow Pip more time to stretch his wings."

It warms my heart that he doesn't just think of my needs, but Pip's, too. No wonder he likes him. I've never had need of using a whistle note before. It's a type of air magic; you whistle, say your message, and focus on the recipients while you whistle a second time to send the message on its way. You feel a tingle on your ear each time the message makes it to its recipient.

It's not a very secure message system because they're easy to intercept and require focus to cast, especially when it's to our entire Zenith. It's convenient for one person and over short distances. I often hear whistles zipping by in the halls of campus.

I pat Scáil goodnight on the chest; when I go to do the same on Calais' leg, she almost snaps my arm off. *Typical.*

I treasure watching them fly together. There's no doubt of their love. They spin and swirl around one another, dipping and weaving amongst the clouds. Surely if someone as rough as Calais can love deeply, so can I.

Inspired by the thought, I intertwine my fingers with Sølas'. He responds with a sweet kiss to the top of my head as we walk back to campus.

# CHAPTER 50

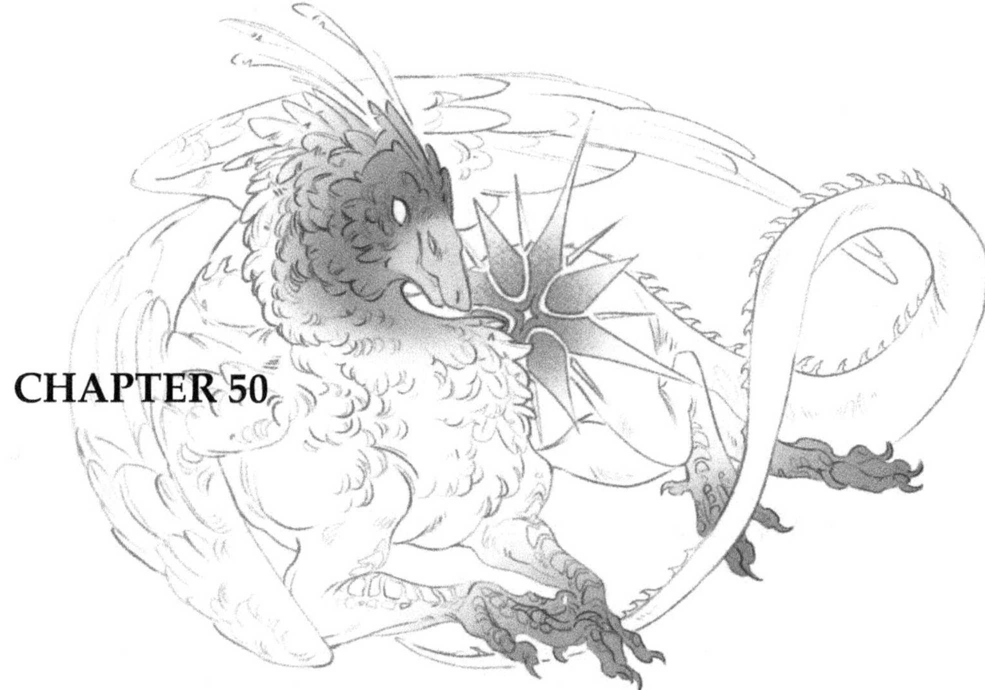

I suddenly remember an important question.

*"How do I reject the bond? Just to make sure I don't unknowingly mess things up,"* I ask along our shared bond.

Sølas flinches at my thought. Instead of letting go of my hand and pushing me away—which is what I would've done—he stops walking. His shadows wrap around me, dragging me into him as he cradles my face in his palms. Two orbs of moonlight scour my soul—in search of what, I'm not sure. A smile creeps its way onto my lips because he can literally read my thoughts. What more information could he possibly need?

*"We are in uncharted territory with the way your bond behaves, but in theory, you would have to say aloud with your hand on his heart: I reject this bond. Truly meaning it with all of your heart and mind,"* Scáil responds.

*"But I don't have to mean it with my soul?"* I enquire.

*"Your soul can never reject a Fated mate bond. You are two halves to a whole, meant for one another in every life, every timeline, and every universe. Sometimes, events happen that can keep you separated or unable to accept the bond in one life versus the next, but the connection to each other's soul is unbreakable,"* Calais answers.

*"If I have already accepted the bond with my heart, shouldn't it be impossible to reject it now?"*

*"It should have been impossible for you to accept it only with your heart and not your mind, too. The Fates are playing a twisted and dangerous game*

*with your bond. The magic is likely unstable as it's not meant to be partially accepted; there could be unintended consequences either way. But yes, it's possible you couldn't reject it now, but with this ancient magic already being disrupted by a partial acceptance, it's possible rejecting it with your mind would stop both of your hearts. For the heart of an accepted bonded mate cannot continue beating if they are rejected, for it is not a life worth living,"* Scáil solemnly replies.

I place my hand on Sølas' chest. Terror and despair flash through the bond. *Maybe* not my smartest move after our conversation, but I'm hoping to give him a piece of what he's looking for since I know he was too lost earlier to hear my thoughts.

"I want you. I want this. I want to try to learn how to love you and be loved by you. I may be shit at it, but you deserve a chance. I'm daring to dream with you. Maybe one day I'll be ready to give all of myself to you," I vow to him with confidence and only a slight tremble to my palm. It's not fully accepting the bond, but it's a promise to get there.

Sølas twirls a lock of my hair in his fingers as he liquefies my soul with his ice-blue eyes.

"You deserve this chance, too. You deserve to be happy. You have to be willing to do this for yourself, not just for me. You need to learn to love yourself first to truly love and be loved. And I'm happy to spend the rest of forever helping you see yourself the way I do. Picking up your shattered pieces, and worshiping your mosaic. You deserve a full life that's more than just surviving. You are worthy of love, my darling," he vows, leaning his forehead against mine.

"The Celestials can keep their heavens, for all I want is you. I can lose myself in your eyes for eternity and be happy. When you are with me, really with me, exposed, with your walls down, not lost in your thoughts, your eyes become the night sky. The golden flecks in your obsidian shimmer, becoming twinkling starlight. I've never seen anything like it. It's the way they shine when you think about the things you're afraid to lose, as if you've forgotten I'd see this whole world burn just to hold you closer." Sølas' eyes match the moonlight casting its glow above us.

"You are my light. My chaos. My soul. My religion." His words give me the courage to dream of the future he promises. Hope spools in my veins, drunk on a closeness unlike any other. My power revels in the heady sensation.

The more I give in, the greedier the bond aches. I unshackle my magic. It pours out, igniting with his shadows, yet it's different this time. Rather than the crackles of destruction of chaos and endings, there's the hum of creation and beginnings.

The entanglement of raw power twists a moan from my throat. Sølas once again captures my pleasure in his mouth. It's all for him, devouring me with his kiss.

My eyes drift open, squinting in the glow of my markings. The light's not only golden, but silver, blue, white, orange, and pink. The warm and cool tones mixing together, ebbing and eddying between the billowing smoke of his shadows. A billowing, vibrant, smoky aurora takes shape.

"Now who's showing off?" He smirks, twirling me around so my back's against his chest, tilting my chin up.

The lights of my powers are fluttering above me, painting the atmosphere with a flowing pastel-rainbow aurora. Little flickers of light cascade down from the heavens. It's snowing shooting stars.

"You are starlight, and I will forever be the darkness of night. Fated together. Bonded from the beginning to the ending of time. Do not let the darkness steal your light. Use it to shine even brighter, *my Luxsula.*" Sealing his whispering words with a kiss on my cheek.

We silently treasure the blessing of the Fates, time and responsibilities lost to the magic around us. A comfortable silence cocoons us as we watch my aurora dance along the meteor shower. It's as if the heavens are anointing our connection, showing us just how powerful we can become as one.

*"You're even more than I ever imagined."* I hear his thought along the bond, but it's different, like it has just slipped out, rather than having direction.

A whistle whips through the air, snapping us back from the empyrean, dissolving the shooting stars and my light along with it. My mind is muddled, like a dream. I'm not completely convinced it was real.

"It was real. This is real," Sølas reminds me as he snatches the whistle message from the air. He always knows just the right thing to say to soothe my soul.

The whistle message speaks:

"You're an ass! Sending us all a message to meet for dinner at *your* penthouse then you don't show up! *And* after another rider attacked you today. *And* without any food, no less! If it wasn't for the shooting stars, I might be worried about ya. They better mean you two finally sealed the deal, or I'm gonna punch the both of ya. Now Shadowwalk your asses over here before I start trying to eat Kivi's mushrooms and you get to deal with me tripping balls. With love, Seraph."

"Worth it," he croons as his shadows consume us, receding to reveal a very aggravated bunch of Fae.

Great. This conversation is already off to a lovely start, and we haven't even said a word.

"*Still worth it.*" I smile up at him, which he returns with a beautiful one of his own.

Then his shadows drape over the western balcony, leaving a banquet brimming with an extravagant amount of food, desserts, and beverages.

Parallel to this stands a long table with seating for us all. Pip wastes no time spreading his wings to devour the feast. I yank him into my arms. He lets out a protesting squeal trying to wriggle free, but I don't relent, or no one will have a chance to grab any food with this scoundrel gobbling about. As soon as I let him go, he plows through the plates, nothing but crumbs left in his wake. I don't even want to know how all that food can fit in a pint-sized dragon.

Sølas pulls out a chair for me next to Kissa.

Seraph chuckles. "He smiled, and he's being a fucking gentleman; that must be some really good snatch. Too bad you're not willing to share."

Sølas lets out a warning growl while I hide my amused smile behind a sip of sparkling Moonwine.

"Must taste better than June berries," Seraph mumbles under her breath, more to herself than anyone else. It's true, though; Elarian pussy does indeed taste like June berries. Each Fae species has their own unique taste.

"What's snatch?" Fenwick beams with an endearing innocence. Seraph is now cackling.

Kissa pinches the bridge of her nose, brows pinched in annoyance. "Will someone please enlighten me on why we are here before I'm tempted to claw Seraph's tongue out... if Sølas doesn't beat me to it." Cleaving Seraph's laughter to an audible swallow. I'm sure several females would be disappointed at the loss of that body part. I don't miss the rumble that thought elicits from Sølas' chest.

Well... time to start facing my fears. If I can defeat monsters, I can manage my way through this. Not sure what it says about me that I'd rather be facing a maw full of fangs than my disgruntled Zenith.

Sølas' hand falls to my thigh with a squeeze that tells me I don't have to be the one to start if I don't want to, supporting my decision regardless.

I need to do this, committing to change, growth, and *him*. Pride paints his face as his shadows wrap around my chair dragging me closer to him. *Celestials, he's perfect.*

I straighten my shoulders and begin. "So… our dragons are not the only ones with a mated bond." A strangle noise tumbles from my mouth, an awkward sound that isn't quite a laugh. Confusion scrunching most of their faces.

Emberhell, I am nervous. I'm not much for public speaking, being socially isolated most of my life. Unless, of course, I'm being reckless, then my mouth doesn't seem to know how to stop. What if this is finally the thing that's too much for them to handle?

Sølas entwines my fidgety hand in his.

These Fae are my Zenith. I need to trust them, and we need to work together to make this work. *We are one or none at all.*

I clear my throat, stirring as much bravado as I can muster. "Um. Well. Sølas and I are also Fated mates, as it turns out. Wild, I know. Anyway… he has already accepted the bond. And, in a unique turn of events, in a Savaé-only kind of way, I accepted the bond, partially. Which means… if I reject it now, we can both die. So, no pressure or anything."

I slump in my chair with an exasperated sigh, bracing for the swift slap I know is coming.

Kivi and Atlas' eyes both narrow, pinning me to the spot in a crumpling mess. I dare say they even show a hint of disappointment on their typically calm, collected faces.

"A simple solution is obvious: accept the bond. We cannot risk losing you both. Not with your powers and your dragons." Gearin adjusts his golden glasses. His logical brain leaving no room for emotional understanding. Sometimes I wonder if he's more Rune Tech than Fae at this point.

"It's not that simple. She deserves the right to choose," Sølas says cooly, but his grip on my thigh tightens. He doesn't like where this conversation is going, and neither do I.

"She already decided, accepting the bond partially. Her choice affects the entire Zenith. So just finish it, and let's be done with this. Her commitment issues don't need to be our problem. I must say, this finally explains the way you two have been acting lately. I guess that means your distracting pheromones in class won't be changing anytime soon. Fan-fucking-tastic," Eko says, crossing his arms.

Sølas tenses at his words. I squeeze his hand, sweeping it into my lap. *"I am okay. Everyone has a right to their own opinions... even if they're not very good ones."*

"Don't be such fucking males. Yes, this affects all of us, but it doesn't mean we force her into something she's not ready for. No matter how much I think Sølas needs to get laid." Seraph winks at me. My eyes roll in response. With a smug smirk, she continues, "As long as you don't reject the bond, we don't lose either of ya, right?"

"Yep. That's the theory, per Scáil and Calais." I nod at Seraph for the support.

Juniper and Fenwick nod at each other. I swear those two can read each other's thoughts.

"We agree. No one should ever be forced into things. Especially something as rare and special as a Fated mate bond," Juniper chirps, springing her dark forest hair over her shoulder.

Pip perches on her head, joining her chirp in agreement.

Juniper giggles, blooming a flower in her hand as a gift to him…Which, of course, he eats, painting a smile across my lips.

"I don't think my ancestors, Gildora and Raeya, would be in support of us forcing a bond. Their love is what inspired the Rune Tech artificial wombs, so no couple was limited. Forcing anything can lead to unforeseen strife and more harm than good," Fenwick chimes wisely.

"I see the points of both sides. However, if the roles were reversed, I would not forgive you all for forcing me into a lifelong commitment of suffering." Kissa rolls her eyes with a sigh before her fangs are ripping into a piece of meat.

"Why would she suffer? They clearly like one another," Eko snips, rubbing his temple, appearing utterly annoyed this is still up for debate.

Highin's feathers ruffle at Eko's remark, talons tapping on the floor. Surprise sweeps our attention to our reserved feathered friend. His quiet nature makes even shy Flint look like a socialite in comparison.

"Aetherhawks mate for life. Distant magic from the original Celestial-blessed Fated mates live on in our bonds. This bond tethers a piece of your souls together. It craves closeness; being separated for long periods of time can cause physical harm, draining their magic, even to the point they can waste away. They can sense one another's emotions, always feeling their presence. They will never be able to truly love another being, the bond making it extremely painful." His hand lifts, weaving into the rust-colored feathers dusting his chest.

A muscle in Highin's jaw ticks, hand dropping. Clearing his throat, he continues, "According to our shamans, if their bond has the strength of the ancient ones, they can hear each other's thoughts and wield magic as one, enhancing their abilities and being able to draw from one another. They are two halves of a whole soul. To force this could cost Savaé her life, and thus Sølas', causing the very outcome you are hoping to prevent. The Fates play fickle games with their sister, Karma. We should not intervene in things we do not fully grasp. Especially when all-powerful beings are involved." Highin's sienna feathers around his neck setting back into place as he finishes, wings tucking tight behind his shoulders.

"Who knew we had a bonded-mate expert in our midst? We should have shared this sooner. Our dragons could only offer speculation." I regret not trusting my Zenith sooner, pledging to myself not to make that mistake again.

"*We offered what knowledge we could,*" Scáil sighs over Calais rumbling in the background of our shared bond.

"*I know. Thank you,*" I respond. Aetherhawks are an extremely secluded culture; I doubt even Atlas knew about this.

Highin's cinnamon eyes swirl to me. "It's natural to seclude this treasure to yourselves initially. Discovering a new bond is a sacred time. Our community supports new mates by allowing them an undisturbed period to be together. Making the choice is a life-altering event and a very overwhelming experience. I do not envy your circumstances; trying to navigate all this during the rigors of our curricular requirements is incomprehensible to my kind."

He sweeps his hawk eyes over the rest of our Zenith before setting on Atlas. "Savaé and Sølas' struggle deserves our patience and utmost support, if we are to be a successful team. We are one or none at all." Highin raises his wing and arm across his chest to honor us in salute.

Flint smiles, his hand landing on Highin's shoulder, while his other arm mirrors the salute. "I agree with his wisdom. You have my su-support." His shy smile is always full of light. I return one in kind.

Vex twirls a black curl framing her vermillion face. "I'm just here for the gossip. Tyranny is going to lose her ever-loving mind when she finds out Sølas is off the market, without a doubt gaining Queen Auntie's attention. No wonder Winx was out to burn you alive, Sølas. If she thought you're a threat just because you're a Bloodline pairing… she'll have a whole new level of determination to end you if she finds out her prized Savaé hasn't fully accepted the bond and thinks there's a chance."

Cinder rolls his amber eyes. "As far as Tyranny and the Queen are concerned, leave that to me. Flint can talk with his cousin, Winx." His irises flaring bright as heat waves warp the air around him. He's awfully disgruntled by a responsibility he volunteered for. For someone so broody, Cinder has a knack for being connected to everyone in power. Freckle-dusted fingers drift over his chin. "But Vex's comment brings up an important point. What happens if Sølas dies with Savaé only partially accepting the bond?"

"I believe the trauma I survived as a child fractured my soul, allowing me to separate my mind from my heart. My heart accepted the bond without my mind being ready. Scáil's theory is that this likely renders the magic unstable, unpredictable. Sølas' death could kill me, I could survive, or something else entirely could happen to my soul. As Highin said, our souls are linked. This power is a combination of deity magic: the Celestials and the Fates. The latter do not favor disruption to their treasured gift."

Atlas' hand rises, our leader signaling his decision. As our Savant, he must consider every possible scenario. His Probabilities Magic is unparalleled in this role, guiding us to the most favorable outcome.

"We will not tempt the Fates. They see all eventualities. To gift a Fated mate bond for the first time in nearly half a millennium suggests there's more at stake than we can possibly comprehend. Savaé is evidently a key component to their plan with her ancient magic and woven gold markings that have never been seen in recorded history. And Sølas' unprecedented power with an unknown bloodline being her mate. The Fates' games of endings and beginnings, the very balance of light and darkness, are undoubtedly at play." Atlas' resolute tone settles Eko and Gearin, who both lean back in their chairs.

"I, of course, am in agreement with the wisdom of Atlas. I did sense a disruption in Savaé's life source when I healed her. Her conclusion is likely correct," Kivi hums.

I'm almost in shock with how surprisingly well this conversation is going. I must admit, my fear was unjustified, giving strength to my vow to face my fears instead of running away or avoiding them altogether. Maybe not all problems need to be stabbed away.

Orion is causally leaning against her chair, looking bored. She's the only one who hasn't voiced her opinion. All eyes shift to her. The silence finally causes her red irises to drift up from fiddling mindlessly with her candy-red nails. Her lips curl into a feral smile. Light shimmers over her teal scales as her head tips back, blotting the air with a smug laugh. The rest of us look to one another, confusion pinching our faces while we wait for Orion to gain her composure.

She tucks her candy-red hair behind her fin-shaped ear. "I don't even know why you are all worried. I can read their Auras. She's going to accept the bond. You could have just asked me and spared us this riveting debate. I'm just glad a Fated mate bond is the reason your auras are intertwined. The other causes are far less… appealing."

"Well, that's not ominous at all," I murmur under my breath, trying to resist the prickling annoyance regarding her mortaring my decision like I'm just another brick in a wall. Her eyes soften as she gleams the shift in my Aura, lazily standing up and sauntering my way.

Orion taps me on the tip of my nose twice as she elaborates. "Don't you worry your pretty little head about it. Just enjoy the intoxicating energy of falling in love that's positively vibrant within your Aura. You can't fool an Aura. The signals come from both your mind and your heart, regardless of their separation from your soul. Your Aura is the least chaotic I've ever seen. It's not uncommon for the mind to play catch-up to what the heart already knows, given its closer connection to the soul."

Orion's final insights are oddly reassuring. Maybe I'm not as bad at this as I thought I would be.

*"Once you set your mind on something, it seems there's nothing you cannot do. Would it be rude of me to kick them out? I'm done sharing you tonight."* Sølas' purr coils around my mind.

*"Can you even be trusted with me tonight? Your desire feels as if I starved you for attention."* I smirk.

*"I guess we will find out, won't we?"*

"Please, you two. Wait until we're out of the room, for Celestial's sake." Kissa sighs as I look up to see Eko already leaping off the balcony to glide to his room.

"See? I told you all." Orion winks, walking with Cinder to the door.

"I need a fucking drink; who's coming with me? Since I won't be prying Sølas away from this one any time soon," Seraph groans.

"I'm in. Let's grab Rizz on our way. Ohhh, Flinnnt, will you be joining us?" Vex jeers.

Flint gives me a friendly pat on the shoulder. "I'm really happy for you! The monsters in your head are the sca-scariest to fight, but you're brave. Use that st-stuborness to beat them instead of letting them wield it against you." He smiles and tips his head before Vex is dragging him out the door.

"Have fun with Rizz," I call out to him before he's whisked out of sight. The mirth crinkling his marble face summons my heart to beat a little fuller; he deserves all the happiness.

Juniper hands me Pip, who's adorned with a handmade flower crown she started crafting after he ate her first gift.

"I'd be happy to dragon-sit this chubby little one any time." She smiles brightly, before linking arms with Fenwick.

"Eek! I'm so excited for you two, no matter what you decide. I must say, you're positively beaming. Are you sure you're not a Radiant, too?" Fenwick giggles.

"Mayybeee." I scrunch my nose with a coy smile. Fenwick does a little clap with excitement, radiating yellow light from her palm as she waves goodbye.

Her childlike joy is infectious, a ray of pure sunlight you can't help but bask in. I hope she always finds a way to see the light and nothing ever steals it from her.

I wonder if I've ever experienced the pure, uninhibited joy of being a child. I was already three years old when I was placed in the custody of my foster parents. Yet only dark memories lurk my mind from that time. Bone-shattering cold. Endless hunger and thirst. Stumbling through shadows to avoid the monstrous male who always found new sick and twisted ways to torture me. Always searching for the crack that would finally break me.

Sølas' rage pours through the bond, a wildfire scorching me from my memories. Before I can even find him, he's wrapped around me. His shadows are always so calm, like billowing smoke from a blown-out candle. Now they are lashing whips. Twisting. Congealing. Clotting into viscous, sticky pitch. The air thickens with an unsettling energy, sending my light magic shuttering beneath my skin. Yet my darkness writhes with my Chaos Magic, gnawing on my ribs, nicking the walls of my veins, craving to mince the pitch to ribbons.

I tug his arms around me, cinching them even tighter.

I'm not going to let fear ruin one more thing for me. *"I killed him. He can't physically hurt me anymore."*

*"But he still harms your mind. That monster shattered your soul, keeping all of you from me."* Sølas' voice slips into an eerily dark undertone, as if he's speaking to his own demons as well. The sick tar that melts off his shadows drips into a puddle, lumping together at his feet. Erratic ripples pulse and throb, melding into a moving, distorted shape.

The flapping of wings pierces the silent night sky. Scáil and Calais dipping down from the blotted clouds overhead. I don't have time to ponder their presence, my hand lifting to sweep raven locks out of stormy black eyes with moonlight irises.

*"I refuse to give him that power over me. He doesn't deserve it, and you will not give him that power over you. If anyone shattered my soul, it was me. So I could leave my body and free myself from his clutches. So I could survive as a child in a world that sought to break me. Calais and you are right. I am stronger than I realize. If I can fight this darkness inside of me, so can you. We'll do it together,"* I command, but his pitch keeps dragging him further away.

He's right in front of me, but there is a chasm of indescribable distance between us, cleaving our world in two. Severing pain lashes through my soul; ache cracks through my ribs as I gasp for air.

*No.*

I will not let anyone make this choice he has gifted to me. I will not let anything take away my dream of what this can be.

Liquid starlight pools in my palms. I grit my teeth, resisting its pleas to retreat. I let out just a trickle of my darkness, spooling around my magic, luring it out with its ravenous thirst for destruction. I think of my cheeks, blissfully sore from all the smiles he's painted across my lips. My heart spills out mirth and light as I recall the night sky set ablaze in a celestial display, beaming from my very soul.

I'll give it all to him. Every last ray, shining bright enough to bring him back to me.

I coax my darkness to rake every happy memory from outside my broken mosaic window. His smiles, like getting drunk on sunshine. When my glittering pools of obsidian and gold locked with his, ice-blue eyes piercing my glacial palace, almost impossible to drag our gaze apart despite the Bone-Thresher lunging for him. The way my gold markings glitter and gleam around him, as if they are actually a beautiful gift. The gift of my mother's love beaming, letting me know I finally found my home.

Every moment we've shared, despite my resistance, has slowly brought us closer and closer together. My mind finally willing to let my heart lead, finally believing I can love and be loved.

The vow of his kiss still hums on my lips, and I know there's nothing we can't conquer together.

Twinkling rays of pastel rainbow light radiate, blinding brightness piercing the night as I release the shackles caging my Chaos Magic. Energy rips out of me, bowing my spine as it prowls. Hunts. Seeking out every molecule of dark matter and siccing my light upon it.

An eerie screech cleaves the air as the pitch seethes into nothingness. My trembling hands, still cast in a faint glow, lift to his face as I bare my most treasured secret.

"You have *always* been there for me, protecting me in your shadowy embrace. When I was young, the shadows were my safe escape, my home, my only solace. You found me long before we ever met. Just as you always will, until the end of time." My whispered words an ancient spell, uncleaving the chasm, the world falling back in place.

Blackness melts from his eyes, revealing a rare glimpse of the traces of crimson. Once, I thought maybe they were a clue about his unknown bloodline, but now I know they're just the scars of his bleeding heart. Overflowing with so much love to give.

I place my hand on his heart.

"My heart accepted the bond the second I let my mental guard down with you because she recognized your shadowy embrace and wouldn't let you get away from me." The words pour like mountain snowmelt in spring, revealing his ice-blue eyes, luminescent and forever reminding me of moonlight.

"I'm so sorry. Sometimes the voice that calls to me gets so loud, I'm lost to it. I didn't want you to have to see me like this. I should go." His head bows, utter defeat marring his features. He takes a step back as shadows begin to envelop him.

I pull him back into me.

"Stay. Let me learn to love you. I never expected love to be easy. If you try to protect me from your darkness, how can I ever give you all of me if you can't do the same?"

He smirks, gliding his thumb across my golden-flecked cheek.

"When did you become so wise, my *Luxsula*? You clearly know more of love than you let on."

"When motivated, I'm a fast learner. I'm sure the fact that I have a hopeless romantic as a teacher helps. Rumor is, he's a shameless flirt, but his heart only beats for one." I wink.

To that, Sølas lets out a deep, genuine laugh, filling my soul and rattling my bones with joy.

I hear Kissa let out her third exasperated sigh of the night. I'd forgotten not everyone has left yet.

"I'm starting to think you enjoy making a Celestials be dimmed fucking scene." Kissa rolls her chartreuse eyes, but it doesn't hide the slight smirk clawing at her lips. My heart flares, realizing she's actually happy for the both of us for once.

"A fascinating display of magic. When did you develop the powers of light?" Atlas asks without missing a beat.

I think about the gold light of my golden marking in the Warded Hollow, the aurora out in the field, the white light when I went to grab Sølas' hand… The glow when I was first close to him, shrouded in his shadows, in a hallway in a pub outside my room.

It's been him all along.

The darkness making my light shine brighter.

"When Sølas first released his shadows around me, after our first trial," I admit, accepting what I refused to then. Shock and hope trickle down the bond from Sølas.

"Fascinating. It would appear you have more than one Celestial Gift. I would say I am surprised, but I do share the same belief as Sølas… You are unlike any other." Atlas bows with deep reverence. Kivi follows suit as they both make their way to exit.

"Watching your magic complete one another is a sacred honor. The

Celestials and Fates without a doubt have blessed you both. Please don't hesitate if you have any further questions." Highin bows before taking flight from the balcony.

At last, we're finally alone. I gaze at Sølas, who's taken a seat, staring off into the distance. His umber skin is three shades paler. It's clear whatever happened drained his life force.

He looks so broken. His mask of effortless perfection and coy flirtation too heavy to wear under the weight of his demons. I sink into his lap, brushing a soft kiss on his arched cheek. My head dips into the curve of his muscular shoulder.

Perhaps I could never fit all my frozen bits back together because I was always missing him. Perhaps our shattered bits will fit just right, finally whole… together.

"Come to bed with me. Even the shadow prick needs rest," I taunt, swirling a lazy finger down the bare part of his chest.

Without another word, he scoops me up in his arms and lugs me, kicking and giggling, to the canopied bed, where Pip's already nestled into his spot.

Sølas moves to curl around me, but I fuss at him, guiding his head onto my chest, my arms weaving around him. Tonight, he needs to feel safe, and I am strong enough to protect us both.

"My heart only beats for you, too," I whisper into his raven waves with a kiss. He weasels his arms around me, dragging me in tight. My fingers dance through his hair, tracing the shadows that swirl down his neck, curling around my golden twelve-pointed star, like the mark is his precious treasure to hold.

Sølas' breath steadies, sleep claiming his tortured soul. My starlight magic spills out, painting the room in fractals of pastel rays, casting away any looming darkness. Tonight, he needs peace. Tonight, he needs me. Under the dancing lights, I drift into slumber.

Daring to dream in a way I've never done before.

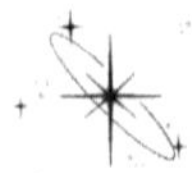

Serrated screams rip from Sølas' throat, clawing me from my dream of exploring a mycelium rift.

"I will not kill her. I love her, with all of me. She is *mine!*" His back arches, body writhing, tormenting pain contorting his limbs.

"I will do your unspeakable biddings, but you *will never touch her. Never harm her. Never have her!*" His shaking cry guts me.

His shadows needle the air around him, whetted blades lashing out at the darkness of night. My hand lunges for his chest, only to be blasted back by an instinctive shield of erupting Chaos Magic.

I dive deep, summoning my starlight. Pastel rays spill from my soul, drenching him in protective dragon scales, the ones I always pretended to morph my rage into. But these ones I've forged for him out of hopes and dreams. His shadows part for my light, letting my fingers curl around his shoulder. I shake him again and again to no avail as his shadows morph, pummeling down, sputtering my light.

Howls of agony lacerate the air. Shadows clot into stringy pitch, coiling around my rays, nipping at my light to snuff it out.

"No! Not again. Mother, Father, I am so sorry. Please, no, not her, too. *Not her, too!* Make it stop!" His rasping pleas whittle at my marrow as my own darkness sinks its claws into his soul, dragging him back from the dark ocean below.

I pour my light into him as I grasp him up into my arms. Drowning him in every happy moment we've shared, every hopeful dream of our future. His head whips violently against my shoulder, his trembling body thrashing me with dredging strength.

"Shh. Just follow my light home. I am here, waiting for you. Sølas, come back to me," I hum, repeating the words over and over again. As if they're a prayer, just for him. Summoning all my strength to keep him close.

Retreating into my mind, I yank open the circular, honey-hewn window. Happiness floods out as I pull him into a golden sea, floating on crested waves of my memories, only the bright and beautiful ones. The ones I've always been too afraid to feel, fearing they're too precious for me to hold, becoming lost to ash in my hands. But I'd gladly lose them all for him. With every intention of making more with him by my side.

Time eddies, carried on the ebbing tide of my focus. My eyes pop open on a rumbling groan from Sølas' chest. His shredded voice cracks, piercing my heart.

"*Luxsula,* what's going on?"

"A bad dream is all. You're safe now. That's all that matters," I hum, wiping the cold sweat from his thick brow while resting his head back on the pillow.

"The light... It was so bright. It reminded me of you... Always of you." His sleepy whispers fraying through the state between twilight and slumber.

Silver weeps from lashes as I trace the edges of his beautiful features, memorizing every line. Even in his nightmares...

He fights for me.

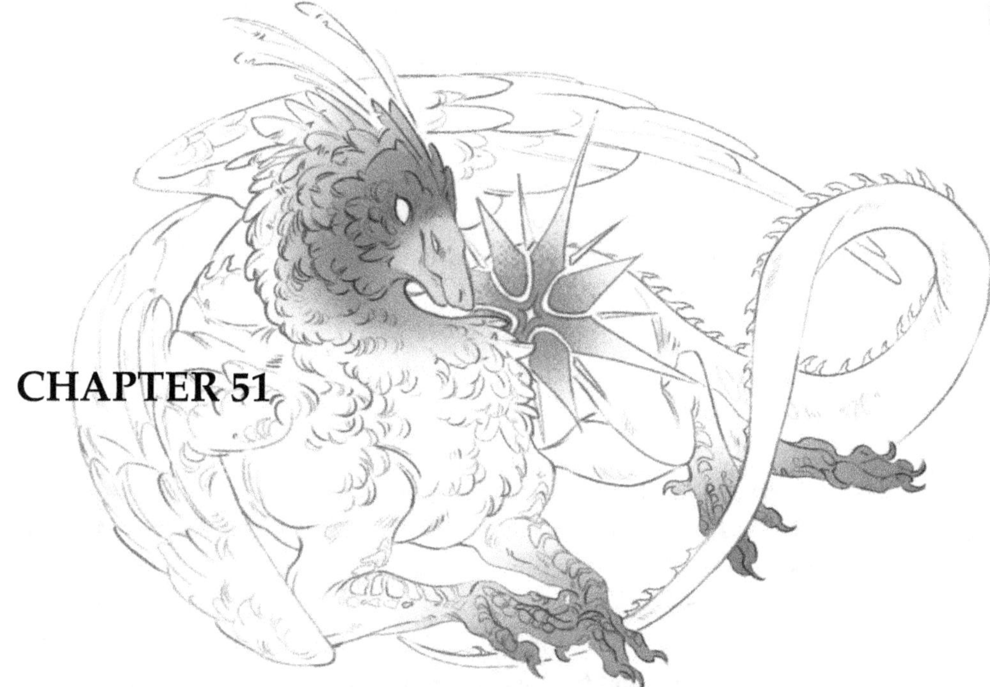

# CHAPTER 51

**M**y night is restless, twisting and tossing. Stoked by the compulsive need to ensure Sølas is okay. I wake frequently, despite his breath remaining steady, features lulled with a sleepy softness.

Since the tumbling boulders of worry bludgeoning my chest refuse to relent, I decide to hop out of bed and start the day. Unlike my handsome shadow prick, I don't have the ability to magically conjure things out of the shadows. At least, not to my knowledge. Rather than wasting time on endeavoring to do so and making a fool of myself, I quickly dress and head to the dining hall. I can't bring back as lavish a breakfast as he could conjure, but I manage enough food for the three of us and two mugs of kahvi.

As I open the door to the Starlight Sanctuary, Pip knocks the dishes out of my hands, lunging for the food. I hiss, hot kahvi scalding my arm. With a crash, breakfast splatters all over me, the plate and mugs shattering at my feet.

Hmm, maybe sitting here trying to magic food into existence would have actually left me looking less foolish after all. My fingers tack together in sticky maple syrup in my futile attempts to pry pancakes and bacon topped in kahvi from my clothes. Berries tumble off me, only to be caught in Pip's happily awaiting mouth.

From the direction of the bed, a deep laugh sunders the early morning air, bubbling one from my own chest as I take in the ridiculous sight of myself.

The sound of Sølas' raspy chuckle curls around my frayed nerves, instantly dissolving the tension pinching my spine.

"This was not the sticky mess I planned to make of you. But if you insist on me eating breakfast off your body, how can I refuse?" Sølas croons. His eyes drift over me, curling his fingers lazily about his chin as a devilish smile twists his lips. "Although I must say, it would be far more delectable if you were… undressed."

I roll my eyes, shaking my head as I march my way to the bathroom. Each step flicking morsels for Pip to scrounge as I go.

My eyes are scrunched tight as I wash the last of the sticky syrup from my hair. I sway into the sensation of thick fingers strumming along my hips.

I turn to find Sølas in the shower with me. Naked. Misty shadows extenuating every valley and ridge of his corded muscles. Dripping. Glistening. I swallow a muffled whimper, breath stripped to uneven pants, the shower no longer the only thing heating my flesh or leaving me soaking wet.

He pins me between his arms against the wall, steam swirling between us.

"I. Want. You," he growls, and *fuck,* do I want him, too. I glance down, stifling a moan as I take in the thick length of him, throbbing hard and ready for me. My core clenches, aching to feel him inside of me. Filling me. Stretching me.

His lips crash onto mine. Hungry. Greedy. Kissing me as if I am the air he breathes and he has been starved for oxygen.

"We are going to lose control," I gasp, using all my strength to nudge his chest back.

"I need to hear my name moaning from your raw lips." His breath fans across my neck in a growl. Each of his next words are punctuated with a ravaging kiss.

"Trust. Me."

I do trust him, in a way I've never trusted anyone else in my life.

Completely.

With the sense of my thoughts, Sølas' hands drift from the wall to my dripping body. His fingers explore, mapping the feminine curve of my hips, the hard lines of my muscles. Delicate ribbons of shadows trace every golden marking, calling upon their light.

Vexing fingers skim down the soft outlines of my abdomen, dipping lower and lower until they're teasing around my clit, enticing rich shivers through every fiber of me.

"You have no idea the scent you are giving off right now. It's driving me fucking mad. Ever since you first laid heated eyes on me, I could smell your sweet nectar. Your heated blood, spilling from your skin, making you sopping wet without me even touching you."

He drags his nose right over my pulse point, releasing a feral rumble. "That wicked scent gets stronger the more you let me in, making me impossibly hard. Every. Fucking. Time. Consuming me in reckless thoughts of claiming all of you…"

Air escapes his lungs in a slow, stuttering exhale, his every muscle trembling with restraint. Shadows waft from the golden star along his corded neck, cascading down my body.

"My shadows are aching to devour you." His rasping purr vibrates against the corner of my mouth, my lips instinctively parting. He quickly takes advantage, torturing my bottom lip between his teeth. That mouth of his is divine, the perfect balance of pleasure mixed with nips of pain.

His shadows swirl down to my breasts. Caressing. Stroking. The thinnest ringlets tantalizing my nipples with a pinch.

A pleasure-filled whimper curls at the back of my throat as warm, velvety ribbons lick their way along my wet inner thighs. Pressing into my skin as they lazily thumb their way upwards. Molten heat rushes through my blood, gushing through my every heartbeat, swirling at my core as my lower belly tightens with need.

Wicked shadows purr along my entrance, lapping at the wetness that pools for him.

He groans at the sensation, grasping my hips tighter, teetering on the cliff of control. His eyes darken as shadows dip beneath the lips between my legs, coiling around my clit as it throbs with an intensity that threatens to unravel me.

He captures my moan in his mouth, groaning into my mine, "Fuck, you are so sensitive. Already twitching beneath me with just the slightest touch."

The shadows continue their onslaught of torture, winding me up tighter and pulling away just as I'm about to come undone. My hips rock back and forward, chasing the fall from the excruciating edge he keeps me on.

"Your sweet little cunt is so needy for my shadows," he purrs as he laps at my neck, his darkness dipping into me, ever so slightly.

The ache between my legs drives to unbearable greed as I whimper softly. Feeling my own control slipping between my fingers, I drag his body into mine.

The sensation of his slick, chiseled core against mine is overwhelming. The carved plateaus of his chest rising and sinking, grinding against mine. The thick, corded muscles of his arms flex around me.

His shadows claw beneath my skin, begging to be even closer to him. To complete the bond.

I moan with pleasure as he pulls my hips to his, moving in just the right way. He rocks me back, spine bowing on an incline perch of his shadows as he drags his thick cock up along my throbbing clit.

The sensation is beyond words as he continues his blissful torture. My head spins as my eyes tumble back, lost in the haze of lust.

He drags out each stroke of his hard length, leaving my body starved and drowning in pleasure at the same time. Trembling with conflict.

My flesh buzzes beneath the tantalizing pressure of his rhythm. Occasionally, his crown slips against my entrance, only to continue to glide upwards without entering me, sinking me in devastating hunger.

I try to remember how to breathe as I drown in everything he makes me feel for him. Beyond the lust, the happiness and light, too. The way he makes me whole, my soul radiating with his.

His cock twitches along my clit, and I want *more*. My hips wriggle, desperately attempting to change the position of my body so that crown of his will slip right inside me.

"Not until you promise me," he roars, placing one hand on my neck in a possessive hold while his shadows twine around me, locking my hips in place so I can't lose control.

My Chaos Magic prickles beneath his bindings, nipping for release. My lips part, nostrils flaring, gulping in air in short pants. Amber, spruce, and something darker saturating my lungs.

The scent minces my thoughts, cinching the promise from my lips.

In response, his shadows become thicker and more violent in their movements. They knead across my sensitive breasts, nipping my nipples. Towing the edge closer to pain without leaving pleasure. The shift only stirs my own darkness. I unshackle her, releasing my chaos to gorge, talons sinking in along his back.

The euphoria of our magic combining sends us both spiraling.

Sølas growls in pleasure along my neck as he takes another painfully delicious and slow thrust along my swollen clit.

His shadows plunge inside me, stretching me, filling me. My body writhes against his bindings as I sink into the abyss of him.

He is all-consuming.

Lashes fluttering shut as a dark moan purrs from my lips, "Sølas."

"Fuck," he rasps, sinking his teeth into my lower lip.

I whimper, eyes drifting down to see his plump crown glistening in precum, tightening the wound-up pleasure within my core to the point of pain.

"Look at me," he grinds out, waiting for my gaze to meet his. "I want to see the starlight in your eyes as I let you fall off the edge into bliss with me." His voice is so feral, I can't disobey, even if I wanted to.

He collides my body against his with violent hunger. His thrusts becoming quick and wild. A commanding moan rumbles from his lips.

"Come with me."

His demand unravels the endless tightening pleasure at my core, coming as I scream his name in ecstasy. Over and over again. Convulsions of pleasure ripple through my body. All the orgasms he kept me on the edge of now shattering through my veins with a vengeance of euphoria that melts the planes of reality.

His cock throbs before he covers our stomachs in his own release, washing away beneath the rain of the shower as he pulls me up into his chest.

The waves of dopamine leave my body shaky and sluggish as he turns off the water.

He lifts me up in his arms. I wrap mine around his neck, my head falling into the dip of his shoulder.

His shadows swirl around us, wicking the water off before placing me in bed. He gets down on his knees. Kissing my hand as the shadows ebb from his eyes, leaving the icy blue of moonlight in their wake. When he's at peace, the flecks of crimson vanish from his eyes, along with the shadows.

He rests his head against my hip, peering up at me as if I'm the only thing in this universe that matters. In that moment, all my fears and worries melt away as bliss lures me into sleep. My heart, body, and soul fuller than I've ever known as a last wakeful thought consumes my mind.

*My mate.*

# CHAPTER 52

Gentle kisses trail down my chest, sinking past my stomach, luring me from sleep just before he stops, right above the slit between my legs. The cessation pries a frustrated moan from my dreamy lips. Eyes fluttering open to see Sølas' fiendish smile between my legs, white teeth dragging across his lower lip with feral desire.

His head dips down, and mine falls back with a moan as his wet tongue lazily licks up the entire length of my throbbing cunt. Legs left trembling on either side of his head from the resounding growl vibrating my twitching clit, deliciously sore and aching for more.

He lifts his head, meeting my stare with dark hunger.

"As much as I would love to savor the sticky mess I've made between your thighs, unfortunately, I need you dressed and fed so we can make it to class," he purrs in pants along my wet, sensitive cunt, ripping a growling screech from my lungs at the thought of having to go to class after he knowingly woke me up like this.

My thought twisting Sølas' lips into a sarcastic pout. "Would you rather I woke you with a cold shower? I rather think you enjoy my form of torture." His smoky voice darkens as he dips his fingers ever so slightly into me to show proof of his statement.

My body's a begging, trembling mess as he slips them into his mouth, groaning at the taste.

"You taste so fucking sweet, it could kill me."

I fist the sheets in my palms, screaming internally, knowing he's going to leave me wanton like this until who knows when.

His shadows swirl all around me, retreating to leave me fully dressed and seated at the table set with breakfast.

I pant raggedly as I narrow my eyes on him. He casually takes his seat across from me. My blood is scorching, bubbling in desire, like it's going to boil right out of my pores.

"You're adorable when you're angry. Now, eat. You'll need your strength to gain some composure before class." He winks before taking a bite of toast. His words do nothing to rein in my temper. He's so *fucking* amused with himself.

I want to smack him, throw him back into bed, and fuck him like a wild animal. That thought gets his attention, arching a brow at me, encouraging the challenge.

"I understand why Aetherhawks are left alone for so long during the bonding process. You look like you'd rather tear down this entire building than go to class right now… and you haven't even fully accepted the bond."

He smirks smugly at my lack of control. Celestials, how did he fucking control himself when we first met and he accepted the bond?

I have never craved chaos so much in my life.

I attempt to cool down by eating the delicious food on my plate, but my body's still blazing. His shadows beneath my skin feel like they are going to crawl their way out if I'm not closer to him.

He scoots his chair closer to me, settling the sensation in my chest. And I swear, I feel him wonder if I've fully accepted the bond by what he feels radiating off me. It's more than the usual emotions I can sense radiating down our bond.

He arches an eyebrow in response, clearly questioning my thoughts as well. I huff, too flustered to think about this. He reaches out to graze a tattooed knuckle against my skin, soothing the roaring flames into humming embers in my veins.

How can his touch change my mood so much? Light me on fire and soothe me without even a thought. My head is suddenly clearer, and I'm wondering where Pip is because he hasn't stolen half my plate yet.

"I fed him before I set the table so you could actually eat for once. I helped him practice his flying while you were asleep. He's taking a nap in the sun on the balcony." Sølas twirls a lock of my hair before leaning over, kissing me on the temple.

All my rage simpers away at his consideration. I know he must be exhausted from his nightmares, but he still made sure to take care of everything so I could rest.

"Ya know… you can be annoyingly perfect, sometimes," I grumble with a smile.

"Well, I will do my best to endeavor to be annoyingly perfect all the time." He winks, standing up, reaching out a hand to help me up. I call for Pip, who raises his head with four sleepy blinks before he prances over to me.

As we walk, the bond aches at the slightest fucking distance between us; it's persisting at an entirely new level today. Sølas intertwines our fingers, and I lean my head against his shoulder. I don't care about the remarks that will surely follow such a blatant display of emotion. None of it matters anymore, *just him.*

Our Zenith nods in quiet support as we walk into the auditorium.

Kissa still can't help but roll her eyes, but she sits one seat over more than typical so Sølas can sit on the other side of me. I'm relieved because this bond would have driven me insane at the distance.

Morning classes go by at a painstakingly slow speed.

Zander Atreides' silver hair glints as he takes the podium to review Combat Physics. The absence of our normal professor reminds me of the threat of the Wuvon knocking at our doors. He reviews the physics of hand-to-hand combat. All points taught to me by Sully.

"One must be mindful of an enemy's center of mass when it comes to grappling and leg sweeps. How to use your own, increasing the force of your hit, shifting your entire weight to add momentum to the strike. In contrast, faster strikes result in less force, allowing for increased speed." Zander paces the stage as he reviews the movements.

I sigh, trying to stay focused, which is a mistake because Zander's silver eyes narrow on me.

"Ensign Savaé, since I seem to be boring you, please enlighten the class on how to use physics to your advantage when targeting kicks."

I'm all too happy to share the teachings Sully imparted on me, no longer pinned by fear of public rejection.

"Powerful kicks take advantage of torque. Using leg and hip muscles in a rotary motion, with the strongest force landing at a ninety-degree angle as the fighter changes their shape, maximizing their moment of inertia. Whereas kicking straight in front capitalizes on the potential energy stored in the muscles of your leg, bursting into kinetic energy with motion."

Pride bubbles in my chest like Sully is looking down on me. Instead of shoving the feeling out my mosaic window, I soak it in, focusing on the happy memories with him. Nodding to my grief without drowning in it. Sølas' head tilts with a heartwarming smile, which I can't help but beam right back at him.

Zander's silver hair tumbles forward with a nod. "Correct. The latter is more similar to the force of a punch, which is dependent on impulse momentum." He continues on how to properly land a punch on your first two knuckles for maximum impact.

His mention of knuckles has me thinking about my favorite pair, covered in dark tattoos.

*"What do the tattoos on your hands mean?"*

*"I had my shadows brand my skin, reminding me of the darkness within me, so I never forget the cost of losing control."* Grief laces his voice, twisting my lips in a frown. I didn't mean to bring up painful memories.

I can't easily touch him in class without drawing back Zander's attention. I think of how his shadows so easily curl like smoke from him, their touch always soothing me.

The swirling aurora from last night spills in through the circular window of happiness in my mind. Hmm, that's more subtle than rays of starlight.

Sølas arches a brow at my thought, which I ignore, calling to my power. It pools at my feet as I focus on how full my heart feels while searching for the one responsible. Wisps of multicolored, liquid light mist around Sølas' ankle, twirling up his leg, intertwining between his fingers.

I peer up to see a smug smirk kicking up the corner of his full lips. *"Impressive. I see you're trying to give my shadows a run for their coin now that you're no longer letting fear hold back your imagination."* His shadows seeping out to do the same.

Kissa huffs quietly. "Of course, sitting next to each other wouldn't be enough for you two." I smile at her because she's right. It's not.

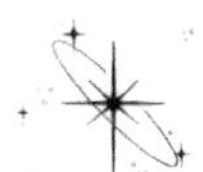

As we saunter into the busy dining hall, the thought of aerial combat lessons this afternoon twists up my stomach into a knot. I'm thankful there will be targets, but worry of Sølas being targeted by Winx again gnaws at my ribs.

We sit down. His arm wrapping around my hip, sliding me closer to him, as if it's enough to cease my worry.

It turns out Winx isn't going to wait until we're in flight to leap at another chance of taking him out of the equation. The air sizzles as violet flames whip out and coil around Sølas, flinging him against the wall.

A lacerated screech rips from my chest, blood blazing with his pain and sudden distance. Before I can stand, she's wrapped his mouth in a cord of flames, along with his wrists and ankles, pinning him so he can't move.

His shadows lash out, but Winx is surrounded in raging fire, levitating off the ground from the heat. As soon as he snuffs out one part, it ignites right back again.

Terror fills his eyes as he gazes down at me. He's afraid she'll hurt me, too. There's also something holding back his powers, preventing him from reaching into his full reserve.

At the smell of his searing flesh, my roar sunders the air as I lunge over the table. Landing in front of Winx and blocking her path to Sølas.

"Stop this!" I growl low, straining against my power threatening to mince her to ribbons.

Her violet eyes are pure flame, not even the whites visible.

"Winx, look at me!" I screech in a panicked plea.

Dark pupils form at the center as they narrow on me.

"I can't stand watching him touch you for one more Celestials be dimmed second. If I kill him, then you'll come back to me." Her voice sounds like the pain of raging wildfires, burning all life in its path.

I've shattered her heart, and she's trying to fix things in her own fucked-up, broken way. She really believes killing him will send me running back to her.

"If you kill him, it will kill me." Terror constricts my heart admitting our weakness aloud for everyone in the dining hall to hear, including Chet. This puts us and our team in real fucking danger. Yet my friends don't balk, my entire Zenith standing in defense around us.

Fenwick casts a golden light shield around us, blocking out the rest of the conversation from prying ears.

Seraphina's water works in tandem with Sølas' shadows to snuff out the flames binding him.

I focus my Chaos Magic, separating the oxygen from the air around her flames that tighten on him, starving them from fuel until he's finally free.

I catch Kivi from the corner of my eye, quickly working to heal his wounds. I'm too afraid to fully look or run to him with Winx casting her full well of power at her fingertips.

Winx's serrated screech frays the air, blasting a shock wave of flames at all of us.

I unleash a wall of chaotic destruction, devouring every particle of her power; not even heat makes it through my shield. I consume it all greedily, my magic vibrating with the extra surge of power. To my knowledge, no one can consume magic but a Siphon. They can wield the magic they consumed. However, my power devours magic and chaos alike, adding to my strength in a different way than a Siphon.

My darkness bucks and thrashes, lashing against my ribs, howling to be unleashed. An insatiable hunger seeking gory vengeance for hurting my mate. I grit my teeth, refusing its pleas. I've already hurt her enough.

My Chaos Magic spreads out, changing the structure of air around her, depriving it of oxygen. Her screech cleaves to a choking gasp as her flames wither away. Crumpling to her knees, struggling for air, which I release back to fill her lungs.

I kneel down beside her, lifting her head up to see her eyes pooling with tears.

"You love him, don't you?" she whimpers.

"I think I do," I whisper.

"I could see it in your eyes when I pulled him away from you. It's why I lost my mind … and control." Her head dips in regret. "I'm sorry. I just feel things so intensely sometimes… It's so easy to give in to the flames. It hurts so much to see him give you what I wanted to." Silver tears paint her beautiful face.

"He is my Fated mate, Winx. There's nothing you could have done. I would've ended up breaking your heart either way," I whisper, hoping the truth will ease her pain.

Her mouth gapes, closing and opening several times before finding her words.

"I never stood a chance, then." She looks down with defeat before meeting my eyes once again. "How is that even possible?"

"I am starting to learn it's unwise to question the Fates. It seems, even with the loss of the Celestials, they still have the power to give this gift. We're connected at the soul; we both die without the other. The bond pulls us together. It's unbearable without his presence. It's why it's so easy for me to be touched by him, even in public. It wasn't that something was wrong with you. But what's between me and him, it's different. Our connection is unlike anything I could ever put into words."

"Well. I guess it turns out he does have something I can never give you," she scoffs.

I laugh in response. "Yeah, and it's not something between his legs." I wink. I do everything in my power not to think about what's between his legs. I don't want to send Winx spiraling again.

Fenwick pops into her light, bubbled around us. "Are you two okay?"

Winx wipes the tears from her face, and I stand up, offering a hand to help her do the same.

"Not really." Winx tries to muster a smile but fails. "I suppose there's no chance for us now."

"As friends, there still is. Now your heart has the chance to move on, and I hope you find someone that matches the fury of your love. You deserve all of that and more." I smile sweetly.

She gives me a side eye before bowing her head and fiddling with her hands nervously. "Sorry for convincing Chet to help me suppress Sølas' shadows. He figured out that smearing his poison on someone without piercing their skin can suppress their magic for about thirty minutes. Not take it away, but weaken it. In my desperation, I said I'd finally give in to fucking him if he helped me. You probably think I'm a horrible person now." I expect shame to pool in her violet eyes, but instead, they're just empty.

"You are fucking wild." I chuckle, trying to cheer her up. With a knuckle under her chin, I lift her gaze back to mine. She rips her face away, and I sigh. "I'm sorry I hurt you so badly, it pushed you to do these terrible things. I'm in a forgiving mood. Why don't we just start over and forget about this whole thing?"

"Really?" Winx's jaw drops, mirroring Fenwick's expression. Apparently, everyone thought I was going to handle this quite differently.

"Really. But if you come after my mate again, I won't be so forgiving a second time." I shoot Winx a knowing look, causing her to audibly swallow.

"You put my magic—at *full power*—out so easily. I think I'd rather not know what your wrath looks like." She shifts her weight nervously at the thought.

"But friends is good!" Fenwick chimes in, trying to ease the new tension.

I smile at them both. "Yes, friends is good." I pause, feeling the profound ache in my chest. "I need to check on Sølas. This bond is threatening to rip me apart if I'm not near him after you hurt him. Please, do me one last thing: do *not* tell Chet about this. He already wants me dead, and I can't have him knowing that taking out my mate is just another way to get what he wants."

"I promise. I don't want to have to deal with that either." She nods and then turns to walk away. Fenwick lowers her shield, freeing us.

Everyone in the dining hall is staring at me. I snarl at them to kindly fuck off, and they quickly go back to doing anything but looking at me. I may have a weak spot for Sølas and my Zenith, but I'm happy to keep everyone else afraid of me, especially if it keeps *him safe*.

I rush over to Sølas, cupping his face in my hands as I look him over.

"I'm fine. Kivi pulled the poison from me and healed the burns. I can't say I'm not proud of how you wielded your magic with perfect control. I guess we'll have more time to ourselves to do other things now that you won't be needing early-morning training sessions anymore." He winks.

I smack him, then crash my lips into his violently.

"What was that for?" He raises his hand to his cheek.

"For reminding me of the frustration you left me with this morning." I smirk, and he smiles in response.

"As much as I enjoy seeing her smack a wink right off your smug face, we need to get to the field for training," Seraphina says. "Unless you're going to keep slapping him because fuck it, I'll grab some more food and stay for the show."

"It's best not to indulge her, or she'll be finding her way into our room hoping to be a third." Sølas tilts his head towards Seraph, suggesting that's something he's experienced before.

"Celestials, you're no fucking fun since ya found her." She waves her tattooed arms up in the air as her blue war braids whip around her, turning towards the door. I let my thoughts wander, exploring what a night like that would entail between the two of them.

He pulls my body back into his with a possessive grip of my hips, growling along my neck.

"Easy with those wicked thoughts of yours. You've lost your mind if you think I'm willing to share you when you won't even let me have all of you yet."

Indeed, a wicked smile curves on my lips. "Leave me wanting like you did this morning, and maybe I'll find myself warming someone else's bed."

He draws me in closer, the hard length of him grinding along my center. He bites into my neck, ripping a moan from my lips.

"*You wouldn't fucking dare. But just in case, I left a visible mark so everyone knows you are mine,*" he purrs with violence.

"Feeling extra possessive today, aren't you? I think everyone already knows that, especially after I saved you." A sarcastic grin curling on my face.

"I'm not ashamed to be saved by you. I loved watching you master your power with ease to protect me. Honestly, it fucking turned me on. You did it so effortlessly. It's beautiful to see you so uninhibited. And don't think I couldn't hear your thoughts through that shield." His smug smile tugs at his lips against my skin, but it does nothing to stop me from stiffening in response.

"Savaé Entropaé actually thinks she might be in love with me," he croons as he kisses the sore spot on my neck, a bruise already blooming. One I have no intention of healing with Sangre magic.

"It makes sense now why the bond has been acting so ferociously today. I was losing my mind holding myself back while you were in the shield with Winx, but I knew that conversation needed my absence to happen." He lays another kiss on my neck before continuing, "I'm proud of you, for forgiving her. I know how hard it is to fight the bond's urge to protect. That night in the Mysticwoods, when Lorgan had you, I thought I was going to destroy the entire forest holding myself back."

I hadn't even thought about how hard that must have been for him, nor do I have time to now as the bells chime overhead. *Shit.*

"*Don't worry.*" He smirks as we become shrouded in shadows. My stomach flips as we appear next to our dragons on the field.

I shove him away, annoyed, realizing he could have done that this morning, leaving more time rather than having us walk to class.

"*That* definitely *wouldn't have been enough time, and you know it.*"

I roll my eyes in response. It's annoying when he's right.

I glide on air magic, mounting Calais.

*"You two certainly took your time swooning over each other. I see he enjoys shamelessly marking up my rider, as well,"* Calais barks in my head.

I laugh in response. "I thought you'd finally be happy I'm no longer fighting this bond."

*"I'll be happy when you are no longer tempting the wrath of the Fates by only partially accepting the bond. I don't enjoy unpredictable magic playing with the life of my rider,"* Calais snaps as we take off.

I smile, wind rushing through my hair. I'm more alive and freer than I've ever been before.

*"You're glowing again. And it's not because of me. I'd be jealous if you didn't look so breathtakingly beautiful,"* Sølas purrs along my mind.

I look down—I *am* glowing, rays of pastel rainbows shimmering around me.

*"As much as I enjoy seeing you shine, Luxsula, you're going to need to know how to control that, or you'll be a beacon on the battlefield."* Worry needling Sølas' words.

I dream up a better idea. It settles on my skin like a second layer as I rip apart the water molecules of the clouds. The mist coats my skin, floating all around me. Every molecule. Then something in me shifts.

I become unbound.

My essence leaking out, forging new polar bonds. I swirl through the air, gliding over Calais' wings, twirling in ribbons along her tail.

*"Where the fuck did you go? I can sense you, but I can't see you."* There's panic in Sølas' voice, fear radiating from all three of them.

*"I'm right here, flying with Calais,"* I say sweetly. Hiding the sarcasm in my voice, torturing them just a little longer.

*"All I see is mist,"* Sølas responds.

*"Exactly. I'm no longer a beacon. I'm hidden but still radiating my light within each water molecule."*

*"That's not possible. Even Seraph can't do that, and she's one of the most powerful Visci."*

*"You told me to dream, and I am. Nothing is impossible anymore."* I drift down, swirling around him, leaving a subtle dampness on his skin.

He smiles, lifting his hand, spreading his fingers through the mist, through me.

*"Look at you, having fun. I hope you can rematerialize in time to cast your magic. I can see the targets up ahead."*

*"A Fated mate bond chooses those who are equal in every way. Now she's showing off as much as you, Sølas,"* Calais grumbles, but I don't miss the undertow of happiness.

I wish I could enjoy this new experience longer, but I'm excited to see what my magic can do now that I'm one with power rather than fearful of it.

I rematerialize without another thought. My eyes gaze over my body, happy to find everything where it should be.

*"Do you feel exhausted after that stunt?"* Sølas inquires.

My power crackles along my skin with an entirely new zeal, no longer feeling shackled.

*"I feel like I'm finally awake, like a shroud I didn't even know existed was holding me back. Now that it's gone, my power feels... limitless."* I smile confidently.

My words a claiming.

Curiosity coils down our bond. Sølas doesn't seem to know what to make of me in this moment.

Targets moving on the ground and whizzing through the air come into view. I wonder if I can use the mist to blink into different locations. The way Sølas can Shadowwalk.

*"Let's not try that here. Maybe another time, when Scáil doesn't have his own rider to mind so he can catch you if I am not fast enough,"* Calais remarks with an unusual gentleness to her raspy voice that I can't disobey.

*"Look at you admitting who the faster dragon is."* I smirk as she grumbles beneath my thighs.

I release my Chaos Magic, static charging the air. I latch onto the electric current, cracking lighting through the targets around us. Conjuring shards of ice down to impale the moving marks near the ground, while others simply burst into dust. Magic flowing through me with ease, leaving me craving something more challenging.

A feeling I soon regret as we hear a blaring sound sundering from Gildorea. The new wards have been triggered.

My heart stills as chaos ensues.

# CHAPTER 53

P rofessor Reska's amplified instructions shout across the wind. "Everyone, return to campus immediately, and head for your rooms."

*"We should stay and help!"* I raise my voice along our shared tether.

*"Absolutely not. Your Zenith is not ready. Don't be foolish just because you can control your magic,"* Calais snaps.

*"She is right. They have well-trained Ellian Knights already on their way. We will just be a distraction and be in the way,"* Scáil remarks.

I think about turning into mist and finding out for myself, but terror rips down the bond from Sølas, reminding me it would be selfish of me to put both our lives in jeopardy because I'm feeling chaotic.

We land in the field, the magic creatures quickly taking off again. It's not safe on the ground, and we need to get inside the wards of campus.

I hear a bone-cracking scream from the eastern edge of the field. My head whips, body spinning towards its direction; before I can see anything, Sølas and Kissa are grabbing both my arms and dragging me to campus.

"You should be running from that sound, not pausing to look!" Kissa hisses in my ear.

"We should be helping, not hiding behind the wards," I snarl back without thinking.

"They're already pushing us through our training faster than ever before. I'm afraid you'll get your wish sooner than you think." Atlas' voice has a slight rattle to it. His rare display of emotion catches me off guard. If he's afraid, I should be too. But for some reason, I'm not.

I shake my head. We are trained to fight, not to hide.

Atlas gently puts his hand on my arm; the powdery softness of his moth-like touch pulls me from my thoughts as I peer into his maroon eyes, framed by iridescent wings.

"Did you ever stop to think that what they're searching for could be you? The stronger your magic becomes, the closer the attacks have been. If the Fates have deemed you a powerful piece in the games they play, they may want to claim you for themselves in whatever battle is coming."

The air whooshes from my lungs, my blood freezing to ice. I suddenly understand why he was so nervous when he heard of the attack that night I had unleashed my Chaos Magic like never before. Calais and Scáil weren't protecting us from my magic; they were shielding it, so others wouldn't sense it. Then my thoughts whip to the time Sølas left to talk to Atlas, when he asked him to stay with me.

Sølas fucking knew, and so did our dragons!

"*Was that what you meant the day we met in the woods, when you said you weren't the only one looking for me?*" I snap at Calais.

"*Exactly. Now please, stay safe. Your magic has been calling them. You have become more powerful faster than I expected, now that the bond has manifested. They are here for you, but you are not ready.*"

"*What do you mean I'm not ready?*" I scowl, my blood radiating as hot as the sun.

"*You need to get her to calm down,*" Calais barks along our tether.

Sølas obeys, pulling me into his arms, but he winces at the heat seeping off me.

"You fucking knew, too! That's why Atlas asked you to stay with me!" I snarl, fighting and kicking to get away from Sølas.

"Yes. I knew. It's our job to protect you. All of us." Sølas' voice is calm, refusing to release me from his hold.

"I don't need your protection or anyone else's. You are not my keeper," I growl as I continue to struggle. My body is so scorching hot, I can feel the pain Sølas is enduring to hold onto me.

"You do not need a keeper, but we are still members of a team. Atlas asked me not to share this with you until he was certain. He didn't want to cause you unnecessary worry."

Them taking away my own choice in the matter sends lighting crackling in the sky all around us. I am livid.

How do they expect me to trust them if they fucking keep things from me?

Sølas' regret and apology pour down the bond, but it does nothing to soothe the boiling cataclysm of my blood.

"We need to get her into the Warded Hollow, now," Kivi hums, as if she's simply talking about the weather and not acting like I'm a ticking time bomb.

Shadows try to wrap around us, sizzling against my skin.

Sølas twists me around in his arms so I'm facing him. Lifting my chin to meet his shadowy gaze.

"I can't Shadowwalk you when you're like this. Can you walk for me?" He gives me a knowing look. "And I mean walk, not run into danger because you're angry and need to punch something."

I nod as my Zenith surrounds me, and Sølas guides me towards the center of the courtyard.

I'm so hot, my vision clouds. My mind minces, wondering: why? Why would they want me? Why could he suddenly not Shadowwalk me? Why am I burning alive, causing my mate pain when he touches me? I know everyone around me is trying to keep me safe, but it's suffocating.

I was finally letting go of all my fear and enjoying life. The thought of being hunted is like my happiness being stolen from me.

I want to make them pay for thinking they can take me, take my magic, take my joy. With each step, the ground trembles beneath my feet.

"*Luxsula, please. I need you to focus on the sound of my voice.*" Sølas' voice trembles with fear. "*You're almost there. Just a few more steps, and you can let go.*" He pushes me gently, urging me to walk faster.

I can no longer see when I hear the door shut behind us.

"Fenwick, Gearin, and I will protect the Zenith with shields. Let your magic free before you burn up," Sølas says as the distance grows between us.

I walk a few steps away from where I imagine everyone else is. It doesn't make sense; using magic is what causes us to burn up, not the opposite way around.

Yet I smell the scent of charred flesh, the bonds of my own skin like the bars of a cage from which I need to be set free. The magic of Warded Hollow senses my power bubbling over and surrounds me in a pink shield.

I let go.

The pink bubble bursts into nothingness as if it was never there. I materialize into mist. Then fire, then snow, then lightning.

*Nothing feels right.*

Nothing seems to ease the endless heat inside me. I whip around the Warded Hollow, each element I turn into smacking against the walls, longing to be free.

Sand, wind, rain, ash.

What am I?

Nothing feels right anymore. I'm not like anyone here, and I guess I never really was.

I need to be… *free.* To be in the heavens above.

I stand in the center of the room, feeling my flesh melt as I gaze upwards, wailing in agony.

The heat finally freeing me from my corporeal form.

Suddenly, I shift into pure starlight, pulling elements from around me to surround myself in a cloud of purple and blue matter. *Stardust.*

Then smoke swirls around me. No. Not smoke. Shadows.

But they're shimmering white.

I twirl them between my fingers as I interlace them with the clouds of dust floating around me. My body forming and unforming, all at once. Then searing pain roars down the bond, thrusting me back to reality as I frantically search for Sølas.

He's on his knees, breathing hard at the very edge of the golden shield Fenwick is still holding up, reinforced by Gearin's glyphs.

Sølas' shadows are nowhere in sight. He feels so weak down the bond, as if he's vanishing.

Everyone gapes at me, eyes wide in terror. Except Atlas, who inspects me with profound curiosity and awe.

Kivi bends down. I can feel her trying to heal Sølas. But from what?

*"From you. You channeled his powers without fully accepting the bond. You're killing him."* Scáil's voice is calm despite the horror of his words, which instantly dissipates the magic in my hands.

*"I didn't mean to hurt him."*

*"I know."* A familiar, smoky voice strains to whisper, coming out more like a whimper.

I try to reach him, but everyone surrounds Sølas, shielding him like I'm the threat. I see Atlas' lips move, but I can't hear what he's saying. In response, Fenwick's golden shield lowers.

I sprint to Sølas, lifting his head to look at me. His raven waves tumbling from his face, but he's pale, his breathing uneven.

"I'm so, so sorry," I whisper as I kiss his clammy skin.

"You just couldn't get enough of shadows, could you? Stealing my heart wasn't enough." A smirk tries to tug at the corner of his mouth, but he's too weak, even for that.

I pull him into my arms. He has never felt fragile to me, but in this moment, I'm afraid of how easily I can break him.

"What the fuck *are* you?" Seraph's fists clench at her sides as she glares daggers at me.

"I don't know."

# CHAPTER 54

**A**rguing erupts all around us. All I care about is taking care of my mate. It doesn't matter what I am; all that matters is him.

Sølas.

I need him safe, where he can rest. Clouds of stardust wrap around us, everyone else lurching back from the blinding iridescent light.

When my eyes open, we're in the center of our bed. I don't know how the fuck I just did that, but I'm happy to be free to rest Sølas' head on the pillow. I grab a cold rag to wipe the sweat from his brow.

Whatever I've done to him, he looks worse than his nightmares.

Pip scurries down and nuzzles his face. He's worried, too.

Sølas starts to shake, his skin becoming ice. There's a pounding on the door, but I'm not leaving him, even for one more second.

If I can pull magic from him, it has to work both ways, right?

I let my Chaos Magic dissolve his shirt, freeing his bare chest. I place my hands over his heart and pour my light into his chest. I spill what I imagine is my love for him into his soul, giving him all the brightness he brings to my world.

"What's she doing to him now!? Get her off him before she fucking kills him and herself!" Seraph yells in panic at seeing her best friend withering away before her very eyes.

"She's trying to channel her magic into him. We should mind our distance, in case his shadows reject her light," Kivi hums as her voice grows farther away.

I know in my heart his shadows won't reject me. They're a part of me, too.

Just in case, I send my darkness to mingle with his, dancing with it, captivating it, entrancing it. His body trembles beneath me, but I keep pushing, praying he will let me in.

I shut my eyes, searching for his black velvet ribbons in my mind. They're in the distance, out the starry, stained-glass window.

I let my starlight reach out to them, twisting and turning into shadows as he consumes it. My teeth grit against the pain searing through me as he takes more and more. Lashes popping open to see dark light radiating off him. His eyes pure white, dark circles spinning within them. His breathing steadies, his umber skin appearing warm once more.

I pull my hands away, and he gasps for air, grabbing my hands, something dark inside him craving more with no intent on stopping. An evil, powerful voice wraps around my mind, fracturing my mental shields.

*"I will destroy you and everything you hold dear."*

I slap Sølas' hands away, and his eyes clear. Terror paints his face, realizing what he's done, as if it wasn't him who tried to take more power from me. The sensation leaves an unsettling feeling gnawing at my stomach.

Sølas sits up, wrapping his strong arms around me. I hadn't even realized I'm straddling him. But I don't care; I'm just so happy to have him back. Tears pool in my eyes, comprehending how badly I could've hurt him without even trying.

He leans back, grasping my hair in his hands to look me in the eyes before catching a glimpse of the black light radiating off him. He smiles, really smiles. The light looks like my starlight but with rays of twinkling, dark rainbows.

"Now you're not the only one beaming, hmm?" he purrs.

A laugh bubbles up. He nearly dies, and it doesn't stop him from endlessly flirting and trying to make me smile.

"Is anyone going to explain what the fuck just happened?" Kissa hisses.

"I don't know that anyone can," Gearin speculates with a thoughtful but disappointed sigh. I doubt he likes the thought of a puzzle he and Atlas can't figure out.

Then we all look at Atlas, expectantly. To our surprise, he shrugs.

"I read about our Celestial living a mortal life in our realm. I thought perhaps you were her descendent when you manifested such strong magic, although the chaos of destruction was not known to be one of their powers. The powers you displayed tonight are far more than anyone would expect from a demi-Celestial diluted by several generations. I am not sure what you are, but I see why you are coveted by our enemy. We must protect you at all costs." Atlas' tone is resolute.

"I need to get fucking sloshed to erase the look of Sølas dying from my mind if I'm going to help you guys protect her after what she did to him today." Seraph turns to the door, clenching her fists.

"Seraph, she didn't know, and she feels guilty enough. Don't you dare make her feel worse," Sølas tries to say cooly, but I can tell he's angry that her words gutted me.

Atlas steps into the center of the room, poised to lay out orders.

"No, Seraphina, I need you to figure out if the threat has been handled. Change into someone important, and do what you do best. Eko, I want you scouting the perimeter; make sure it's safe and no one snuck past the wards. Highin, I want you on the roof with Cinder looking for anyone in the distance. Gearin, Fenwick, and I will work on warding your room. Juniper, Orion, Vex: I want you three to get food. Flint, stand guard at the door until the wards are finished. Kivi, please check Savaé and Sølas over to ensure they are both okay," Atlas commands, snapping into his role as leader.

Everyone quickly gets to work. It's silly, sitting next to Sølas in bed, doing nothing other than letting Kivi's spores tickle me.

"Your bond feels different, stronger. Did you accept it?" Kivi hums with eyes shut, waving her hands around us, but with her question, I see one of her eyes peek slightly open to peer at me for my response.

"No," I grind out. "If I had, I wouldn't have nearly killed Sølas channeling his shadows."

She seems disappointed in me, as if I should have accepted it immediately after to ensure this won't happen again, but goes back to humming with her eyes closed.

Sølas curls his arm around me. I'm annoyed he's selflessly trying to comfort me after what I did to him.

"You saved me, too. Twice in one day. Give yourself some credit." He lifts my gaze to his.

"I put you in danger twice. If I wasn't a part of your life, neither time would have happened." My brows pinch with anger, lashing it at myself.

"Don't think like that. I'd rather die being your mate than not have you in my life," he whispers with a kiss on my cheek. I'm too angry at myself to enjoy him.

"Stop that. Don't you dare think about pushing me away because you lost control tonight. I told you to let go. When I felt you pulling on my powers, I could have stopped you, but you finally looked so at peace. You turned into pure starlight. I've never seen anything like it. I'm finding it harder and harder to deny you anything. Plus, I did promise you all of me." He smirks.

I smile at his ridiculous comment. "I suppose you have more of me now, too." I run my finger through the black rainbow rays beaming from him.

He tilts my chin back up towards him. "I'm still waiting for all of you." He moves closer to kiss me, but Kivi clears her throat, reminding us she's still there.

Blood rushes to my cheeks as she glares at us like two younglings being caught in a salacious act.

"Sølas' power is restored, and then some. As for your power, it appears you barely tapped into your reserves tonight. Which suggests Atlas' claim has merit. Just a fraction of what you demonstrated would have drained the rest of us. Now I understand why you survived wounds you shouldn't have. I believe you are not mortal," Kivi hums with a flat tone.

I'll never get over how she can say world-altering things as though they're nothing. I'm lightheaded taking in her words.

"How can I not be mortal if Atlas believes my mother was?" I ask hesitantly.

"I suppose that answer lies with who sired you, your father," Kivi hums with a gentle peace about her.

This is too much. I've never really thought of my parents, and I don't care to now, no matter who or what they were. They abandoned me. They don't deserve anything from me. So, I ask a more important question, about the one person in the world who does truly love me. Who stays hopelessly in love with me, even after I almost accidentally killed him.

"Does that mean I can live if Sølas dies?" I shudder at the thought. I don't like the idea of having to spend eternity without him. That'd be an awfully cruel punishment, to have a Fated mate between a mortal and an immortal.

I hold my breath in the pause before Kivi answers.

"I am not sure Sølas is entirely mortal, either." Kivi's words fill my lungs with air once more before she continues, "According to the conversation I had with Highin, after we left last night, you should have killed him channeling his magic without accepting the bond. Even a partially accepted bond should not have made a difference. Your souls need to be one to pull from one another. He's not nearly as strong as you are, but appears to have something else running through his blood that is not just Elarian. It appears to be blunted, though, like it's… trapped, deep within him. Your unique bloodlines, whatever they may be, are no doubt why the Fates blessed you. You both appear to be otherworldly. Linked in a game beyond our realm. I must go discuss this with Atlas."

Kivi bows and heads to the balcony, where Atlas is working with Gearin and Fenwick.

This is too much. Fear curdles in my chest, latching its way up my ribs, threatening to pull me under. I don't know what I am, and I'm possibly not even from this world now.

*Great.*

I'm ready for this day to end. I want to go back to this morning when the biggest upset of my day was the aching between my legs. I let out an exasperated sigh.

"*I'm happy to indulge that thought once everyone is gone,*" a smoky voice purrs along my mind.

"*How can you think of that when she just told you that you are not entirely mortal either?*"

"*I didn't know my birth parents, and neither did you. It doesn't change anything. I'm just happy to be alive. I'm not going to let something I can do nothing about ruin my day. Are you?*"

"*I hate it when you're right.*" I smirk.

"*You secretly love it. Except this morning. You* really *did hate it, then.*" A devilish grin pulls at his lips.

The door bursts open as Orion, Juniper, and Vex carry in food, setting it on the table. Seraphina and Flint arrive next.

"The Wuvon attack was handled. It was a small scouting party. Easily dealt with." Seraph sighs with disappointment to see there's no liquor on the table.

"We are done with the wards!" Fenwick claps with excitement. "No one but members of your Zenith, or your dragons, can get in here unless they can survive a burning blast."

Highin and Cinder return next.

"We didn't see anyone who wasn't friendly." Cinder leans against the wall, flicking dust off his uniform.

"Good. Let us eat, and then we all need to get some well-deserved rest," Atlas says calmly.

It's uncomfortably quiet as we eat. I think we're all at a loss for what to say after the events of the day. As much as I appreciate the help of our Zenith, I can finally breathe once everyone leaves. Sølas falls asleep as soon as his head hits the pillow. He tries to pull me into him, but I can't lie still.

I twist and turn restlessly, wondering what I am, wondering who the dark voice that threatened me from Sølas' head belongs to.

Eventually, sleep comes for me, too.

I'm awoken by a kiss on my cheek. I vaguely recall muttering something in my sleep to Sølas. A sense of peace and happiness flowing through my soul at the words he said in response. His soft, full lips leaving another kiss on my temple before sleep claims me once more as he wraps me tighter in his arms.

# CHAPTER 55

Strange voices echo from around the corner of a crystal wall. Endless light spills through the refracting prisms of the entirely crystal facade, igniting a sea of glinting rainbows.

I step quietly, leaning closer to hear, stopping just outside the door.

"She grows more and more powerful by the day," a bright, feminine voice says.

"But will she be enough?" a darker female voice responds, silky with the cool undertones of a winter's night.

"She cannot take her final form until the bond is complete, to ensure she cannot be corrupted," gleams the bright voice, melodic like spring and sunlight.

"I am glad she's finally daring to dream. Her mother would be proud," a third, younger voice says, an odd undulating balance ringing within it.

"She has her mother's beauty and her father's temper," the darker voice responds.

"If she had killed him today, what would have happened, Endara?" the voice of life and light asks.

"She wouldn't have. However, we are lucky that, in his moment of weakness, he was not corrupted. Her light should keep him protected, although he almost used him to devour her," Endara responds. That name. I know that name from somewhere... It's the name of one of the twin sisters, the Fate of Endings.

*"He grows restless. We cannot lose this game, sisters," the younger voice responds. She must be Karma.*

*My senses prickle as a sudden silence clots the air.*

*"I sense her presence. The clever being has learned to Realmwalk. Shall we go meet the youngling?" The light voice has to be Baeságe, the Fate of Beginnings.*

*Realmwalk? What's that? And are they talking about me, or is there someone else here, too?*

*Padded footsteps resonate through the crystal floor, their vibrations moving towards me. The thundering beat of my heart drowns out the sounds around me as I lurch up, spinning into a sprint. Even if this is just a dream, the thought of meeting the fickle Fates and Karma doesn't sound like a good ending for me.*

*My darkness gnaws at my ribs, clawing at my mind, like she's trying to tell me something is off... like this may be more than a dream.*

*I dart around corners of endless hallways, not daring to stop. The crystalline architecture shifts into gold as I dash down a grand corridor. Two steps at time, hurtling down a gilded stairway. Right. Then left. Then right again. The gold vanishes, the walls and floors seamlessly transforming into black diamonds. Serrating pain nipping me beneath gasping inhales, yet I press on.*

*A bright light pierces the walls up ahead to my left, calling to me as I force my legs to expand their strides. I slide around the corner to a balcony, and without another thought...*

*I jump.*

*I fall through fluffy pink and blue clouds, spinning to take in the building I leapt from. A castle suspended in the air. One side: crystals of light and rainbows; the other: darkness and black diamonds. Pinned in the center is pure gold, a waterfall of starlight cascading down the middle. There's nothing else in sight; I can't even see the sun, yet everything is bright.*

*I tumble through endless clouds shifting colors. It would be beautiful if I could fly. I find myself wishing I was back in bed with Sølas, praying to any Celestials left I don't fall to my death.*

"Wake up!" A smoky voice whisks me from my dream. No. Not a dream. From walking in another realm? Ugh. So much for things going back to normal.

"Are you okay? You were burning up again." Sølas' voice is laced with fear. I rein in my magic instantly, terrified of potentially hurting him.

My magic scrapes along my veins, violently resisting being trapped more than ever before. Rippling waves of magic erupt along my skin. Patches of chaos, lightning, the elements, and starlight burst and disappear. Like they're trying to find a way out.

"Well, that's new," Sølas croons watching the various forms of magic crackle along my skin.

His fingers reach out, and I lurch back. "Don't touch me! I could hurt you again," I snap as the bond in my chest burns against the words that just left my lips.

"Asking me not to touch you hurts more than your magic ever could. I've treasured these last few weeks where you've let me in and dared to let me dream what it'll be like to have all of you. If you push me away now, I don't think I'd survive the heartbreak. I would bear it, though, if you decided you didn't want me... but I would have to leave. I cannot stomach the thought of being near you and not being able to touch you, to hold you, to kiss you, to love you with all of me." Longing and grief bleed through his voice, as if he truly believes I can ignore this bond after everything that's happened between us.

I lie down beside him, peering up at the storm of shadows torrenting in his moonlight eyes. The glow of black light has receded, just barely visible now. I reach out, tussling his loose curls to the side, then cupping my hand to that perfectly handsome face.

"I don't think I could stand the thought of you out of my sight for even one second. If you thought what I did was powerful yesterday, I would destroy entire worlds to bring you back to me. *You are mine.*"

"Destroy worlds for me, huh? May the universe find mercy when I have all of you. You will be a force unlike any other," he purrs with a smug smile that I steal right from his lips in a kiss.

We tumble around the bed. Our hands greedy and wild, as if we have never touched before, each kiss feeling as if it's the air we need to breathe. Like our lips hold the map to something ancient and trembling.

My hand drifts beneath his loose-fitting pants, and he stops me. Brows pinched with confusion, I meet his gaze, the bond telling me he desires me just as badly as I want him, if not more.

"I still feel your power coursing through my veins. It wants to come back to you; it doesn't care at what cost. As much as I love hearing my name breathy on your lips, I don't think I have it in me to stop when you want more. And I know you *always* want more." A sad smirk tugs at his lips as he looks up at the stars, lost in conflict.

"How can I promise you all of me if I don't even know what I am?" I murmur, admitting a new reason swirling around my head, since I can't blame it on not knowing how to love anymore. How could I after I felt like I was going to die watching the light fade from his soul when I took what was not mine to take?

"Apparently, I don't know what I am either. You'll need to come up with a better excuse than that, *Luxsula*." He gives me a knowing look, telling me he isn't going to let this revelation change anything between us.

"I nearly killed you." Guilt hangs heavy on each of my words.

"You wouldn't have if you had already accepted the bond, so don't even try to make that an excuse with me." Solas' tone needles at me with an unusual bite to it.

I push off him, lying beside him, staring up through the glass ceiling to the heavens.

"For someone who is so brave, ready to leap into danger, you certainly seem to enjoy acting like a coward when it comes to emotions. I was hoping you admitting your feelings out loud meant you'd finally be willing to give me all of you. Yet you seem insistent on tempting the Fates at this point."

"Things were so wonderful. And now, with everything that's happened, with not knowing who or what I am, what you are… everything feels so different and strange."

"It doesn't appear that our hearts feel any different to me. Dare to dream how even more lovely things could be. Do not let the darkness of the unknown smother you. I will keep reminding you until my last breath. Use the darkness to shine brighter, my *Luxsula*."

"That feels impossible now, knowing that I am hunted."

"Another excuse," he says dryly before pulling me in close to him. With his chin on my head, he continues, "I suppose I should be grateful that I will have more years than I ever expected to convince you to give me all of you. To help you face your fears until you run out of excuses to accept what I know you already know."

I can tell he's trying to be patient, but there's a loneliness in his voice that twists my heart.

He's right. I am a coward.

Kivi's remark about not knowing who my father is lashes my mind. This, combined with the ancient text from Emberhell that Atlas read, citing only one with demonic blood could wield Chaos Magic… suddenly, things make sense.

The blackness to my eyes, that darkness within me, why my Chaos Magic becomes empowered by destruction. I think about the odd dream I had that felt nothing like a dream. Their words about how we both are at risk of corruption. What if I accept the bond and our darkness together becomes too much?

I am a coward, paralyzed by fear.

One who isn't ready to know what it's like to love him as much as he's hopelessly in love with me, for I am afraid it may make me a monster. Or, even worse, make him the monster, like the evil voice vowing to destroy everything I hold dear when Sølas tried to pull power from me tonight without my consent.

What if my starlight isn't enough for the both of us?

# CHAPTER 56

"That smile of yours
Captivates my soul
Lost in your beautiful darkness
Seduced by spellbinding starlight eyes
Oh
But when you laugh
Not even my demons
Have a place to hide.

And when my own darkness threatens my soul,
You are my guiding light.
I will always be with you,
Until the end of time.
Instead of letting fear pull you from me,
Let our demons dance together.
For stars cannot shine without darkness."

Yours always,
Solas

My heart swells at the words etched on the parchment resting on my pillow, yet it does little to quell the aching bond with his distance. He does have a way of always making me shine brighter. I wonder where he's run off to; it's unlike him not to be here in the morning.

I rouse from bed, a smile kicking up on my lips. Sølas, of course, left breakfast warm on the table, more than enough for me and Pip, with hot kahvi on the nightstand beside me. It certainly would be easier not to fall for him, to keep him safe from me, if he wasn't so fucking perfect.

Pip zips around the room. His grace with flying almost rivals his skills of stealing almost every piece of my bacon. The rascal. I can't believe how much he's grown since I first met him; he's now the size of a small fox. I wonder how big he'll become.

A knock at the door jolts me from my thoughts. Before I can get up, Kissa barges in.

Her chartreuse eyes immediately dart to the note left on the bed. I lunge in front of her, trying to interrupt her view.

"Is that from loverboy? I can't *wait* to read it and find out why he can't walk you to class himself when he bloody shares a bed with you. Instead, waking me up early to come grab you. Since everyone is convinced you're a valuable weapon, I don't think they give you enough credit, insisting on an escort once more," Kissa snarks, prowling to get around me.

"I don't need an escort. I am no one's weapon but my own. Plus, it's not like Calais wouldn't be happy for some extra snacks if anyone makes a move against me. And that note is none of your business."

Using her feline grace, she dashes past me, snatching the note before leaping on top of my armoire, crouched and out of reach while she reads. Her cackle grates my ears as I shoot her a scowl.

"Of course he writes love poems to you. I'm surprised your distant, cold ass isn't suffocated by him. I'm starting to think the Fates gave you this Fated mate bond as a cruel joke!" She snickers, jumping down, tossing the poem at me.

I stuff it into the drawer of my nightstand, clenching my fist at her remark. Perhaps she's right; that would be more typical for my life. The ominous words from my dream last night bludgeon my brain on repeat. *We cannot lose this game.*

Fear seeps into my veins, constricting my breath in its grip, whittling at my marrow as it sinks into my insecurities. I'm terrified I'll fuck up in some important game I don't even know the rules to, potentially destroying Sølas' soul in the process.

His power may be shadows, but he's my light, my darkness to shine within.

Corruption. That was the word they used. Sølas' vibrant shadows turning to putrid pitch floods my vision. A silent scream notches in the back of my throat as I recall the ancient, dark voice carving my flesh from sinew, claws burrowing into my power with an endless hunger. What if it's all me? What if I'm what destroys him?

The brewing fear in my blood recoils, scattering. A splintering cry splits my lips as my world goes silent.

My eyes pop open, blinded by beams of endless light, fueled by a primordial energy surging down my throat, spitting acid through my vessels before igniting my golden markings ablaze. My feet lift off the ground, flesh liquefying before melting off my bones to reveal pure starlight. A voice that's not my own thrashes up my throat. Foreign, ancient, omnipotent.

*"Fear is the only limitation to your power. Fear will feed the corruption you dread. If you allow fear to control you, you have already lost the game before you've joined the fight. The fate of the universe rests in your hands. The choice is yours: fill it with your light, or watch as nothingness consumes it."*

The crushing power rips out of me, dumping me on the ground on all fours. My chest almost cleaves in two as I retch, hacking up increments of stardust, white shadows, light, and darkness.

Kissa pounces to my side, twisting my hair back. I suck in a treasured breath between spewing up more magic. That voice was unlike anything I've ever heard, the very lifeforce of everything coursing through me.

"Well, that wasn't ominous as fuck," Kissa hisses as she whistles, likely sending a message to our Zenith.

Shortly after, my assumption proves correct as the sound of my retching is interrupted by the voices of Atlas and Kivi, among others. The hair sways on my neck, and strong arms are instantly around me, brushing my sweat-matted hair.

"Who the fuck did this to her?" Sølas growls at Kissa. Shadows appear in front of me, leaving a bucket and cleaning up the mess on the floor.

"Don't you fucking growl at me! She's your fucking mate, not mine. You shouldn't have left her," Kissa sneers with a hiss.

Kivi tries to approach me but is met with a primal growl from Sølas.

My eyes snap to his, scrunched with annoyance. His outrageous need to protect me is understandable—I know it too well after yesterday—but he isn't helping.

His stiff shoulders relax, and Kivi dips over me. I'm back to vomiting, struggling to think through the pain of my guts writhing inside out and the magic pounding against my skull.

"It's natural for a mate to overreact seeing his bonded harmed." Highin preens his feathers nonchalantly.

"Well, it wasn't my fault. I was doing him a favor, escorting her to class." Kissa waves her hands dismissively.

"Kissa, please explain what happened since Savaé is clearly not well enough to do so." Atlas' calm tone eases the chaos.

"I made a joke about their mated bond being a cruel joke from the Fates, since she's always so cold and distant, and Sølas is leaving love poems on her pillow. Then… she looked bloody possessed. Light was coming out of her eyes and mouth. She was levitating off the floor. Her skin turned dark blue, except for starlight radiating from her golden markings. An ancient, powerful, and fucking terrifying voice spoke through her. It sounded… feminine. Talking about how fear is the only limitation to her power and something about the fucking fate of the universe being in her hands. Then, when the voice stopped, she started vomiting up pure magic. I've never seen anything like it before."

"Hah! Kissa pissed off the Fates before I did. You're wilder than I give ya credit for, kitty cat," Seraph mocks, quickly regretting it when she finds her neck in Kissa's claws.

"Call me kitty cat one more time, and you'll be meeting the Fates," Kissa hisses.

"You two, settle down. Don't make more healing work for Kivi. We are a team. Act like it," Orion snaps.

Kissa releases Seraph with a snarl. Orion stands over me with an assessing look on her face.

"Her Aura is a mess. The power radiating through it makes what she did yesterday look like child's play. No wonder she's vomiting up all that excess power: it's too much for one body to contain," Orion claims sympathetically.

"I warned you all not to tempt the Fates," Highin scoffs as he continues to preen his feathers, unamused.

"It wasn't the voice of the Fates. It was a warning from something else. Something… more powerful," I manage to whimper out between heaving up every shade of the rainbow, mixed with every known element.

"How would you know it was not a voice of the Fates? Perhaps Karma, then?" Atlas enquires.

"I heard them last night. In a dream," I mutter weakly.

"Kivi, what is she sick with? She sounds delirious." Kissa huffs, crossing her arms.

I stab her with a glare. After what she just witnessed, she has the nerve to call me delirious.

"She was burning up last night when I awoke her from a nightmare." Worry forming between Sølas' brows.

"Whatever is going on with her is beyond my powers to heal." Kivi's melodic voice trembles, racing my pounding heart even more. Nothing ever shakes her.

"Tell us about this nightmare," Atlas beckons.

In response, Sølas voice turns feral. "You can't be seriously asking her that when we just watched her vomit up a fucking piece of dirt that grew a flower and then died! Meanwhile, she's beyond Kivi's help. As our Savant, I thought you were the smartest one of us."

"I understand your need to protect her, but we have minutes to figure out what is going on before we have to get her to class."

"You've lost your mind if you think I am taking her to class like this!" Sølas roars.

"The last thing we need is the Chancellor's attention on us, any more than it is already. I doubt after Winx's display yesterday she's willing to help us again. What do you think they'll do if they discover she is an immortal being? Do you think they will care that you are her Fated mate? They will keep her locked away. I shudder to think how valuable they will consider her for *Bloodline pairings*." Atlas' voice wavers on his last words, sending a cold shiver crawling like a spider down my spine.

Sølas' arms tighten around me as he whispers, "You don't need to tell them anything." His closeness settles the bond in my chest.

"Why can't you just read her thoughts?" Highin asks.

"Her head's been fuzzy and hard to read since I woke her from the nightmare. I was on my way to find Kivi to ask her to examine her during lunch today. Then, I couldn't feel her for a moment. I imagine that's when whatever took over her body happened. I rushed over here as quickly as I could. All I can sense right now is her pain. It just sounds like… rushing water roaring through her thoughts."

"Savaé, how did you know it wasn't the Fates' voices?" Orion says softly. She's now down by my side, thrumming small circles on my back. My shields are down. I'm unable to focus keeping them up through whatever's going on with my body. This allows Orion to send soothing energy into me. She's taking on some of the pain I'm experiencing to help make things more manageable, so I can speak. Another thing Sølas would be able to do if I accept the bond.

"I thought it was a dream, but it felt like I was actually there. I heard the voices of the Fates and Karma." My voice barely a whisper. The vomiting stops, and I curl up into Sølas, whose back is leaning against the bed.

He continues to stroke my hair, lowering his head over mine. "Why didn't you tell me last night?"

"Too much has changed already. I just want things to go back to normal. I was hoping it was just a strange dream," I muster out through chattering teeth, my skin frosting with a thin layer of ice.

Sølas quickly pulls down the blanket from the bed and wraps it around me.

Pip also jumps in, curling into a scarf around my neck, while Cinder heats the air in the room.

"We will continue this discussion later. Get her up and dressed for class. Sølas and Seraphina, combine your magic to get her cleaned up," Atlas commands.

"She's shivering and looks pale as a ghost," Sølas snarls, pulling me in tighter.

"So far as we can tell, she is an immortal being. If she's strong enough to survive whatever happened to her, she should heal quickly enough," Atlas replies dryly, clearly done with Sølas' protective nature.

"And whatever being left her like that was ancient and even more powerful," Sølas grumbles, more to himself than anyone else.

"It is my job to think of all possible outcomes of our actions as a Zenith. To ensure all of our safety, including hers. That's an order, and I expect you to obey it. If she's going to cause you to be insubordinate, we have an entirely new issue to discuss." Atlas' maroon eyes narrow on Sølas.

"I'm okay. I'm sure with their help I can make it to class. We don't have much time. Let's not waste it arguing," I muster, wobbling as I try to stand.

Sølas helps me up, and Seraph grabs my other arm, leading me into the bathroom. They snap their fingers, and I'm being bathed and dressed at the same time. I brush my teeth quickly, glancing up in the mirror to confirm I look as great as I feel. *Like shit.*

"You look stunning, as always," a smoky voice coos from beside me with a kiss on my temple. I can't help but lean into him.

I tap Pip; four cobalt eyes open along my scarf.

"I need you on my wrist, little buddy." A raspy whisper leaves my lips. Pip scurries to grab Dream Singer, and in a blast of light, he shifts into his typical bracer on my wrist.

"Has Calais said anything?" Sølas asks.

"*I am sorry, Nebulight. Even Scáil and I do not know what happened. My bond to you was also disrupted during the event. Which, to our knowledge, should not be possible.*" Calais' tone is all too gentle. When she chooses to be kind, I find it off-putting, so unlike her. It also doesn't make the blow of her words any less. I'm suddenly going to be sick again. Too much is unknown. Too much has changed too quickly.

After losing Sully, my life plan was simple: become an Ellian Knight, and die on the battlefield in glory. I wasn't meant to be some unknown immortal being. I definitely wasn't training to save the universe. I didn't even have lofty goals for my career in the Golden Legion. I just wanted to slaughter monsters until they were all gone or I died doing what I was good at. But I know if Sully were here, he'd tell me that nothing has really changed in my plan. He'd give me some smartass, sage comment.

I can hear his husky and warm voice now. "*Your mission is still the same; the timetable and extent have just expanded. I trained you to become a weapon so no one would ever hurt you again. Defend those who cannot defend themselves, as you once couldn't. Fight for a better tomorrow. Fight for the light beaming within your darkness. This is just another monster to slay. Find its weakness, and do what you do best. Unleash your fury.*"

The thought kicks up my lips at one end.

"There she is," Sølas' smoky voice muses next to me. I can hear the smug smirk on his lips without even looking at him. He's drawing idle circles on my lower back, inspecting me, trying to figure out what I'm thinking now that my thoughts are unclear.

I straighten my shoulders and gaze at myself in the mirror. I drag my power from its infinite well, reinforcing my veins, my bones, my muscles to give me strength for today.

As my magic courses through me, my translucent hair begins shimmering. Appearing to move on phantom winds, twinkling like starlight. *Mmm, that's a little too much.* I rein in my magic, my chest-length hair returning to its typical, unnatural, wraith-like demeanor.

A wraith. Hmm. I suppose I am more like one than I realize. Perhaps that's where my darkness comes from—an ethereal harbinger of death. A weapon for the Fates to wield in their endless games.

If they want me to become a wraith, a weapon? *Done.*

"I'm not gonna lie. That feral look she has is turning me on," Seraph says with a rakish grin teasing her lips.

Sølas curses under his breath, knowing his best friend all too well.

In being born female, I've learned to hone more than just metal and magic into weapons.

I prowl right up to Seraph, tracing my finger down the corded muscle of her neck, my voice sultry and low. "He gets rather possessive over me, particularly when thoughts of all three of us in a bed run wild through my mind. Luckily for you, he can't read my thoughts right now." I smirk with a wink.

Sølas is immediately behind me, growling down my neck, "That wicked mouth of yours is going to be the death of me. Where has this sudden surge of energy come from, my starlight?"

I turn in his arms to face him. "If the Fates want me to be a weapon in their game, then I shall become one. Yet I shall be my only wielder."

"I would expect nothing less. And where does this game leave me?" Sølas purrs, eyes darkening with desire and pride.

"Beside me, I hope, continuing to sharpen my edges and inspiring me to see all that I can be."

"Consider it done." Sealing his promise on my lips with a burning kiss, withering all my fears into nothingness.

"As much as I hate to break up this skraith, tender moment… We need to go, unless you want to find out what Atlas' wrath looks like." Seraph arches a brow.

I huff a laugh, trying to envision an angry Atlas as I follow her out of the bathroom.

Kissa links my arm as we make it out the door from my room. "Glad to see you have your color back. Next time we hang out, can it be just us, without an all-powerful being possessing you?"

I shoot her a side-eyed glare, letting her know exactly how unamused I am with her unreasonable ask.

Kissa cackles. "It was worth a shot. I never thought I'd prefer going back to a time when finding you covered in others' blood was a preferable outcome."

"I have a feeling that'll still be a regular occurrence, don't you fret," I sarcastically croon, tapping her cat-like nose, rousing a hiss from her lips. A giggle bubbles from my chest before it's muffled by the blooming aching of the bond.

Without even searching for him, Sølas is instantly by my side, soothing my soul.

"Missing me already, *Luxsula*?" he says with far too much confidence in his tone. I know whatever I feel is tenfold for him.

"Wouldn't you like to know?" I taunt. It's obvious he doesn't enjoy the lack of being able to read my thoughts clearly.

"Be careful. I'd hate to see you trip and stumble down these steps." A devilish grin curls on his face.

"You wouldn't dare! If I died, so would you," I say with shock those words even left his mouth.

"Apparently, you're immortal." He winks. "However, I'd happily follow you into death... but you're right, I wouldn't. I could never hurt you. I'm slightly appalled you thought I would."

"I didn't."

"The shock in your face says otherwise." He smirks.

"Careful, or maybe I'll slip just to torture you," I snark as I pretend to stumble.

Sølas panics, encasing me in shadows. The rest of the walk, he stubbornly refuses to uncoil his arm from around my waist.

# CHAPTER 57

A symphony of anxious chatter clots the auditorium's air after yesterday's attack. I plop down, melting into my seat, grateful to be off my unsteady feet. I almost throttled Sølas after the sixth time he asked if I was sure I didn't want him to carry me. I'd never fucking live that down, being carried into class like a princess or someone too weak to merit being here—never mind being in the leading Zenith Wing assignment.

Dread curls along my spine as Professor Gloomnight's parchment and gold wings flutter frantically, like she's readying herself to lurch from a predator's maw.

"Good morning, everyone. We have decided to move up Fortress Battle… to today. Given the scouting party that occurred last night, we think it's safest to move this event up even further. This way, you will not be so close to the wards when there's a chance of another attack."

Murmurs crescendo into an uproar, curdling the room with palpable panic. Typically, this event is held as a final at the end of the school year, assessing our progress and team dynamics.

Professor Gloomnight raises her pale, dusted hand, conducting the crowd into silence.

"This battle pits each Wing against one another. The goal: whoever brings the spelled flying Golden Pearl to the top of Rayea's Fortress wins. However, your Chivalry cannot simply fly it to the top. It must be passed off to your Ground Units battling in the field in front of the fortress. This is a test of your ability to work together as a team."

Sølas grips my hand. "If you are not feeling up to this, I will find a way to get out of it."

I shrug in response. "I suppose it's time we figure out how strong I really am."

"There's that reckless confidence from when we first met. Glad to see it's finally back. Celestials, it's sexy," he purrs with a smirk I'd love to kiss off his full lips.

Professor Gloomnight continues, "There will be no deadly blows. This is about magical restraint, flight dynamics, and team coordination. Primary Command will go first. Please note, there is a patch of Blackwood near this location. Should a member fall into the area, there will be no search and rescue; consider their life forfeit. Summon your flying magical creatures to the southern field. Professor Reska will lead you to the northern region around the stronghold and release the Golden Pearl. This will signal the start of the game, which is meant to be competitive and fun. There's no benefit to losing your life in this battle. You are dismissed. May the games begin!" She bows before darting off stage. Clearly having no intention of answering questions about the attack last night.

We make our way to the field, my Zenith encircling me, adopting a new walking formation, as if someone might spring an attack at any moment. Just as I'm about to sling a snide comment, Calais's unease washes over me, twisting me up with worry the closer I get to her.

She flaps her four enormous wings, constantly shifting her weight like a pinned-down, wild animal.

I stroke the iridescent scales of her leg, shifting colors with her every movement.

*"We will be okay,"* I hum, trying to soothe her.

*"They are being reckless. I have half a mind to set your professors and the Chancellor on fire in the hope their replacements have more sense."* She huffs, smoke billowing from her nostrils. *"Let's go before I lose my last thread of control and do exactly that."*

I laugh while summoning my air magic to glide onto her back.

"Save that fury for the battle. I want to win this game today," I say, giving her a reassuring pat on the neck. Which I immediately regret as she takes off like a bat out of Emberhell towards the sky, almost catapulting off with only one hand gripping on. I cast air magic to brace myself down towards her body against her breakneck speed.

She finally slows down, and the rest of our Zenith catches up, shifting into formation once more. Calais and I are at the top, drifting in and out of the clouds dotting the sky, her iridescent scales shifting to blend in. I set my Chaos Magic free, charging the atmosphere. Hot air smashes into cold; lightning erupts, weaving into Calais' conductor spikes.

I tip over to see Sølas in the middle of our five-pointed star. To his right is a red wyvern with an elongated snout, giving it a mixed look between a wolf and a lion. Its warm red colors match its rider, Vex, with her vermilion skin. Her horns of her Infernai descent are rounded to her skull compared to the long straight ones of her wyvern. In its merlot mane, bat ears twitch in all directions.

Vex is positioned with the best tactical view to ensure the best use of her Battlesense Arcane Glyph, marked by a silver infinity symbol on the back of her neck. She coordinates her random glimpses of battle with Atlas to determine our next move. Reserving her rare Chronosense for only the direst of circumstances, given how draining it is on her magic.

Just below whirls a mess of forest-green braids perched on an eddying kaleidoscope of colors: Juniper flying on her Hypnosis Drake. She's situated closer to the ground to make use of her Naturalist abilities.

Cleaving the air next to her is a chimera of teal and indigo with Kissa's feline form on top. Above her, to Sølas' left, Cinder rides a black phoenix. An epic, fire-powered assault team. But for today's game, he'll be playing a more defensive role.

Professor Reska commands the Chivalries to hold their current positions while the rest of the Ground Units are dropped off by Pegasuses at the edge of the battlefield clearing before Rayea's Stronghold.

The point of this Fortress Battle game is to work together with your Wing as a cohesive air-ground team, outsmarting your opponents to win. No one strong player can triumph; it takes each member working in seamless tandem.

*We are one or none at all.*

Normally, we'd have multiple drills in mock scenarios in the Warded Hollow prior to the game to prepare us as a team, learning how to play to each other's strengths and weaknesses in a fight. This year, we won't be gifted that luxury. Instead, we'll be relying on a handful of practice sessions in the Warded Hollow combined with everything my Zenith has already faced because of me.

The corner of my mouth kicks up. We've been forged into more than just a team by facing those challenges together. In my newfound, reckless hope, I see us more akin to a family, bound together by adversity rather than blood.

I raise my golden mental shields, reinforcing them while only partially shielding my Fated mate bond to Sølas. It will only serve as a distraction to feel each other's emotions during the battle and risk faltering our mental shields for a Persuasive to take advantage of.

Crisp air charged with electricity puffs up my lungs, arcing lightning through my veins, mind poised to strike. The weight of the universe may be on my shoulders, but today… today is a game I know the rules to. Today is a game I know exactly how to play.

Time to make Sully proud, using everything he taught me.

I press my button on my Rune Tech ring. Magic zaps a communication link to my brain, allowing us to speak at will to our Zenith.

"Reska is behind us. When she releases the Golden Pearl, Sølas should Shadowweave with Scáil to claim it, then portal it to me. I've charged the clouds with lightning, and I doubt anyone will risk getting too close. I'll get it to the field. Cinder, Juniper, and Kissa should fly ahead to prepare for when I descend from the clouds, losing my protection," I suggest with the few minutes we have to plan.

Juniper replies hesitantly, "We shouldn't break up. Your plan puts too much risk on you. Plus, you can't strike a deadly blow, which means they'll be willing to risk your lightning."

"They'll be expecting us to stay together as trained. Splitting apart allows us the advantage during descent. Sølas will be with me. Have Cinder stay slightly behind you two, giving me extra cover." Attempting to reassure Juniper before continuing my plotting.

"Orion, can you create an illusion as I fly out of the clouds?"

"If you're close enough, I can. Whatcha have in mind?" Orion's voice curves with a devious smirk.

"I want you to create as many copies as you can of Calais and I. Every other Wing will be gunning for me once I leave the protection of lightning-charged clouds."

Atlas interjects, "Clever. However, I'm wary of it being just you and Sølas. You are both driven to protect one another by the bond. If something were to happen, you could lose sight of the objective. Kissa, stay back with them and shift into the form of Calais; her natural form will absorb any lightning. This also adds another target to throw them off—one that can actually interject if something goes wrong, unlike Orion's illusions."

It's a good idea, a great fail-safe for my plan. My team continues to impress me with our abilities to complement one another, forging us stronger as a whole.

"Why do I always get stuck with the lovebirds? Sitting next to them in class is punishment enough," Kissa groans.

"Quit your whining, pretty kitty, or we'll find out how powerful my shifting powers are," Seraphina teases, only to be met with a growling hiss from Kissa.

I roll my eyes. "You two really need to fuck and make up later. Sølas, cover us in shadows. Kissa, fly up here, and shift. Orion, can you create one illusion of Kissa riding in formation while Fenwick shields you so you can focus?"

"You sneaky little vixen. This way they'll think Kissa as Calais is the illusion," Orion muses.

"Precisely," I purr.

"*Fuck, you're sexy right now,*" a smoky voice growls along my mind.

A lethal grin pins my lips. "*I do love to play... and win,*" I purr right back as shadows cloak our entire Chivalry, and Kissa joins my side.

My powers seep out, clotting the clouds to veil her Chimera. Kissa bounds off, blinking into an exact replica of Calais soaring next to me. Kissa-as-Calais sends us a wink.

The dragon below me rumbles.

"*I am one of a kind,*" Calais growls.

I laugh. "*You still are. Don't worry; Scáil won't be running off with her.*" In response, Calais rolls, sending me spiraling to hold my grip. "*Okay, I deserved that.*" I smile as the shadows retreat.

"Let the games begin!" Professor Reska's voice howls on the wind. She slings the Golden Pearl high into the air. Wings burst from the sides as it whizzes about.

The fastest riders from every Wing dodge and dive for it, erupting a cacophony of roars and snappy maws. But they're no match for Sølas. He and Scáil blot out of the shadows, snatching the orb with a sly wink.

I bite my bottom lip, concealing my blooming smile. *That's* my *handsomely smug mate.*

Sølas unfurls out of a cloud of shadows below me. "*Miss me?*"

"*Hardly.*" I smirk, the bond in my chest beaming at his proximity.

He tosses the Pearl to me, and I quickly tuck it under my arm. Calais shreds through the sky, wings beating furiously towards our target.

"Several attacks incoming," Vex signals.

My lashes drift shut, power rippling out, undulating around each ensign colliding into my sphere of chaos. I meet their advances with crackling lightning and hailing ice daggers, just close enough to injure without risking deadly blows.

A ball of fire sends Calais dipping into a coordinated trap of vines curling up her legs. Before they have a chance to cinch down, Cinder's amber flames lick up, nothing but ash left flitting in the gust of her wings.

Seeing the almost-success of a coordinated effort spurs the other Wings to work in tandem to take us down. The smell of singed hair clots my nostrils as I duck, narrowly missing a volley of blue flames as Calais spins, and Sølas sends out a shadow shield to block both versions of Calais' wings from a blast of wing-freezing ice. The world whirls around me as I grit my teeth, fighting the Persuasive clawing at my mind while manipulation magic yanks at the Golden Pearl my arm flexes around.

Patience fraying, I unshackle my Chaos Magic. Devouring power rips out of me, greedily feasting on the slew of magical attacks slung at me. Nothing makes it through my aura of destruction.

Until one particularly brave ensign appears behind me out of a water portal. I spell the Golden Pearl to lock into Calais' riding spikes as I bound to my feet.

"Seraph, way to not tell me Visci can portal. Why are you always using Sølas' Shadowwalking?" I grit out, turning to face my new opponent.

"C'mon, it's way more badass appearing out of the shadows. Plus, it's not worth the power sink. Push that sneaky bitch to use her magic, and she'll tire out fast," Seraph responds.

A petite female slinks towards me, whipping navy curls framing a round face of deep brown. Her eyes flare dark blue, giving her away as a Visci, as if the water portal hadn't already. My blows need to focus on making her bend her body like water, draining her magic reserves.

Lightning arcs out, reinforcing my shield of Chaos Magic to prevent any attacks from distracting me, leaving all my focus for the tricky-as-fuck opponent before me.

The air cries, cleaving along the blades of my slinging daggers, testing her skills. Her body warps, bending into liquid, contorting into hollow spaces as my blades zip through without a drop of blood marring their edges. *Fuck. She's good.*

"*Unleash your wild darkness, Luxsula,*" Sølas beckons, stirring my darkness from her slumber, unfurling ravenous chaos to course through my veins, steeling my nerves.

As the Visci solidifies once more, a maniacal smile crooks up, twisting her face, which I return, sinking into the well of darkness I reserve for fighting.

My head snaps to the side, a rush of air nipping at my cheek from the dagger slicing by. I leap up, dodging two more aimed for my legs, instead clinking off of Calais' scales. Chaos lashes out around my arm, obliterating her next blade as I knock it away, barely in time to see another one heading straight for my abdomen. My spine snaps back, bending into a back handspring, narrowly missing my guts being skewered.

Not wasting another second, I lunge for her, ripping my short swords from my back. Each strike is met with a *clang* of her own blade or the cool whoosh of air as she melts her body away from my piercing blow.

Back and forward, we dance, weaving between Calais' lightning-rod spikes, each of us equally trained. Our chests heave in short pants of exhaustion. My nostrils flaring on the metal tang from the few nicks that mar our forearms.

"*We're approaching the field. Act fast, or I'm spinning you both off of me and winning this game myself,*" Calais grumbles.

I spare a glance to take note of our position. We're getting close to the field. Too close. *Son of a bitch.*

I need to end this.

My darkness scrapes along my veins, lashing my insides in its plea for boundless release. I can't strike her with lightning without risking her life and forfeiting our win. I just need to slow her down.

Frost prickles out from my boots. Creeping and crawling along Calias' scales as I distract the Visci with a volley of sword strikes. Her eyes go wide, watching my exhale billow a white puff in the frigid shift. Ice races up her legs as I coat Calais and myself in starlight to keep us from freezing.

I plunge the temperature further and further; snow hardens to hail, pummeling us in its onslaught. The Visci backpedals, ice splintering in her attempt to flee, but her movements are too sluggish, her flesh taking on a blue hue as blood retreats to her core.

A serpentine smile coils on my lips as I revel in the pure horror frosted across her features. I summon a cloud of purple and indigo stardust, beckoning it to twist and swirl around her.

*Hope this fucking works.*

Her wriggling ceases, too cold to move from my icy grasp. I imagine the courtyard of Gildorea, shooting her a knowing wink as she vanishes before my eyes into the stardust.

I pray to the Celestials that she ends up where I want her. I've only used my ability to portal once. If I fail and hurt her—or even worse, lose her— we'll lose the game, and I'll be facing expulsion.

"Celestials, you're more of a show-off than the shadow prick!" Kissa snarls but fails to hide her amused undertone.

"This shadow prick needs you two to focus. We're almost at the field," Sølas tsks.

I return them both a wicked grin as I slide into my seat and prepare for descent, placing the Golden Pearl back under my arm for quick maneuvers. I drag down the clouds with us, providing as much cover as I can for as long as possible.

Then, five illusions of Calais appear around us, spurring several grumbling huffs of annoyance from my dragon. I give her ego a sardonic pat.

*"Insufferable."*

My chuckle falls silent as the battle ensuing below me bleeds into view.

A dome of green light erupts from Gearin's palm, a runic protection shield covering him, Kivi, and Orion. The latter is deeply focused on maintaining the illusion of multiple replicas of Calais around me.

The skies above them blaze in amber and orange fire, Cinder and his black phoenix single-handedly controlling the air from Wings trying to halt our Ground Unit's advance.

On the battlefield, Flint lands a devastating side hook, knocking out a Pyro casting for Cinder. He smashes through a stone wall blocking my Zenith's path like it's glass. A sword slashes down on Flint's shoulder, fracturing as it ricochets off his marble skin. Leaving the ensign distracted as

Eko appears out of his spectral form to knock him unconscious before shifting back into the ether.

Flint's advance is met with a wall of vines, expanding to encircle my Zenith. Juniper races ahead but won't get there in time. Fenwick casts a wall of plasma to scorch the twisting roots.

"Wait!" Vex's shrill command freezes Fenwick. "Ugh, those brats are waiting in ambush on the other side. They're using the fog to hide their movements. My Battlesense is leaning to them trying to take out sweet baby Flint first."

Atlas relays orders. "Let Flint be bound, keeping them occupied while Seraph catches up. Highin, set him free while Juniper controls the crowd, creating a straight path towards the tower. Then, Juniper, you need to find the other Naturalist and use your hypnosis flowers to stun them, taking them out of play so they can't reverse your magic."

Golden plasma waves over the wall, leaving nothing but ash in Fenwick's wake. A group of ensigns leaps out of the smoke. Vines whip out, coiling around Flint's wrists and knees, crumpling him to the ground. The brunette female with buzzed sides from my third trial prowls out of the fog while a male lassos his neck in a chokehold.

I use my Rune Tech ring to warn my team. "The female approaching Flint is a Persuasive. Don't let her get her hands on him!"

Highin hovers on his wings above our Zenith, dodging attacks while nocking five arrows in quick succession. The first arrow lands at the toe of the Persuasive, her scream piercing the air. The rest of the arrows perfectly slice through Flint's bindings while Eko's spectral blades tear through the vines that snap up to replace them.

Meanwhile, Seraph sneaks in, bashing the hilt of her war axe over the male restraining Flint. Rays of light whip out from Fenwick, holding back the attackers from advancing as the entire ground before Rayea's Fortress starts to shift.

Towering walls of thorny vines erupt, caging the other combatants, weaving them off in a maze of blooming hypnosis flowers. Fenwick bubbles a shield of golden light around Flint, Eko, and Seraphina, protecting them from the floral hypnosis scent now permeating the air.

"Why stun just one when I can stun them all?" Juniper giggles.

Atlas sighs at his plan going awry, but luckily, Fenwick's shield holds as our team quickly advances to the door of Rayea's Fortress.

"Savaé, duck!" Vex screeches. My eyes snapping up to see Chet on his Poison Dart Draco hurtling towards us. A storm of venomous quills blot the air, raining in all directions to weed out the illusions.

Calais banks left to avoid the barrage of quills coming for us. Her new position leaves them aiming for her chest. A flashing memory skitters across my mind. The new, small scale on her chest, exposing her soft flesh below from giving me her old one to forge the greatsword.

I summon Dream Singer from my bracer with a tap, channel all the wind I can from around me through her blade, and aim it down on Calais' wings, sending us spiraling right. I hear her snapping something at me, but I quickly slam the crescent-moon window of our bond shut in my mind.

I have to stay focused. Chet has already caught us off guard once.

Chet's now fully aware of who his real target is, but instead of coming for me, he's set on a new prize.

I follow his line of sight to Sølas, whose previous position below me is now exposed from our new flight adjustment. His gaze is locked on me—like an idiot too focused on the survival of his mate!

*"Shadowwalk now!"* I scream down our shared tether. I glimpse the poisonous quill bead in crimson as it hits Sølas' face right as he and Scáil disappear into the shadows.

I frantically search below me, lowering my shields to figure out where he portaled to. The poison will disrupt his magic, rendering it hard to control, if he can at all.

I can't see his velvet ribbons to lead me to where he is, but… *I feel him.*

I gaze down to my right to see him and Scáil tumbling out of control towards the Blackwood.

*No!*

This is fucking terrible. An absolute living nightmare.

Chet is hurtling right for them. *Okay, worse than a nightmare.* Why is he after him? My heart pounds into my throat. Did he somehow find out he's my mate?

I send a gale-force wind ripping with ice daggers at Chet and his Draco. A curdled shriek frays the air as icicles shred its wings. They flail. The Draco's tattered flesh beats frantically but fails to generate lift. They spiral off course, crash landing on the outskirts of the Blackwood.

"Kissa, think fast!" I chuck the Golden Pearl towards her, catching it in her talons as she blinks into a large white hawk.

"What the fuck are you doing?" she growls.

"Saving my mate… again." A humorless laugh escapes me as I yet again put him in danger.

"Absolutely not! Sølas and Scáil are strong. They will fight their way out or be lost to our Zenith," Atlas commands.

*"Your Savant is right. As long as they stay together, they will escape,"* Calais barks, but her terror bleeds through the bond.

Before I can think about it, my mental shields thrust up, blocking everyone out as I dissolve into mist.

Every molecule of my being vibrates in the shattering roar Calais unleashes. I know she wants to save her mate too, but I'm still struggling with the guilt from almost killing Sølas yesterday. I can't fail him today. I won't survive it. I can't fail him like I failed Sully.

I float down to the patch of barren forest, ripped raw from where Scáil crash-landed. A lacerated wail rips from my throat as I combust back into my corporeal form.

Blood and feathers. So much blood drips down the snapped corpses of tree trunks, smattered in frayed and fractured raven feathers. My heart pounds, bludgeoning itself in bruises against my ribs. I worry my bottom lip, fighting the tears prickling at the back of my eyes.

This is bad.

Really bad.

My legs break into a sprint, following the path of caved-in, broken trees, slinging Dream Singer back to my bracer to pick up speed. I let my shields fall once more so I can feel Sølas while stuffing my Rune Tech ring into my pocket. The team is already poised to finish their objective without me.

Sølas' velvet ribbons flutter distantly in my mind. I gasp in relief, knowing he's alive.

*"Savaé, get out of the Blackwood this fucking instant!"* Calais roars.

*"I'm coming, Sølas. Just stay safe until I get to you,"* I plead down our bond.

*"Savaé! No! You can't be here. Get out now."* His words are drenched in desperation. I have to tell him.

I have to make him understand why I came. The moment his perfect blood glimmered on that quill… I felt it. I knew it.

My world unraveling before me, all my dreams fading into grey pastel.

My heart was so lost, deep in a bottomless pit of darkness, hidden in a prickly maze of ice. Yet he never gave up. Slowly weaving unconditional warmth and light between my ribs, curling it around my soul in his protective embrace. Despite my protests that I could never be loved, he cracked my chest open anyway. Showing me my limping heart still beats, still loves. And when I held her in my hands—wrapped in a stringy, golden mess of Sølas' attempts to heal her—I gazed down to see she had been painfully waiting for him all along.

His icy moonlight eyes, the reflection of my soul, my other half looking back at me. While the gold in mine is his endless love for me.

I've always had to be strong, but with him… He pinned my fears against the wall, creating a safe place for my soul to breathe, to rest. In the sanctuary of him, he stripped me of my armor and snarling mask, baring everything I can be, a version of me I never dared to dream of. He's shown me how to swim rather than drown in the darkness, wielding it to create my own light, shining even brighter.

He lets me know what it is to be loved. Unwaveringly and unconditionally.

To live rather than just survive.

I've had just a taste, and now I can't imagine a better way to spend my newfound immortality, loving the darkness like only the stars know how. Endings and beginnings. Light and darkness. Shattered and whole.

I know now why I've always felt fractured, until I let him in. He is my missing piece, my other half, and with him, he shall have all of me. Silver tears stream down my cheeks as my lungs burn and ache, craving to be filled with the scent of amber and spruce.

To feel the home we share in one another's arms.

To be blessed by his rapturous kiss on my lips.

*"I love you. I promise all—"*

The silent words fall from my mind as the Blackwood morphs and whirls around me, revealing a dense canopy of crimson strangling the light above me.

Oh *no*.

He's fucking right.

I should not be *here*.

# CHAPTER 58

No. No. *No.*

I reach for my mental shields as realization sinks in.

*Snap.*

I whip around to the sound of the breaking branch behind me, throwing everything I have into my shields…

But I'm too late.

*Too fucking late.*

A fanged leer hangs like a crescent moon in the shadows. Painted across the plumb lips of the pale figure prowling from the darkness… as day becomes night.

Black mist coils around me, seeping into my pores. I try to run, only for my eyes to widen. I'm frozen, every single muscle in my arms and legs unmoving.

My eyelids clasp shut on prickling tears as I reach for my power, only to find it just out of reach. All the windows in my mind are sealed shut, a black mist hovering over the locks. I can't even move my body within my own fucking mind.

Talons pierce into the moonlight, retracting into nails along a pale hand; shadows of twisting vines in crimson and black snake along her flesh. I swallow the terror racing through my veins.

*Wuvon.*

Her eyes meet mine. No pupils, just crimson dusted in flecks of light, as if the night sky were drenched in blood. Long, black, metallic hair dips into the light, sharp as the features it frames.

She's stunning.

Ash flints on a black mist, ebbing and eddying, like a rolling fog around her. Her voice severs the silence. Smooth as silk. Fine as ash. A lulling, venomous entrance.

"My, oh, my. Look at what a pretty thing I've found! Lurking far too deep in the Blackwood. What do we have here?"

I try to wriggle out of her compulsion, but her grip only tightens. Talons tap and scrape my golden mental shields. Gouging in. Cracks splintering across gold, like too much pressure on thin ice.

"Get the fuck out of my head!" I snarl.

"Tsk, tsk. Don't bother, my pretty little thing. I've caught you in my spiderweb, and you have nowhere to run."

The tone of her voice curving up at the end with pure delight, knowing I'm trapped. Perfectly matching her serpentine smile, revealing sharp, pronounced canines, leering to carve me up for her feast.

Something coiling around my ankles drags my gaze down. Vines mirroring the crimson night sky reflected in her eyes twist into chains protruding with thorns. Yet the spikes don't bite into skin as they curl and crawl up my body. Snaking around my neck, they wrap around my face, suffocating me.

A serrated gasp slits up my throat, flesh-searing pain whipping and ripping through my mind, my golden shields blazing to ash. My lashes pop open to find myself in the crimson night sky of her eyes, teleported into another reality altogether, another dimension.

A mindtrap.

Thorny chains retreat, binding my wrists and ankles as I'm splayed apart.

She circles me, a sea serpent stalking its prey. Her presence presses into mine, dominating me. Her silky hum slithers down my skin in a wicked caress.

"My, what an interesting catch I have here." Her voice low and sultry as she purrs with delight.

Eyes wide, screams trapped in my frozen throat, I watch my armor fracture off my body, shattering into a thousand pieces. Leaving me with nothing but the bands around my breasts and the briefs on my hips.

Her nail elongates into a talon, scraping into the gold marking my flesh. She twirls her finger through my iridescent hair as she looks me dead in the eyes. Her irises take shape. Gold slit with vertical pupils, swirling with ash. A golden blaze of wildfires, destruction. Endings.

"Lumaé Nasceá. Our little immortal Celestial has come to claim her reign once more," she hisses through a maniacal smile. Followed by a cackle that has me questioning her sanity. Her words mince my brain. Is she talking about our prior Celestial or me? I'm still not entirely sure what I am.

I summon just enough movement to spit out, "If you're going to kill me, get it over with. I don't like being played with." Banking on Kivi's theories about my being immortal.

"Oh, but I do so love playing with you. The games we shall play! The wars we shall wage," she croons, stepping around me like a vulture ready to devour its carrion prize.

She sucks on her fang, pausing before she tsks, tapping me on the nose. "My, oh, my, you have no idea what you are."

My lip curls into a snarl. I open my mouth to respond that I don't need to know what I am to kill her, only to find it frozen, too.

Her head leans in, lips brushing against my ear. My nostrils flare, drowning in her scent of wood ash and moonlight magnolias.

"Oh, but, my dear, you are far too valuable to kill! And much more meaningful *alive*." Her sultry voice of silk licks down my bare skin, crackling my power, but I can't reach it. This dimension seemingly keeping it out of reach. I can feel the separation while my magic struggles to fight its way back to me.

She grasps my chin with her fingers, yanking my attention back to her.

"We have been waiting many millennia for you. Icarus felt your presence come into the world. We searched but couldn't find you. As if you were hidden from us." She snarls the last words, clearly disgruntled about that bit.

"No doubt the work of Seer. Tricky little fucks can even hide from the Fates." She clicks her tongue before her voice slips into silk and sultry. "And then your magic called to me, drawing me to you. As we are made for one another. Now here you are, having walked right into my beckoning lap."

A growl rumbles from my chest. She's not made for me! How dare she? Her words pinching my heartbeats in palpitations of terror as I think of Sølas, my mate. If I'm facing her, he's no doubt dealing with a Wuvon of his own. I need to get to him.

The lady of silk and night stiffens at my thoughts, gaze drifting down to his mark of shadows swirling beneath the bands of my chest.

"I see someone's already marked your heart, but it's so new… and you haven't accepted it yet, have you?"

She tsks again. "Naughty little thing, rejecting a Fated mate when there hasn't been one in half a millennium. You are so very fun, aren't you?" She twirls with delight before returning to her prowl, stalking around me, a panther poised to pounce.

"Don't worry, my darling Starfire. It's almost too easy for me to remove. Can't have someone else marking my precious gem."

Her sultry voice dips into a possessive growl. "I want him to smell me on you. I want him to taste me on you. To know what he holds precious and dear no longer belongs to just him. I will ruin him—for you, for him, for what he is. Then perhaps, you'll join me in my darkness. No rules, just pure mayhem. I will give you my rebel heart and savor you in chaos like he never can."

I want to scream and thrash at her words. The bond gnaws on my ribs, shredding the flesh in between, ripping me apart to seek vengeance at her threats. My resolve crumbling as I'm able to do absolutely nothing. Of fucking course, once I'm ready to accept the bond, the Fates would send someone to destroy everything. Kissa is right. They are cruel, cackling themselves silly on the sick joke they've weaved into my fate.

I may be their weapon, but I will wield myself at them for this twist.

The female before me prowls closer, her presence cold as the night dripping off her in a fine black mist. Her scents lingers, like crisp winter air with a hint of moonlight magnolias and burning wood, perhaps from the bits of ash that float in her dark mist.

No matter how alluring her presence is, I refuse to let her spin me in her silk. I will not give in. I focus my thoughts on Sølas. How my starlight shines brightest in his dark embrace. My love. My mate.

Her hand collides around my neck. Her grip bruising. She licks up the side of my face, her tongue sharp as a whetted blade. Her fangs nip along my jaw.

My heart screeches in my chest. Her touch is pure ice compared to the flames Sølas ignites. Yet something builds deep inside me, uncurling from the darkness I keep buried away, the feral part of me that enjoys my own pain as much as others, reveling in her grip.

I want to hate that hidden part of me. The one I've created to survive the atrocities of my childhood. The part of me that finds a unique pleasure and thrill in pain and blood. With the shields of my mind quivering at bay, I have no control over the things she brings out in me.

I wonder if accepting the bond would quiet the darkest parts of me, filling them with light? Or would it starve them until they lash out and hurt someone? Hurt *him*.

"Let those damaged parts of you lash out and whip me raw. Your depravity is safe in my midnight. For stars shimmer brightest in the deepest dark," she growls as her fangs plunge into the side of my neck, exactly where the bruise from Sølas healed.

The pain and pleasure mix along my nape, stirring the darkness in me, stretching its reach for her. *Traitor*.

I curse myself for the shiver she lets escape her control. Warm crimson trickles down my chest, curling a whimper from my throat as I listen in horror.

She laps my blood up, purring like a kitten drinking warm milk, a sound and sensation I don't want to admit has heat pooling between my legs.

I'm never one to kink-shame, but knowing my Fated mate is somewhere in these woods—potentially *dying*—while my darkness enjoys this depraved moment twists my stomach with sickness. If anything, it's becoming a fucking big red flag that I can't give him the love he longs for, the love he deserves. Nor do I deserve the boundless, wild, soul-crushing love he promises me.

I know he has a darkness in him, too, but his heart is so full of love, it makes even his shadows appear vibrant and full of color to me.

She hisses, "Don't you dare think of him when you are with me. You'd choke on your own thoughts if only you knew his true darkness." Her manic cackle curls around my throat.

I muster enough strength to pinch my upper lip into a snarl at her suggesting I don't know the true darkness of Sølas when he so intimately let me see his darkest depths the night by Emerald Lake.

She snaps at my bottom lip like a plump blackberry. A metal tang filling my mouth.

A traitorous moan erupts from the stinging pleasure. I hate not being in control, feeling things that make me feel wicked. The shame I'll carry looking into Sølas' eyes, knowing I felt pleasure in a touch that wasn't his. How can she even do this to me when I have a Fated mate?

*Fuck.*

I need to get the fuck out of here. I need to save him. I may not be able to love him like he deserves, bright and beautiful, full of light, but I can save his life. Even though I know, without me, it isn't much of a life worth living.

A sharp slap to my cheek snaps me from my thoughts. A harsh *tsk, tsk* at the cusp of my ear. "Naughty, indeed. I am so very lucky you've been stubbornly resisting this bond that mars your heart. Let's take care of it, shall we?"

A wicked grin kicks up her midnight lips. "How foolish you are, loving him while still refusing this bond. Pretending you don't know how to love when you can't help but do so for that wretched nothingness," she hisses, prowling around me.

Her words punching the air from my lungs. I thought I loved him, but how can I if I feel fucking pleasure from her? She thinks I love him? If anything, this little escapade has taught me I don't know the first thing about love.

With my shields down, she has access to all my memories, all my emotions, my thoughts. Wuvon use the power of crushed skulls and brains of the strongest telepathic magical creatures to heighten their powers. So how can she be wrong? Perhaps I can still love him.

Just as the stars love the night: impossibly and hopelessly.

I decide being stuck in a mindtrap with a deadly Wuvon isn't the safest place to continue my contemplation of love. Especially of someone who I'm failing miserably at saving currently.

The female saunters in front of me with a wicked smile as she licks my blood from her canines with wild amusement. Her golden eyes shifting to molten silver, swirling with ash.

And then I remember.

Those silver eyes, haunting my dreams.

A dagger of pure nightshade wisps into her hand out of nothingness. Terror stilling my heart as I put her abilities together.

She's a Nightlancer—and something else, given the ashes emanating from her black mist. She controls darkness, can Dreamweave and create all manner of weapons to wield. Her imagination is the only limit to her power.

Her touch is as cold as fear itself. Her abilities drag up your deepest terrors. Mental demise is a certain fate when getting caught by one with your shields down.

The hairs along body prickle at the realization. There are some ancient texts that suggest Vyzon, the first leader of Wuvon and corrupted Ellian Knight, who Gildora and Reaya killed, was thought to be a Nightlancer. The information around the first five corrupted Ellian Knights is heavily redacted. When I asked Atlas about it, he said it was due to the shame the five uncorrupted Ellian Knights had of not being able to save them, failing to notice the darkness corrupting their Chivalry.

Her metallic black hair has the same sheen as the blade in her hand. She cuts the bands wrapping my chest from the bottom, hissing as she watches Sølas' shadows swirl beneath my skin.

"I should cut these evil things right out of your flesh." A thousand wraiths screech within her threat. The bloodcurdling sound chills my bones to ice. I thought sounds like that only came from monsters.

"Mmm," she purrs, "I have something much more devious in mind. A love note for your prince of nothingness."

She grips my throat again, twirling the nightshade dagger through her fingers as her eyes shift once more, the night sky drenched in crimson, dusted in silver, gleaming like stars.

Darkness creeps in at the edge of my vision, a heady sensation taking over before I hear her sharp *tsk* as she loosens her hold.

"Now, now. I want you awake to feel the pleasure of my craft. My artwork." Her cold silk voice is against my neck, each breath more chilling than the last.

Her dagger plunges into my chest as I choke on silent screams.

Burning frost seeps through my veins, biting into the skin under my breasts. My heart stutters, icy tendrils spooling out from her blade, coiling around it, thorns sinking deeper with each beat.

With the next movement of her blade, I watch misty darkness pour down her, plunging into me with searing waves of pleasure. Crisp, cool night fills me, spurring the faintest crackle of my power betweeen my fingertips.

Before I can latch onto the spark of magic, she drives the blade deeper into my chest.

Straight into my heart. I gasp as her black magic gushes into the next beat of my heart, filling my veins with ice and the darkest thrill.

I wait for my last heartbeat to come… It's only a matter of time with an injury of this degree. Fear pelts through me in a torrential downpour. I've failed so utterly. I put my entire Zenith at risk to go into the Blackwood to save Sølas. Now, they're not just losing one of us, but both of us. I let whatever I feel for him cloud my judgement. I refused to listen to Calais, who knew I sought death running into these woods, woods even she didn't dare venture into with her mate injured here as well.

I failed to save Sully. And Pip! She's likely captured him, too. He'll end up dissected in a million pieces to give unfathomable amounts of power to the Wuvon.

I'm a fuck-up, just like my foster father said I was. Curseborne. Everyone who cares about me, telling me I'm stronger than I know… Now look at me. Proving them all wrong.

Perhaps Chaos Magic is more fitting than I thought, with my reckless ability to destroy everything I touch. Maybe this female isn't Wuvon at all; she very well could be death herself. My jealous lover, finally come to claim my soul as her own. It would certainly explain how the darkest parts of me swirl in delight around her magic coursing through my blood.

A raspy cough pierces my thoughts, the onyx shade lifting from my eyes as her black magic doused in fear retreats from my veins. I watch her wipe away thick, tarry mist, dripping from the side of her mouth. Her face suddenly paler as the blade evaporates from my chest.

My power buzzes beneath my skin in her moment of weakness. This time, I grab the spark and hold it in my hand, imagining it in a box of nothingness, so neither I nor her can sense it.

Her molten silver eyes lock onto mine, widening with a flash of fear or defeat before her face hardens back to ice and malice. Her eyes returning once more to gold as ashes swirl in violent storms.

"This pesky bond is tied to something ancient, something much more profound than an unaccepted Fated mate bound." A sadistic pout tugs on her lethal lips, stained in a poisonberry hue.

She clicks her tongue, as if pondering what to do with me next. Then an opulent throne of black glass appears with crimson velvet cushions. The legs and arms made out of vines covered in a thousand thorns. She drapes her legs over one side and props her elbow up on the other, resting her chin on her hand.

For a second, I wonder how she isn't bleeding before I remember we are in a pocket realm, a mindtrap, a shared space between our minds. She has complete control with my shields down. If she wants things to bleed, they will. If she wants pain and pleasure, it happens with just her mind willing it into existence.

We're taught about this ability of the Wuvon. I never thought I'd so stupidly let myself fall prey to being caught in a mindtrap.

I'm not sure what she seems to be waiting for. Perhaps for reinforcements to arrive, collecting my physical form? She's made it clear she wants me alive, not dead.

"Oh, my precious little Starfire," she purrs while looking at her nails, as if bored by the inconvenience of whatever she's waiting for. "I took care of that little pest that's always seeking to kill you."

Chet. She must be talking about Chet, who also crashed into the Blackwood.

Before I can even blink, her lips are a mere whisper from mine, digging her talons into my chin, ensuring I hold her gaze. She twirls a strand of my iridescent hair around the finger of her other hand.

"I left his brain a spindly mess of fluff. It was pure delight. You should find him... much improved." She lets out a wicked cackle.

A thousand whispers echo through my mind all at once as I watch the Nightlancer's head snap to the direction they come from. I can only make out bits and pieces of the eerie sounds.

*He comes... He's near... He hungers.*

I use her distraction to let my chaos escape the box of nothingness I hid it in. In this mind realm, there are no molecules or particles for me to sense. But there's energy. The magic of her Persuasive powers, which require control.

I close my eyes, reaching out, sensing for her control, and it's all around me. I imagine that spark turning into an arched web of lightning and release it. Blue light cracks apart the tightly wound power of her control.

Her eyes whip to meet mine. "Clever little minx, hiding things from me. I'll make sure to punish you later for that." She winks with a devilish grin that tells me she'll make true on her threat as she vanishes through the black mist that emanates off her. I glimpse a room of red marble surrounding her before the darkness fades to nothing.

I look around to see myself exactly where she found me; the only trace she'd even been there at all are the specks of ash rising towards the now night sky. Apparently, in a mindtrap, time works differently.

All my armor and weapons are in place, except Dream Singer lies at my feet, which doesn't make sense unless… Pip.

He's gone.

I crumple to my knees in horror. She took him. That must have been what she was waiting for, someone to grab him while she had me distracted.

I have to get him back, my innocent, pure companion who never abandons me. I pray to the Celestials his dragon fire is strong enough to melt whatever metal they've caged him in. I'll see the entire Blackwood burn to ash before I let them hurt him—even if I burn right along with it.

I tremble, the feral darkness in me reveling in the idea of carnage, right along with my Chaos Magic, nipping at my skin to be released. The clear night sky suddenly clots with clouds. Howling winds whip through my hair as the static charge of lightning builds.

My chest is hollow, the warmth once kindling there now left suffocated. Only cold coals remain. The thoughts of my utter failure spiral like a cyclone above me. The earth beneath my boots fractures, mirroring my soul at the realization of what my actions have cost me.

The gale whispers. A familiar chirping sound, freezing my power in my veins.

It can't be, can it? I close my eyes, listening to the frequency, honing my senses in on it like a beacon. I lunge towards the sound of snapping branches, raising Dream Singer as my magic crackles along its blade. Ready to destroy whoever's chasing Pip.

A blur of orange and blue whirls through the darkness, knocking into my chest. A large slobbery tongue licks my face, smelling of bacon. I drop my sword and squeeze Pip tight in my arms, spinning with relief and joy.

A set of strong, familiar arms wrap around me as the scent of spruce and amber fills my lungs. I almost cry for the happiness of it all, but something's off.

Something is different.

I hadn't felt Sølas approach. I can't feel his emotions. I close my eyes, searching for his black velvet ribbons that shimmer like stardust in my mind.

They're gone. And so is the beautiful, starry, stained-glass window that tethers them to my mind. No. It's not gone.

It's shrouded in fucking black mist, with ashes dancing on an invisible breeze. *That fucking bitch.*

What did she do? I try to reach for the latch of the window, but black mist sears my flesh like frostbite, turning my fingers black.

A little tag hangs from the bottom of the window on a thin silver ribbon, twirling on an invisible wind alongside her ashes. Thankfully, the tag is right outside her midnight mist.

I grab it to read:

# BONUS CHAPTER 5

## SØLAS

Her hand reaches out towards me, an irresistible tether, tugging me like a thread across the seams of the very universe. My heart crumples beneath a distance too heavy to bear. I weave through voids of darkness, faster and faster, until time and space bleed together, my soul starving for her, sundering the heavens in pursuit of her.

Her eyes, shimmering pools of gilded obsidian, glinting above cheeks flecked in gold. My guiding constellation through the night sky. My north star, guiding me home, to her. Always her.

Golden threads weave around my heart, curling tighter. A lover's embrace. Warmth, light, love, creation—she is every page of my story, her heartbeat the hum of eternity echoing between my lines.

She is everything to me, and yet... all we have ever had is the moment between the stars. Forever dancing in my dreams.

Her stardust aura gleams into view, her power threading with all the vibrant colors of the universe. A serrated wail lacerates my throat. Tar dips down her neck, swallowed whole in endless pitch. No light ever escapes. Not even hers.

I'm always too late.

Her starlit face cracks at the sight of me, golden eyes wide as a silent, heart-wrenching scream echoes through my chest, shattering my ribs into shrapnel, mangling my bleeding heart to a bloody pulp.

Her scream, always a warning. To stay away, and that's exactly why it *guts me. Rips me to ribbons. Leaving me bleeding, lanced on her warning cries, while my very soul wails to collide with her.*

*I fracture under the weight of her plea, tangled up with longing in her eyes, the promise of a love to reforge the universe.*

*You're sacrificing yourself to save me. And that... that crushes me, gutting me into nothingness.*

*My shadows dissolve away, and I am nothing other than the gaps where light cannot touch as I race for you.*

*I do not exist without you.*

*We are together, or we are nothing at all. Together, we are everything.*

*No.*

*No. No.* No.

*I am never fast enough.*

*Always too late. Only ever arriving to see the gluttonous pitch consume your last ray of light. Emptiness is all that is left. An emptiness I clot with my bellowing agony as my soul shreds apart, my heart blazing away into ash.*

*I am nothing without you.*

*There is no universe within which I am willing to exist where there is not a me and a you. You are love and light.*

*You are everything that is beautiful and bright. Your stardust, the woven threads that string me together, making me whole. Giving me my corporeal form.*

*Existing without you is an Emberhell all its own, a cruel joke even for the Fates.*

*A dark cackle gloats in the distance, slithering around the ashes that are left of me, yanking me back from joining her in the Ever After.*

*"You were never meant for her. You have always been mine."*

"No!" A rasp claws up my raw throat, tossing me from the haunting dream. Cold sweat slicks down my body as I clasp my hand over my chest.

It's still there. Still beats.

But it feels different.

An unfamiliar... radiance. Spooling inside me. A ray of starlight, weaving its way between my ribs, lassoed around my heart, tugging at my chest.

*Well, that's new.*

The beautiful female with iridescent hair has haunted my dreams for years now. But this… I have never felt this. The tether from my dream blooming to life.

For years, she has nicked herself into my very marrow, strung herself into my sinew. We are made of the same stardust. Always trying to find our way back home to each other.

Seraph thinks I've lost my mind, thinks all the poetry I feed my soul has muddled my brain. Some days, I wonder if she's right. Once, I even convinced Eko to use his spectral form to sneak deep within the catacombs. He scoured the well-kept birth records, but no one has ever been recorded with translucent hair that glimmers like liquid starlight.

Some days, I wonder if I've gone mad. What a surreal feeling.

To miss someone you haven't even met yet.

Yet everything in my dream is too visceral, too real, leaving echoes of her in every part of my very being. No other dream or nightmare has stitched itself so deeply into my essence.

She is real. I know it.

And this new radiance in my chest is more than just an echo—it's tangible; it's gravity.

It's *proof.* The pastel rainbow light curls around my heart, tugging at my chest. I let her lead the way. Let her guide me home, to her. Maybe this time I can find her before it's too late.

Celestials, it better not be too late. I shake my head, flinging that thought from my mind. I choose hope. Daring to dream of beautiful endings, just like my adopted mother and father taught me.

I stretch my muscles, sore from training with Maiden Zenna yesterday, adjusting myself as I stand.

"Alright, light, I'm listening," I say aloud, hoping to summon this new force in my chest. It beckons me, and I follow, heading to my balcony on the north bay of the golden arched windows. I fling the doors open. Late spring air inflates my lungs, sunrays sprinkling my skin in warmth.

The radiance snags on my ribs, dragging my attention to the Dragon Spine Mountains. The skies are so clear today, you can just make out the glinting, icy tip of Eldoria, a frozen star, glittering with guiding light.

Could she really be tucked away, deep within the Highlands, all this time? The string slung around my heart hums in acknowledgement, sending starlight skittering through my veins. My soul soars on wings of unbridled hope, gliding through clouds of possibility.

I will find her.

I will find *you.*

I spin around, drunk on optimism as I head to my dresser to get ready for a new day, a new dawning. I've spent years flying with Scáil, scouring the continent, searching for any sign of her, while Calais hisses cryptic Ritherin-shit about me needing to be patient. At least they always believed me when I told them it was more than a dream.

*"I felt it too, through you. Let's find her. I am ready to fly when you are."* Scáil's ancient voice has a subtle mirth to it as it glides across my mind. Our connection grounds me. I wouldn't have survived that day I lost everything without him. His training, his words of wisdom taught me that my power is not the curse I believed it to be. My powers do not define me; they are not inherently evil, like so many Fae here think.

I used to wish on the stars I could've just stayed with Scáil. Wishing he didn't bring me to the Maidens, where the other Faelings feared my shadows, convinced I'd grind up their bones and eat them just because the most recent Shadowmancer was Wuvon and my bloodline is unknown. Gildora was a Shadowmancer, too, and she defeated Vyzon with her powers, wielding alongside Rayea.

Even if I am related to the last Wuvon, it's about how I *choose* to use my magic. I have more power than I know what to do with. A power I have trained endlessly to control, even when it threatens to rip me apart, craving release. I persist. I define it. I can't fathom the desire to add black magic to the torrent of shadows and pitch that already hurricanes beneath my seams of control.

My adopted parents filled me with so much love and light, and yet, I was their ruin. Their ending. I was just as terrified of my magic as the other Faelings were. I hated myself, hated that they'd never accept me because of my shadows, but now I realize individuals who fear me aren't worth my time.

I am worthy of more than their expectations of me. I am worthy of all the love and light my parents gifted me. But I have learned not everyone is worthy of the real me. So, I hide behind masks, only a select few knowing the breadth of color and radiance beneath an exterior shrouded in shadows.

Footsteps shuffling across the white marble floor snatch me from my thoughts. Dishes *clang* against the silver tray as Maiden Hera's time-shaken hands set it down on the table.

She's draped in her typical golden robe with modifications to cover the lower half of her face. Typical attire for Maidens, their form hidden. Their only focus is to prepare us to be the best we can be for the Golden Legion. Almost all Faelings raised by the Maidens make it into a Wing assignment. Slabs of young clay, slowly molded over time until we're old enough to be fired in glaze, hardened into the perfect weapons.

"Always with your head in the clouds, so full of daydreams, it's a wonder you haven't floated away on them," Maiden Hera tuts as I bend down to press a gentle kiss to her head, bowed with the posture of old age. I was a terrified ghost of a child when they assigned her to raise me when I was eight years old.

She never feared me. Even when my shadows lashed out with lack of control, lost in my grief of losing my family, frozen in fear from my own magic. She'd just sit in the room with me and read from my favorite poetry books until I exhausted my powers. Then she'd hobble over with cookies and tea, letting me know it was okay to feel everything I was feeling. She told me all that mattered is what I chose to do with those feelings.

*To let them break me, or let them remake me.*

Hera was the one who brought me and Seraph together. Two broken souls, who understood each other, and in our own way, figuring out how to heal together.

Fingers crooked with wisdom pat my face.

"Out of the clouds with you! Eat your breakfast, Sølas, then you'll meet Maiden Zenna for combat training."

Her craggy hands lift the silver cloche, revealing a balanced breakfast of protein and vegetables. I run my hands through my hair, unsettled energy suffocating my hunger as the tug within my chest grows restless.

She clicks her tongue, knowing me all too well.

"Maiden Hera." I bow my head as a sign of respect for her life's dedication and a desperate plea for her cooperation. "Can you get me on the list for the first trial in the Highlands?"

"Now why would you want to do that? The trip to Snomas is abysmal, even in the spring. Plus, it's too late now. You know that."

"I have to go to the Highlands as soon as possible, even if I miss my own trial in the Midlands."

Maiden Hera lifts the back of her hand to my head, checking for a fever. Then sighs, as if she was hoping illness could be the cause of my madness.

"Is this about the lady from your dreams, Sølas? It's just a dream. No Celestials exist in our world. You need to let this foolish notion of finding her go and focus on your real future. Why don't you take Tyranny on a walk tonight after training? It would do you good, spending time with a nice Fae like her."

"Tyranny! That's a great idea." I grab her hand, stamping it with a kiss before I dart out the door. Hera's disgruntled words fading off behind me.

I breathe deeply. Donning my mask, playing the part others expect to see of me. Cloaking the real me safely behind shadows as I wait along the wall outside of Tyranny's room.

"Sølas!" Tyranny startles. "What are you doing here so early?" She smooths down her golden tunic uniform before flipping her long blonde waves over her shoulder. After months of avoiding the snare she's tried to slither around me, I swallow hard at what I need to do to obtain what truly matters.

"I had a dream last night."

"Oh?" Tyranny flutters her eyelashes, feigning innocence over her conniving core.

The words pool like bitter poison on my tongue. "You and me, alone in a cabin in the Highlands. By the fire."

She walks her fingers up my chest. "While I'm glad you have finally come to your senses about indulging me," she pouts, "we have the trials next week." She flicks me on the nose and turns to make her way to our training session.

I grab her wrist, spinning her into my arms. The tether lashing the inside of my ribs until my chest is a bloody mess, seething at Tyranny's closeness. I know I'm an absolute piece of shit for using Tyranny like this, but I will go to any length necessary to find the female that clutches my dreams. Even if it's feigning interest in the vile succubus before me.

"Talk to your aunt. Get us on the list for the trial at Snomas, and you can have me all to yourself."

Tyranny looks me up and down, tasting my proposal. I grip her hip just a little tighter, pulling on just the right strings.

"Consider it a date. One I expect you'll make well worth my efforts." She snags my jaw in her hand, giving me a shake before trotting off down the hall with a sultry sway to her hips, like she has just won the game she's been playing for far too long.

The all too familiar *clink* of my best friend dressed in far too many weapons stiffens my spine. *Shit.*

"What the fuck did I just witness? There's no way after all these years you're finally giving in and fucking Tyranny." Seraphina lengthens her stride as she roars down the hallway.

"I can feel her. She's somewhere up north. Indulging Tyranny is a means to end. The only way I can get my name on the list for the Highlands trial. I have to find her."

Seraph pinches the bridge of her nose in a long sigh. "Not this again. Sølas… ya know I love ya; you're the only wretch in this gilded shithole I give a damn about, but… it's just a dream. She doesn't exist."

"Seraph, she does! I can finally feel her, a light in my chest leading me to her. Scáil felt it, too. What if she's in trouble and needs me?"

"Okay, okay." She takes another deep breath, trying to piece herself together to be the responsible one for once. "Let's assume she does exist. What if she doesn't recognize you? What if ya go all the way north and actually find this magical being from your dreams and she wants nothing to do with you? Now your heart is broken, and ya have Tyranny trying to pry a vow proposal out of ya. What if you go off the deep end and lose control and the dark voice that calls to you finally gets what it wants from you?"

"I have failed saving her in my dreams for years now. I have nothing to lose if I find her and she doesn't feel the same. But if I do find her, at least there is a chance to build the love story that is tattooed into my marrow and branded into my soul."

"Celestials," she sighs, fingers grazing over her face as she shakes her head. "If you do find her, promise me you'll chill it with your hopeless-romantic poetry Ritherin-shit. You'll scare her right the fuck off."

"Or maybe it will positively woo her?" I croon.

Seraph smacks me over the back of the head. "I'm serious. I don't want to have to go pulling ya out of a broken-hearted pit of despair. Ya know I fucking will, but they are finally giving me reprieve from mission now that I have the trials and will be at Gildorea. I plan on fighting and fucking my way through my newfound freedom."

I wrap my arm around her shoulder. "I wouldn't expect anything less."

"I was planning on doing it with you, ya fuckwit."

"As much as I enjoy pleasuring females by your side, imagine what you can do without me getting in the way." I wink.

Seraph elbows me in the gut and chuckles as we stroll together to magic combat training. I know she's angry I'm leaving her. She needs to unpack the shit that's been eating away at her soul for months now. The unspeakable things she has to do on her covert missions.

Her powerful Visci abilities to shapeshift into any form had her put to use as a weapon way too young, stealing her innocence. Her brash humor and shit coping skills are her own mask, keeping the broken girl that falls asleep crying in my arms hidden from the world. We are each other's anchor in the storm. Always there for one another, sweeping up the broken pieces left behind and gluing them back together again and again.

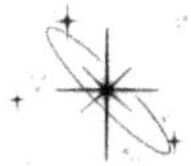

I SHEATHE my swords along my back, dressed and prepared for the first trial today. Hera was right. The trek to Snomas was abysmal, especially having to tiptoe a very delicate line with Tyranny. I retreated so far beneath my mask, I worried I'd lose myself completely. But that ray of light kept weaving around my heart. Tethering me to reality. Reminding me why every tortured scrape of Tyranny's affection to get here was worth it. Once the trial is out of the way, I'll have time to search for her.

I check into the pit without grievance from administration, thanks to the queen's intervention. I turn on my heel to join the other trialists before my assigned slot.

My knees buckle. Air punching from my lungs, radiance cinching my heart as I gasp.

Long translucent hair glimmers like liquid crystal in the sunlight. No. *Starlight.* A female perched on the bench, like a falling star frozen in place.

Gravity crumbles beneath my feet, her orbit swallowing me, spinning me off axis, pummeled in a storm of unrelenting emotion, threatening to shred my last thread of restraint. My shadows lacerate my veins, gnawing their restrained bars of my marrow, roaring for release to suss out if it's truly *her*.

*"Ground yourself. You control your magic; it doesn't control you,"* Scáil reminds me, commanding me to retreat to the library of my mind. I cradle the book that contains my power, thumbing the worn parchment pages as I settle my shadows.

I steel myself, rethreading the binding of my composure, slinking to the top row of seats. Fear and doubt rattle from their books on the shelves of my mind, begging me to read their poison, let their black words seep in to control me. I know better than to give in. I am afraid, afraid it's not her, but what if it is? Hope has always been my greatest power.

A wisp of shadows curls like smoke from my fingertip, spilling down the ledges beneath the amphitheater seats. Zigzagging strategically, so as not to draw her attention.

Her muscles stiffen, my powers freezing out of sight, yet her head snaps to their location. Her gaze latching onto my shadows when they should be invisible in the shade, as if she can sense my magic. They recoil, retreating back into me.

No one has ever been so aware of my powers. The thought chisels at my fear and doubt, releasing a landslide to bludgeon me, to suffocate my hope. What if she hates me, rejecting me for my shadows like everyone else? What if I'm not worthy of her? What if the dark voice is right, and I am only ever meant for him? My shadows rive, clotting into dark pitch with my spiraling thoughts.

*"You are no one's but your own making, Sølas. Do not forget you are worthy of all the love and light your parents beamed into you,"* Scáil beseeches.

*"I would be lost without you, my dear friend,"* I respond back down the bond.

*"No, you wouldn't. You already know these wisdoms. Sometimes you just need reminding."*

*"You need to stop coddling him. He needs to learn to remind himself,"* Calais' sharp voice grates along the shared tether to my mind.

*"Always a pleasure, Calais."* I roll my eyes.

"Sølas Zyon," the announcer rings out overhead, and I Shadowwalk down to the pit floor, the burst of magic taking the edge off my power gnawing for release. I saunter to the center, faltering a step.

The radiance spooling around my heart… *tugs.*

I suck in a breath, letting it lead my gaze. Time slows down. My attention dragged into the inescapable orbit of the frozen, fallen star.

Our eyes collide, unraveling reality as I *fall.*

She is everything, and yet no one, for I know her deeply and not at all. But she is here. Truly here. In front of me, finally within reach, and I will never be far from her again.

I soak in her every detail, savoring them like I'm sipping on her sunlight.

Her skin is olive and sun-kissed, so simple compared to the starry heavens I've seen gleam upon her flesh, ensnared by gold markings as if they are holding her corporeal form together. I find myself jealous of the wind weaving its breeze through her iridescent hair, imagining my idle fingers lazily twirling through it. Her eyes are softer than the golden supernova gaze of terror in my dreams. Younger, not yet deep with wisdom.

The way she looks at me like a stranger cleaves my soul in two. The Fates have always been cruel in the games they play.

Ache gnaws at my heart. I gasp in the undercurrent of the crash of my warring emotions. Pain in her lack of recognition. Hope in all the chances we now have to know one another. Every precious moment I'll gladly spend unraveling her story, soaking her up, drowning in every hidden corner of her soul.

Her confident perusal undresses me, leaving me barer than I've ever been. Can she see the obsession carved into marrow, me kneeling at her feet, offering her my bleeding heart, my soul, everything I have to give? Can she hear my silent words whispering to her, written on the seams of every timeline, of every universe?

You are the female from my dreams, whose screams haunt me, devour me. You've threaded into me, across space and time. A connection transcending the rules of reality, forever intertwined, two parts of a whole. Have you felt my shadows searching for you, calling for you between each beat of my heart?

And now after all these years, here *you* are.

Drowning me in the golden pools of starlight shimmering in your obsidian eyes. I gaze over the gilded flecks along your cheeks, lingering like echoes of kisses I left there in another lifetime. If only I could graze my finger across your soul, drawing you to our love story permanently inked along my aching bones. My groaning bones, bowing under the resistance to run to you, take you up into my arms, and never let you go.

A smile kicks up on your lips, a fleeting glimpse, some deep part of you flickering in recognition of me. Your soul speaking to me. And, just like that, everything clicks into place.

My mate.

My love.

My sacred light.

I will always love you, even if you do not love me.

No other has meant anything to me because I have always been waiting for you. Now so close… closer than you've ever been. Yet so far away.

Farther than you've ever been.

You no longer know me, the love in your eyes gone, replaced by so much darkness. Darkness I will cast away with my shadows as I wrap around you with all the love and light you are worthy of.

Searing pain etches across the side of my neck as I impossibly pull my gaze from hers. My attention ripping towards the creaking gate. Not before sending her a sly wink filled with promise.

First, I survive this trial, then I find her.

Find *you*.

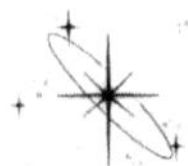

CELESTIALS, the way she looked at me after I slayed the Bone-Thresher fills me with hope the female I love is hidden somewhere within her, hidden behind a maze of walls she's built to protect herself. From what, I don't know, but I will find out and wage war against every demon who has ever harmed her. My nostrils flare. A feral need to protect her boils over in my blood.

A name is called overhead: "Savaé Entropaé."

My heart stills as she stands up. I swallow her name like it's holy, weaving it into my marrow. She walks like someone who's never been allowed to fall. Every cell in my body acutely aware of her presence.

Her face softens, flickering with light as she hands her cloak to a giant male with a beard, beaming at her with pride. As he turns, his glare stakes me to the spot with warning fury. I blaze in recognition of his face, ex-Commander Sully Stonewall.

His hatred boring through me, recalling his heroic defeat over the last Shadowmancer. Yet this is more than the loathing people usually spit at me when they think I might be Wuvon spawn. It's a deep-seated knowing, like he can see the pitch that mars my soul, the dark corruption I struggle most to control.

I rip my eyes from his to focus on our shared affection, moving with the grace of a warrior, no doubt thanks to Sully's training. He may hate me, but he has all my gratitude for being the one who taught her how to defend herself. Bringing her here today.

I grapple with the heat rising in my blood. The potential of my mate getting hurt prods my powers into a ravenous beast, nipping for release, to shield her. My knuckles go white under the strain buckling my spine, resisting this new, incessant need to protect.

I tremble, heat quickly shattering to ice as the fourth gate creaks open, the one out of place. My shadows pour out, sinking between the beams. Exploring, investigating. Frost shivers down my spine. The shape they reveal can only be one thing.

*Ritherin.*

Its talons might as well be wrapped around my heart as visceral fear slithers along my marrow. How am I supposed to sit here and watch my mate die?

*"Fated mates can talk to one another through the tether that connects their soul. Find it, and use it, young one,"* Scáil urges.

My eyes slam shut. I race deep inside myself, scouring my soul for the bond that connects us. She may not have accepted it or even know it exists, but something stronger than gravity led me to her.

There!

My shadows are thickly braided, shimmering like velvet ribbons attached to a beautiful iridescent silk that glimmers with pastel rainbows. Her starlight.

I let one of my black ribbons twirl along her silken light, following it to Savaé's mind, just like I followed it north, to her, to my Fated mate. I'm met with a thick wall of golden light. I cast my shadows out, cloaking the orb, searching for a way in through her mental shields. To no avail.

Yet, somehow, I hear a single thought escape her shields: *surprise or distance.* I pour my power, my inexplicable love, my very soul down our connection, urging her to pick surprise. I pray to the Fates and the Celestials that she can feel me. I open my eyes, gaze fixed on her, unable to blink, forgetting how to breathe in wait to see what she'll do.

Savaé darts for the side of the gate, choosing surprise. My rigid posture unravels, air filling my lungs once more. A brief reprieve before the bond claws through my muscles, ripping at my sinew, begging me to be closer to her, to protect her at all costs. I send my shadows trickling out, subtly expanding the shade she's cloaked in, deepening them, easing the raving pain tearing through my being at resisting the bond.

*"Fated mates are equals in every way, but I can sense her power from here. It is sleeping beneath her veins, waiting to be awoken. Do not risk yourself to save her. I know it is hard to resist the bond, but if she needs power to defeat the beast, it will awaken to protect her. I promise you."* Scáil's ancient voice curls around my mind, easing the burden.

He's always right; never once has he lied to me. I rub my chest, gritting my teeth. The pain mincing through me is more than I've ever experienced. An aching, a longing, a feral rage to protect and be united with the other half of my soul.

The Ritherin prowls out of the gates. My hands dart out, grasping the wooden bench beneath me, holding me in place, my umber knuckles blanching under the force threatening to shatter my soul. Each click from the monster's mouth, another dagger dragging across my skin, scouring me in marks of my every failure to protect her.

Savaé leaps from the shadows, timing her steps effortlessly with its clicks. Undetected, a predator of her own making. My boiling blood turns to molten lava, smirking as I watch the lethal beauty before me meld into a weapon unlike any other.

She soars, swinging her arms up like wings with dagger-like edges, stealing the breath from my lungs once more. Her shifting force through the air signals to the Ritherin something is behind it, twisting towards her as her eyes go wide. She misses her mark, her grasp landing in the zone of a thousand mouths, nipping at her beautiful flesh. Each bite burns into me, branding me each time I don't protect her from pain, a tally of all the things I will spend the rest of my life making up to her.

Smoky shadows curl up from my shoulders and pool at my feet, taking all my focus to rein them back from reaching for her. They no longer feel as if they are my own; it's as if all of me belongs to her, even my magic. And I will gladly give it all to her. But if I help her now, she'll be disqualified—and with the way she moves like a wraith among the shadows, I know she'd never forgive me for saving her life. She is darkness incarnate. Yet all I see is hidden starlight shimmering beneath glacial ice, begging for someone to break through, setting her free to shine.

The sound of claws ripping into flesh shreds me from my thoughts. I stifle the growl serrating my throat as the Ritherin's claws dig into Savaé's back. The muscles in my legs flex, bow strings ready to be released. I start to stand, set to sail to her just like an arrow, but Calais' sharp growl cleaves my head in two.

"*Sit. Down. Now. She does not need your help. You must resist the bond. She is no damsel. Did that bond searing into place spoil your brain? If she rejects you, it will kill you. To be fair, if she dies here, it will also kill you, but I know she will survive. I have overseen her training from afar. Despite what she may think about the Fates, they will not let their champion perish.*"

"*How do you know her thoughts already?*" Realization spews my blood into liquid fire. "*You fucking knew where she was the whole time and didn't tell me?*" I have always known Calais to be the icy lightning to Scáil's grounding calm, but I never believed her capable of such cold, striking betrayal.

"*Sølas. We know a great many things, but when it comes to the games of the Fates, we are not allowed to intervene. I swore a blood bargain many years ago; the cost of the deal seals the fate of our eggs. Calais can Dreamweavve; she has been guarding Savaé's mind while she sleeps. She is destined to protect her, just as I am destined to protect you from the dark voice that calls to you,*" Scáil responds, his voice always a soothing balm to my storms.

The snap of the Ritherin's neck is music to my ears as they tumble forward. My anger is forgotten as relief melts over me.

Celestials, she is beyond beauty, victory cascading off her like ribbons as she stands. Black blood is splattered across her face, but she shines with a subtle white light when her gaze meets mine. I sense her shields are down. My shadows instinctively slink along the bond in a warm caress as my eyebrow kicks up with pride and amusement.

She didn't need me. Maybe she never will.

But I need her, like life needs breath.

I will have all of her or die in the beautiful pursuit of her.

# BONUS MOMENT CHAPTER 54

## SØLAS

She awoke with stardust flickering from her sleepy eyes.

In the vulnerable moment between sleep and wakefulness, she gazes up at me through thick lashes.

"Do you still love me today?" she mumbles.

With a soft kiss on her cheek, I reply, "I still love you today. Tomorrow. And every day after that."

She hums sleepily in response before her breath shallows once more.

I press another kiss to her temple.

"I will forever love you, like the night loves the stars. Impossibly, yet full of hope. All the way through the darkness, until we shine with a light all our own."

I drink in the way sleep softens her face in the most beautiful way. Intoxicating me with a deep starvation to know every soft piece of her she has hidden away, to guard it with all of me. To be the place where she can strip away her armor, her walls, her strength, and melt into me. One day. One day, I will be that for her, but for now, I am thankful for every piece she is willing to give to me.

I pull her tighter into my arms as she naturally nuzzles into me. My other half. Two perfectly fitting pieces of a celestial puzzle.

Shadow and light.

Darkness and stars.

Chaos and control.

# ACKNOWLEDGMENTS

Wow. What a journey this has been. I wrote the first version of my prologue after receiving some terrible news. The big emotions threatening to unravel the remains of my crumbling mental health. I needed something to hold on to, something to keep me from going under. So I wrote. And I didn't stop for months until the first draft of AOTS was done. Emberhell, I didn't even chapter the book! And then I re-wrote it again and again.

It feels so surreal to put down the pen and finally be done. Welcome to LuxsulaVerse, a world I created where I had all the control to prevent the real world from breaking me. Well... other than Savaé, who holds the plot at dagger point, and I just try to work around her. *Awakening of the Starborne* is book one in the series, The Game of Endings and Beginnings, an epic dark trilogy that keeps getting darker. Sorry, y'all, book two is gonna wreck us all. I have several other series planned for the universe, including Nyxara's very own prequel series!

Alright, time for the sentimental shit Savaé and I hate, but through lots of therapy, I have learned not to throw it all out a window... *Coughs loudly at Savaé, who just flips me a middle finger* *The cunt we all know and love.*

Thank you to my dogs for putting up with me while I tucked away in my chaos-writing den. Thank you to my friends and family, who supported my very rough first draft of AOTS. Thank you to my amazing writing partner, who was there from draft one, to all my endless messages of line changes, to the final version before you! You believed in AOTS when I almost gave up on her during the editing process, always my cheerleader, lending me strength when I was struggling to find my own. Thank you, MM Parks. AOTS wouldn't have made it through my own darkness without you, and some days, neither would I.

Thank you to my amazing PR team, who helped bring my story to life on social media, helping organize my chaos dragon nature behind the scenes.

Thank you, Rachel, for seeing my dream and believing in me with just a pitch before even reading my story. You fell in love with Cascara and all the characters, and it truly shows with all that you do for me! I can't wait to see all that you make of Quilibré. We reach for the Celestials and fall on the clouds! Thank you, my Lock Ness monster, for keeping me organized and dealing with my random streams of consciousness. Thank you to my alpha readers and my developmental editors; you all pushed me to lean into my poetic voice and make AOTS uniquely me.

THANK YOU TO MY AMAZING STREET TEAM!!! My Celestial dragons, who spurred me on, kept me hydrated and fed, despite insistent grumbles that energy drinks and gummy candies were enough to satiate my wild brain. You all are the light that kept me going through the last leg of my journey and made my life falling apart bearable as I continued to muster my dragon strength to finish this book for all of you. You are all a dream come true, and I am so honored to have all of you in my den!

To my passionate Patreon subscribers! Thank you for supporting my chaos dreams of transitioning to writing full time. Especially to my top-tier subscribers! Nyxara's very own Naughty Brats: Bree, BookishPsychWard, AJ my Giggle Dragon, Cat my Pastel Dragon, Kasey Darling, Ashley and Andrea!

Thank you, READER! I am so honored you took a chance on my debut novel. You are why I do this. My words are my magic, weaving a piece of my soul around your mind, one I hope you treasure.

Are you salivating and begging for more!? That's my good girl (or good boy, Savaé doesn't discriminate). Let me tease you, leaving you on the edge as I write book two by subscribing to slow burn newsletter, full of WIP snippets, concept art, and bonus scenes. Now type LouveCH.com into your cellphone browser… Good, just like that. Click the subscribe button… you're being so good for me. Now fill out that form… look at you, so fucking perfect for me.

Now that I've gotten you all sweaty… The Game of Endings and Beginnings series continues! We'll be Shadowwalking back to Cascara as chaos unravels it all. I can't wait to see how beautiful you look, holding FOTS in your hands in 2026.

# ABOUT THE AUTHOR

Louve -ch is a queer indie author, utter chaos dragon, unapologetic hoarder of your tears while crafting slow-burn yearning that will edge you until you want to scream. Her debut poetry book released in July 2018. She is now bringing her lyrical prose to the romantic fantasy world with her debut Epic Dark Romantasy: Awakening of the Starborne.

How to support this unhinged CHAOS DRAGON?

1. Leave a review so the algorithm Fates don't banish her to the void.

2. Shove this book at your friends like it's contraband fantasy crack.

3. Post your feral screaming online & tag @UniqueRandiace (Instagram) or @Louve.Author (TikTok) so she can cackle in the shadows.

Join the Celestial Dragons Newsletter: if you want bonus chaos, sneak peeks, art reveals, and even more emotional damage.

Indie authors don't have marketing armies—we have readers like YOU. Thanks for fueling the dragon hoard.

APPENDIARY
AWAKENING
OF THE
STARBORNE
LOUVE·CH

# APPENDIARY CODEX

Wondering where the APPENDIX is!?

Use the QR code above of head over to LouveCH.com for the full virtual Appendix, Bestiary (with tips from Sully and Professor Yuri), Fae Species and color map!
Celestials Blessings
Xo Louve -ch